MORE *of* US TO THE WEST

Book One of the Adrift Series

TRINITY DUNN

Copyright

I dedicate this book to my husband.
You have made me everything that I am.
Thank You.

THE ADRIFT SERIES BOOKS
(IN ORDER):

Book 1: *More of Us to the West*

Book 2: *Feathers Floating Through Ember*

Book 3: *Remnants on the Tides of Time*

Book 4: *A Reflection of the Sky on the Sea*

Book 5 (Final): *The Stars that Call us Home*
(Coming Spring 2023)

PART I

Stranded as we were.

Chapter One

It was 3:30 in the morning and ours was the only vehicle on the road. The absence of other travelers left me with an eerie feeling that was both calming and terrifying as we merged slowly onto the snow-covered freeway.

It was early March, and the blizzard was an unexpected and unwelcome surprise; a stark contrast to the warm spring weather we'd been counting down the days to.

The radio was off—as it was Chris's habit to turn off the music whenever weather conditions were treacherous—and the only sounds between us were the crunch and hum of the layer of snow giving way beneath our tires, the hiss of snowflakes hitting the windshield, and the low whistle of the truck's heater.

Snowflakes danced infinitely in the headlights as we navigated along a set of tire tracks another brave traveler left just for us. Without those tracks, I had no idea where the highway ended and the median began.

Now, I'm not entirely sure when it happened, but somewhere during the past ten years of our relationship, I'd transformed into a nightmarish passenger. Where I'd once simply trusted my husband to get us to our destination in one piece, it was now my instinct to grab the handle of the door in a panic, point at things on the road as if Chris hadn't seen them—*the man had never been in an accident, of course he'd seen them*—and drive a hole into the floor where an invisible brake pedal might be.

I could sense my body tensing up and preparing to become that monster of a passenger as I squinted to see through the veil of thick gray that enveloped the windshield.

'You're going to make it worse, Alaina. Just shut up and let him drive,' I told myself, forcing my back all the way against the seat.

Glancing over at him, Chris's demeanor was the opposite of mine. He showed no signs of anxiety despite driving under some of the worst conditions I'd ever seen.

I laid my hand on the console between us and he interlaced his fingers in mine, smiling while he casually steered us along with only the palm of his other hand.

My fearless husband.

I internally rolled my eyes for allowing myself to get so anxious. Of course, he would get us there. He always did.

Slowly letting my shoulders relax, I laid my head back and closed my eyes to picture the warm sunny beach in Bora Bora that was awaiting us. I envisioned the quiet calm of the ocean at my feet; the sun on my face, legs, and bare arms—the totality of warmth it would bring—a much-needed break from the never-ending Chicago winter. I imagined lying still and warm in an oversized beach lounger, a Piña colada in one hand, a book in the other, and not a care in the world.

Most of all, though, I pictured Chris.

I saw him the way he'd once been—long before we'd settled into our routine—when he'd kiss me just because the urge hit him, or would make love to me because he needed to.

We'd gone too long as familiar strangers, and I was desperate for the affection we once shared; anxious to touch him with the familiarity we'd had years ago, before we'd let ourselves become physically estranged and shy with one another. I was eager to be kinder, happier, and not always consumed with unspoken resentment toward him.

I was sure this vacation would fix all we'd let become broken. It *had* to.

'We need to talk,' he'd said the day I suggested the trip, and those four little words had sent my entire existence spinning out of control. Where I'd always been so sure of our marriage, those little

words made every bit of my certainty crumble into a thousand pieces.

In an attempt to prevent what I was certain he would've said next, I rambled on about a getaway to "reset" ourselves and our relationship; a honeymoon we never got the chance to take.

Since I hadn't given him much room to speak, he'd agreed to it and the conversation ended there. For the months that led up to our departure, however, there was a constant nagging thought in the back of my mind. What would he have said if I'd let him talk? Would he have asked me for a divorce? Had we really let our relationship get so bad?

"What's this?" he muttered to the silence, shaking me from my thoughts and back into an anxiety-ridden state as a red and blue light appeared in the haze of snow ahead of us. I let go of his hand so he could steer with both and held my breath, reaching to touch the small pendant on my necklace—a habit I'd formed over the years to calm myself.

As we slowed to an almost stop, I stiffened from both the fear of what we might see ahead, and what might not see us from behind. Clutching the handle of the door, I leaned forward as if those couple inches would magically make the scene ahead clearer.

Moments later, the police car came into focus, as did the bright pink flames of the road flares. The flares overlapped the tire tracks we'd been driving in and I realized as we approached, the car which had left them was now upside down in the median.

A police officer signaled us through, and we passed slowly, watching a man and woman as they knelt in the snow to search for their belongings from the overturned car's driver-side window.

Glancing around the cabin of the truck, I wondered what I would need if it were us in that situation?

My purse, perhaps?

No.

Phone?

Not important.

I smiled at the man in the driver's seat. I would only need Chris. Nothing else would be so important I couldn't leave it and get off such a dangerous highway.

Despite the distance between us, he was my home and my best friend. It was only him I needed.

After all we'd put each other through, I wondered if he felt the same about me? Would this trip really mend us the way we both hoped it would or would the *'we need to talk'* conversation continue when we arrived back home?

I couldn't imagine a life spent without him—didn't want to imagine such a lonely existence. Sure, we'd grown apart, but even at a distance, we meant something to each other.

There was a desperation in me to prevent a life spent without him. I couldn't let that conversation happen. I'd fix what I broke; I'd make him love me again. Coming home to a divorce couldn't be an option.

With no tire tracks to guide us through the blinding pink orbs of snow, we drove on in silence for a short eternity, both of us sobered for entirely different reasons.

It was only when we merged onto the I90 expressway leading into Chicago's O'Hare airport that we were joined by other vehicles. The appearance of other drivers brought a sense of relief, so much so that, all at once, my body relaxed, and I let out a long breath I hadn't realized I'd still been holding.

The world was alive once more.

The roar of departing and approaching planes, the scrape of snowplows, and the constant "SWISH" of passing cars in the slush drowned out the silence that had once been between us. We exchanged relieved smiles when we pulled into the parking lot and he placed the car triumphantly into park.

I touched his arm. "Thank you for not killing us, love."

The corner of his mouth curled upward and he ran his hand down my hair to cup my cheek. "If I were going to kill us, Al, it'd be much more exciting than a car accident."

I chuckled. "Oh yeah? You think about killing me often?"

He shook his head, but his eyes were alight with mischief. "Never."

Laughter burst from me. "Oh, bullshit. You know you've thought about it at least a few times in the past ten years. How would you do it?"

His lip twitched. "We'd have an accident at the zoo. You'd *accidentally* fall into the lion enclosure."

I gasped in fake outrage, adjusting my cheek against his palm where he was still holding it. "That is a very distinct answer, Mr. Grace. You really *have* given this some thought. I never took you for a *feed-her-to-the-lions* type husband. I thought you'd shoot me maybe... or a good honest strangling even. Not *lions*. Would you watch them devour me?"

"Oh yes," he said earnestly, his eyes wide. "And then I'd spend years telling everyone about how I'd witnessed it and it was the most dreadful moment of my life. No one would suspect me of a thing. How would *you* kill me?" He raised his brow. "Poison?"

"Do you even know me at all?" I grinned. "I'd stab you, of course, then I'd hide your body in another state... I'd even organize the search parties that would never find you."

His mouth opened in shock, but he was still smiling. "You're brutal!"

I shrugged. "I've been married too long to be soft."

With a chuckle, he leaned in and pressed his lips to mine.

The moment was much more short-lived than I'd hoped. His eyes darted upward through the passenger side window behind me toward the airport shuttle. "Ah crap," he muttered, and I heard the screech of the train coming to a stop.

"It's only a five-minute wait," I assured him. "We'll get the next one. We've got plenty of time before the flight."

"*Flights*," he corrected, opening his door. "And I don't like waiting to wait. Since *somebody* wouldn't let me sleep an extra twenty minutes, I want to get to whatever seat I'll be waiting in and take a nap."

We were going to be flying first on the 6:40AM flight to L.A., and from there, we'd have to endure a four-hour layover to then catch the 12:40PM flight to Bora Bora. Neither of us was particularly excited about the flights, but both of us were anxious to get to our destination.

Working our way through security in record time, we arrived at our gate to find only ten other people there.

"See!" He glared down at me. "I told you we could've slept a little longer!"

It was rare for us to be this early for a flight. Chris was always a last-minute person, and as a result, we'd missed two flights during our relationship. Because of the snow, I'd insisted we leave earlier.

"Oh well." I yawned. "We'll sleep on the plane."

We found a seat and I laid my coat across us, resting my head against his bulky shoulder while attempting to ignore the metal arm rest dividing my seat from his digging into my ribs. Just as I started to close my eyes, a shrill female voice came over the intercom in our gate.

"This is an announcement for passengers on United Airlines flight number three thirty-eight to Los Angeles. The flight has been delayed due to snow. Our new departure time is 9:50 AM."

"9:50?!" I sat up and frowned at Chris, the neurotic side of me taking full control. "That's going to leave us with..." I groggily crunched numbers and time differences in my head, "less than an hour from landing to board in LA. No way we're going to make it onto our next flight!"

"We'll make it," he said, his tone entirely too calm for the amount of panic I felt the situation warranted. "Don't get all worked up. It'll be fine."

He laid his head back and closed his eyes.

Annoyed, I huffed and hoisted myself up out of my seat. "I can't sleep in this chair. I'm going to find something to read... or do... or eat... You want anything?"

He opened one eye, yawning as he stretched his long legs out in front of him and pulled my coat up toward his chin. "See if you can find me a neck pillow."

Before I could answer, he closed the eye again and smiled.

'How can he be so calm right now?' I asked myself as I made my way down the terminal toward the smell of caffeine and cinnamon. *'We are definitely going to miss our second flight. No doubt about it. And he's not even worried. Of course he's not*

worried. Why would he be? He didn't even want to come on this trip. Not really.'

I turned to the left and found a small gift shop. Irritated, I spun the rotating book stand a few times, skimming the titles without really reading them.

'He doesn't care about the delay… just like he doesn't care that I'm walking around the airport by myself! God forbid he walk with his wife and strike up a conversation! Oh no, we can't have that.. especially not on our would-be honeymoon!'

That was the thing about the neurotic side of me. She tended to make Chris out to be a monster when she was awoken. Any little thing could set her on a crash course of unwarranted blame and complete outrage.

I, of course, could've asked him to join me—*should've* asked him to join me if the purpose of the trip was to mend our marriage. I knew he would've been happy to walk with me. Instead, I found an excuse—much as I always did—to be angry at him; an excuse to hold onto the contempt bottled up inside me. Maybe I wasn't quite ready to let go of the hurt. Or maybe I needed an entirely different landscape in order to even begin to relinquish the weight of all we'd gone through.

I snagged a bright yellow book off the rack, half-read the description, and grabbed a second in case the first was bad. I pulled two neck pillows down from the wall behind it, painfully aware of how many we had at home, and tossed them onto the counter at the poor little cashier whose head barely made it over the display case.

Bags in hand, I sulked across the hall to a little coffee-shop that was not Starbucks, knowing even before I ordered us both coffees I'd be disappointed.

Yes, I was a thirty-one year old, neurotic, husband-loathing, passenger-seat-driving, Starbucks snob. My twenty-one year old self would've never recognized the adult I'd become.

With two boiling hot coffees burning my hands, two bags stinging the ring finger I'd looped them around, and my purse—loaded with toiletries—weighing down my shoulder, I was seething by the time I got back to our seats.

"I got you a stupid coffee and neck pillow, here!" I managed, handing him his coffee and finally setting mine down on the table next to him to relieve my hands of the heat. Dropping the bags and purse onto the floor, I slinked into my seat. "Ugh. I've worked myself up into a frenzy, love."

He eyed me with an amused expression, taking the lid off his coffee to blow on it before taking a very loud sip.

'Always the loud sip. Always...'

I reminded myself why we were there and adjusted my mental outrage. Honeymoon... Mended marriage... If I didn't change myself, I was going to lose him. I couldn't be a *single,* neurotic, passenger-seat-driving, Starbucks snob.

His mouth twitched, and he used his free hand to pat my leg. "It's alright Ally, we'll get there. Might not be when we wanted to, but we'll get there soon enough."

I straightened and reached down to fish out the cinnamon roll I'd picked up for us, opening the little box and holding it between our knees. He immediately pinched off an enormous bite as I took my first sip of coffee, cursing myself for not walking a little farther to Starbucks.

Despite the less-than-pleasant taste, I devoured the coffee and, with Chris's help, the cinnamon roll in quick time. Laying my head against him, I forced my shoulders to relax.

Why *did* I let myself get so angry so often?

'We'll get there soon enough,' I thought. But I couldn't wait to get to Bora Bora. For some reason, fixing our broken relationship in Chicago—or even the United States as a whole—seemed impossible. The pristine beaches of Bora Bora, on the other hand, would be far too perfect a landscape to stay angry once our feet could land upon them. I couldn't wait to get us back to being us again—to the couple we'd been before we hurt each other over and over. The truth was, I missed my husband, and I couldn't wait to get him back—to view him the way I once had.

I wasn't always so angry, and he wasn't always so distant. We'd been great once.

Closing my eyes, I drifted into a half-sleep, smiling as I allowed myself to be transported away from the cold air of the airport to the warm summer night we first met.

Chris and I met each other at a concert ten years prior. I was there supporting my then-boyfriend Kevin, a drummer in the headlining band.

Kevin had big dreams of rockstardom and I, being freshly twenty-one, an aspiring singer-songwriter myself, and *highly* impressionable, was completely enamored with the idea of him. It was a fast-paced and young lust that had kept us together for the couple of months that led up to that night.

I was four vodka-cranberry drinks in, after having arrived with the band while they set up and sound-checked. Painfully, I'd endured the first two acts and found myself standing in a long line for the women's restroom. I had one hand propped on the sticky painted concrete wall to keep my balance while the other was fastened around a plastic cup housing the fifth vodka-cranberry of the night. Despite my desperate urge to pee, the straw kept finding its way to my mouth.

The hall was dark except for the light that would spill out of the bathroom along with a wave of female chatter each time the door to the restroom would open and close. Across the hall from me, the light came more frequently, and I watched men going in and out of the men's room with no line or chatter whatsoever.

I danced from toe to toe, wondering why the gap in the light was taking so long on my side of the hall. What compelled women to chatter in the bathroom while other unfortunate souls pee-danced in the hallway?

The sudden muffled vibration of bass and drums and the sound of cheers from the crowd overhead told me Kevin's band had taken the stage. Eager to join them, I threw caution to the wind and launched myself across the hall, plowing into the men's bathroom door and directly into the arms of a somewhat baffled Chris.

We fell, entangled, directly onto the men's bathroom floor, my drink spraying out in an explosion of ice and pink.

He'd taken the brunt of the fall, shifting his weight so he hit the ground with an "oof" and with me lying haphazardly on top of him.

I lifted my head, and that was it. My heart stopped, and I lost the concept of time, space, and that mere moments prior I had been willing to sacrifice all caution just to release the pressure in my bladder. All I could do was swim in those big green eyes.

He smiled up at me, making no move to unlock his enormous hands from my sides. "Well, hello."

I smiled an awkward "hello" back as reality returned and, with it, the realization that we were lying on the bathroom floor, the door jammed against our sides, with a crowd of men cheering obscene gestures over us.

"Oh my God, I'm so sorry," I huffed, my cheeks burning with embarrassment. With trembling legs, I stood, extending my hand to pull him up as I pushed the door away from his body.

He took my hand in his, the size of it making mine seem frail and very feminine. He hoisted himself to a sitting position, the wicked smile remaining on his lips. "You frequently burst into men's rooms? I can be more cautious when exiting from now on."

I didn't care that he was cheesy. I was in awe of him.

Keeping hold of my hand, he stood, towering a good foot above my head as he did so; his bright white teeth still on display.

I took it all in as he stood; those long legs, the broad shoulders, the slight waviness in his dark hair, the way his plain black t-shirt hugged his biceps, and the very slight dark hair of a five o'clock shadow on his face. I'd never seen anything so manly—so handsome. He made every other guy I'd ever dated or shown interest in seem like a boy. This exquisite creature that stood before me was a *man*.

"Oh God, no, I'm so sorry. I just—

Three men slid around us on their way out, one bumping into my back and forcing me, once again, to plunge head-first into his very sturdy chest. My cheeks on fire, I pushed back rapidly only to nearly knock over two men coming the opposite direction. "I'm so sorry, so sorry." I looked back at him. "I'm sorry."

His smile remained unchanged. "I'll forgive you if you let me buy you a..." He paused, his gaze running the length of me to observe the bright pink spatter of my cranberry drink covering the majority of my once white Social Distortion t-shirt. The corner of his lips curled slightly higher. "Coffee perhaps?"

I was mystified. This beautiful man was looking at me in a way I knew meant trouble. I'd never considered myself unattractive, but I'd never had a man who looked quite like him regard me in such a way.

"Oh... ah... yes... ok," I managed, following him out the door.

"What were you doing bursting into the men's room, anyway?" he asked as we entered the blackness of the hallway.

"Oh! I had—*have*—to pee. Just wait one minute." I glanced at the line for the women's bathroom—it'd grown to about twenty-five women deep—then back at the men's room.

"Here," he smirked, "come with me." Seizing my hand, he pulled me behind him.

There was something about my hand in his that sent a jolt of electricity through my body. I blindly followed, beaming at the women whose heads turned to get a second look at him while we made our way through the crowd to a hallway on the opposite side of the stage.

He was beautiful, and as far as every other woman in that place knew right then, he was mine. I kind of liked the idea of that, however short-lived whatever was about to occur might be.

He led me down a set of stairs and through a door opening up to a brightly lit hallway. The contrast had me squinting as I heard him cheerfully boast, "Hey Chuck! This one's gotta pee. Mind if we use the one back here?"

"Not at all," shouted a deep male voice from far down the hall.

He placed his hand on an unmarked door and held it open to reveal a private bathroom. Winking, he grinned down at me and said, "I'll just wait here and protect any other unsuspecting saps from risking the same fate by getting too close to that door."

I laughed—the sound foreign as it hit my ears. I'd never made a sound quite so nerdy in response to a line quite so cheesy. Cheeks on fire, I hurried inside.

'Oh. My. God. Alaina,' I thought to myself, leaning against the door as it closed and taking three deep breaths. I stepped to the sink and squinted at the Picasso of a reflection looking back at me.

'Get it together, woman.' I braced the sink with both hands. *'Don't be drunk. Please don't be drunk right now.'*

My hair had already started to curl and the fluorescent light of the bathroom amplified every wisp of the fiery red chaos I'd spent hours straightening earlier that evening. My eyes were definitely glossed over and…

'Is that… smeared mascara under my eyes?? Seriously?!'

I grabbed a handful of paper towels, running them under the sink water and wiping my eyes while I hobbled into the single stall to pee.

'Be cool. Say nothing until you've drank an entire cup of coffee… Coffee… They don't serve coffee here… That means we're leaving… And what about Kevin?'

Bladder pressure finally relieved, I stumbled out of the stall and walked back to the mirror. I washed my hands and ran them, still-wet, over my hair in an attempt to smooth it.

'Good as it's gonna get. We're going to get coffee, and that's that… We don't really like Kevin that much, anyway.'

Part of me expected—maybe even hoped—he'd be gone when I opened that bathroom door. I mean, who was I next to this charming man? He could've had any woman in that club. What in the world was he doing escorting an awkward, half-drunk, freckle-faced redhead to a private bathroom, anyway? But there he was in all his glory, leaning against the wall and smiling directly at me.

He stepped forward and offered me his arm. "Shall we?"

I blinked at the offered arm, and despite my best judgement, slurred out, "Well, wait juss a second cheesy-mystery-bathroom-man. I have questions."

"Oh?" He chuckled. "Please do fire away."

'Shut up, Alaina, please shut up,' I thought, but the words kept coming. "One." I leaned exaggeratedly forward as I pressed my

pointer finger into the air. "How does one just magically have access to inaccessssssssible bathrooms down mystery hallways and yet chooses to use the filthy public ones?"

"Well," he said, smiling and wrapping my arm in his to turn me back the way we'd come. "That's easy. The owner of this venue is a friend of mine and I come here often to hang out with him. It just so happens I was closer to that hallway than this one when the urge hit me to pee. Next question?"

I let him lead me, leaning slightly more on him than I'd have preferred. "Alright then, *TWO*..." I had lost control of my volume and the word "two" was shouted, echoing across the fluorescent concrete hallway we walked down. "Where in the hell do you intend to buy me a cup of coffee and are you some kind of outrageously good looking axe murderer who plans to get me all hopped up on caffeine before you chop me to bits?"

He gave my arm a little squeeze and opened the door back into darkness and loud music. At least my volume control wouldn't be an issue. He leaned down to shout in my ear, "There's a little diner one block over I'm quite partial to, although I'm afraid I've left my axe at home this evening."

We were working our way through the crowd arm in arm and I stopped, placing my hand on his chest so I stood in front of him, dancing concert-goers bumping roughly into each of our elbows. "Alright fine, I will *let* you buy me *a* coffee, but don't get any ideas. I'm a lady, ya know."

At this, he smiled wide and his hand worked its way down my hair to cup my cheek, loosening a frenzy of butterflies in my stomach. "You're adorable. Where in the world did you come from?"

Adorable? There was that word. My entire life I'd been called *adorable* or some version of it. Just once, I wanted to be "sexy" or "seductive."

Rolling my eyes, I looped my arm back through his and turned toward the exits. "I come from Hyde Park, and we'd better hurry before the band sees us. I was sorta dating that drummer."

Chapter Two

We'd stayed up all night to avoid oversleeping. Between the cold, the tension of the drive, the first flight, and the complete lack of sleep, my body was done with me by the time we stepped off the first airplane. Once again, I found myself tensed and shivering, but this time from utter fatigue.

We were late arriving, and if we were to have any chance of catching our next flight—which was on the opposite side of LAX —we would have to run.

I hoped to God Chris knew where we were going. He was a good twenty feet ahead of me—his legs being longer than mine— and I focused on the back of his head while I panted and struggled to keep pace with him. He slowed long enough for me to catch up to his heels as we turned into the escalators which would take us out to the shuttle.

Taking the steps two at a time, we caught the shuttle just as it pulled in. The time was 12:15. Boarding had started five minutes ago. I sat down near the doors, panting with my hands on my head. "We're never going to make it now," I managed.

"We'll make it," he assured me, rubbing my lower back as I steadied my breathing.

The shuttle ride was all a blur of panic and panting, followed by more sprinting once we reached Tom Bradley. By the time we arrived at the desk, my side ached in a cramp, and I had to lean on the counter to catch my breath.

'Alaina, we're getting on the treadmill every day when we get back home. This is ridiculous.'

"I'm sorry, sir, you've just missed it," I heard the woman explaining to Chris once I straightened. "I can put you on a flight out tomorrow afternoon at 12:40 or I can place you on standby."

Chris looked apologetically at me.

"Standby," I grunted. "I just want to get there." The idea of wasting a night of my hard-earned vacation time stuck in a Los Angeles hotel room did not appeal to me. I was eager to get to the beach and, after the music industry there broke my heart, I wasn't a big fan of Los Angeles.

"Alright," the woman said. "We'll call your names if something opens up for you. In the meantime, make yourselves comfortable and don't venture too far."

Utterly defeated, we turned. Near our gate was a Starbucks, the familiar coffee bean and hazelnut aroma beckoning me toward it. "Well…" I pointed, "Coffee?"

He yawned. "Yeah, I guess."

"You want me to find you a book to read?" I asked, gesturing for him to find us some seats.

"Nah." He smiled, pulling his phone from his back pocket and sitting. "I'll see if I can find us some much-needed good luck." He winked at me, and I turned toward the warm promise of a vanilla latte.

'Of course he would pull out his phone,' my neurotic inner voice complained. *'He would literally prefer to scroll aimlessly for hours through social media or play poker with complete strangers than to converse with his wife. Have I become so boring or have we just run out of things to say to each other? If we can't even talk in the airport, how are we supposed to enjoy this vacation?'*

Fixing things was definitely going to be a challenge if I continued to interpret every action of his as an attack on me. Of course he was unaffectionate. Who wouldn't be when their wife was always so bitter?

A proper coffee in hand, I took my seat next to him, noticing—despite myself—he didn't take his eyes off his poker game as I did so. Shaking it off, I sipped my coffee and pulled out one of the two books I'd picked up in Chicago.

For as much as he'd been caught up in his poker game, I was whisked away into a romantic fantasy where the novel's lead male would never forget to look up from his phone at his lonely wife in an airport.

So enraptured was I in the story, I might've forgotten I was stuck in the airport had it not been for the chair serving as a constant reminder, forcing me to shift my legs every few minutes to give each side of my butt equal opportunity to go completely numb.

At some point around chapter twenty, Chris had fallen asleep and his head was rested heavily on my shoulder. The warmth of his breath on my arm was a welcome heat to my exhausted body. I wondered how he could sleep in such a position, but was glad one of us was getting some rest.

At 10:30pm, I was pulled from my book by the call we'd been waiting for over the terminal speakers.

"Christopher and Alaina Grace, please report to Gate 155."

I nudged Chris back to consciousness. "They've called our names."

Gathering our luggage, we headed back to the gate's desk.

"Mr. & Mrs. Grace, I've got some good news for you."

I sighed with relief.

"We've got two seats available on the 11:40pm flight. Unfortunately, I can't seat you together, but one of our openings is a first-class seat, which we'll upgrade you to free-of-charge."

Chris and I looked at each other, then back at her.

"Yes, great, we'll take it," Chris said. "Give her the first-class seat, I'll take whatever."

"Alright then," she said, handing me my ticket. "Mrs. Grace, here is your ticket: seat 2B... and Mr. Grace," she batted her eyes at him like most women tended to do, "here you are. You're seat 28C."

Spirits lifted, we took our new tickets and sat down inside the gate's seating area. I laid my head on Chris's shoulder and yawned as he once again pulled the iPhone from his pocket.

That's when I spotted him. Jack Volmer... *The* Jack Volmer.

Almost fifteen years ago, Jack had been on the cover of virtually every teen magazine, and assuredly hanging on a poster in every 16-year-old girl's bedroom—*myself included*. He was the tall, blonde-haired, blue-eyed, perfect-bodied star of the then-popular teen drama series *'Fairview Nights,'* in which he played the role of Elias Phillip, a handsome teen who'd spent nine seasons falling in and out of love with the show's lead female. I'd all but forgotten him until he stood in my gate looking rather impatient.

The last decade or so had been kind to Jack. He had to be close to my age and he still looked fantastic, perhaps even better than he'd looked as Elias. His shoulders seemed wider and more muscular than I'd remembered. He towered over the surrounding men, and he'd grown a short beard which suited his rugged adult appearance well.

I found that watching him and contemplating his mood was the only means I had with which to stay awake. Chris was enthralled with his poker game next to me, thoroughly unconcerned that his wife was eye-stalking a handsome man across the room. So, I observed Jack Volmer for the better part of an hour while he ignored the men standing with him, snapped a photo with three women who entered the terminal and recognized him, and ultimately resigned to sit in one of the gate's chairs and struggle, just as I had been struggling, to find a comfortable position in it. I watched him until he caught my eye and I was forced to look away.

I focused, instead, on a mother and daughter directly across from me in our row of seats. The daughter—at-most five years old —laid atop her mother, who was stroking the girl's long golden hair. My heart warmed at the sight of them and I reached for my necklace, longing for a child of my own I could never have.

A few seats down from them was a young woman with silky dark brown hair. Her phone was pulled outward and upward as she adjusted her facial expression to snap selfie after selfie. Scanning the rest of the row of seats, I found every single person staring at the screens of their various devices.

My career relied on technology but I abhorred it. I yearned for the simplicity of earlier decades when people would actually talk to each other. Over the past year, I'd made it a point to keep my own phone buried deep in my purse to avoid the addiction to mindless scrolling we all tended to suffer from. Unfortunately, the clarity did very little to make me more sociable. If anything, it made me more bitter and judgmental of people who were merely passing the time. At thirty-one, my inner thoughts were more resemblant of an eighty-year-old; cursing technology for making us unsocial but having no desire to actually converse with anyone.

Jack stood and paced with his phone pressed to his ear, drawing my eyes, once again, in his direction. He had an arrogance about him when he walked, standing taller than the people he passed with an expression that exuded immediate dismissal to anyone who might try to approach with small talk.

He sauntered to the large window overlooking the tarmac and stood with his back facing me, the tensed shoulder blades beneath his shirt defined and easing in response to the hushed conversation he was having.

I wondered what it might be like to be the woman I imagined was on the other side of that phone... Would Jack Volmer neglect his wife in an airport to play poker with strangers or would he be so consumed by her that he wouldn't even notice his flight had been delayed? Would he ever tire of her stories? Or forget to notice her when she'd put on something seductive before bed? Was he sweet and romantic or did all men lose that intensity over time? Would I have been doomed to be in the same situation regardless of who I'd married, or had I just married the wrong man? Or maybe he'd been the right man, but I hadn't been the right woman... Would Chris have been better off with another?

'We need to talk,' my mind reminded me, forcing my eyes to Chris's phone as he opted to fold his two-pair when a flush showed on the table.

What if *'the talk'* would've led to him confessing he'd met someone else? It wouldn't have been the first time he strayed. Was my husband considering leaving me for another woman? Perhaps one that didn't loathe his every move and drool over handsome celebrities in an airport? Could I really blame him if he did?

I shook the thought from my head. That was not the way I'd start this trip. We were far away from Chicago and I'd sworn when the first flight took off I would leave our issues there. I was going to put everything I had into fixing this relationship. Everything.

I inched my body a little closer to him and laid my cheek on his shoulder, watching as a new hand was dealt. "I love you," I whispered.

"Mm, love you too," he grumbled absentmindedly as he raised the bet.

"Chris, do you think—"

"Good afternoon passengers," a female at the desk announced. "This is the pre-boarding announcement for flight 89B to Bora Bora. We are now inviting those passengers with small children, and any passengers requiring special assistance, to begin boarding at this time. Please have your boarding pass and identification ready. Regular boarding will begin in approximately ten minutes' time. Thank you."

Anxious travelers began to stand all around us. Jack hung up with whoever he'd been talking to and hovered near the desk.

Abandoning whatever sentimental garbage I might've spewed out prior to the interruption, I gathered my carryon, purse, books, and neck pillow, opting to end our time at the airport on a playful note. "You gonna miss me all the way back there in coach?"

He lowered his phone to his lap. "Al, I'd miss that face even if you were seated in the row in front of me."

I stood and stretched upward. "Wake me up when we get there." I bent to kiss him on the lips, hoping he might touch my face or pull me into the kiss the way he used to. When he didn't, I forced a smile, kissed his forehead, and hurried onto the plane, swallowing the lump in my throat hard.

Upon boarding, I found my seat in 2B was next to *The* Jack Volmer, who was looking all too comfortable with his long legs spread out in front of him in 2A.

Lifting my carryon into the overhead bin, I hurried to take my seat beside him, allowing the agitated looking man behind me room to take his.

I extended my hand as I sat. "Alaina," I said in introduction.

Jack observed me with a half-smile but didn't take my offered hand. Instead, he crossed his arms over his chest, laid his head back against the seat, and closed his eyes. "Jack," he responded, the corner of his lip raised in a smirk, "That's some hair you got there…"

I touched my head and realized all the hard work I'd put in to taming my curls twenty hours prior had come undone and my head was two times larger than it had been upon arrival.

"Oh, God," I laughed, pulling it all to one side and pinning it against the seat. "It's been a very long day. We've been on standby since this morning and traveling since 3:30 AM."

He smiled with his eyes still closed. "Sounds dreadful. Who's 'we?'"

"My husband and I. We missed our connecting flight because our first flight got delayed. They didn't have any seats together, so…" I shrugged, realizing I was rambling. "Here I am, hair and all."

He grinned, but did not respond.

I'd never flown first-class before—never saw the value in spending that much more on a ticket to get to the same destination. As I reclined back and stretched my legs out in front of me, I decided I might have been wrong all those years flying coach.

Amid the sea of passengers flooding the plane, I spotted the emerald eyes of my husband and smiled. As he passed, I exaggerated my stretch, sticking my tongue out at him and wiggling my fingers in an innocent wave.

"Yeah, yeah," he said as he slogged his way past me, looking back over his shoulder to add, "I'll see ya in a few hours."

I watched him disappear into coach—well, all but a forehead and one long leg poking out into the aisle.

Happy to have the opportunity to finally close my eyes, I did so, and only opened them again as the plane navigated away from the terminal and the flight attendant began her safety presentation.

"Newlyweds?" Jack asked, eyes still shut.

I laughed at that. "Hardly. We've been together for ten years."

He opened his eyes at that and whistled a sarcastic *"impressive"* note. "No wonder you didn't give up your first-class seat."

Taken aback, I turned toward him. "Excuse me?"

"I'm just saying… you could've offered whoever had the seat next to him your fancy first-class seat. They probably would've loved to trade. Why didn't you?"

I paused. I really hadn't even considered it. I could've traded, and ten years ago, that would've been the first thing on my mind. Why hadn't I thought of it now? I pursed my lips and spun to look down the aisle, thinking about whether to run back and attempt a sudden trade.

"Only messing with you, Red," he said lazily and poked at my elbow between us.

I frowned. I hated being called *'Red.'*

"Do you think they'd trade me now if I ran back there?" I half-stood and bobbled with the plane as I faced coach. There was a middle-aged couple sitting next to him sharing a magazine. I wondered if I could convince them to separate.

A soft hand touched my elbow. "Ma'am, please take your seat."

I twisted back to see the scornful look of a very pretty flight attendant, her dark brows furrowed over brown eyes.

I sat down to avoid her scowl. More than I hated being called Red, I loathed being called *'ma'am.'* It was a new term for me as I'd hit my thirties and one I couldn't get used to. I clasped the seatbelt on and, after a moment, looked over at Jack.

He even sat with arrogance. His eyes were closed, arms were crossed over his chest, and his legs were sprawled out wide in front of him. Even with the legroom of first-class, he was taking up my personal space.

Annoyed that he'd made me feel guilty for no reason other than boredom, I stretched my legs, forcing him to adjust his position as my boot grazed his.

This might've given me some semblance of self pride had the airplane not vibrated in preparation of takeoff to remind me I was a *very* nervous flyer.

Much as it always did, my mouth became dry, and my heartbeat quickened. As the plane sped forward, forcing my head back against the seat, I clenched my eyes tightly shut.

In what might've been the single most mortifying moment of my life, I realized, as my stomach floated up toward my throat, that where I would normally squeeze Chris's hand on takeoff, I was now squeezing Jack Volmer's hand... *hard*.

But as we ascended at what felt like ninety degrees, I couldn't let go.

'*Oh God, level out... level out...*'

On the verge of hyperventilation, I squeezed harder, gritting my teeth, and begging myself not to throw up as my stomach lurched.

'*Oh, please level out... please...*'

The sounds around me grew more and more muffled as the pressure filled my ears. I swallowed several times, but they only grew more clogged—more painful. A cold sweat washed over my skin.

'*Don't you dare throw up, Alaina... You're a grown woman... please don't throw up.*'

Every muscle in my body tightened as the plane climbed higher. '*That's got to be the clouds... we've got to be leveling out soon. Oh God, please don't let me throw up in front of Jack Volmer. Alaina, you are so ridiculous.*'

The world around me continued to shake and I could feel my head starting to swim; moisture forming at the back of my mouth. '*Get it together... Jesus. Please level out!*'

As if to oblige me, we leveled out and my stomach returned to its appropriate position. I opened my eyes and turned my head to see the very amused expression of Jack Volmer—his fingers still locked in my fist. I let go and reached up to turn on the overhead fan.

'*Oh dear God, air...*' I took several deep breaths as it washed over my face, letting my heart rate settle.

Jack had said something, but my ears were too clogged to make it out.

"WHAT?" I asked too loudly.

"ARE YOU GOING TO THROW UP?" he shouted, turning everyone's heads around us in my direction.

"No," I snapped, lowering my head between my knees to catch my breath. *'Maybe... Jesus Alaina, what is wrong with you?'*

I opened my mouth wide and closed, wide and closed, swallowing over and over until my ears finally popped. Slowly, I unfolded and laid my head back against the headrest, feeling him observing me the entire time.

Cheeks on fire, I tried to compose myself. "I'm so sorry... I'm a nervous flyer... I didn't mean to... touch you."

He rubbed his fingers where I'd nearly broken them. "You've got a hell of a grip, Red... This actually kinda hurts..."

"Don't call me Red," I growled, taking another deep breath.

"Won't happen again," he assured me, placing both hands up in surrender.

"Sorry about the fingers," I attempted to recover. "What... ah... what are you going to Tahiti for?"

"My kid sister's getting married."

"Oh, that's sweet." I faced him. "We're going for our honeymoon and—"

"Sounds thrilling," he interrupted, my cheeks turning red with embarrassment as I realized he was annoyed and silencing me. "I'm going to try to get some sleep now."

He produced a set of earbuds and popped them in his ears before I could continue. "Night... Red."

'You smug bastard,' I thought, closing my own eyes as I reclined back. *'Hope those fingers bruise.'*

I heard the familiar *'ding'* of the seatbelt sign turning off just as I drifted off to sleep.

Chapter Three

In dream, I was transported to the diner the night I'd met Chris. Billie Holiday was playing from a radio in the nearby kitchen. The restaurant was small, and its only inhabitants were Chris, myself, a cook, and a waitress.

The booth he picked was well-worn, showing tears in several spots on the fabric where I sat nervously peeling at one. Chris was seated across from me, not breaking his gaze, even when the little waitress came over.

She was all of five feet tall, a hundred pounds if she was soaking wet. Her skin was leather. The boxed blonde hair on her head had grown out about three inches to expose gray and dark roots, and her voice was low and full of grit I could only imagine came from a lifetime of cigarettes and parties. "Can I get you two somethin' to drink?"

Still staring at me, he said, "Two coffees and a couple of menus please."

Ears and face on fire, I smiled, shifting my focus from him to the tear in the seat and back. "You're making me very uncomfortable staring like that."

"I don't mean to make you nervous, it's just really hard to look away. You're very wonderful to look at."

'Say something witty, you fool,' I thought, but my mouth wouldn't form words. The only sound that escaped it was an awkward, "meh heh heh."

"Do you really not know how beautiful you are? I mean, look at you."

"Oh, well, I…"

I sighed, having no idea how to even respond to those kinds of words in my drunken state. "Listen, cheesy-mystery-man, I'm gonna be honest, I'm not my best self right now and until I've had that coffee—*and maybe some eggs*—I'm probably going to say something awkward and stupid that I'll be embarrassed for later."

"Well, I don't mind if you do, so long as I can sit here lookin' at you. My name's Chris. Christopher Grace, if you'd like the whole thing."

He stuck his massive palm out toward me.

I took it, happy to shift the conversation away from my looks. "Alaina McCreary." I shook his hand, squeezing too hard and regretting it almost immediately. "What's the deal with you, anyway? Where are you from? What do you do? How often do you steal women away from concerts to woo them over coffee?"

"This is a first," he admitted, and paused while the waitress clumsily laid out our coffee cups and poured too much coffee into each.

"Soups tonight are cream of broccoli and chicken noodle." She laid a menu out in front of each of us. "I'll be back momentarily to take your order."

As she walked away, I reached for the cream and sugar, adding what I could before the cup would overflow. Without a thought to gracefulness, I leaned my head down to the mug where it sat on the table and sipped—loudly. I became painfully aware of his eyes on me long before I raised my head back up.

'And that's the night. See ya later, Chris Grace.'

He smiled in wonderment rather than running out the door, and continued on with his story. "I'm from Arlington Heights. Started out as a construction worker for my dad's company, got my general contractor's license and now he and I build houses side by side as Grace Construction. That's how I came to know Chuck Miller next door. Built his house for him. Gave him a good deal, too."

Holding my coffee like a human being now, I decided not to speak until I'd finished the entire thing. I made it a habit to raise the mug to my lips whenever I thought he might pause in his story to potentially ask me any questions.

"Your eyes are going to kill me by the way," he noted, and continued, "I moved to the city about a year ago, an idea that I thought was good at the time, but I can't wait until my lease is up so I can move back. Too much noise here. I want a yard and a neighborhood and the freedom to drive and park my car with ease. Are you ready to talk yet or do you want me to just keep going?"

I brought the cup back to my lips and looped my pointer finger around in a circle to signal him to keep talking.

"Alright then, well, let's see, I was a baseball player in high school, ran a little track, started college—decided it wasn't for me —learned my dad's trade, moved here, went to that damned bar almost every night waiting for you to bump into me, and here we are. Did you know your eyes are both blue and green depending on which way you look at them?" He tilted his head.

I swallowed hard and set the mug down on the table. Glancing around the room to test my vision, I decided I was headed towards sober faster than I thought.

"Track, huh?" I smirked a little.

By the time breakfast arrived, I felt like myself again, and conversation flowed freely.

"Well," I was saying, "I put off college to pursue music. I'd even gotten a producer interested in recording me one night after one of my acoustic gigs." I poked the eggs with my fork. "But it didn't really lead anywhere so here I am, twenty-one years old and in my freshman year of college."

"Did you end up recording anything?" He smiled, holding a piece of bacon. "I'd really love to hear it."

"I did." I scooped up my hash browns as I fumbled around my purse. "And I still play sometimes." I took a bite, producing an iPod and earbuds. "I'll always have music but a design degree will pay the bills."

I thumbed through the songs for a moment until I landed on my personal favorite. "You really want to hear it or are you just being nice?"

He glided across his seat, circling around the table to slide in next to me on my side of the booth. He picked up one earbud and placed it in his ear, handing me the other. "Show me."

"Oh."

I was immediately intimidated by his presence near me. He excited and scared me all at the same time. Feeling self-conscious, my thumb hovered over the play button. "I mean... it's not... it's ok... it's..."

His hand curled over mine and forced the thumb down, inciting goosebumps up and down my arms as acoustic guitar and piano filled our ears.

I watched his face as he listened and his lips curved upward when my vocal began. He said nothing, just stared at me while the song continued.

As the last notes of the piano rang out, I pressed the "Stop" button and pulled the earbud from my ear, rambling, "It still needs some work, and I don't know if I like the second chorus.... I wasn't feeling that great when I sang it, and —"

He touched my hand over the iPod and my stomach danced. "It's beautiful," he said softly. "Very sad, but very beautiful. Who made you feel this way?"

"Oh." I blushed. "Thank you... Just some boy once."

Some boy being my on-again-off-again high school boyfriend who had just recently proposed to a girl he'd only been seeing for a few months... I decided to leave that little detail out of the conversation. I shuffled the iPod back into my purse.

"Well, whoever he is, he's a complete idiot. Just look at you!"

And he *was* looking at me... the same way he'd been all night, only now he was inches from me. "You're amazing."

I laughed nervously, "Ah... Well, you haven't seen my temper."

He raised one dark eyebrow, tilting his coffee mug in my direction. "I look forward to it."

We stayed just like that, on the same side of the booth, talking until 7am. He told me about his mother, an artist who struggled with depression, and his father who doted over her. I told him all about my own mother and her challenges raising two girls all by herself. We shared our dreams of the future—both of us wanting children and a home far outside city living. He showed me pictures of his work, and I shared two more of my songs with him.

When people started to pour in for breakfast, we decided to part ways. Standing just outside the door, he placed his hands on my face.

I'd been waiting all night and morning for that very moment. My stomach filled with excitement. Everything quivered in anticipation. His face drew closer to mine, and he whispered, "Wake up, Alaina."

When I looked up at him, I saw that past him, the clouds had grown dark. Rain began pouring on us, and a crack of thunder nearly swept me off my feet. He clasped my face and shook me... hard. "WAKE UP!"

I was jerked awake by the plane lurching and a squeeze of my hand so hard I thought it might break. My eyes opened to stare into the wide, fear-ridden, blue eyes of Jack Volmer.

Around us, the plane was a blur of flashing lights and shaking colors. I couldn't focus on or hear anything around me. There was a stabbing sensation ripping through me, and my seat was shaking so hard I was sure my insides might spill out. The scene around me had erupted into a trembling chaos, but what stood out was that there was no sound at all.

I realized, in a haze, we were crashing... rapidly. I could see the oxygen mask already on my face; bits of pink and yellow flipping through the air in the quick flashes of light that flickered around us.

Was I still asleep? I should've been afraid, but I wasn't. The silence made it all feel like a dream.

Jack Volmer was gripping the seat in front of him, mask on, temple pressed against the seat, eyes wide and staring at me.

I was sure he was screaming beneath the mask, and I found myself squinting at his mask to verify it when a sharp pain ran across my skull. Dazedly, I blinked, my eyesight blurring as Jack reached out to touch my forehead and it all turned black again.

I knew the impact woke me. After having fallen in complete silence, my hearing returned, and the world around me became deafening. I could hear the water rushing in, the loud creaking of the sinking plane, the shouting of men, the shrill screaming of a woman, and a sobbing child nearby.

I felt every inch of whatever damage was done to my skull, wondering in those few seconds if my head was split open and if I might die in the coming seconds.

My mind moved to Chris, and I twisted in my seat, the motion sending a stabbing pain up my left side. Bright yellow fuzz filled my vision.

As it cleared, I noticed the back of the plane was gone, and there was only an infinite blackness where it once had been. Violent waves reflected in the lightning flashes from the gaping hole that had replaced the back of the plane. We were floating in the nose. There were maybe five rows of seats left. Where were the rest? Where was Chris?

The water was rushing all around me, pulling my body upward. I needed to get out.

'I'm going to die here.'

My hair was drenched and wetness dripped down my face as I fumbled with the seat belt beneath the water. I couldn't get it unlatched. It was stuck.

'I'm going to die here!'

Panic ran up my neck along with the ocean as it reached my mouth. I took one last gulp of salty air and felt a hand on mine beneath the water.

"I've got you," a man said, pulling the seatbelt loose.

Whatever was wrong with my head was playing with my consciousness. I attempted to focus on the man who was freeing me, but my eyesight went dark once more. I knew he'd lifted me, but everything faded into a steady static as I found myself drifting back into the diner once more.

'No, no no,' I thought. *'I can't pass out now. I can't die like this. I have to get to Chris.'*

Forcing my eyes open, I woke in a raft in the blackness. I noticed the pressure of an inflated life vest around my neck and shoulders, bodies all around me—on top of me even—and we rocked so violently I had a constant feeling of falling. My stomach in knots, I reached out for something to grab on to. I touched an arm and followed it outward to a rope. My other hand found an ankle as we slid downward for what felt like an eternity.

I was pinned beneath two male bodies lying face down in a pool of saltwater. There was water coming in from every angle. From above, it was pouring rain, and the waves would lift us and spill over onto us every few seconds.

I shifted a little beneath the weight of the men on top of me so I could try to get a glimpse of what was going on. A flash of lightning above lit up the wall of water approaching us.

'Chris!' I thought, trying to wiggle free to search for him.

"Stay still," said a man's stern voice, breath hot against my ear, "or we'll all fall out."

"The back of the plane!" I yelled atop the roaring ocean. "Does anyone see the back of the plane?"

No response.

"Please!" I shouted, attempting to be heard over the storm. "The back of the plane! Do you see it?"

The steel voice returned to my ear. "It's gone, stay still."

"But my husband!" I sobbed. "Please look! Please! My husband was in the back!"

An enormous wave took us then, and we rode it partially up, my stomach sinking as we reached our stopping point and it rolled us back down to crash over us. As we tumbled, those on top held the ones on bottom tighter. We all clutched the ropes and a leg locked around mine. We were under water for a second, then back upright.

My side and my head stung. Sharp pains washed over my entire body. The men on top of me pressed down harder, pinning me against the bottom of the raft. I lifted my face so I could inhale, then lowered it into the flooded floor to exhale. Over and over, I did this, just barely breathing.

Up a wave we'd go, and bodies would stiffen. We'd all hold on as we traveled up, praying we'd make it over and not tumble back down. Once over the top, on the way down, we'd all shift. Legs and elbows bruised and bloodied all of us as we rolled and bounced through the storm, kicking, kneeing, and elbowing each other on every rise and fall of the ocean beneath us.

Lightning danced across the blackness only to make the blackness that was swallowing us more terrifying. Giant black waves pushed us out into more blackness. We were tossed up and down, forwards, backwards, upside down, and sideways. There was no break; no time to exhale.

As our bodies were jostled around, I realized there was another woman pinned to the raft next to me, and between us, a little girl. I adjusted my grip so one of my arms crossed over the child to a rope. This did very little for my breathing situation—my face pressed even deeper in the growing puddle—but the position secured her better between us. Feeling my arm near her head, the woman next to me did the same, draping one of her arms across mine atop the girl to grab a rope near my head.

We flipped again, this time going deeper under the water. I struggled against the men pinning me to the raft; the threat of drowning urging me to fight on instinct, but we came up again and I settled back down. Everything was stinging now.

"Hold on!" the man shouted above me, and as suddenly as he'd shouted, his weight shifted, lightened, and he was gone.

A knee came down beside my face and I stretched my neck to see what was happening. I didn't dare let go of the ropes. Without the man's weight to hold me in, I wasn't sure I could stay in the raft on my own.

We dipped hard to one side, and the sound of skin sliding against wet rubber reverberated in my ears. "Don't let go," the man panted. "We're going up again, I'll pull you in as we slide down. Just hold on tight. I won't let you go."

Up we went, and without his body atop me, I floated upward, stomach feeling as though it had made its way up to my throat as I begged myself not to fall out. Just as suddenly as we'd gone up, we sped back down.

Evening out with a crash, I heard a male scream in agony. A heavy body came down across my back and rolled across my legs, followed by the familiar weight of the man who'd been there before. The heavier man adjusted his position, grabbing hold of the raft's rope nearby and pinning my legs beneath the bulk of his weight. The other man took his place over me, chest pressing down against my back to keep me from falling out.

Over and over we fought the waves until, after what felt like hours, we were reduced to a soft bobbing on top of the water. Collectively, we all released our grips on the rope and each other. The men who'd been holding us down shifted, and we all sat upright for the first time in hours. It was pitch black, so dark, I couldn't see my hand in front of my face.

Exhausted, I leaned back against the rubber, all my muscles giving way as I did so. "The back of the plane," I whispered, my voice practically gone from me. "Did anyone see the back of the plane?"

Someone's fingertips found my shoulder.

I jumped at the touch, looking out for some sign of Chris in the darkness. "Who's that?"

"Your head," a man said, his words cut short by an outburst of violent coughs. "You're injured." He struggled to clear his throat as he tightened his grip on my shoulder. "You should lie down until daylight."

Sliding closer to me, he wrapped his palm tightly around the top of my head. "It's Jack."

"I'm fine," I argued, trying to wiggle free of him to look around. "Did anyone see the back of the plane?"

"You're not fine," he hissed, his voice hoarse as he stifled another cough. "Your head is cut bad. Stay still."

He positioned his body behind me, coughing with the effort, and pressed my head back against him.

"I *am* fine!" I squirmed, but the quick motion shot pains up and down my body, "Ahh…" I straightened against him in pain, and he placed his palm back over my forehead, urging me to lie back.

"My husband was seated in 28C, towards the back of the plane," I persisted, giving in to my physical predicament and laying my head against his foreign chest. I could feel the rattling in his lungs as he laboriously inhaled. "Did anyone see what happened to it?"

"Storm took us by surprise," a man said at my feet. He breathed heavily between words. "Tried to get up above it, but we were already in the thick of it." He let out another deep, rattling breath. "Lost the tail, and I tried to level us out. The back of the plane broke off long before impact... We got lucky..."

"Mama?" cried the small girl. "Mama?!!" Panic setting in, she grew louder, her words cracking as she worked herself into a wail. "MAMA?? MAMA??!"

"Shhh..." a woman soothed, and I could feel her movement nearby as she comforted the girl. "It's gonna be alright, hush now."

The child whimpered, but quieted.

"You're the pilot?" Jack asked over my head.

"Yes, sir," the man managed. "I'm so sorry. We had no warning, no signs... It just formed right over us all of a sudden. There was no storm in the forecast. No rain... no clouds... I don't know what happened."

"That wasn't no storm," a man with a thick southern drawl said softly. "There wasn't no sound to it... no sound at all... and the lightning... It hit us over and over—I saw it hittin' us—and it didn't make no noise."

"There was no turbulence either," a deeper voice added. "No wind... even when the back of the plane broke off... Did you notice? There was no wind."

"No sound even then," the southern man continued. "Like someone hit the dang mute button. I don't know what in the hell that was, but it wasn't like no damn storm I ever seen."

We rocked along then in silence with only the occasional cough from Jack or sniffle from the little girl. None of us would sleep, I knew, not with all we'd just been through.

In a daze, I leaned back into the chest of the man holding my forehead and longed for the man who should've been in his place. I wrapped my fingers around the pendant on my necklace and closed my eyes.

'Where are you, Chris?'

Chapter Four

The sun crept up on the horizon, offering us all our first opportunity to see one another. In the gray purple of the morning light, the raft was a terrifying site. Blood floated all around us in the pool of water that had filled the bottom, shading the once bright yellow rubber in a dull red-orange.

Groggily, I searched for the primary source of blood.

In front of me was a tiny blonde woman, pale, with large blue eyes. She had the look of a true introvert, like she would sport a tweed skirt and thick glasses outside this particular setting. She appeared unscathed and sat inspecting the side of a heavy-set unconscious man.

From his attire, I gathered the man she was examining was the pilot; his white shirt and black pants were soaked with shades of pink and red. His belly protruded high over his belt and his breathing was labored. I couldn't see the side of him she inspected, but I could only assume he was bleeding from it based on the distorted expression on her face.

Behind them, sprawled out with his arms hanging slack at his sides, was a lanky man in his mid-thirties. He wore a black t-shirt under his open life vest, and I could just make out the words "Mama Tried" in big white letters. He had dark hair with big brown eyes and bushy dark eyebrows. His mouth was set in a far-off grin as he stared out at the ocean. Although he appeared shaken and exhausted, he showed no signs of bleeding.

Clinging to him with one arm wound around his neck was a young woman. Her thick straight chestnut hair spilled over his shoulder like silk. In stark contrast to his tall, rugged appearance, she was tiny with bright pink nail polish on her fingers. She'd removed her life vest in the night and wore a flowy white tank top speckled with blue flowers over light khaki shorts that had become pink from the bloody pool of water she sat in.

"Lilly?" A shaking female voice called out from the opposite end of the raft, cut short by a painful sounding coughing fit. I shifted my gaze to the far corner where I could see two bright white heads of hair huddled together. A man had his arms wrapped around the woman who spoke as she coughed to a choke, then laid her head back on him as she settled.

"Lilly, honey?" she continued, evening out her voice as she focused on the brunette who had her face buried against the *'Mama Tried'* t-shirt. "Are you alright?"

At the sound of her name, the woman unwound her arms from the man and looked up. "Gramma?"

Her eyes welled with tears and the raft lurched as she scurried across it toward the couple.

This sparked a miserable groan from a man lying in front of them. He was face up with a sizable gut protruding from underneath his turquoise and yellow flowered button-up shirt. He held one hand to his lower back, and couldn't appear to move anything beneath his waist.

"Gramma?! Grandpa? You're alright!" Lilly sobbed happily, embracing them both.

The old man's eyes watered, but he smiled genuinely, caressing the woman's dark hair. "Are you hurt?"

She shook her head, "No. Are you?"

"We're alright, honey." He pulled her into his arms, weeping as he held her. "I'm so glad you're okay."

Next to them sat a large native-looking woman with long, thick dark hair streaked with silver. She smiled at the joyous reunion, her arms coiled around a little girl with golden curls. It was the same girl I'd seen in the airport tucked in her mother's arms. She seemed that much smaller surrounded by the endless ocean around us. The woman coddled her sleeping body closely, then matched the gaze of Lilly and her grandparents as they all stared silently back at *me*.

My eyes followed theirs, traveling up my legs where I found the blood grew darker at the top of my jeans and up my white t-shirt; darker still against the bright yellow of my life vest. I shuddered at the thought that *I* could potentially be the primary source of blood.

I reached up, with some effort, to feel around Jack's fingers where they were still plastered to my forehead. Holding my hand in front of my eyes, my stomach twisted in a panic as my own fingers came back red.

"This is bad," Lilly said, her brown eyes wide as she looked around. "*Really* bad. What do we do now?!"

"S'gonna be alright," the thin man said in his thick southern accent. He bent his legs and pushed himself to sit straighter, arms unmoving at his sides. "They'll come a-lookin for us. Just gotta' wait it out for an hour or two. It'll be alright."

"How do you know?" She scanned the ocean, her pitch raising. "What if they don't find us? What do we do?" Tears formed in her eyes as she lifted up on her knees, spinning in a circle to search the infinite blue surrounding us. "Are we going to die out here?" She looked back at me. "Is *she* going to die out here?"

"Ay, hush now," the man insisted. "Ain't no sense in panicking. Ain't gonna do nothin' for nobody."

"Hey sweetie," the blond woman cooed, her voice as delicate as her small body appeared. "There's a bag by your feet. Take a look inside and see if there's a first aid kit in there." She glanced at me worriedly, then up over my head. "Is she warm?"

"Yes," Jack said, his voice vibrating through me where my back rested against his chest.

"I'm alright," I offered, trying to prove it by turning toward him—an act which sent a sharp pain up my side. I cried out, and my hands moved to my ribs. The adrenaline of the crash and the storm had worn off, and I could feel the extent of the damage to my head and my side.

Jack's other hand followed mine to my ribs and he peeled back the vest and blood-soaked tank to reveal the very dark blue and black skin on my abdomen. "Her ribs are bruised."

"Might be broken," the blonde added. "Try to sit up straight as you can, okay?"

I closed my eyes and straightened my back uncomfortably against Jack's chest, very much aware of the way he kept his palm sealed around my forehead.

My mind raced, my vision blurred, and my eyes grew heavier with the rising fever.

'I wonder how bad could it be? Is my face mangled? Am I going to die out here? Am I already dying? Is Jack Volmer really holding my head right now?'

"How are we looking over there?" the blonde shouted over us to Lilly.

Lilly untied a yellow survival bag and peered inside. "Water... *lots of it...* paddles... flares," she dug around, "and a first aid kit!" She extracted a large white box and waved it at me, her hands shaking as she did so.

"That's great," the blonde encouraged her. "Now see if there's a stitch kit in there."

Lilly popped the lid open and went straight to work examining its contents.

I smiled to myself, recognizing the blond woman's attempts to keep Lilly occupied so she couldn't panic.

"Bandages... gauze... sunblock... scissors... tape... arm splint... oh, wait..." She pulled a small white and purple packet out of the box. "Zip stitch? Is that right?"

"That'll work on her." The blonde smiled at me. "But not on him." She diverted her attention back to the large man that laid before her. "There's nothing else?"

Lilly returned her focus to the white box and rustled around it once more, pulling out a small black zipped bag and studying it. She unzipped it and grinned. "Yes! This is it!" She scrambled on her knees across the raft, extending the kit to the woman.

"Perfect. Thank you, Lilly. Now..." The woman removed a few packets from the case and brought them close to her face to read the labels. "I'm going to need you to take the zip stitch and close up her wound." She tilted her head in my direction. "I've got to get this man stitched up before he bleeds out but I'll walk you through it."

Lilly blanched. "Oh..." She surveyed me cautiously, shaking her head. "Oh, I don't think I can."

"Miss, I'm gonna need stitches too." Beside us, a man shifted uncomfortably. Beneath a head of blonde and white hair, his expression was twisted between agony and anger; thick brown eyebrows furrowed above the rims of his cracked glasses, causing the lines in his forehead to deepen. He leaned to one side, holding both hands over a wound in his abdomen. "And my son too." He motioned to the teenager at his side.

"I'm alright," said his son—a scrawny teenage boy covering his arm just outside my view. His cheeks were spotted with acne and his hair was a dusty brown color that curled upwards in spots. He breathed heavily through parted lips, exposing teeth that were a little too big for his mouth. "Are you a doctor?"

The blonde proceeded to dab a wound on the pilot's side with alcohol. "I'm a nurse. My name's Anna. I'll be right with you both." She refocused on Lilly. "Lilly, honey, you can do this. It's not hard. I'll talk you through it."

"You don't understand." Lilly looked from me to the packet in her hand and back. "I have this thing about blood..." She glanced at the thin man and held the packet out toward him. "Here, *you* can do it."

The man grinned at her, "I cain't move my arms else I'd do it for ye.' Ye' gonna have to suck it up, Cupcake. Else she's gonna bleed to death real fast."

Resigned, she swallowed and took a deep breath, bravely sliding across the raft to sit in front of me.

As she opened the packet and inspected the contents, I focused on her face and noticed, for the first time, how incredibly beautiful she was. Her skin looked like porcelain. It was smooth and flawless. Her eyelashes were long and dark over huge brown eyes. She had bright white and straight teeth encased inside full pink lips. She was in her early twenties, if I had to guess, and the picture of perfection.

I envied her at that moment. I wondered what I must look like in contrast—bloody, hair probably triple in size with curls poking out in every direction. I was sure my freckles were doubling by the minute and my skin was turning hot pink under the rising sun.

Despite my condition, I found myself smiling at the poor girl. How on earth had she come out of that crash looking so flawless?

She turned toward Anna. "Do I just...like this?"

Over her shoulder, I could see the thin man nod. "Yeah, ye' put the sticky part on each side, probably gonna need about three of 'em side by side, clean it off with the alcohol first and dry it... then stick it on, pull 'em strips and it should pull closed."

"That's right," Anna conceded, threading her needle. "Used it before?"

The thin man laughed, "I been cut up purdy good a time or two."

Lilly turned back toward me and I took a deep breath as I met her panic-stricken eyes. She opened another packet just outside my field of vision and the smell of alcohol burned my nostrils.

"Ready?" She asked nervously.

I closed my eyes and Jack released his grip on my forehead. I felt the tickle of blood as it raced down my right eyebrow, then tasted the familiar metallic tang when it slid down my nose and reached my lips. My consciousness threatened to slip away again but I fought to stay awake.

"Oh God," Lilly whispered under her breath. "Oh Jesus... Oh God..."

"You can do this," Anna assured her.

The icy sting of the alcohol swab made me stiffen, and the quick motion shot needles down my side. Jack's hand squeezed mine where it sat over my ribs. The action itself brought a strange sense of comfort that I would've felt guilty for in any other circumstance. In this one, I was glad for something to hold on to.

As she made her way along my forehead with the alcohol, I focused my thoughts on Chris.

The pilot said we lost the back of the plane long before we hit the water. Could he have survived it? We survived after all. Was there a chance he was out there too?

She dabbed with a soft gauze, and I tried to remember the crash. Had I looked back for him? Was he in his seat? Would he have tried to come to me when the plane began to go down?

This thought conjured up a barrage of nightmare scenarios where Chris had unfastened his seatbelt and died violently. Image after image of possible deaths plate on repeat: Chris crushing his skull as the plane lurched forward, Chris being sucked out into thin air or being engulfed in flames...

I'd spent the night convinced he was alive somewhere on the ocean nearby, but as the daylight showed an infinite vacant blue surrounding us, I couldn't help but picture his death over and over.

I was jerked back to the present when Lilly pressed the sticky edges of the zip stitch to each side of the gash in my forehead. From the placement, I gathered the cut had gone from the center of my forehead all the way to my temple.

Again, Jack squeezed my hand, and as she pulled each zip closed, I squeezed back; the sensation of a million tiny needles piercing my skull.

"Ok." She exhaled as if she'd been holding her breath the entire time. "What now?"

"See if ye' can warsh 'at blood off her face and then put one of 'em bandages over the stitches."

She looked back at me, lightly touching the stitching. "Does it hurt?"

"No," I whispered, attempting to make a face that appeared unscathed by it all. "Thank you."

She dipped a piece of bandaging into the salt water and used it to wipe the blood off my forehead, eyebrows, cheeks, and nose. "That's a lovely necklace," she said. "My name's Lilly. What's yours?"

I wrapped my fingers around the small pendant. "Alaina."

She looked up over my head. "And you?"

"Jack."

She narrowed her eyes at him. "Don't I know you?"

He coughed gently, my ribs protesting at the motion. "No."

I'd forgotten Jack was the same person I'd watched in the airport; the same smug celebrity who'd been short with me on the airplane just hours prior. How irrelevant his fame was out here.

"I'm Bruce," said the man who'd been lying belly up in the raft's floor, raising one arm up in the air. "Bruce Dietrich."

"Dietrich?" the man with cracked glasses echoed, breathing heavily through his nose. "As in Dietrich's on Fifth?"

Bruce smiled. "That's me."

"Phil Ramsey," he said, "from Ramsey and Wendell. Our law firm often has you cater our events. This is my son Kyle." He patted the leg of the curly haired teenager at his side.

"Almost finished," Lilly assured me, taping a fresh bandage over the stitching.

I'd watched her confidence grow as she'd worked on me and was proud of her for so swiftly transitioning from the shivering girl afraid of blood to the polite caretaker.

Once the tape was secure, she spun around and made her way back to the first aid kit in the raft's corner, tilting her head toward the older couple next to her. "These are my grandparents, Bud and Bertie." She inspected the thin man who'd talked her through the stitching. "What's your name?"

"Jim." He wiggled a little where he sat. "Will somebody come over here'n take this damn thing off me?" He nudged the life vest with his chin. "I cain't move my arms else I'd do it myself."

The large woman on his left unwrapped her arms from the little girl and gently laid her off to the side. The raft lurched as she moved to sit in front of him, and he raised his face off his chest to smile up at her. "Well, haaay big mama."

"My name is Magna," she scolded with a deep Polynesian accent, carefully choosing her words as she spoke them. "Are you sure you want to be taking this off right now? What you going to do if you fall out?"

"PFFT. I'll be just fine, thank ye' verra' much. I cain't breathe with this damn thing on. "

"What's the matter with your arms?" she asked, eyeing him warily.

"Well," he closed one eye, "I don't rightly know. Cain't move 'em so I'm thinkin' they're broke."

"I don't know if you should be sitting here with no life vest on and two broken arms," she said, feeling around for broken bones.

"You're prolly' right." He winced as her fingers worked down his forearms. "But I'll take my chances breathin' in here and risk drownin' out there at another time."

As Magna and Lilly removed his life vest, I let my eyes close and my body unclench, realizing as I did so I was still squeezing Jack's hand. For the second time in twenty-four hours, I released my death grip on him.

"Sorry... I can move," I offered shyly, "if you're too hot."

His voice was warm against my ear as he whispered, "I'm fine. I've broken my ribs before, and you need to stay upright. I don't think you're in any condition to be able to do that on your own. Really, I don't mind."

I sighed in relief. I didn't want to move. My ribs ached, my head was split in two, and despite the rising sun, I was freezing. Jack's body was the only sense of comfort I had to cling to, and despite the guilt I felt for being pressed up against a man that wasn't my husband, I was grateful for his body heat in that moment. I laid my head back against his chest, noticing the faint rattle in his lungs with every inhale.

"Your lungs sound terrible," I said between us.

"Just took in a bit too much water in the storm." He coughed softly. "I'm fine."

I took my own deep breath, grateful for the ability to do so smoothly, and felt something different about the air. It seemed somehow lighter than it ever had before. It tasted different and it smelled... like nothing. It was strange to me that the air—air that I'd never noticed as having a distinct smell—was now so suddenly devoid of its scent. I took another deep breath, basking in the cleanness of the oxygen as it filled my lungs.

"There's something in the water!" Lilly screeched, causing all of us to jump.

I tried to focus in the direction she pointed, but the sunlight blended with the fever and forced my eyes shut. *'Please, let it be Chris,'* I prayed.

"Grab 'at paddle, and see if ye' can get us closer, darlin. They's another paddle in the bag!'"

I heard the sliding and shifting of legs against rubber and felt the raft pull in a different direction. "What is that?" Lilly panted. "Is it people? HELLO?!"

'Oh, please, let it be Chris!' I pried my eyes open and squinted as we paddled toward several dark specs on the water.

"It ain't people." Jim wiggled up onto his knees, causing the little girl to stir. "It's... luggage."

Lilly and Magna paddled harder. Through my blurred vision, I could just make out the distinct square edges of several suitcases bobbing against the raft.

"Get evra one of 'em you can," Jim said, his arms still slack at his sides while he watched Lilly pull in a large black suitcase. "We'll be needin' anything and everything we can get if they don't find us soon."

'If they find us at all...'

The little girl frowned, her eyes filling with tears as she scanned the raft over and over. "Ma—Mama? MAMAAAA?!" She burst into screaming tears.

"Ay Sis," Jim sat back down beside her with a thud that rocked the raft to one side. Lilly grunted as this caused her to lose her grip on the second suitcase. "It's alright, hush 'at hollerin' now, come on. You're alright."

But the girl didn't quiet, nor did she acknowledge him. She let her head fall back and wailed hysterically.

"Come on now, sugar," Jim cooed, leaning over to nudge her with his shoulder. "It's gonna be alright."

She remained unaffected by Jim's attempts to sooth her and proceeded to sob, her breath hitching between each howl.

Lilly pulled in a third suitcase. "Hey," she called breathlessly. One hand still on the case, she reached over to touch the girl's foot. "Hey sweetie, can you tell me your name?"

The girl wouldn't acknowledge her, either. She cried even louder, raising an octave and splitting my already aching head in two.

Magna slid over to her, scooping her up against her chest. "It's okay. It'll be okay. Shhh…" She rocked gently, and while the girl continued to sob, her volume gradually decreased. "Your mama's probably out there right now looking for you, my sweet girl. She'll find you soon, and until then, we'll take care of you." She spoke tenderly, rocking back and forth until the girl's cries were reduced to small sniffles. "Let me see you." She pulled the girl away to look at her face. "What's your name, baby?"

The girl stared at her, bewildered.

Lilly smiled sweetly, pulling in another case. "My name's Lilly. Can you tell me your name?"

The girl again said nothing and Lilly's eyes shifted to me as she raised her shoulders, resigned and confused as to what to do next.

The girl's attention followed and her eyes grew wide as she took in my blood soaked clothing.

I smiled in an attempt to neutralize my appearance, but it was too late. Her lip quivered and fresh tears spilled down her cheeks. She didn't bellow this time, but whimpered pitifully, terrified to be left alone with strangers.

"Ay," Jim nudged her again with his shoulder. "Looky here."

At this, she looked up at him, cautious as she curled both arms around herself.

He crossed his eyes and grinned at her, then let one eye navigate around in a hilarious circle while the other held still.

She studied him, unsure of how to respond.

"I know you's fixin' to smile." He grinned wide. "Come on, let's see a smile." He went cross-eyed again, rotating the other eye in a loop.

The corner of her mouth raised ever so slightly at this, but then she let it fall.

Lilly wheezed as she pulled in two suitcases; one a bright pink hard case and the other navy blue.

"Mi—MINE!" The girl reached both arms out toward the pink case, her eyes lighting up at the promise of something familiar.

Lilly examined the tag on the handle. "Isobel. Your name is Isobel?"

The girl didn't respond or look away from the baggage, but only stretched her arms further out and grunted.

Lilly slid the suitcase over to her and she hastily unzipped it, pushing the top open with both hands and rummaging through a mountain of pink, yellow, and purple fabrics. She combed quickly through the clothes and pulled out an unraveling flowered blanket.

Inhaling the fabric deeply, the tension faded from her little shoulders. Apparently deciding Jim wasn't a threat, she nestled her head against his side, pulled the blanket to her cheek, stuck her thumb in her mouth, and closed her eyes.

Jim smiled at her. "There ye' go, lil Sis. Ye' gonna' be alright now." He smirked at me, one thick brow raised high on his forehead. "Ay Hoss, that purdy wife of yers is gettin' a ginger tan if ye' know what I mean... We don't get some shade on her soon she'll be laid up with a sunburn for days."

"He's not my husband," I corrected defensively, squinting until the throbbing that speaking had caused eased.

"Was there a—"

Jack's words were cut short by a coughing fit he couldn't stifle. He held me away from his chest as he choked to a gag. Evening out his breath, he cleared his throat and proceeded hoarsely, "Was there a canopy in that bag?"

I shivered at the sudden loss of his body heat. He kept me upright by my upper arms while he tensed in preparation of a potential new cough attack. Recognizing my chill, he moved his hands rapidly up and down my bare arms, attempting to warm me.

It was a sweet gesture and I felt suddenly guilty for having been so defensive for being mistaken as his wife. He didn't owe me his care, but he gave it nonetheless, and I needed to be grateful for whatever kindness I had in these dire circumstances. I could feel my fever rising. Without their help, I wasn't entirely sure I'd live through the night.

Magna plucked up the bag from her side and rummaged through it. She pulled out a clear plastic bag with a red fabric wound tightly inside. "This says canopy." She held it out toward him.

"Ay Hoss, why don't ye' trade places with me. I can keep her from tumpin' over for a bit. Ye' can help get that canopy on 'for we all get burnt to shit."

Chapter Five

The morning turned to afternoon quickly. We all rocked on the water, listening for sounds of a boat motor or helicopter while Anna finished stitching up our pilot and Phil. Jim had wiggled his way around me so Jack, Magna, Bud, and Lilly could attach the raft's canopy. He'd remained there, too exhausted, I assumed, to relocate again.

Both of his arms were splinted at the elbow, thanks to Lilly, and he balanced them on his bent legs on each side of me to keep me from falling over. I was appreciative for the solidness of his chest beneath my head as I teetered in and out of consciousness, my eyes closing and long gaps of time being lost in what only played like seconds.

"Yer hotter than Satan's house-cat, ye' know that?" he whispered, pulling me from my befuddled state and breaking what felt like hours of silence between us. "Ay Princess," he called to Lilly, "look in 'at first aid kit again and see if they's any kind of Tylenol. She's burnin' up."

"Oh my God," Anna gasped beside us, staring wide-eyed down at the teenage boy. With his lack of complaints, we'd assumed Kyle's injuries were minor. Anna had made the rounds and saved him for last. Now she sat, holding her hand to her mouth as she inspected what once resembled an arm. Bits of bone, flesh, and muscle protruded from his thin lower arm.

The sight made my already dizzy head spin even further.

She swept her palm over his forehead. "Jesus, you're burning up. Why didn't you tell me you were hurt this bad?"

His voice wavered from high to low as it battled against pubescent hormones, thirst, and a rising fever. "I didn't know. I just thought I cut it. Is it bad?"

She clicked her tongue and shook her head, grimacing at the arm. "I don't... I don't know if I can fix this..."

"What do you mean you can't fix it?!" Phil asked hatefully beside her. "Just set the bone and stitch him up. I thought you said you were a nurse?"

"Take it easy," Jim warned behind me. "She's doin' the best she can."

"*You* don't tell me what to do!" Phil's voice raised as panic swept over him and he returned his attention to Anna. "Tell me you can set the bone and stitch him up?"

"It's not that simple." Her voice quivered. "This is more than just a broken bone and a cut. The tendons.... The muscles... it's all severed... and with what I have here... there's no way for me to reattach it... We're gonna have to..." She swallowed hard and met Phil's eyes.

"No. Absolutely not!" Phil shook his head, pointing his finger at her face. "You have no right to make that decision."

"Phil, I understand you're concerned, but if I don't, he could die. Would you rather your son died?"

"If you don't what?" Kyle looked up at them, his tired blue eyes begging for relief.

"Kyle, honey," she softened her tone, "your arm... we—"

"I said NO!" Phil grabbed her by the upper arm and pulled her away from Kyle, positioning himself between them on his knees. "We'll wait for rescue."

"Hey now." Jack slid across the raft, resting his palm at the center of Phil's chest. "There's no need to put your hands on her." For the first time, I noticed just how large Jack was as his massive upper body towered over Phil's.

Phil smacked his hand away, but wisely adjusted his tone. "That's my son. It's for me to say what happens to him. I can't just let her... No. We'll wait for help to come."

"Phil," Anna insisted calmly, "if we don't—

"It's okay, dad." Kyle swayed with the raft, blinking until he could focus his eyes on Anna. "You have to cut it off?"

Anna nodded, careful not to make eye contact with Phil.

He swallowed. "Will it hurt?"

Anna again nodded her head. "Yes. But if I don't do it, you could die."

"Well…" He sighed, incredibly calm for a boy his age to have been handed that kind of news. "I don't want to die."

"And we can't hold off for rescue?" Jack asked. "Wait a day or two? Surely, someone will find us by then?"

"No," Anna said. "We could risk infection and more complex circulatory issues the longer we wait. If I do this now, he'll only lose his lower arm. If we wait, he could lose far more."

There was a long silence as we all processed the weight of what was to come.

Kyle broke that silence, putting on a brave face. "Let's get it over with then."

"Ye'r one tough sonofabitch." Jim joked, easing the tension in us all. "Balls of steel, kid. I couldn't do it. Ye'd have to pin me down and knock me out."

Kyle laughed at that, showing his big crooked front teeth as his eyes darted to Lilly and back. "I wouldn't mind being knocked out."

"Lilly," Anna cleared her throat, "did you find any pain killers or fever reducers in that first aid kit?"

Lilly once again rummaged through the first aid kit, squinting to make out the labels in the poor lighting. The daylight beat down on the red fabric, cloaking us all in a dim pink hue. "There's some Ibuprofen, but only four of them."

Magna perked up, touching a suitcase at her side. "Maybe there's something in these bags. Tourists always bring a pharmacy with them."

"Good call." Anna nodded. "See if you can find anything that might knock him out and any kind of fever-reducer for Alaina."

Bud and Bertie both reached for suitcases and began unzipping as Lilly and Jack did the same.

Within seconds, the raft became littered with suits and skirts of all colors, bikinis and swim trunks, toiletry bags and hair dryers— the personal belongings of people less fortunate than us.

They found a few bags of soggy chips and a bottle of Dr. Pepper in one, a carton of cigarettes and a lighter in another that Jim drooled over, lots of travel sized soaps and shampoos, and an inventory of brightly colored flip-flops.

"Jackpot." Lilly grinned, pulling a freezer bag full of orange and white prescription bottles from the front compartment of a red suitcase. She fished the bottles out one by one, holding them against the light to read each label until she found what she'd been searching for. "Hydrocodone Acetaminophen.. Isn't that Norco?"

Anna smiled in relief. "Yes. That should do it *and* knock out the fever. Give her a half of one and some water." She tilted her head toward me. "And give me the bottle."

Lilly followed her orders, breaking a pill in half, then extending her arm to me with the pill and a small silver packet with a label that read *"Emergency Drinking Water."* She crawled to Anna and handed her a bag of water along with the pill bottle.

As Anna administered the pills to Kyle, Lilly stared at the water in my hand, pulling her lips in to wet them. "Can I have one of these waters, too?"

"We need to figure out how we want to ration these," Jack said beside her. He sat with his forearm rested on one knee, carefully breathing between words to avoid coughing. With the heat, he'd removed his life vest, as had the rest of us—excluding Phil, who appeared more terrified of the water than his injuries. "We all need it. I've been taking inventory. There are thirteen of us here and ninety-six of these little four-ounce bags. We can go roughly seven days on a bag each per day or fourteen on half a bag a day with a few bags left over for emergency rations. How do we want to ration them?"

"Seven days…" Lilly repeated in a daze, her hands hovering over the bag. "Do you really think we could be out here that long?"

Jim huffed. "They'll think we're dead, princess. We've drifted too far. No ones findin' us in this Got damned water."

Jim's mood had gradually grown sour as the temperature in the canopy rose higher—even higher for him with my fevered body pressed up against his. "Half rations and pray the Good Lordt pushes us across a shipping route."

At this, Lilly's eyes grew wide. "They'll be looking for us... Won't they? They can't just leave us to die out here. My dad wouldn't let that happen. They'll send a search party..."

"You can bet your ass they'll send a search party, sweetheart," Jim continued, "but they won't be looking for us. They'll be lookin' for the plane or parts of it. If I had to guess, it's about half past three, and the search party done found whatever parts could be found since I ain't heard nothin' but ocean and ain't seen nothin' but ocean all day. They ain't found us by now, they ain't gonna."

"Jim," Jack cleared his throat, "maybe just a hint of compassion." He glanced at Lilly, whose expression had shifted to complete trepidation.

"Now, I ain't gonna' sit here and sugarcoat it for nobody, Hoss." I could feel his body tense up behind me. "We gonna' have to fend for ourselves now... figure out a way to get *ourselves* out of this hellhole."

Lilly slowly shook her head in disbelief. "But... there's barely any food... how are we supposed to survive out here on two ounces of water a day? That's not enough... is it? We'll die out here... They've got to find us. They've *got* to."

"Listen sugar, *they* ain't comin." He sighed, "We're in the middle of the Pacific and the odds are against us. We gonna' need to figure out a sense of direction and head in one. While we do, you go on ahead and do what you want with your water. I'll do what I want with mine."

"Easy now. You know that won't work," Jack argued, his raised voice forcing a single gurgling cough to escape as he reached over for the survival pack. "We all take equal amounts and we have to determine what those are. If one has more and we run short, it'll be a fight for water that won't end well for anyone involved. I say half rations unless it rains, then we recalculate. If one person drinks more, we all do."

"The middle of the Pacific," Lilly repeated under her breath, eyes still wide as she wrapped her arms around her knees. "We're going to die and no one's going to find us."

Feeling the situation going south fast, I leaned forward and reached over—wincing as I did so—to touch her arm. "No one's dying today, love." I forced a smile, despite the burning pain in my ribs. "Look at us. We survived an airplane crash. Anyone should be so lucky to beat those odds. If we can survive that, we can survive this."

As I said the words, I swallowed them *hard*. It was highly unlikely we had survived; it'd be unlikelier still that the people in the back of the plane would be as lucky.

In all the time we'd been floating, even with visions of him cracking his skull or burning in his seat, I'd never fully accepted that Chris was actually dead. He *couldn't* be. My fearless husband couldn't possibly be killed in that crash while I lived through it. Could he?

I could feel the panic welling up in my throat but forced it back down. Now wasn't the time to fall apart—not yet.

Jack reached into the pack and pulled out several bags of emergency water. "Are we all agreed on half?"

Those that could all nodded in agreement, and he handed out one bag per person, the raft lurching and bobbing as he made the rounds. Bruce couldn't raise himself up and lifted only his head to take a few sips before laying back down.

Jack stopped last in front of us with Jim's share, eyeing his splinted arms. "How do you wanna do this?"

"Don't reckon ye' got a straw now, do ya?"

"Nope." Jack ripped the bag open. "You... ah.... You want me to just pour it?"

I felt Jim raise his shoulders in a shrug, and Jack brought the bag to his lips.

"Little more," he breathed, and Jack indulged him, tipping the bag up and back, his eyes meeting mine for a fleeting instant when he sat back on his heels. Resealing the bag, he began to return to his spot when Jim interjected.

"Now hold on one second there, Hoss. Where ye' goin' with my share?"

Taken aback, Jack spun on his knee. "I'm taking it back to the bag with the rest of them. You got a problem with it?"

"Who the hell made you head bean counter?"

Jack laughed. "Head what now?"

"Ye' know, the head honcho, big Kahuna, Grand Puba."

After much struggle with my wet fingers, I managed to get my own bag open. I popped the half tablet into my mouth, brought the bag to my chapped lips, and drank.

Water had never tasted so heavenly. I held it in my mouth, letting it moisten my dry tongue—my dry *everything*—and closed my eyes when I swallowed, goosebumps running over my skin as it wet my aching throat. It took all my willpower to stop halfway and zip the bag closed.

Jack tilted his head to one side as the squabble continued. "Well, I don't think you're in any condition to play *Grand Puba* at the moment, Jim, but I'd be happy to relinquish the title. I'm just trying to look out for us all, and someone needs to be managing the rations to keep track. Should we put it to a vote?"

"Just give him the damn water," I groaned, my eyes so heavy with the headache I could barely hold them open.

"No. You go right on ahead and ration the water, but you set mine right here where I can see it."

Reluctantly, Jack placed the water down next to his feet. "Fine, but if it turns up missing, you won't get another until the day after tomorrow." He took my offered bag, spun on his knees and resumed his place across from us.

Behind me, Jim mimicked him, "iF iT tUrNs uP mIsSiNg…"

"Stubborn sonofabitch," Jack muttered.

"Was there a compass in the bag?" I asked, as much to neutralize the situation as to get a sense of direction and a plan to return home.

Jack abandoned the tiff and reached into the bag, rummaging through it for a moment before pulling out a hard plastic case. He popped the lid to reveal the white face of an embedded circular compass. "There's some fishing gear in there too."

"And what in the Sam Hill we gonna' do if we catch a fish, huh?" Jim scoffed behind me. "Not evra' fish is edible raw, ye' know. 'Side's that, with barely any water, eatin' is only gonna' dehydrate us more."

Lilly ran her palms down her cheeks. "So what do you suggest we do then, smart-ass?"

She lowered her voice to match his tone, tilting her head as she echoed his words, "If *no one's findin' us in this Got damn water*, and *not evra' fish is edible…* and if we *ain't rationing the dang water…* what the hell do you suggest we do???"

"Hell," he blew out. "I don't know."

"He's asleep now." Anna interrupted, checking Kyle's pulse with two fingers at his throat. "I need everyone who's able to help Phil hold him down in case he wakes up. And Lilly, I need you to get fresh bandages ready. I have to do this quick."

Magna, Lilly, Jack, Phil, Bertie, and Bud sprang into action, readying bandages, needle and thread, and positioning themselves around them to take hold of his small body.

Jim and I sat helplessly at the side of them watching with Bruce as they prepared for amputation. The pill I'd taken was beginning to kick in and I could feel the raft spinning around me; my head growing heavier on my shoulders as the tension in them eased.

"Okay," Anna's voice quivered from behind the wall of bodies that obstructed her from my view. "Here goes."

I heard Kyle cry out; an unearthly, guttural scream that made my entire body stiffen. The raft jounced heavily as the group scrambled to keep him held down. I heard them scuffling, could feel the movement of the raft beneath me, but their voices became further and further away as my eyelids grew heavier—shades of yellow taking over my vision. This time, I welcomed the dark void of unconsciousness, hoping to find my husband inside it.

Chapter Six

I was in my apartment, pacing back and forth from the small nook that was considered a kitchen to the adjacent living room and back. Chris would be there any minute.

It'd been three days since we'd parted ways at the diner and my stomach had been in knots for the hours leading up to that moment.

We'd spoken, of course. He'd called five minutes after I'd left the diner.

"You didn't kiss me," I'd said when I answered.

"What's that now?" He half-laughed.

"I wanted you to kiss me," I insisted.

"Oh… well…" he paused, "where are ya? You can't be far. I can fix this."

"No no," I joked, "It's too late now. I'm already getting on the freeway."

"Well then," he cleared his throat, "I guess I'll have to drive fast."

"You'd never catch me. I'm too fast. You're just going to have to ask me out again."

Without a pause, he answered. "How's Tuesday?"

For the three straight nights in between we had talked, staying up late into the morning hours with the phones pressed to our ears. The anticipation of seeing his face was almost more than I could bear. I fluffed the little blue and yellow throw pillows on the couch for the fifth time, straightened the scented candles on the coffee table, and checked the roast in the oven for signs of burning just to be safe.

After so many nights on the phone, I'd decided to surprise him by cooking what I'd learned was his favorite meal—pot roast—and hoped the gesture didn't seem too forward for a first date.

I lit the candles on my tiny two person table, turned on some Billie Holiday, and stood looking around the confined space that was my kitchen-living room.

'He builds houses, he's going to hate this place,' I thought as I observed the fake parquet linoleum floor that divided the kitchen from the living room carpet. The baby blue kitchen cabinets had definitely seen better days. Two of them, I noticed for the first time, were hanging slightly crooked.

The carpet was thankfully spotless. I'd borrowed my mother's carpet cleaner and, cutting our call a little shorter the night before, stayed awake turning what was once a dull tan back into white.

On top of the carpet, I'd placed a simple blue and tan Persian rug I'd found at a thrift store, an off-white couch adorned with yellow and baby blue pillows, a mismatched table to each side and an antique coffee table with several candles as a centerpiece to bring it all together. This all sat in front of a built-in entertainment center which housed a TV that was about two times too small for its opening, and shelves overflowing with my extensive collection of books.

There was a knock at the door and my whole body tingled with anticipation.

I ran toward it and stopped short at the foyer. By foyer, I of course mean more fake parquet linoleum to separate the entry from the living room carpet. I checked the mirror to tame the wisps of hair I had worked so hard to keep straight.

Hair intact, *and looking quite good*, I walked to the door, caught my breath, and opened it.

I inhaled, and before I could exhale, he stepped forward, one hand sliding down my hair to rest on my cheek as the other slid round my waist and scooped me up toward him. He pulled my face an inch from his, and I could feel his breath warm on my lips when he whispered, "I wanted to kiss you too."

His lips met mine immediately, tender at first, but as he parted them, they grew warmer. Wrapping my arms around his neck, I let out a sigh against his mouth, letting him guide me out of the doorway to the middle of the living room.

His hand glided from my cheek to the back of my head, and he wrapped his fingers in my hair to deepen the kiss. My body formed to his—my *everything* melted against him—and he wound his arm around my back to pull me closer.

I was lost entirely in him; every sense heightened as he took over my mouth. He smelled like aftershave and freshly cut wood, tasted like limes and ginger. His height and mass was more significant than I'd remembered, but I fit against him perfectly.

His lips pulled away, but he held my head in place and those deep green eyes searched mine. "Dear God," he said breathlessly, "I'll never not kiss you again."

Not quite ready to be done with the moment, I pulled his mouth back to mine, standing on my tiptoes for better leverage, and softly ran my lips over his once more. "I'd have turned the car around if I knew that was what I was missing." I smiled against his lips, and although my body protested, desperate for more, I released him and stepped back.

He really was beautiful, towering over me in his white button-up shirt and dark blue jeans, looking at me like he was about to devour me. My tiny apartment looked that much smaller with him in it.

'Don't mess this up,' I thought to myself, *'Do not sleep with this man... yet. Three dates, Alaina. Three dates minimum.'*

He was holding yellow lilies—my favorite—in his left hand that I hadn't noticed. "You brought me flowers?" I asked.

He stared still, but his mouth curled into a smile. "You made me pot roast?"

I batted my eyes and nodded.

"You're a hell of a sight to take in, Alaina." He offered the flowers to me. "Those eyes, I've dreamt of nothing else since Saturday."

I blushed a little and took the lilies, waving him to follow as I took the couple steps to the kitchen to fill a vase. "You had the same effect on me, ya know." Turning the sink on to fill the glass vase I'd pulled from the cabinet, I smiled. "I don't think I've ever looked forward to anything more than opening that door and finding you on the other side. I'm afraid I've become slightly enamored with you, Mr. Grace."

He sat down at my kitchen table and let out a long breath. "Oh good, so can we just skip the whole cat-and-mouse bit?"

Without making eye contact, I set the vase on the table and spun round to take the roast out of the oven.

"I'm not patient enough to play the mouse," I said matter-of-factly, setting the little dutch oven on the counter with my back to him. "If I want to be caught, you'll catch me."

He laughed at that, the deep sound igniting a fire deep inside my core. I definitely couldn't play the mouse with *him*.

"So what happened to the drummer?" He asked as I pulled the lid from the pot to release a rolling plume of steam along with the aroma of beef and rosemary.

I giggled, placing a serving of meat and vegetables on each plate. "The poor guy didn't know what hit him. He got off the stage and was so confused when I wasn't there to tell him what a superb job he did."

I pulled out the silverware drawer, wincing as it fell off its track like it tended to do daily. "He called several times while we were at breakfast."

Digging out two knives and two forks from the drawer, I jiggled it loudly back on its track until it closed with a thunk.

"I don't think he was too concerned, though." I circled him to place the two plates on the table. "I do believe I heard a woman's voice in the background when I finally called him back the next morning to let him down."

He stared at me with the same intensity he had the first night, his attention unwavering while I took my seat across from him and picked up my silverware. "Sounds like a real winner. Glad I stole you away."

Picking up his fork and knife, his attention was pulled from me only once he'd taken a bite that forced his eyes closed. "Oh my God, that's good."

"Oh, I know." I grinned. "Lucky for you, your favorite food is the one thing I actually know how to cook."

"That's fine by me, Ally. I could eat this meal every day for the rest of my life and be perfectly happy."

I tilted my head. "Ally?"

He sipped his wine. "You don't like it?"

"Oh no, it's fine." I smiled. "No one's ever called me that before. I like it, though. Much better than some of the other pet names I've been called."

"Such as?"

I laughed. "So many... let's see... there's been the classic *'babe'* a few times, Lainey, A.J., Mac, Freckles, and the *dreaded* Red."

"Don't ever call her Red, check," he said playfully, scooping up another bite. "And A.J.?"

I sipped my own wine. "Alaina Jane. My family calls me A.J."

We ate slowly, talking about past loves and adventures for hours, searching each other's eyes and body language for confirmation of feelings we both already knew we had.

I knew I loved him right then, sitting at my kitchen table. I loved him completely. But the little bit of mouse in me told me not to say so just yet.

The conversation and the wine flowed hours past dinner, and as the kitchen candles burned low, he stood and held his hand out to me. I took it and he pulled me into a very close and slow dance while Billie Holiday's *'I'll be seeing you'* poured out of my small kitchen speaker.

"Stay with me," I whispered, standing on my toes to reach his ear.

"I don't wanna rush this," he said back in mine, turning us slowly.

"Not for that." I laid my head against his chest. "Just stay and be next to me. Nothing more."

I could feel his lips press against the top of my head, then he laid his cheek against my crown. "I don't think I could resist the possibility of more."

"I can, though." I lied, "I'm not ready to say goodbye to you yet."

He held me closer, resting his head on mine for the duration of the song. As the final notes rang out, he spun me out of his embrace. I held his hand and leaned over to blow out the candles, tugging him toward the bedroom door.

"I really shouldn't stay," he said, stopping us before we could cross to the other side. "But, I'm not ready to say goodbye to you, either. Wait one second."

Grabbing the throw blanket from the back of the couch, he draped it over my shoulders. "I have an idea."

He plucked up the wine bottle and our two glasses from the table. "It's a beautiful night. Let's take a walk."

Without a moment's hesitation, I snagged my keys, pulled the blanket tight over my shoulders, and led him out the door.

We walked arm in arm the few blocks from my apartment to the lakefront and found a quiet little spot in the sand near the museum. He poured us each a glass of wine, and we huddled together under the blanket, looking out at the lake as the city behind us fell asleep.

The moon's reflection danced on the water as we opened our hearts to each other, talking about family and philosophy until the rising sun's orange glow replaced the moon's silver glimmer on the water's surface.

He made his way to a sitting position behind me and wrapped his arms and the blanket around me. I laid my head back against him and shut my eyes, completely content in the moment. I drifted off to sleep while listening to the waves as they rolled gently to and from our shore.

As my mind slipped into sleep, I felt my heart screaming out to him, *'I love you,'* and on a sigh, just as I drifted away, my mouth exhaled the words—too faint to be audible, but loud enough to warm my entire body.

Chapter Seven

I could still hear the waves when I began to rouse. The sun was warm on my eyelids and I felt his breath rising and falling against my back. My head was pounding, and, not quite ready to open my eyes, I sighed and turned my cheek a little to rest more easily against his chest, running my hands up his arms where they encircled me.

I felt like I was floating…

Wait… I *was* floating, and I tasted… salt?

My eyes opened abruptly, and I jerked myself forward in a panic, escaping the arms of Jack Volmer, pain running like lightning down my side.

"What the hell are you doing?" The raft bobbed in protest as I spun around to face him.

Jack blinked back, startled and looking somewhat annoyed. He cleared his throat and responded in a low gravelly voice, "Keeping you upright."

"You passed out and have been asleep since yesterday," Anna informed me, suddenly at my side with a hand on my arm.

The raft rocked again as I dodged her hands, ignoring the pain in my side as I crawled haphazardly to the canopy's opening and leaned out toward the water; feverish emotions surfacing and rendering me delusional.

"Chris?!" I shouted out to the nothingness, feeling my head split in two as I did so and ignoring it.

"CHRIS?!" I screamed frantically, a lump forming in my throat as fresh, warm tears spilled down my cheeks. I leaned over the side of the raft to get a better look out, nose running and sobbing desperately now.

'You can't be gone. You can't. You're my home, my whole life... Please, please... I promise, I'll be better... please...'

"CHRISTOPHER??!!!" I screamed at the top of my lungs, and my vision blurred—from the tears, and from the sharp pain that had filled my head, my throat, and my heart.

Hands were on my back and arms, softly urging me back. Muffled voices surrounded me, but my eyes darted from one side to the other of the emptiness I looked out into.

'I can't lose you. Not now. Please.. Please come back.' My hands shook and my body shook with them. I inhaled deeply and screamed once more, "CHRIS??!"

I collapsed to sob uncontrollably on my side, not caring who witnessed it. People were touching me—their voices speaking softly above me—but all I could think of was him; all I could hear was him.

'I'll never not kiss you again...'

I still smelled his aftershave in my nose, still tasted his warmth on my lips.

How much time I'd wasted being angry at him... Years we'd both wasted... Precious years I'd never get back now.

I closed my eyes tight and wrapped my arms around my shaking body, trying to conjure up his face in my mind; the strong jawline, the pointed nose, his big green eyes—but every time the image became clear, his face was set in terror as he tumbled in a free fall in the dark storm.

'No, this can't be real. Wake me up, Chris. Please God, wake me up from this.'

With my eyes squeezed shut, I waited for someone to wake me, but no one did. The hands on me caressed, and the voices soothed, muffled and distant as I pressed my eyes tighter shut. I tried to picture him alive on another raft somewhere in the ocean, searching for me as I was him.

'I'm right here. Come find me, love, I'm right here. Come find me and let's not waste another second. I'm so so sorry.'

My body was trembling, and I wept like a child; loud and without restraint. The numbness that had taken over me dissolved into sharp pains down my side and across my eyelids, and I sobbed harder—in pain, both physically and in every depth of my soul.

'I'll never not kiss you,' he'd said, and it echoed in my mind over and over.

"Shhh," said a voice above me, stroking my damp hair as it pooled in the inch of water on the raft's bottom.

Larger hands gripped my arms. "We have to set you upright now." This was said by the all-too-familiar voice of Jack.

I didn't want to be set upright. I didn't want to *be* anything. All I wanted was my husband, my life; my heart. I wanted to shut out the world around me and go back to the lakeshore, but I couldn't get back. I couldn't shut off the sounds of their voices, the pull of Jack's arms, or the taste of saltwater on my lips.

I allowed myself to be dragged into the present and this new, harsh reality I was trapped. inside. Opening my eyes, I found myself face to face with Jack.

Maybe it was the fact that I'd watched him for nine seasons as a teenager, or maybe it was that we'd sat together and crashed together that made him less a stranger to me than the rest. Whatever the reason, I didn't like how familiar we were becoming; didn't like the feel of his arms around me where Chris's should've been; didn't like his eyes on me right then, watching as my heart shattered to pieces.

It was irrational to be angry at him, but I was, and because I needed to feel any emotion other than the devastation that had been consuming me, I let it all spew out right then.

"You," I narrowed my eyes at him, "don't touch me again."

Taken aback, his face turned stony. "Excuse me?"

I huffed and wiped the tears from my face, well aware of the others' eyes on me. "You heard me."

"You can sit right here, pretty lady." Jim winked, showing his teeth in a wide crocodile grin.

My face was on fire and my eyes remained locked with Jack's. "You don't know me and I don't know you. You don't get to touch me." My voice cracked as tears overtook me. "Not like that."

"Hey..." He held his hands out in front of him, his voice hoarse. "I wasn't the one snuggling up against you and moaning in *my* sleep."

My face flushed and my nostrils flared. "You son-of-a—"

"Alright, alright," Anna placed her hand on my back. "Just sit back now, Alaina." She led me up against the raft, opposite Jack. "You've still got a fever and you need to keep those ribs straight. I'm pretty sure you also have a concussion so try to calm down now and relax."

Lilly slid to my side, smoothing the hair from my face. "It's alright now," she cooed, smiling. "Tell me about Chris. Who is he?"

I exhaled, shivering as I straightened my spine. The canopy was hot and sticky, but my bones were cold and limp. "He was—*is* my husband. We got separated on the plane. He was sitting in the back."

Her expression shifted to pure terror, and she quickly looked down at her hands.

"What?!" I demanded. "Did you see what happened to them?"

She shook her head but would not meet my eyes. "No..."

"You saw something... tell me." My heart raced. "Please."

She spread her fingers out on her lap. "I can't..."

"Please," I begged, "just tell me if you think they could've lived?"

She shook her head. "I don't—I don't know..."

"You know something, though. Please don't leave me wondering if there's a chance he's out there... I'm begging you. Not knowing if he's alive or dead is eating me alive."

"He's dead," Phil interrupted, staring off at the horizon. "The back of the plane broke off and exploded. I saw it all, like it was in slow motion. No one could've survived that explosion."

"Oh." I nodded in understanding, swallowing the lump in my throat and lowering my eyes to hide the tears that welled in them.

Try as I might not to picture Chris burning in his seat, it was an image that played on loop in my mind.

'And there you have it, Alaina. Chris is dead. And it's all your fault.'

I closed my eyes and imagined his face. I saw his eyes as he reluctantly agreed to the trip—knew it was a last-ditch effort to salvage our marriage before we would get the divorce I was sure he wanted.

Maybe I should've let him talk that day. He'd at least be alive... I'd at least get to see him on occasion in passing.

The thought of never looking upon his face again felt like someone had placed my heart in a vice and twisted its lever until all the blood spilled out of me.

Who was I without him? Did I even want to know?

For the past few years, I wasn't sure I could keep living with him, but now, I was pretty certain I couldn't go on living without him.

Feeling everyone's eyes on me, my cheeks burned hotter. I stared down at my hands, pleading in my heart they'd let me be.

The pointed edge of a cowboy boot slid into my field of vision and the foot flexed to nudge mine. I looked up at Jim, and he bobbed his eyebrows at me. "Ay, ye' wanna see what I can do?"

Without waiting for my response, he opened his mouth and rolled his tongue in a circle, straightened it, and rolled it again in the opposite direction. Again, his big bushy eyebrows bounced and he grinned widely at me. "Eh? Ye' wanna come sit next to Jimbo? Ye' can moan in your sleep all ye' want an' you won't hear nary a peep outta me."

At this, the tension in my shoulders eased, and I laughed a little, despite myself. Kyle, who was seated next to him, laughed as well, the remaining upper part of his arm wrapped tightly in bandages.

"Oh, Kyle!" I blinked back the tears and attempted to compose myself, feeling even more embarrassed for having caused such a scene after all he'd been through. "You're okay?"

Jim beamed at him. "This little summbitch is tougher than a two-dollar steak, I tell ye."

Kyle giggled, lowering his eyes. "I'm okay."

My cheeks were officially on fire. "Does it hurt? I'm so sorry! I didn't mean..."

Jim winked at me. "He's all hopped up on the good stuff. Been high as a Georgia pine all day."

At this, I observed Kyle's overall demeanor. He was far too relaxed and had a euphoric, far-off grin affixed to his face. "I feel good. Got a good story to tell, too!"

"The ladies will love it." Lilly made a kissy face at him. "You got a girlfriend back home?"

He blushed then, looking down at his lap. "No."

Phil shook his head. "What about your wedding date?"

"A date?!" Lilly echoed, "Oooh! Who is she? What's she like? How'd you meet her? Tell me everything."

"Not just any date," Phil mocked. "His *first* date."

"Dad!" Kyle frowned, his embarrassment showing in his reddened complexion. He rolled his eyes and continued, "Just this girl from school. She's really sweet. We were supposed to go to homecoming together, but I had a dirt bike accident and had to miss homecoming, so dad said I could invite her to the wedding instead. She flew out with her parents separately."

"Aw," Lilly swooned. "Well, now you'll have this really amazing story to tell her."

"Whose wedding?" Anna asked, tilting her head to one side.

Phil straightened. "Oh... what was her name... my wife went to college with her..." He twisted his mouth to one side as he thought about it. "Macy something and..."

"Robert," Anna finished for him, smiling as she attempted to wedge her palm beneath Bruce to get a feel of his spine. "I was going as well."

"You know Robert Harris?" Jack finally spoke, coughing as he did so.

"Oh, yeah." Anna grinned. "Well... sort of. There's a doctor in my ER that I've been seeing, Ben. He and Robert are close. We've gone on a few double-dates with him and Macy. Macy insisted I come to their wedding. Wouldn't take no for an answer. Ben bought me a ticket and here I am. How do you know him?"

"Macy's my sister."

"AH HA!" Anna clapped her hands together. "I *knew* you were Jack Volmer!"

"Wait a minute…" Lilly sat forward, her eyes narrowed in his direction as she put the pieces together. "Jack Volmer…. OH!!!! That's how I know you! You're the guy from that show! Fairview something!" She smiled and batted her eyes. "You're *famous.*"

He lowered his lashes as the entire raft zeroed in on him. Kyle grinned even wider, leaning forward to get a better look at our celebrity.

Jack waved them off. "Not anymore."

"Fairview *Nights*," Anna corrected, her tone just as flirtatious as Lilly's had been. "Elias and Maggie were one of my favorite couples growing up."

He half-smiled, his eyes watering with the effort of holding back another cough.

Lilly grinned, leaning over to touch his arm. "Didn't you date that girl in real life?"

This was news to me and I couldn't help but look at him then, picturing the two of them on Maggie's iconic front porch locked in a kiss. I knew he was uncomfortable, and I felt horrible for contributing to his current predicament, but I was curious too.

He sighed. "Unfortunately."

"Elias?" Jim scoffed. "What the hell kinda name is 'at? Is 'at one of 'em heathen teenage vampire shows?"

"No." Lilly laughed, squinting while she tried to recall the storyline. "They were just regular teenagers… With superpowers?"

Jack blushed, nodding as he rolled his eyes.

Lilly flipped her hair over her shoulder. "Olivia Bishop. That's her name. She was in that movie that won all the awards last year, wasn't she?" She bit her lower lip. "God, she's beautiful. You guys dated for a while, I remember. Why did you break up?"

Kyle perked up at this, swaying heavily as he did so. "You dated Olivia Bishop? She's… like… *ridiculous* hot."

Olivia Bishop *was* ridiculous hot. She had that perfect shimmering hair that was just the right blend of brown and sun-kissed blonde, gorgeous golden tan skin that seemed to glow in even the dullest of lighting, and the biggest brown eyes I'd ever seen.

He shifted uneasily. "It's a long story. I don't really want to talk about it."

"Oh, come on," Lilly pleaded, wrapping both hands around his bicep. "What else are we going to talk about out here?"

Jack shook his head. "Really, it was a long time ago. I don't want to talk about it right now."

"Pleeease?"

"No," he snapped, jerking his arm free of her, and leaving her with a somewhat bewildered expression. "Talk about something else." At this, the coughing fit he'd been holding in took over. He coughed until he gagged, then leaned out the opening of the canopy to spit over the edge.

"Ay Princess," Jim called, "I's on TV once too, want me to tell ye' about it?" He narrowed his eyes at Jack who was concentrating on his breathing.

Anna hovered beside Jack, mindful not to touch him. "Jack, that cough is getting worse. I'm afraid you might have pneumonia or even a punctured lung. You need to sit up straight and relax as well."

Jack nodded, but waved her off as he settled himself against the raft's edge.

"It was the channel five news..." Jim continued even though no one appeared to be listening, "A tornado had come through town and I's caught in the middle of it..."

Chapter Eight

That night, the air was cool and crisp, and the moon shone brightly down on us, illuminating the raft in its blue light. Lilly and Anna sat across from me, leaning against each other under a large men's sweater.

I shivered, bones achy and weak, and I shifted incessantly to find a comfortable—*and warm*—position against the cold wetness of the raft's edge. I felt a soft fabric drape over my arms then, and pulled it around myself as Jack moved to sit propped up beside me.

"I'm sorry for lashing out at you," I whispered.

"Mmhmm," he mumbled.

"No satellites," Jim announced to no one in particular, looking up at the sky.

"What are you talking about now?" Lilly looked up.

"There ain't no satellites. Ye' can normally see 'em on a night clear as this—tons of 'em—soarin' through the stars… I ain't seen a one."

I looked up then, remembering the crystal clear sky in Minnesota and watching satellites as they glided across the infinite canvas of stars. He was right. There wasn't a single satellite up there. Where were they?

"Ye think," he sighed, "well, that wasn't no ordinary storm that hit us… Ye' think we got sucked up into some kind of Bermuda Triangle? Or… ye' think maybe we're dead?"

"I don't think it'd hurt this much if we were dead," Kyle noted.

"Oh, honey." Anna unwrapped herself from the sweater and moved to sit beside him. "Is it bothering you? I think we can give you another pain killer now if you need it."

Kyle nodded.

"Jim," Lilly said, still looking up at the sky while Anna fumbled with the pill bottle beside her, "I have a question I've been meaning to ask you."

"Fire away, darlin.'"

"Well," she hesitated, "I don't mean for this to sound rude, but... what were you doing in first class? Doesn't seem like your style."

Phil laughed haughtily, bulldozing his way into their conversation as he'd tended to do throughout the day. "Don't mean it to be rude?! What else could you have meant by that? Of course it's rude!"

"No," she stuttered, "I meant—

"You meant he didn't belong there," Phil snapped. "You're stuck up and judgmental and that's a very rude thing to ask someone."

"I didn't mean it like that." Her voice raised as she tried to explain herself. "I just meant that he... well, he doesn't seem like... Oh, forget it."

"Oh, no ya don't," Phil continued his barrage. I didn't like his tone, but I didn't entirely disagree with him. "You finish what you started."

"He just," her voice quieted, "doesn't strike me as a person who would pay extra for a first-class ticket is all... I'm sorry, Jim."

"How's your head?" Jack whispered in my ear, his shoulder touching mine when he leaned in.

I jumped at the touch.

"What?" I whispered back, feeling unnerved by his sudden interest in my well-being. He'd remained to himself throughout the day, opting to stay quiet while the rest of us attempted small-talk to pass the time. "It's fine... I'm fine..."

Phil laughed as the conversation continued around us. "You can't follow up a judgmental statement like that with *'I'm sorry.'*" His condescending tone grew louder and more animated. "*Oh, hey guy I just met, you don't seem like you belong in first class... oh, but I'm sorry for saying so.* It's so petty!"

"And your ribs?" Jack asked me in what he evidently hoped would become a private conversation. "Are they still bothering you?"

I shook my head. "Not as much as they were."

"I SAID I DIDN'T MEAN IT LIKE THAT!" Lilly screeched.

"Didn't you?!" Phil countered.

I could see the silhouette of Phil's head across from us, and although I couldn't see them, I could sense his eyes on us—on *me*. Looking for... my approval? I swallowed, suddenly grateful for a private conversation to escape to. I focused on Jack and whispered, "I'll be alright. What's with the nice-guy act?"

Jack tilted his head to one side. "What's that supposed to mean?"

"Well," I turned to face him, "you don't say much, and when you do, you're not very friendly."

"Lilly, honey," Bud said softly, "it *was* a rude question."

Jack cleared his throat and leaned closer. "I didn't realize one was *supposed* to be friendly after their plane crashed out of the sky and left them stranded on the ocean."

"This has been hard for all of us." I let my eyes meet his. "You could at least pretend to be interested in the small talk here and there and stop dismissing anyone who shows an interest in you."

"OK FINE!" Lilly's voice quivered as she broke into tears. "I TAKE IT BACK! I DIDN'T MEAN IT, OK? ARE YOU SATISFIED? I'M A TERRIBLE PERSON FOR ASKING IT!!"

"When have I ever dismissed you?" Jack hissed.

I smirked. "You dismissed me almost instantly when I tried to converse with you on the plane. And then today, you nearly bit poor Lilly's head off when she asked you about Olivia Bishop."

"It's difficult for me to talk to people I don't know."

"You?" I scoffed, "Jack Volmer?! Shy?! I don't buy that for one second."

"Not shy... just cautious I guess." He struggled with a cough that tried to escape him but contained it and continued. "People have never been exactly genuine in wanting to get to know me. Trust doesn't come easy."

"Lilly," Bertie's voice soothed, "don't get so worked up, dear. Sometimes you say things you don't realize are hurtful."

I narrowed my eyes at Jack. "Trust has got nothing to do with being friendly. You don't have to trust us, but you could at least be civil. Who knows how long we'll be stuck together?"

"Jim," Lilly sobbed, "I'm sorry."

Jim smirked. "Oh, it's alright. Ye' ain't exactly wrong, sweetheart."

There was a long silence then. The only sounds between us were the sniffles of Lilly and the water brushing against the edges of the raft as Anna returned to her seat beside her.

Jack sighed and cleared his throat, raising an eyebrow toward me as he announced loudly, "Olivia Bishop had the most rotten breath I've ever smelled."

"GROSS!" Kyle shouted, howling with laughter.

We all laughed out loud and Lilly sat forward, forgetting her exchange with Phil, too excited at the opportunity to gossip. "Really? Is that why you broke up?"

He smiled. "No, but it should've been. We actually had to cut before any kissing scenes so she could rinse with mouthwash first. She smoked like a chimney and drank coffee all day and night to keep herself from overeating. She was a lunatic about her weight... come to think of it, she was a lunatic about most things."

Lilly giggled. "So... why *did* you break up?"

Jack blew out. "Well, she got cast in this independent film, and she left for about a month to shoot in Edinburgh while we were in between filming seasons five and six. I got a call from her about six days after she left saying she'd met someone else."

Lilly gasped. "What a hussy!"

Jack laughed. "I figured out later that the woman's got a nasty habit of sleeping with her co-stars. She was madly in love with the guy in the film... until they were done filming, that is. Since then, she's dated five other actors throughout her career. Even tried to get back together with me when we resumed filming. Made for a very interesting season six."

"Does that happen often?" Kyle asked. "Actors and actresses thinking they're in love or whatever?"

Jack's shoulders rose and fell. "I couldn't say for certain, kid, but it sure worked on me."

Jim tilted his head to one side. "Was it like... a shit smell? Or a sour smell?"

Jack laughed heartily. "Mix both together and you've got Olivia."

Lilly sighed, "I don't think I'll ever be able to watch a movie again without thinking about their breath." She cuddled into Anna beneath the sweater as the wind picked up. "I think you just ruined Roman Holiday for me."

"What's Roman Holiday?" Kyle asked.

Lilly scoffed. "Just the greatest movie ever made."

"Pfft, that ain't the greatest movie ever made, darlin'." Jim shivered. "True Grit, John Wayne. Now *that's* a great movie."

"You're so weird." She opened the sweater and motioned him over. He inched closer and let them cover him with the fabric. "What about you, Jack?" Her teeth chattered between words. "Got a favorite?"

He smiled, shaking a little against the cold himself. "Hands down, the Godfather."

"Ooh, that's a good one." Bud nodded. "One of my favorites."

Lilly giggled. "But not *the* favorite. Their favorite was always Casablanca." She beamed at him. "What about you, Magna?"

Magna wrapped a t-shirt around Isobel and pulled her closer as the wind blew even stronger, the waves gaining strength and rocking the raft. "Gone with the Wind."

Kyle groaned. "Chicks always say that movie. I don't get it."

Lilly rolled her eyes at him. "Ok fine, what's your idea of the perfect movie, Kyle?"

He tilted his head for a moment as he considered. "I don't know. I don't really watch a lot of movies."

"Bullshit," Phil bantered, holding the raft's rope with a death grip as the waves grew more intense. "You watched Indiana Jones on repeat until you were fourteen."

Anna laughed. "Liam recently discovered Indiana Jones. He's obsessed. It's a great movie. I mean... it's no Star Wars, but it's nothing to be ashamed of!"

"And Liam would be...?" I asked.

"Oh, I have a son," she said proudly. "Liam. He's five." She paused and looked out at the water, then quickly shifted the conversation back away from her. "What about you, Alaina? What's your favorite?"

I pulled the dress tighter around my shoulders and shivered. "Jurassic Park."

"Really?" Jack smirked beside me.

"Yes *really*. It's a great movie."

"Hmmf." Phil adjusted his grip on the rope and laid on his side. "Took you for more of a Notebook type girl."

"Oh, the Notebook!" Lilly swooned. "Oh... the breath..." She laid her head against Jim's shoulder. "They're all ruined now."

We all sat in silence then, staring up at the undisturbed sky overhead.

After a while, Bud and Jack clambered around the raft, reattaching the canopy, and everyone gradually lowered themselves to lie on the floor.

Lilly and Anna made a play out of creating a *"Jim Sandwich,"* lying on each side of him and pulling the sweater over the top of them, all three giggling as they adjusted their positions. Bud and Bertie curled up together in the far end of the raft, Magna and Isobel at their backs. Phil and Kyle laid at the opposite end while Bruce and the pilot took up the center.

Since neither of us could lie down, Jack took his seat propped up a few inches from me. I could feel his body shudder every few minutes against the cold. Despite the canopy blocking the wind, it was still chilly.

He'd been kind enough to warm me when I'd needed it. As the most familiar stranger of the group, the least I could do was return the favor. I slid the few inches between us to come shoulder to shoulder with him and moved the dress to cover both his arms and mine.

"I'm sorry about your husband," he whispered against the top of my head.

I nodded, closing my eyes. "I'm sorry about *nine* seasons of bad breath."

He gasped. "You watched it?"

I tucked my hands under my cheek and let my head rest against his shoulder. "Oh yes. I waited for each episode with... *bated breath.*"

"Oh ha ha." He coughed. "So you knew who I was the whole time?"

I opened one eye. "I knew what you did for a living, Jack. I do not presume to know who you are."

He adjusted the dress over my shoulders. "Few people can differentiate between the two. I'm sure you've heard the rumors, though. Is that why you recoiled when I touched you?"

I sighed. "No. I didn't mean to *recoil.*"

"Because I'm not that guy," he murmured, lowering his head to rest against the top of mine as we floated quietly on the water.

Intrigued, I poked further. He was notorious for his dubious love life and had always come across as someone who was too confident to care about being judged for it. "You're *Jack Volmer*. Why would you care what *I* think of you, anyway?"

He cleared his throat. "Despite popular opinion, I happen to care a great deal about what *everyone* thinks of me."

"You know," I whispered, "you're not so bad when you're civil. You should try it more often."

I felt him chuckle before he stifled a cough. "I'm sorry if I was a jerk on the plane. I didn't mean to be."

I nodded, inching my body closer against his for warmth. My eyelids grew heavy when he slid an arm around me, and my body relaxed for the first time in days. "I'm sorry if *I* was uncivil to *you* today. I just..."

"I know," he whispered. "You don't have to explain it. I can't imagine how hard this must be for you."

I adjusted my head against his shoulder. The human side of him had completely surprised me. He wasn't arrogant, but guarded, and I'd been too quick to judge him. In fact, where I'd accused him of being cold and unfriendly, it was I that had been cold with him while he'd been caring toward me.

"Just so we're clear," Jim said into the darkness, "I *ain't* the type of man to buy a first-class ticket."

Lilly giggled, her face nuzzled in his side. "So why did you?"

"Funny ye' should ask… I won the lottery." He closed his eyes, grinning.

She began to shriek in disbelief, but he quickly silenced her with a: "night y'all."

Chapter Nine

The next morning, I woke very much aware of the raft wobbling under my soaked back. At some point, I'd slid down to the floor and my ribs ached for it. The sun had started to rise—I could feel it on my eyelids—and the sound of sliding skin on wet rubber near my face told me the raft's inhabitants were awake and removing the canopy.

There was a smell coming off us now. Not just sweat and blood, but something more stagnant—more rotten. I could taste its tang on my tongue. I opened my eyes and pushed my stiff body upright.

Anna was sitting at the pilot's side, a look of horror on her face.

He was still breathing, but it came as a gurgle more than a breath—forced and strangled in his throat.

Her eyes met mine, and she shook her head. He wasn't going to make it.

Jim sat across from me and had managed to work his t-shirt up over his nose and mouth. His eyes were wide where he stared at the pilot's nearly gray skin.

Despite the man's impending death, it was hard not to notice the scenery as the canopy was lowered. The ocean was still, calm, and windless. The sky reflected on the water, and it was hard to tell where one began and the other ended.

If it'd been me dying, I imagined this was the backdrop I'd want around me as I went.

Throughout the morning, we endured the heat as the sun rose higher, not wanting to contain the smell. It felt wrong to converse while the man that'd saved our lives laid dying between us, so we sat listening to each of his struggled breaths, holding our own in between as we waited for the next.

When the sun was at its highest, Jack reached for the bags of water, quietly handing them out to each of us. As he passed her, Lilly made her way over to me.

"Do you think…" She looked at the pilot then out at the water, chewing her lower lip. "Do you think we'll die out here too?"

"No, honey," I lied, taking a small sip of water and holding it in my mouth, pleading with my stomach to let the moisture be enough to erase the hunger that had taken permanent residence there. "I think we're going to be alright. Someone will find us."

It'd been days since we'd crashed and we hadn't seen a single sign of rescue; not even a plane far up in the sky. As far as we could tell, we were completely removed from the world.

"I'm scared and I wanna go home," Lilly breathed, her eyes welling with tears. "I don't know how much more of this I can take."

'Me neither.'

I took her hand in mine and squeezed. "Someone will find us. We just have to be patient. Now, on a much more serious note," I leaned in, "what's the first thing you're going to do when they find us?"

"Ugh," she sniffled and blinked the remnants of her tears away. "I'm going to take a very long, very hot shower."

I smiled as she changed her tune, whispering close to my ear, "No… First I'm going to drink a glass of very very cold water… with ice. Then I'm going to eat a giant cheeseburger…. *Then* I'm going to take a very long, hot shower."

She laid her head on my shoulder, then sat back up and returned to my ear. "Do you think Jack's single?"

There was a hint of possession that swept over me. I noticed it and was taken aback by it. Jack had been kind to me and had held me through the night, but it wasn't flirtatious. It was necessary. Crashing together had made us more familiar, secure enough with each other to seek comfort in each other's body heat, and that was all there was to it. I belonged to Chris and had no reason to feel possessive of any other man.

I dismissed the notion, whispering casually back, "Only way to know for sure is to ask him."

She smiled over at him, leaning her hot head against my already hot shoulder.

There was something about her sudden interest in him that had me unsettled, and, despite my desire to suppress it, I couldn't shake it. I didn't like that she began flirting the moment she found out who he was, creating ways to graze his shoulder with hers when she'd move around the raft or leaving her hand over his slightly too long when he handed out the water.

I'd witnessed the more human side of Jack the night before. I'd met the man who was self-conscious about the tabloids, who, likely as a result, had a hard time trusting the authenticity of the people around him.

'No wonder,' I thought, *'if all women were always so quick to throw themselves at him because of his fame.'*

Perhaps I wasn't being possessive but *protective*. Jack had been my only real friend on the raft, and there was nothing wrong with protecting a friend. This was an emotion I *could* own; *this* feeling didn't conflict with my love for Chris.

Internally, I laughed at my tangled web of imaginary conflict, grateful no one but me was aware of it. Who cared if she flung herself at him for the wrong reasons? None of this mattered. We were either going to die in the raft or be rescued. Either way, none of us would see each other again when it was over.

If Lilly wanted a fling in her last days here, who was I to judge her for it? Or anyone?

Looking around the raft, I wondered if we all weren't feeling some kind of pull to another; seeking out one person to share our dying moments clinging to, no matter if they were a complete stranger. No one wanted to die alone.

Kyle certainly had chosen Lilly. She might've caught him drooling over her had she not devoted so much of her time to seeking Jack's attention.

His father, I was pretty sure, had selected me as the person he wanted to die beside. Phil stared unabashedly where he clung to the ropes across from me.

Jim and Anna had spent the night shoulder to shoulder, and Bud and Bertie had hardly let go of one another since we'd crashed. Magna held Isobel tightly.

Every day that passed without rescue seemed closer to our last.

Maybe that same desire to hold on to someone was why I felt so protective of Jack. He had quite literally been the man of my dreams growing up. Maybe some part of me had chosen him as the person I'd cling to when death found me.

Suddenly, the pilot let out one long rattling breath, forcing everything to pause and the raft's inhabitants to become quiet. Another inhale did not follow, and we all waited as Anna felt around for a pulse that would not come.

We'd known it was coming, but now he was gone and none of us could find the words or the actions that needed to follow. We just gazed at his lifeless body until Jack finally moved on his knees toward him.

"We'll have to put him in the water," he coughed out. "It's not going to be easy, but we can't keep him here."

"Ye think we orta' say somethin?" Jim tilted his head to one side. "Don't seem right to just dump a man who saved our hides and not say nothin' over him."

"Like a prayer?" Jack asked, his nose scrunched up a little at the idea.

"Ye'd rather just quietly toss him in the water like some kind of garbage?" Jim huffed. "Say nothin' at all? He's the only reason any of us is still sittin' here."

Jack blinked. "I wouldn't know what to say."

At this, Bertie slowly rose to her knees and shuffled over to him. She placed her hand on top of his chest and squinted her eyes in thought. Softly and a little choppily, she recited, "Then I heard a voice from heaven say, *'Blessed are the dead who die in the Lord from now on. They will rest from their labor, for their deeds will follow them.'* Amen."

Jim nodded in approval. "Amen."

After a few moments of silence, Jack tested the man's weight, lifting from the man's midsection to determine if he could raise him out of the raft. "He's too heavy. We're gonna' have to slide him out."

"Now hang on a minute," Jim said. "Check his pockets for an ID. We'll want to tell his family when we get somewheres."

Jack stared at Jim for a second, bewildered, then at the lifeless body. He closed his eyes in resignation and reached into the front pocket first, pulling out a wallet, keys, and, much to everyone's surprise, an iPhone.

"Oh my God." Lilly bounced beside me. "He's had that the *whole time*?"

The only people on the raft who'd managed to escape the crash with their phones were Jack and Lilly. Jack's phone was shattered to pieces and Lilly's wouldn't turn on despite days of attempting.

"Here." Jack handed it to her. "See if you can get it to work."

Lilly snagged it out of his hands and pressed the side button while he checked the other pockets. Finding the man's pockets empty, Jack opened the wallet. "Frank Reynolds from Garden City, Idaho."

He sighed as he stuck the wallet in his own back pocket. "Well, Frank, sorry it had to end like this. Thank you for keeping us alive." Jack placed both hands on Frank's side and rolled him. As the body fell onto its stomach, Jack collapsed in a nasty coughing fit.

"Hold on, Hercules. I'll help." Jim wiggled sideways along the raft, propping his back against the edge as he bent both legs and wedged his heels into Frank's side. While Phil clung to the raft's ropes opposite me with his eyes tightly closed, Bud and Magna also positioned themselves at the side of Frank. "Alright, on the count 'a three...'"

Jack evened out his breathing and ran the back of his palm over his mouth, straightening and repositioning himself alongside them.

"One... Two... Three!!"

They pushed, and the raft dipped hard, threatening to tip us all with it as Frank's body hit the water with a splash.

I knew he wouldn't, but part of me expected his body to sink deep down into the ocean immediately, far from our line of sight. He didn't, of course. His body floated on the water, right where they'd cast him.

"It works!" Lilly shouted, her face illuminated by the bright white phone screen as it turned on.

We all huddled around as it finished starting up. She touched the *"emergency call"* button and held the phone out in front of her, then half stood to hold it up higher, then out over the ocean. All of our eyes remained glued to her.

"No service." She hobbled to the other side and repeated the process.

"Get the paddles and move us outta here, Jesus God, Ay, Ay sweetheart..." Jim yelled, and we all turned our attention to Isobel, who stood at the edge of the raft staring wide-eyed at the dead body floating behind us.

Despite Jim's calls, she didn't look away. "Ay... You hear me, lil' sis?"

Magna scooped her up against her shoulder, turning her face away from Frank's body. Without a word, Jack picked up a paddle and began paddling us in the opposite direction.

I looked over Lilly's shoulder, frowning at the little battery icon that touted 63%.

"Lilly," I said softly as she wobbled back and forth with the movement of the raft, "let's turn it off for now. Save the battery. We'll check it again tomorrow."

She stared down at the screen and I reached into her hands, pushing in the side button and watching the screen return to black.

She collapsed against my shoulder, and I held her tightly as Jack and Bud paddled us away from the death at our backs.

I could feel her crumbling. The phone had been the first small bit of hope we'd had in days. Within minutes, that hope disintegrated and all we had was each other. With one of us already dead, what good was it to have each other if we all were headed toward the same end? Hope felt so very far away.

Exhausted after several minutes of hard paddling, Jack leaned in, suppressing a cough. "I can't paddle anymore."

We all looked back and saw the body—still as if it had been lying on solid ground where it floated on the surface. My heartbeat quickened as the water stirred around it—as *something* stirred around it, a fin shaped silhouette skidding across the water toward him. Then another.... And another.

"Is that... a..." Jim's words were cut short as we all watched the splash of water when one dark figure came out of the water, then the other, and the flash of red as they tore, tugged, and—

I forced myself to look away just as Jim shouted, "OHH SHIT!"

Our raft bobbed violently to one side, forcing me nearly overboard, and Phil screamed out, latching his arms once again around the ropes. Just before I'd pulled my upper body back in, I caught the sight of a large, dark shadow below the water's surface gliding toward the frenzy.

"Shark," I said to myself, then watched as another came by, "SHARK!"

The raft lurched again, and a large arm snagged me by the life vest and yanked me off to one side. Jack and Jim huddled together where I'd been, leaning over the side to get a better look.

"What the hell are you doing? Go sit back down." Jack scolded Jim, not looking away from the water.

"My legs ain't broke and I'll do what I damn well—THERE IT IS!!" Jim shouted, and just as he did, something bumped the opposite side, raising the raft nearly up in the air.

I wrapped my arms around Isobel and Lilly before they could topple over the side, pulling them both against me despite the stabbing pains it forced up my insides. I winced, the sound of Phil praying for his life filling my ears, and when I opened my eyes, Jim was gone.

Before I could shout, Jack ripped his life vest off and was jumping in after him, leaving us all at the edge in a stupor.

We watched the water; all of us hanging over the side in search of signs of them—all but Phil who curled into a ball in the corner, too terrified to open his eyes.

I held my breath and waited... waited...

'Oh please, please come back...'

I searched the ocean, but only saw my own distorted reflection on the surface.

'Please... Please come back.'

Jack was the only person on the raft I'd felt even remotely close to. The thought of being stuck out here without him made me feel suddenly alone and panicked.

I didn't want to die alone.

I watched the water, my heart racing, and then, with a splash, two heads emerged in a massive gasp of air.

"COME GET ME YOU SUMMBITCH!" Jim kicked his feet as Lilly and Bud grabbed him round the waist to hoist him back inside, his arms lifeless at his sides. Jack leapt in behind him, looping a thumb around Jim's belt to pull him the rest of the way in. He then collapsed on the floor and began coughing uncontrollably.

"The sons 'a bitches been followin' us this whole time!" Jim shouted, drops of water seeping from his hair and down his forehead, forcing him to blink heavily. "Waitin' for one of us to fall in!"

Jack's hands were shaking—his entire body was shaking, and the cough was only getting heavier.

Magna snatched the life vest and placed it over Jim's shoulders, whacking him over the top of his head with it as she did so.

"DAMMIT WOMAN! I didn't fall off the dang thang on purpose."

Isobel crawled across the raft and into Magna's arms, avoiding the chaos that was erupting before us.

Beside me, Jack coughed to a gag, choking and spitting over the edge, his face red and eyes watering once the cough eased. His eyes bored into Jim and he wheezed, hyperventilating between words, "You…. Fucking….. Idiot….. Hillbilly."

Jim crossed his ankle over his bent knee in front of him and faced Jack matter-of-factly. "First off, I ain't no Got damned hillbilly. I'll knock you on your ass you call me that shit again. And TWO: I said I didn't fall off the dang thing on purpose. What ye' so worked up about anyway, Hoss?"

But Jack couldn't catch his breath enough to retort.

I touched his heaving back, smoothing over his spine, grateful beyond words he was back in the raft. I watched my hand as if it were someone else's, and I wondered what had made me reach out to touch him so effortlessly. I didn't know this man, but he was familiar to me. I owed him nothing but found myself increasingly concerned over his wellbeing, protective of him even.

I'd spent the entire day creating conflicts and excuses for those conflicts with him instead of thinking about my husband.

Maybe we didn't want someone to cling to in death. Perhaps we all just wanted to be distracted from death entirely.

"Shhh," I whispered. "It's over now. Come on, sit back." I pulled at his shoulder and he obliged, sliding back to the edge of the raft to lean against it.

"Forget about him." I patted his shaking hand, glancing over at Jim, who had already forgotten the fight and was grinning happily as Lilly dried his hair with her shirt. "Your breathing is getting worse. You need to relax. Lest we all end up…" I swallowed, looking out toward where Frank's body had once been, "out there."

Chapter Ten

That night was the hardest night we endured together. The reality that rescue would not come seemed to have hit us all. The events of the day mixed with the unrelenting hunger, thirst, and the endless movement of the raft, and we all unraveled slowly.

Under a moonless, cloudy sky, the raft was cloaked in darkness. It was the darkness that offered us the security to break down where we hadn't before.

Anna was the first to break.

She was seated next to me and I heard her hitched breathing followed by very soft sniffling.

Lilly, oblivious to Anna's attempts to mask her tears, made it known to everyone. "Anna, you're crying?!"

"I'm fine," Anna said softly, her wavering voice a dead giveaway she wasn't.

"Don't cry," Lilly pleaded. "It's going to be okay. We're going to make it home. Is it Liam? Are you worried about him?"

"OF COURSE I'M WORRIED ABOUT HIM!" Anna snapped, her sudden outburst plunging her the rest of the way over the edge. She broke down emphatically, wailing and sniffling. "I've never left him before. Never been away longer than a workday. Certainly never overnight. I knew it was a stupid idea to fly out here. I even told Ben I didn't want to come. But, he bought me a ticket so stupid me felt GUILTY if I didn't come... Stupid stupid STUPID woman!!! And now..." Her voice hitched and she took a quivering breath. "Now I might never see my baby again!"

"It'll be okay." Lilly's own voice shook.

"HOW?! How will it be okay?!" Anna wept. "Jim's right, no one's going to find us out here! I haven't even seen a single airplane, have you?!"

"...no." Lilly's voice became smaller.

"No," Anna repeated, "I miss my son. I'm hungry and tired and miserable and stranded with a bunch of strangers. I will probably die out here because I'm an *idiot* woman who makes *idiot* decisions. Stop telling me it'll be okay because it won't!"

Lilly went silent then, but I heard her weeping in between each of Anna's sobs.

I wanted to cry with them but I couldn't. I needed to cry; needed to break down under the blanket of darkness, masked by the sounds of their sadness, but I couldn't.

I tried. I pictured Chris. I pictured the devastation on his parents' faces when they found out their son was gone. I tried to imagine my life back home and all I'd lost... but still, the tears wouldn't come. I didn't *feel* the loss. Instead, I felt like he was within my reach. I tried to persuade myself he was gone, tried to force myself to feel it, but I couldn't. He didn't feel gone.

I heard someone else crying now, a third set of sniffles and uneven breathing—masculine this time—and I wondered who it was. Phil, perhaps? He seemed the most likely to break first of the men on the raft.

I shook my head, disgusted with my own judgement of them. Who was I to judge anyone for breaking now? Even if it was Phil?

I slid back to prop my back against the raft's edge, my body aching in every way it could—hunger eating away at the last reserves of energy I had to fight off the pain in my head and ribs.

I begged my mind to let me have this moment to come undone... this moment when no one could see... I *too* was hungry, tired, stranded, missing my family, mourning my *husband*...why? Why couldn't I have the same relief? Was I reverting to the Alaina I'd been? The numb, lifeless shell of a human I'd once walked around as? Why didn't he feel gone?

'Feel something!'

I squeezed my eyes shut, trying to force tears to the surface, but my cheeks remained dry.

The sounds of sorrow surrounded me as everyone else had their own breakdowns. Some wept, some just lay in silence, letting the desolation of the situation inhabit them. Even Jack emitted a sense of despair seated next to me. He was silent and still, lost in his own mind. I could hear his long, drawn out breaths every so often as he struggled with our situation.

"I never should've left your mother," Phil murmured from the far end of the raft. "She was the only one who ever really loved me."

"Don't talk like we're dying," Kyle said softly, "we're not... not yet, anyway."

"But we might," Phil tried to whisper, but his own tears made his voice shake and his words became more pronounced. "And I need you to know that I did love her... once."

"Then why'd you treat her like you did?" Kyle hissed back.

"I don't know..." Phil sighed, "Because loving her wasn't enough..."

"Grandpa?" Lilly whispered, her hand reaching out in the blackness and touching my arm, making me jump.

"We're over here, baby." Bertie answered.

"Can I hold on to you for a while?" She pleaded, sounding like a small child.

"Of course you can," Bud assured her, the raft quavering as she found her way to them.

The movement of the raft under us sent Jack into a new coughing fit. This one was the worst we'd heard. His lungs gurgled when he tried to inhale between outbursts and it went on for several minutes before he got it under control.

Anna sniffled. "We need to do something about that cough. And don't fight me on this. There's an inhaler in the pack. It might help."

He breathed uneasily out. "Okay."

"Who has the pack?" Anna shuffled around, searching.

Again, he launched into a terrible hacking cough, shaking the raft with him as he battled to get above it. For the second time that day, I reached out and caressed his back, hoping it would offer him some kind of relief.

"It's here," Lilly said.

"Ye' sound like shit, Hoss."

He wheezed and gradually regained composure. "I'm fi— fine."

"Shhh." I inched closer, absentmindedly running my palm in circles over his back. "Try not to talk. You'll only make it worse."

Then, much to my surprise, he leaned into me, resting his very heavy head against my shoulder and groaning as his body shook to fight off a renewed wave of coughing. "I… hate… this…." Again he choked, but only for a few seconds.

"Shhh." I laid my cheek against his head, smoothing my hand over his tensed back muscles. "We're ok," I whispered very quietly, begging myself to believe it. "We're ok."

I could hear the shaking of pill bottles and the crinkle of papers as Anna dug through the first aid kit in the darkness. "Whenever you have those fits," she advised, still rummaging, "you need to make sure you spit it all out."

He nodded against my shoulder as if she could see him.

"Ok, I've got it," she announced.

I reached out my free arm, feeling her shoulder and working my hand down until I touched the hard plastic container. "I got it," I took the inhaler. "How many?"

"Start with one," she instructed. "Jack, inhale as deep as you can to make sure the medicine gets there. Then wait a few breaths and do it again."

"Okay," he breathed, raising his head from my shoulder. I pulled my arm from his back and drew out his hand so that I could place the inhaler into it. "You need help?"

He coughed again, shaking it off. "No."

I heard the familiar "tsk" of the inhaler and listened as he breathed it through rattling lungs, holding it deep before exhaling. Again, he pressed the inhaler, wheezing as he drew it in. On his exhale, he returned his head to my shoulder. I felt the plastic as he laid it in my palm, his fingers curling over mine momentarily before retreating to his lap.

There was something about his presence that comforted me. Stuck as we were, his body was constantly in close proximity to mine, and the moment he'd jumped off, I felt a panic I couldn't explain, a loneliness that only his reappearance erased. It didn't make sense, but I couldn't shake it. The truth was, instead of mourning the loss of my husband, I was finding solace in the nearness of him.

'We need to talk.'

Those four words played on repeat in my mind, and I realized I'd been mourning the loss of Chris since long before we crashed. Maybe I didn't feel the loss because it had been there for years. Instead of crying now, I was searching for relief from my constant grief. I laid my head over Jack's and closed my eyes, transporting myself to a time before I'd lost him, to a time long before I'd forgotten what it felt like to be truly happy.

I'd endured three hours of hair and makeup, then squeezed myself into the yellow chiffon bridesmaid's dress my sister had insisted I wear. In that time, I'd also drank my fair share of mimosas. I stepped out of the bridesmaids dressing room—only slightly off balance—and into the bridal suite where my mother stood buttoning the last two buttons of my sister's wedding gown.

"Oh, Cece!" I gasped as she turned. "You are ravishing!"

She'd chosen to wear her hair down and the long loose curls in her bright blonde hair shimmered in the sunlight. She had a single yellow flower tucked behind one ear and her makeup made her hazel eyes pop against her porcelain white skin.

The dress was a long princess cut gown, a mixture of tulle and white lace that cascaded down from the lace corset top. She spun in a circle, laughing as the skirts flowed out around her. "I know, right?! I told the makeup artist I'm taking her home with me." She grinned in the woman's direction. "She thinks I'm joking."

I wrapped my arms around her waist. "My little sister getting married before me. I'm *so* not jealous of you at all right now!"

She pried my arms off her. "Oh quit, A.J., you're going to make me cry before I even get out there." She fanned her eyes with her hand, taking a sip of her mimosa before yelling back toward the makeup artist, "Is this gonna run down my cheeks if I cry?"

The woman grinned. "No, honey. It's waterproof."

"Oh," she blew out, "thank God."

She poked my side. "Get a load of you, hot stuff! I told you that dress looked fabulous." Turning me toward the large mirror to stand next to her, she placed her hands beneath my breasts and bounced them once. "It even makes it seem like you have boobs." She laughed loudly as I smacked her hands away. "Where's this Chris guy? I want to meet him!"

I turned to one side, then the other. The dress was long and flowy, strapless with a built-in bra that miraculously did make it appear as if I had *boobs.* She'd insisted I wear my hair pulled up to one side in a braided bun.

The makeup artist had also done a fantastic job on me, airbrushing the freckles away to make my skin appear silky smooth. My eyes were dramatic, and I did in fact look quite fabulous.

I smiled at her in the mirror. "I didn't want him sitting around while we were getting ready. He'll be here soon, I think."

I was eager to see him and slightly unnerved that he'd be meeting my entire extended family on just our second official date.

"Both of you quit hogging my mirror." My mother stepped in front of us, posing as if she were having her photo taken for Vogue. "You can have the makeup artist, darling," she shifted to another overly dramatic position, letting her leg kick out in front of us, "but *I'm* keeping the hairstylist."

She slowly shook her head from side to side to show off the glow of perfect curls in her bright red shoulder length hair. She wore a long, sparkling silver dress that made the red hair stand out.

Her hair had turned grey years ago, of course, but she was too much of a diva to let anyone see. Only Cece and I knew she dyed it and we were sworn to secrecy lest we be murdered in our sleep.

She noticed me in the mirror and tilted her head. "Oh wow, Lainey, you do have boobs!" She turned again. "Does this dress make me look fat?"

Cece giggled and pushed her out of the way. "Oh God, mother move, you haven't looked fat a day in your life." Following suit, Cece posed the same way our mother had, turning from side to side, and making fierce faces at herself.

"Celia Bug," our mother handed her a mimosa, tearing up a little as she met her eyes in the mirror, "I'm going to miss this."

Cece took a large drink and exhaled loudly, setting the champagne flute down near the window "Nope. Nope. We're not doing this right now, ma. You've got me here for another three months. We'll talk about it then. Not today. I'm not crying right now." She fanned her eyes. "A.J., make her quit looking at me like that!"

I rolled my eyes and laughed. "Alright ma, let's go see if Chris is here yet. I want you to meet him."

Cece pouted. "But I want to meet him toooooo...."

I snickered. "I swear to God, I'm adopted. You two are so dramatic, you know that? You'll meet him right after, I promise."

She made a face. "Fine. Hurry, though. I haven't had my *'Oh my God, I can't go through with this'* moment yet that you see in all the movies... As my sister and best friend, it is your duty to give me one extremely profound bit of sisterly wisdom that makes all the reasons *I can't go through with this* seem stupid. You have ten minutes. Go."

I escorted our mother to the balcony that overlooked the country club's outdoor wedding venue. Rows of white chairs adorned with cute little bunches of yellow and white flowers sat in front of a white arbor covered in similarly flowered ivy. There were only a few guests in their seats, so I looped my arm back through hers and hurried toward the front entrance.

"Slow down, Legs!" she complained. But I spotted him walking toward us as we came out of the French doors, tall and gorgeous in a crisp dark navy suit, and I sped up to the edge of the steps.

"There he is." I grinned and motioned toward him.

"*That's* Chris?" My mother's mouth fell open. "Jesus Lainey, does he have a brother?"

"Behave, ma." I whispered, stepping off the steps to greet him.

"Ally." He leaned down to kiss my cheek, "You look…" He inspected me, then frowned. "Wait… Where are your freckles?"

I laughed. "Buried under about an inch of makeup."

He shook his head, smiling. "Well, you look amazing, although whoever thought you needed an inch of makeup over that masterpiece of a face needs a lesson or two in beauty." His eyes shifted to my mother. "And this must be Cece? Shouldn't you be wearing a wedding dress?"

My mother batted her eyes and giggled as she examined him top to bottom. "Yes Lainey, I think you can keep this one."

I rolled my eyes. "Chris, this is my mother, Sophia. Mom, this is Chris."

"Mrs. McCreary." He took her hand and kissed it. "You're looking very lovely this afternoon."

"Oh," she laughed and placed a palm on his chest, her eyes going wide as she did so. "OH!"

I shook my head and covered my mouth, stifling a laugh. "Mom."

She looked back at me, hand still on his chest. "What?"

I raised my eyebrows.

She sighed, removing her palm and adjusting the shawl over her shoulders. "It's very nice to meet you, Chris." She turned to head back inside, mouthing to me *"OH MY GOD"* before she moved on to greet my cousin near the door.

I wrapped my arms around him and raised up on my toes to kiss his lips. "You're going to be so sorry you agreed to this. They're all going to do that."

As if on cue, my aunt appeared at his side, her short bright white hair teased high. "Well, I see you've met my date," she announced, grinning up at him as she looped her arm around his. "Hello handsome, miss me? Come on, let's go find a seat. Shew." She flapped her hand toward me. "Go on, get."

"Chris, this is my aunt Betty." I exhaled. "And this is her husband, Don." I presented the tall, smiling, grey-haired man behind them. He was one of my favorites, always happy, patient, and collected where aunt Betty was loud, cranky, and wildly unpredictable. "Don, Betty, this is Chris."

Betty looked at Don and pursed her lips, then she tilted her head back up at Chris. "I don't know who that man is. Come on, let's run away together." She winked at me, letting him go to wrap her arms around me. "You know," she pulled back, looking me over. "I don't like this color on you. Makes you look too pale."

Don shook Chris's hand and laid a hand on Betty's back. "Don't listen to her, A.J. You're perfect. Come on Betty, we'd better head down there now so we can get you to a seat before it's all over."

"Oh, hush." She smacked his hand as she hobbled slowly toward the door. "I'm coming. Soph! That dress makes you look old!" She cackled as my mother glared at her.

I looked up at him. "You know… you could run. No one would blame you."

"Are you kidding?" He draped his arm over my shoulder, watching as aunt Betty insulted two more people before she'd gone through the door. "I love her."

I giggled. "She's something. I have to head back now. I feel terrible throwing you to the wolves like this. Are you going to be okay?"

He winked at one of the flower girls who'd been standing on the stairs admiring him, sending her scurrying with a giggle back inside. "I'll be fine."

I raised on my toes and kissed him one last time. "I'll see you shortly. And if anyone starts to tell a story about the Easter ham, none of it's true."

I spun around and hurried back inside, my stomach a flurry of butterflies.

When I returned to the bridal suite, Cece smiled at me through the mirror as she fastened her pearl earrings. "Alright, give it to me. Sisterly wisdom."

I furrowed my brow. "You don't look like you have cold feet."

"And *you* don't look pretty when you make that face. My feet are freezing, what do you got?"

I smirked and stood behind her, curling my arms around her waist. "Owen is smart, handsome, funny, and wildly rich. He's the full package and you know it, too. If you don't get your scrawny butt out there and marry him, I will."

She gasped, "You wouldn't dare!"

"I would too. And he'd be sorely disappointed since you got all the blonde and boobs."

She snickered. "That's your wisdom?"

I rested my head on her shoulder. "No. My wisdom is simple. You're too smart to have agreed to marry someone you wouldn't love your whole life. You know you will and that's why we're standing here. You're also too smart to think I'd have any kind of worldly wisdom, and this is obviously all a ploy to make me uncomfortable."

She rested her head against mine. "You better come visit me all the time."

"I promise I will."

Sighing, she looked at her reflection one last time. "Alright then, let's get this over with, yeah?"

The ceremony and dinner went off without a hitch, and as the dance floor opened and the guests flooded the bar, I stole a bottle of champagne from the table and dragged Chris outside. "Come on handsome," I whispered, "let's go see if we can get in trouble."

"Where are we going?" He chuckled as I pulled him with me, peering across the golf course in search of witnesses.

"Shhh." I slid into a golf cart, "Get in. Let's blow this joint."

He climbed in beside me, scanning our surroundings as if we might get in trouble. I, of course, knew that Owen's parents had rented the entire course along with the clubhouse for the duration of the evening, but I pretended it was a scandal. I enjoyed watching him squirm as I drove off to the green of the tenth hole, far from the noise of the reception.

Stepping out of the cart, I grabbed the two golf balls and putter I'd strategically placed there ahead of time. The moon was bright overhead and illuminated the green beautifully.

"Alright, Christopher," I handed him the putter and dropped one of the balls, "make it and I'll kiss you. Don't make it, and you drink." I popped the cork off the champagne bottle and took a swig.

"Oh?" He laughed. "From here? Piece of cake."

He lined up carefully, gauging the distance, adjusting his feet and hands, lined up the shot against the darkness, and with a "clonk," tapped the ball. It skipped across the green, then veered to the left as it approached the hole.

"Oh no," I pouted, holding out the champagne bottle and swaying it back and forth. "Drink!"

He took the bottle from me and drank, wrapping an arm around me when he'd finished and hovering near my lips.

"Na ah ah." I pressed my finger to his lips. "No cheating. It's my turn." I dropped the ball. "What do I get if I make it?"

He grinned mischievously.

"Hey now," I chuckled, "it's gotta be something I'm up to, otherwise I'll just launch it the other way and take a drink."

"Ok gorgeous, we'll keep it classy. If you make it, *I'll* kiss *you.*"

"Amateur," I snorted, taking the putter from him to line up my shot. I shifted my grip, bent my knees and "clonk." I watched as my ball curved out and back in, effectively disappearing when it reached the hole. I jumped and spun around, raising both arms up in a victory dance. "Yessss."

"You're good, kid," he slid his palm up my cheek, "real good." He took the putter from me and let it fall as he wrapped his arm around my back. My toes curled the moment his lips came down over mine. He parted my lips and I gladly opened for him, his mouth warm and sweet from the champagne.

His fingers slid down my neck as I let mine spread wide over his chest. He broke the kiss, his lips lingering an inch from mine. "Did you want to keep golfing or…"

I locked my hands behind his neck and pulled his mouth back over mine, letting each pass of his tongue stir up new butterflies in my stomach. My heartbeat quickened and my breathing grew more labored as he dragged me further into the euphoria of him. I gasped when his mouth moved to my neck and curled my fingers into his dark hair. Closing my eyes, I let my head fall back.

I was pulled from my ecstasy when the sound of another golf cart came roaring up from behind.

"A.J.!" My sixteen-year-old cousin yelled out as he hung over the side of an overloaded golf cart that screeched to a stop two feet from where we stood. His two older brothers and their dates remained inside, cackling with drunken teenage laughter. "A.J.!" He hiccuped, looking up at Chris, "Ooh, man, you're gonna be in trouble if uncle Bill sees *you!*"

I huffed. "What do you want, dorkus?"

He giggled. "We're gonna go skinny dipping in the pool!"

"We're not going skinny dipping with you, Tommy." I shook my head. "Go on."

"GROSS! I don't wanna see you naked." He snarled. "No, I came out here cause your mom's looking for you. She wants you to take pictures or somethin."

I sighed, "Ok. I'll head back momentarily."

He lingered, swaying as he stared at us.

"Okay, I said! Go on before I call your mom and tell her you're wasted!"

He jumped back in the cart. "Alright, I'm goin, but if you tell my mom I'm drunk, I'll tell uncle Bill you were out here doin' the dirty!"

They took off in a hurry toward the pool house.

Chris curled his arms around me and laughed, pressing his forehead against mine. "Probably for the best. I definitely don't want this uncle Bill character after me for *doin' the dirty* on a golf course."

I smiled up at him, "Thank you for coming to this."

He ran his hand down the side of my hair to cup my cheek. "I like seeing you here. With them. Every time I think I've got an idea of how incredible you are, something more amazing about you surprises me and makes me want you that much more."

I blushed. "Oh. Well, I mostly wanted you to come so you could see how amazing I look in this dress." I swung it around.

"Ally, I'm not likely to ever get the image of you in *this* dress out of my head."

Chapter Eleven

It was the next morning when the blessed cry of "LAND!" emerged from Jim, waking us all from our sleep. "JUMPED UP JESUS ON A HICKORY STICK! LAAAAND!!!" He threw his head back and laughed hysterically.

"Where?" I asked, blinking the sleep from my eyes as I scanned the horizon.

He raised one splinted arm toward a tiny black speck in the distance, so small we might've blinked and floated right past it.

Every hair on my body stood at attention. That little black speck meant life where we'd all spent the past few days convinced death was a certainty.

With trembling hands and star-filled vision, I grabbed a paddle and started paddling, hard and fast as I was able, smiling to myself as the others spotted our salvation for themselves.

"Oh, thank you, Jesus," Phil breathed beside me, his body relaxing for the first time since we'd crashed.

"Here, let me do that." Bud took the paddle from me and matched my enthusiasm. Jack had grabbed the other and was on the opposite side of the raft rowing as hard as he could.

Before long, the little speck became gray, then spots of green became trees climbing up a volcanic cliff, the peak towering high above the clouds, and then we saw sand... and we were going to live!

The acceptance of my impending demise had created a sort of fuzz around my mind. Nothing mattered when you were dying slowly of dehydration. I'd stopped thinking about Chris and my family; stopped hoping I'd actually see any of them again, and had been just barely living from one minute to the next.

Seeing that island, however, the numbness in my heart and mind gradually fizzled out, and the sudden onset of hope was like a warm blanket being wrapped around my body.

I could see my family again. I could hope to see Chris again; could allow myself to believe he might still be alive.

As soon as the water turned a lighter shade of blue, Jack jumped in, running as best he could with us in tow. Too excited to sit still, I jumped off too, the soft, solid ground beneath my toes a welcome change to the constant movement of the raft. One by one, we all jumped into the water to run, even Jim, despite his barely functional arms, all of us pulling only Isobel and Bruce to the shore.

I collapsed in the sand when we arrived, my eyes full of tears, and basked in the glory of lying perfectly still for the first time in nearly a week.

Around me, I heard Jack, Jim, Phil, Lilly, and Bud shouting out "HELLLOOOOO" from various parts of the beach.

With newfound hope still thrumming through my veins, a thought occurred to me. If Chris *had* somehow survived and ended up on another raft, might he have drifted in this very direction? Could he be on this very same island waiting for me?

The notion, though I knew it was far-fetched, stuck, so I wiped my tears and leapt up to join the search.

"HELLOOOO?!" I shouted toward the towering trees, hands cupped around my mouth.

There was only wind and the sound of the leaves swaying in it as a response.

Not so easily defeated, I plucked up my socks and boots from the raft and hurried to shove my feet inside them.

Jack was jogging down one side of the beach and Jim the other, his splinted arms stiff at his sides. Bud walked along the water's edge, peering up at the summit with his hand over his forehead to block out the sun. Bertie, Magna, and Anna were positioning Bruce and the raft under the canopy of a large palm, Isobel at their heels.

Phil was inspecting Kyle's arm while Kyle watched Lilly, who had turned the phone back on and was walking along the shore with it held out at different angles.

If Chris was there, he'd have climbed up to get a better vantage.

Partly delusional from a lack of food and water, caution was the furthest thing from my mind as I darted into the tree line ahead of me.

"HELLLOOOOO!!" I shouted, scanning the wilderness of rock, sand, and trees for signs another survivor had made it there ahead of us. "ANYBODY THERE?"

I looked up toward the summit, high above where I stood, and back to the beach.

'What if he's here and he's injured? What if he can't get to me?'

He would go higher to search for me. That would be his instinct. I'd go higher too.

I worked deeper into the brush, struggling to find a manageable path as it grew thicker the deeper I went. Thoughts of plunging head-first into Chris's outstretched arms forced me onward where I might've otherwise had the sense to turn back.

"HELLLOOO???" I called desperately, praying Chris would somehow materialize from behind the next bush or rock.

My boots were heavy in the clay, and my shorts and shirt grew damp as I navigated clumsily through dew-soaked vegetation.

Ribs nagging, I pushed myself forward.

The canopy above me grew thick enough that the entire ground became shaded with a green hue, the island's wilderness transforming into a tangling jungle of vines, moss-covered trees, mud and overgrowth the farther I traveled inland.

"CHRIS??" I shouted out, urgency cracking my already hoarse voice.

The ground inclined and my heels slid in the mud, but I kept going, climbing uphill toward the side of the summit in the hopes of getting a better vantage.

In my mind, it was no longer a question of *'if'* he survived. If I survived, he had to be alive too. I just needed to find him.

My sides ached as the trail grew steeper and steeper, so much so that I had to use my hands and knees to continue upward.

Muffled voices shouted from somewhere below me, also searching for signs of life.

I climbed until the brush and clay gave way to jagged mossy rock that eventually shot straight upward. When I looked up, it appeared as though I'd barely climbed at all. The summit towered high into the sky above me, so high the top was hidden from view.

It was quiet, I noticed. *Eerily* quiet. There were no familiar sounds of birds or bugs, no noise but the leaves in the breeze, the waves coming in to kiss the shore, and the occasional muffled "hello" or "Alaina?" coming from far down below.

They were looking for me, and that realization brought back a bit of clarity where I'd otherwise been madly searching for a husband everyone else knew was dead.

My side was on fire, my head was pounding, and my lips and throat were so dry I struggled to breathe through them. We'd had no food other than some soggy chips on the raft and very little water. The lack of food and the exertion of climbing caught up to me, forcing my legs to give way beneath me.

I sat with a thud on a large flat rock that jutted out between me and the solid wall of the mountain at my back. The ever-present lump expanded in my throat.

'He's not here.'

I was covered in dark black clay—my hands, forearms, and the bottom half of my calves and boots were caked with it. It was hardening and beginning to crack in the folds of my palms. My vision blurred for a second, then steadied.

From my rock, I could just see our beach above the tree line I'd come through. I slowly stood on top of it and peered out, shaky as I was. Upon standing, stars danced across my eyes, but then cleared. There was nothing there but our motley crew—spotted dots on the sand from where I stood, a canvas of trees separating us, and the ocean as far as the eye could see.

'There's no one here.' I thought, defeated, as I lowered myself back down to a seat.

'But if Chris lived, he might still be on the water... maybe he's on a raft. Maybe I could see it if I get high enough.'

I looked up the massive barrier of jagged black rock as my mother's voice came to me. *'He's not on the water and you know it. You should get down and go back to the others before you get hurt. They're looking for you.'*

I often had conversations with loved ones in my head, and, tired as I was, arguing with my mother's voice of reason came easily.

'I'm already up here and I could find a way to get the rest of the way up... I could search for a way around... What if he IS on the water? What if he's hurt?' I closed my eyes and could just see him, floating far out on the ocean in a life vest, his body covered in burns, barely hanging on.

My mother's voice came again. *'Lainey, honey, he's not there. He's gone. And you're going to get hurt up here all by yourself.'*

The sound of her voice in my mind made me accurately aware of just how alone I was; in a foreign place and injured. I longed for her so much that my eyes welled and a tear slid down the side of my nose.

'Mom, I don't think I can go on without him, without you... There's so much I needed to fix... with both of you. I can't give up looking for him now.'

I knew I should get down and join the others, but the image of Chris would not leave me—the guilt of our unfinished business would not let me surrender. Giving up on the search felt like giving up on him. I took a deep breath, looked down at my clay blackened hands and decided to explore just a little further for a way up.

I peeled the thick mud from the bottoms of my boots as best I could, stood, and with one hand on the black rock, I followed it, working my way back, farther and farther away from our beach and into the island.

'He doesn't feel gone,' I argued with myself, my sadness turning to anger. *'And what if he doesn't feel gone because he's been out there this whole time while I've been snuggled up with a stranger on the damn raft?'*

"ALAINAAAA?" I heard someone call out far below me.

'Who are you anymore, anyway?' I asked my subconscious, ignoring the sound of my name from the person I least wanted to hear it from just then. *'And what do you think you're doing snuggling up with Jack Volmer? Flirting with him, even, just days after you were separated from your husband? Like all these years with Chris meant nothing?'*

'It's nothing,' I assured the half that was asking. *'I had a crush on him when I was a kid and those old feelings are just surfacing as a coping mechanism. It doesn't mean anything.'*

I kept walking because it was the only thing I could do to silence my mind. The sun grew higher in the sky and the clay on my arms tightened. I walked for—Well, I didn't quite know how long I'd walked. Was it 30 minutes? Two hours? I'd completely lost track of time. I walked until the rock opened up to a lush green slope of trees, leading higher than my eyes could see.

Ready to climb, a noise caught my ear. Mixed into the constant static of leaves blowing in the breeze and the random muffled cries of *"Alaina"* from below was a new sound... a rushing sound... a rushing *water* sound.

It was downhill from me.

'He's not out there,' my mother's voice reminded me, and my dry lips ached at the promise of an unrationed supply of fresh water. I could drink and drink and drink until my tongue no longer felt like cotton.

I needed water... but I also needed to find my husband and tell him all the ways I was sorry.

I looked up once more. It'd take hours to reach the top—possibly more in my condition. A sip of water might carry me the rest of the way...

'He's gone, Lainey.'

I could almost hear my mother next to me.

I knew the decision was made as my body turned toward the sound of the water. With bent knees, I leaned back and descended through the rock until it became clay once again, staying low to the ground in case I lost my footing.

"ALAINA!" Jack's voice was getting closer.

'Stay the hell away from him, Alaina. This is not the time or place to be living out some childhood fantasy.'

The water grew louder in my ears the further I descended, and back under the green canopy, I increased my speed, anxious to silence my guilty conscience.

Too confident, I was all but running toward the sound when the ground gave way, forcing my legs to slide out from beneath me.

I rolled to my stomach as I slid down a muddy slope, gaining momentum despite my attempts to slow myself; grabbing at branches that snapped instantly as I free-fell through the sludge.

"HELP!" I cried out, praying someone would magically appear with something to hold on to.

The slippery surface grew wetter, colder, harder, and as it pushed my tank top upwards, I could feel the fire of sharp rock scraping my stomach and chest.

This was how I was going to die. I was going to tumble off a cliff and crack open my skull.

All the hope of finding land had been wasted on a putz and the fuzzy numbness of my inevitable extinction returned as I fell uncontrollably.

I would die, not from a plane crash or from dehydration or starvation, but from being completely irrational and reckless. Seemed like a befitting end.

Mud in my eyes, I held the pendant of my necklace in one hand as I grabbed blindly for anything I could with the other.

Just as the rock gave way to nothing at my feet, I locked my fingers around something solid with my right hand.

I held so tight, I was sure the bones in my hand would break under the squeeze of my own muscles.

There was guilt in that hold; guilt in the realization I hadn't died after all. Holding on meant I *wanted* to survive; wanted to hold on to hope even when I knew, deep down, Chris was dead.

I'd fought to remain alive when my whole world was gone.

Why?

I freed my left hand and wiped the mud from my eyes to get a look at my surroundings.

I'd grabbed hold of a thin tree that was protruding out of the crevice of a *very* jagged and steep rock.

My upper body was on a solid flat ledge but my legs hung off the edge of a cliff that dropped at least a hundred feet below me. Uphill, I saw the path I'd slid down. A single muddy trail zig zagged down an almost vertical slope.

'Idiot,' I said to myself.

Pulling my legs up, I tested the rock I laid on before letting go of the tree.

My body was on fire.

Everything hurt.

'I told you you'd get hurt out here. I told you to go back,' my mother's voice taunted me.

Ignoring her, I peeked over the ledge. Just below and off to my left, a massive waterfall spilled over into crystal clear water a hundred feet below. Luscious trees lined the pond and, the rushing water, so close to my ear drowned out all other sounds.

I laughed despite myself.

Water. I'd found water by sheer accident and had nearly killed my stupid self in the process.

How did no one think to lock me up years ago for being a danger to myself?

And moreover, what kind of God thought it was a good idea to reward my idiotic behavior with fresh water?

To my right, a much more manageable hill sloped down to the water's edge, and with painfully chapped lips, I couldn't very well walk away from the promise of relief now. Once I'd had a few sips, I'd go find the others and act like a functional—*and rational* adult.

Very, very warily, I inched down the hill with my legs in front of me and my butt on the ground, crab-walking my way to the bottom. I crawled to the edge, jerked off my caked boots and soaked socks, then began to tiptoe inside when a stern voice called out from behind me to stop me in my tracks.

"What the hell is wrong with you?"

I turned just as a seething, panting Jack came stomping out of the tree line. He scanned me from head to toe and I became disturbingly aware of what I must look like, standing there covered from top to bottom in mud, with leaves and twigs poking out in every direction from my clay-soaked hair.

"I…" I swallowed.

Looking at his perfect, angered face, the guilt of our time on the raft resurfaced, and my cheeks flushed as my temper caught up to his. "What the hell do you mean, *what's wrong with me?* What the hell's *wrong with you?*"

"I'll tell you what the hell's wrong with me," he ground out through gritted teeth, the defined muscles on his chest tightening under his open button-down shirt as he balled his fists at his sides.

"I can't turn my back for two seconds without one of you," he broke to cough to one side, then straightened and continued hoarsely, "injuring yourselves, falling overboard, or wandering off… Did you not hear me calling after you? I've been…" He hacked and wheezed again. "I've been chasing you for almost two damn hours!" He ran his hand down his face and through his beard.

I clenched my own fists as heat rose in my throat. "Where the hell do you get off? You don't own me, you don't *own* any of us. You don't hold some kind of superior power over us that allows *only you* to go off and explore the island for life. What do I look like to you? Some kind of child in need of constant supervision?"

He moved closer, eyes narrowing, and spoke in a low voice. "Yes, as a matter of fact you do."

He took two long strides toward me. "Look at you, covered in mud and blood and God knows what else. You've been in and out of consciousness for a week with a fever and you think you don't *need* to be supervised?"

He took two more long strides. "You haven't eaten a thing in days, barely had the strength even to sit upright, and *you* don't need to be supervised? You think you can just disappear for almost two hours in a completely foreign place and no one would think to go searching for you? That *I* wouldn't go searching for you? What the hell were you thinking?"

My jaw clenched, I closed the gap between us, lifting my chin so my face was inches from his. "I was thinking I had to get up high to search for life; to search for *my* husband. I had to know if he made it here; had to at least see for myself."

My lip quivered as I said the words, but I inhaled deeply and straightened. "I was thinking it was the only thing I *could* do. I can't lift anything or treat injuries. I can't build a shelter or get the damned phone to work, but I *can* still walk, dammit."

I raised up on my toes to meet his eyes. "I was thinking there might be something or someone out here—some sign of life... and maybe *I* could be the one to find it."

His nostrils flared, and he took a deep breath, his expression softening slightly as his attention moved from my eyes to my lips.

For a single, fleeting moment, I wondered what it might be like to be kissed by him, and I loathed myself for allowing the thought to surface.

I was a tightly wound ball of contradiction. I'd spent the past two hours convincing myself my dead husband was on this island, and within seconds of coming into contact with Jack Volmer, I'd imagined myself kissing him.

There was something severely wrong with my head.

I should've been locked up for more than being a klutz.

Shaking myself of it all, I took a step back, frustration nearly exploding from my pores. "I didn't find any life..." I cleared my dry throat and motioned behind me, "but I found water."

For the first time, he looked past me, and I saw his throat move, his own thirst erasing the harshness in his features. His eyes went wide as he stared up at the massive waterfall.

"Now," I said pointedly, "I'm going to have some of it if you don't mind."

I turned on my heel, stomping through the water toward the waterfall. "You can keep yelling if you want, but I'm thirsty."

I dove down and came up in the waist deep water, opening my mouth to let the cool fresh mist tumbling off the rocks moisten my tongue.

I climbed up onto a rock just at the waterfall's edge where the main stream of water shot a separate blast of overspray, and I opened my mouth.

I'd never felt more refreshed.

I stood, letting its water beat down on my head, neck, and arms to wash away the clay, sweat, blood, guilt, and anger. Closing my eyes, I let its drum beat in my ears and drown out the rest of the world.

I drank until I could take no more and opened my eyes to see Jack next to me doing the same. His eyes were closed and his mouth was open, the water flattening his hair and darkening his beard, forcing his shirt to mold to his body.

I might've been a contradictory asshole for thinking it, but, my God, he was gorgeous.

This is why he'd hung on posters in my bedroom. Broad shoulders topped a swelling chest and finely chiseled abs. His beard was short but full—a weave of perfectly even gold and brown that matched the couple of inches of thick straight hair on the top of his head. He had a small scar just above his eyebrow that split the hairs ever so slightly, and his legs were long but thick— his jeans soaked and pressed against them to show the outline of hard-worked muscles on his thighs and calves.

I looked away before he could catch me mid-gaze. Once again, guilt stabbed at my heart for looking too long; for having craved his mouth on mine just moments prior.

I dropped down into the water, saying nothing, and trudged back through until only my toes remained in the mud of the creek's edge where I waited.

Everything inside me was a juggling act as I tried to work out what the hell was going on with my brain.

In one hand, I tossed around memories of the early, happy days of my marriage. Chris and I had loved each other fiercely once, and I was feeling the loss of the younger him more and more each day as I struggled to accept he was dead.

In the air, however, was the question of whether or not that marriage would've survived beyond the trip. Did Chris want to divorce me? In the aftermath of the crash, the feelings of abandonment and loneliness hadn't just magically disappeared. My husband hadn't touched me—not really—in years. He hadn't wanted to. And whether he was dead or not, the craving for physical interaction was still very much there. All our unfinished business remained unfinished and waiting for a resolution.

In the other hand was a handsome stranger I'd once dreamt of endlessly who'd made it a point to seek out my attention above all others. Affection starved as I'd been before the crash and feeling the devastation of the loss of my husband, it was only natural to crave something resembling tenderness... Wasn't it? It didn't have to mean there was something wrong with me. I'd been through a lot the past week—hell, I'd been through a lot the past decade. Maybe I was just coping in some bizarre way.

Kicking a rock near my ankles, I focused on the herculean source of my quandary where he'd dropped down from the rock.

"We should tell the others about this place," I called across to him as he walked toward me in waist-high water. "They'll all be thirsty. We should bring them here right away. We'll have to figure out a way to transport it back to the beach."

"There are bags we can refill in the pack," he said, walking past me through the mud to his own pile of shoes and socks. "I can go get them and the others. You stay here."

"I certainly will not," I informed him, standing. "We'll have to set up a camp. We'll need to build a shelter, a fire... explore the island for food. I can do no good sitting on my ass out here."

Not sitting, he hopped from one foot to the next to force each foot into socks and shoes, looking back at me as he did so. "*You're* gonna build a shelter? Start a fire? Hunt? Fish?" He laughed haughtily.

I narrowed my eyes and set my jaw, pushing my damp hair back from my face. "Are you implying that I can't do any one of those things?"

He smiled a deviant smile. "Oh, I'd sure like to see you try, sweetheart."

And just like that, the smug and arrogant Jack Volmer I'd sat beside on the plane returned. I saw red, and the words spilled out beyond my control. I heard them as they did, as if someone else were speaking. "And *you* could do better? *You,* hacking up a lung every time you speak? *You,* a washed up Hollywood snob who's had his life served up on a silver platter for the past ump-teen years? *You're* gonna build us a fire? *You're* gonna build a shelter?"

I laughed just as arrogantly as he had, regretting the choice of words, but unapologetically standing before him with my hands on my hips.

I could see his throat move as he swallowed the words, his body stiff as he glared at me. I prepared for the worst and stood ready to go toe to toe, but he only said, "Keep up," then spun round and stormed off into the tree line.

His long heated strides ate up more distance than three of mine, so I had to run every few steps just to keep him in view. I kept pace though, and I dared not wince, complain or let him catch even the slightest hitch in my breath—despite the fire that was burning across my entire body.

We walked for a short eternity in silence. Having come from a different direction, we were lost in the jungle terrain, and our only tool of navigation was the sound of the ocean. We struggled through the heavy, wet brush, its branches unrelenting as they slapped and stung my bare arms and legs.

In a clearing, he stopped and leaned against a tree, panting with his back to me as he fought the cough that wanted to come.

When I reached his side, my mood shifted from pride to panic. His color had gone ghostly pale, and he was struggling hard to get air. His chest heaved and his body trembled.

"I didn't mean any of that." I fumbled in my pocket for the inhaler I'd placed there the night before, praying it hadn't been damaged in the water. "Here." I held it out to him.

His eyes remained on mine as he took the inhaler, shook it, then brought it to his lips. I was relieved when it appeared to work normally.

"Please don't be angry with me," I begged. "I didn't mean those things. I'm just... I just..." My eyes watered and my shoulders sank. "It was stupid for me to run off like that, but I really thought Chris might be here. I know that sounds ridiculous, but I couldn't help myself. I lost my mind looking for him. And I feel like an idiot. I'm this ball of sadness and anger and bad decisions... and that shouldn't be your problem."

He took the second puff of the inhaler, still watching me as he gained control of his breath.

"I know he's not here," I rambled. "Deep down, I think I know he's not *anywhere*. And I feel like half a person—guilty for everything I ever did wrong to him; guilty even for living now without him. So I need to do something. *Anything…* to feel like I'm whole. I didn't mean to take that out on you. I've made you come all the way out here when you should be resting and healing. You don't need to be dealing with my stupidity."

He nodded, placing the cap back on the little yellow inhaler.

Without warning, he laid his hands on my shoulders and turned me completely around.

"Look," he whispered close to my ear, making my hair stand on edge.

"What?"

"Up."

I shifted my gaze slowly upward and, high in the trees over my head, in bunches of green and bright orange, were clusters and clusters of bananas, all growing upward toward the sky. Hundreds of them surrounded us.

The world's problems forgotten, I laughed as I circled, my eyes darting from one tree to the next to the next. Jack did the same beside me, both of us mesmerized as we took in the welcome sight of much-needed food.

"I've never seen bananas that color," I breathed, my stomach growling and my mouth watering.

"Me neither." His focus danced from tree to tree as he licked his lips.

"How do we get them down?"

"They're not too high," he said, "and the trunk isn't too thick. I could try to climb part of the way up and break it."

"Jack." I looked at him. "You can barely breathe. And…" I glanced back up at the bananas. "*I* need you to get better. You're the only person I…" Thinking better of the sentimental words that might've spewed out of me toward a man I had no right to share them with, I waved a hand to dismiss it. "Forget it, I'll climb."

He laughed. "And you're the only person *I*," he mocked. "Do you really think you're in better condition to climb a tree? With broken ribs and a concussion? Not happening, Red." He sauntered ahead of me toward the shortest of the trees—one we'd both had our eyes on.

"Jack, I can—"

But it was too late. He was already wrapped around the trunk, the tree shaking in protest as he worked his way up—hands first, then feet coming together against the thin base.

About halfway up, I heard the crack of the limb breaking, and watched with my breath held as he pushed the top half one direction and then the opposite, wiggling it loose until, at long last, it crashed to the ground, bright orange bananas with it.

He gracefully slid down the trunk and hopped off, coughing only for a second before he cleared his throat and joined me at the canopy of the fallen half. "These will need to be cut loose as a bunch if we want to keep them all. We'll have to drag it back to camp. It's too thick to tear off."

"Should we...?" I raised an eyebrow, my stomach once again vocalizing its desire to be filled.

He pondered for a moment, his own stomach echoing mine, then knelt and broke off a single banana, unwrapping it and splitting it in two. He grinned as he handed me part of it, then "toasted" the occasion by tipping his half toward me before we each took a bite.

I was... surprised.

It wasn't sweet, but it wasn't unsweet either. It was semi-hard, semi-soft, and had an almost starchy, tangy taste where I'd expected the familiar banana flavor. My mouth watered painfully at the promise of sustenance, and I closed my eyes as I swallowed and bit off another chunk.

Next to me, Jack laughed with bulging cheeks, his breath rattling in his chest.

"What's so funny?" I asked through my own mouthful.

"This is the best-worst tasting banana I've ever eaten," he said, shoving the last of his half in his mouth before kneeling to tear off another.

I chuckled, sitting down next to the fallen tree, my mouth still full. "It really is."

Once again, he tore the banana in half and handed me the larger portion. "Maybe it's like a plantain?" He turned the white fruit over in front of his eyes. "Better cooked?" He popped the entire thing into his mouth.

I ate mine slower, savoring the flavor—oh, to taste something after having gone so long without any kind of food! I didn't care that it was the best-worst banana. It was food, and it was wonderful.

"We should get back," he sighed, extending a hand to me. "We'll need to set up camp, make another hike back to get more water, and get a fire started before it gets dark."

I nodded, taking his hand so he could pull me to stand. "I didn't mean to wander so far. I really am sorry."

He pulled me to my feet and, much to my surprise, into a side hug. "Stop apologizing, Red. You did what you thought you had to do. I can't say I'd have done anything differently if it were me in your situation. Besides, you found water and food. You're our hero." He pulled away and winked, grabbing the trunk of the fallen tree. "Come on, let's get back."

With quite a bit of effort, we managed to pull the several feet of tree and bananas through the thick jungle and down the beach. I kept pace all the way, ribs on fire, refusing to stop unless he needed to—and he didn't until our group came into focus several hundred feet ahead of us in the sand.

We made the last bit of trek through the sand, meeting Lilly, Bud, Jim, and Magna about halfway where Magna and Bud relieved us of the tree.

"Y'all look like you been ate by a bear and shit over a cliff!" Jim grinned.

"We found food," I said proudly, pointing at the bananas.

"Oh, these are Fe'i bananas!" Magna informed us. "They're wonderful boiled!"

"Hopefully they taste better cooked than they do raw." Jack smirked.

"There you are!" Anna embraced me as we reached her.

"We were wondering where you'd gone!" Bertie smiled.

Scattered in the shade of a large palm, our group had created a little camp. The raft was leaning against a smaller palm, its shade offering protection to our stash of suitcases, the dwindling provisions from the survival kit, and Lilly's stiletto heels.

Phil, Bud, and Magna had spent the day gathering fallen palm leaves and bamboo, and they'd already created a frame for a shelter high on the beach.

"We found a waterfall," I beamed.

"*She* found a waterfall," Jack corrected. "*I* found her. We need to get together anything and everything we can store water in. We'll take a trip back to gather water for camp before it gets dark."

"The rocks over there had a bunch of old glass bottles and rope," Lilly said, frowning a little as she did. "They look old—*really* old—but they seem like they're all still intact. I'll take one of the cases out and grab as many as I can."

"I'll come help you." Bertie knelt at the suitcases and emptied the contents of one of the duffel bags. "Thank the Lord. We might just make it through this after all."

"See," Jack whispered, nudging my elbow with his. "You're our hero."

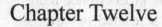

Chapter Twelve

I was propped up against the far wall of the shelter wrapped in a jacket, bodies lined up deep in sleep on either side of me when my eyes popped open. I thought I'd heard someone scream, but couldn't be sure, in my debilitated state, what was real or what was a dream.

We'd all been exhausted after a long day on the island. Collectively, we'd managed to get the shelter together enough that we had a solid roof over our heads and were sleeping up off the ground. We'd used the lighter to get a fire started and had boiled several of the Fe'i bananas. They were indeed delicious when boiled. We'd gathered about twenty glass bottles of water at the fall, refilled all the emergency bags, and cracked several coconuts. Without a word, we all conceded to sleep and collapsed in the shelter, all of us too depleted of energy to do much else.

From the blackness beyond the fire, I heard another blood-curdling scream—the scream of a child far ahead on the beach—and realized it wasn't my imagination.

"Isobel!"

I scrambled up out of my seat and sprinted toward the water.

The moonlight shone brightly on the sand and I could just make her out, about a hundred yards down the shore, her tiny silhouette facing the water.

She screamed again.

I slowed my pace and crept closer, observing her as I did so. She faced the ocean, bellowing at the top of her lungs while she covered and uncovered her ears.

I could hear voices coming up behind me, and, with the knowledge she wasn't in immediate danger, I motioned with one hand for them to slow down and watch.

"What is it?" Magna asked on one side of me.

"Is she hurt?" Jack asked from the other while Lilly and Bud caught up.

I watched the small girl go through the process once more—covering and uncovering her ears as she screamed out over the ocean, my theory confirmed. "I think she's lost her hearing."

We inched closer as she wailed again into the night sky.

Just as her breath ran out, the thuds of bare feet racing across sand came up behind us so quickly I barely had time to move out of the way.

Jim, wearing only a pair of bright white boxer shorts, darted past us at full speed, splinted arms flailing behind him. "I'm comin' for ya! Hold on, lil sis!"

He ran splashing into the water in front of her. "What is it? Where is it?" He looked around frantically, then back at her, his hair standing straight up from sleep.

We caught up, and I waved him in. "There's nothing out there, Jim." I rested my hands on her shoulders. "I think the crash damaged her hearing."

Kneeling, I turned her body toward me. Her big hazel eyes were swollen, her cheeks covered in the streaks of tears, and her lip quivered. I smiled as warmly as I could and wiped both cheeks with my thumbs.

I pointed at my ears and then to her, asking the question I already knew the answer to.

She stared.

I covered my ears and then covered hers, showing her I understood what was happening.

She slowly nodded, and her eyes filled again.

I laid my hand on her cheek, then brought her into my arms. I held her tight, and I could feel the warmth of her tears sliding down my shoulder.

I was an adult and this whole experience had completely knocked me on my ass. I couldn't imagine being a child, separated from my family with strangers after such a crash, and with no hearing on top of it. She had to be terrified.

My heart broke for her and, not wanting to let her go, I tried to raise her up to carry her back with me. As I stood, my bruised ribs —re-injured from my earlier fall—reared up in protest, and I was forced to lower back down to my knees.

I felt a hand on my back and straightened, allowing Jack the room to bend down and replace me. He scooped her up into his arms, petting her golden hair as she nuzzled her head against the crook of his neck.

"It's alright," he murmured, caressing her back. "We're all going to take care of you for now. We'll get you home soon. It'll be alright."

He carried her back to camp, and we all followed quietly. I wasn't sure which emotion was stronger, my empathy for her or my surprise at Jack's gentleness with her.

Jim walked alongside me and, in the softest voice I'd ever heard come out of him, said, "Bless her little heart." Had the moon not been at our backs, I could've sworn his eyes had teared up.

We entered camp and a concerned Bertie reached out to stroke her hair. "What happened?" she asked, raising on tiptoes to peer at her face in Jack's arms.

"She can't hear," he said back.

"Oh." She made a "tsk" noise and laid her hand on the girl's back. "We'll have you conversing in no time, my little angel."

Jack knelt inside the shelter and gently laid her on a large men's sweater. My heart warmed as he ran his hand once more over her hair and covered her with a t-shirt.

Absentmindedly, my fingers curled around the little pendant of my necklace while we watched them from outside. He remained kneeling beside her for some time—until he was sure she was asleep—then rose and joined us by the fire.

"What are we going to do with her?" he asked, sitting down and crossing his long legs in front of him.

Bertie, seated on a suitcase with an oversized jacket wrapped around her shoulders piped up. "Well, do any of you know sign language?" She peered around the fire. "I thought not. We'll develop a language—essentials first—hungry, thirsty, hurts, danger… then we'll grow it from there day by day. We'll all have to learn it." Her eyes met mine. "She'll be fine. She's young and this won't debilitate her. We'll get her talking. You'll see."

"If anyone can do it, Bertie can," Bud assured us, glowing with pride as he sat in the sand next to her case and laid his hand over hers. "Bertie was a schoolteacher… Prettiest and smartest schoolteacher any one of those kids had ever seen."

"Oh, Bud." She giggled. It was a flirtatious giggle that could make me almost picture them young and madly in love.

"Well, you were!" he continued, giving her hand a small shake.

"How'd yuns meet each other?" Jim asked, falling onto his butt in the sand beside Jack.

Bud beamed. "Oh, we were teenagers when we started dating. She'd come walkin' past ole' Bill's garage—that's where me and the boys would meet up before headin' off to school—wearing her little red polka-dot dress and fancy shoes, carrying her books… and every single one of us'd go quiet and just stare. We'd stay just like that, heads turned, watchin' all five-foot-two of her until she'd round the corner. Every. Single. Day."

"I never wore a red polka dot dress."

"You did too. I remember it clear as day."

"Bud, you're as colorblind as the day I met you. That dress was orange." She laughed heartily.

"Anyway," he grinned, "I worked down at my dad's shoe store after school, and one day, I caught her coming back the opposite direction." He waved his free hand out to pause the story, "Now, keep in mind, I'd been tellin' the boys for months this was the girl I was gonna marry… so," his eyes went wide, "there she was coming toward me. She had on a little blue dress."

"It was green."

He let go of her hand and held both out in front of him to better tell the story. "She had on a little blue dress, and a little red hat, and it was like God himself came down and answered all my prayers because right as she was coming up to pass me, the heel of her shoe broke and she fell—God as my witness—straight into my arms."

We all leaned in, fascinated.

"So there I was, standing out on the step in front of my store, my future wife in my arms with a broken shoe. And do you know what I said to her?"

We all held our breath.

"He said," Bertie interrupted, pausing for effect, "why yes, I would love to dance. And proceeded to spin me round!"

"I did!" He smiled, and not quite finished with the story, he raised his hands again. "But the thing is, I was so proud of myself for thinking of such a great line that I'd forgotten her heel was broken and I spun her around and flat on her bottom into the street!"

Bertie laughed hard at this, wiping tears from her eyes. "Oh, it's true! And it was a fairly busy intersection at that time of day. He came flying off that sidewalk to my rescue!" She looked affectionately at him and couldn't find the next words for laughing.

"And got hit by a damn Buick!"

She bent with her laughter, waving him off. "Just barely. It nudged him in the behind!"

"It hit me nonetheless! So... she pretty much had to go out with me after that. I fixed her shoe and asked her to the movies that night. We've been inseparable ever since."

He took her hand then, locked their fingers, and pulled their entwined hands up to his mouth to kiss them. "That will have been fifty years ago in a few months."

There was a moment of quiet and then Jim sniffled. "Hot damn, yuns got me sittin' over here grinnin' like a possum eatin' a sweet potato!"

And for the very first time, we all *really* laughed out loud together.

"Wait a minute…" Bruce frowned in thought, looking from Bud to Bertie to Lilly. "You said you worked at your father's shoe store? I knew you looked familiar… Are you… Buddy and Alberta Renaud?"

Bud smiled, nodding at that.

"And your son is Richard Renaud. I knew I'd heard that story before! I read it in Time magazine last year… how you two built the Renaud Boot Factory into the staple it became after the war… and then Richard… with the hotel chain."

I grinned. My own Renaud boots sat feet away in the shelter behind us.

Bud sighed. "That's us." He smoothed his hand over Bertie's knee. "Although Time tends to make the story much more glamorous than it was."

"You'll have to share it with us."

Bertie yawned, a cough escaping as she did so.

"A story for another night," Bud promised, standing and extending his hand to her. "Come on Bert, let's get you to bed now. We'll get started with Isobel first thing in the morning. Don't worry. Children are resilient. With Bertie's guidance, she'll be talking up a storm before you know it."

Hearts full, one by one, our little island crew made their way back to the shelter.

I remained in the sand, legs stretched out in front of me, staring into the fire.

I'd always pictured Chris and I growing old together, and I'd always imagined we'd be as happy as Bud and Bertie; sharing stories of our first meeting with that same level of affection. It was hard to think he was gone forever. He really didn't *feel* gone. He felt distant—like he'd just gone away on a trip and would be back any minute; our problems still right there for us to solve when he returned.

And that was the thing that nagged me most. The problems were still as present as if he were. I still felt the resentment, the hurt, and the desire to make things right between us. If he were gone—*really gone*—those problems would've died with him.

Wouldn't they? Surely, a widow didn't still harp on her dead husband's past mistakes?

"You alright?" Jack's voice came low and hoarse from across the fire, shaking me from my thoughts.

I jumped at the sound. "I thought everyone had gone to sleep."

In the distorted air over the fire, I watched him stand, stretching tall before he moved around the flames. He sat down next to me, extending his legs and leaning back against his forearms, coughing to one side. "Couldn't sleep."

"Me neither."

"You probably should," he said, motioning to the scrapes on my knees. "You've had a busy day."

We both stared at the fire for a while, listening to the crackle and pop of the wood as the flames danced over it.

"You wanna talk about whatever's going on in that head of yours?" he asked, his eyebrows raised as he looked toward me.

"No."

I didn't want to talk to *him* about it. How could I? He was part of the problem; most of the reason I was revisiting our marital problems. That split second at the creek where he'd glanced at my lips had sent me back through the years of pain Chris and I had delivered each other. Of course I couldn't talk to him about it.

There was a much longer silence between us then that was only broken by a sudden coughing fit that overtook him. His eyes watered as he sat up and bent his head over his shaking body.

"That cough is getting worse, you know."

He nodded, wheezing as he steadied his breathing. "I'll be fine." Leaning to one side to spit, he took the inhaler out of his pocket and pressed it to his lips.

"You really should take it easy for a few days. That inhaler is only going to last so long."

He shook his head. "It's fine, really."

"It's not fine and you know it." I snapped, leaning in. "You're getting worse, not better. If we're going to stand any chance of getting off this island, we need you healthy. You're the biggest and strongest of us all."

"I can't just sit back and do nothing right now." He stifled another cough, placing the inhaler back in his pocket before he leaned back on his hands. "We need food and a large platform for a signal fire ready to go if a ship or a plane comes looking for us. We need to stock more water and prepare to get back out on the raft if a ship or plane doesn't come soon. Everyone here is injured in some way or another, and with no doctor among us, who knows how bad those injuries actually are? Have you seen Kyle's arm? Or Bertie's cough? And you? You aren't exactly the model of health right now. There's too much at risk to sit and do nothing. And we need to get up on that summit to look out. Sooner than later."

I shook my head. "That cough sounds like pneumonia. You keep going at the rate you are and you'll be dead long before anyone else."

He lifted his palm to silence me. "I'll worry about me."

I rolled my eyes and focused my attention back on the flames, allowing the silence to return.

"You're not a good liar, ya know," he said finally.

I laid back on my forearms next to him and raised an eyebrow. "Excuse me?"

"Easy, easy... not picking a fight, Red... Just saying, you probably shouldn't play poker for a living."

"Please don't call me Red," I said, tipping my head back to look at the stars. "When have I ever lied to you?"

"I asked if you wanted to talk because I could tell you did."

"Hmmf." I laid back on the sand, folding my arms beneath my head. He followed suit beside me, our elbows nearly touching. "And you're suddenly what... this island nice-guy who's sweet to little girls and cares about people's feelings?"

"Do you argue with everyone naturally or is it just me?"

"I'm not arguing," I sighed, "I just miss—well, I'm *trying* to miss my husband."

I stared up into the sky, searching for the movement of a satellite or airplane, and saw nothing but the infinite stillness of the stars. "He was my entire world once. I don't even know who I am without him... like he's..." I turned my head toward him. "You really wanna talk about this?"

His eyes stayed on the sky and he nodded. "I'm all ears."

I shifted my gaze back upward. "It's like he's a part of me… a part of me that doesn't *feel* gone—just far away… does that make sense? I miss him… not the way you'd miss someone who's died, but the way you miss someone who's left… Like all the unfinished business is still here waiting for him. And today, when we got to the island, I don't know… something came over me… like I had to look for him. I know the back of the plane exploded and I should know he's gone. He just doesn't *feel* gone."

His head moved a little in acknowledgement.

"And I don't know what to do with myself now. How do I mourn someone whose loss I can't feel? It's eating me alive. I should feel something… Shouldn't I?"

He turned on his side and propped his cheek up on his fist. "You want me to answer or do you just want me to listen?"

I blinked. "An answer would be helpful if you have one."

"You just survived a plane crash," he said, running a finger through the sand. "Your head was split open and your ribs have been badly bruised, if not broken. You've endured a massive storm in a raft on the Pacific and lived through days of non-stop bobbing on the water… You've been struggling to recover from a concussion, and been in and out of feverish dreams. You've witnessed death, been set upon by sharks, haven't eaten, barely slept, and you're surrounded by strange people in a strange place." He cleared his throat. "Your body and your brain are in survival mode. You can't feel anything outside of attempting to stay alive. None of us can. The loss will come when your body and your brain have had a chance to heal."

I could feel a lump forming in my throat, but I swallowed it down and rolled back to gaze upward. *'Maybe,'* I thought. *'Or maybe I am entirely and inappropriately distracted by the nearness of you.'*

Chapter Thirteen

In a dream, I found my husband once more… Only he wasn't my husband yet in the memory I landed upon. We were young and full of life; our problems hadn't become an immovable stain upon our hearts just yet.

It was our fifth official date, and he'd taken me to a state park an hour and a half outside the city. The air was clean and the birds surrounded us in song. We walked for hours and never saw another soul.

Chris was holding my hand, and the heat of the day's hike had formed perspiration between our palms. Neither of us dared let go of the other. Every touch was coveted—magical—and as we walked, I would feel my hand shift a little in his, and my stomach would dance.

"Just a little farther," he said over my head. "I promise it's worth it."

We'd detoured off the main trail—one that was lined with man-made wooden railing and wooden beams underfoot—to trek through a small dirt path in the trees. A bit too used to city living, I was concerned about finding our way back, but the promise of a surprise ahead and the ease with which this man was leading me to it suppressed any anxiety I might've had.

We came out at a clearing that overhung a miniature waterfall, spilling out over a wall of rock into a creek about thirty feet below us. On the rock cliff, he'd spread a blanket with wine, two glasses, and a little wicker basket.

"M'lady." He smiled, gesturing toward the little picnic.

I'd never been *"romanced"* before. I didn't know how to respond. My cheeks hurt from smiling, and I couldn't help but feel a little ridiculous. Men in the real world didn't do these kinds of things.

"You take all your women out here?" I joked.

"Never liked any of them enough to bother with even a second date, let alone enough to invest in a *wicker* picnic basket."

I let go of his hand and knelt to inspect the contents of said basket. He'd made us ham and cheese sandwiches, wrapped in wax paper, inside a ziplock bag, and pressed up against a chilled ice pack. He'd bought a couple bags of kettle chips—my favorite, a pack of strawberries, and filled a plastic container with assorted cheeses and crackers. He'd picked up my favorite wine from the first date, and there was a little iPod positioned alongside a single yellow lily resting on one of the place settings. "When did you— how did you?"

He knelt beside me, his finger running up my spine to my neck and circling round to tuck my hair behind my ear. "You like it then?" His eyes met mine, and I could tell he was genuinely searching for my approval.

"Are you kidding me? I... I'm speechless. Normal people don't do this kind of thing!" I touched his chin. "I love it."

He grinned, his bright white teeth a beacon of pride. "Well, I'm not normal. And I'm glad you like it." He laid a kiss on the top of my head and shuffled into a sitting position beside me.

Pulling out a little utility knife from his pocket, he unfolded a corkscrew and went to work on opening the bottle while I took in the magnificence of all he'd done.

As he poured a glass of wine and handed it to me, I blurted out, "Funeral flowers..."

"What?" he laughed, his focus following mine to the lily I was staring at.

"My mom always said they reminded her of funerals. But I always loved them." I looked back at him. "I haven't really been to many funerals so I suppose they haven't been ruined for me yet."

He took the lily and positioned it behind my ear. "I don't suppose I've been to many either."

He contemplated it for a minute. "Actually, not one, and I like lilies. They suit you."

"Not one?" I echoed. "I remember being at my grandpa's funeral as a kid. I don't remember much though, certainly not the flowers anyway. I remember seeing my uncle tear up though, and I never saw that before."

He was engaged and listening, so I continued. "My father wasn't around, so my uncle Bill helped raise me. Never saw anything in him but strength... and I remember seeing his eyes water that day and that broke my heart. Was the only time I ever saw him vulnerable."

He touched my leg. "I wish I would've met him at the wedding. Tell me your favorite memory of him."

I grinned. "Christmas. His face on Christmas when he'd hand my sister and I our presents. He was always so happy to watch us open them. We didn't have much money-wise, but between my mother, him, and their sister, we had plenty of gifts. I hate that you didn't meet him. I think I'd like you to."

His face lit up at that. "I think I'd like that very much."

We ate our sandwiches and drank our wine, chit-chatting casually over the next hour until he said, "Let's climb down," and motioned toward the cliff.

I peered over at the jagged rocks and back to him as he stood and extended his hand to me. "Are you crazy?"

"I've done it at least..." he looked up in thought and back down to me, "once before, trust me. I won't let you fall."

A normally very level-headed person, I don't know what compelled me to take his hand then and follow him to the edge of the cliff, but I did.

"I'll climb down to that ledge there." He pointed at a small ledge about ten feet below us, big enough to barely hold both of us. "And then I'll guide you down—I'll catch you if you fall," he winked, "and then we'll both jump to that one across from it, I'll lead us down that ledge from there.."

"This is nuts," I said under my breath as he disappeared over the ledge.

'You're going to fall and crack your head wide open and bleed to death in the middle of nowhere,' I heard my mother's voice assuring me.

But I stood at the edge and watched as he gracefully hopped down onto the ledge and lifted his arms to me. "Okay, come on!"

'Oh Alaina, you're not seriously about to climb down this waterfall?' my mother's voice persisted, even as I slowly slid my legs behind me and over the edge.

I worked my legs downward, holding onto the rock for dear life until I felt his hands slide up my legs to my waist. "I've got you," he said, and I let go for him to lower me down, smiling all the way until my feet touched the rock.

"It's fun, right?" He grinned down at me. "Now's the tricky part. We're going to jump there." He pointed to a much larger rock ledge about five feet across and three feet down from our rock, near enough to the waterfall to show droplets of water dancing across its face. "I'll jump first, then I'll catch you when you come over."

He jumped down, swiftly and gracefully, his long legs making it look more like a step than a jump. I looked around me.

I didn't think I was capable of climbing back up the way we'd come, so it was either jump or live on this rock forever. Gathering what courage I was able to muster, I jumped down into his open arms.

I held him tight, letting the cold mist dance on my cheeks for a minute, grateful to still be alive.

"Okay," he said, motioning toward the slope of rocks that led the rest of the way down to the creek. "The rest is easy."

Hand in hand, he in front of me, we carefully worked our way down to the creek bottom where we removed our shoes and socks to walk along the rocky water. We stood just outside the waterfall so stray droplets of cool water kissed our faces, arms, and legs.

The water was freezing in contrast to the hot summer, and my toes were delighted.

He wrapped his arms around me and kissed my mouth, warm and soft, pulling away to brush the hair from my face with one hand. "Alaina." He blinked and swallowed. "I..." Pausing, he tucked my hair behind my ear and adjusted the lily he'd placed there.

He looked back to my eyes then, and the words came fast and shaky and without room for breath in between. "This whole thing... Today... I wanted it to be special because I needed to tell you I love you, and I'm sorry. I know I should wait, it's too soon, and all the other reasons why, but I love you and that's all of it. I love you, and I couldn't stand the words being held up inside me any longer. I love you with everything I've got and you don't have to say it back, you just have to know it, and know that I'd do anything, absolutely anything, to make you happy. I'll climb up there and dive head first if you tell me that makes you happy. It's absolutely insane, but that's how I feel about you."

His eyes darted from left to right, searching my eyes. "So there. You have it. I love you, and now I've said it five more times than I've ever said it to anyone in my life and I know I should stop talking now but I'm slightly terrified of what you might say, so I ⸺"

I pulled him to me, kissing his mouth and immediately parting his lips. Pressed against him, my body prickled at the feel of his hands on my skin, soft and vulnerable as they ran up my arms, down my back, into my hair, then growing more and more comfortable; more and more anxious as they began to pull.

I'd never had a man do so much to show his love. The picnic, the scenery, the way he kissed me... I felt like I'd been whisked away into some romantic movie. Surely, this was too good to be true...

I ran my palms down his chest, separating our bodies as my fingers found the edge of his shirt and worked their way beneath, pushing it up until he broke away from the kiss long enough to pull it over his head with one arm.

With our foreheads pressed together, my gaze followed my hands up his bare torso, watching as I felt my way past his abdomen, up across his wide solid chest, along his neck and shoulders to slide the fingertips back down his back. I looked at him then, our foreheads still touching, and as though I couldn't contain it any longer either, I exhaled with a smile. "I love you too."

He came alive then, his arms circling around me to lift me up to his mouth before I could even finish the breath.

He led me backwards to the edge of the water; our lips locked in a kiss that grew hotter, wilder, and more desperate for each other. As my feet hit solid ground, my knees bent on their own and he lowered me down to the grass while I reached, pulled, and grabbed at every part of him, entirely unconcerned that we could potentially be discovered by other nature-lovers.

This was my great romantic moment. To hell with onlookers.

His mouth released mine and I gasped for breath while his arm beneath me pulled me closer, arching me upward so his lips could find their way to my neck.

We were absolutely mad with our desire for one another, and I was relatively certain any unsuspecting nature-lovers were going to get quite a show if they lingered too long. Nothing would've stopped either of us in our determination to have the other undressed.

"Oh god," I whimpered softly when he pressed his full weight against me once, hard and wanting, then back as he worked his way down my neck to my shoulder.

With one arm locked around me, he slid the other up my torso, pushing my tank top up and over my head. He groaned in approval as he looked down at my bare breasts.

Before I could make a sarcastic comment about being braless in the wild, his mouth took them, one at a time, claiming them as his from that moment on.

I was his. I didn't rip my clothes off in public places... but for him, I didn't care. He could do with me whatever he pleased because I was entirely possessed by him.

I tangled my fingers in his hair, urging his lips back to mine, and he obliged, his mouth covering mine, thick and wet, both of us breathing heavily, our bodies moving against each other.

He kissed me deeper, his hand skidding downward to my shorts, and I whimpered once more against him as he found me, wet and aching, his long fingers sliding inside while his mouth found my ear.

"Say it again," he commanded in a raw, low voice, biting delicately at my earlobe.

But my mind was blank and there was nothing but the feel of his fingers inside me, the need to feel more, the torturous wanting.

I pulled at his shorts, but his free hand came out from behind me, forcing me back to lie flat on the grass as he grabbed both of my hands and pulled them over my head.

"Say it again," he breathed more desperately into my ear, removing his fingers only long enough to pull down my shorts before resuming.

I couldn't think. My body begged him further. I panted and my legs trembled as his fingers slid deeper.

He let go of my hands and kissed my lips harder, reaching down with his free arm and shifting his weight. I could hear the zipper and the sliding of fabric on his skin. I was shaking, trembling, teetering on the edge of reality when he moved to my ear once more. "Say it again."

I shook and arched against his mouth on my ear; his fingers taunting me, rising me up and back in a constant battle. "I love you," I breathed, and his fingers left me empty only for a moment before he pushed himself inside me.

And he filled me entirely.

I was his.

I was his and he knew it. He claimed me with every thrust and every touch of his lips to my skin.

When it was over, the full weight of him lay on top of me, and I basked in the feel of him, exploring the skin of his torso with my fingertips, both of us breathless and limp.

"Dear God, woman." He lifted himself up to look at my face. "You're going to be the death of me, I just know it."

Chapter Fourteen

The next morning, returned to the reality of being deserted on an island, tempers ran hot. The excitement of finding land had worn off and the realization that we may be stuck on the island indefinitely kicked in. We had fire and the shelter was coming along, but surviving long term *together*... Well, that was something else. Something a few of us couldn't quite come to grips with.

"Now, Got dammit, there ain't no reason we cain't load up as much water and food as we can carry and get back out on that dang raft!" Jim insisted. "We cain't just sit here and wait!"

"Jim," Magna argued, "it's the Pacific ocean. That storm we took on the first night is nothing compared to what's possible. It's the rainy season and storms much larger than that are known to hit this area. We're safer here. We'll make signals. Big enough for a plane to see."

"Ain't nobody findin' us out here, woman! Look around ye! We got better luck out in 'em waves comin' across a shipping route than we do sittin' here with our thumbs up our asses."

"I think that's an unnecessary risk to take at this point," Jack said. "Do you remember the first night? Frank was a big man and fell out of the raft. We barely made it through that storm."

"You ain't the boss of nobody, Hoss." Jim narrowed his eyes at him. "What you know about survivin' in the wild anyways? Anything? What you gonna do out here? How you gonna eat? Huh? You gonna bat 'em purdy blue eyes at the fish and pray they come a-floppin??"

Jack balled his hands into fists.

"That's right, you cain't do diddly squat without me! You don't know shit from shinola, and you Got damn well know it. Soon as my arms can move, I'm takin' my happy ass back out on that water. Y'all be damned."

"I know the land," Magna said softly, placing her hand on Jack's arm. "Plenty here to eat. Plenty more to catch out there. We can survive here…" She looked at Bertie and Bud where they sat on the sand. "*They* can survive out here… long as it takes."

Jim interrupted before Jack could speak. "Well, yeah we can *survive* out here, but what in the hell's the point of just survivin? Dammit, woman, if we get back out there, we can find ships. We can go home!"

"He's not wrong," I added, looking at Jim who flashed a smile in my direction. "No one is."

His smile promptly disappeared.

"We should consider staying for a while… until the rain season is over and everyone has had time to heal at the very least. We could stock up on food and water... *maybe* consider getting back out there if no one finds us in a certain amount of time?"

Lilly paced near the shelter. "How long? A few months? A few *years*? How long do we wait?"

"I don't know…" I sighed, looking around us. "But we've got time to figure that out. There's no sense in us standing here arguing about it now when none of us are in any condition to go anywhere any time soon." I eyed Jim's splinted arms. "Especially you."

Jim rolled his head back and groaned. "Lordt help me." Kicking the sand at his feet, he looked back at us and I watched his surrender change his entire posture. "Welp, come on wit' yas then. Since y'all ain't got the sense GOD GAVE A GOOSE, might as well teach yuns a thing or two about catchin' fish. Cain't just sit here eatin' bananas for months on end."

"I'll come with you." Bud stood. "I haven't been fishing in years. Lilly, you should learn this."

Lilly stopped pacing. "You want *me* to catch a fish? Grandpa, you can't be serious."

He frowned. "You're gonna have to carry your weight here, sweetheart. I'm very serious."

She swallowed. "Do I... do I have to touch it?" She looked down at her perfectly pink nails.

Bud laughed. "Oh honey, it's not gonna bite ya. Come on."

Lilly looked at Jack, batting her eyes. "Are you going?"

Jack crossed his arms over his chest. "No. I've got to work on the signal here."

Phil stood from where he'd been sitting next to Anna. She'd peeled back the bandage on Kyle's arm and was examining it. She'd been wrought with concern over it potentially getting infected. He cleared his throat. "I'll stay too and work on the shelter."

Lilly looked at me, desperate. "Alaina? Come with? Please?"

I smiled. "Sure. I haven't been fishing in forever."

"Oh, thank God." She sighed, wrapping her arm in mine and leaning against my shoulder as she turned us to follow Jim and Bud down the beach. She leaned into my ear. "Are they slimy?"

"Lilly," I squeezed her arm in mine, "you'll have to touch one and see."

Fishing in the ocean was interesting. First, Jim had us all pick out long branches from the tree line. With the utility knife, we cut two of these into spears. We wound the fishing line around the other two to create poles, cutting a small "V" shape at the top to control the pole. We had hooks, but with nothing to use as bait, we decided upon lures and fashioned two out of Lilly's dangly silver feather earrings. She wasn't thrilled about losing her favorite earrings to a fish.

Once Jim had set Bud and Lilly up on a rock, he followed me down to the shore to practice spearing.

"First things first." He plopped down in the sand and stuck his booted foot out toward me. "Help me take these off and roll my pant legs up."

I raised my eyebrow but obliged, pulling the boot off to release the very pungent odor of socks that had stayed wet for too long. "Oh dear God, Jim." Holding my nose, I pulled the sock between my thumb and forefinger and rolled his pant leg up, repeating the process on the other side.

He smiled. "Whooooo Lordy, feels good to get them sumbitches off." He wiggled his toes and dug them in the sand. "Now, let's get started."

He rocked side to side until he got his feet under him and stood up. "Now…" He looked at me, still holding my nose. "Well get the stick, woman! I ain't got all damn day!"

I collected my spear and we waded out knee deep into the water. "Now," he said softly, "you stay still as you can... so still they'll think you're part of the landscape, see... And you hold the spear out... No... not like that…"

He groaned in frustration. "OUT woman, hold the stick OUT, like you gettin' ready to stab somethin' with it! Come on."

I adjusted my grip.

"There you go. Bend your knees a lil' bit so ye' don't tump over... good good... now stay still and if something swims up, stab down in front of the summbitch." He turned to walk back to the shore.

"Jim?" I called back, staying frozen in position.

"You keep quiet now. I'll check in on ye' later."

At that, he walked off to leave me alone with absolutely no clue what I was doing.

I stood there and watched the water…

'*Well, this is pointless,*' I thought as I stood perfectly still staring at the same bit of sand for a short eternity. '*If he wanted me to do absolutely nothing today, he's definitely made that possible. This would've been a much better job for Lilly.*'

Five minutes passed, then ten, then twenty, and my arm was starting to burn when a little flash of white caught the corner of my eye.

'*Okay Alaina, be still... wait for it... wait for it...*'

As it came close, I stabbed down right in front of it, only to watch it dart out of reach before the spear could come anywhere close to touching it.

'*You sneaky little bastard.*'

I resumed my position, excited to try again.

Another twenty minutes passed before a shadow in the water nearby moved toward me. '*Okay, here we go. This time let it get closer.*'

Again, I stabbed and missed.

On the third attempt, a big dark fish came in from the nearby rocks.

It swam toward me, slowing as it got closer.

'*Come on, big guy... nothing to see here... come on...*'

It cautiously moved forward and, just as it swam beneath my spear, I stabbed down with all my strength.

At my feet there was a flurry of sand and... movement!

"JIM!!!!" I screamed, "I GOT ONE!! I ACTUALLY GOT ONE!!"

I was terrified to move, horrified that if I lifted the spear, it might get away. It was thrashing wildly at my feet and bigger than I thought it was, forcing my arm to vibrate as it fought against the spear.

Jim appeared on the beach. "You serious, sis?"

"YES!!!! WHAT DO I DO NOW?"

He came splashing into the water toward me. "Well hell, I don't know, lift the pole up."

"It's big though... What if it... Idunno, flops off?"

"Woman, where's it gonna flop off to with a big ole' hole stuck through the middle of it? Lift the dang pole up."

I adjusted my grip and pulled the pole out of the water. Floundering on the end was a massive spotted fish with sharp looking fins.

"Well, I'll be a son of a bitch, that's a damn grouper!"

I laughed, inspecting the wriggling fish as I struggled to keep the spear steady. "Is it edible?"

He smiled. "Sweetheart, that one'd feed us all. Hell, I didn't think you's gonna actually catch nothin'… You're a dang natural! Come over here and whack it in the head and see if you cain't catch us another one!"

"WE FOUND SOMETHING!" Lilly shouted from down the beach, hopping from toe to toe. "COME QUICK!! YOU'RE GONNA WANT TO SEE THIS!"

I rushed out of the water, lowering the fish down onto the sand and pinning it there.

"WE'LL BE RIGHT WITCHA!" Jim turned his attention back to me. "Put yer foot on it, then pull 'at spear out and whack it with the dull end."

I did as I was told, closing my eyes as I jammed the dull end of my spear against the head and the fish stopped moving.

"Alright, we got dinner. Grab it by the gill there and let's go see what kind of nonsense Princess thinks she's found."

I slid my fingers into the fish's gill, lifting it with some effort. I grinned, pride sweeping over me as I took in the sheer size of it.

We hurried down the beach to the rocks where Lilly danced impatiently.

"We got one too!" She motioned beyond her where Bud stood holding a white fish by the gills.

"Oh, that one's kinda pretty!" She hopped around mine. "Look how big it is, grandpa!"

Bud whistled, "Oh that's a beaut!"

I held it toward Lilly. "Wanna touch it?"

She cringed, "No, thank you."

"Come on!" I wiggled it. "It's not even slimy."

She raised an eyebrow. "It's not?"

"Nope."

Reluctantly, she reached a single finger toward it, and just as she laid the finger on the fish, Jim crept up behind her and barked in her ear. She screamed an ear-piercing scream and jerked away.

"Jim, you asshole!" she shouted when she'd recovered, knotting her hands into fists and stopping just short of punching him in his broken arm.

"Oh, come on now, Sis, I's just havin' a little fun." He grinned.

"Come on." She climbed over the rocks and motioned us to follow. "You have to see this!"

We followed as she skipped excitedly down the beach and turned into a small cove between the rocks. As I turned the corner, my mouth dropped open.

Pulled up high on the sand and wedged between two towering rock faces was a small wooden boat lying upside down. Its white paint had faded and peeled over the years and the wood had decayed heavily but was still intact. It was about twelve feet long and maybe four feet wide with two very decrepit paddles lying at its side.

"Well, that's an old lifeboat," Jim marveled. "Wonder if she'll still float?"

Lilly clapped. "That's not all! Look at this!" She crawled around the side of the boat and pulled out a small wooden box, standing and presenting it to us. She popped the latch and opened it, revealing a perfectly preserved brass spyglass collapsed inside a red velvet mold.

"Oh wow," I sang, handing my fish to Bud and reaching in to pull the small telescope out and extend it. "Lilly, this is amazing!"

I held it up and pressed the eyepiece against my eye, closing the other as I scanned the farthest reach of the horizon. "We can search for ships."

"Someone's been here, on this island!" she said. "You think they got rescued? You think we could use this boat to go home?" She glanced between Bud and Jim.

"No honey." Bud smiled affectionately at her. "It's too rotted out and small for that ocean."

"*But*," Jim interjected, "we could use it for fishin'—we'll have to patch it up a bit first—and if we did spot a ship, we could use it to paddle out closer to it."

She looked down and twisted her lips, disappointed. "Oh… alright."

"Ay, we'd best get out of the sun for a while." Jim hid a smile as he looked at me. "We'll come back out here tomorrow, see what we can do about this boat."

Lilly nodded, taking a deep breath in and out as I collapsed the spyglass and set it back in the box in her hands.

"Ay Princess, since ye' ain't carryin' nothin' big, come over here'n grab my boots for me." Jim looked back at me and winked.

"You're gonna want to take your fish back now," Bud said, extending the grouper to me. "Wouldn't want anyone thinking I'd caught it, would you?"

I happily took the fish as we headed back over the rocks.

When the rest of our crew spotted us coming down the beach, I couldn't help but smile.

A very excited Anna met us halfway. "Oh my goodness! That's huge! Magna got us some weird-looking algae to go with it. She says it's full of nutrients so... Oh, I'm so excited! We'll eat an actual hot meal tonight!"

It was nice to feel proud of myself for a change. Knowing that I'd caught the hot meal we'd all share made me feel accomplished and worthy of the life I'd somehow managed to escape with.

By the time we'd reached the camp, my arm was on fire from carrying the grouper. I made sure everyone saw it before I set it on the flat rock where Magna had set up a space to clean them.

"Oh honey," she looked up at me and shook her head. "You are going to be hurting tonight."

For the first time, I noticed the stinging sensation that ran across my nose, along my shoulders, arms, and down my back. I extended my arms out in front of me. "Oh... crap."

I'd burned a little on the raft but stayed mostly out of harm's way under the canopy. The fluorescent pink that now covered my arms, neck, back, and face made the sunburn from the raft look like a walk in the park.

"There's a small travel bottle of aloe vera in one of the carryon cases and some sunblock too," she said in her deep voice, raising one of her salt and pepper eyebrows at me. "If anyone on this island's going to need it, it's going to be you."

Anna was at my side. "I'll grab it. You should probably get out of the sun."

I sighed and walked over to the shelter where Jack was securing the side wall. He saw me and stifled a laugh that in turn forced his words to come out in a cough. "Holy hell, Red!"

I sat down on the bamboo boards beneath the shelter's canopy and leaned back, basking in the cool of the shade. "Yeah, yeah."

"Impressive fish." He tightened the rope he'd been tying and came to sit next to me. He hid a smile as he inspected me. "That's gonna hurt like hell."

"It's not that bad," I lied.

"And those freckles! They've multiplied!"

"They do that." I looked out over the beach to see the very large SOS signal they'd formed out of logs and rock along the sand. Near it stood a giant fire signal platform, a tall pillar of twisting branches. Inside the shelter bordering an entire wall was a line of old glass bottles that were filled to the brim with water.

"I see you've been busy." I grabbed one of the bottles. "Do you mind?"

"Take it." He leaned back and watched me, an apologetic grimace affixed to his features.

"How's the cough—

Lilly hopped into the shelter and sat down hard between us with the aloe. "Here." She shoved the bottle in my direction and focused her attention on Jack. "Hi Jack!" She rolled a strand of hair around her finger. "Did you see our fish?"

He nodded, looking out to where Magna was cleaning them. "Yes, very impressive." He frowned at her. "*You* caught one of those?"

I could see it in her face that she considered taking credit, but she took the high road and I was proud of her for it. "No. I was fishing with a lure… didn't catch anything. Alaina *speared* the big one!"

He smiled in disbelief, coughing before looking back at me. "You speared that thing?"

I stopped smearing the aloe long enough to catch his eye. "I got lucky." I continued over my cheeks and forehead and down my arms, struggling to reach the center of my back.

"Here, let me do it." Jack reached for the bottle.

Lilly snatched it up quickly. "I'll do it."

She spread the aloe across my back a little forcefully. The coolness of it on my hot skin sent a shiver up my spine, and I was thankful for what I could get. I closed my eyes and sighed with relief as she crossed over my shoulders.

"Thank you, Lilly." I smiled up at her.

She softened as she came back around to sit between us, letting the little hint of jealousy melt away. "You're welcome." Her long, now tan legs stretched out in front of us and she flexed her bright pink painted toes. "Jack, did she tell you what *I* found?"

"What'd you find?" He raised his eyebrows, pretending to be interested.

"Oh, just a boat." She grinned. "And this." She pulled the spyglass out of its box and handed it to him.

Chapter Fifteen

That night, as we all sat around the fire to share our first warm meal, Magna stood, a white flower tucked behind one ear with a small basket of more. "Tonight we celebrate," she said, somewhat ceremonially in her deep voice, calling us all to attention as the fire danced across her face.

"We celebrate our good luck—surviving, finding this island, Anna's incredible work saving us all, Lilly's amazing find, and all of us finally sitting down together to a warm meal."

She walked around the fire, stopping at each person to hand them a flower. "In the islands, we all wear the tiaré when we are celebrating. Both men and women wear them."

She smiled as she knelt to tuck one behind Isobel's ear. "If you wear the tiaré behind your left ear, you tell the world you are taken." She rose and continued, stopping at Jim. "If you wear it on your right ear," she pulled another and tucked it behind his right ear, "you are available."

"Ay momma," he grinned and winked, "how you know I ain't got some supermodel waitin' for me back home?"

"Oh Magna, I love that!" Lilly clapped next to me as Magna circled to our spot, handing us each a flower. Lilly slid hers quickly behind her right ear and smiled at Jack.

Bruce positioned his flower behind his right ear despite the gold wedding band around his left finger, and his large features made the flower look that much more fragile. "Well, since we're celebrating..." He held the bottle of Dr. Pepper out. "Who wants some?"

This was met by a barrage of "ME!" from all of us. He took a swig and passed the bottle along.

I twisted the flower in my fingers for a minute. *'Left or right, Chris? Are you out there?'* As Magna took her seat, I fastened it behind my left ear.

We'd sent Isobel on a task to gather large sea shells and twigs earlier in the day. Anna and I had then shaved the twigs down into chopsticks. We used the large sea shells as plates to hold our fish and algae dinner.

The first bite was glorious. I rolled my eyes back as the warm, salty fish touched my tongue. I held it there and savored it.

"Oh my Gooooood," Lilly groaned next to me as she did the same.

"Alaina," Phil called across the fire, mouth full of fish, "if I thought I could get away with it, I'd come over there and kiss you right now."

I smiled. I was actually proud of myself for the first time in as long as I could remember... I'd provided the fish *and* helped build the fire that cooked it. I just wished Chris could've been there to see it. Then again, I thought, *'I wouldn't have done either of those things if Chris had been here. I would've relied on him to do them...'*

"MMM MMMMM! Put that on top of your head and your tongue would beat your brains out trying to get to it," Jim informed us after Anna had placed a piece in his mouth with her own chopsticks. "Thank ye' blondie." He winked at her when she raised the sticks again.

Lilly furrowed her brow as she looked at Jim. She turned to me and Jack and leaned in scandalously. "Hey," she whispered, "how's he been... you know... going to the bathroom this whole time if he can't use his arms?"

Next to me, Jack began to cough violently. It wasn't his normal cough. This one was pure embarrassment.

I bit my lip, handing him my water, and watched Lilly's face as she very slowly put it together. Her eyes went wide after a moment. "Oooooh..... eeeeeew."

He chugged the water as she stared at him, his cheeks turning shades of red.

"Oh, don't look at me like that!" he hissed between us. "It was either *I* do it, or one of you. You're welcome!"

She looked down and poked at her fish with a chopstick, lips twitching as she held back her laughter. "That's so sweet of you. Thank you, Jack."

"Yes." I held my own amusement, looking over at him and nodding. "Thank you, Jack."

Her eyes met mine, and we both curled over in stitches.

"Ay! Ay!" Jim's head lurched to one side. "What are you two over there carryin' on about now?"

We both straightened. "Nothing, Jimmy," Lilly said innocently, looking back to me and shaking with the chuckle she held in.

"Shut up," Jack snarled as we both burst into uncontrollable laughter once more.

After a minute, we both straightened and I wiped my eyes, catching my breath and avoiding eye contact with Lilly, who was adjusting her flower and taking deep breaths.

"Magna," Lilly finally said as she wiped the mouth of the Dr. Pepper bottle and took a drink, swallowing and exhaling hard, "tell us more about Tahiti."

Magna smiled, rocking back a little to think for a moment. "Well, you know they call it the friendliest place on earth." She paused, carefully choosing the English words. "It's much different than anywhere else. Not so busy. It's simple. You go to the states and everyone's busy with their phones and their computers and their jobs... No one talks to each other in the states except through their phones and their computers... even when they're sitting next to each other."

She closed her eyes. "Not on the island though. Every morning Enoha, our local baker, makes baguettes and his son Metua comes round before dawn to deliver them fresh on our doorsteps. Haunui —that's my husband—and I," she smiled and touched her flower, "we would sit outside under our porch to share coffee and bread with our neighbors long before the sun ever came up."

She bit into a piece of fish and waited until she'd finished chewing to continue. "It's a beautiful place. Everything is either green or blue depending on which direction you look. And everyone knows you there. We talk to each other a lot. All day, everyone is always talking to someone. We have a lot of surfers who come. We often invite them to our homes for dinner. We show them the island; make friends with our visitors."

I took a drink of the warm Dr. Pepper and passed it over to Jack, enthralled in the story as it fizzed down my throat, leaving a trail of sweet cherry flavor in its wake.

"And we have one road that goes across the whole island. You never really see cars on it—well, except for the surfers—the rest of us all ride our bicycles or walk. Many of us work the resort or the charters so we all go together down to the water as the sun comes up, and we wait for each other to return home as the sun goes down."

"It's very beautiful. You see children outside playing all day and all night and if you want to close your store and go swim with the dolphins, no one complains. It's a simple life and a very happy place."

"Dolphins?" Lilly hopped in her seat. "Do you often see the dolphins?"

"Oh yes. All year we have dolphins, and so many different beautiful fish and turtles. If you stand at the water and look down, you could get lost for days in the life below you... Oh, I wish you could all come see it with me. I would show you all the best places."

"That sounds wonderful, Magna." Lilly smiled.

Magna looked beyond us to the water. "I will see it again." Her dark eyes shifted back to us. "But until then, we should be grateful for this place. It's just as beautiful. We found our own *private* paradise right here. We are here for a reason. We should learn from it... enjoy it... while we have the opportunity... before we are all pulled back to our busy lives."

I think we all collectively sighed when she'd finished her story to return to her meal. She was right. The island we'd found was very beautiful—all green or blue depending on the direction you looked... still... my heart ached for Chris. Had he been sitting there next to me, I might never want to leave. I might hide away with him and stay there forever. As it was, I was anxious to leave paradise; anxious to know if he was truly gone forever.

I reached down to the small wooden box between myself and Lilly and pulled out the telescope, pressing it to my eye and looking up at the stars. Through the magnified lens, the sky was picturesque.

"Jim," Anna said sweetly as I scanned the sky for the movement of a satellite. "What about you? Tell us where you're from... what brought you out here."

"And we wanna hear *all about* those lottery winnings," Lilly added.

Jim sighed. "Oh well... they's not much to tell really..."

'Where are all the satellites?' I frowned, lowering the telescope and rejoining the conversation.

"Don't be shy now." Bertie laid her hand on his shoulder, her shaking voice warm with affection. "We've all been sharing our stories since we met dear. Good and bad. You've been the loudest among us and yet we know the least about you."

"Well..." he started, clearing his throat. "Where to start..."

"Why don't you start by telling us where you're from, dear," Bertie encouraged him. "With an accent like that, I've been curious to know."

"Well, you wouldn't of heard of it, small town in Oklahoma. If you blinked you'd miss it." He bit into the fish Anna offered, continuing on with his mouth full. "All poor folk, mostly. We started out in Arkansas. My daddy run off when I was about ten, and my momma' moved us near her brother in Oklahoma. I ain't sore about it. Made me into a good man and I didn't like him much, anyway. Always comin' in drunk and beatin' on my mama."

"Anyways," he stretched his legs out, straightening his back as he took a deep breath in, "mama used to buy a lottery ticket—same numbers evra' few days. Well, when she passed, I kept on playin' those same numbers evra' few days. Then one day, BOOM. I won me some money."

"How much money did you win?" Lilly asked, eyes wide.

He looked over the fire at her. "Now don't go eyeballin' me now, sweetheart. I ain't no go-zillionaire or nothin, but I won some money, 'nuff to pay for a trip and come back and buy my own rig. Maybe start my own truckin' business and buy some land. Mama always talked about goin' to Bora Bora if she ever won." He frowned. "She never did make it... she never made it anywhere outside Arkansas and Oklahoma... so I thought I'd come see it for myself straight away. Hoped maybe she might somehow be able to see it through me. Ye' know?"

He paused in thought and blew out. "Ain't it a bitch though? I went my whole life being poor as old Job's turkey, finally come into some money and the Good Lordt strikes my plane out the sky so I cain't spend a damn penny. Me and Him's gonna have words when I get up there."

"If you get there before I do," Phil teased, "you tell him I've got some words for him as well... not so much about this as it would be about my second wife and whether or not she really was the devil incarnate."

Jim laughed at that. "Ay, ye' know I believe I might've met yer second wife, myself?"

Jack cleared his throat. "Me too. Got real bad breath?"

The three of them laughed thunderously, a peaceful quiet coming over us all when they'd settled.

"Bruce," Anna looked toward him, offering Jim another bite of fish, "what about you? Tell us about your wife." She glanced at the wedding band.

Bruce frowned. "No, no." He pushed a piece of algae around the shell with his chopsticks. "That's not a pleasant story and I don't want to spoil the mood."

"Don't be silly," she insisted. "There's no mood. We're just getting to know each other. You two separated then?"

"Oh... Well... We..." he started, setting his shell down and clearing his throat, "She, ah..." He looked down. "Well, I suppose separation is a good enough word as any. I always knew she was too pretty for me. Everyone said so too… She's thin and fit… Beautiful blue eyes… the cutest dimples right here." He pointed to each side of his own cheeks. "No idea how she ended up with someone like me…" He presented his belly as if that were the only explanation needed.

He blinked. "For whatever reason, she married me. I made her laugh, she said. We bought a house… and things were good for a year or so… A few weeks ago, she asked me for a divorce… said she met someone else... I knew she had. Could tell by the way she was acting… She stopped laughing at my jokes… Stopped looking at me altogether."

Once again, my thoughts returned to Chris. He hadn't laughed at me in ages. He, too, had stopped looking at me, and I couldn't help but wonder if he would've asked for a divorce the same way Bruce's wife had. Did he meet someone else? Was he only going on this trip to appease me with one final attempt to salvage what we once had?

Phil made a noise. "*Sounds* like my second wife." He raised the Dr. Pepper to Bruce. "Count your blessings buddy, sounds like you dodged a bullet."

Bruce turned his hand over in front of him, letting the light from the fire dance across the gold band. "I tried to take the ring off…" He laughed then. "It won't budge though."

Anna set her shell on the ground, leaving Jim, who'd been sitting with his mouth open for another bite, with a disappointed look on his face.

"Let me see that." She snatched his hand and inspected the finger. "I can get this off." She rubbed his fingers for a moment, then rose to her feet.

As she disappeared into the shelter behind us, Bertie laid her hand on Bruce's. "All part of a bigger plan, dear." She shifted her eyes toward the shelter and back. "Better days are coming to you, you just gotta have faith."

Anna reappeared with a coconut and dental floss. "You know," she knelt in front of him, "you could've lost your finger like this."

As she covered the finger in coconut oil and began to wrap it with floss, Jack mumbled behind me.

"What'd you say?" I asked.

"I said," he leaned toward me, "women are heartless."

I pursed my lips. "Lots of them, yes," I agreed, talking in a whisper as we watched Anna pull at the floss. "Not all." I smiled as the ring slid with ease up and off the finger.

"There! See!" Anna beamed. "You should've mentioned it sooner!"

He sat rubbing his finger, staring at her. "That's so much better. Thank you!"

"It's no problem." She smiled, holding the floss out as the ring dangled between them. "I had to do it for myself just two years ago… What should we do with this?"

He touched it lightly with one finger. "Idunno… I'd throw it in the ocean but I'm sure we could make something out of it."

"Alright." Anna stood. "Do you want to hold on to it until we do?"

He shook his head. "Nah. You keep it. Good riddance."

She tucked it into her pocket and bent to whisper something in his ear. As she came back, they both laughed.

Lilly nudged my shoulder, whispering in my ear, "Oh Bruce," she giggled, doing her best impression of Anna, "I'd be happy to keep your ring… Take me now… take me now!" She laid her head on my shoulder and sighed.

I smirked. "You're terrible."

She curled her arm around me, looking back at them. "You have no idea." She pulled me closer. "They'll be madly in love by the end of the week once I'm done here."

I felt suddenly at ease with the group. I'd never had close friends before—just family and Chris, but I felt connected to these people like I'd never felt connected to anyone outside my family. We'd gone through hell together and come out alive… come out still able to laugh together somehow.

"Ay Hoss." Jim tilted his head to one side, peering through the fire in our direction. "Let's me and you take a walk. I got somethin' I need to talk to ye 'bout."

At that, Lilly curled into me and we burst into uncontrollable laughter once again.

Chapter Sixteen

"Marry me." Chris said, his chin rested on my chest. We were lying in my bed in my apartment, only a thin sheet between our naked bodies as the morning sun spilled in from the corner window.

"What?" I laughed back at him, running my fingers through his hair. His knees were bent behind him, and I could see his feet dancing back and forth in my peripherals.

"Marry me," he repeated, his big green eyes sparkling.

"Are you serious right now?" I asked.

"Well…" he lifted his chin and laid a soft kiss where it had been, then met my eyes. "Yeah." He bent his arms on each side of me to prop himself up a little higher and I let my hands fall from his hair down his back.

We'd been dating for only six months, but I'd fallen so madly in love with him in those six months, it felt like I'd known him for years.

I paused, searching his eyes. "Chris… You're serious?" I laughed.

"Yes, ma'am."

"*You* want to marry *me*?"

"Yes, *I* want to marry *you*. Right now." His hand slid back from under my pillow and came up holding a small black box.

My face lit up. "Right now?" I ran a finger down the velvet box and he popped it open to reveal the most beautiful diamond ring I'd ever seen.

"It was my grandmother's ring," he said, watching as my finger ran along the center diamond. It was a stunning princess cut, one enormous diamond housed among a circle of smaller, all surrounded by an intricate silver braid that wrapped seamlessly into the band.

My mouth dropped open, and I looked back at him, tears in my eyes. "Of course I'll marry you!" I pulled him to me and kissed his lips.

He broke away and rose to sit back on his calves, straddling me as he placed the ring on my finger.

"This means you belong to me now." His voice was low and thick.

My eyes fixated on the ring, I smiled. "I've always belonged to you, love."

He lowered himself, arms on each side of my face, and hovered just beyond where my lips could reach. His eyes possessively scanned my face. "All mine."

"All yours, love." I wrapped my arms around his neck, but raised an eyebrow when he continued to study my face.

"Tell me what I can give you, Ally. What should our life look like ten years from now?"

I ran a finger down his arm, observing the shine of the diamond as the light from the window danced off it. "Well," I smiled, gazing back at him, "we live out in the country—small town, but not so country that we can't still come to the city easily…"

I pondered, shifting my gaze back to the ring as I ran my fingertips over his shoulders. "And we have a little white house with black shutters… and a porch that wraps around the front, with an old-fashioned swing like gramma's have… with big tall trees that circle the whole property."

I slid my hand over his jaw, and he turned his head to one side to kiss my palm. "Mmm, what else?"

"And three kids. Two boys and a girl—the girl is the youngest so the boys will watch out for her… Obviously."

"Obviously," he echoed. "What else?" He kept his eyes concentrated on me as his lips worked down the side of my wrist.

"And..." I breathed out in a sigh as his mouth came to my shoulder, his breath near enough to my neck to send a shiver through my body. "A big fluffy dog..."

"And?" He breathed against my ear, lowering his mouth to my neck.

"And," I panted heavier, tangling my fingers in his hair to pull him further up my throat, "and we sit at a table to eat dinner as a family every night... no matter how busy we are..."

His lips, now wet, worked downward, pulling the thin sheet with him as he moved his way along my collarbone. "What else?"

I closed my eyes. "And... we take the kids on vacations every year... no matter what. They need adventure so they don't get restless."

His hand slid down to cup my breast, his breath teasing as he hovered over it. "What else?"

I arched, begging him for more, but he waited there, torturing me with each exhale. "And... I... sing to them." The warmth of his mouth came down over my nipple then, and I gasped, pulling him against me.

His tongue grew heavier as I arched into him, my head swimming, heart pounding.

"What else?" His hand came up to warm the chill his escaping mouth had left on me, his nose teasing as he slowly dragged it along the center of my abdomen toward my belly button.

"And..." I pulled at his hair, begging him back to me... "and... you teach them how to build things..." He moved lower. "How to..." His breath taunted and his arms curled over my abdomen as he moved lower still... "fix... things."

He hovered, pressing me to lie flat as my body protested, shaking against him. "What else?" He asked in a long airy whisper that had my body screaming around me.

"And we... do this... every morning." My knees bent and my body curled around him as his mouth came down to find me.

"We'll fight you know... at some point," he said afterward into my shoulder. His hot skin stuck to mine as he lay lifeless and heavy across me, my insides still throbbing as we both caught our breath.

I smiled at the ceiling, running my fingertips up his back. "Yes, love, I know that."

He raised up on his forearms over me, his expression turning serious. "You and me, this isn't like everyone else. You don't get to walk out on that. You don't get to give up on that. No matter how bad the fight."

I tilted my head to one side, and I could see that he was legitimately terrified of the thought. "I won't. Not ever. I promise."

Chapter Seventeen

It'd been a few days—I'd already lost track of time—since we'd discovered the island, and our group had fallen into a sort of routine; waking up and fetching water, heading out to the rocks to find crab, stalking fish with our spears—with no additional luck there—and working on our various distress signals.

Magna, Kyle, Jack and Bud had flipped the boat over and found the wood inside more rotten than they'd thought. It would need a lot more patching before we could attempt to take it on the ocean.

Jack and Jim had grown restless with waiting. They'd insisted we climb the summit and prepare a signal on top of it. I'd argued, Anna had argued, even Bertie had chimed in, all of us insisting that neither of them were in any condition to make the climb. Both of them were stubborn and, once they had made up their minds, there was no talking them out of going.

Jack knelt in front of the inventory of colorful glass bottles and resealed emergency bags, draping the duffel bag across his chest on one shoulder and packing the opening with empty survival bags.

"We should start from the waterfall, fill these back up and go from there." He spoke past me to Jim and coughed before he focused his attention back to me. "You found the waterfall on your way down, so there's a way up from there, yes?" His voice was gruff and fatigued. He'd been coughing more regularly in the night.

"It's steep." I touched the cut on my cheek in memory. "I lost my footing and slid down it. Wouldn't be wise to take that path up even if we were all healthy. Jim definitely couldn't make it up from there without the use of his arms. I'll come with and help navigate."

He rose to tower over me, looking back at Jim. "We know the path up is on that side of the island. We'll start there, fill up and see if we can find a more manageable trail nearby."

"I'm coming with," I repeated, waiting for approval.

Jack ran a hand over his face and beard. "It's not for me to tell you what you can and can't do, Red. You wanna' come with, that's fine. Are you sure you're up for it?"

I nodded. "I'm fine."

"Alright," he ducked as he exited the shelter behind Jim, "you ready?"

"We cain't go up without fire, numbnuts," Jim scolded, nodding toward the fire. "Ay freckles, grab 'at lighter in case we need to spend the night. The rest of yuns make sure you keep that fire good 'n stoked while we're gone."

I shuffled around the campfire where we kept the lighter, feeling around in the sand. "Umm... Where is it?"

"Whatcha' mean, where is it?" Jim barreled toward me. "I saw it last night. It was lyin' right there!"

I felt around, shaking my head. "Well, it's not here now."

"Somebody take the dang lighter?" Jim shouted out.

"Don't look at me." Jack raised his hands in surrender. "I haven't touched it."

"The last time I saw it, it was sitting right there." Magna motioned to where I was standing.

"I didn't touch it," Kyle confirmed. "Dad?" he called behind him. "Did you take the lighter?"

"Why would I take the lighter?" Phil appeared from behind the shelter, zipping his sand covered dress pants and adjusting the waistband.

"Well, I didn't take it," Lilly said.

"Me neither." Anna stood, joining me to circle the fire. "Would Bud or Bertie take it?"

Lilly shook her head. "No. They didn't even come near the fire last night or this morning. Went straight out on their walk."

Bud and Bertie walked the beach every morning to catch the sunrise together, collecting any litter that might prove useful along the way.

"Well, hell," Jim frowned, "I certainly ain't got it. It's got to be around here somewheres."

"Could it have…" I swallowed, looking over the smoking coals, "gotten too close? Maybe caught fire in the night?"

Magna followed my gaze. "Surely we wouldn't have left it that close…"

"*Somebody's* got to have it," Jim said matter-of-factly. "Princess, run down 'er and find the ole' man and see if he didn't grab it up for somethin.'"

"He wouldn't take the lighter," Lilly argued, rolling her eyes.

"Just go look." His pitch raised. "Jesus woman, it ain't gonna hurt ye' to get off yer ass once in a while."

Lilly scoffed at him. "Excuse me?"

"Oh, don't start. Just go see if he's got it. I ain't got time to sit here arguin' with ye."

She raised up off the sand, blowing out and rolling her eyes before she stomped down the beach.

"Ay momma." Jim looked at Magna. "Ye' gonna have to keep this fire alive if we don't find it. Might wanna' throw a few logs on now. It's gettin' awful low."

Magna nodded and headed for our firewood.

"Everybody check yer pockets," Jim ordered. "Maybe one of ye' put it in there by mistake."

We all followed his orders and all of us came up empty.

He sighed. "The old man's *got* to have it."

Jack walked the circle around the fire, moving sand with his foot and inspecting the area thoroughly. Simultaneously, Magna tossed a few logs onto the fire and thick plumes of white smoke wafted off the semi-wet wood and straight into Jack's face.

This was the nail in the coffin I was sure would've been his undoing when we'd headed up to the summit. He coughed violently, stumbling backwards away from the smoke, where he collapsed to his knees, unable to catch his breath.

He coughed a thick wet cough over and over, placing both fists down on the sand as he attempted to get through it. Reaching one hand back to his pocket, he pulled out the little yellow inhaler as he shook with wave after wave of unrelenting coughs. He brought it to his lips and pressed the canister, but couldn't stop choking long enough to get the medicine down. He tried again… and again.

"Alright, that's it!" Anna placed our makeshift pot on the coals —a tin bucket we'd found near the trees—and filled it with water. "Nobody's going anywhere."

Anna pointed to each of us, divvying up orders as Jack shook and coughed without end behind her. "Kyle, you go through the suitcases again and see if we missed any kind of cough syrup or lozenges. There's a bottle of amoxicillin in the large freezer bag marked *'Dennis Gonzales.'* Grab that."

"Phil, I need you to gather as many smooth, dark rocks as you can carry and put them in this fire immediately."

"Alaina and Magna, I need you to take the canopy from the raft and turn it into a fully enclosed tent over the sand. We're gonna make a little steam room and see if we can't get him breathing."

We all sprang into action as Anna knelt beside Jack's writhing, wheezing body.

My hands shook as we unfastened the bright red canopy from the deflated raft.

I looked across at Magna, who was unclasping the fabric on the opposite side of me, her eyes watering as she looked from the canopy to Jack and back.

"He's gonna be fine," I assured her, trying to convince myself. "He's big and strong… He'll get through it."

She stared at him wide-eyed as he wheezed loudly. "I didn't mean to…"

I shook my head. "It's not your fault. This was going to happen either way. The man's a stubborn fool and should've been taking it easy like we all told him."

Magna and I went straight to work securing the canopy over the sand, the entire time listening to Jack choke behind us.

"Come on Hoss, spit that shit out! Come on buddy," Jim encouraged, helpless as to what he could do.

"HE DOESN'T HAVE IT!" Lilly shouted from down the beach. "I TOLD YOU HE DIDN'T HAVE IT!"

"GET YER SCRAWNY ASS UP HERE 'N HELP!" Jim yelled back.

"What's going on?" Lilly panted as she rushed into camp. "Jack... JACK!"

"We're making him a steam room," Anna informed her. "Lilly, I need you to go help Phil gather rocks."

"But... is he going to be okay?" she whimpered, kneeling beside him to run her fingers over his hair.

"If you do exactly what I say, he might," Anna ordered. "Now go get rocks. Big ones. Smooth, black ones if you can find them. Get as many as you can in that fire right away."

"Come on Jack," Anna cooed. "Breathe with me... come on... breathe with me."

Jack's lungs fought as he hacked and choked, gasping loudly for air.

"Alaina, Magna... Let's get him inside."

Neither of us spoke, but immediately scrambled to kneel on each side of him, each of us draping a heavy arm over our shoulders as we lifted him up, bending as he coughed out of control. We walked him slowly to the little red hut and, once we unzipped the flap, he collapsed inside.

"You stay here." Anna looked at me. "Help him breathe."

She turned toward the fire. "Magna, I need you to help me find something that we can turn into tea."

"Wait. What do you mean, *help him breathe*?" I asked, terrified.

"He seems to listen to you—won't listen to me at all. Lean him against you so he can breathe with you, coach him. And keep yourself and him calm. If he doesn't stop panicking, his throat will tighten even more. I'll be right back. I'm just going to get everything ready. "

Frazzled and nervous, I crawled into our little shelter where he writhed and wheezed under the dim pink light, a constant gurgling now present with each hysteric inhale.

"Okay, Jack," I soothed, climbing over him and pulling him back toward me. "Come on, sit with me. You're going to be okay. Come on, sit up with me. Since you won't listen to anyone else, I suppose you're stuck with me."

Ignoring my burning ribs, I wrapped my arms around his massive chest, bending my knees on each side of him for extra support. "God, you're heavy. Come on, inhale with me before I suffocate with you."

I took a deep breath in and he attempted to follow, the liquid in his lungs audible as he did. He burst into a new coughing fit, shaking us both.

I had no idea what I was doing so I rubbed his back until he spit and leaned him back again.

"I can't breathe," he managed.

"Yes, you can," I assured him. "You *are* breathing. It's just a little harder than normal. Nothing to get upset about. Come on now. Inhale." I took another deep breath, and he tried again, once again bursting into a coughing fit.

He bent and I rubbed his back until he spat.

"See?" I said calmly, praying he couldn't feel my heart racing. "You're alright." I ran my hands up and down his arms. "Come on, do it again."

"I… can't." He gurgled.

"Yes, you can." I pulled him back against me, inhaling. "I need you here, okay?" I leaned closer to him, whispering in his ear, "You're the only friend I've got. If you go, I'll lose my mind. So breathe with me, okay?"

I inhaled, and he followed, the liquid in his lungs babbling before he choked again on the exhale.

'Keep him calm.'

I could feel him shaking, panicking further as he struggled more and more to get air. "I have a sister, you know," I said, breathing in and waiting until he had gagged and wheezed through the exhale to continue. "Cece... If she were here, you'd all be chasing after her."

He inhaled, coughed, and spit...

"She came out with the most beautiful, natural platinum blonde hair and it only got thicker and more gorgeous as we got older."

Another inhale, cough, gag, and spit..

"Our mom was Irish. Dad was bright blonde. I looked more like mom where Cece got the perfect mix of the two. Tall-ish, blond, with mom's figure and dad's blue in her hazel eyes. I'm pretty sure the only thing I inherited from our father was a flat chest." I giggled as we inhaled and he coughed violently.

"Anyway, Cece had a little girl a few years ago. Madison— Maddy." I smiled.

Inhale... small cough...

"Maddy's five now. She got the same bright blond hair, but it's curly like mine... with the most adorable little freckles."

Inhale... cough, spit...

"She likes bugs... and Barbies." I laughed, thinking of her little body bent over a Barbie playhouse filled with black beetles.

Inhale, gurgling, struggling exhale...

"And *she* got pneumonia once." I remembered her tiny outline under the blankets as she lay in that large hospital bed, tubes and machines hooked up to her.

Inhale, violent coughing....

"She was so small, Jack. I was terrified for her. Her little lungs sounded just like yours."

Inhale, choke halfway....

"Cece was an absolute mess. She never left the hospital."

Inhale, cough, spit...

"But, you know... that little tiny human came out of it grinning and giggling. The whole family had been there... showering her with gifts... and she just ate up all the attention."

Inhale, cough...

"They kept her in bed for a week with her chest elevated... gave her antibiotics... and she was good as new... Outside collecting beetles in her little purse by the next week."

Inhale, cough...

"So..."

Anna crawled in with the pot of boiling water, setting it in the center of the shelter before she disappeared again.

"Inhale, sweetie," I reminded him, and he obliged, coughing again on his exhale.

"Here's what I think. If that little tiny human can get through it, then the massive and infamous Jack Volmer can too."

We inhaled again, and he grabbed my hand, squeezing as he struggled through another coughing fit.

"There's a bottle of antibiotics in one of those bags. We've been giving them to Kyle but there's enough to split it between the two of you. We'll get you started on them and you'll stay in the shelter for a week. Me and Magna and Phil and Lilly and Kyle can do all the heavy lifting while you rest... And then, after a week, you should be good as new too." I leaned in. "Promise you'll rest? Even if you feel better? I can't have my only friend out here die now."

He squeezed my hand again.

The flap opened again and Anna crawled inside, a pair of makeshift tongs in one hand and a second metal bucket full of rocks in the other. She zipped the canopy's zipper and spun to face us. "Okay, here comes the steam," she promised him, taking the two sticks and picking up a large rock, then dropping it in the boiling water.

The water hissed and thick plumes of steam rolled off it.

I pulled him against me and took a deep breath. He followed, coughing immediately before he could exhale.

"Come on, Jack," Anna encouraged him. "You're tough. You've got this."

He straightened against me, both of us inhaling again. The air was thick with steam and I sighed audibly when he finally exhaled with me.

"Again, go again!" Anna cheered, dropping another rock into the water.

We inhaled and exhaled again. He coughed softly, but was able to breathe through it. The air was heavy and hot and I began to sweat, but I dared not stop.

For fifteen minutes we breathed the hot steamy air and at the end his breath came easier and easier.

"Okay, that should be enough for now," Anna said finally. "We'll keep the rocks hot and the pot here in case of another attack. But that doesn't mean you're in the clear, Jack." She unzipped the flap so the light shone in.

"Look at me," she demanded. "You are drowning. Your lungs are full. You have to get it all out and that means more coughing. When your throat gets tight, you come up here and we'll throw the rocks in this water. But you're going to have to relax. NO physical activity whatsoever. And you need to keep your chest elevated. Do you understand?"

He nodded, breathing carefully.

Chapter Eighteen

Despite my attempts to separate myself from Jack, the pneumonia had brought me back sleeping shoulder to shoulder with him at night. I was too concerned to sleep anywhere else.

Lilly took notice of our sleeping arrangements and hadn't been thrilled about it. She'd gone out of her way to dote over Jack over the course of the week as he sat in the shelter, frustrated with his circumstance. She'd brought him tea, sat beside him, massaged his shoulders, would even eat dinner next to him at night, avoiding any physical labor while we all gathered food and improved the shelter around them.

Jack wasn't interested in flirting. He was miserable and wanted to be left alone. He'd cough and hack randomly, but with the steam and the antibiotics, the fits came less frequently. Restless and cranky, he would have outbursts aimed at Lilly that would send her scurrying down the beach in tears. Her sadness was always short-lived, though. She'd return an hour or two later, full of forgiveness.

I spent my days far from the shelter, busying myself at the water and avoiding the awkwardness of watching her flirt with a man I was becoming more and more attracted to.

Determined to perfect the art of spearfishing, I enjoyed the solace of being alone with my thoughts. I thought about home... about my mother and Cece... tried to work out what I'd do with myself once I'd gotten there. I couldn't imagine going back to my house without Chris, so I told myself I'd go to Cece's for a while and tried to develop some sort of plan for my life once I got there.

Would I go back to work right away? Would I even need to work? Surely the airline would compensate us for the crash... Would I sell the house? Would I ever even be able to go back to Illinois? To pass by all the places we'd once visited together? Could I look at his mother the same after this? Could she ever look at me the same for having survived without him?

Amid the sea of questions I'd go down with, there was one subject that would interject itself into every attempted answer: Jack Volmer. I found myself increasingly infatuated with him; the childhood crush I'd once held returned to infiltrate my thoughts and linger significantly longer than any other.

Sleeping next to him meant I dreamt more frequently about him, often losing control of myself in those dreams when his lips were covering mine; when his hands skated over my skin and through my hair.

I'd tried to fight the attraction; shaking the dreams off whenever common sense would return to me. I wasn't proud of it, but I craved the familiarity of his body next to mine in a world so completely foreign to me. I longed for his arms around me to stave off the loneliness of being stranded.

I promised myself I wouldn't act upon the impulses that filled me, but I wondered how much restraint I might be capable of should his hands become more exploratory; should his eyes offer something more than flirtation. Would the promise of a physical connection, however short-lived it may be, be too tempting to turn away stranded as we were in this unfamiliar place?

I knew I was deflecting, much like I'd always done when faced with realities I didn't want to deal with.

When my relationship with Chris faced hard times, I would become withdrawn, living alternative versions of my life in daydreams rather than fix the issues that stood in the way of the perfect life I dreamt of.

Now, I was finding distraction in an imaginary fling I played out in my mind, all the while evading the reality that Chris was dead. I knew I would have to come face to face with it—*and soon* —but given the way things had been between us before the crash, mourning him would be more than just the acceptance of his death.

It would be reliving words I should've spoken and actions I should've taken. Mourning him would mean facing the injustices I had dealt him that led us to board that airplane in the first place.

Mourning him would mean accepting the blame that I'd ruined my relationship with him and inevitably caused his death. I couldn't will myself to face it. Not yet, anyway.

So, I propped myself up next to Jack at night and dreamt of him, pushing any guilt that attempted to surface as a result into the far recesses of my mind.

It was easier to be distracted.

"Did you catch anything today?" he whispered, his breath warm against my temple and awakening a frenzied reaction from the hairs on my arms.

"I did," I sighed. "Just one, but I'm getting better at it." I pulled the sweater up toward my chin to hide the smile that being close to him tended to place there. "How are you feeling?"

"Tired of being in this damn shelter. I can't stand it much longer."

"Hmmf." I shifted my back against the hard bamboo wall behind us. "I'm tired of being on this *damn* island."

He adjusted the sweater over his shoulder. "Me too. I swear, if I have to listen to one more of Phil's stories I'm going to explode."

Phil tended to ramble on for hours about places and people we'd never met, speaking of them without introduction or explanation as though we should simply understand what the names meant. He'd go into exhaustive detail about things like what he'd eaten for breakfast on the day in question or how he'd woken up late but still taken a shower before he went to the place or met with the person whose name we'd never heard of.

I laughed. "Oh, it's Phil's stories that are driving you nuts today? Yesterday it was Lilly's back rubs."

He grunted. "Can you believe she actually kissed my earlobe today?"

"She didn't!" I smiled, looking over at her small body where it was curled into Jim's side. She was maybe the most mischievous human I'd ever met, and I'd grown to love her for it. "What'd you do?"

"There was only one thing I *could* do. I called for Phil to come join us. Even went so far as to ask him about his ex-wife."

Through all Phil's ramblings, there was one common theme: his ex-wife. He loathed her and, once on the subject, would itemize for hours all the reasons why she was evil.

"That sent her away *real* quick."

I smirked. "She's relentless."

"She's bored." He stifled a cough, clearing his throat. "She needs something to keep her occupied and *far* away from me."

I yawned. "You're gonna miss her when we get back home."

"Doubt it."

"What *will* you do when you go home?" I asked. "I mean, obviously after you've eaten everything you can eat and taken a hot shower... Do you think things will ever be the same after all this?"

He paused for a moment. "I hadn't really thought about it... No, I guess not... I don't really know what I'll do."

I laid my head against his shoulder. "Me neither."

"Where are you from, anyway?" He asked, sounding genuinely interested.

"Just outside Chicago, but... I don't think I can go back there —not without Chris—not for a while, anyway. You?"

"I have a house in L.A. I guess I'll just go back to it. It'll be strange getting used to the quiet after being out here with all of you... Phil and Bruce's never-ending stories... Jim's loud mouth... Lilly's incessant flirting... you..."

I uncrossed my legs in front of me and crossed them the opposite way, my knee burning from being pressed against the solid bamboo floor of the shelter night after night. "You don't seem like the typical L.A. type."

"Far from it," he chuckled. "I was born and raised in Branson, Missouri. My mother pushed me into acting and after a while it just became more convenient for us to live there. Always hated the *typical L.A. type*—avoided them like the plague."

"Ah, that explains the random accent."

"Random accent?" he scoffed. "Madam, I think you're mistaken."

"Oh, I assure you I am not," I giggled, leaning into him as the wind picked up and it started to rain lightly on the shelter. "When you talk to Jim, hints of an accent slip out. It's quite endearing, actually."

He slid an arm around me and pulled me closer, covering my body with the length of the sweater as the rain grew heavier, "Do you know how many years I spent getting rid of that accent?"

I snickered, closing my eyes to listen to the rain as it grew into a gentle percussion against the palm fronds above our heads.

"Do you think we'll stay in touch?" he asked.

"Maybe." I wrinkled my nose. "I imagine we'll want to talk about what happened and it'll be hard to relate to anyone who wasn't here with us. I'm sure Anna and Bruce will insist on keeping us all connected, and Lilly might just follow you home."

"I mean *me and you*, Red. Do you think we'll still talk when we go back?"

"Oh..." I fumbled with the sweater, reminding myself not to indulge in fantasies only I was aware I was having. "I... Well, I hope so."

"Me too."

We sat quietly then, and I watched the firelight dance across the walls of our shelter; the flames straining as they battled against rain that threatened to put them out. I looked around at the sleeping bodies. Would I see them again once we'd gotten back home? Would we get together once a year to reminisce about our time here... gradually dropping off one by one each year with excuses until we just lost touch all together?

Lilly would likely go back to her upper east side New York lifestyle. I doubted we'd see much of her. Jack's celebrity status would undoubtedly be elevated when he returned from the dead. I imagined he would probably be too busy for us with all the press he'd get from it.

Bertie and Bud... they might keep in touch but traveling would become harder for them with age. Phil and Kyle would just go on with their lives. Phil didn't strike me as sentimental, and I couldn't see him making any effort to get together.

Magna... she might try to keep in touch, but after what happened to us, I doubted any of us would be ready to board another flight to Tahiti any time soon. Izzy was too little. I was sure she'd go home to a relative and gradually forget us all. Which left me, Anna, Jim, and Bruce. I could just see the four of us sitting in a restaurant, struggling to strike up meaningful conversation and ending up small-talking our way through a painful dinner.

No. We wouldn't keep in touch once we got home.

Jim moved a little and a small "toot" escaped him.

"Ope." He grinned, his eyes still closed. "Must be a duck around here somewheres."

"That's disgusting!" Lilly scoffed, rolling away from him.

Phil, Kyle, and Bruce howled with laughter. I giggled too, pulling the sweater against my cheeks.

I would miss them.

"Hey Red?" Jack said softly as the rest of the shelter settled.

"Yeah?"

"Maybe you could come stay in L.A... just until you figure things out."

I sighed, knowing I wouldn't—*couldn't*. Flirting on the island was one thing. I could fantasize here because it's all I had and fantasizing wouldn't hurt anyone. Going home with him would be something else entirely, and that could hurt plenty of us.

"Maybe..." I let my eyes close. "Assuming there's even an L.A. to go back to."

"What do you mean?" He laid his head against mine, an action that never ceased to make my shoulders relax and my heart beat a little faster.

"Jim was right that night on the raft," I stuttered, feeling foolish for buying into Jim's paranoia. "There are no satellites. And I can't stop looking for them. It's like they just disappeared after the crash. Where did they go?"

I felt his head shift as he looked out at the sky above the ocean. "No planes either."

"Or boats." I curled my body toward him as the rain intensified and brought a chill with it. "Just feels like something bigger happened when we crashed, you know?"

He nodded a little against my head. "There's really no precedent to compare surviving an airplane crash to, so to say it feels like something bigger might've happened… Idunno, it's a pretty big thing we went through as it stands. You know?"

I shrugged, letting my eyelids grow heavier. "I know." I yawned. "But something just feels… bigger."

Chapter Nineteen

"And you're sure you can't see anything?" Chris laughed from the driver's side of his work truck. I could see nothing but the red of the bandana around my eyes as the truck bobbed softly back and forth, the cool autumn air blowing in through our partially open windows.

"Is this really necessary?" I moved my fingers up to touch the fabric.

One big hand wrapped around mine and pulled the fingers away. "Don't even think about it, Ally. You'll spoil the surprise."

The road beneath our tires grew bumpier, rocking me from side to side. "How much longer do I have to wear this thing?"

"Almost there." He spread his fingers out on my knee, giving it a little squeeze.

After a few minutes, I could hear rocks and dust as the truck slowed to a stop. "Okay," he said, excitement in his voice. "Don't you dare take it off yet."

I smelled the musky-sweetness of fallen autumn leaves as the icy breeze from his open door filled the cab. I heard his boots crunching on leaves and the shifting gravel underfoot as he came around the front of the truck to open my door.

One hand came around my upper arm and the other took my hand, leading me out of the truck. He moved behind me, guiding me with his hands on each of my shoulders. "Just a few more steps."

My feet moved over leaves and loose rock, then grass, and his hands tightened on my upper arms, stopping me and turning me slightly to the left. His breath was warm against the chilly October air on my cheek. "You ready?" He whispered.

"Yes! Please!" I laughed.

His fingers fumbled with the knot and the red fabric gave way to reveal a white house with a big old-fashioned wrap-around front porch. The white siding stood stark against the lush orange, red, and yellow of the towering maple and oak trees that surrounded it.

The front yard sloped down toward us—a wide open canvas of green grass littered with bright yellow, orange and brown leaves, split in two by a stone walkway that led up to the porch steps.

"It needs work, I know," he said, still standing behind me and wrapping his arms around my waist. "I'll add the black shutters, wash and paint the siding… But what do you think?"

My nose burned and my eyes welled. My throat locked up, and I sniffled.

"I had one of the realtors we use hold off on showing it," he panicked, coming round to stand beside me to get a look at my stunned face. "We can keep looking, I just thought…."

"It's perfect."

And it was. I could see us there on the porch drinking coffee while it rained around us… kids playing at our feet… I could picture us, on a similar chilly autumn evening, sitting on the porch steps carving pumpkins.

He exhaled. "Well, don't say perfect yet. There's more to see still." He took my hand and led me up the little bumpy walkway to the porch steps. As we stepped onto the porch, I noticed the paint was peeling on the columns that supported it. I looked up to see aging beadboard lining the porch ceiling, thick cobwebs dusting all its corners and crevices.

"I thought we'd sand all this down, re-stain what we could, replace what we can't. Any color you'd like. Maybe add a little lantern above the door." He jogged down the porch to the end and spread his arms wide. "And a porch swing here…"

My heart burned with affection for him. How had I gotten so lucky?

"And I'll add shutters here..." He touched the window as he passed it. "And over there."

He came to the door where I stood, and bent, checking scribbled numbers on his wrist against the dials on the lockbox until it popped open and he produced a key. "We'll replace the front door, of course." He placed the key in the lock and pushed the door open, resting his hand on my back to lead me inside.

The foyer held a wide, dark wooden staircase on the left that curved upward along a wall that disappeared into the ceiling over our heads. "Now, we can do anything you want here. I was thinking," he ran his fingers over the spindles on the railing, "I can pull all the old trim and replace it or paint it white... and over here..." He rushed ahead of me to the living area, placing his hand on a wall. "We'll tear out this wall and open it up to the kitchen so you can have your open floor plan."

He moved ahead and disappeared to the other side of the wall as I stood taking the room in—the large picture window, the tall ceiling, the stone fireplace off to one side. I could just picture it in my mind: furnished, shiny, dark wood floors with bright white trim and mouldings; the two of us curled up on the couch together reading a book.

I made my way into the kitchen where Chris was anxiously waiting. "We open up that wall there, don't worry about these cabinets—we'll tear these out and get new ones—fridge here." He hopped excitedly from one end to the other. "An island here that looks out to the living room and double ovens here?"

I smiled wide, still unable to speak, and pressed my hand to my heart.

"Oh! And here!" He dashed to the French doors behind him, opening them up to a dining area with sliding patio doors on the far wall. "We can open this up too so it feels like part of the kitchen, and we'll put a table here and look!" He opened the patio door, motioning me behind him as he dashed out.

I crossed slowly through the kitchen, imagining the island, rich with granite, looking out on the living area. I could see myself there, preparing a thanksgiving dinner for the family who were cheering loudly for their football team—the sounds of its whistles and commentators coming alive in my mind—from the tv mounted over the living room fireplace.

I stepped out of the patio doors to a large shaded back porch, grass poking through the brick pavers underfoot. It looked out on a wide stretch of grass with large maples enclosing it, their leaves bright yellow and orange covering the ground and leaving very little green to show through.

There was one oversized oak tree sitting in the middle. Framing the house and porch were overgrown lilacs and peonies. I could just smell the last of their blooms on the breeze.

Chris ran to one side of the oak, leaves spraying out under his long legs as he crossed and shouting back, "We could build a swing set here." He took a couple more noisy strides to the oak, slapping a large hand on it. "And maybe a tire swing—no, a treehouse here!"

He half-jogged to the other side. "And maybe a little garden here?"

I smiled at him as he came back to stand next to me on the porch. "And it's not too far from the city. From our parents…"

Emotions filling me, I wrapped my arms around him as tight as I could and tucked my head into his chest. "I love it. I love it so much."

He kissed the top of my head, and swept both palms down my hair. "But wait til you see the best part."

He unwrapped me and pulled me back into the house, dragging me behind him through the living room and up the stairs, down a hallway of doors, where he opened a set of double doors to the master bedroom.

The light in the room was as bright as if we'd just stepped outside. High ceilings and vintage wood flooring stretched wide enough to house a king sized bed, dressers, and a sitting area. Directly across from me, the wall was lined with two sets of French doors which opened out to a balcony that sat atop the back porch. It looked out over the yard into the thick forest of maple, oak, and pine trees that sat beyond the property's edge. It was more than I'd ever dreamed of.

He walked slower now at my side as he watched me take it in. "This is the best part," he said, eyes still fixed on me. "This is where we'll make our family, Mrs. Grace."

PART II
Bigger even than that.

Chapter Twenty

With no signs of rescue, we'd fallen into a daily routine. The days all bled into each other, and although we hadn't been keeping track, we assumed we'd been stuck on the island for about three months.

In that time, Jack's breathing had slowly returned to normal, and he resumed his role as the alpha male of the group, barking orders and leading expeditions deeper into the island or out into the ocean on the lifeboat.

Lilly had gradually lost interest in trying to win his affection and deferred to being worshipped by Kyle instead, eating up his willingness to do anything for her and doing very little for herself as a result.

Kyle's arm had healed but was awkward. He was able to use the nub minimally, which proved much more challenging for Phil than it was for Kyle, as he pushed him harder each day to gain strength in the other arm. Kyle seemed unaffected by it as he gathered coconut on Lilly's behalf, brought her her share of the water, and made her stay on the island resemble that of royalty as opposed to someone stranded.

When Lilly grew bored with being spoiled, she attached herself to Jim, enjoying the play of constant banter that a day with him would almost always produce.

Jim, impatient as he was, had insisted we remove his splints early and regained movement and strength in his arms through sheer will, I was sure. With his heart set on catching a boar, he spent countless hours setting traps for them.

He'd dug pitfalls and had even managed to catch one briefly, only for it to claw a path in the mud and escape. He then returned with a vengeance and dug the pits so deep that no amount of clawing would allow for a boar to escape; just getting himself out required a ladder to be fashioned out of bamboo.

We spent weeks searching for the lighter and had never found it, which meant we were constantly having to stoke the fire. We had a smaller shelter built beside our primary one, a large piece of metal that had washed ashore placed in its center where we would keep burning coals when the rain would come in heavily.

Bertie spent her mornings with Isobel in the shelter. Armed with a small sketch pad and a marker we'd found in one of the carry-ons, she developed our own island sign-language and was teaching her the basics of how to read and write.

Lilly, myself, and Magna would gather fallen coconuts from the tree line, then work our way to the opposite side of the island where there was a small tide pool. We'd wade out early in the morning to gather what Magna called "Spaghetti Algae"—a bright green, very fine algae that grew en masse in the tide pool. It was rich in vitamins and we collected as much as we could every morning.

When we'd returned from the tide pool, Kyle and Lilly would go out to collect Fe'i and guava from the canopy while Magna and I gathered breadfruit.

In the afternoons, Bruce would take whatever we'd caught and foraged and obsess over the ingredients; blending, tasting, and perfecting our nightly meal while Phil hovered nearby, always quick to taste and critique his work.

Phil had a knack for setting us all on edge. He wasn't particularly strong or handy, which made him a nuisance to the other men when he'd tag along to fish or explore the island. He talked incessantly and frequently complained, which meant he was often sent to join the women while we foraged. He'd spend hours flirting with us and staring in a way that made us uncomfortable. He was harmless, we knew, but he was unnerving nonetheless.

Jack and I would gather firewood and retrieve water from the waterfall in the late afternoons. My infatuation with him came in waves at first, and I'd told myself in the instances it would flare up that it was strictly my mind's method of coping with our situation and nothing more.

Outside of innocent flirting, I remained faithful to my dead husband, never acting upon the attraction, and over the months, the flirting gradually turned into a strong friendship—one where we bickered almost constantly.

We'd argue about just about everything. My contribution to these small arguments came as a complete surprise to me since I'd always been one to stay silent rather than pick a fight with the men in my life. There was something about Jack, though, that brought out a much more argumentative side of me than I was accustomed to. I enjoyed it though. It kept my mind off the direness of our situation.

We all were desperate to keep our minds occupied the longer we went without rescue.

In the evenings, we'd talk around the fire, enjoying whatever dinner Bruce mustered out of the day's work. Magna would weave baskets and fish traps while Lilly ripped apart clothing from the carry-ons to fashion new clothes for Isobel. Isobel would teach us all her new signs and we'd go over old ones to keep them fresh in our minds.

While the rest of us spent time collecting fruit or catching fish, Jim was out exploring. He knew the island better than any of us. One night he ventured so far out that he didn't return until the following day, leaving all of us worried sick about what might've happened to him. He found a way up to the summit and needed to gather supplies so he could return for an extended stay and setup a proper lookout.

We'd been gathering his provisions the day all hell broke loose.

"Ship," Lilly said across from me as I stood to toss a coconut in our basket. Her eyes were fixed on the water behind my head. "SHIP!" she said again and took off toward camp at full speed.

I looked out at the ocean and saw nothing.

I walked toward camp. "Lill, honey, I don't see—"

And then I ran. As fast as I could run, I ran toward her. "Lilly, no. Lilly, don't!"

Before I could get to her, her arm shot straight up in the air and a small plume of smoke erupted as the ball of pink flare danced upward and out over the water, barely visible against the bright blue sky.

"AY!" I heard Jim long before I saw him come barreling out of the trees. "What in the SAM HILL'S GOIN' ON?"

My heart ached for the verbal lashing he would undoubtedly deliver her.

"There's a ship," she said, looking out at the ocean in a panic, holding the telescope in one hand.

He stood beside her, squinting out over the water. "Where?" He jerked the telescope out of her hand and extended it.

"Right there!" She pointed.

"That ain't..." He pressed the glass to his eye and looked out, then erupted. "THAT'S A GOT DAMN SHIP!" He looked again, "SMOKE! WE NEED SMOKE!"

He ran to the fire and pulled out a smoking branch, lighting the tall signal platform we'd made on the beach before turning with the smoking branch toward the trees.

Jack came out of the tree line as Jim sprinted toward him. "What's going on?"

"There's a Got damned ship out there's what's going on, and he cain't see us! Dammit, I knew I should've stay up 'er!"

Jim ran at full speed, and Jack spun on his heel to follow him, both of them headed for the summit.

We all rushed to pile green leaves on the platform. Lilly fanned it with a large palm frond, sending billows of smoke high into the air.

I turned back to the ocean, squinting hard, and could just see a small dot the size of a speck of dust on the horizon.

'Oh God, please let them see us.'

I paced to the trees and pulled more fresh palm, launching it onto the blazing fire—now burning too hot to get close to.

What could I do? There was nothing I could do but wait.

I stood at the water's edge, and knowing it was useless to do so, I waved my arms and shouted. One by one, the others joined me, all of us yelling at the top of our lungs and waving our arms, checking behind us every few minutes for signs of smoke above.

After a while, I couldn't see the speck on the water anymore, but I yelled and waved anyway. We all screamed into the ocean, arms flailing, running back to pile more leaves on the fire every few minutes until our voices were gone and the sky turned dark.

We spent the night awake and on edge, all of us staring between the ocean and the sky, throwing leaves and branches on the fire every ten minutes and praying.

The hours passed, and no fire shone above. We kept our fire on the beach burning until the sky turned shades of purple as the morning creeped in.

When the first signs of light rippled on the water's edge, Jack and Jim came sulking out of the trees.

Jim's eyes watered and he dragged a branch behind him. "The damn fire went out before we got to the top... couldn't get a new one started... shoulda' lit the whole dang island on fire while I had the chance."

He threw the branch to one side, kicked the sand, and sat down, pulling his knees to his chest to rest his head on them. "If someone hadn't lost the GOT DAMN LIGHTER, we'd be on that ship right now!"

Jack walked to the shore, hands on his hips, looking out as he exhaled heavily. His clear blue eyes showed signs of red at the corners from a night of no sleep. "If there's one, there'll be another."

Jim rocked back and forth, cursing under his breath.

"If there's one, there'll be another," Jack yelled back to him.

"Oh, horseshit," he spat, leaping to his feet. "There ain't gonna be no other. We had one shot, and we blew it. *I* blew it, Got dammit."

He stomped and kicked, eyes red and watering as he paced back and forth, his arms clasped and resting on the top of his head. "That ship shoulda' seen the beach fire. Shoulda' seen that smoke and turnt..."

Lilly danced nervously around his pace, "Jimmy… it's ok… there'll be another one."

"Oh, get off me, you dim-wit. Who wastes a Got damned flare in broad daylight?" he paced and turned, "on a ship that's too far out to see it…" he paced again, spinning back, "when we only have three flares?"

Her eyes watered. "I'm sorry… I… I thought…"

"Sorry? You're sorry?? Get the hell outta here with your *sorry*…" He paced again. "Sorry, I oughta show you sorry…" He spun and blew out in a growl.

Lilly's lip quivered and she collapsed on the ground in tears.

Jim continued to march behind her, his eyes darting down to her and back up as he grumbled to himself… but he slowed his pacing each time he'd look down and he held his scowl until he couldn't take any more. "Oh, stop carryin on."

He knelt down beside her. "I'm sorry, alright, it's me that's the dim-wit. Alright? Hush up now." He patted her on the back. "There'll be another ship, hush… we'll be ready for 'em next time."

"The summit takes too long to climb," Bud said. "We can't go racing up there fast enough if it comes back."

"We'll need to set up a watch," I offered. "Someone needs to be on that summit looking out for ships at all times."

"We'll go in shifts," Jack added. "Two go up at a time and don't come down until two go up to replace them."

Jim nodded. "We'll take the flares up with us, keep our eyes on the water day n' night for a ship. Have a signal fire ready to burn."

I moved closer to them. "We'll need to build a second shelter up there in case of a storm. The two who go up will have to take turns sleeping. There should always be someone monitoring the water."

Jim nodded. "Now… way I see it, there's only a handful of us able to go up right now. Bertie cain't make the hike, Isobel's too young, and Bud," he looked at the old man, "I know you could do it old-timer, but I ain't gonna' let ye. Now… Who wants to go first?"

"I want to see it." I raised my hand. " I'll go."

"Oh, me too." Anna hurried over. "I want to go."

Jim pondered it and shook his head. "Listen, I know you got your women's rights and whatnot, but the truth of the matter is I don't wanna be sittin' down here on my ass knowin' there's two women trekkin' up that mountain by themselves. I think one of us and one of you ought to go."

He held up a hand before any of us had a chance to protest. "And don't go gettin' your panties in a bunch over it, neither. We're bigger and stronger." He paused and inspected Magna. "Well, except maybe for you Big Mama, but anyways, if we're gonna put a shelter up there, you're gonna need us."

"Actually, I agree with him," Jack chimed in. "At least until the shelter's built."

"It's a long trip up," I noted. "It'd be a waste of resources and energy to have people moving up and down it frequently. The ones who go up should stay up for…"

"A week?" Jim suggested.

"Can we gather enough provisions for two people to live on for a week at a time up there? And can we store them?"

Jack ran his hand over his face and beard, looking up at the summit with his eyes squinted.

"I could smoke fish. Lots of it," Bruce said. "With the Fe'i bananas, algae, guava, breadfruit, and coconut, it shouldn't be too difficult. But we don't have enough to send someone up today."

"We should go up today, as soon as possible." Jack motioned toward the ocean. "That ship was headed somewhere and maybe it's going to head back the same way it came. We could get lucky and catch it on the way back."

I nodded. "He's right. I think we should go right away. What do we have right now?"

Bruce furrowed his brow as he thought for a moment. "Well, there are several filets of the grouper fish I smoked yesterday. Enough for two, *maybe* three days if you eat it sparingly. I can give you all the spaghetti algae—that'll be enough for the whole week. I've got five coconuts de-shelled and maybe a dozen Fe'i bananas. The guava's not going to be ready for another few weeks. You can grab some breadfruit on your way up."

"It'll do." Jack turned toward me. "I'll go up with you on the first shift." He raised a palm toward Jim, whose mouth had started to open in protest. "We should get packed and head out before the sun gets too high."

"Did ye' get a look at that ship?" Jim asked as we headed toward camp, scratching his head as he stared out at the water. "It was older than sin. I couldn't see it real clear, but it looked like a dang pirate ship from here. What ye' reckon a ship like that's doin' all the way out here in the middle of the Pacific ocean?"

Lilly frowned. "Maybe they're shooting a movie?"

Jack peered out. "They wouldn't venture this far out for a movie. They'd shoot it close to shore." He squinted his eyes, twisting his lips as he considered it. "Has to be something else..."

Chapter Twenty-One

We loaded up one of the carry-ons with food and bags of water we'd filled from the waterfall. Magna and Lilly had added two fabric straps to a basket Magna weaved and we very carefully placed hot coals from the fire into three separate tin cans we'd found on the shore inside. We wrapped the cans loosely in a t-shirt and would have to constantly stop to check them along the way to stoke them as needed.

I strapped the wicker basket to my back as Jack looped rope through the suitcase's handle, fashioning a cross body strap and pulling it over his head to one side. Armed with spears that would double as walking sticks, the utility knife, phone, and wind up flashlight from the survival kit, we prepared to head out on our journey.

Before we set off, Jim drew us a map in the sand.

"Now," he said, "looky here." He pointed with his stick. "We're here, see… what you gonna' wanna do is go arooooound," and as he dragged out the word, he circled the map's edge with his stick, "to the other side. About two hundred yards ahead of the tide pool, I left a stick poked up in the dirt. That's where you'll wanna go in."

"Dammit, I know how to get there," Jack snapped, starting to rise off his knee.

Jim kept his stick where it was and eyed him, "Ay, we ain't got time for ugly right now so pay attention cause this is important."

He looked back to his stick in the sand and dragged it a little further toward the center.

"Right here you'll start to see some of 'em boar tracks." He lifted the stick and pointed off his trail a few inches. "I think they's a family of em livin' somewhere in here. You'll wanna steer clear of this area." He circled it and returned his stick to its path.

"If you go in like I told ye, and keep a straight line," he dragged the stick slowly inward, "I've got traps set here," he drew an "X" for each along his line, "here, and here. You'll see a stick poked up outta place on each as a warnin' sign that there's a pitfall underneath so you make sure you walk wide around it."

Jack leaned in as Jim continued.

"You'll come out here to a clearing before you hit the second canopy." His stick was about halfway to the middle. "If you go through the canopy this a-way, you'll hit a straight wall of rock, and you ain't gonna be able to get up from there. You gotta go to the right and make sure you keep right all the way till the path upward goes from black rock to green trees. Once ye' get up through them trees, it's a steep climb but one ye' can do on your hands and feet. That'll take you up as far as I been. Didn't wanna' make the climb by myself, figured I'd probably bust my head open with my luck. From there, you're on your own."

At that, we said our goodbyes and walked together, side by side, down the beach toward the opposite side of the island. It was hot but my body held a chill from the exhaustion of being up all night.

As we got farther and farther away from our camp and its noises, the sound of the waves in the silence between us became louder in my ears. Desperate for interaction, I tapped my left eyebrow where a scar split Jack's in two and asked, "How'd you get that?"

He looked forward, his eyes far off in the distance. "Car accident."

I kept pace—which was more difficult in the sand. Every few steps I'd have to take a hop-step just to stay at his side. "What happened?"

He didn't meet my eyes but kept his on the path ahead, glancing down at his feet every so often. "Car flipped..." He peered off into the trees to my right, continuing his long strides. "My face hit the driver's side window and it split open."

I waited for him to say more as I struggled to keep our pace. I could already feel my lungs burning and we'd barely started. When it became clear he wasn't going to, I poked further. "How'd it happen? The accident, I mean... What caused you to flip?"

"You gonna ask questions the whole way up?" he snapped, a little too cold for my liking.

"Oh, no, I prefer to be completely silent and docile when going on long walks with other people."

"You can talk, Red, just drop the interrogation."

I huffed and bit back. "I've told you to stop calling me that name. And I'm not interrogating you. I asked you a simple question!"

"And I don't want to answer it."

"Why not?"

I was definitely going to have to slow down. My lungs were on fire, and my side was starting to cramp. I hated myself for not working out more often.

He stiffened. "Because I don't. End of story."

"What's gotten into you?" I asked, spinning in front of him to walk backwards, legitimately confused at his crankiness toward me.

"Are you kidding me right now?" He shook his head. "We had one ship in three months. *One* ship and we missed it. I should've been on that fucking summit the first day, but we waited. Got too comfortable and now I'm going to be stuck on this damn island forever... and you wanna have small talk? How can you possibly be thinking about anything other than the fact that we missed our single chance at getting off this island?"

"So what, we just trek up angry and bitter for the next several hours about something we can't change?" I panted with the effort of keeping up.

He rolled his eyes, hurrying past me. "I'm sorry I'm not in the mood to do small talk."

I groaned. "I just wanted to know more about you."

"It was an uncomfortable question and I'm in no mood to answer it. You want *me* to start asking you uncomfortable questions? Huh? Come to think of it, it's really been bothering me that you never answered *my* question. How'd you end up sitting next to me instead of your beloved husband? Eh?"

I felt as if I'd been slapped in the face; the question was delivered with such venom, it caught me dead in my tracks. I glared up at him, and through gritted teeth I seethed, "I told you, we were on standby and couldn't get seats together."

He glared back down at me. "Yes, and I asked why you didn't trade. You never answered. What's the matter? Don't like being interrogated?"

'A week with this jerk... I'm going to spend a week with this sonofabitch, arrogant prick, this big fucking.... Creaton!'

My breathing grew heavier, both with the pace and the anger. "You can really be a prick when you want to be, you know that?"

The fatigue from the night before forced a lump in my throat I couldn't swallow. My eyes welled and my nose burned. I could sense the tears wanting to come, *needing* to come, but I stared at my feet and continued on.

He increased his stride, and I let him walk ahead of me, slowing my own steps just enough to avoid further interaction.

We passed the tide pool and I could see the marker Jim had mentioned up ahead. Jack reached it first and stopped until I caught up. As I did, I raised my chin and passed by him into the shade of the trees without meeting his eye.

'Walk in a straight line,' I could hear Jim say, and I did so, very much aware of the eyes boring into the back of my head from three steps behind me. *'Prick.'*

As I walked, though, his words clawed at my mind and, having lost the distraction of lusting after him in that moment, forced me to ask myself the questions I'd been too distracted to ask before.

'Why didn't I even think to trade my seat? Why hadn't Chris? Were we so far detached from each other that neither of us cared to make the effort to sit next to each other on the way to our would-be

honeymoon? Is that really how we envisioned fixing our relationship would start?'

I was caught completely by surprise when I felt Jack's arm wrap around my waist, jerking me off my feet as we both fell to one side, landing with a thud, he on top of me, in a heap of leaves, clay, and broken twigs.

"What the hell do you think you're doing?" I demanded, pushing at his chest. "Get off me!"

He sat up, his heavy legs bent and locked on each side of my torso, pinning me to the ground. He didn't say a word, just took my face between his thumb and forefinger to turn my head so I was forced to look in the direction we'd just been.

I could see the shaved wooden stick poking out of the ground precisely where Jim had told us his pitfalls would be. *'You idiot, Alaina,'* I thought. *'You stupid, stupid idiot.'*

Jack grunted and stood, extending an arm to me once he'd risen. His clear eyes met mine, and I couldn't make out what would come next. Yelling? Scolding? Would he storm off? Berate me?

Reluctantly, I took his hand and he pulled me to an abrupt stand. Just as I straightened, he spun me around. The straps pulled at my arms as he jerked the wicker pack off my back, roughly raising my tank top along my back and pulling it back down. He knelt as I turned back, head bent over the smashed wicker pack, pulling each tin can out to check its contents, then setting them back in place and covering them up again.

Satisfied, he pressed the sides of the wicker basket, forming it partly to its original state. He stood then with the pack in one hand, his eyes—still unreadable— met mine once more.

Without a word, I turned around and let him place the straps back over my shoulders.

'He checked me for burns...'

I spun slowly back to face him, the thumb of one hand tucked into the strap of the basket. "I'm sorry."

I saw his shoulders raise up as he breathed in, running his hand over his face and through his beard as he exhaled. "I'm sorry, too. I'm just tired is all."

He stepped in front of me, taking my free hand in his, and led us wide around the pitfall and back up our straight line. When he released my hand, I followed, silent and docile, feeling like a child who'd wandered off toward danger.

We hiked for what felt like hours in silence through the trees into the clearing. We'd kept right until we could see green in place of black above the canopy, then continued forward. He'd led us, shifting the rope from one shoulder to the other every fifteen minutes. All the while, I'd replayed the events over and over in my mind.

'He checked me for burns... He checked me for burns before he checked to make sure we still had fire... Oh! The fire!'

I broke our silence then, calling up to him, "We should check on the coals."

Under the green canopy, the air was thick and damp. The clay was heavy on my boots and my legs were on fire. I motioned toward a large rock a few feet ahead of us as I caught up to stand next to him. "My feet could use a break too."

Still saying nothing, he nodded, and as we came to it, I sat down with a thud on the rock, letting my feet swing out in front of me.

'Oh, thank god.'

I removed the wicker pack as he slid the carry-on from his shoulder. I could see the relief in his shoulders as he set it on the stone surface.

"We should trade for a while," I said up to him.

He stretched his arms and sat next to me, bending to the opposite direction to check the coals and poke through the carry-on bag.

I cleared my throat. "We should trade for a while," I repeated loudly.

He produced two bags of water and handed me one. Eyes focused on the bag he held in his lap, he said, "It was my fault..."

I looked up at him. "No, it was my fault. I'm tired and I wasn't looking where I was going. It was stupid—"

"The accident," he interrupted as if he hadn't heard me, taking a sip of his water and peering out at the canvas of green below. He exhaled and his shoulders eased. "It was my fault."

"Oh…" I breathed, not daring to ask him what he didn't want to offer.

"My kid sister, Macy, was with me… in the passenger seat." His nose twitched a little.

"She was seventeen." He set the bag down on the rock, stretched his arms out behind him and leaned back, gazing at the leaves overhead as he continued on. "I was driving her out to this little dress shop in the middle of nowhere to pick out a prom dress. All she talked about for months was the prom, and if she wasn't talking about the prom, she was talking about the boy who was taking her. Danny O'Conner."

His eyes narrowed as he said the name. "We were going up the coast, and…" He blew out. "I didn't see the truck until it was too late."

"It had come over into our lane, and last minute I jerked the wheel to the right so the truck hit my side of the car." He touched the scar. "But we flipped to her side and rolled several times until we were upside down at the bottom of an embankment. I forced my way out of the driver's side and went running over to hers. She was pinned and unconscious."

His eyes ventured further off into the memory.

"They got her out, took her to the hospital, but the damage was done. The car had crushed her left leg and left a scar from one side of her beautiful face to the other. The leg never fully healed, so she'll walk with a limp for the rest of her life. And the scar… well… Danny O'Conner didn't stick around to see how she recovered. Took some other twat to the prom and broke Macy's heart."

Snapping back to reality, he sat forward, looking down at me. "And I quit the show after that. Stopped acting altogether. See, *and here's the kicker*. I'd been out late at a party the night before. I hadn't slept. Not even for an hour. I still had drugs in my system. I still had drugs in my system and I put her in my car. I nearly killed her—maimed her for life."

I raised my eyebrows and moved my hand to touch his, but before I could, he grabbed his water and downed half of it, hopping off the rock as his face changed back to business. "Anyway… I'm sorry for being short with you. It's a sensitive subject for me. We should get going."

I sat there looking at him as he returned the bags to the case, hoisted the rope of the carryon back over his shoulder, and bent his legs to adjust the weight.

I'd watched the show, of course, and like many of my female counterparts, I'd hated the way it ended; was angry, devastated even... but I'd never known he quit. And now that I knew why, my heart hurt for him, and I felt a stab of guilt for my year of complaining about the show's ending.

He held out the straps of the wicker basket to me, small puffs of smoke dripping out of its folds, and I slid off the rock to let him place it on my shoulders.

We climbed for another hour before the shade of the trees gave way and we stared up at the jagged black rock incline that led to the peak.

We couldn't see the very top, but it wasn't much farther. The incline was steep but manageable with careful footing. Fatigue was getting the best of me, and I was eager to reach our destination.

"You should go in front of me," he said, shading his eyes to look up toward the summit. "Use your hands before your feet to get up. I'll be right behind you in case you slip."

"I'm not going to slip," I yawned.

"Test for loose rock with your hands before you set your feet," he added. "I don't wanna take a boulder to the head today."

I nodded, stretching, and yawned again.

"Just a little farther and you can sleep first," he said, pushing my back lightly to encourage me forward.

"I'm goin,' I'm goin.'"

I started up, hands before my feet.

'Oh wow, he's not kidding, he's literally right behind me.'

I looked over my shoulder to see his face at eye level with my behind, arms to each side of my ankles on the rock. "A little close there, don't you think, Volmer?"

"If you slide, it'll be easier to catch you." His matter-of-fact tone left me no room for sarcasm.

'So bossy.' I continued up, feeling for loose rock with my hands before I moved upward.

As we worked up at a snail's pace, my mind began to roam.

'One week up here... What the hell are we going to do all day? I wonder how far out we can see... Oh, I hope we spot a ship... What if we do? What if we're rescued?'

"Slow down a little," he muttered.

I rolled my eyes in front of me. *'I wonder what he's like under all that attitude? Beyond the flirting and cuddling... when he's stripped down and his heart's exposed... I wonder what it's like to be loved by him? Trusted entirely by him?'*

'What the hell are you thinking about, Alaina? You're married to Chris, remember him?'

'Chris is dead.' I argued with myself.

'Oh, he is, is he? Fine job you're doing mourning him!'

I looked back over my shoulder to see the top of Jack's head over his broad, exposed shoulders. There was definitely an attraction there, denying it wouldn't do me any good, it'd been there since I was a teenager. I was curious about him, that's all.

'That's all.'

We reached a ledge in the rock. I felt up with my hands first and touched a solid platform. Carefully, I pulled myself to it and looked into the wide mouth of a cave. Toward the back of the cavern, I could see a bit of light shining through. I waited for him to pull himself up and turned. "I think we've found our shelter."

Dropping my pack at my feet, I edged deeper into the cave toward the light while Jack checked the coals. "It leads out to the top from here!" I shouted back to him, my words bouncing back at me off the rock walls.

He moved toward me, inspecting the ground with his toes as he did. We both stood looking up through a two foot wide, twenty foot long tunnel that gradually led up to clear blue skies.

"Should I try it?" I asked him, head already stuck into the opening, peering around at what the light bounced off—praying a bat wouldn't come flying toward me.

"Go slow... *extremely* slow... I'll watch until you're through and then I'm right behind you."

I climbed in. It was damp and dark; the rock was cool. For a moment, I was reminded of being a child at one of those play-places, crawling in my socks through colorful twisting tunnels, a ball of static-electricity for anyone who dared get close enough for me to touch.

I crawled now, on hands and bare knees over sharp rock, slowly inching my way closer to the clear blue sky.

"What do you see?" His voice echoed through the tunnel below me just as my head popped out to take in its splendor. I crawled all the way out and stood on a massive landing, its bottom covered in bright, soft green moss.

What I saw was ocean and blue sky as far as the eye could see. There were a few trees that grew higher still, an opening to one side where the moss gave way to a rocky ledge, and bright pink, purple, and yellow flowers grew in abundance near the cave's opening.

"Oh, you're gonna have to see this for yourself," I yelled back, treading lightly toward the edge of the landing and peering down on our island.

It seemed surreal. Blue danced with white and became turquoise as the waves rolled over into the copper colored sand. Further down the beach where the sand gave way to rock, the waves crawled and crashed against the stone peaks in an elegant exclamation of teal effervescence. Treetops formed like flowers, a symphony of greens and reds that crawled all the way up to where my toes were planted. The breeze held me and I swayed in it as I let the fatigue and the ache of the trek fall away.

"Oh, wow." He stood beside me, his eyes drinking it all in.

"Isn't it just breathtaking?" I sighed.

"It's beautiful," he said, and I turned to see his gaze shift from me to the ocean.

I stepped back a little from the ledge and stretched, yawning as I did so.

"You should get some rest," he said. "I'll wake you in a few hours."

At the promise of sleep, my body grew heavy. "No," I yawned again, "I should help you get the fire going, and we have to test the phone."

"Alaina." It was the first time he'd ever actually said my name directly to me, and my heart fluttered at the sound of it on his lips. "You're going to fall where you stand. Lay down over there." He motioned toward a large shady tree, its long spidery branches littered with green leaves and fluffy red flowers. "I can handle this."

Resigned and thankful he hadn't taken me up on my offer, I walked to the shade and curled up into a ball on the moss facing where he stood. "Jack, what do you think that old ship was doing out here?"

He expanded the telescope and pressed it to his eye, looking out at the water. "I've been thinking about that almost the whole walk up here."

"And?"

"And..." He frowned, lowering the telescope as he glanced back at me. "It doesn't make any sense. Maybe it's some kind of attraction at a resort? But if we're in between Hawaii and California, I don't know of any resorts that would be in this area. That's the only thing that would make sense, though. No matter how crazy the director, they wouldn't pull a wooden ship this far out to sea for a movie—at least not without an accompanying boat and a helicopter—and no one in their right mind would venture this far out in one of those just for sport. So it's got to be some kind of resort attraction. Which means it's on a schedule, so it'll be back."

My eyes grew heavy as I watched him disappear back into the cave's tunnel to retrieve the fire wood, supplies, and phone.

'Alaina,' I heard his voice again in my head as sleep overtook me.

"Alaina," his voice came to me again and I smiled.

"Alaina," and I could feel his hand on my shoulder.

I blinked my eyes open.

Behind him, he'd lit a small fire and in its light I could see the signal platform not far from it—a wide pillar of twisted twigs and branches climbing up each other. He'd unfolded the carryon and organized our food neatly inside it.

I raised up a little, squinting in the fading light. "How long have I been asleep?"

"Couple of hours. You should eat something."

I sat up and stretched. "What are we having?"

He turned and rummaged through the case, returning to sit across from me cross-legged.

"For starters," he joked, handing me a half of a coconut, "we have a creamy lobster bisque."

He laid out a half of the smoked grouper. "Then, for the main dish, we have a tender filet mignon, seared in garlic and crusted to perfection." He sprinkled the fish with the spaghetti algae. "Paired with garlic red potatoes," he handed me my bag of water, "and a 10-year-old cabernet."

I laughed, my mouth watering. "Oh God, this sounds just wonderful. What are you having?"

"For me..." He raised and turned back to rustle through the bags, returning with a much smaller piece of smoked fish and two of the Fe'i bananas. He handed me one before he continued. "I'll be having a half-pound cheeseburger, cooked medium, with bacon, bleu cheese, red onions, lettuce and tomatoes."

He pulled two shaved twigs from behind him. "And for dessert..." He handed me the makeshift skewer as he stuck his own through his banana and balanced it on the fire. "French silk pie."

I smiled, and as we dived into our dinner, I could almost taste the garlic potatoes.

When he'd finished his fish, I stuck out half of mine. "Here, have some of my *steak*, that's not enough food for you."

"I'm fine." he said, sipping his water.

"You're not," I insisted, pushing the fish toward him, "Eat... before this turns into another fight."

He smiled at that and took it, sighing heavily as he bit off a chunk. "Why *do* you fight with me?"

"I don't fight with you, Volmer… I *respond* to you. "

He smirked, "I've never had anyone *respond* to me quite the way you do."

I batted my eyes at him. "Well, that's probably because *they* have never been trapped on an island with you having to listen to you boss everyone around all day."

He leaned back to pull his banana from the fire, setting it on the rock beside him to cool. "I'm not that bossy."

I laughed out loud at this. "Yeah, okay, and I'm not the slightest bit Irish."

Although it was too hot, he still attempted to peel his banana with the tips of his fingers. "Oh, but those freckles…" He jerked his thumb back from the heat and brought it to his mouth.

"Can you hand me mine, please?" I motioned to the skewered banana still on the fire. "*Carefully?*"

He obliged, and I set it down on the rock next to his. "So… your sister." I leaned back. "She was getting married?"

He leaned back as well, smiling affectionately. "Oh, yeah…" His brow furrowed. "I hope so anyway… I don't know now… I hope I didn't ruin it."

"Tell me about him. The guy."

His face lightened, and the smile returned. "Robert… really great guy. Dotes on her. I was so worried for her when she went off to college. But he never even blinked at the scar or the limp. He said it was love at first sight."

I grinned. "Sounds like you couldn't have ruined it then. How did they meet?"

He frowned. "Hmm… I don't really know. They met in college. I guess I was too busy giving him the stink-eye over Thanksgiving dinner the year she brought him home to have paid attention when they told the story."

I raised my eyebrow. "Protective?"

"With Macy? Oh yeah. She was always so sweet and naïve. Somebody had to be watching out for her. And now she's got Robert to do that."

I smiled at that, thinking suddenly of Chris.

He noticed the shift in my mood and changed the subject. "Okay, let me show you what I've got going on so I can take a nap." He stood and extended his hand down to me.

I took it and he pulled me to a standing position next to him. The night breeze was cool and refreshing, the stars filled the sky above us, and the moon danced brilliantly across the water. Goosebumps ran over my skin as he placed his hand ever so softly against the small of my back to point me in the direction of the platform.

"It's not much yet," he said, "but it's all we had on us. I figured, each time we come, we can bring more wood, and we'll grow that to be about five times that size so night time ships can see it from miles away."

I nodded.

"Daytime ships will be harder." He turned me toward a small pile of green palm fronds off to one corner. "We'll need smoke and lots of it. We can pull branches from these trees up here, but when we go back down, we should collect what trash we can from the beach—plastic, rubber, anything that can help us darken the smoke."

I paused in thought. "You would think we would've found plastic or rubber on the beach by now. I haven't seen any. Have you?"

He furrowed his brow. "Actually no. You're right... we should've found something by now. We've had plenty of rope and glass wash ashore. Why no plastic?"

I looked up at the sky. "Why no satellites?"

He stretched, standing on his toes as he let out a yawn and looked up at the sky.

"Get some rest," I offered. "I can handle it."

"If you see a ship, wake me up."

"I will."

He lingered for a moment beside me as we looked out on the night sky, then he turned toward the tree behind us.

I stayed, staring out into the darkness, letting the breeze rouse my sleepy body, the hairs on my arms slowly rising as I let it envelop me.

"I shouldn't have asked you that," he said behind me.

I turned toward his voice. The light from the fire outlined his body where he laid on one side, one big arm folded beneath his head, the other curled up and resting on the ground in front of his chest. His bright blue eyes reflected the orange of the flames as he looked out at me. "About your husband. I had no right to ask you that."

I'd forgotten about the fight and was taken aback by the sudden tenderness in his tone. He'd been different with me since we'd arrived at the summit.

Instead of his usual casual flirting, he'd been tender, thoughtful, and now apologetic. The shift in our general demeanor toward each other was uncharted. I raised my shoulders and let them drop. "You were tired. I was tired... And it's a question..." I looked out to the black ocean behind him. "...that's haunted me since you asked it on the plane."

I could still feel his eyes on me as I scanned the ocean for lights. In the corner of my eye, I could see him shift, adjusting his arm a little under his head. "It was a mean-hearted question I never should've asked you. Knowing I'd asked it before all this happened..." he waved his arm out in front of him. "Knowing you struggle with it... It's haunted me too."

I sighed and looked down at him finally. "I'd have struggled with it whether you'd asked it or not. I struggled with it long before," I waved my arm out around me, "all this."

My eyes watered. "Since..." the words stopped short, and I said no more. I turned my back to him and stood silent for a long while, wrapping my arms around myself and listening to his breath as it slowed into sleep.

'Since... Evelyn.'

Chapter Twenty-Two

I unfastened my seatbelt and hugged my mother from the passenger seat of her car as I looked up the hill at my charming home. Chris had finished the siding, porch, and black shutters the year before and had been working tirelessly to make the interior perfect.

My mother and I had driven up and spent the week in Minnesota with my sister and Owen to meet their new baby girl, Madison, and while I'd been happy to spend so much time with them, I was anxious to be back home with Chris.

"I love you, ma," I said, squeezing her tiny body. "Don't be sad. We'll go up again soon."

She nodded against me. "Don't forget dinner next Sunday."

"I won't." I kissed her cheek and opened the door, circling back to the trunk of the car to grab my suitcase.

As I pulled the bulky case out and onto the ground, I caught sight of Chris hurrying down the hill toward the car, his broad shoulders shimmering in the August afternoon sun over a damp white t-shirt that was plastered against his chest, a full tool belt at his waist over his paint splattered blue jeans.

"Hey mom." He grinned at her as he approached, pulling me into a bear hug and squeezing the life out of me while he walked backwards toward the passenger window. I giggled as he held me there against his oven of a body. "How's Maddy? Did you have a good time?"

"It was wonderful," my mom answered, her voice muffled in my ears as I was smothered by his arms. "It's your turn now. I want at least two more grand-babies that I get to see regularly!"

"I'll get straight to work on that, Soph." He eased his grip and ran a hand over my hair.

"Dinner Sunday," she reminded him. "I'm making chicken and dumplings and we're playing euchre with uncle Bill. Don't you guys forget. I love you. See you then."

"We'll be there." He smiled as she drove off, then focused his big green eyes on me. "I've missed you."

He cupped my face in his hands and bent to kiss me. Breaking the kiss, he lingered there, inspecting my face as I smiled up at him. "You're so beautiful. And my God, you smell amazing."

I laughed, stretching my arms out and yawning. "Love, I smell like strong coffee and ten hours of leather seats. I need a long shower." I raised on my toes and kissed him, inhaling deeply. "Oh God, and so do you!"

He chuckled as he knelt to pick up my heavy suitcase with ease. "Well, I wasn't expecting you for another couple of hours. I'd planned on taking a shower."

"Mom let me drive," I beamed at him. "I made record time."

He led me up to the house. "I have a surprise for you."

"You do?" I leaned against him as we climbed the porch steps. "What is it?"

He opened the door and motioned me inside. "You'll see."

I stepped across the threshold onto the plastic I'd come to accept as part of my life living in a construction zone. The entire main floor smelled like freshly cut wood and paint as Chris and his father spent their evenings and weekends building a new kitchen, running new electric, patching drywall where they'd ripped out walls, and painting.

A stack of boxes full of hardwood flooring towered high in what would someday be my living room. Chris and I spent what little time we had not working on the house confined to the one room in the house that was finished—our bedroom.

He moved in front of me and led me up the stairs. "This way."

I let him lead me up the stairs—also covered in plastic, and he paused at the first door on our left. "Ready?" He raised his eyebrow at me.

I nodded, eager to see what he was up to.

He turned the knob, and the door opened to an elegantly finished office overlooking our backyard. He'd painted it in a warm gray with white trim and lined one wall with white built-in shelving and cabinets. My entire book collection was thoughtfully placed on display throughout the shelves, small plants scattered throughout.

He'd refinished the wood floors in a dark stain and built a large custom white executive desk in the center of a bright white and gray rug in front of the window. On the desk was a brand new laptop with a second monitor and a new set of unopened file folders, pens, and paper neatly stacked on one side. A big tufted leather chair was pulled up to its center.

Behind the desk, beneath the window, was more built in cabinetry below a tufted window seat lined with a dark gray cushion and light gray, white, and rose-colored pillows stacked neatly to each side where two tall cabinets lined the window.

On the opposite side of the room, he'd set up my acoustic guitar on a stand and my keyboard on a smaller white desk. A comfy little chair sat in the center.

"Happy birthday, Ally. I know it's been hard to focus around here, and I want you to know how proud I am of you for getting your degree. I know you're anxious to have your own space with this new job." He ran his hand over my back. "Do you like it?"

"Do I *like* it?" I crossed the room to run my fingers over the shelves, stopping at the desk to marvel at its detail. "Honey, I *love* it. It's..." My eyes watered. "It's perfect." I gazed up at him. "*You're* perfect. What did I do to get so lucky?"

He shook his head lackadaisically, his lips curling to a smile as he beamed at me. "No Al, it's me that's the lucky one. I only want to make you as happy as you make me."

"Love," I took the few steps back to stand in front of him and wrap my arms around his waist, letting my forearms rest on the tools that overflowed from his belt. "We could live in a cardboard box and I'd be happy so long as you were with me."

He bent to kiss me, and I laughed. "Although, that box might need a shower cause you stink!"

He smirked and backed up, pulling me with him out into the hallway, cupping my face in his hands as our feet hit the plastic noisily and we rustled down to the master bedroom.

"I hated being here without you." He backed us into the bathroom, releasing my face with one hand to turn the screeching knob on the shower without looking away from me. The water beat steadily into the porcelain tub beside us as I squeezed the latch on his tool belt and set it gently on the floor. "I don't know what to do with myself when you're gone."

We'd been estranged physically over the past several months, working late hours on the house and tending to fall into bed when we were both too exhausted to move. I was eager to feel his skin against mine—desperate even for it. My body shivered as his palms smoothed down my arms, his thumbs hooking in my tank top and pulling it up over my head.

"I promised your mother a grand baby," he whispered.

"Oh?" I pushed his white t-shirt up and he raised his arms, laughing as I stood on my toes to pull it over his head.

His hands came down over my hair while his eyes gazed into mine. "What do you think? Should we start trying now?"

I unbuttoned his pants, biting my lip as I slowly pulled the zipper down and moved my hands around the back of him to squeeze his bare bottom, pushing the pants and boxers down. "Okay. Let's do it. Let's have kids."

He stepped happily out of his pants, pulling off his socks with one hand, as the fingers of his other curled around the elastic of my shorts.

His mouth moved over my neck, sending chills down the length of me as he pushed the shorts down my legs. One arm curling around my back to pull my bare body against his, the other smoothed up my thigh.

He stepped into the tub, dragging me with him to let the warm water spray over our shoulders.

"It's been *far* too long," he groaned in my ear. Without wasting a moment more, his fingers slid inside me, forcing me to gasp and cling to him, pulling at his neck, hair, shoulders whatever I could grab on to. "I miss my wife."

He moved his mouth hungrily over mine, demanding my lips open as he pressed me against the tile wall. His fingers moving inside me, my knees buckled, and both of us slid down to the floor of the tub.

Shifting his weight, he pulled my hips up, removing his fingers so he could slide himself in, hard and in a hurry.

His breathing thickened, and he thrust harder, faster, his mouth growing heavier on mine as the water sprayed over our faces; skin sliding loudly against the porcelain. His fingers curled into the hair at the nape of my neck, pulling tightly as he drove deeper and became more impassioned.

He groaned heavily against me, breathing harder as he released my mouth and latched onto my neck with his tongue and teeth. I pulled at his hair as my hips rose to keep pace with him, crying out as he penetrated deeper, moving more urgently as his body began to shake.

His hand gripped my thigh hard, forcing it higher as his fist in my hair pulled harder. He pressed his mouth to mine, and I pulled him deeper... deeper... harder until he convulsed and cried out, then collapsed heavily on top of me, heaving as the water sprayed over us.

He raised up quickly and searched my face. "Oh my God, Ally, I didn't mean to... did I hurt you?"

I smiled and shook my head, "No, love."

"I don't know what got into me." He slid himself out of me and pulled me up into his arms. "I didn't mean to be so rough with you."

I laughed, blushing slightly, "Oh, but I liked it."

"You did?" He held my shoulders out to look into my eyes.

I nodded, passing a hand softly over his cheek. "Love, I'm your wife. Whatever you feel, and however you need to express it, I want that. You never have to apologize for it. I want to feel what you feel, however passionate it may be. I prefer that to whatever you *think* I want to feel. I'm your wife, not some stranger who's going to judge you for it. I felt loved, missed, and wanted more than I've ever felt, and I love you that much more for it." I slid my hands down over my stomach. "And who knows? Maybe we'll have a little human as a result."

He chuckled, pressing a kiss to my brow. "We might if I'd suggested it a little sooner."

I hid a smile. "I stopped taking birth control while I was on the trip... Mom kinda' got to me... and seeing Maddy... well, I was hoping you'd be ready to start trying too."

Chapter Twenty-Three

Through the night I'd paced, watching the water, waiting. I'd circled the fifty feet of our ledge at least a hundred times. I'd tried to relive the plane crash, tried to see more—*had I looked back for Chris? Had I seen him?*

I thought about music and wondered where I might be had my musical career led me down a different path. *Would I be on this island? Would Chris have been on that plane?*

It was easy to avoid dealing with the loss at camp. There was always something that needed to be done and I could keep myself occupied all the way until it was time for bed, where I could snuggle up with Jack to keep my mind occupied further.

But on the summit and alone with my thoughts, I was balancing on the edge of an emotional breakdown. Reality had hit me overnight.

The crash, losing Chris, the years I'd gone without his affection, the sudden reality of Jack and the craving for a closeness with him that made me disappointed with myself; it all hit me like a ton of bricks.

The sun was slowly coming up over the water and I sat with my bare feet and legs hanging over the ledge, watching as the sky turned from navy to violet to shades of lilac, pink, and orange, and in the quiet light of morning, I closed my eyes, fingers curled around the little glass globe pendant of my necklace and spoke to him.

'Chris...'

'I don't know if you can hear me but... I don't know who I am without you... or who I even became with you... and I'm mad... I'm mad at you, mad at myself, and I'm so damn mad at God for taking any chance I had at saying so away from me I can't breathe...'

'What am I supposed to do now?'

I turned to look at Jack; the sunlight was just starting to touch his face. The faint morning glow made the bits of blonde in his beard and on his head sparkle. His eyes shut, mouth curled upward in a half smile, I couldn't help but wonder who he was under it all.

Lying there, looking so peaceful, the worried lines on his brow erased, I realized I was eager for him to wake... looking forward to him in a way that was more than the distraction I'd normally looked to him for.

'What the hell am I supposed to do now?'

I turned back to the ocean, scanning the water for any signs of life.

"You're crying," Jack said huskily behind me.

"I'm not." I wiped the tears off my cheeks in a hurry, relieved to finally be freed of my own thoughts as I turned around. "You want some breakfast?"

He was still lying just as he'd been the night before; on his side with his arms curled up by his head, his clear blue eyes staring at me. The worried lines returned as his brow furrowed and he studied me with suspicion.

I stood, straightening my tank and shorts. "I'm fine."

I padded barefoot over the soft moss to the case, bending over it with my back to him, "Did you get enough sleep? Coconut or banana? I've been thinking... there's a very small opening on the other side of the cave that looks like it could—"

I was stopped short by his sudden appearance at my side. His worried eyes scanned my face.

"Looks like it could..." I continued, clearing my throat and looking back down at our food, "could maybe lead down to a wider space. I..."

I grabbed a half coconut and met his concerned expression again. I could feel my cheeks flush as my eyes lingered on his for slightly too long.

'Oh, please don't look at me like that,' I thought. *'If you touched me, I'd fall to pieces.'*

I broke away again, shaking it out of my head. "I was poking around down there for a minute last night. I didn't want to go in alone."

Not making eye contact, I handed him the coconut and stood, escaping to where I had been seated near the ledge to grab my boots and socks. Devoid of personal contact on the island and fraught with emotion, the warmth his eyes offered this morning had my insides reaching for something to hold on to so I could be pulled away from the breakdown I was teetering on the edge of.

I sat and pulled my socks and boots on, lacing them back up before looking back to where he knelt over the food, holding the coconut, still watching me with concern painted on his face.

"I really wish you wouldn't look at me like that." I hugged my knees to my chest. "I don't need your sympathy right now... I don't want it."

He sat back, planting his feet in front of him and letting the coconut rest between his bent knees. He cleared his throat. "Would you prefer me to look at the trails of tears on your face and feel nothing? Just pretend I don't see it and go on with the day?"

I swallowed, looking down at the slight rip forming in my sock. "I don't know how to do this with you... This... whole... new type of flirting you're doing with me."

I ran my fingers through my hair as I resigned myself to pick a fight instead of continue on uncharted water. "The bickering and mean words—the fighting—I can do that. I can even do the flirty conversations and snuggling at night. But this sudden nice-guy act —bringing me pretend dinners, and looking at me," I made eye contact, "like you're looking at me now... I don't know how to do that, and I don't really get your angle. Why *are* you being nice to me, anyway? You don't owe me that."

I shuddered as I forced myself to continue, lowering my tone and raising one eyebrow. "Unless you're after something... What are you trying to get out of this? Are you looking to continue your movie-star lifestyle out here? What's the matter, Jack? Not enough girls on the island to allow you to sleep with someone new every night?"

I saw his face change—watched his throat move as he swallowed the words. *'There. Mission accomplished Alaina. Satisfied?'* He lowered his legs to sit cross-legged, holding his untouched coconut in his lap. Looking down, he twisted the words around in his mouth before he looked back at me. "This is your opinion of me?"

Defiant, I raised my chin and looked off toward the ocean. "I'm not some naïve kid. I've seen your face smeared across the tabloids enough to know better than to trust nice words in the night from *'Hollywood's playboy.'"*

He straightened, leaning to one side to pull the utility knife out of the pocket of his jeans. Quietly, he shaved off a piece of coconut, holding the knife in place when his eyes returned to mine. "If that were what I was after, I'd have insisted Lilly come up with me." He balanced the piece of coconut between the knife and his thumb, smirking as he raised it. "Much more my type," he added, popping the coconut into his mouth.

A ping of... *jealousy?*... stabbed at my heart for a moment and I shook it off. Standing, I snatched the flashlight from our pack. "I'm going down to explore the cave."

He stayed in place, leaning back on one arm, chewing slowly, head turning and eyes following me as I moved toward the opening. He said nothing in protest as I lowered myself down into the damp darkness of the tunnel.

I crept down slowly on my hands and knees, keeping my stomach low across the jagged cool rocks that led to the cave's floor.

'What the hell are you doing, Alaina? Is this really how you want to spend the rest of the week up here? Fighting? Insulting each other?'

My knee burned as my weight crossed a protruding rock, *'And now you're gonna go down by yourself—he's certainly not coming now—to squeeze, and probably get stuck, in a creepy dark cave?'*

I came out of the tunnel to the brightness of the sun shining into the cave's mouth. Across from me, I could see the narrow crevice—about a foot wide. I walked toward it, shining the flashlight inside.

Just as I'd noticed the night before, the passage slanted downward. It remained about a foot wide as far as I could see and disappeared into the blackness beyond the flashlight's beam.

'I'll just go in a little, see if I can see further. I'll go up and apologize after... maybe he'll come down then...'

Just as I began to shift my body, two firm hands gripped my upper arms and spun me abruptly around, pushing my back flat and hard against the rock wall.

He pinned my arms against the wall and I could see the temper in the light that shone on half his face as it hovered inches from mine. His nostrils flared and through gritted teeth he hissed, "You want to fight? Fine. Fight me."

I squirmed in his grasp, panicking as my hands pushed against his chest but could get no leverage. My shoulders and upper arms were stapled against the cold, damp rock behind me. The sudden touch had me coming apart at the seams. I could feel the tears forming as I swallowed hard, fighting to free myself.

"Fight me. Come on, that's what you want... To be mad, isn't it? Go ahead fight me."

I squirmed harder, balled my hands into fists and tried to punch, but he slid his grip down to my elbows and pressed harder. "Come on, show me how mad you are."

I clawed at his forearms, "Let me go!"

"I will not." He leaned closer. "You wanted a fight, and you got one. Come on then. Insult me. Tell me what you really think. You think I enjoyed the women? You think I enjoyed the superficial smiles of women who were only after their moment in the spotlight?"

He let go of my arms and put his hands on the rock to each side of my head, his eyes piercing through me. "You think I enjoyed being used, over and over, so they could go back and say they'd slept with Elias Phillip?"

I turned my head to one side, closing my eyes against the tears that were filling them, and pushed as hard as I could against his chest. He didn't budge.

"You think I want to be stuck on this island? With you? Stuck up here? With *you*? Unable to feel anything but guilt for not offering to trade my own damned seat? That's why you hate me, isn't it?"

He reached over and jerked my chin so my eyes were forced to meet his. "That's why you fight me, *isn't it?* It should've been him up here with you, not me... Isn't that it? Go ahead, fight me dammit."

And the breakdown I'd been holding found me. All at once my body stiffened, and I screamed at the top of my lungs, beating his chest with all the strength I had, tears streaming down my cheeks as incoherent sobs echoed through the cave.

In my head, I screamed, *'Yes! Yes! It should've been him here, not you! He could've loved me here!'*

But in reality, I punched him, kicked him, and clawed until my arms fatigued. I relived, frame by frame, every opportunity I blew to make things right with Chris; every cold word I ever spoke to make myself the martyr.

I felt every fight I walked away from, every moment I chose to ignore him, and every unhappy thought I'd allowed my mind to think about him. I'd let myself get so angry at him that I'd even gone so far as to kill him in my daydreams with a freak car accident or heart attack that would set me free of the bad marriage I'd created.

I sobbed violently as the world around me blurred and I remembered the worst of it. I watched my marriage crumble night after night as I crawled into bed and turned my body away from his. All I had to do was reach out. That's all I ever had to do. And I hadn't. I waited. I waited and held onto a grudge that I created in my head until it was too late to make it right.

I clawed blindly as I replayed the crash, relived the moment I opened my eyes to stare into Jack's instead of turning in my seat to check on the only man who had ever truly loved me; the man who couldn't love me anymore because of all that I had put him through.

Succumbing to the devastation inside me, my body gave out and went limp against the wall.

I'd pushed my husband away until he didn't love me anymore. Now I could never fix it. I shook with tears as my mind echoed, over and over: *'He didn't love me anymore.'*

Much to my surprise, and despite the claw marks streaking both his biceps, Jack pulled me softly into him and wrapped his arms around me, holding me against his chest and stroking my hair while I shook and wept against him.

His arms around me made me painfully aware of just how long it'd been—long before the crash—since I'd felt comforted, touched, loved... I buckled then, and we slid down to the cave floor. He kept his hold on me as I curled into him, tears wetting his shirt as I buried my face in his chest.

He held me there, rocking us gently, until I was drained of tears, caressing my hair even after the sobbing had stopped. I sniffled, and trying to regain my composure, pushed myself slowly apart from him.

He wiped the tears from my cheek with his thumb. "Better?"

I inhaled deeply, noticing the wetness of my tears on his shirt. I dabbed at it uselessly. "I just can't seem to get a grip."

"You will," he said, rubbing my back. "And until you do, you can beat me all you want."

I ran my hands back to smooth my hair, trying to steady myself. "Thank you." I laid my head back against the cool rock wall and blew out. "I don't know why you're being nice to me after all that, but thank you."

He bent his legs to push himself upward, grabbing my hand to pull me up as he did. "Well, it was either be nice to you, or hike three hours down to trade you in for another model."

I laughed at that, realizing I actually did feel a little better. I'd been holding onto the breakdown for years and now that it was out, my chest felt a little lighter for it.

"There's the smile," he said, bending to pick up the flashlight. "That." He straightened, winking. "That's why I'm nice to you."

He turned then toward the cavern and shined the light inside. "Now… should we go see if we can't get trapped and perish together in this death tunnel you've discovered?"

After he made a quick run back up to the top to scan the ocean once more, we headed into the narrow passage. He slid in first, back against the wall, and inched sideways, flashlight pointed ahead of him. I inched in beside him, shoulder to shoulder.

As we side-stepped farther away from the light of the opening and into blackness, he took my hand in his.

"Just in case I fall," he whispered.

There was a curve as we crept downward, turning the crevice completely black aside from the small beam of light shining from the flashlight. One hand in his, I held the other out to slide along the wall of rock in front of me.

Gradually, the wall grew farther and farther away so we were able to walk forward instead of sideways, then wide enough that we could stand side by side.

The light danced from the left wall to the right. Shiny black rock surrounded us and led downward like stairs into blackness. "Stay slightly behind me," he said in a low, quiet voice, forcing me to pause to let him step ahead.

He kept my hand in his as we walked downward in the dark for a short eternity. After a while, a small bit of light shone ahead of us, growing brighter and brighter until we could make out a gap in the rocks about two feet tall and two feet across.

Still holding my hand, despite the light from the opening, he knelt and climbed through, tugging my hand to indicate the coast was clear. With one arm being pulled ahead, I awkwardly knelt down and crawled into the light.

I came out standing on a ledge overlooking a massive cavern two hundred or so feet below us. On the far side from where we stood, a large opening shone its light through bright green vines that hung over it like curtains, painting the entire cave shades of emerald.

Below us, black and brown boulders tumbled toward the cave's giant mouth, growing hints of bright green moss that grew thicker the closer they got to the entrance. Just beyond the opening, we could hear the sound of running water.

On my side there was a slight decline of smooth surface that wound around the wall of rock to the floor. "Look," I whispered, pulling at his hand and pointing to the path down.

The ledge we stood on along with the path down was only about a foot and a half wide. With the path being on my side of where we stood, I started toward it, only for him to pull me back.

"I'll go first," he whispered.

"Seriously?" I rolled my eyes.

Letting go of my hand, he turned himself to face the rock at our backs and inched toward me.

"I can just go back—"

He laid a hand on my stomach and pushed me back against the wall.

"This'll be more fun." He smiled as one leg and one arm came around to the other side of me, forcing his entire body to press against mine as he shifted his weight. A momentary rush came over me at the feel of him against me—a feeling I'd been starving for.

Without realizing, my eyes closed, and I breathed out a soft whimper. Reality returning to me, I opened my eyes to meet his. With his forearms at each of my ears on the wall behind me, he hovered, eyes shifting from my eyes to my mouth and back.

He lingered a moment longer until I turned my gaze away from his. He shifted his weight and brought his shoulder to the wall where he whispered in my ear. "Way more fun." He then swung his other arm and leg around to the opposite side.

He took my hand in his and we made our way down to the cave floor, over the rocks, and we peeled back the vines to look out.

The mouth opened up to a small oasis, trees and palm circled and shaded a pond that water spilled into from two tall cliffs crawling with green moss standing side by side. Bright pink and yellow flowers littered the ground. Above, hints of blue shone in small gaps between the palm trees. Two large banana trees grew high to one side. Beyond the pond was a straight narrow path down into the canopy near the trail we'd taken up.

As we stood with our feet on the rocky edge of the creek, we could see large fish in abundance just beneath its crystal clear water.

"What do you think, Red?" He tugged at my hair. "Take a swim with me before we head back up?"

"Don't call me Red," I laughed. "We've been gone a while," I said, despite my desire to stay and be flirted with. "Should probably get back."

"Probably should," he said, pulling his shirt off over his head. "But I'm not going until I've gotten you in that water." He kicked off his boots and unbuttoned his jeans, his eyes full of menace. "You'd better get those boots off, *Red*. You're going in whether you want to or not."

I took a few steps back from the water's edge. "Seriously," I backed up more as he started toward me, "stop calling me that name. And why do you want me in the water so bad?"

"Well," he smiled, "frankly, you stink, and if I'm gonna spend a whole week with you, we're going to have to remedy that."

I took two steps back, laughing genuinely as he followed. "I do not!"

"Last chance, Red, better get those boots off."

"Ok, stop," I said as he closed the gap between us. "Stop, I'm taking them off! Wait wait!" And that was all I could get in before I was hoisted over his shoulder.

"Jack I swear if you throw me in…" He turned us around and started toward the water. "Just let me take my boots off, please!" I squirmed, laughing, but his arm tightened around me and he froze.

He bent to set me back on my feet, eyes locked straight ahead.

"What?" I asked, still smiling, following his gaze toward the stream of water rolling off the rocks.

He started toward whatever he'd focused on, bare feet crawling over the rocky ground, arms and back stiff, and I followed cautiously.

Then I saw it. My mind tried to rationalize, tried to make it out to be an animal, but the skull was definitively human affixed to a definitively human body, lying on its side against the cliff.

The skeleton had become a part of the landscape. Wild grass, weeds, and flowers had entangled their roots among its rib cage, through its femur, and bright green vines had worked their way along the arms and legs.

Around its waist was a fabric that might have once been pants torn into shorts that appeared now, as if they would crumble to pieces if we touched them. Off to one side of it was a very worn, cracked leather-like shoulder bag—whatever color it had been had faded to almost white from the sun.

"I wonder if this is the owner of that boat down there?" I asked as we stood above it. "How old do you think it is?"

He knelt, opening the flap of the bag next to it to peer inside at its contents. "Old."

He used both hands, digging around in the little fragile bag. "I... don't believe it." As he said so, one hand emerged from the fold holding a very large knife protected by an intricately patterned brown leather sheath.

He popped the snap of the sheath open with his thumb and the sun glistened across the mirrored edge as he pulled out the blade— still sharp and pristine. It was a bowie knife, about a foot and a half of blade protruded from a wooden handle, one curved edge came up to meet a dip in the other side that slid back to the full width as it wound back toward the handle, sharp on all sides.

I knelt beside him and he handed me the knife. I was surprised at the weight of it as I held it forward and touched the tip with my forefinger.

As I placed it back into its sheath, Jack's attention returned to the bag and he grinned as he pulled out two fat glass bottles, one half full, the other filled to the top with a golden brown liquid. He pulled the cork from the half full one and sniffed, smiling as he handed it to me to do the same. Whiskey—very potent whiskey.

He re-corked the bottle, set it on the ground at our feet and dug back in to produce a leather-bound journal—its pages filled with blurry scribble, years of water damage rendering the words illegible.

"Oh, you wonderful man," he laughed to the skeleton as he pulled out an old folded straight razor, a hatchet in decent condition and a little piece of thin gray metal I didn't recognize. Its design looked like a boat—two edges curled up and around to form hooks the width of a finger on each end. He held it in his palm toward me as he reached back in the bag with his other. "Do you know what this is?"

Satisfied with whatever he'd been digging for, he outstretched his palm to present two white rocks. "It's an old flint and steel." He smiled and looked down at his open hands, eyebrows raising to his forehead in amazement.

I watched him. He was squatting with one knee on the ground, keeping his body still, his bare feet curled beneath him. His bright blue eyes blinked in awe of the flint in his hand, the hatchet and knife at his feet. His broad bare shoulders and chest glistened in the bits of sunlight shining through the trees on him as he shifted back toward the bag, peeling it up from the ground to place the items back inside. Happiness was lovely on him.

"Should we..." I swallowed, looking at the skeleton. "Should we bury him, you think?"

He draped the bag over one shoulder. "Not today, but maybe we can come back here when Jim comes to relieve us and put him to rest. We should really be getting back."

He stood then, grabbing my hand to pull me up beside him. "But first," he bent and quickly hoisted me back over his shoulder, "we've got unfinished business."

"Jack, seriously, no," I squealed, pounding playfully at his back. "Come on, please!"

He turned and headed back toward the pond, one big arm holding my legs in place as he pulled off my boots and socks, letting them fall on the ground in his path.

I was laughing uncontrollably. "Seriously, don't you dare!"

He moved quickly. I heard the 'thunk' of the bag sliding to the ground and the splashing water as he stepped with me still over his back into the water and walked us deeper, "No, no, come on, please don't!"

Then he let himself fall backward, forcing me to dive head-first into the cool water.

"Thank you for today," I said that night as we sat by the fire under a blanket of stars to eat the fish we'd brought back with us. "For forcing me to face it and being there so I didn't have to face it alone. I needed that."

He laid back on his elbows across from me, his long body stretched out in front of him. "What was he like? He must've been quite the guy to warrant that kind of..." He casually swept his palm over the scratches on one arm, "...reaction."

My cheeks flushed as I noticed the thin red streaks my nails left on his upper arms. "Oh, I'm so sorry—

He waved it off, smiling. "I'm fine. I wasn't trying to make you feel guilty. I'm just curious about him. All this time, I can see your mind going to him, but you've never really described him as anything but your husband. Who was he? What was he like? Is he like me or...?"

"Oh, er...." Caught off-guard, I stuttered, trying to find a way to navigate this unfamiliar ground with a man my mind seemed so determined to replace him with. "In some ways, yes... In some ways, no... He was..."

I squeezed my eyes closed, wading through the past few years of hurt to find the person I wanted to describe him as; the person I wanted to *remember* him as.

"He was the kind of man who, instead of using words or affection, would go to extremes to show me he loved me. He'd build me my dream home, surprise me with the perfect dinner, would drive for days just to spend a few hours with me..."

I swallowed a lump in my throat. "And it took his death for me to see it... I'd be standing in that dream home he built me looking at that perfect dinner and only notice that he didn't say the words or offer affection."

I swallowed. "He kept his emotions guarded, even from me. He didn't talk about them, wasn't a particularly affectionate man, but he showed it in his own way. He worked harder than he needed to to make sure I could have the life I'd told him I always wanted. He built me things, bought me things, and showed his love through his support of me instead of in more traditional or even superficial ways."

"And you wanted the traditional," he said softly.

I nodded. "I was blind... I was... awful."

He gazed up at the stars and leisurely shook his head, "It's not awful to want the physical touch... to want the words, even if they *are* superficial... It's why I lived the way I did... woman after woman... it's human nature to want to be touched—*loved*—in a certain way. A person can have great intentions, but without the intimacy, what's the difference between a lover and a friend?"

"Did you love any of them?" I poked lazily at my fish with my chopsticks, happy to deflect the conversation away from my marriage. "The women?"

He smiled. "I wanted to. I wanted that kind of connection so desperately; wanted one of them to be that perfect match, that soulmate I couldn't live without. But no, I never did love any of them. It was all superficial, all lacking real substance. They didn't want me. They wanted the character they knew and loved; a made-up person that I wasn't at all. And so none of them were interested in talking or showing me any part of their true selves. It was always about Elias."

I glanced at him then, noticing his normally confident shoulders shrink inward as though he were sheltering himself from the cruelty of the world. "That's not fair."

As I'd said the words, I wondered how my own behavior was any better than that of the women who'd made him feel that way. I'd been using him, just as they had, as a distraction from reality. He was familiar to me as Elias, and I'd taken just as much advantage of his character, flirting and curling comfortably into his arms to play out my own selfish fantasy.

   Unlike them though, I justified, I'd had more time than a one-night stand allowed for. In that time, I'd been forced to see him, and as he exposed those innermost, vulnerable parts of himself, I was more intrigued by the person beneath the character.

   He shrugged, "Maybe that's just life, you know? Maybe years of romantic movies and television have set unrealistic expectations of what love should be."

   His head came forward, and he tilted it to one side, eyeing me. "I mean, even someone like you had a relationship that fell short of expectations. If *you* can't find happiness, where does that leave the rest of us?"

   "Me?!" I scoffed. "Whatever pedestal you've just placed me on, I urge you to pull me right back down. I'm not exactly a walk in the park, you know."

   He smirked, displaying the red scratches that lined both of his arms once more. "Oh honey, I'm very much aware of that fact!"

   I laughed out loud at that, and his expression softened. "You know, you're very beautiful when you laugh."

   I blushed a little, looking back up at the stars. "It's been a long time since I've laughed."

   "And even more beautiful when you blush," he added. "You should get some sleep."

Chapter Twenty-Four

"I'm so sorry Mr. and Mrs. Grace, but I'm afraid I have bad news."

My breath hitched and Chris's hand reached down to settle my shaking leg as we sat in front of a wide mahogany desk.

I looked up then at the little plump woman sitting across from us. Her cheeks were red beneath her glasses, and her nose was a little too big for her face. Her dark brown hair had wisps of gray sprinkled through it, and her facial expression told me she was as uncomfortable giving the news as I was about receiving it.

I'd been working as a designer for a large marketing firm for three years. The house was finished and felt empty without children to fill it. We'd tried to conceive for three years, but no children came. Each month, I'd tracked my cycle and had done everything by the book. After much debate, we decided to go through a rigorous and extremely invasive testing process.

"Well," Dr. Moore continued, "Alaina…"

I closed my eyes as she said my name. I knew it was going to be me. Years and years of painful periods had always made me suspicious.

"You have what's called a unicornuate uterus. It's a relatively rare genetic condition where only half of your uterus has actually formed. This means yours is smaller than a typical uterus and has only one fallopian tube. A unicornuate uterus is going to affect your ability to get pregnant or carry a pregnancy to term."

Chris placed his hand on the desk, fingers spread wide. "Are there numbers? Percentage odds?"

She sighed, "Again, it's not a common condition so I can't say for certain but I was able to pull some figures and the chances of conceiving and actually delivering a healthy baby are slim."

"How slim?" I begged, feeling guilty for making her continue on with the very uncomfortable news.

"I'm so sorry." She paused and blew out. "I'm afraid you're not likely to conceive at all. And if by chance you did, you are much more likely to miscarry or go into preterm labor."

Chris took my hand in his and squeezed. My heart sank in my chest.

"How likely?" I asked.

She shook her head. "On the off-chance that you were able to get pregnant and I don't know that percentage but I know it's not much," she glanced down at the stack of papers on her desk, "the live birth rate in women with your condition is only about twenty-nine percent."

I inhaled, straightening my back against the stiff fabric chair in an attempt not to break down right there in her office.

"I know that's not the news you both were hoping for." She opened a manilla folder and pulled out a stack of papers and pamphlets. "I've gathered some information on adoption for you."

I noticed Chris's hands were shaking as he reached out to take the papers from her, setting them in his lap and thumbing through the first few.

"There's a slight chance though, right?" he asked, his voice pleading for hope. "It's a slim chance, but there's still a chance there?"

Dr. Moore pursed her lips for a moment and looked at both of us with an apology in her eyes. "I can't say that it's entirely impossible, Mr. Grace. It has happened, yes, but it's highly unlikely. I think you'd both make wonderful parents, and it'd be a shame not to share that with a child. Think about adoption. Take your time with it. Give me a call when you're ready and I'll help connect you with an agency."

I could feel my eyes burning as I looked at the stack of papers on Chris's lap. Without glancing back at her, I shakily said, "Thank you, Dr. Moore. We'll consider it."

We said nothing during the entire hour drive from the doctor's office to our house. Chris held my hand the whole way, squeezing it every once in a while.

As he pulled the truck into the driveway, he drew our entwined hands to his lips and kissed my knuckles. "I know how much this is hurting you. I can see it. Tell me what you want me to do and I'll do it."

I sighed. "Well, right now I just want to go inside and take a bath... forget it for the night." I glanced at the papers between us. "I don't know if I'm ready to give up entirely just yet... Maybe there's something we can do... some weird hippie herbal nonsense we could drink or something... I know the odds are against us... I'm just not ready to accept it yet."

"I will drink any weird hippie herbal nonsense you tell me. I'll stand on my head if they say it'll increase our odds. Whatever you want, we'll do it."

He opened his door, wrapped me up tight against him and carried me out of the truck and up the walkway to set me on my feet at the front door.

Unlocking the door into our pristine foyer, he nudged me inside, the rich dark wood floors and winding white staircase sparkling as he switched on the overhead chandelier.

"I'll go run you a bath," he said sweetly. "Do you want anything else? Are you hungry?"

"No, love." I squeezed his hand. "Thank you."

Really, all I wanted was to curl into bed alone and cry loudly, but that would have to wait until he went back to work the next day.

He kissed my forehead and ascended the stairs. I listened for him to cross into our room and heard the screeching of the knob as he ran the water for a bath.

I sighed, walking slowly into our kitchen and flipping the light on. I admired his craftsmanship as I looked around at the tall white shaker cabinets, the large dark wooden beams that ran from kitchen to living room, the vast glistening white and gray granite countertops that sat atop the gray bottom cabinets and the large island that sat in the center.

How I would've loved to see children here—*our* children, faces that resembled our own, learning to walk and growing to peek at me over the counter as I prepared dinner. I pulled a glass from the cabinet and filled it with water, drinking it all down quickly to calm my nerves.

'Highly unlikely.'

I wanted to cry but I couldn't. I could feel the tears in there somewhere, even tried to force them out, but they wouldn't come.

I flipped through the mail that sat on the island, then walked over to the patio doors to look out. Would I be able to adopt a child? To love a child that wasn't my own? Could I handle the waiting that came with adoption? How long could I wait? What was the point of living in this beautiful house and working so hard if we didn't have children?

I heard the knob squeal as he turned the water off above me. I set the glass in the sink and made my way into the foyer and up the stairs.

He wanted children too. Would he also cry when we were apart? Why did I feel the need to cry only when he couldn't see me?

I crossed through our bedroom and into the bathroom to find him rummaging through the drawers of my vanity, two candles in each hand.

"Do you want lavender, chamomile, or eucalyptus?" He stood and turned, holding them out to me. He'd filled the large tub, the lavender bubbles fizzing at the water's surface.

Overwhelmed, my eyes filled with warm tears and I threw myself into him, folding my arms around his neck and squeezing him tightly.

Still holding the candles, he pressed his forearms against my back and pulled me close. "Hey now." He laid his cheek against the top of my head. "It's alright. We'll be alright. We'll figure this out like everything else."

I let the tears fall as we held onto each other. "You wanted them too. You don't have to be strong for me. Not over this. You're allowed to cry if you need to too."

"Shhh." He kissed the top of my head. "I'm alright. Come on, let's get you in the tub before it gets cold."

He slowly let go, and I wiped the tears from my eyes while he turned to light all four candles.

I stripped off my clothes somewhat shyly. "Come in with me?"

"You sure? You seemed like you wanted to be alone." He looked so self-conscious as he asked it.

I shook my head. "No, I want to hold on to my husband. It's been a hard day for you too."

He nodded, pulling his shirt over his head. I flipped the switch to turn off the overhead lights, letting the candles dance across the white tiles as he stripped down quickly. We eased ourselves into the hot water and I pulled him to lie back against my chest, wrapping my arms and legs around him as I tucked my chin into the crook of his neck.

He exhaled, taking both my hands in his. "Maybe they're wrong. We could go to another doctor."

"I don't want to hear another doctor tell me the same thing." I squeezed him tightly. "We're not giving up yet. We're still young and we have time. We'll keep trying for a while and see what happens."

Chapter Twenty-Five

"Checkmate!" I said for the fourth time that evening. I stood and strode arrogantly toward the fire where I had two fresh white fish we'd caught in the creek grilling across three metal pipes we'd balanced between rocks.

The week had gone by slowly on the summit. Through the day, one of us would keep an eye on the ocean while the other went down to spear fish in the creek and gather firewood. We found small ways to keep ourselves occupied.

One day, we played baseball with rocks and a large branch. Another, we weaved baskets out of palm fronds, formed a handful of clay bowls, and carved a small chess set out of wood.

With nothing to distract us, we talked a lot. He told me all about Hollywood—the ups and downs, the show and the short-lived fling he had with Olivia Bishop. He talked about his sister and I about mine. We talked about our lives outside the island—my music, his acting. We shared horror stories from high school. We flirted and laughed, and I felt lighter for our time together.

Now that we'd come to our last night on the summit, I was a little sad to leave it. I wondered what we'd be like once we returned to camp.

Would we be closer for it, or would we return to the routine we'd had? Would we continue to dance around the infatuation we'd developed for each other, or would there be more?

Was it only infatuation between us? He flirted with me more frequently... and I with him, but there was a little more there than just that. He was no longer a means to distract myself from my thoughts but someone I genuinely was interested in. There was more than attraction there. There was an emotion attached to him now—an emotion I wasn't quite prepared for so soon after losing Chris.

"How do you keep doing this?" he laughed, staring down at the chessboard in amazement.

I pulled the fish from our makeshift grill and placed them into clay bowls with the spaghetti algae. I turned back and handed him one, along with a pair of chopsticks. "I'm just that good I guess."

He took the bowl, still gazing at the board. "I guess..."

I took my seat across from him as he cleared the board, both of us placing our bowls on top of it.

"Red..." He cleared his throat, readjusting his chopsticks between fingers. "There's something I've been meaning to ask you about and I'm pretty sure you'll tell me to piss off if I do... I'll be alright if you do, but I have to at least ask..."

I inspected him suspiciously. His playful demeanor had been replaced by a seriousness I hadn't seen from him since the night after my meltdown. "What's that?"

"Well," he pushed a piece of fish around his bowl. "A few days ago... when you beat me up..." He grinned at that. "You said something that's sat with me for a while."

"Oh? What did I say?" I hadn't remembered actually speaking —only screaming and sobbing incoherently.

"You said..." He frowned. "*He didn't love me anymore...* and if you don't want to talk about it, that's okay, I just... haven't been able to shake that. I was curious to know what you meant."

"I said that out loud, huh?"

He nodded, swallowing.

"Well..." Did I want to talk about this? I hadn't recalled saying it, but since it was out there, I might as well talk to someone about it. It had been eating me alive for the past two years. "I... well, I don't think he did."

I looked up from my bowl at him. He'd set his chopsticks down and was listening intently with a hand on his chin.

I looked out over the water as the setting sun cast a bright orange glow over the ripples on its surface. "There was this day… he came into the kitchen and he said we needed to talk… and," I huffed. "Well, I looked at him and I just knew he was going to ask me for a divorce. So I didn't let him talk. *I* talked. I suggested the trip to Bora Bora… to fix us. A honeymoon we never got to have… hoped we could fall back in love there. He was hesitant, but he agreed to go… and never did say what it was we needed to talk about. In the months that passed between the suggestion and the trip, I kept kicking myself for not letting him speak first. What would he have said? Not knowing if your husband wants to divorce you or not while you're trying to get him to fall back in love with you is a very bizarre feeling to have. And now I'm left with so many questions I'll never know the answers to."

He shook his head. "Christ. Do you think the trip would've fixed things?"

"I really hoped so." I picked up a piece of fish, "But I don't think it would've." I sighed heavily, holding the fish over the bowl. "Neither of us cared enough to consider trading my seat… and even before that… we barely said two words to each other in the airport. I think the damage was too much to repair."

I brought the fish to my mouth, closing my eyes as I chewed.

"I don't buy it," he said, picking his chopsticks up and launching a piece of fish into his mouth.

"Don't buy what?" I asked.

"That he didn't love you. I don't buy it." He shook his head, moving the fish to one side of his mouth. "Had to be something else."

"Ha!" I scoffed. "You have a lot of confidence in a man you never met!"

"Well, I *am* a man sitting here looking at you and I'm telling you, no man in his right mind would stop loving you once he started."

"Oh." I blushed, diverting my eyes to stare down into my bowl. "Well, you—"

"The music. Do you still write?"

"Um..." I was taken aback, and I found myself suddenly nervous with him. "Well... no. Not really."

"Not really?" he echoed, raising an eyebrow.

I sighed, taking another bite of my fish and waiting until I'd swallowed to continue. "I mean, I kind of got caught up in life I guess. Between work and bills and cooking and cleaning... It just got lost after a while."

He lifted a piece of his own fish and chewed, closing one eye as he observed me. "You should sing something right now."

I laughed. "No."

"Why not?" He grinned. "You've got no work, no bills, no cooking or cleaning to distract you up here. Come on, Red, sing me something."

"No." I smiled shyly. "It'd be weird."

He raised his eyebrows. "You watched my horrible season six. Nothing is weirder than that. Come on." He nudged my foot with his toe. "If you sing me something, I'll tell you something embarrassing about myself."

"I don't know... how much would I have to sing in exchange for this kind of information?"

He chuckled. "Depends on what level of dirt you want."

"I can sing anything I want and you'll tell me something embarrassing?"

He leaned back. "Anything you want."

"Alright then," I giggled. "Close your eyes. I can't sing if you're looking at me.."

He snorted, closing his eyes. "So exciting."

I took a deep breath and proceeded to sing the opening lines to the Gilligan's Island theme song.

He opened one eye as I continued, and as I reached the climax, I raised my arms wide, holding out the final note for effect.

He clapped. "Beautiful. Absolutely amazing." He fanned at his eyes. "You really made me feel it."

I bent over in a bow and sighed. "I know. I know. I'm really that good." I picked up my chopsticks. "I held up my end of the deal. Your turn, Skipper."

"My mom made me take ballet when I was a child."

He said it so suddenly and it caught me so off guard that I coughed a little as the fish I'd been chewing got lodged in my throat.

I brought my bag of water to my lips to wash it down while he continued.

"Don't laugh, it's hard work!" He smiled, poking at his fish. "God, that woman was so convinced I would be a child star. She had me in six different classes before I started kindergarten. Modeling... tap dance... child acting... singing lessons... *and* ballet!"

"Oh, you poor thing!" I joked, laughing harder. "I can just see you in tights doing a pirouette!"

"Hey now." He straightened, stifling his own laughter. "A pirouette is no laughing matter."

"Oh, you have to show me now!" I set down my bowl and placed my hands together at my lips. "Please, please do one!"

He slowly took a bite of his fish. "That's not why I brought it up..."

"Oh, but you *know* how to do one..." I clapped my hands. "Please, Volmer, please do one! Just one. For *me*."

"I'll do you one better," he said, smiling mischievously as he raised up. "Come stand here."

I happily obliged.

"Okay," he took my arms in his hands and lifted them over my head, "curl your arms like... no, come on, Red, have you *never* seen a ballerina before?"

I curled in laughter. *'Graceful'* was not a word often used to describe me. "Okay, okay. Like this?" I did my very best impression of the traditional ballerina stance.

He staunched a laugh as he circled me, adjusting my posture, lips twitching as he tried to maintain a straight face. "Yeah, sure. Put your feet together, though... no, don't try to get on your toes... just keep your feet straight."

He stepped behind me. "Okay, now, stay as straight as you can, and when I lift, arch your back just a little. DO NOT bend forward. Then, when I tell you to, slide this leg back about a foot. Got me?"

"What?" I laughed. "Are you serious?"

"Yes."

I felt his fingers wrap around my waist on one side as the palm of his other hand found the small of my back. Goosebumps formed up and down my arms. Effortlessly, he lifted me above his head. "Okay, arch and slide your foot back slightly," he ordered, and I awkwardly did so.

Then his hand at my waist released, and the hand on my back lifted me higher. "Are you impressed yet?"

I was, actually... I was more than impressed. Held high in the air by only a hand on the small of my back, I was completely captivated. "Uh huh..."

"Ready for the best part?" he asked.

"Uh huh," I breathed, trying to remain in the delicate position.

"Bend your knee."

"Which one?" I closed my eyes, trying not to laugh.

"The one in back," he answered patiently. "Slowly bend it toward me."

I bent my knee, and as I did so, he spun me around and down, looping an arm around my leg as one of my arms instinctively curled around his neck. He held me up with an arm around my waist and my leg, his face hovering inches over my own.

In such close proximity, his eyes lured me into trance as they danced to my lips and back. His mouth lingered so closely over mine I could feel his breath on my lips, and I closed my eyes in invitation.

He made no move to indulge me, but laughed, pulling me from my rapture and forcing my eyes open.

"*That's* why I brought it up."

"You sneaky bastard." I smiled abashedly up at him. "You baited me!"

"It worked though." He grinned, raising us up to set my feet gently on the ground. "I was wondering what you looked like from that angle."

I punched him on the arm as we returned to our little table.

"You're impressed though..." He smiled, picking up his chopsticks. "Admit it, just a little."

"Actually," I took my seat across from him. "I was just thinking... they don't teach children *that* kind of ballet... so... how long exactly did you take those classes?"

He bit into his fish. "Long enough."

I bit into mine, heart still beating a little too fast.

"If you tell anyone about this, I'll kill you," he added, poking around his algae for another piece of meat.

"Don't want Jim to know you're a secret ballerina?" I hid my smile with my bowl.

"Very funny, Red." He scooped up his last piece of fish, exhaling. "I'm going to miss this."

"Miss what?" I set my bowl down, stretching as I leaned back.

"This view. The quiet... You... The way you are up here... It's been nice."

"Oh." I looked around, sighing. "Me too."

There was a long silence then as we both looked out on the setting sun. The week had been a wonderful distraction from reality. The flirting, the stories, the games to pass the time... I too was sad to leave it.

After a while, I stood. "Jack?"

He looked up at me. "Yes?"

"Can you," my lips twitched as I cleared my throat, "can you do that pirouette now?"

Chapter Twenty-Six

"Haaaaay good lookin'!"

I was startled from the journal I'd been attempting to decipher and spun around to see Jim's head protruding from the opening of the cave's tunnel.

He made a long whistling noise as he looked around, clambering out of the hole. "Some view we got here. What y'all been up to all week?" He looked at me and bobbed his eyebrows. "You miss me?"

His eyes darted to the signal fire platform, and he shook his head. "Six days y'all been up here and 'at itty bitty thang's all ye' got to show for it? What in the Sam hill you been doin' all day? Y'aint been up here bumpin' uglies, has ya?"

I laughed at that. "It's good to see you, Jim."

From the tunnel below, I heard the echoes of a raucous female voice. "Eeeeew, Jim! Kill it!"

He grinned and winked at me, looked mischievously at Jack, and then turned back toward the opening, poking his head inside. "Oh, for the love of Pete, it ain't no bigger than a popcorn fart. Squish it and come on."

A very distinct whining sound erupted from the hole. "Jim, seriously, kill it!" This was accompanied by an ear-piercing shriek. "It's coming toward me! Jimmy! Hurry!"

"You know…. If it ain't one thing with you, woman," he started back down the hole, his voice echoing back, "it's another.

Look, there. T'ain't nothin but a itty bitty lil' thing, prolly more scared of you than you are of it. Come on."

Jim crawled out with said *"itty bitty lil' thing"* still between his fingers, Lilly in his wake.

He held the spider out toward us. "Now would you look at this." He shook it. "Whole way up here, had to stop 'n kill somethin' or wait for her to clean mud off her shoe." He looked back at Lilly. "What kind of idjit stops in the middle of the mud to clean off mud? Before they're through the dang mud in the first place??"

She dropped her small pack and dusted off her shirt and shorts as she straightened, rolling her eyes at Jim and extending both her arms toward me. "Alaina." She grabbed hold of me and squeezed. "I missed you!"

"You know what she got in that lil purse there?" He raised his brow at Jack. "A Got damn toothbrush and shampoo. You know what I got? The fire AND the Got damn supplies. Food, water, wood, all strapped to my back while Princess here carried a dang toothbrush—and *yammered on* about it the whole way."

Lilly narrowed her eyes playfully at him. "You spend three hours walking uphill next to Clod Hopper and see if you don't complain. My God, he talked the whole way up. The Whole. Way. Up."

"Anyways," he held his hand up to Lilly to silence her and focused his attention on Jack. "It's gettin' a little late in the day for y'all to be headin' down tonight, and that first hill's slicker 'n dog snot on a doorknob. Best you hold up here with us for tonight, get some rest and head down in the..." He stopped short, walking over to our case and examining its newest additions. "Is..." He licked his lips, bending gently to caress the glass bottle. "Is 'at hooch?" He looked at me, hope washing across his face.

"If by hooch, you mean whiskey, you would be correct, sir."

He cautiously picked up the bottle, held it against his cheek, and caressed it with one hand. "Oh dear sweet Jesus, thank you Lordt."

"Now, wait a sec..." I started, and he shot me a look that resembled a child who was about to have his favorite toy taken from him. "We'll want to bring these to Anna. We might need them for medicinal purposes."

He looked back at the bottle, lower lip protruding slightly. "Cain't we just have a little? Before she sees it? Lordt knows that woman'll hide it the minute she gets her grubby little hands on it."

I wasn't altogether heartless and we could all use a drink. "Perhaps just a little." I smiled. "Along with those, we've got a knife, a hatchet, and get this—flint and steel. We found an easier way up and down too. And we won't need to haul supplies up next time. You're definitely going to want to see this."

We scanned the water quickly and led Jim and Lilly down the passageway, a trail of complaints echoing in our wake.

"Oh god what's that... Ew... Something touched me... It's in my hair..." I got a pretty clear picture of what the hike up must've been like.

We gave them a tour of the cave and the oasis, finishing it off with the bones.

Jim whistled. "Well shit. Poor summbitch. How old ye' reckon he might be?"

"Not sure," I said, "I haven't been able to decipher much from the journal, but I think a shipwreck brought him here."

He poked at the rib cage with a stick. "It'd have to be close by... looks of that knife up 'er, I'm gonna guess late 1920s. Maybe a merchant? If we can find 'at shipwreck out there, might be some stuff we could use... for..." he coughed, "*medicinal* purposes."

"You think?" Jack asked, taking the stick away from him.

Jim straightened. "Well, a man don't walk around with a purse full of whiskey so 'at tells me he might've been transportin' some. If it was in the twenties like I reckon, he's probably got all sorts of it, bein' prohibition and all... Might be a ship out there full of all sorts of supplies. Cain't be far off."

I hadn't thought of that. Intrigued, I moved forward to stand on the other side of him. "If it was close, he might've pulled some of it to shore. He might have a shelter somewhere on the island..."

"If he did," Jim continued, "it'd be up here somewheres. If he was alone, he'd be up here watchin' same as we're up here watchin' now. Might not have hauled all the supplies up here, but some of em, I'm sure." He peered around. "Maybe down in that cave somewheres. Lots of corners and crevices to hole up in."

Jim's eyes narrowed, and he knelt down over the bones, reaching down to the ground beneath them and producing a very rusty shell casing between his finger and thumb. "Somebody else was out here with him."

He stood, inspecting the bullet. "And whoever it was didn't care much for him at all."

Lilly, who'd stayed near the pond and shivered at the mention of "dead body" inched a little closer, standing on her tiptoes to catch a peek at it. "What if there were lots of them? What if there are still some of them left on the island?"

Jim made a *tsk* sound. "I'd have seen somthin', woman. I been up and down that tree line and all over 'cept up here. We'd have seen 'em, or they'd have seen us."

Her shoulders relaxed, but she crept closer to us and kept a wary eye on the cave.

"We could spend the rest of the day down here," Jack said, glancing at me. "See if we can find his shelter while you guys keep an eye out. We'll come back up when it starts to get dark. You think you can manage the path back up without the flashlight?"

"Does a bear shit in the woods?" Jim grinned, turning back toward the cave as he shoved the casing into his pocket, "Shake a leg sugar britches, I ain't got all day."

Jack turned to me and with a wave of his arm said, "Shall we?"

The four of us walked back to the cave—the odd couple splitting off to go up as we turned left to venture into a tunnel on the other side.

"Ye' know," Jim's voice echoed behind me as he ascended the rock ledge, Lilly trailing far behind him. "You're slower than molasses in January, woman."

I laughed as they disappeared into the small opening in the rock that led back up, some part of me wishing I could be a fly on the wall to listen in on their interactions while they spent a week alone together.

We reached the small tunnel on our end of the cave, tall and wide enough that we could comfortably walk it. Jack shined the light inside and, grabbing my hand, led us along.

The tunnel was a labyrinth of twists, turns, and forks. Several small caverns branched off it, and we used the utility knife to mark the paths we'd taken to serve as a guide on our way back.

After an hour of searching nearly every turn, we were about to give up when we spotted a stack of cases in a small crevice around a turn in the rock.

Whiskey and port wine. Three cases of each were stacked against the wall.

"Oh dear sweet Jesus, thank you Lordt," Jack joked, doing his very best impression of Jim—and doing the accent entirely too well.

I laughed and examined the bottles. "I think he might die of happiness with this find. Oh God, can you imagine what Anna will say?! Or Bruce?!" I smiled as I pictured Bruce's big cheeks lighting up at the promise of wine as an ingredient.

"It's cooler down here, might've kept the wine preserved. Wouldn't want to move it until we need to use it. We'll bring a bottle of each out with us," Jack said. "It's getting late, we'll want to get back. I'll mark a trail so we can find them."

We emerged a half hour later onto the summit with a bottle of whiskey and a bottle of port.

"Anybody want a drink?" I called out from the tunnel's entrance, shaking the whiskey bottle toward them.

"I's right, wasn't I?" Jim grinned, standing up from his place near the fire to come examine the bottles. "Let's get this party started."

We opened the port while Jim uncorked the whiskey, taking a swig and informing us all it was "so good it'd make you push yer grandma in the creek!"

We took our places around the fire, passing the bottles around and telling stories about the week.

As the sun set, Jim, a passed out Lilly snoring softly across his ankles, motioned to us, slurring ever so slightly as he said, "Y'all should get some sleep, looks like there's rain a-comin,' go lay down in the cave."

I yawned and stood, stumbling backwards a little but catching myself. The world around me spun, and I blinked my eyes hard to clear it.

A hand on my back steadied me. "Come on, Red," Jack whispered in my ear. "You think you can make it down?"

"PFFFT." I bobbled, grabbing his hand to stabilize myself as he led me toward the tunnel. "Probably…"

He went down ahead of me and I clambered down awkwardly at his heels.

Inside the cave, I stumbled to the wall and slid down it, closing my eyes tight to try to clear the fuzziness in my head.

"Lightweight," he said, wavering a little himself as he came to sit next to me.

"Shhhhh," I leaned up against him and laid my head on his shoulder.

The rational, sane person I'd been only a few hours prior was gone and in her place was a stranger… A stranger who was running her fingers up the length of Jack Volmer's arm.

"What are you doing, Red?" he asked in a low voice, grabbing my hand and placing it in my lap.

But she didn't stop. She reached down to slide her palm up the inside of his leg.

Again, he removed my hand and placed it in my lap. "Seriously Alaina, you're not thinking clearly."

I heard the stranger's voice coming from me and could do nothing to stop her. "So?" She walked my fingers down his arm toward his hand. "You think you're the only one who gessss to flirt?"

As my nails danced across his knuckles, he flipped the hand, curling his fingers through mine and holding it to the cold floor. "It's not the time. Go to sleep."

I felt my body raise up from the wall but again could do nothing to stop it as she led me around to face him, "Donnn't wanna." My free hand reached out to touch his face and his other hand came up to grab it promptly.

"Thisss'll be more fun," I mocked him, pressing myself up against him as I leaned to whisper in his ear, "way more fun."

In one quick motion, I was pinned to the floor with him above me, his fingers locked around my wrists as he hovered there. "I said knock it off. This isn't happening."

I softly bit my bottom lip and I watched him notice as the moonlight highlighted the frustration on his face,

"Whass-a-matter Jack?" the stranger asked softly. "Don't want me?"

His face lowered inches from mine. "Oh, I want ya," he breathed, his lips lingering over mine. "But not like this."

She whimpered and squirmed, fighting to reach his lips where they remained inaccessible to her. She moved my hips against his, her appetite growing ravenous as she recognized the conflict her movement stirred up inside him. He trembled with the effort and therefore she persisted, moving tauntingly against him.

He remained there, breathing heavily until the affection-starved stranger began to give in to the sleep-deprived woman she inhabited. Slowly his grip around my wrists softened and just before I drifted off to sleep, I felt him roll to one side, draping one heavy arm over me.

Chapter Twenty-Seven

The snowflakes hissed gently on the picture window above us as I lay wrapped in a blanket against Chris's chest, his arms circling me on our couch, the only light coming from the Christmas tree near the lit fireplace.

We laid for a while, listening to the snow and the crackle of the fire. I ran the tips of my fingers up and down his forearm at my waist where the sleeves of his sweater had been pushed back.

"I have one last present for you," I said softly, smiling to myself as the anticipation of handing him the box I'd had hidden in my left hand under the blanket ate away at me.

His face came in close, the hint of stubble on his chin rubbing against my temple as he kissed it. "Oh?" he whispered, pulling me tighter against him.

I rolled over in his arms, resting my chin on the soft fabric of his sweater at the center of his chest and looked up at him. "Yes." I grinned. "And I think you're going to like it."

He reached out and ran his hand down my hair and along the side of my face. "I'm sure I will."

I pulled myself up to straddle him, producing a thin gold-foil wrapped box with a bright silver bow.

"Ooh, is it a…" he turned the small rectangular box in his hands. "…diamond necklace?" He laughed.

"Maybe," I teased. "You'll have to open it and find out!"

He meticulously removed the bow, slid the ribbon off to one side, and unfolded the crease in the wrapping. I bounced with anticipation. "Just tear it, man!"

"Shh, I like to take my time." He smiled, delicately running his thumb along the seam and unfolding the wrapping to reveal a long black velvet box.

"It *is* a necklace, isn't it?" He popped the box open and froze as he stared at its contents.

I held my hands together against my mouth, smiling behind them.

He stared, eyes filling with tears, and finally his voice came shakily. "Are you..." He swallowed, blinking the tears away before he looked back up at me. "Are you sure?"

I nodded, my own eyes filling.

"You're..." He reached inside, letting the velvet box fall. "You're pregnant?!" He held the little white and purple pregnancy test I'd wrapped in plastic between his two hands, staring at the two little pink lines on its window.

"Mmmhmmmmmmm." I nodded again, tears streaming down my cheeks.

"I..." he looked at me and back at the test, "...how..." then back to me, laughing as his words got stuck in his throat. "When?"

I sniffled. "I took the test two weeks ago." I wiped at my cheeks. "It's been the hardest secret I've ever had to keep from you!"

He sat up and wrapped his arms around me, burying his face in my shoulder and shaking with both tears and laughter. I kissed the top of his head and ran my fingers through his hair.

He pulled back a little, eyes swollen as they met mine. "I'm gonna be a dad..." He twisted his lips upward at the word. "Oh, thank you, my beautiful, perfect wife. This is the best gift..." His voice cracked and instead of finishing the sentence, he reached up and pulled me to him, his mouth finding mine softly, the salt of both of our tears on our lips.

He pulled back. "Wait... but your condition... How do you feel?"

He inspected me thoughtfully, and I touched his cheek. "I'm fine, love. I have an appointment next week to get checked out. We'll be careful. We'll do everything they tell us to do."

He wrapped an arm around my back, the other under my legs, and scooped me up off the couch as he stood.

"What are you doing?!" I laughed, resting my head against his shoulder.

"I haven't the faintest idea. I'm just so damn happy... like a kid on Christmas... who suddenly wants to protect his gift from the rest of the world."

I chuckled, placing my palm against his chest as he turned toward the stairs. "Let's stay here tonight. By the tree."

He sat and curled me into his lap. "What should we name him?"

"Him?" I snickered. "He could be a *Her,* ya know."

He rocked me softly. "Even better. What should we name her?"

"Well," I traced his collarbone, "I've been thinking about that... How about Evelyn... after your mother? Maybe Pearl for my grandmother? Evelyn Pearl Grace?"

"I love that." He kissed the top of my head. "What if she's a boy?"

"Hmm..." I closed my eyes. "I'd like to use William after uncle Bill... and I thought, maybe, Christopher William Grace?"

He ran his hand up my back. "William Christopher, maybe."

I sighed against him. "Perfect."

I laid there for a while, letting the rise and fall of his chest lure me toward sleep, then his breath stopped abruptly. "What if it's twins? Or, more?? Didn't you say twins ran in your family?"

I giggled, interlacing his fingers in mine. "We'll handle it and love them just the same, even if we have octuplets."

I pulled our entwined fingers close to my face and snuggled into him.

We sat peacefully listening to the crackle of the fire and envisioning our future until sleep overcame us.

Chapter Twenty-Eight

A nearby strike of lightning jarred me awake.

I was staring up at the black rock of the ceiling, one massive arm wrapped around me. Rain poured just outside the mouth of the cave.

My back ached from the hard stone floor and my head—

'*Oh God, the drinking... last night... What I said... what I did...* 'I squeezed my eyes tightly shut, willing myself back to sleep so I could stave off the embarrassment just a few hours more.

'*You idiot. You stupid, stupid idiot...*'

Another roar of thunder shook the cave around me. Knowing sleep would not come, I slowly opened my eyes again, exhaling and turning toward the large body that held me captive. His clear blue eyes were open, and he smiled, raising his scarred eyebrow.

I squeezed my eyes closed. "I'm an idiot." I opened them again as he smoothed his hand over my bare arm.

His expression softened as he scanned my face. "It's alright," he whispered, thunder rolling behind him as his palm worked up and down my arm to warm it. "You were funny."

"No, I was an idiot." I turned my face down to the icy floor as more memory came to me. "Thank you for..." I looked back at him, "for not...."

His hand stopped and slid up to my forehead where he ran his thumb along the small scar that had formed there. "It's not my style, Red."

I looked down at his chest. "I really do wish you wouldn't call me that," I said softly.

He pulled at a piece of my hair where it draped over my shoulder. "I like it, though. Gets you all agitated every time. You're fun when you're annoyed."

I smiled for a moment. "You do annoy me… quite often."

He flashed his white teeth as he smiled, turning the hair in his fingers. "You like it."

I squinted at him. "Not really."

"No?" He let the hair fall and slid his hand back to the ground near his face "That's not the impression you were giving off last night with your whole *'you're not the only one who gets to flirt'* bit."

I rolled my eyes and turned away from him to lie flat on the floor. "I knew it. This will never go away."

"Nope." He sat up, looking down at me, his face shifting from playful to serious as he raised his knees and wrapped his arms around them. "Be warned though, Red, if it happens again, I won't turn you down a second time."

I covered my face with my arm. "Oh, believe me," I said, "I won't be drinking like that ever again."

He leaned closer to my ear. "Who said anything about drinking?" Then he rose to stretch, bending his back as his arms nearly reached the cave's ceiling.

"Don't think we're gonna be able to go back down today." He gracefully changed the subject as the rain poured steadily at the mouth of the cave. "We could do some more searching, see if we can find our friend's actual shelter."

I pressed the crease of my elbow tightly over my eyes. "As soon as my head stops pounding."

I heard him cross the cave to one side, then back to me, placing a bag of water in my hand. "We should go up and check on Jim and Lilly. Drink that."

I sat up slowly and drank the water, closing my eyes and listening to the storm as it poured down on our cave. I hoped the people down at camp were doing ok.

I stood and stretched, and despite my protesting muscles, got on my hands and knees to climb up the tunnel to the summit, Jack at my heels.

When I emerged, I had to stifle a laugh as I spotted them under the big tree.

Jim, whose hair had grown to almost shoulder length in the time we'd been on the island, was looking miserable with small braids shooting out of his scalp in all directions. Lilly, soaked to the bone, hummed happily behind him as she finished the final braid.

I crawled out silently and, turning to hold my finger to my lips, motioned for Jack to do the same.

We knelt there at the opening, rain pouring on us, watching as Jim's head bobbed back and forth with the braid until, unable to take any more, Jack cleared his throat and I burst into laughter.

"Oh, hush." Jim hissed, eyes darting to us but remaining still in his seat, head down as she finished the braid. "You try tellin' this one no and see where that gets ye.' She'll just hoot and holler and carry on till she gets her way, anyway."

Bent over with laughter, we made our way out of the rain to the shelter of the tree beside them.

"You laugh, but you'll be the one sittin' on this rock all gussied up with no place to go next, Hoss." He squinted as she knotted the end of the braid.

"All done!" She stepped back to admire her work.

He rolled his neck from side to side, his braids dangling hysterically. "Don't reckon you'll be wantin' to head down in the mud. Thought I might ask one of yuns to stay up here with Princess so I can get a good look in 'em caves."

Head still pounding, I was relieved at the thought of not going on an adventure. "I'll stay. You guys go ahead."

"Oh, fun," Lilly said, picking up a small toiletry bag and leaning over to speak closer. "You'll never guess what I found in one of the cases."

I looked down at Jim's bare feet as he wiggled his toes, each sporting a shiny new coat of bright red polish. He winked at me before he rose, sliding his pretty toes into his socks and boots.

"You're gonna go… like that?" Jack hid a smile as Jim grabbed the flashlight and knife, delicately tapping his braids in realization.

"Well, I ain't sat my sorry ass on that rock for three damn hours just to take 'em out now, did I? Come on then."

As Jack and Jim hurried down the tunnel, Lilly leaned in to nudge my elbow with hers. "So… what's going on with you two?"

"What?" I laughed nervously.

"I'm not mad. He's not my type, anyway." She smiled, sitting down on the rock and crossing her legs. "But I'm not blind. I saw you two all snuggled up together. What happened up here?"

"Oh, nothing." I looked back toward the cave's entrance.

"That didn't look like nothing." She extended her fingers out in front of her, wiggling them as she checked out her nails. "I know something when I see it. And *that* was definitely something!"

"Flirting is all, brought on by too much alcohol… completely harmless and definitely not enough to be considered s*omething*." I sat on the rock beside her.

"You're allowed, ya know." She turned her hand, curling her fingers toward her to check the nails from a different angle. "You're still a woman after all."

"Lilly, it's nothing," I insisted. "Now, are we going to do my nails or not?" I held my hands out in front of me.

She took them roughly, pulling them close to her face. "Oh my God, Alaina. Have you *ever* had a manicure?"

I rolled my eyes as she pulled a smaller case from the toiletry bag, out of which she produced a thin nail file and bright red nail polish.

As she filed, my mind couldn't help but wonder, *'there was definitely something…'*

"Well, then…" she huffed, "if you're not going to give me juicy gossip, tell me about home."

I don't know what it was about the girl, but I liked her. She was snotty, spoiled rotten, and could even be rude on occasion, but beneath it all, there was a sweet side I adored.

Maybe it was the lack of female companionship I was missing without my mother and sister, or a need to talk to someone who I wasn't physically attracted to, but as she filed and painted my nails, I told her everything.

I told her about Chris—how we met, fell in love, the fireworks. I told her about our wedding and the house and my career. I told her about the divorce conversation that never happened. And I talked about the crash and all that I'd felt afterward. All the while, she listened closely, shaping my nails into perfection.

Finally she spoke, head still down, as she brushed the final coat on my left hand. "You know what I think?" She didn't wait for my response, but continued, "I think you've been beating yourself up long enough. It's time for you to stop now. There's nothing you can do to change any of it, is there?"

I thought about it for a moment. "Well... no."

She blew on my fingers, "Don't touch anything..." She moved to untie my boots. "Well, then..."

Mortified, I pulled my feet back. Her reaction to my fingers was one thing. My toes would maybe send her over the edge.

She pulled my leg forward. "Alaina, I painted Jim's toes. There's absolutely nothing that could be worse."

I surrendered and closed my eyes as she removed my boots and socks.

"Anyway," she continued, pulling her file out again, "I think you should ask yourself what Chris would want for you. Would he really want you moping around this beautiful island, scared to feel something other than guilt because... he's not here? And although I can't imagine anyone could ever stop loving you, let's say you're right and he did... do you think he'd be disappointed if you found some bit of happiness, even if it wasn't with him?"

I shook my head.

"Do you really think he'd want anything but for you to be happy?"

I sighed. "No."

"Well, there you have it. I'd give my right arm to have someone on this island look at me the way Jack's looking at you. Let yourself feel wanted, even if it's just momentarily."

I scrunched my nose. "You really think he looks at me differently than any of you?"

She rolled her eyes. "Alaina, he never takes his eyes off you. And if he's not looking at you, he's figuring out some excuse to touch you... I'm pretty sure I could shave my head and he wouldn't notice. Flirt with the pretty man, enjoy paradise, maybe even sing to your friends once in a while."

The rain cleared, and the sun turned the air muggy as the evening crept in. Lilly and I had just finished boiling the bananas when we heard laughter coming up the tunnel.

We heard Jim's voice first echoing across the stone walls, "Ooh boy and I tell ye', she was sweatin' like a pregnant nun in the front row of a church meetin!"

They both howled with laughter that became louder as they made their way out of the opening and toward the fire where we sat.

"Wooh wee," Jim said, running his hand over his braids as he inspected me. In the hours that passed, Lilly had braided my hair to one side, painted my nails, and forced me to put on eyeliner. "Damn woman, you look finer than a frog's hair split four ways!"

Jack stopped in his tracks, making a guttural noise in his throat when he saw me.

Lilly grinned, teasing. "Doesn't she look beauuuuuutiful?"

He swallowed, nodding slowly.

I smiled, flashing my teeth at him.

"My head's itchin like a summbitch," Jim announced, scratching at his braids. "Sugar, you gonna have to help me take 'em out now."

"Or..." she pursed her lips, "I could just cut them out."

He sat down by the fire and she handed him the fresh filet we'd prepared. "Woman, you're nuttier than a squirrel turd."

I laughed out loud at that. "Jim, how many sayings do you think you've got on queue in that head of yours?"

Jack sat down next to me, *still very much checking me out*, as I handed him a piece of fish.

"Oh hell, I could go all night. Try me." He winked, scratching at a braid before biting into the fish. He rolled his eyes back as he chewed. "Oh Lordt, that's good."

"What was the one you said on the way up?" Lilly asked. "About it being too hot out?"

He grinned wide, patting her on the head. "You do listen, bless your heart. Hotter than a mess of collard greens on the back burner of a two-dollar stove?"

I laughed. "Where do you get these?"

He chewed, closing one eye as he thought for a minute. "Don't recollect... Just a part of growin' up in the sticks I reckon."

"Tell me about home," I said, feeling guilty for knowing so little about him. "Did you always want to drive a truck?"

"Pfft, no." He grinned. "I's gonna be a civil engineer, just like my uncle. Ye' wouldn't know it to hear me now, but I had the brain for it back then. Numbers just made sense to me... problem was people didn't."

He shook his head. "I couldn't help that I was poor. And them other kids, well, they couldn't help remindin' me of just how poor I was on a daily basis... and well... I'd get mad and bust 'em up for it."

He took another bite, chewing to one side as he continued, "I'd get suspended and come right back and do it again... them kids wouldn't quit... and I wasn't one to be made fun of."

"Anyways, 'for long, I just got too far behind. My grades started slippin' and them numbers quit makin' sense... After 'while, I just give up. Dropped out and started doin' odd jobs—ye' know... paintin' houses or hangin' drywall and the like... makin' just enough money to load up on cigarettes and booze, maybe buy a sammich here and there."

"You could go back," Lilly suggested. "I mean... you won the lottery... you wouldn't need to work. You could go back and finish school still."

"Bah!" He waved her off. "Too late for that."

"Why?" she demanded, frowning at him.

"Well, see, 'em kids grew up, and they didn't get any nicer. People... well, they ain't nice to folk like me out there in the real world. Like to remind me where I don't fit in... like first class."

"Jimmy, I didn't mean that. I'm sorry."

"It's alright, darlin.' I'm alright in my place away from people. Never needed 'em much, anyway."

"How much money *did* you win, by the way?" She leaned over, nudging his shoulder with hers.

"Why? Ye' wanna run away with me now?"

She laughed and punched him in the rib. "Not unless you let me cut your hair."

He laid his cheek on her head. "I just knew we's meant to be, you and me. Grab the straight razor and let's get on with it."

As Lilly hauled Jim off to the last bit of sunshine on the ledge, I turned to Jack. "You're awfully quiet. How was the search? Find anything interesting?"

He cleared his throat. "No. I wonder if he didn't build a shelter somewhere else close by. We walked down just about every crevice we could find. No signs of life other than the whiskey and wine. We gave up after a while, but we buried the bones near the creek. Didn't seem right to just leave him there as he was. I like your hair like that."

I touched the braid that ran down my shoulder. "Thank you."

"And the nails..." he added.

I wiggled my fingers in front of me. *'Flirt with the pretty man. Enjoy paradise.'*

"I thought you might."

"Ouch, I swear to Got if you cut my ear off with that thang..."

I laughed to myself, turning back to Jack. There was a familiarity that was missing after spending the day separate and I could feel myself dancing around it with small talk. "How was it, being alone all day with Jim?"

He scanned me from head to toe and back. "Well," he sighed, "not the same as being alone all day with you... on the plus side, he didn't beat me up, not even once. How was it being alone all day with the Princess?"

I stretched my legs out in front of me, showing off my toes. "Well, we did mani-pedi's and talked about boys all day. It was actually kinda nice."

"I missed you." He looked down, clearing his throat.

My heart warmed, comfort slowly coming back. "I kinda missed you too." I leaned back on my palms. "I didn't have anyone to punch or call names. Lilly's much too fragile."

"You look… good," he said after a minute. "I mean, not the hair and makeup… you look, I don't know… happier."

I sighed. "Lilly's got ways of making people talk. I actually feel kinda… happier."

"It looks good on you." His eyes lingered for a moment too long before he blinked, abruptly changing the subject. "Anyway, I think there's something near the pond we're not seeing. Jim was right, he'd be up here watching for ships just like we are. He's got to have a shelter somewhere close by."

I turned to face him, curling my knees up and wrapping my arms around them. "Or maybe it's on the way down? We could go down through the trail that's off the oasis. Poke around that route on our way down to camp?"

He nodded. "I wanted to talk to you about camp." He flicked a twig off his pant leg. "The trek down is going to be muddy tomorrow. I'm up for the trip as long as you are. It's not going to be easy in the mud."

"I think I can handle it."

"Good. I'm worried about them after that storm. It'd be much worse on the water than it was up here." He straightened one of his legs and bent the other knee to his chest, casually wrapping an arm around it.

"Jim and I have been talking… With the oasis, we'd be much safer camped up here and wouldn't need to hike three hours to look out."

"But Bruce…"

Jack put his hand up. "Not right away. We'll want to explore more of the island and get Bruce healthy before we even think about moving."

"And Bertie?"

"Well… Bertie's…." He gazed at the ground beneath him. "I talked to Bud, Bertie doesn't have long. She has lymphoma. The doctors didn't give her more than a few months when they left for the trip. We'd wait…"

"Oh." I looked out to the water. The sun was disappearing, and the sky was becoming a deep shade of violet.

After a few minutes, I snapped back to reality. "It's a good plan. And with the cave, we could all spread out… have some personal space. Not be sleeping on top of each other."

"Woman, you cut my hair plumb off!"

We turned to see Jim and Lilly walking back toward the fire. Jim was running his palm along the inch of hair that remained on top of his head.

"It's so much better, isn't it?" Lilly skipped, looking to me for affirmation, then back to Jim. "You look ten years younger! Tomorrow, maybe we'll shave your face!"

Jim ran his hand over the short, dingy beard that had formed in splotches around his lips and chin. "That's where I draw the line, Cupcake. You ain't touchin' this masterpiece of a face."

He winked at me and took his seat near the fire.

As the night rolled in, we talked about the bones and theories about them, about moving camp and where we'd shelter. We talked about foods we missed and people we didn't. And we talked about losing Bertie and how much we all loved her.

Jim insisted on taking the first watch, *even though none of us had seen him sleep in the last twenty-four hours*, so after much argument, resigned, Jack, myself and Lilly all found our places in the soft moss under the tree.

As I brought my fingers to the braid, Jack touched my arm. "Leave it." He smiled, lying down on his side between myself and Lilly.

Behind him, Lilly, who'd been brushing her hair religiously, paused and gave me a wry grin before she crawled to the other side of the tree, turned herself to face the opposite direction and laid down.

I let my hands fall away from the braid, and lowered myself down to lie on my side in front of him, a foot of ground between us.

Lilly had been right. He hadn't taken his eyes off me since they returned.

The moonlight outlined his face as he gazed at me, and my heart beat a little faster as I took him in—the strong jaw and almost clear blue eyes... his perfectly rugged beard and chiseled nose... The shape of him... He truly was picturesque in the moonlight and I wondered what on earth I had done to have deserved any of his attention.

"Hey Red?" he asked softly, his eyebrows high on his forehead.

I sighed. "Why do you insist on calling me that name?"

He propped his head up on his fist, grinning down at me. "Why *does* it bother you so much?"

"I don't know... it's always made me think of some old, fat, raggedy hound dog... which isn't really the most flattering image to have of one's self."

He chuckled. "Well, that's certainly not what the term conjures up for me at all."

"No?" I knew I was fishing for the compliment but I asked anyway, enjoying the intimacy of the moment. "Tell me what it *conjures* up for you then."

His expression shifted from playful to sincere. "Well, I've been thinking about how to answer that." He adjusted his head on his hand, leaning ever so slightly over me as he spoke low enough that only I could hear. "I call you Red because it's beautiful."

I snorted, covering my eyes "Yeah, okay."

"It is. This week, every night, you and I have sat on that ledge to watch the sun set and turn the entire sky red... and we've marveled at how unbelievably beautiful it is." He gently pulled my hands from my face. "Red *is* beautiful... and sexy... and fun when it wants to be. And on you?" He lightly touched my braid, "It's perfection."

My cheeks burned and my heart raced. It was much more perfect than the compliment I'd expected from the question. *'Too perfect,'* I thought, and, not being a natural romantic, I, of course, sabotaged the moment. "How long have you been thinking about..." I hid a smile, "*those* words specifically?"

He laughed out loud. "For a day or two... waiting for the right opportunity to say them to you. Did it go over well?"

I smiled at that. "Yes, very."

His attention shifted from my eyes to my lips and back. "I know it's a little rehearsed and corny, but I'm an actor, not a poet... and," he sighed, "I think you're beautiful. I think you're beautiful in every way a person can be and you deserve perfection."

His lips curled upward. "The idea of clamoring awkwardly through an *'I really like you'* speech just didn't seem fitting. Didn't seem like enough... Not for you. And not for the way you make me feel. You're the type of woman *worth* rehearsing for. I know we crashed and we're lost and I should be in a state of complete panic... but, I can't seem to feel anything out here but you."

I could feel my throat tighten. There were emotions sweeping over me that I couldn't quite get a handle on and they were far more than just the attraction I knew I already had toward him. I'd dreamt of this man when I was a teenager. I dreamt of him now.

I dreamt of him with my eyes open and him staring right back at me... Longed for his lips on mine in that very moment—in almost every moment he was near enough—could almost feel them... but was I ready to close that small gap between us? To cross that line and never be able to go back?

To touch him would mean I'd have to let go of the weight I was carrying... to let go of Chris and the guilt that came with... was it too soon? If I touched him, it wouldn't be just a momentary satisfaction... This man could be much more than that. I'd been so ready to feel loved again when I'd boarded that plane... what if that love was offered by someone other than Chris? Was I ready for that?

I reached out to touch his face, but stopped short, wary of what it would lead to if I did. We'd been familiar together... We'd flirted and touched each other playfully, we'd cuddled when the nights got chilly. I knew what his body felt like against mine, knew what his fingers felt like on my face, but the thought of those things now and what they might mean made me suddenly terrified. "Jack, I—

"Shh." He shook his head, placing his hand over mine to lower it on the moss between us. "I just needed to say that before we went back down. I don't expect anything to come from it... not now, anyway."

I sighed as his thumb ran softly over the side of my wrist, unleashing a wave of butterflies in my stomach. "I really like you too, you know." I bit my lip to hide the awkward smile. "And you're right... that doesn't seem like enough."

Chapter Twenty-Nine

My stomach was in knots, the excitement forcing my hands to shake as I pulled the lasagna out of the oven. Since our mothers' birthdays were so close together, Chris and I planned a family birthday dinner where we would finally announce our pregnancy to both families. Having made it successfully through the first trimester, and after Doctor Moore had assured me everything looked healthy and normal, I finally felt safe to say the words out loud.

Those months had taken forever keeping such a large secret from my mother and Cece. Every time I'd spoken to them, it was all I could do to hold it in. I was starting to show the slightest bump now, and I had seen my mother eyeing it on more than one occasion. I was sure she'd already figured it out.

Cece couldn't make the trip, but we'd be conferencing her in on a laptop already set up at the head of the dining room table.

I took down a stack of plates from the cabinet and hurried to the dining room to set the table. For the hundredth time, I adjusted my sweater in the reflection in the patio doors, turning from one angle to the next to make sure the bump was well hidden.

"Hellooooo?" my mother shouted theatrically from the front door.

I smiled, glancing once more at my reflection before hurrying into the foyer.

"Helloooo," I answered back, grinning. "Happy birthday!"

"Eve and Mike just pulled in too." She rolled her eyes half-jokingly as she dropped her coat on the couch and crossed into the kitchen. "Holidays are one thing, but I can't believe I even have to share my *own* birthday now!"

"Yeah, yeah. Where's gramma?" I looked back toward the door. "I thought she was riding with you?"

"Don't get me started on gramma." She opened a cabinet and pulled down a wineglass. "She's driving herself because she wants to *'leave when I damn well please.'*"

I laughed at that just as Chris's parents came through the door, smiling happily in my direction as they took off their coats.

"Hey!" they said almost in unison when they'd entered the living room, causing my mom to take a large sip of the red wine she'd poured before she forced a smile and responded in the same jocular tone.

"Hey! Long time no see!"

"Happy birthday!" Eve laughed as she came around the island to hug my mother.

"Happy birthday to you too!" My mother accepted the hug and patted her back awkwardly until Eve released her. Affectionate was not quite the word I'd use to describe Sophia McCreary. Well, at least not toward anyone who wasn't her child.

"Hey Mike." I smiled at Chris's father. He was tall and lean with salt and pepper hair, and I imagined, aside from the brown eyes, was the portrait of what Chris would look like in twenty years. Eve was short and petite with Chris's big green eyes, always bubbly and happy to see everyone.

"Hey Ally Cat!" Mike slung an arm over my shoulders. "Bill here yet?"

"Not yet." I giggled as he walked us to the kitchen island. "I've got bruschetta, cheese and crackers, and I made some fresh bread with garlic oil just for you." Mike was a sucker for anything with garlic. Normally, so was I, but the baby didn't care for it so I had to make Chris put together the oil.

"Oooh." His eyes went wide as he hovered around the appetizers.

Behind us, I heard the door. "A.J., I almost broke my damn neck coming up that driveway. Where the hell's Chris? He don't have any salt? Where do you want me to put my coat? Doctor says I can't drink with my pills, but wine is just old grapes, so pour me a glass, will ya?"

Gramma had arrived.

"Pearl!" I heard Eve greeting her in the foyer. "You look lovely!"

"Oh, shut the hell up, Eve. I look exactly how I feel. Old, fat and sassy." Gramma cackled with her smokey laugh as she stormed across the living room, her bright white hair perfectly curled and teased high. "I swear to god that woman'd smile and compliment a mountain lion just before it bit her head off!"

Eve rolled her eyes but kept her smile affixed as she took a seat at the island.

"Soph," gramma sat down next to Eve, "pour me some wine."

"Ma, you're not supposed—"

"Don't tell me what I'm supposed to do. If I want to have a glass of wine, I'll have one. I'm a grown ass woman." She spun in the barstool from one side to the other. "Happy birthday. You know," she met my eyes, raising one eyebrow, "this should really be a celebration of me. I did all the work pushing her out that day. She didn't do a damn thing."

I circled around my mother. "Go sit. I've got this." I pulled a wineglass from the cabinet and poured a small bit of wine in it. "Here ya go, gramma. That's all you get though."

"Pfft."

"Hellooooo!" Uncle Bill stood in my living room, his cheeks bright red from the cold.

"Oh look," gramma sipped her wine as she spun all the way around in her chair, "you're not dead after all." She sipped again. "I assumed, since I'd called several times and not once gotten a call back from my only son, he *must* be dead."

"Hello mother," Bill said sarcastically. "So nice to see you. You look very nice today."

"Do you hear that smart mouth? Toward your own mother. Your father ruined you," she teased. "All that work I put in trying to raise you up right and look at you, just like him."

"I'm starving!" Chris appeared in the living room, collecting my mother's coat from the couch and extending an arm to take Bill's. "Pearl, mom, mom, dad, nice to see you all. Let's eat!"

I wondered how he could disappear like that every time people were arriving, avoiding the bickering and sarcasm until it was time to eat.

We ushered our guests into the dining room, gramma falling behind to sneak a quick refill on her wine before she joined us at the table. I laid out the lasagna and salad and fired up a Skype call with Cece on the laptop as everyone filled their plates.

"Happy birthday, momma!!" she shouted as soon as she answered, a two-year-old Madison skipping around in her background. "And Eve!!"

"Hey Cece!" Eve beamed. "How's the campground?"

I filled my plate and took a seat at the opposite end of the table, squeezing Chris's hand beside me.

"Well, we've got the last of the ice-fishing this week and then we start prep-work for the spring and summer camps. Lots of work to do!" She grinned. "A.J., did you give mom my present yet?"

I laughed. "No, not yet. Presents later."

Cece growled. "Oh my God, you guys, eat faster!"

While we ate our dinner, Cece put Madison on screen to jabber incoherently, then filled us in on the two new cabins they would be building the following month. Gramma snuck back into the kitchen mid-meal and returned with another full wineglass, and Bill and Mike sat huddled together to one side talking about trade work.

"Alright," I said excitedly after I'd cleared the plates from the table, "time for cake and presents!"

"Finally!" My mom tapped her fingertips together greedily. "Bring on the presents."

I chuckled and collected the two large silver foil wrapped presents from Cece, handing one to Eve and one to my mother. "From Cece."

They went to work ripping the pristinely wrapped gifts open, Eve delicately untying the ribbon and unfolding where my mother tore violently at the paper. Inside, they both found brand new Coach purses and Marc Jacobs perfume sets.

"Oh, thank you Celia! It's the one I wanted!" My mother held the purse out to show off.

"Celia!" my gramma teased, "Where's mine?"

"Thank you so much, Cece, you shouldn't have!" Eve grinned as she ran a finger along the stitching.

I reached down and grabbed the two gold wrapped boxes from myself and Chris, handing one to each of them. "From me and Chris."

Once again, my mother ripped wildly and Eve carefully unfolded. They popped open the boxes, and I watched their faces as they pulled each identical gift out in order.

"Reading glasses?" My mother frowned, eyeing me suspiciously.

"Oh, reading glasses!" Eve smiled. "I needed some of these!"

My mother pulled out the next gift, narrowing her eyes. "Hair curlers…"

Eve stared confusedly at the little pink curlers, "Oh… thank you."

"Cookie dough…"

Chris disappeared into the kitchen as my mom pulled out a ball of yarn and knitting needles. She looked at me and I could see it in her expression that she'd figured it out, but she waited graciously, looking across the table to Eve, who was trying to look grateful as she pulled her own ball of yarn from the box.

As she sat contemplating, Chris appeared with the cake, a few candles lit on each side and we all erupted into the 'Happy Birthday' song, Chris and I replacing their names with "Grandmas" as he sat down the cake to reveal the words: "Happy Birthday Grandmas!" written across the center.

"Are you serious?" My mother's eyes watered.

"You're pregnant?!" Eve teared up as well, jumping from her seat to wrap her arms around me.

"Yes, aaaaand..." I grinned as my mother rose from her seat, "it's a girl."

"Oh!" My mother hugged Chris and then me. "I knew it!"

"I just thought you were getting fat." Gramma grinned from the rim of her wineglass, winking at Chris.

"She's due in August. Evelyn Pearl."

My own eyes watered as I said her name.

Chapter Thirty

We woke to a frenzy. "Wake up! Wake up!" Lilly was screaming. "Isobel! Isobel's missing!"

I jolted upright to see a red-eyed, panting, and mud soaked Anna pacing the landing. Her thin blonde hair was caked with clay and plastered to her head. She looked like she hadn't slept in days.

Jim had jumped up and was hopping from one foot to the other, hastily putting on his boots. He plucked up his shirt and slung it over his bony shoulder as he reached for the knife and flashlight.

"What do you mean, she's missing?!" I sprang up and jerked my socks and boots on as Jack darted past me to grab his own.

"When the storm hit, she disappeared," Anna sobbed. "We've all been out looking for her all morning and night. When we couldn't find her, they sent me up here to get Jim." She turned to him. "We figured you'd be the best one to track her."

"You shoulda' come sooner—ain't no matter… I'll find her. You stay up here with Lilly and keep an eye out. I'll come back for yuns after I find her." He bolted to the tunnel, stopping to look at Jack. "Come on!"

Jack and I were on his heels, rushing through the tunnel, sprinting down the narrow path to the oasis and down into the canopy.

"Alright," Jim said, eyes scanning every direction. "Spread out. Anna came up from the west so I'll go east, you go north," he pointed at Jack, then me, "you go south. Work slow toward the coast. Yell as loud as you can if—*when* you find her."

He sprinted to the east side of the canopy, shouting "IZZY!" even though he knew she wouldn't hear it. Jack turned to circle toward the north as I went forward hurriedly, my boots already heavy as I hit the mud.

I headed down and slowed, scanning every tree, leaf and rock, trying to think like a five-year-old girl.

'What would cause her to wander off? Was she sleep-walking? Looking for one of us? Following a bug and got lost?'

I scaled up trees, slid down in holes, and I moved every dead palm leaf in my path.

As the hours passed and I got closer to camp, I grew more desperate. *'What if she's in the water? What if she got washed out to sea?'*

I veered off course and came to our waterfall. I splashed into the creek, my eyes burning against the murky water as I searched for her there. I walked directly into the jet of the waterfall's primary stream, burning my face and shoulders with its force as I crossed behind it into a small cave.

I had no flashlight, only the very dim light shining through the fall, so I got down on my hands and knees, propping one palm against the rock as I shuffled around the tiny cavity. Once I'd circled it and gauged the size, I stood and walked around it, feeling around for any sign of her.

'Not here. What if she climbed up?' Memory of my discovery of the waterfall came to me and I raced out of the fall into the creek to look up to the crest. I could see the steep incline to the rock wall of the summit, but no signs of her feet in the mud.

I ran back the way I'd come.

Back on the southern path, my clothes drenched and plastered against my body, I asked myself, *'What if she went looking for her mother? Tried to swim out in the ocean?'*

Panicking, I began to sprint, fast as I could toward the beach. *'Maybe she's out there, floating in the water… why didn't we think to look out from the summit?'*

Then I saw it out of the corner of my eye—the partially sunken ground with a shaved twig poking up at the side of it. *'The pitfall. She's fallen in the pitfall!'*

I ran as fast as I could toward it. *'How had no one thought to check the pitfalls first?'*

As I reached the ledge, I could see her curled into a corner. Her little eyes were closed and she laid on one side.

'Is she hurt? Is she breathing?'

I looked around and saw the discarded bamboo ladder lying about five feet from where she'd fallen. I'd run so fast and so hard toward her that I hadn't noticed anything else—*including* the boar, until its tusk dug into my upper thigh, sending both myself and the pig tumbling into the pit among a shower of dead palm fronds and twigs.

I cried out as my right foot hit the ground first, ankle sliding sideways as my weight fell down on it. The pig landed a few feet from me, in between myself and Isobel. It let out a high pitched, blood-curdling scream that made me cover my ears as I saw Isobel's eyes open on the other side of it.

'Isobel.'

Despite her lost hearing, she screamed, drawing the boar's attention—its twisted, broken back legs dragging on the ground as it turned to face her, flailing and squealing as it bucked in her direction. I shouted at the boar while I felt around on the ground beneath me for some kind of weapon.

In the rustling leaves, my fingers wrapped around a branch about three inches thick and three feet long. I raised it and brought it down as hard as I could on its twisted back legs. It let out a sharp-pitched wail and thrashed, whirling its body around to face me, its black eyes meeting mine.

I could feel its breath, hot and wild and mixed with the distinct stench of filth-covered livestock. I pressed one hand against the dirt wall behind me and the other held out the branch, ready to fight. Its breath came thick in a grunt, and it charged toward me. I jumped to one side, hitting it on its head as hard as I could with the branch.

My ankle burned as I landed on it but I forced myself upright, determined to keep the boar's attention on me.

"I FOUND HER!" I shouted as loud as I could while the boar recovered, dragging its legs and turning its body to prepare the next charge. "JACK!!! I FOUND HER!!!!"

'Jack, where are you??'

I held the branch with both hands, swinging it like a baseball bat as the pig lunged again.

"WE'RE DOWN HERE!!!"

This time, I hit it in its snout, forcing it to fall on its side as I retreated to the other corner. *'How the hell am I going to get out of this???'*

Isobel screamed again as the boar's body rolled toward her. I leapt in front of her, pressing her against the mud as the pig thrashed and squealed. It rolled from one side to the other, trying to get its hooves back on the ground, and I threw myself on it, pinning it between my knees.

I pushed the branch against its throat with both hands, hopelessly trying to crush its airway. "ANYBODY??! HELP!!!"

The pig bucked, and the branch snapped in half, knocking me off to one side as it came upright behind me. "HELP!!!" I screamed out at the top of my lungs, forcing myself up just in time to push Isobel out of the way of its charge. "WE'RE DOWN HERE!!!"

I pulled her behind me as I danced with the panting boar. It grunted wildly as it turned, trying to pull its broken back legs upward as I circled the pit. "JACK?!! I FOUND HER!!!"

'I think you're beautiful. I think you're beautiful in every way a person can be and you deserve perfection.' I could hear Jack's words... see him lying across from me in the moonlight. *'I have to get out of this... I have to get back to him.'*

With two broken halves of the branch, I swung violently at it. "ANYBODY?!!"

I glanced up. Could I lift her out? The pit was a little under six feet deep, and while I'd risk getting maimed in the process, she could run for help. If I could get it on its back again, I'd lift her out.

The boar let out a cry I knew meant it would charge, so I adjusted my grip on one of the halves, and as it came barreling forward, I stabbed down with the sharp edge into its eye.

It bucked its front half and roared—half the branch stuck in its eye cavity. With all the strength I could muster, I rammed myself into it, forcing it back on its side.

Quickly, I stood and lifted Isobel as high as I could against the mud, keeping one eye on the screaming, writhing pig.

She pulled at the mud, trying to get a hold on the ground above. "GO! COME ON, IZZY, YOU GOT IT!" Her weight eased as she found a grip, and I lowered to push her legs upward as hard as I could.

In the corner of my eye, the boar was rocking, flailing, screaming as it tried to get back upright. Isobel's feet went over, disappearing above my head.

"ANYBODY????! HELP! I'M DOWN HERE!!!!" My voice was beginning to crack.

The boar pulled itself over and dragged its body back to a lunging position. *'Dammit, Alaina, this is not how we're dying... not after everything we went through... not after everything Jack said to us last night... we're not dying down here...'*

I adjusted my grip on the half branch I had left, ready to fight for my life. "I'M DOWN HERE!!!!"

It lunged toward me again and I jabbed at its other eye, missing and hitting its ear as I leapt out of the way, but I landed on my right ankle and lost my balance, coming down on one knee against the wall. It turned quicker than I'd expected, charging again before I could get fully upright, its tusk digging into my upper arm and tearing as it shook violently. I screamed out in pain as I felt my muscle shred beneath its tusk.

I was quicker than the boar and rolled out of its grip to the opposite side as it dragged the full weight of its body on only its front legs.

"ANYBODY???" My voice was gone, and the words came out as barely a whisper.

I braced for another round as its one eye focused in. It was panting wildly and I could feel its breath from the several feet away I stood.

On the other side of the boar, up high, I saw the bright yellow bamboo of the ladder crossing over the ledge. It bobbed and tilted and finally came down with a thunk, Isobel standing wide eyed above it.

'Oh, you sweet little genius.'

With one hand on the wall of dirt behind me, I slid along the wall, working my way around the edge toward the ladder. Halfway there, the boar let out a scream, and I jumped toward the ladder as it charged into the wall.

I sped up two steps at a time and the ladder tilted and shook beneath me from the charge of the boar below, threatening to topple me back in. When I reached the top, I rolled onto the solid ground, away from the opening to land on my hands and knees, panting as I stared back toward it.

Isobel's arms curled around my neck instantly and I raised myself up to sit on my knees, wrapping my shaking arms around her as she whimpered softly against my shoulder.

I slid my hands to her shoulders and pulled her back, frantically signing, "Why? You Go. Why?"

Her face formed into a pout as her lower lip jutted out and her eyes welled with tears. She signed back, "Saw pig. Surprise Jim." And then the tears took her over.

I pulled her back to me and collapsed to a sitting position, rocking her softly, as much to calm her as to calm myself. "I've got you. Shhhh, I've got you." I pet her head, letting my own tears fall as the boar squealed below us.

As the pig settled into heavy breathing, my heart rate slowed down enough to become aware of the damage it had done. My arm was on fire, and my right leg was shooting pains all the way up to my stomach.

I gently pulled Isobel away from me and motioned for her to sit at my side. For the first time, I looked down at my body. Thick red blood and dark black clay covered my yellow tank top, blood running heavily down one arm where a massive gash ran the length of my bicep. My leg bled just as much, if not more, from a very deep wound in my thigh, and the ankle below it throbbed beneath my boot.

'I went south... and they went east and north. No one's coming south. No one's coming to get us. You've gotta get yourself back, Alaina... Get yourself back before you bleed to death.'

Despite the need to collapse, I gathered my strength. I pulled my tank top over my head. Using my teeth to tear it into two long strips, I wrapped the first around my thigh, pulling the knot until my leg throbbed. The second, I wrapped and knotted around my upper arm, having Isobel pull one end so I could force the other tight.

Standing was another thing altogether. With the adrenaline worn off, my leg could bear no weight. I tried once, then toppled over.

I pulled Isobel to face me and signed, "Look" and I pointed toward the trees. Then I plucked up a twig and demonstrated a walking stick and the size it should be.

She disappeared behind me, and I leaned back, closing my eyes. *'Don't fall asleep. You can't fall asleep, dammit. Open your eyes.'* And I did, forcing my attention on the husky breathing of the boar below me.

I could smell it, below me and on my skin, the stench of manure and piss, sweat and the mixture of its blood and mine, and I grew angry. I crawled on my belly to look over the edge. "I hope you enjoyed your last fight, you disgusting piece of shit."

It squealed and writhed.

"You filthy sonofabitch, I'm going to slit your throat. I'm going to slit your ugly throat and make bacon. You hear that?! I'm going to eat you. Then I'm going to find the rest of your family, and I'm going to eat them too."

I could hear Isobel's little footsteps coming back so I leaned in. "And I'm going to enjoy it."

Chapter Thirty-One

Even with the walking stick, we made very limited progress. The sun was setting and my body was starting to shiver despite the heat. Isobel stayed at my side the entire time, taking a step, then pausing to allow me to catch up. We'd headed east toward the beach and our camp, hoping we'd run into someone along the way.

I had no voice left to cry out when I finally heard their voices far off in the distance.

"Izzyyyyyy?" Jim called, overlapped by Jack's panicked voice shouting my name.

I reached down and shook Isobel, pointing toward their voices and signing, "Jim."

She stopped, looked outward, and screamed at the very top of her lungs. Then she looked at me for reassurance and I smiled, nodding for her to continue. She screamed again, and their voices grew closer.

"Izzyyyy?!"

"ALAINAAAA?"

One last time, she yelled and I could see them, Jim and Jack, barreling through the trees ahead.

Isobel grabbed my hand and squeezed as we hobbled toward them.

I could see the fear in their faces as they grew closer, and I could only imagine what we must look like. Though Isobel wasn't hurt, she was covered in mud and my blood, holding my hand as I limped in only a bra and shorts, covered from head to toe in the same.

As they reached us, Jim wrapped Isobel up in his arms, holding her tight. Jack reached me just in time for me to collapse into his chest.

'Safe.'

The immediate relief brought on by their presence was overwhelming.

Jack was frantically inspecting me, feeling my face, my hair, and surveying my arm and leg. I looked past him to see Jim doing the same to Isobel.

"Sh-she's f-fine," I said, my voice barely squeaking out. My throat was dry and I was trembling. "We're okay."

"What happened?" Jim asked, scanning the trees behind us.

My body was giving out, and my vision tunneled. "She-she wa-as in the..." I swayed heavily against Jack as bile rose in my throat, "the pitfall."

Jim held her tightly against him. "Oh, my dear sweet baby girl... Where in the hell was the ladder?"

"O-Outside." I swallowed, knees buckling as Jack held me up. "I... I was going to grab it, pull her up... but there was a boar..."

"How'n the hell did the ladder get outside?" Jim demanded. "I always leave it—what you mean, *a boar*... A boar did this to you?!"

"She's bleeding bad," Jack interjected, sweeping my legs up into his arms and curling me into his chest. "We've gotta get Anna."

As he turned, Jim got a glimpse at my arm and leg. "Aw Jesus. Oh Jesus, God, that's an artery there. I'll get Anna, you take 'em back to camp." He'd already set Isobel down and was running toward the summit. "Wrap 'at up good 'n tight!!"

As Jack started toward camp, my body gave in against him, and feeling finally safe, I let my eyes close.

"No no no," he begged me, doubling his speed. "Don't fall asleep, Red. Come on, stay with me. You're alright... You're alright.... open your eyes... Look at me."

I knew I needed to stay awake and I tried. I forced my eyes open, but they were too heavy and proceeded to close despite multiple attempts to keep them open.

"Stay awake, please please stay awake."

Again I tried to hold my eyes open, but they fell shut and the world around me went quiet and dark.

When I woke, I was freezing. I couldn't make out where I was or what was happening. My eyes were too heavy and I couldn't seem to get them open. I could hear voices, lots of them over me… arguing? I tried to make out the words, tried to push myself awake, but I couldn't quite get there. I shivered and tried to turn… I was stuck. My eyes grew heavier and as I tried to make out the words above me, a familiar voice came to me.

"Alaina," he called. "Alaina, stay with me."

Chris? He was here? Had I dreamt it all? Panicked, I tried to reach for him, tried to sit up, tried to force my eyes open, but something was pushing me—pinning me back down.

The boar… was I back in the pit? Was I dying?

"Alaina?" he called again.

"I'm right here!" I called out. "I'm right here! Where are you?"

"I'm here," he said and suddenly I was standing on the edge of the pitfall looking down into blackness. I could hear the strangled breathing of the boar below.

"I'm coming!"

I saw the bamboo ladder lying on the ground at my feet. "Hold on!" The breathing got louder in my ears as it struggled harder to get air.

"Alaina," he called as I pulled at the ladder. It was heavy and I could barely slide it, but I yanked and pulled, my arm burning until it slid into the pit.

"Alaina, can you hear me?" he asked from below as I climbed down onto the ladder.

The ladder shook beneath me, and I knew it was the boar. "Chris!" I called to him, forcing my way down the trembling steps.

I looked down. Blackness. No matter how many steps I took, I could see nothing but blackness, hear nothing but the heavy slow breaths of the boar ringing loudly in my ears as the ladder quivered against my hands.

"Are you there?" I shouted, pushing myself down further. "Are you here??"

"Right here." His voice was soft and close.

But there was no end to the ladder below me. I climbed and climbed downward with no bottom in sight. The pig's breath grew louder and closer, and its labored attempts to breathe began to rattle.

I could hear water. I could feel water, cold on my arms... on my legs... on my face. *'He's drowning,'* I thought, and I let go of the ladder to let myself fall into the blackness. As I fell for what felt like an eternity, the wheezing breath filled my ears, and I recognized it as my own.

I fell into water, panic washing over me as my head went under. I pushed and fought until my head was back above it, and realized I was waist deep, not in water, but in mud—mud that was pulling me deeper, threatening to swallow me whole.

I could see Chris then in the mud, strapped to his seat with an oxygen mask over his face, sinking rapidly as his bloodied arms fumbled with the seatbelt, big green eyes wide with fear. I tried to push my stuck legs against the cold mud, tried to reach for him as my body sank lower.

The mud was at my chest now, and across from me, Chris had sunken in deeper. The seat had disappeared, leaving only his head above ground. I shouted for help... for Jack... as I reached with all my strength for Chris.

"Jack!" I screamed frantically as I watched his head go under the mud. "Jack!" I sobbed, reaching out to where he had been, suddenly able to move and digging for him. "Jack, help me!"

I grabbed hold of something and pulled. I pulled with all the strength I could muster. It was heavy, and it dragged me over with it, but it came up—*she* came up, and as I turned her, Isobel's little hazel eyes found mine.

"Mama," she whimpered.

"Izzy?" I wiped the mud off her little cheeks.

"Mama," she cried again, and my mind recognized her as my own child... as Evelyn.

"No, you can't be Evelyn." I wrapped my arms around her as if she were, pulling her tight to me.

"Alaina," a voice called from above. I knew it was Jack, but I focused on the little girl... scanning her face for any resemblance.

"Evelyn?"

She said nothing as her big tear-filled eyes looked up at me, only nodded slowly. I wrapped her in my arms and sobbed. "Oh, my sweet baby girl! I'm right here! I'm so sorry!"

"Alaina, open your eyes." Jack's voice came closer, but I squeezed my eyes tightly shut, holding onto my daughter before she was gone. There was a panic in me that told me she'd be gone if I opened them... if I let go... so I held her tight against my breast, letting the mud swallow us both.

I felt the cold wet grip of the mud on my throat, chin, and then felt it fill my nose as it washed over my head. I felt it fill my lungs... and realized my arms were empty... I was in the dark... alone, I couldn't breathe, and Evelyn was gone.

I tried to scream out but could get no air. I choked against the mud in my throat. I tried to pull myself up but my arms wouldn't move against the thickness of it. I writhed and shook, desperate to get out, to go back... to breathe...

The rattled breathing that had filled my ears was gone, and I kicked and clawed with all my might to get air, to get above the mud... to get to Jack.

I slashed and raked at the clay, kicking my legs against its thickness, shouting without breath, begging for life.

And just as suddenly as I'd sank, I resurfaced and a calmness came over me. Weightlessness washed over my body as the mud gave way to warm water...

I opened my eyes to find myself floating on the calm water where Frank had been, the ocean around me a mirror to the lilac sky overhead. Evelyn was with Chris now. Would I be joining them soon?

It was silent and still for a good long while and I wondered to myself if I had died, but then a ripple in the water caught my eye… then another, and another, as they circled me.

'Sharks,'

I panicked, searching for air that would not come, trying to turn to my stomach to swim but finding my body frozen.

"JACK!" I tried to call out, but my voice didn't work. *'I'm not ready yet!'*

The edges of the water went white as it started to surface, and I closed my eyes as a mouth came over mine. I could taste the faintness of coconut, smell the saltwater with a hint of campfire, and air filled me. Fresh warm breath filled my burning lungs again and again and I gasped as my lungs came to life. My eyes fully opened and I could see the blurry figure over me—the bright orange light of a fire dancing around him.

"Jack," I whispered softly.

"Alaina?" Jack's panicking voice rang out. "Alaina, oh thank God. Stay here with me."

My eyes burned and my lungs were heavy, but I focused on him, squinting in the dim light to make out his face.

He was kneeling over me, eyes bloodshot. One hand was squeezing mine, and the other was caressing my hair. "Can you hear me?" he asked, his eyes searching my face.

My throat was tight and I couldn't speak. Slowly I nodded my head, an action which sent needles through my skull, forcing my eyes back shut.

"No, no no, stay here. Look at me. Please open your eyes," he begged, squeezing my hand harder as his breath shook. "Please Alaina, I need you to stay."

But I couldn't. I tried to stay, tried to will my eyes open. I tried to reach out for him, but I was falling backward, farther away, the darkness around me spinning beyond my control.

"Dammit Alaina, open your eyes!" He shouted, squeezing my hand so hard it felt it might break.

And I did for a moment. I saw him there, sobbing as he shouted past me, "She's going again! Please don't go… stay here with me."

And then I *was* with him. I was standing on the summit staring straight into his eyes, a blood red sunset behind us.

"I'm asleep again…?" I asked him.

He nodded.

"I'm not ready to die… am I dead already?"

He shook his head, stepping closer to me, and wrapped his arms around me, curling me tightly into his chest.

"Jack… Don't let me die yet."

I closed my eyes against him, letting my tears fall down his shoulder, and when I opened them, I was back in the dim firelight, still wrapped in his arms. "I won't. I promise," he whispered against me.

I could feel small hands on my neck, my forehead, and running along my arm. I could hear Anna's voice and could just make out a few of her words, "infection… done all I can do…."

Despite her ominous tone, a calm came over me. I was in Jack's arms, and I was going to be okay. I was going to be okay because I'd found the love I'd desperately been hoping for when I'd set out on this trip. I loved *this* man, inexplicably and entirely, and as the realization swept over me, I let my eyes close, unafraid for the first time of the dreams that would come, however terrifying they might be. I would wake, and when I did, everything was going to be different.

Chapter Thirty-Two

I sat on the sofa surrounded by pink and tan baby items. Scattered throughout the living room and stacked nearly to the ceiling were boxes containing diapers, a crib, car seat, high chair, baby bath, a changing table, and clothes to last for at least a year. There were toys, bottles, baby wipes, rattles, and decor littered throughout the house.

Still smiling, I laid my head back and folded my fingers over my seven-month-pregnant belly.

For the most part, I'd really enjoyed being pregnant; feeling my body change as she grew inside me, talking to her throughout the day and night, feeling her little legs as she responded to me. But the gas... I'd never been able to get used to the gas and the cramps that came with it.

Most days, the familiar dull ache would creep up and make my life miserable for an hour or two. That afternoon, it'd shown up in the middle of my baby shower and was still lingering, stabbing at my abdomen as I sat on the couch watching my mother and sister clean up.

"Some shower!" Cece shouted from the kitchen as she closed the dishwasher and started it up. "You need anything while I'm in here?"

She'd surprised me the previous morning, showing up at my door with a suitcase and a crib—not just any crib, mind you—the top of the line, eight hundred dollar crib she'd special ordered along with a luxury organic baby mattress that brought the grand total to somewhere around twenty-five hundred dollars, more than I'd paid for my entire bedroom set.

Despite June being the start of the busy camping season, Cece had insisted she come and host my baby shower herself. She and Chris had planned her week-long stay. They went straight to work painting the nursery they were determined to build me while she was here.

She was champing at the bit to get upstairs and finish putting it together.

I loved having them both under the same roof, but they both babied me and refused to let me even pour my own glass of water. I was afraid I might get too accustomed to be catered to.

"Actually, can you bring me one of those chocolate cupcakes?" I asked. "Oooh, and some ice cream."

My front door opened. "Helloooooo?" Uncle Bill had arrived.

"Hellooooo," my mom answered with the same exaggerated cadence from the kitchen.

I dragged myself off the couch, my back protesting and tightening while I straightened and he entered my living room, a massive box in his arms wrapped in pink and white paper.

He bent to set it gently on the floor and raised, holding his back as he bent back and poked his own enormous belly out in front of him, mimicking me. Waddling in theatrically, his big red cheeks raised high under his eyes as he flashed his teeth and rubbed his hands over his stomach. "Oh," he froze, his eyes opening wide, "I think I felt it kick."

I giggled, eyeing the box. "What is this?"

Cece crossed into the living room, a saucer containing my cupcake and ice cream in one hand, as she hooked the other around our uncle and squeezed. "Hey Unc. You need to come up and see Maddy! She misses you!"

I heard the door to the garage open and smiled to myself as I heard Chris drop his keys on the kitchen counter. "Holy hell!" He laughed, snatching a cupcake as he passed the island to eye the overflow of gifts that littered the living room.

"I know, right?" Cece smiled at him, setting the saucer down on the coffee table in front of me.

Bill pulled a smaller box out of his pocket. "I got something for you too, Chris."

"Oh, hey!" Chris exclaimed through a mouth full of cupcake. He quickly navigated through the labyrinth of gifts to take the box from him. "Thanks man!"

Chris set the remaining half of his cupcake onto my saucer, wiping his palms on his pants before he delicately unwrapped the box, careful not to actually rip the paper as he unfolded it at the seams. He pulled the wrapping back. "Cigars! Nice!"

"I'll be having one of those with ya when the baby comes." Bill smiled and patted Chris on the back.

I took a quick bite of ice cream and waddled around the table to the giant box. "Can I open it now?"

Bill rolled his eyes. "Well, I didn't personally bring it over so you could open it later! Open it, woman!"

I laughed and ripped madly at the paper, gasping when I saw the picture on the side of the box showing the little white and tan glider ottoman set I'd seen online but refused to put on my registry because of its price tag. "Oh, it's the one I wanted!!"

I jumped up as quick as a pregnant woman could "jump" and wrapped my arms around my uncle. "Thank you! Thank you!!! I love it!!!"

"Let's build it!" Cece was already peeling back the tape on the box. "And the crib!" She looked back at Chris. "And the changing table and dresser! Come on Chris, make a pot a coffee and let's pull an all-nighter!"

I yawned at the thought. "Oh Cece, I don't have that kind of energy. I'm already ready for bed and it's only, what? 6:30?"

"I wasn't talking to *you*, was I?" She stuck her tongue out at me. "Uncle?" She looked at Bill. "You wanna stay and help? Mom? Let's put it all together and stay up late watching old movies." She looked over at our mother, who was happily singing along to Patsy Cline as she wiped down the countertop of the kitchen island.

Bill yawned in response. "I'll stay for a while. Here, grab this box Chris, let's get the big stuff upstairs. Soph," he gave my mother a mischievous look, "since you're not doing anything, make yourself useful and put on a pot of coffee for *the men*."

Bill loved to annoy my mother with chauvinist comments. It always worked. She stopped wiping the counter long enough to raise one perfectly arched eyebrow. "You boys let me know when any men show up and I'll get right on that."

I laughed, bending slightly as my stomach and back tightened. "Oh…"

"What's wrong?" My mother dropped the dishcloth on the counter and ran over to support me, placing a hand on my back and gripping my upper arm until I had straightened.

"It's nothing," I assured her. "I think I just need to sit down for a minute."

She helped me back down onto the couch, eyeing me cautiously. "Doesn't look like nothing. Tell me what's hurting."

"Just gas, ma." I sat back. "I'm so tired of having to fart and not being able to."

"She alright?" Chris asked. He and Bill had frozen on their way to the staircase, each of their arms loaded with boxes.

"I'm fine," I snapped, exhaling and reaching out for my saucer that was too far from reach, pouting at my mother as if I were a child again until she handed it to me.

Bill and Chris lingered a moment longer before disappearing upstairs. Cece kept her eyes on me as she loaded her arms with boxes and bags, far more than she could carry. "When I was pregnant, I farted constantly. Poor Owen. He always had to take the blame for it in public." She grinned and headed toward the stairs.

I balanced the saucer on my belly and unwrapped my cupcake, very much aware of my mother still hovering over me. "Ma, I'm fine. Really."

She glanced at her watch, then back at me. "If it happens again, you tell me."

"It's cramps, it happens constantly." I bit into the cupcake, rolling my eyes back as the chocolate icing hit my tastebuds. "I'll tell you if something feels weird," I added with my mouth full.

Satisfied, she returned to the kitchen, glancing back at me every so often as she counted scoops of grounds into the coffeepot.

'It was different from my normal cramps,' I thought to myself, *'but it didn't hurt. It would hurt if it were something else, wouldn't it? It's got to just be gas.'*

Cece reappeared several more times, each time loading her arms with boxes and bags until they reached her chin and hauling them upstairs. I let my head rest against the couch, closing my eyes to listen to my mom sing along to the kitchen radio beneath the overpowering sounds of swear words, power tools, and laughter from upstairs as Bill and Chris assembled baby furniture.

My mom had pulled out four mugs and was pouring coffee when it came again. My stomach and back clenched suddenly like a fist, holding tight for only a moment before returning to normal.

"There it is again," I said, this time much more concerned. I'd read all the baby books and wondered now if Evelyn wasn't dropping down. The sensation lined up with early labor symptoms and I was at a high risk for early labor.

But I'd just been to see Dr. Moore, and she'd said everything looked surprisingly good.

My mom set the coffeepot down and rushed to my side. "It's been twenty minutes. Is it like a tightening or a cramping feeling?"

"Tightening." I sighed. "But it doesn't hurt. Could it be Braxton-Hicks, you think?"

"Maybe." She frowned. "We'll keep an eye on it. If it's not, they'll get stronger and closer together. Maybe we should have Chris get a bag together, just in case?"

"No." I touched her hand beside me. "Not yet. It's probably nothing. I don't want to worry him."

Above us, there was a loud clanging noise resembling that of several pieces of crib falling against hardwood. This was followed by a series of curse words from uncle Bill and uncontrollable laughter that was distinctively Cece's.

"They're gonna tear up my floors up there," I said. "Someone really needs to be watching them."

My mother would not be distracted. Her expression concerned me more than the contractions. "I'm going to have Celia get a bag together." She raised up her hand so I couldn't protest. "Secretly. Just in case."

"It's too soon, though." I frowned, panicking slightly by her persistence. "Isn't it?"

She patted my hand. "Hopefully it's nothing." She stepped to the edge of the living room, shouting up toward the landing, "Cecelia! Come down here and grab these coffees."

I heard Cece's footsteps on the stairs and my mother disappeared into the foyer, speaking in a hushed voice outside my earshot.

"WHAT?" Cece responded incredulously. Our entire life, Cece had never figured out how to control her voice. They'd both been pregnant before and their reaction had me on-edge.

'Should I be worried? What if Evelyn is coming now? It's too soon. Way too soon. She couldn't be coming now... could she? Mom looks worried... Mom would know. But shouldn't I know? Wouldn't I be able to tell the difference? It's my body...'

My mind raced as they entered the living room, Cece looking worriedly in my direction as she passed to the kitchen and loaded up the mugs.

"Not a word to Chris yet," my mother insisted as Cece turned to head back.

"It's too soon, though." Cece looked at me, carefully balancing the three mugs between her fingers. "She's got almost two months left!"

This time, there was pain. My entire body tightened and a sharp stabbing pain in my cervix forced me to cry out.

"Forget the bag." My mom took the mugs from Cece and dropped them quickly on the counter. "Go get Chris." She hurried into the living room, grabbing my hand as I attempted to breathe through the pain.

"Mom," I pleaded between breaths, my eyes filling with tears. "She can't come yet."

"I know baby, it's gonna be alright." She rubbed my back as the pain gradually settled. "Lots of women go into preterm labor and the babies are just fine. Look at Tommy. He came early. Evelyn's going to be just fine."

Within seconds, everyone was in the room, dashing madly to gather keys, put slippers on my feet, and find my purse. But it was all a haze.

Evelyn was coming. It was too soon and in my heart, I knew something didn't feel right.

Chapter Thirty-Three

My eyes opened to the bright light of the sun beating down on me. I was staring up at the bamboo of our shelter, lying flat on my back. Small bits of sunlight danced across wisps of smoke that curled into the crevices between the bamboo above. I could hear voices outside the shelter, talking softly.

My body was heavy but my eyes were lighter than they'd been, and as they adjusted to the light, I looked around me. The shelter had caved in on the opposite side, broken bamboo had fallen and leaned heavily upon itself against a palm tree just outside the shelter.

At my side was a pile of shirts... a clump of navy, white, and green, all soaked and turned mostly red and burgundy with dried blood.

I could smell the campfire burning nearby; could feel the salt breeze against my legs and arms, on my chest and in the wisps of hair that tickled my face as it blew over me... bringing the hair on my arms to life, bringing *me* back to life. I inhaled deeply.

My lips were chapped and my throat was dry. I swallowed roughly, small bits of thick phlegm offering slight relief.

I raised a finger, then another, and pulled my heavy arms over my chest to look at my hands.

I had died; I knew this much. Chris had been there. I felt him there in the water with me. Evelyn had been there, too. I could still feel her in my arms, could feel the pull of the mud, remember the desperation as I suffocated... I inhaled the fresh air again, pulling it deep into my lungs as I spread my fingers out against the sunshine in front of my face.

I was so close to them... I was so close to being home... to being whole again... But I was back on the island now. Why had I come back?

I closed my eyes and I could recall the weightlessness... the peace of it all. Any doubts I had in my mind about Chris dying in that plane crash were gone from me. I knew he was dead and he was with Evelyn. My family was waiting for me... calling for me... and I'd come back.

Outside the shelter I could hear clanging and shuffling, I could hear sizzling and smell... barbecue. I could smell *barbecue.*

I slid my arms down to my sides and pushed myself up with my forearms. I was heavy and my arms shook with the effort, but I could see them all... the reality I'd come back into.

In front of me, just outside the shelter, Anna and Bertie were bent over something, their backs to me as they spoke softly to each other. Beyond them, Magna was ladling liquid into a clay bowl.

At the water, I could see Lilly and Jim walking along the shore. Lilly was pointing out to the water, nodding as they carried out what appeared to be a heated conversation.

Lilly's head turned toward me and I heard her scream, "She's up!!! She's awake!!" just before she came running toward the camp, bare feet sending sand in every direction.

The light from camp was momentarily blackened by the large silhouette of Jack rising and filling what was left of the shelter's opening as he rushed in, falling to his knees at my side and placing his arm around my back to support me. "Oh, thank God," he breathed, wrapping his other arm around me and pulling me softly against him as he laid kiss after kiss on my temple.

Before I could process the tenderness of the moment, I was bombarded. The shelter filled instantly with bodies and voices.

"Oh, Lainey!" Lilly's voice was at my ear, her bony arms around my neck pulling me to one side. She'd never called me Lainey before—no one but my mother had—and it made me long for her then. "I was so worried!"

"Haaaaay good lookin!'" Jim's head emerged at the shelter's opening. "Well, butter my butt and call me a biscuit, you're sittin' up!"

Anna shoved through them with a steaming clay bowl between her hands. "Everybody back up," she commanded with an authority I'd never heard from her. She'd always seemed so frail—like she would crumble if you touched her—but her voice was stone cold and the bodies around me fell back to let her through.

She held the bowl near my head, and Jack's arms at my back raised me up a little further.

"You need to drink some of this down," she said softly. "Just a bit. I've got water too."

I squinted hard, and my stomach growled at the sudden enticing aroma of broth.

"It's bone broth," Bruce bragged behind her. "I made you some soup."

"Me n' Jack went back an' killt that summbitchin' pig," Jim assured me. "Although they wasn't much left to kill once you was done with him."

I let her bring the bowl to my lips and sipped. The hot liquid overwhelmed my senses. The taste of salty pork danced across my dry tongue, down my throat, and warmed my stomach. Realizing I was starving, I raised my own hands to the bottom of the bowl, helping Anna as she tipped it again... and again.

"Okay, okay, slow down a little," she whispered, removing the bowl as her palm curled over my forehead. "How do you feel?"

Disoriented, I looked from her to Jack, then out to the crowd gathered at the entrance. "What..." I coughed and gurgled, trying to clear my dry throat.

Jack brought a glass bottle of water to my lips and I drank, the water washing the warm salt down and allowing my throat to finally swallow with more ease.

"What happened?"

Anna raised the bowl to my lips again. "You've been in and out for a week with fever. That cut in your thigh was deep, and you lost a lot of blood. It got infected. I stitched it up as well as I could. We've been treating it with the alcohol, but we couldn't get the fever down. Even with the antibiotics, it wasn't healing. Your arm wasn't any better. That boar did a number on your bicep. You may have pain for a while in it. Limited range of motion. And you can't lift anything for a while."

I looked down at my arm, wrapped tightly in a bandage now. I continued downward where a fresh oversized black t-shirt hung in place of the blood-soaked bra and shorts I'd come out of the pit with. My legs were propped up on a case, one heavily bandaged and swollen at the thigh and ankle, bright red toenails still intact despite the yellow and purple bruising around them.

My fingernails hadn't fared as well. The polish had chipped and most of the nails were broken, ragged, and scabbed over.

I shook my head, blinking hard, "Is Isobel ok? Is everyone ok?" I looked over to the caved-in half of the shelter.

"Everyone's fine, darlin.'" Jim's voice came closer as he knelt at my feet. I noticed his eye was black on one side. "We been eat up worryin' over you is all. You scared the bejesus out of us." He looked at his hands and back to me. "I cain't tell you how sorry I am. I promise ye,' I'll go out first thing and fill evra' one of 'em holes."

I tried to sit up more, and Jack slid in behind me, letting my back rest against him.

"Who's at the summit?"

"Phil and Kyle," Jack said behind me. "They've been up for a week."

"No one wanted to leave you." Lilly smiled at me. "You stopped breathing, Lainey. We were all terrified."

Magna's deep voice came over me, instantly comforting me. "Relax now, you just concentrate on getting better. Come on," she turned to the others, "we've got work to do. You let her heal."

One by one, they turned to follow her, leaving me alone with Anna and Jack.

"You think you can eat a little more?" Anna asked softly, placing her hands around the bowl.

In truth, I could've eaten the whole pig right then. My stomach was begging for it. I nodded and as she raised the clay bowl to my lips, I took it in my own hands and drank the warm broth independently.

"That's good," she said as I handed her the empty bowl. "Do you want more?"

I nodded, letting my head fall back against the rise and fall of Jack's chest.

"I'll heat you some more. I'll be right out there if you need me." She rose and tip-toed out of the shelter.

As she knelt by the fire, Jack's arms came around me and he rested his cheek against my temple. "I should've been there. I never should've let you out of my sight."

I huffed, resting my arms on his against my waist. "I'm not a child..."

He ran his fingers along my wrist. "Indeed, you are not. I saw what you did to the boar. You put up one hell of a fight."

I closed my eyes, remembering it.

"But," he continued, pulling me against him. "The thought of it —of you fighting that monster down in that dark hole with nothing but a stick—it's an image I can't shake. I should've been there... should've been there fighting it instead of you. Should've never let you leave with no weapon... no way to defend yourself."

I blew out, frustrated to be playing the injured damsel in distress once again. "The boar didn't win."

"It came damn close," he growled, "And the whole time, I had the knife that would've stopped it... Alaina, I..." he wrapped his fingers in mine, squeezing, "I couldn't live with myself if I lost you... I—

"My necklace!" I screeched when I'd reached for it and come up empty. I looked around, tears spilling out of me. "Where's the necklace?!" I tried to raise myself up to stand, but Jack put a hand on my shoulder and pushed me flat on my bottom.

"Calm down," he started, but I was in a frenzy.

"Don't tell me to calm down! Do you have any idea what that necklace means to me? You don't understand, I have to find it! I can't lose it!"

His eyes darted around the shelter. "I'll find it, just calm down..."

"I need that necklace! It's all that I have left of her! I can't..."

"Oh, no ya don't." Anna's stern voice bounced across the surrounding bamboo, and I turned to see her carrying the steaming clay bowl back in. "Jack. Out."

He reluctantly rose to go as she knelt beside me. I watched him as he made his way out into the sunlight, my eyes locked with his. "I'll find it. I promise." He turned on his heel and headed toward the trees.

"You should cut him some slack," she whispered as we both watched him go.

I turned my head back to her as she lowered herself to sit.

"He hasn't slept. Hasn't eaten. Hasn't done anything but dote over you." She stirred the soup with a make-shift chopstick, eyes still fixed on where he'd once been.

"You called for him... in your sleep." She raised her eyebrow toward me, making eye contact once again. "Over and over. And it broke him... He cares about you, ya know."

She handed me a full bottle of water. "He was wild with grief that first night," she continued, pushing the water bottle until I took it and drank. "When we came down through the trees, he was unrecognizable... eyes wild and red as he ran toward us."

Her eyes ventured off in memory, then returned to me. "That's how Jim got that black eye. Jack was in a rage—blamed him for the ladder... came up the hill swinging at Jim. Turned out Isobel's the one that pulled it out."

"Isobel?" I asked, wiping my cheeks.

"Oh yeah. Bertie got out a pencil and paper and got the whole story out of her. She'd seen the boar near camp during the storm and followed it. When it got near the trap, she was scared it might escape like the last one, so she pulled the ladder out. After she'd pulled it, she couldn't see where the edge of the pit started in the dark night. Lightning struck a tree in front of her, scared her, sent her jumping back... straight into the hole."

"Jesus," I said under my breath.

"Meanwhile, the storm blew in strong here, scattering our supplies and blowing over half the shelter. We'd been out trying to recover the cases when we realized she was missing."

I looked out to the fire where I could hear Jim speaking low to Bud, their heads huddled together in some sort of scheme. "And Jim? He's ok?"

Anna smiled, looking out at them. "He's fine. Blamed himself for it. Didn't put up a fight... not that there was much of one. Jack was far more concerned with your wellbeing than revenge."

"Hmmf." I resigned, finishing the water.

"Anyway, we've decided to move camp as soon as you're well enough." She replaced the bottle with the bowl, urging me to sip. "Not up to the summit—that's too far still for Bertie and Bruce, but further up, maybe near the waterfall."

I forced a smile. "Speaking of the summit... Someone should relieve Phil and Kyle."

She rose to her knees with the empty bottles in each hand. "Magna and Jack are already packed—started packing when your fever broke last night. They're planning to head up tomorrow. He saved your life you know... when you stopped breathing... it was him who brought you back."

Chapter Thirty-Four

That night, I lay wide awake in the shelter, shoulder to shoulder with sleeping bodies, waiting for the sound of Jack's return. He'd left that morning promising to find my necklace, and he hadn't come back. I was worried sick.

My bones ached and my mind raced. I needed air. I'd been cooped up too long.

Carefully, I raised myself up and stumbled out. The fire was burning low, but just enough for me to see the outlines of Jim and Lilly lying asleep in the sand near it. I navigated my way past them toward the ocean and into the darkness past camp.

The weight on my ankle stung as I limped along slowly in the sand but the breeze on my bare legs felt amazing so I forced myself down the beach about fifty yards, stopping just before the rocky inlet, and I sat in the sand at the water's edge.

I was still wearing only the oversized black t-shirt and the sand on my thighs was cool and welcome on my exhausted skin. I stretched out my legs and let the tide come up to dance around my ankles as I inhaled deeply.

The air smelled like salt and fish mixed with the sweet scents of the island flowers, palm leaves, and just a whiff of campfire from farther down the shore. The slightest sliver of a moon shined high over the water, sending hints of its light across the ripples of the ocean whenever the surrounding clouds would allow.

My body was weak and my muscles were heavy, but my lungs rejoiced as the cool night air filled them. I spun my wedding ring

on my finger and remembered the struggle for air, the burning of
my lungs, the shaking and panic as my body begged for oxygen
that would not come. I recalled the warmth of Jack's mouth over
mine, the taste of coconut on his breath, and the sweet relief of his
air as it filled me.

I remembered grabbing on, fighting my way back, scratching at
the mud to get back to him... to open my eyes. I relived that first
gasp of my own air as my eyes found him against the orange light
of the fire—panicked and worried as he hovered over me. And I
remembered feeling safe, feeling loved. I'd come to him... and left
my family in the mud... in death.

I wanted him, and maybe that was selfish, but I wanted him
with an entirety I couldn't explain. I wanted to know what it was
like to feel his lips on mine, to hear his voice say the words *'I love
you,'* and to feel his hands on me and know they were exclusively
mine.

It was wrong. I shouldn't want him, but I did. I should've
wanted to stay in that water, in the calmness of death, but I
didn't...

I should've been grieving for Chris, but I wasn't.

I felt someone watching me on the beach, and my heart skipped
a beat in anticipation of Jack's presence. What would I do when I
turned to find him? Would I tell him I loved him? Should I? Would
I collapse into his arms and never look back? Would I instantly feel
differently? I turned toward the shadowy figure that stood a few
steps behind me.

"Ay sis," Jim said, walking closer so I could see his face. "I
didn't mean to sneak up on ye.' You mind if I sit wicha' for a bit?"

I patted the sand next to me, exhaling the breath I'd been
holding, a sense of relief washing over me that I wouldn't be
obliged to answer the questions that raced through my mind just
yet. "No." A knot had formed in my throat and forced the word to
shake.

Jim sat down beside me and laid his arm across my shoulders.
"I came out here to tell ye' how sorry I am... bout the pit, but then
I saw ye' here cryin' and... well, you go on ahead and lay your

head on my shoulder till you're good 'n done. I ain't here to stop ye."

I growled in frustration as the arm over my shoulder forced the tears to come. "I'm so sick of crying, Jim. Sick of my own thoughts most days. You know I never used to cry? The past few years, I feel like it's the only thing I *can* do."

He squeezed my shoulder, "T'aint natural not to cry. Reckon yer probably just catchin' up is all." He smiled. "It's alright, go on ahead then."

"That's the thing Jim, I don't want to... I'm so sick of walking around here feeling this... this... GUILT!!! I feel guilty if I smile, or laugh... guilty if I enjoy myself a little too much... because my family is gone. THEY'RE GONE AND I SHOULD FEEL GUILTY!!" I sobbed uncontrollably.

He drew me closer, rocking us as he stroked my hair. "That's alright now, I got ye, you go right on and get it out of ye."

"God, I was right there. I could feel death right there if I just let go. If I'd just let go, I could've gone to my family... to my husband... to my daughter... the guilt would be over... and instead of going to them... I chose to come back here! For what?"

He rubbed my back as he continued to rock us gently.

"I'm supposed to choose them! I'm supposed to be there! But I chose to come back to this island while they waited for me in death... chose to come back to a... a... PRACTICAL STRANGER instead of my family... A stranger that I shouldn't want to be with... shouldn't let myself be drawn to... but I am and I do... And now I feel so goddamned ashamed of it, I don't know what to do with myself."

He rocked me quietly until the tears wouldn't come any longer. I laid my head on his shoulder. "I wanted to go home, Jim... And then it was right there in front of me... pulling me toward it... and I didn't *go* home... What does that make me?"

He stopped rocking to look down at me. "I suppose that makes ye' human like the rest of us. We're all fightin' death no matter what's on the other side waitin' for us. It's in our nature to wanna carry on all the way up till we cain't."

He took his thumb and wiped my cheeks, "Now," he continued, "I don't know about your husband and your daughter and I ain't gonna ask what ye' don't wanna say right now, but I am gonna say this. You got family right here that loves you. I know it ain't the same, but it means a good deal to me that ye' know it. We all love you. The big man 'specially. He was right sick over it when you come back bloodied and beaten. Mad with worry. I saw it myself. He jumped down in that pit and stabbed that pig to death before I could even get on the ladder."

I turned to speak, but he raised his palm. "I ain't the smartest man in the world, but the way I see it is this... Bein' happy *now* don't mean you wasn't happy *then*. Don't mean you won't see 'em again someday and be happy then neither. What you had might've been mighty fine. But that *cain't* be the extent of it... otherwise the Good Lordt wouldn't have put ye' on that raft. Wouldn't have put ole' Hoss in there at the side of ye' neither. There ain't nothin' wrong with lettin' yourself be loved—ain't nothin' in it to to be sorry for. Besides... What you gonna do when you get up there with no stories to tell 'cept how ye' set down here mopin' around waitin' for the Good Lordt to come get ye?"

I wiped my cheeks with my palms and sniffled, taking a deep breath. I could feel the weight lifting off my chest. "You're right..."

"I'm always right," he whispered close, squeezing my shoulder.

We sat for a minute, quietly looking out at the black water, listening to the waves as they tumbled toward our feet. "Had me this girl once... name of June."

I looked up at him and he smiled at me. "Itty bitty thing with bright blonde hair and freckles like yorn." He affectionately touched the tip of his finger to my nose. "You'd look at her and think she was sweet as pie, but oh she was meaner than a two-headed snake when she wanted to be."

He sighed, looking back at the water. "Me and her, we'd fuss and fight and carry on like two hens fightin' over a worm. She broke my nose twice—and one time I hadn't even said nothin'...

Told me I didn't have to say nothin'... said she knew I was thinkin' it!"

He grinned at the memory. "Oh, but if we wasn't fussin, we'd be tangled up somewheres goin' at it like a couple of rabbits. Hell, sometimes I'd pick a fight just so we could make up later. Lordt knows I couldn't keep my hands off that woman."

He laughed a little. "See, I knew she's bad for me, but I loved her for it anyways. Lil' spitfire of a thang... smart mouthin' all the time... made me laugh like a hyena."

"Anyways," he blew out, "one day she come up pregnant. Hollerin' bout how I wasn't fit and how am I gonna' support this child and so on."

"Ooh boy, and you bet your ass I went out and got me a job faster than a duck on a June bug. I'd be driving a rig five hundred miles a day, from one end of the country to the other. Sold my pickup and my best huntin' dog. Moved her into my trailer and I hit the road."

"My first run took me out west and I'd be gone for two weeks before I came back through. I spent evra day on the road thinkin' about that child. How I's gonna' be different than my daddy... how I's gonna do right by him... raise him up right. Evra place I stopped, I'd grab up a teddy bear or a lil trinket... even picked up a pair of itty bitty cowboy boots. Didn't matter was a boy or a girl... I's tickled pink either way."

"Well," he sighed, running his hand through his hair, "I got home and she's gone. Packed up her thangs and run off. Didn't tell a soul where she's goin' neither. I searched for her, best I could, for a year... then two... then three... She plumb disappeared. I never did see hide nor hair of either of 'em. That baby'd be about seven now."

He squeezed me tight against him. "See, thing is, I kept on drivin' that rig. Kept on buyin' trinkets and savin' my money... I knew I'd see 'em again someday. That child would grow up and come askin' round, or June'd change her mind like she always did and come creepin' back someday. So... after a while, I just kept on. I met other women... let myself go out and have some fun. I never stopped waitin' for 'em, never stopped lovin' em or lookin' for 'em. They were always right here with me… but I didn't stop livin' my life neither."

He took my chin between his fingers then and turned my face up toward him. "Let me get a look at ye." He wiped the tears off my eyes and smoothed the hair from my forehead. "It ain't my place to tell ye' so, but I'm tellin' ye' anyways. There ain't nothin' wrong with bein' happy while you got the chance to be. Lettin' yourself love somebody don't mean you stopped lovin' the ones waitin' for ye.' There ain't nothin' in it to to be sorry for. What I'm tryin' to say to ye,' is… he's a good man, Jack, and if ye let him, he'd be good to ye." He looked past me toward camp and lowered his voice. "Now, let him take ye' back to camp and try not to fuss."

He rose then and as he disappeared into the shadows in the direction toward camp, I closed my eyes.

I'd been carrying the loss of Evelyn and the guilt that came with it for years before the crash. Now I'd added the loss of Chris and it'd been more than I could bear. He'd been right. Happiness here didn't mean I wasn't happy there… didn't mean I didn't love them. It was alright to want to live… to want to feel something new… and as I heard their muffled voices exchange passing words behind me; I *did* feel something new.

'We all love you. The big man 'specially…'

When he'd said it, my heart stopped. What had I done to deserve love from any of them? I'd been so caught up in my own grief that I'd looked past them. I had been ungrateful for this life; for these people who called me family. I spent most of my time longing for what I'd lost and not nearly enough time being grateful for the life I'd been granted.

And Jack… I heard his feet in the sand behind me and I couldn't help but see him down in the pit with only a knife against the boar that had nearly killed me. I couldn't help but feel his breath in my lungs, his arms wrapped around me, his hand squeezing my own… Couldn't shake the words he'd said when I woke… *'I couldn't live with myself if I lost you…'*

Quickly, I moved to stand up, shifting my weight to my left leg and balancing as I rose myself awkwardly off the sand. Before I could straighten, he was there with a hand on my back and at my elbow.

His sudden touch on my skin brought all the emotions I'd been both feeling and fighting to the surface. My heart raced and a new lump formed in my throat. I rapidly spun around to face him, wrapped my arms around his neck and, without thought to what I was doing, pulled him down to my lips.

He inhaled deeply and for a splitting second I wondered if I'd been too forward. But then he pulled me up on my toes and deepened the kiss I'd initiated, parting my lips and forcing tears of relief to pour past my closed lashes.

I let the tears fall as his arm circled round me, and the life I'd lived before that moment fell with them. Evelyn, Chris, the crash, the boar—all of it fell away and there was no more guilt, no more hurt or resentment or blame. There was only the two of us.

I'd fought falling in love with him for months, but with his lips growing more passionate against mine, I knew I couldn't fight anymore.

Beyond my control, I let out a sigh against him where, completely enveloped in the moment, I breathed the words my heart had been screaming, "I love you."

I froze in a panic, my entire body stiffening in his arms. "I shouldn't have said that... It just slipped out and I—"

He pressed his forehead against mine and laughed. "Alaina, with every ounce of my being, I love you, too."

"You do?"

He nodded. "Of course I do."

I saw his eyes water. Mine filled as well, and I pulled his collar, meeting his lips halfway and kissing him with every bit of strength I had left in me. His mouth drove deeper against mine and, as I slid my palm up to rest on his cheek, I could feel the wetness of his tears on his skin.

"I'm so very in love with you," he said against my lips, "and I have been almost since the first day I held you in my arms on that raft."

I half-laughed as the realization that *the* Jack Volmer had just told me he loved me, and I might've been waiting my whole life for just that. "But I've been so… neurotic and uncertain. I've been a lunatic half the time we've been out here. Why? Why do you love me? How?"

His lips found a path down my jaw to my ear. "Because from the moment I met you, you've made me feel like more than just the man that *played* a good man on t.v. You make me feel proud of myself, flaws and all. No one has ever looked at me and seen me the way you do. And I see you. I love that you're neurotic and uncertain and have been a lunatic at times. It makes you real. It makes this real."

He pulled me against him, his fingers sliding down my arm to interlace with mine.

"And not being able to tell you that," he whispered, pulling our joined hands up to his lips, "watching you fall apart for a man I could never be and knowing I couldn't comfort you the way I wanted to… the way I *needed* to… I thought that was the hardest part of these last few months."

He lifted me off my feet and knelt in the sand to pull me across his lap, combing back the hair at my temple.

"But then you stopped breathing and I would've given anything to have the torture of not being able to comfort you back. I would've been happy even if you'd never spoken to me again, just to know you were alive."

He kissed me again, forcing my eyes closed as his fingers swept over my cheeks and he parted my lips once more. "If you need time to mourn him still, I'll wait. I'll wait as long as it takes. Whatever you want."

I let my palm glide up his throat to circle his jaw, then ran my fingers softly over his lips. "I want you."

"You do?"

I nodded. "Very much."

He swept the hair from my face with one quick motion, cupping my face and pressing his lips against mine again.

"You have me." He kissed each of my temples, then returned to my lips again. "You have all of me." He worked his way down my neck. "For as long as you can stand me."

I drew in a breath as his mouth grew warm and frantic against my neck, the soft hairs of his beard dancing across the thin skin and awakening every nerve in body. Selfishly, I surrendered to the moment and pulled him closer, urging him further as my hands balled into fists in his hair and I leaned backward so we fell over onto the cool, soft sand.

I hadn't felt loved like this in so long—maybe not ever—and I clung to him, terrified for it to end too soon.

My legs floated upward so I could feel him through the thin fabric as his body responded to our mouths, taking on a rhythm of its own against mine.

I was warmed by the weight of him; whole where I'd been wandering around as a fraction of a person most of my life. He fit so perfectly against me, as if he'd been molded exclusively for my body. I wasn't sure I'd ever felt so exactly in the right place.

His palm slid up my bare leg and came to a halt once it reached the bandage on my thigh.

"I don't want to hurt you," he whispered, freezing in place.

"You won't." I moved my hands down his back, pulling his collared shirt up so I could feel the bare skin along his spine. I needed to feel more of him. I needed to bask in this moment for as long as possible. His back muscles were tensed and shaking as the tips of my fingers danced over the surface.

"But you've barely had any food," he said softly. "Your leg is still in bad shape, and your arm..." He tried to even out his breathing as he pulled his chest from mine to look down at me, but he was trembling with the effort.

I pulled his shirt up the length of his back and, despite his attempts to settle us, he let me pull it over his head, raising one arm, then the other to shake it off.

My more rational mind knew, deep down, we needed to stop. My leg was throbbing, and we both needed to rest. But my heart beat loudly in my ears, drowning out all logical thought, and my body moved on its own, pleading to be connected to his.

"I should take you back," he whispered, closing his eyes as I brought my lips to his chest above me.

"Not yet," I breathed against him, feeling his muscles tense along the trail my mouth took up his throat.

He was leaving the next morning to spend a week on the summit and I wouldn't wait that long to have him.

With one arm looped around his neck, I reached down with the other to drag my t-shirt up and over my head, lying back in the cold sand so he could see me.

And I loved the feel of his eyes drifting over me; loved watching him admire every inch of my skin in the moonlight.

"I have only just realized I love you," I whispered, tracing the scar on his eyebrow, "and I want this more than I've ever wanted anything. You won't hurt me."

I guided his fingers down my side and his body fell back into its dance with mine, shaking now and more anxious as I placed his palm on my breast.

I arched, letting out a soft whimper as his mouth replaced his hand over my breast, warm and wet as he explored me for the first time, learning all the ways I would melt beneath his lips.

His fingers slowly drifted lower, sliding down my abdomen, then lower still, gliding gently over the thin cotton of my panties until he could feel the excitement he'd left on my body.

He made a low, guttural noise against my breast before he released it and covered my mouth with his.

I reached for the button on his jeans, unable to live another moment without him inside me. His hands followed mine, assisting in the process as his breath came once again to my ear. "Are you sure?"

"Yes."

He examined me for a second to be sure, then pressed his lips to mine as he removed the fabric barriers that separated us.

There was some far off understanding between us that neither of us wanted to play. This wasn't an act of pleasure or teasing, but necessity. We needed each other—had needed this almost since that plane had gone down.

I gripped his shoulders tightly as he entered me, easing himself in inch by inch.

There was nothing but relief in that moment.

He caressed my face and he pressed his forehead against mine as he moved inside me, slowly at first until my body urged him further.

His mouth came softly over mine and he grew harder, steadier, and his kiss grew deeper and more passionate as I moved with him.

I pulled him further into me, my legs shaking as the realization came over me that he was mine, entirely and completely mine. That knowledge filled me just as much as the scent and the taste and the feel of him did in that moment.

Jack Volmer was mine. He loved me and I loved him and nothing would ever be the same about my life after this monumental moment.

We moved in tandem; slow, rhythmic, and gentle as we learned how to love each other. Then we climbed faster and hungrier... panting against each other, our foreheads pressed together as we moved in perfect rhythm. His lips became frantic over mine as his body began to shake.

He wrapped my hair in his fist and gently pulled me upward toward him, his mouth covering mine as I released and he followed.

He held me there in the darkness, unmoved and pulsing inside me, his arm around my back and his fingers in my hair as he kissed my lips once more. "I didn't hurt you? Your leg—it's okay?"

I ran my fingers up his arms, sighing. "I'm fine."

He lowered me back down to the soft sand, remaining inside me as he balanced on his forearms over me. He softly kissed my palm as it slid across his cheek, closing his eyes as I traced the outline of his beard.

The faint blue light from the moon glistened against the whites of his eyes and I noticed for the first time the bags that had formed beneath them... the complete fatigue in his shoulders. Anna had told me he hadn't slept, but it hadn't really registered until now.

"You should sleep," I whispered, glancing toward camp to make sure no one had seen us. The fire was a small yellow dot far down the beach where no one appeared to be stirring. "Anna said you'd been up all night... and then I forced you to go back and—

"I found it." He smiled, leaning to one side to reach for his jeans with one hand, the thumb on the other lazily tracing my collarbone. He produced the necklace, holding it up against the moonlight and inspecting it before he balanced on his elbows to unfasten it and refasten it around my neck. The soft graze of his wrists against my skin sent shivers down my spine, and the tenderness in his eyes as he did it made my throat tighten.

Once the clasp was fastened, he traced the silver chain. "You said it was all you had left of her... Who was she?"

I laid my fingers over his atop the little glass pendant. "My daughter."

I was surprised at how easily the word came, surprised more at the sudden need to tell him about her. I had never spoken about it before to anyone—not even Chris.

"Evelyn." I sighed. "She came eight weeks too soon."

My gaze followed my fingers as they ran casually down his forearm and worked their way up his shoulder to finally rest over his heart.

"There are no words to describe the relationship you build with a child as it grows inside you." I could almost feel her familiar weight in my lower abdomen where Jack was still inside me.

"I knew her... long before she came. I talked to her, all day and night, both out loud and in my head... dreamt of her... and she knew me. She knew the most intimate, secret parts of me. The inner thoughts that never made it out... The me that no one else could ever know... And I loved her more than I have ever loved anything."

I drew a circle around his collarbone with my thumb. "When she came, she didn't cry. They rushed her out before I could even look at her. I waited for hours and hours while they worked on her... not knowing if she was alive or dead."

He slid his hands over my hair as he hovered over me, watching me closely. I felt so very safe to be vulnerable beneath him.

"Then the doctors finally came in." I chewed my lip, remembering it. "They'd set her up in an incubator on a ventilator in the NICU on the far side of the hospital and I could go see her, but before I did... they had to warn me. She wouldn't make it. Her little lungs couldn't hold on their own and even if they could, her intestines weren't working properly. She couldn't breathe and she couldn't eat. She would either asphyxiate or starve."

I blinked the tears from my eyes, moving my fingers up to comb through the stiff hairs of his beard as his thumb wiped away a stray tear that slid down the side of my nose.

"I refused to believe them, of course... Had heard too many miracle stories of premature babies... my own cousin being one of them. Everyone tried to prepare me for it, but I held out hope. I lived in the NICU. Sat beside her and never took my eyes off her, praying for a miracle. I didn't eat... didn't sleep... I just prayed... prayed and begged and tried to bargain with God... I just couldn't believe that beautiful little creature could come into this world only to be pulled right back out of it. She held on for a week... which was a whole week longer than they told me she would. Despite the doctors' constant warnings she still wouldn't make it, I never could've been ready for it when she finally went."

I shook my head slowly. "They let me hold her then... she was so tiny. I remember sitting there and raising her little limp fingers and toes, committing her every inch to memory, waiting for her to miraculously start breathing on her own."

I finally met his eyes. "She never did."

"I fell apart." I took a deep breath. "Shut out everything and everyone. Couldn't bear the thought of being happy while my baby was dead. Felt guilty to feel anything, really. I..." I swallowed. "I pushed the world away from me. Wouldn't let anyone back in... not even my mother... and Chris..." It felt only a little strange to say his name. "He tried for a time, but then even he stayed away. We lived like strangers for years after that... Even after I'd gotten over the worst of the grief... the damage was done. That's why... on the plane..."

He closed his eyes and shook his head as I continued. "Anyway, I saw them—both of them—when I stopped breathing... I knew I was dead and there was peace in knowing he was with her... knowing she wasn't alone anymore..."

He took my hand in his and raised it to his lips, kissing my fingers softly. "Alaina, I'm so sorry."

I traced the side of his face with my other hand and smiled. "I was there with them… in this weightless euphoria and the peace it brought me is something I've needed for a very long time. And I had to tell you all that so I could tell you this. I heard your voice there calling for me. I heard it and knew I had the choice to stay with them or come back to you. I was right there and I couldn't go with them. I wasn't done here. I *had* to know what this was… I had to know what these feelings I've been fighting meant… So I *chose* you. I chose to live… I chose to live because for the first time since they took her little lifeless body from my arms, I feel like I've got something worth living for."

He exhaled shakily, wrapping both arms around me, his weight over me offering more comfort than I could've asked for. He kissed my temple. "I can't imagine how heavy that decision must weigh, but I'll do everything to deserve it. I'll do *anything* to deserve it."

I kissed his shoulder as I exhaled heavily. "I wish I were going up with you tomorrow. I don't think I can stand to be apart from you now that I've had you."

He rose and kissed me again, softly, pulling me against him before he eased out of me, leaving my body empty and wanting without him. "The thought of having you to myself for a week up there sounds heavenly. I don't have to go you know… We could just stay here… forever. To hell with the ships."

He adjusted himself to sit on the sand, pulling me into his arms as he reached for the black shirt I'd been wearing. I wrapped both arms around him and laid my head against his shoulder, "If it were just the two of us, I'd never leave… But we can't do that to Isobel… or Kyle… or Anna… We have to stick to it. I hate that I can't go up… I miss you already."

He laid his cheek against the top of my head, pulling me tighter and pressing me against his bare chest. I felt him exhale, and I softly traced the lines of his collarbone as I closed my eyes and did the same. After a moment, he placed the shirt over my head and I managed to find and pull on my sand covered underwear.

He stood with me, holding me in place with one hand and then the other as he stepped into his jeans and pulled them on. He shook out his navy shirt with one hand, then wrapped the fabric around my bare legs and lifted me back up, turning toward camp as my arms wrapped around his neck.

"'*I love you*' isn't enough either," he said. "It's bigger even than that."

I sighed. "I'll take it though." I let my eyes close and the weight of the world fell off my shoulders as he carried me back.

'Bein' happy now don't mean you wasn't happy then.' Jim's words echoed in my mind as the smells of our small campfire grew stronger. Being happy with him wouldn't negate the happiness I'd had before. I loved him and I wouldn't let myself feel guilty for it any longer. I wasn't replacing my life… I was going to live it.

As the warmth of the fire reached my toes, I placed my hand on his cheek, whispering softly, "Not in the shelter. I can't breathe in there. Sleep out here with me."

He slowly knelt down, balancing me there as he reached back to grab two t-shirts from the case at his side, spreading them out on the sand before lowering me down onto the fabric. He adjusted his shirt around my legs, tucking it securely around them before he laid down on his back beside me in the sand. I curled into his chest as his arms came around me.

While his fingertips brushed lightly along my forearm over his chest, I listened to his heart beating, his breath rising and falling with my own, and I smiled as my eyes closed.

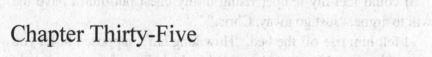

Chapter Thirty-Five

"Ally, honey, please come out. Everyone's here," Chris pleaded behind me from the doorway of our bedroom.

"I don't care." I covered my head with the comforter. "I told you I didn't want to see anybody. Just leave me alone."

"Baby, you've been in here for weeks. Please," he sat down on the edge of the bed, running a hand down my arm over the blanket, "you gotta find a way to get above this."

My eyes burned as I curled the blanket closer to my face. "I can't." I swallowed the lump in my throat as the tears rolled down my nose. "I can't ever get above this."

"Why don't you just come out for a little bit?" he begged. "Eat something. Your uncle's grilling and my mom made the pasta salad you love. Your mom made you a cake."

"I can't."

"Ally, they're all here for *you*. For *your* birthday." He tugged at the comforter. "They know you're hurting and they want to be here for you. What do you want me to tell them?"

I rolled away from him. "Tell them I lost my child and I'm not in the mood to celebrate my birthday... like I told you to tell them in the first place."

"Ally," he sighed, "she was my child too."

"It's not the same." New tears welled behind my closed eyelids. "I don't want to talk about this right now. Just leave me alone."

"You never want to talk about it." He pulled at my shoulder, but I resisted, keeping my body faced away from him. "Please talk to me. At least let *me* be here to comfort you."

"Not now." I jerked my shoulder away from his touch. "I don't want to talk, I just want to lie here and be left alone with my grief. Grieving is all I have left of her. Can't you just give me that?"

"You think I'm not grieving her too?" he snapped. "You think I'm not hurting too? I lost my daughter *and* my wife."

I could feel my temper rising in my chest but didn't have the will to argue. "Just go away, Chris."

I felt him rise off the bed. "How long am I supposed to let you go on like this? Months? Years? What the hell am I supposed to do here?"

"Just go away," I pleaded softly.

He breathed out. "It's not fair to me that you're shutting me out like this. I'm hurting too, ya know, and *I* need you."

To this, I didn't respond but instead waited quietly until I heard his footsteps retreat and the door close behind him.

The tears spilled warm down my nose and cheeks as I listened to his muffled voice in the hallway explaining to his mother that I wouldn't be joining them. How could he expect me to just pick up where we'd left off? To go on with life as if she'd never existed? As if I'd never held her in my arms?

'I'm not being fair to you?! You're the one who's not being fair. I carried her inside me. I knew her and you didn't. And now you want me to what? Just get up and force a smile on my face because people are here? People I told you not to invite over? People I insisted I didn't want to see?'

I squeezed my eyes tightly shut as I heard his mother offer to come talk to me.

'No Chris. Please don't let her in.'

I held my breath as Chris responded in a hushed voice and sighed in relief as I heard them make their way back down the hallway toward the stairs.

I laid lifeless, begging for sleep, while my birthday party continued downstairs without me. I could hear them talking, laughing, doors opening and closing, dishes being brought out, and the sounds of dinner conversation just beneath me. I listened to his dad telling stories with my uncle, my mother randomly interjecting. I could hear them outside as the night came, and could see the light of the fire they sat around dancing on the glass of the French patio doors in our bedroom.

Would I ever be able to join them again? Would I ever feel whole again? It felt like she'd been ripped from me, taking half of me with her. My insides begged to have her back, and my hands frequently went to the spot she'd once been, coming up empty, a constant reminder of the loss.

I listened as the night grew late and the voices outside got a little louder as the wine and beer flowed more freely. He'd be drunk again when he came to bed.

He'd come to bed smelling like alcohol nearly every night since it'd happened. I knew I should be worried for him, but it was a relief to me that he would come in and pass out instead of trying to talk to me about it. He'd returned to work right away, staying away later and later the longer I stayed in bed, returning more and more drunk each night.

As I heard our parents and friends saying their goodnights at the front door and then his footsteps heavy on the stairs, I waited for the familiar dip of the mattress on his side of the bed. Instead, the door was flung open; the knob hitting the wall with a bang as he fell into the room. I could smell the bourbon long before he reached the bed.

"Get up," he growled as he dropped heavily onto the bed, crawling over me and pulling my shoulder to force my back flat on the bed. "Get up, I said."

In the blackness of our room, I could barely make out his face as it hovered over mine, the smell of whiskey emitting heavily from him. His eyes were glazed over and his body was heavy as he climbed onto me. I tried to jerk away but was pinned.

"Get off," I snapped, pushing at his chest.

He lowered his mouth near my ear. "No."

"Chris, I'm serious." I pushed at him as his mouth came down forcibly over mine. Panicked, I squirmed and kneed him hard, hitting him in the groin and forcing him to roll off to one side. I stood abruptly. "Are you fucking crazy?" I screamed, "What the hell did you think you were going to do? Force me?"

He was curled over in pain, holding himself protectively. "Jesus Christ, Alaina," he managed through gritted teeth, "I just want to touch my wife. I *need* to touch my wife. To have you touch me... to make me... to make *us* both feel something else, just for a minute."

I jerked my pillow off the bed. "I don't want to feel something else. I'm not like you, I can't just shut it off."

"I didn't shut it off! It's always there." He sat up, his jaw set. "And the minute I think it might be gone, YOU remind me it's still there! Dammit, she was mine, too! I lost her too! I didn't do this to you, you know. It just happened. We did everything right and it still happened. It happened to both of us. Why are you punishing me for it?"

"Oh, don't act like you're the victim here," I snapped. "Nobody's punishing you."

"No?" He gripped my wrist and tried to pull me toward him, but I stiffened. "Then what is this? Why can't I touch you?"

"Because I don't want to be touched!" My eyes filled. "I don't want to be consoled. And I especially don't want..." I narrowed my eyes, swallowing, "to *feel* something else."

He let go of my wrist, letting it fall to my side. "And what about what I want?"

I shook my head, squeezing the pillow against my chest. "I'm not going to sleep with you just so you can feel better about it." I turned away from him and headed toward the door.

"That's not what I wanted," he said softly as I closed the bedroom door behind me and headed down the hallway.

I hadn't left our room in weeks and had returned in a haze after being in the hospital for a week before that. Chris had been bringing dinner up to the room nightly and I would pick at it here and there, my appetite being completely nonexistent.

As I walked down the hallway for the first time since returning home, I noticed everything was just where it'd been when we'd rushed out that night. Boxes of diapers and gifts lined the hallway just outside the nursery. A paint roller still sat in a tray of now dried paint against the wall near the cracked open doorway.

I pushed the door to the nursery open and my heart shattered at the sight of it—light gray walls with a half built crib on one side, my rocker built in the opposite corner with a plush pink pillow sitting at its center, bright white cursive letters spelling *"Evelyn"* stitched into it.

On the far wall, a bookshelf littered with children's books, a little white dresser next to it with a pink elephant lamp on top, and the little silver spoon my mother had bought sitting just beside it, still elegantly wrapped in its box. The closet doors were still open and inside hung two perfect rows of pink, yellow, purple, and white baby clothes.

I looked back down the hall toward our closed bedroom door. *'Why wouldn't he clean this up? Close this door? Did he want me to look at it? Did he want me to pass by it and feel this loss all over again?'* I shook my head and closed the door. *'Why wouldn't he pack it all up by now? Return it all?'*

I squeezed the pillow to my chest as I forced myself to continue past the nursery and downstairs.

I navigated past the remaining baby gifts and boxes that were stacked at the bottom of the staircase and into the living room. On the coffee table, there were three glasses and a bottle of bourbon, an open bag of chips, and two dirty plates. The pain in my heart gave way to rage as I looked around the room.

Half-empty glasses, plates, and bowls sat dirty on nearly every surface. *'Why wouldn't he clean this up? Why hadn't someone cleaned this up? Mom would've cleaned... oh God, was it like this when they got here?'*

In the kitchen, beer bottles lined the counter to one side of my sink. With them, two bottles of bourbon sat empty, one tipped over and dripping its final drops onto the granite. Inside the sink, several coffee mugs sat with thick grime coating the insides.

I felt my insides boiling. *'What kind of person does this? Who the hell did I marry?! Had he told mom not to clean? Why would he do that?'*

I stomped barefooted into the dining room where a half-eaten cake boasting "thday ina" sat in the center of six dirty icing-covered place settings.

And that's when my rational mind shut off and all the pain inside me took over. Without consciousness to what I was doing, I swung my arm across the table, sending several plates over the side to shatter on the floor amid the loud clanging of bouncing silverware on the hardwood.

Heart racing, I worked my way around the table, grabbing each plate and launching it at the wall to shatter. As I did so, I screamed at the top of my lungs, tears spilling out of me. I flipped the chairs, flung the cake, ripped a framed picture of us off the wall and launched it through a glass cabinet.

As I stood panting wildly in the center of the dining room, searching for something left to break, my eyes spotted a small box inside the busted glass cabinet wrapped neatly in a gold box with the words "Ally" written on it.

Consciousness returning suddenly, I tiptoed around the broken glass on the floor to the cabinet and pulled it out. I ripped the paper off quickly to reveal a black velvet jewelry box. I popped the box open and pulled out a piece of paper, and my heart sank as I read the scribbled words.

"Happy birthday, my love. I had this made for you. I know you miss her and I know I will never know the loss of having carried her with you for so long. Perhaps you can still carry a piece of her with you now."

I raised the necklace from the box and held it out so the light could dance off it. It was a shining thin silver chain boasting a perfectly clear, thick glass globe pendant. Inside the glass were several small wisps of very fine, light red hair. My hand shook as I held it and my body felt suddenly too heavy for my knees as I collapsed onto the floor with it cupped in my hands. I held it against my chest and sobbed uncontrollably.

"Jesus," Chris muttered from the doorway, looking around what was left of our dining room.

I peeked out over the table that sat between us. "I…" I struggled to get the words out between sobs. "I'm sorry."

"Jesus!" He spotted me and leapt over the broken glass, circling the table to sit on the floor across from me. "You're all cut up."

I squeezed the necklace tightly against my chest as he inspected me, unable to stop the tears that overtook me.

He pulled my foot into his lap. "I was going to clean it up," he assured me as he pulled a small piece of glass from my heel. "Your mom fought me, but I wouldn't let her. I didn't think you'd be down to see it and... I just... I just haven't had the will to do much of anything."

He pulled another small piece of plate from near my toes as I held out my palm to reveal the necklace.

He paused, holding my foot in his hand. "Is it okay? I didn't know if I should..."

I nodded as another wave of tears came over me.

"Oh Ally." He wrapped his arms tightly around me. "I'm so sorry. God, I'm so sorry. I wish there was something I could do."

I rested my head against his shoulder and let the tears fall as I squeezed the necklace against my heart.

"I'll clean this up," he said after a bit, pulling back and running his hand down my hair. "Tell me what I can do... to make you feel better."

I shook my head, "Love, I don't think I'll ever feel better."

Chapter Thirty-Six

In the days that followed, I built up my strength. My right ankle had only been sprained, and with it wrapped, I was able to walk with very little discomfort.

I spent my days with Lilly, Bertie and Isobel, falling back into a routine of gathering food, washing clothes, and packing up our supplies as I waited anxiously for Jack to return.

Bruce worked his legs day and night, pushing himself to walk with Anna always at his side. Bud and Jim would still go out in the morning to catch fish—despite the smoked pork we had in abundance—and in the afternoons they'd team up with Kyle and Phil to search near the waterfall for a suitable spot to build a new shelter.

I welcomed the distraction the routine brought me. However hard I tried to focus, my thoughts were always on that beach with Jack. He'd left early the following morning, wrapping me in a shirt and kissing my temple before he'd risen to go, and my heart ached for his return. I longed for just one more kiss... to feel his arms around me for just one minute more.

"I have an idea," Lilly was saying as she sat behind me, vigorously trying to brush my curls. "I've been trying to figure out what day it is. I know we crashed on March third and I've been slowly recollecting the days we've been here. I think it's somewhere around July fifth. Which means grandma and grandpa's anniversary is sometime around now. I want to plan something for them."

July? Had we really been here that long? I tried to smile as the brush ripped through another knot. "I think that's a wonderful idea Lill," I sighed.

"That's it!" She darted around to face me, tapping the brush against her palm. "Spill it. That's the fifth sigh in three minutes. What happened?"

"What?" I started, but before she could call my bluff, Jim came darting through the trees, grinning from ear to ear, Kyle at his heels.

"Y'all ain't gonna believe what we found up 'er!"

"What?!" Bruce jumped from the small rock table he'd made to clean fish.

"We found ole' Willy's shelter!" Kyle beamed at Lilly. Jim had taken to calling the bones we'd found "Ole Willy" and so we'd all adopted the name.

Our faces lit up and Jim grinned. "I's runnin' all over hell's half acre up 'er and boom, there it was, a jagged rock cliff, few hundred yards from the creek. A big ole' tree'd grown up smack dab in the middle of its opening. I almost missed it. By Got, it's a damn cave! Right there under our noses. Covered in moss and trees. And I tell ye, it is full of all kinds of supplies—books, journals, markins' on the walls, it's got an axe and a bed and it's plenty big enough for the whole lot of us!"

Eager to see it, we all jumped from our spots.

"Now where in the hell you think you're goin', Sis?" he asked me. "You ain't fit to travel yet."

"I'm fine," I assured him, grabbing up two bottles as Lilly wrapped her arm around mine. "I gotta see it. And I could use the fresh air."

"Now, Got dammit, woman," he scolded as we skirted past him toward the tree line, "if you get yourself hurt or rip one of 'em stitches, ole Hoss up 'er's gonna come down and black my other eye."

He hopped a few steps out to walk backward in front of us. "And believe you me, it ain't gonna be all sunshine and rainbows this time around. No ma'am. Now, you'd best get on back, 'for you start a Got damn war."

"Oh, hush." I smiled at him. "I won't get hurt. I've got *you* here, don't I?" I batted my eyes at him and Lilly giggled.

He paused and grinned, then skipped forward to keep pace with us. "Well... I ain't gonna let nothin' happen to ye... Still... slow down." He looked up to the sky. "Oh Lordt, please look down on us poor sinners and don't let this woman do nothin' stupid like to get us killt."

I wrapped my free arm around him and kissed his cheek. "My hero."

He looked back up. "And Lordt, don't ever let ole' Hoss catch her callin' me that again."

We walked arm in arm, the three of us, the rest of our lot following closely behind, as Jim led the way toward our new home.

"Ye' know," he leaned into me after a while, "a man could get used to havin' his arm around such a fine lookin' woman. You reckon I could take him?" He looked up toward the summit.

"I'd have to fight dirty," he joked, pondering to himself. "Use my teeth... bet he'd go down faster than green grass through a goose if I pulled that purdy hair on his head."

Lilly cleared her throat on the other side of me. "Replaced me already, Jimmy?"

"Oh hush, woman." He grinned around me. "You know you're my number one."

She laughed and pulled me away to gossip freely as she let the rest of our group pace past us. "Alright, woman, you've been smiling for two days and you don't smile." She leaned scandalously in. "Did something happen with Jack?"

I blushed and looked down.

"Something did happen!" she hissed, hopping with excitement. "When?! How?! Oh, you hussy! Don't you dare keep good secrets from me on this island where nothing exciting ever happens!"

I laughed out loud, slowing our pace to whisper, "Yes, something happened."

"I knew it!" She grinned. "Where? When?!"

"Shhh." I glanced up toward our group then back to her. "Two nights ago... on the beach."

She pulled my shoulder closer against hers. "Oh, how exciting! Did you sleep with him? You did, didn't you?! I want all the details. Starting with who kissed who. Wait.. no... were you sitting or standing when you kissed?"

"Seriously?" I chuckled. "Why would that be more important?"

She laid her head on my shoulder and sighed. "Lainey, the most action I've gotten on this island was when a crab pinched my butt cheek while I was sleeping. Just give me this one thing."

I squeezed her arm. "Standing... *I* kissed him."

Her head lifted. "What? Why you sneaky little minx! Go on..."

Despite my desire to keep the details hogged to myself, the girl pulled every last one out of me as we trekked up to the creek. By the time we'd reached the clearing, her eyes had glazed over and she sighed against my shoulder. "C'est l'amour..."

Jim wedged himself between us with an arm around each of our necks. "Now, look there, you see it?" His arm squeezed around Lilly's head as he pointed out into the trees.

I followed his hand as Lilly snorted, wiggling free of the headlock. I squinted, searching, and there it was, camouflaged by the trees that surrounded it and grew out of it, a big pointed rock wall, covered in green with a crack running down its center—a big tree nearly blocking the opening entirely from view. "I see it!"

We hurried over and stepped inside where Phil was already immersed in a book on the floor, a bottle of port in his hand.

The cave was beautiful. Its ceilings were high, and it was deep enough that we could spread out comfortably, each having our own personal space. The ground was soft and full of moss that grew wide from the opening. The opening was about as wide as a single person and as it shot up halfway to the cave's peak, the crevice narrowed down to about an inch.

The sunlight bathed the cave through the tall crack, making it warm and cozy. I walked along one wall, running my fingers along the cold rock, tracing the carved lines Ole' Willy had left behind. A few hundred of them marked one wall, each line neatly grouped into four with a single diagonal line across them.

He'd made a small platform for a bed. Remnants of old dead palm leaves were littered across the bamboo planks and beneath them sat a large metal pot inside a metal skillet inside a piece of thick fabric, both perfectly preserved.

Next to the bed were books, at least thirty of them, and several journals. I flipped one open and was ecstatic to see the handwriting had been preserved as its elegant black cursive spelled out "Zachary Charles William - 1928."

"Man was a merchant." Jim grinned, coming up to stand behind me and look over my shoulder at the journal. "Look here." He reached around me and flipped through several pages before landing on one dated September 3rd 1928. "He was importin' textiles and fine china from a port in Hawaii when he came up on a storm just like us. Listen to this." He cleared his throat and read the journal entry out loud. "*The night was clear and the ocean was calm when suddenly everything went quiet. The wind stopped and bright blue streaks of lightning struck the ship multiple times. I watched as the entire boat became surrounded by the lightning. It danced across the water but made no splash. It cracked open the hold but the shattering of the steel made no sound.*"

Jim shook his head. "Same exact thing. What the hell ye' think it was?"

My eyes were wide as I re-read the words and shook my head. Whatever happened to us had happened to him and he died here. Would we suffer the same fate?

"I ain't read much further than that but I intend to." He waved at the large stack of books and journals to one side of the bed. "The man had a lot to say... I do know one thing though..." He grinned.

"Ye' see, hidden beneath all this..." He motioned around the room at the various trunks and boxes that lined its walls, "...was the real merchandise..." He took my hand in one of his and Lilly's in the other. "Come on!"

He dragged us to the back far corner of the cave where he led us down a narrow passageway much like the one we'd found up on the summit. He let go of my hand once we were completely enveloped in darkness, and the small beam of the flashlight flickered on as he led us out into a second, smaller cave.

This one was lined with large sealed barrels of what I could only assume was more whiskey against one wall, casks and casks of more port stacked up beside them. "It was prohibition, see." He winked at me. "...and he had the mother load."

I turned slowly in a circle, holding the journal against my chest as I followed the beam of light and took it all in.

"Alright, come on back to the main cave," Jim said excitedly. "There's somethin' yer gonna' wanna see, Princess."

As Jim hauled Lilly off to a trunk near the entrance of the cave, a large blue and white trunk against the far wall caught my eye. I rushed to it and flipped it open. Inside was perfectly preserved fine china stacked as tall as my hip—plates, bowls, saucers, teacups, and glasses, all wrapped in straw that crumbled as I touched it. On each plate, bowl, and cup, was an intricate weave of blue ink. A small swirling braid grew into flowers around the rim. Larger versions of the flowers sprinkled the center of the bowls and fashioned the side of the matching teacups.

The silverware was well preserved in a smaller box. Actual silver, I noted, delicately wrapped individually in a silk cloth and still shining after all the time that had passed.

In another box, wrapped individually, were about five hundred white candle sticks—with them, at least a hundred separate crystal holders.

I closed the trunk and continued along the rock wall, noticing a stack of tools just outside a long, worn wooden box. A very worn axe, a small shovel, a chisel, and a machete were spilled out on the ground. I thought of the boar and pictured how different things might've turned out had I had the machete in my hands.

"Oh, it's perfect!" Lilly's voice shrieked from behind me. "It's perfect!" She jumped at Jim, wrapping her arms around him and kissing him loudly on the lips.

"Well, ain't you sweet," he laughed, spinning her around and out of his arms.

I peered around them and saw what she'd seen. An open trunk overflowed with fabrics, some intricately patterned, others solid. I stepped closer to inspect it and found tightly wound rolls beneath the loose fabric of silk, linen, wool, and cotton.

"What's this?" Kyle asked next to me, his hand raising slowly to present the slightly rusted metal of an old revolver.

"Careful with that, son." Bud dropped the book he'd been inspecting and walked to Kyle's side. "That's an old Colt .45." He slowly took the gun from Kyle, holding it down and releasing the cylinder to expose bullets still in each chamber. "It's still loaded. Might come in handy for the pigs."

"Lainey, look!" Lilly laughed, wrapping a patterned red and cream silk robe around her body and dancing from side to side. "It's like I've died and gone to heaven."

I laughed, joining her at the box she'd been emptying to fish out a very beautiful, blue, silk dress with a high collar and sleeves. I held it against my body. "What do you think? Too much?" I giggled.

Lilly ran her hands down the sides of the dress. "Oh, it's beautiful... I could make this look amazing on you..."

My eyes narrowed in on a small case in the shadows just behind her. I knew what it was just its shape, and the hairs on my body prickled with excitement.

I let the dress fall into Lilly's hands and drew closer, my hands shaking with anticipation as I reached the small case, flipped the clasps and pulled out a pristine violin. I had no idea how to play one, but I missed music in a world so devoid of it and decided right then and there I'd practice night and day until I'd learned.

Bruce spotted it too, awe spilling over his expression as he whispered, "Oh my God." His eyes watered. "May I?" he asked, reaching for it.

I handed it to him and watched as he gently turned the pegs, plucking the strings with his ear to one side. Much to my surprise, he laid it across his shoulder, closed his eyes, and played the most beautiful sounds I'd ever heard.

We all stopped everything and watched him—except for Isobel, who'd found the trunk of fabric and was pulling each one up to rub against her cheek. My soul warmed with instant comfort as he drew out each note.

Closing my eyes, I let the music pull me away, and lost in those long, haunting notes, I thought of Jack. I felt his arms around me, his lips over mine, his breath against my cheek... I could hear his words in the melody as he'd said, *'I love you...'* and I missed him... longed to share this moment with him... to dance with him, and to feel his hands on me now.

I was pulled from my daydream when Lilly slid down the wall beside me, her shoulder brushing up against mine. "Oh, Lainey, I have the greatest idea."

Chapter Thirty-Seven

I paced the dimly lit cave of our new shelter in my bare feet, wringing my hands to keep them from shaking. I was excited, scared, and anxious. Jack and Bud would be there any moment.

It was the first time I would see him since the beach and Lilly and I had planned an elaborate anniversary party for Bertie and Bud that would serve as a backdrop to our reunion.

Despite disapproval from Jim, Lilly had convinced him to let us stay in the new shelter—using my ankle as an excuse—so we could work on the preparations.

For Lilly, no detail would be left undone. It was to be an elegant soiree—all of us dressed to the nines—with dinner and dancing, candles and wine. This meant we were all put swiftly to work.

Anna, Lilly, and I stayed up late into the night altering dresses and jackets both from the suitcases and from the trunks. This could only be done while Bud and Bertie were kept occupied at our old camp by Bruce and Phil.

We'd informed them we were preparing the new shelter and would need time to make it comfortable for them. Jim and Kyle were tasked with fashioning beds, tables and chairs out of trunks, boxes, bamboo, and fabric. Even Isobel had a chore—she was to gather fresh flowers for centerpieces and tiarés.

Having a girlfriend on the island to confide in and plot with proved to be invaluable. I'd never had a best friend before; never had a female I was close to aside from my mother and sister. Lilly had filled the void losing them had left. I loved her, even more so after we'd planned the evening. In addition to the party, she'd helped me plan a romantic homecoming for Jack.

She'd secretly altered the dress I'd found, a stunning silk navy that she cut and reshaped to drape loosely over my shoulders, fitting snug at the waist and flowing softly as it wound around to kiss my knees. It scooped down low at the back with a slit purposely placed on the left side.

She'd handed it to me a few hours prior along with a razor from a toiletry bag, "You're gonna want him to see those legs as soon as he gets back." She winked before turning her attention to Bertie.

We'd had to give Bertie a few details. Lilly was too excited to get her dressed. We'd spent a small eternity putting together a red dress with white polka-dots and we were all anxious to see her in it. None of our fabric came with polka-dots, so this meant Anna and I spent an entire day dotting the red fabric with a bleach pen that we'd found in one of the cases.

Lilly had jumped up and down at the opportunity to style our hair and put eyeshadow, eyeliner, and lipstick on all of us—including Isobel, and had gathered little white flowers for us all to place behind our ears.

She'd pulled my hair into a loose braid that ran down my left shoulder. I'd then added my tiaré to my *left* ear.

Jim and Anna were to go up and inform Jack and Magna of our plan. They would all then come down together in the jackets and dresses we'd made for them. The summit could wait. Tonight was more important.

They were to meet Bud on the beach—he was clueless and assumed he was just waiting there to lead them back to our new home—where they would dress him in his new jacket and escort him back.

Everything was going to plan. Bertie was glowing in her red dress and lipstick as she patiently waited in her seat at a small table in the center of the cave. The table was draped in white fabric and adorned with pink flowers, a single candlestick in the middle of two proper place settings to make it that much more romantic.

Bruce had prepared steamed crab and smoked pork with boiled Fe'i. I could smell it from where I paced. Food prepared and ready to serve, he was off to one side, tuning the violin that would provide the evening's entertainment.

The sun was setting outside, and the last few beams of its warm orange light trickled in through the crevice at the top of the cave's opening. They would be here any minute. My heart beat faster.

"They're coming," Lilly whispered as she snuck back in, uncorking the wine and pouring two glasses at Bertie's table. She hurried around me to the long table we'd fashioned out of wooden boxes on the far end of the cave, covered in white fabric.

On top of the table, we'd placed bundles of pink flowers and candles that lined up from one end to the other. We'd pulled several of our newly fashioned box chairs up to it, each adorned with a small bouquet of flowers tied to the back.

On the table, she'd laid out wine glasses for the rest of us along with a water bottle for Isobel and perfect place settings with the fine china we found in the trunk. She filled the glasses quickly, then snuck in beside me in the shadows to hand me mine. "Good luck."

Bruce stood and pulled the violin to his shoulder as Lilly rushed outside to greet our guests, her little white dress flowing wildly around her legs.

The first notes of the violin rang out as Anna, Magna, Jim, and Jack hurried through the mouth of the cave to stand patiently on each side and make way for Lilly and Bud as they appeared arm in arm. He was looking quite dashing in his Khaki pants and navy blazer. His eyes fixed on Bertie and his face lit up in a smile. Lilly's did too as she escorted him to the table.

Lilly released him so he could bend down to kiss Bertie's bright red lips. Her hands came up to cup his face as he did so, and I heard her shaky voice say joyfully, "Happy Anniversary, my darling."

Touched by their interaction, I focused my attention on the cave's opening where Isobel was dragging Magna further inside while Anna, Jack, and Jim took in the room around them. We'd draped ruched fabric, pinned with bouquets and carefully placed candles all along the cave walls. The candlelight danced across the shiny rock walls, and the light bounced down from the rock above.

I grabbed a second glass of wine from the table and stepped out of the shadows. Jack's eyes instantly met mine.

He swallowed as I approached, scanning me from top to bottom. I'd altered a black blazer under Lilly's direction that made him look intimidatingly handsome. He had shaved his face smooth, and it was all I could do not to wrap my arms around him and pull him into the darkness outside as I came close.

His mouth was slightly open as I offered him the glass of wine in my hand. "Care to join us, Mr. Volmer?"

He blinked, looking down at the wineglass with its finely engraved stem. "I..." He looked back at me. "You..."

I took his free hand in mine and turned, purposely giving him a glimpse of the open back of my dress as I pulled him toward our table.

Lilly winked at me as she passed by, holding a platter of steamed crab in one hand, boiled Fe'i in the other.

When we'd reached our table, I pulled out a box chair and motioned for him to sit. He obliged, twisting uncomfortably to prevent from taking his eyes off me while I circled around.

I found my seat to the right of him, and, crossing my legs to show the slit that ran up the left side—my good leg—I watched his eyes follow it to my thigh just before he took a large drink of wine.

'Thank you, Lilly.'

"You look stunning," he breathed into my ear as Lilly worked her way along our table to serve steaming crab and pork, placing bowls of Fe'i and breadfruit in the center.

The corner of my mouth turned up as I sipped my wine. "Oh? You like it?"

"Mmmhmm," he grunted, turning the end of my braid between his fingers. "How are you feeling?"

I picked up my fork and knife, delicately cutting into the pork. "I feel good as new. How was the summit? Anything new?" I took a small bite, enjoying his eyes on my dark red lips, praying the lipstick wouldn't spread all over my teeth before the night was done.

"No, it was fine..." he said in a daze, eyes glued to my mouth, then shifting lower. "Where did you get this dress?"

"Lilly made it. Do you like it?" I smiled and batted my eyes as Bruce sweetly transitioned into another song, momentarily forcing my eyes closed to take it in.

"I think I'll need to thank her personally." He smiled, picking up his fork for the first time and turning it in his hand with amazement before grabbing the knife and cutting his own pork.

"What do you think of our new camp?" I asked, sipping my wine.

He looked around. "This place is amazing, I'll give him that." He gazed up to the rock ceiling high above us as the violin bounced off its peak. "Jim filled us in on what he'd found, but... wow... it's really..." he looked at me, "breathtaking."

I smiled, leaning close to his shoulder to whisper, "I've missed you."

His fingers slid up the back of my shoulder, sending chills down my spine.

On the other side of me, Jim caught both of our attention.

"Jesus Lilly," he was saying, keeping his voice low enough so only we could hear as he squirmed in his gray blazer. "It's hotter than two rats fuckin' in a wool sock. For the love of Christ, why cain't I take it off now? They've done seen me in it!"

"Not yet, Jimmy, and it's not that hot." She daintily cut her meat from across the table.

I felt Jack's fingers climb up to circle the nape of my neck and goosebumps ran the length of both my arms.

"Not that hot?" He pointed at her with his fork, "Y'aint wearin' nothin' but a Got damned piece of torlette paper. Of course *you* ain't hot."

"Jim," she narrowed her eyes at him, "please act like a normal human being just this one time... for me."

He stabbed his fork down into his pork to pull the large piece of meat up with it. The fork wobbled with the weight of the meat, and her eyes went wide with horror as he bit a chunk off and grinned at her.

All the while, Jack's fingers danced lightly down the center of my back.

"You're an animal," she snarled, but she was stifling a laugh.

"You bet yer ass I am." He wiggled in the jacket, resigning to pick up his knife and eat normally as he mumbled to himself, "Thirty-eight years I gone never wearin' one of these damned monkey suits... And it'll be ALL TOO SOON if I can go another thirty-eight 'for I put one on again."

Conversation at our table returned to a normal flow and Jack leaned back in. "It was torture being away from you." His knuckle brushed down my arm. "It was all I could do not to sneak back down just to kiss you one more time." As his knuckle reached my palm, he curled his fingers around mine.

"If I could've made a break for it, I'd have followed you up the first day," I whispered, squeezing his hand.

His breath against my ear sent shivers up my spine. "I dreamt of you... every night."

I turned my body slightly toward him, leaning in. "I did too."

He rubbed my wrist with his thumb. "I dreamt of what I'd do to you when I saw you..."

I smiled mischievously, raising one eyebrow as I brought my wineglass to my lips. "So did I..."

He coughed and took a big drink of his own wine while I returned to my dinner.

When dinner had wrapped up, the violin stopped. Lilly skirted around the table to us, kneeling between us. "Look at them, look at how happy she is right now! Oh, she has no idea... It's time!"

Right on cue, the violin pulled the soft notes of the intro to Nat King Cole's "For all we know," the first song Bertie and Bud had danced to—a small detail Lilly was bursting at the seams to watch play out.

Bertie and Bud both looked toward Bruce, then back to each other. Bud rose, extending his hand down to her. Softly, she took it and stood.

They walked together just past their table and came together as if they were made to do so, so swift a movement it seemed like second nature as their hands met and his arm came around her.

The violin slowed and shifted back and forth between the lead vocal and the melody that moved it. I could see Bud's lips moving as he sang it to her while they rocked back and forth, turning ever so slightly along the way.

Lilly rose and walked past us. "Dance with me, Jimmy," she insisted, pulling at his shoulders, "and I'll let you take that jacket off the minute we're through."

He jumped up and escorted her to our makeshift dance floor, making a show out of extending her arm wide to one side and shuffling her dramatically in an awkward waltz.

Isobel pulled Magna to the floor as well, hopping from side to side and grinning despite her lack of hearing.

Without a word, Jack raised us by our joined hands, placed his hand on the small of my back and walked me toward the floor, settling on a spot closest to the cave's opening before he stopped. Keeping his palm in place, he drew me toward him and took my hand in his as we began to dance.

We danced slowly, staring into each other's eyes through the song and into the next one as Bruce transitioned into "The Very Thought of You."

He slid his hand up my back and pulled me closer, forcing my arm to curl around his neck and our faces inches apart, "Tell me…" he said quietly, "…about your dream."

I smiled, shifting to his ear. "Well, it starts off a lot like this… we're dancing…"

His breath found my ear. "And then what happens?"

"And then you lead us outside…"

He spun us gently, moving us closer to the exit, forcing me to giggle as he continued, "And then what happens?"

"And then I take this hand," I unclasped our joined hands, letting mine slide up his arm to curl around his cheek, "and softly cup your face…"

I could feel the cool night air against my back as he spun us outside. "And then?"

"…well, by then, given our history… you would've already backed me up against…" my bare back hit the cold rock exterior on the side of the cave, "…this wall."

"And now?" he asked, propping both forearms on the wall behind my ears, his mouth hovering over mine.

"Well, this is where..." I bit my lip and pulled the sides of his jacket so his mouth could come down over mine.

His kiss was urgent and his hands were desperate as they slid down the silk at both my sides. His breathing was heavy, and he pressed up against me, gripping my face as he parted my lips.

I wrapped my arms around him, pulling him closer as I slid my foot up against the cool damp rock, bending my knee against his thigh, begging him closer with the same urgency.

He brought one hand to the hair at the nape of my neck and gripped tightly, forcing me to moan against him as the fingertips of his other hand found where the silk gave way to the slit at my raised thigh.

Panting, he released my mouth, "I never want to be away from you again," and then his lips came down on my neck, hot and wet, his fingers spreading wide against the bare skin of my thigh—

"....now dammit, I told ye I'd do it in a second, woman!" We froze in place as Jim's voice crossed from the echoing cave to the night around us. "But first, I gotta see a man about a horse."

I laughed quietly, burying my face in Jack's shoulder to stifle the sound as we stayed perfectly still. I held him against me as he did the same and we all but lost it when we heard the distinct stream and a very long sigh of relief from the bushes on the opposite side of where we stood. He curled his arms around me, and we convulsed quietly with uncontrollable laughter.

Once we heard Jim's footsteps return to the cave, we both cracked, letting the laughter pour out as we held onto each other. His still watering eyes met mine, and he ran a hand over my hair, "I got a little carried away and I—

I raised on my tiptoes and pressed my lips to his. "Don't you want to know what happens next?" I asked, "in my dream?"

Before he could answer, I grabbed his hand and headed in the direction of the waterfall, forcing him to spin on his heel as I pulled him behind me.

Chapter Thirty-Eight

When we reached the creek, my ankle was on fire, my heart was beating out of my chest, and I felt I might burst without his lips on mine. I spun around once my feet were on the cold, damp rock of the water's edge and pulled him to me.

His kiss was passionate. He cupped my face in both his hands, his lips moving feverishly over mine as he inhaled my scent. I breathed him in and let his breath fill me, warming my soul and muting the world around us.

There was only him—his mouth, his warmth, and his fingers tangled in my hair.

I'd spent every second of the week dreaming of only this.

I pushed the jacket off his shoulders and as his arms released me to let it fall, my fingers went anxiously to work on the buttons of his shirt.

"So impatient," he growled, taking my lips again.

While each button gave way, my mouth on his grew more emboldened. The last button surrendered, and I pulled the shirt from his shoulders, driving my palms over the warm skin of his chest as he rushed to shake the sleeves from his arms.

The feel of him was like a drug. It didn't matter how much of him I had, I still needed more. I wanted to experience him in every possible way; wanted to shut out the world and explore each other for months on end.

His bare arms wrapped tightly around me, pulling me up to him while his mouth swept down, consuming the skin along my jaw until he reached my neck.

His lips, tongue, and teeth commanded me and I submitted as he worked downward, his arm sliding up my torso to arch my back while his mouth came down over the silk at my breast, soaking the thin fabric that separated us.

He leaned over me, pulling me closer while he shifted to the other side, groaning deep in his throat when he took my breast fully into his mouth through the delicate silk and forced me to cry out.

"Christ," he purred, "I can't tell you how much I've wanted this... How every waking moment of this past week has been torment waiting to get back to you..."

His palm slid down the length of my side, then circled to return upwards when it reached the bare skin at my thigh.

I took his mouth in a hurry and raised my knee against his outer thigh, placing my hand over his and urging his fingers onward. He obliged, leaning over me while his palm slid the length of my skin beneath the fabric, circling upward to cup my bare breast as his mouth devastated mine.

Tilting me further, his hand beneath the fabric drifted up to slide the sleeves of the dress down my shoulders. In one quick move, his mouth released mine, the fabric at my breasts gave way to the night air, and his lips encircled my nipple. I arched back in a gasp of ecstasy, fingers forming fists in his hair and begging him further.

A breeze swam across my skin, and with it, the faint sounds of violin and laughter from the party in the distance.

He made no move to slow us as his palm ran down my stomach to rest at the edge of my panties, but he breathed against me, "Not here."

Still pulling him against my breast, I slowly straightened us, panting as his fingertips danced along the elastic waistband. "Behind the fall," I managed, gasping for air as his hand slid further down beneath the cotton, inches from me. "There's a spot behind the fall..."

His mouth returned to mine, and as it did, I loosened his jeans, peeling them back as his middle finger came lower to tease, lightly caressing me.

I pushed the jeans down, and as he kicked his boots and pants off, his hand retreated, sliding upward to push my dress up with it and over my head. His kiss returned, tender on my lips, while he tossed it to one side.

Wrapping an arm around my back, the other came up under my bottom and he raised me up to wrap my legs around him. Feeling the full hardness of him against me, I coiled my arms around his neck, bare chests coming together as he walked us into the cool water.

He led us toward the fall, kissing me ardently as we crossed the water, my legs wound tightly around him. When I could feel the mist on my skin, he tucked me into him, shielding my head with his arms as we passed under the rush of cold water and into the complete darkness behind it.

I could see nothing but blackness, hear nothing but the fall behind us, feel nothing but his hardness between the soaked fabric that separated us.

He walked us deeper until my bare back pressed against the cold damp wall of rock and the full weight of him pressed against me.

He breathed heavily against my ear as I let one foot come down on the rock below us. "Would you like to know what I dreamt of?"

He pulled his weight from me and I reached for him in the blackness but came up empty as he knelt to slide the cotton down my legs. His lips skimmed my inner thigh causing my body to shake, then his breath reached the wetness between them.

His thumb traced lightly over my center as his breath came closer to my core, sending a chill up my spine. "I dreamt of tasting you."

And then his mouth was on the sensitive flesh, and I was grateful for the rush of the waterfall that it would drown out my cries from the party beyond it.

I buckled, my knees trembling as he took his fill, his palm on my stomach forcing my back to remain stapled to the stone wall.

He took me rapidly up and over the edge, and waited until I was flinching to stand and bring his lips to mine.

"I never want to be apart from you again," he said, lifting my legs and sliding inside me.

I held his kiss to mine, moving with him in the darkness as my heart beat faster.

We moved softly, slowly, and quietly together, our lips locked as we both held on to each other. He pulled me from the wall and lowered me onto the stone floor, careful to keep our lips and our bodies connected as we both gave everything to each other.

He kept his lips over mine, kissing me long after we'd each finished, the fingers of one hand caressing my forehead while the other skimmed the length of me as if he were trying to commit every detail to memory.

I ran my palms down his shoulders, doing the same. I whispered softly into the darkness, "If we hadn't crashed, we'd have never known each other."

I drew a circle around his collarbone with my thumb. "...or if I'd traded my seat..."

His hand found mine, and he curled his fingers around it.

"Or if I'd let him talk first that night instead of begging for the trip..."

He squeezed my hand as I continued, "...or if our marriage hadn't fallen apart..."

He raised our hands to his lips and kissed my fingers softly.

"...or if I hadn't given up on music... had never met him..."

I ran my thumb along his lips. "I really, *really* loved him... and never stopped. I love him *still*... I will always love him..."

I let my fingers glide down the smooth surface of his jaw where his beard had once been. "But this... the way that I love you... It's something else entirely. This love showed up and made sense of every other moment in my life."

I traced the outlines of his face. "Everything in my life... every decision I did or didn't make, every tear I cried, and every breath I took brought me here to you. Brought me here to find this love that I can't seem to function without. And there is nowhere else I ever want to be."

He kissed my palm, then lowered himself to kiss my lips. "Me neither."

He sat up and pulled me into his lap, curling his arms around me and rocking me softly. We sat there for what felt like hours, listening to the jet of the waterfall echoing on the rock walls around us, both of us entirely content to be still together.

"Jesus, you're shivering," he said after a while, kissing my forehead and tightening his hold on me. "Should I take you back?"

I nodded, nuzzling myself against his warm skin. "They'll probably be wondering where we went."

He ran his hands rapidly up and down my arms. "And where do we tell them we've gone?"

I smirked. "I don't think it's much of a secret, you and me. They'll know exactly what we were up to when we both come back soaking wet and smiling." I straightened, kissing his lips ever so softly. "I don't think I'd want to hide it, anyway."

I felt him smile against my lips. "Thank God. I don't think I could keep my hands off you if I tried." He stood, scooping me up in his arms as he did so. "Ready for a swim?"

Once we'd crossed back to the rocks at the creek's edge, we both put our clothes back on as we shook from the cool night air. Jack cloaked me in his jacket and we headed, hand-in-hand, back toward the cave, the sounds of violin and conversation still very much alive as we got closer.

He stopped us just before we got to the opening and spun me to face him. The blue light from the moon fought with the orange glow from the cave as they lit his face to show his eyes gazing down into mine. "I don't deserve you," he said, taking both my hands in his, "but I—"

"There you are!" Lilly came skipping from the cave toward us. "You should sing for—OH MY GOD!" She reached us and inspected our wet hair, our joined hands, and something on my face caused her to laugh. "I'm so sorry... didn't mean to interrupt..."

She lingered, a very strong smell of port wine emitting from her as she raised her thumb to my face and wiped beneath my eyes. "Everyone wants you to sing something." She grinned, looking back up to Jack. "You've hogged her long enough."

Smoothing a hand over my hair, she made a face. "And look what you did to her hair... fix it and come sing." She spun on her heel and hopped back toward the cave, announcing loudly as she entered, "I FOUND THEM! AND I WAS RIGHT!"

As she disappeared, his hands went to my hair, gently unwinding the loose and soaked braid that had once been perfect. I watched his face as he concentrated on the braid, relief pouring over my scalp as the knots gave way, and I could see the words he'd said to me in his eyes as they followed his fingers. For the first time in a long time, I *felt* loved.

The loose curls fell damp against the jacket on my shoulders and his fingers curled around my neck as he raised me on my toes to kiss me one last time. I didn't want to go in; didn't want to share him with the others. I wanted to steal away to some place quiet, wrap his arms around me, and never leave.

"I'd like to hear you sing," he said softly, pressing his forehead against mine.

My heart sank. I hadn't sang in years—hadn't wanted to. Did I even know how to anymore? What would I even sing if I did? His arms folded around me, and as he pulled me against him, I exhaled. If this man wanted me to sing, I'd sing... whether I remembered how or not.

One arm draped around me, he turned me toward the cave and escorted me slowly inside.

Inside, the camp was filled with music and laughter. Bertie and Bud were laughing with Magna and Phil while Anna slow-danced with Isobel. Lilly was giggling as Kyle attempted to lead her in a dance. A grinning Jim greeted us, a bottle of whiskey affixed to one hand. "Go for a swim, did ye? You, ah..." he tapped the corner of his mouth while stifling a laugh, eyes shifting from Jack to me.

"Y'all both got a little somethin'..." he cleared his throat, "...right here."

I looked up at Jack who was smiling widely back at me, bright red lipstick smeared across his lips and halfway to his cheeks. I imagined I looked somewhat similar as he laughed apologetically down at me. "Hang on." He touched my lips with his thumb. "I'll get something."

He walked off toward our table and Jim's arm came hard around my neck. "Woman," he slurred loudly in my ear, "I'm happy for yuns." He looked in Jack's direction, then back to me, attempting to lower his voice and doing a poor job of it as he returned to my ear. "I could take him though, if'n you ever change your mind." He giggled and hiccuped. "Wouldn't have to though." He squeezed me tighter as Jack walked back in our direction. "One night with me and ye'd be throwin' rocks at ole' Don Juan there."

As Jack approached, Jim raised his arm, winking at me then focusing on Jack. "Best you keep her close, Hoss," he hiccuped again, "else someone more *experienced* might just steal her away."

Jack half smiled and went hastily to work rubbing my lips with a wet piece of silk. As I took the cloth and returned the favor, I could feel the eyes of the entire room on us. "I do believe..." I said softly between us, "...the cat's out of the bag."

"Well then," he grinned as the silk passed over his lips, bending down to kiss me softly, "might as well give 'em something to talk about."

"Ay!" Jim wandered off and yelled toward Bruce. "You know any Charlie Daniels?"

Jack held me there a moment longer, smiling down at me as I wiped his lips one last time. The bright red lipstick was tough, and a soft pink hue remained around his lips.

As Bruce teased with the opening notes to 'Devil went down to Georgia,' Lilly appeared with two wine glasses at our side. She handed one to each of us and waited until we'd both taken a drink before she focused on me. "Lainey, Jim's been singing loudly for at least an hour. Please end my suffering."

I smiled at her and nodded, sighing, "Alright Lill." I sipped heavily from my wine. "I'll sing."

She hopped up and down, clapping excitedly as I crossed the room toward Bruce.

'What do I even sing? I've never really done cover songs... just my own. Can't expect Bruce to play one of those... Or can I?'

I walked slowly and worked out the lyrics I had been toying with in my mind over the past week.

Quickly, I thought up a chord progression and pulled Bruce to one side—interrupting the Charlie Daniels song and getting a few choice words from Jim.

As the violin drew out the long slow notes, my knees shook beneath me, my palms began to sweat, and my stomach knotted. I'd never been nervous to sing before, but suddenly I felt terrified.

I closed my eyes and let the notes fill me; let Jack fill me. I could still feel his hands on me, taste his mouth in mine, and as I remembered the sensations, I began to sing.

"The sky cracked wide open...
and it pulled me straight through...
Then it shook up the ocean...
and it sailed me to you."

As I carefully navigated the words of the verse, eyes tightly shut, I let myself be transported back to the waterfall. Felt his body over mine and the song poured out of me.

"And we danced on black water...
Until the sun intervened...
And under red skies, you offered...
To fade away here with me."

As the song reached its chorus, I opened my eyes and focused on him. He was watching me fixedly and I let the rest of the world fall away so there was only him as I sang louder.

"I would stay faded away...
I would stay forever with you...
I would wait...
Wait here for days...
I would wait forever for you."

I sang the words and I meant them. I was in a paradise and it took these people to open my eyes to it. I was happy here.

As we lowered back down to the verse, I let my eyes wander from Jack to the others. Jim had one arm wrapped around Lilly and they swayed from side to side, smiling proudly at me while Kyle, frequently jealous of anyone who touched his precious Lilly, glared at Jim from a distance.

Phil was beside him, watching me as he topped off his wine glass yet again. Bertie and Bud were sitting together, their fingers entwined, looking at me affectionately. Anna and Magna were dancing in a circle with Isobel.

I realized I was *very* happy here. This group of strangers had become my family, and I was grateful for them... I loved them all.

The violin rang out the final note and I wiped my eyes as they all clapped and cheered.

"You've made a fat man cry," Bruce whispered in my ear. "Thank you."

"More!" Lilly clapped. "Do one more!"

"Oh," I laughed shyly. "I think we should give Bruce a rest for a while." I looked to him at my side, his eyes still full of tears. "I think he could use a drink."

"Here, let me." Bertie rose and crossed slowly over to us, carefully taking the violin and laying it across her shoulder. "I haven't played since I was a girl," she announced, closing her eyes and pulling the bow elegantly across the strings, the opening notes to 'This Magic Moment' bouncing off the cave walls.

We danced, and I sang late into the night, until one by one, we all worked our way to the fire just outside the cave's opening. Bruce and I were the last to join and as he found his place next to Anna, I found mine in front of Jack, letting him wrap his big arms around me so I could lay my head back against his shoulder.

"Thank you," Bud said softly, his arms wrapped similarly around Bertie. "Tonight was more than I could've ever asked for."

"Yes." She smiled, nuzzling her head into his arm. "Thank you. It was perfect."

Jack squeezed me tighter and whispered softly in my ear, "It *was* perfect."

"What in the Sam Hill you think ye're doin' woman?" Jim had laid down flat at the opposite end of the fire, and I could only see the ends of his pointed boots along with a pair of small bare feet.

"Snuggling. I'm cold," Lilly said.

"I don't snuggle, dammit. Go on."

"Oh, come on, Jimmy, it's cold." I could hear the rustling of bodies against the dry palm on the ground.

"Then go put on some dang clothes. Now I done told ye, I ain't snugglin.' Get off wit' ye."

Kyle coughed. "I'll keep you warm, Lilly."

I laughed to myself as Lilly ignored him, whining at Jim in protest. Jack found my ear again. "I think I've shared you long enough now. Come to bed with me?"

I sighed, leaning back to whisper as Lilly stomped off into the cave. "Where?"

He kissed my neck softly. "You're not the only one with dreams, you know. I set up a little something."

He bent his legs and rose, pulling me up with him. "Bertie, Bud, happy anniversary." He smiled fondly toward them, "We'll see you all in the morning."

Lilly reappeared near the fire wearing a black t-shirt over her white dress with the bold, white *"Mama Tried"* lettering and a piece of wool fabric draped over her shoulders. "Night lovebirds." She grinned, resuming her position next to Jim.

Jack grabbed a smoking log from the fire, then turned us toward the trees and led me into the darkness. "Here." He handed me the log, one end still burning a bright orange against the velvet night. "You should get off that ankle."

He scooped me up against him and carried me uphill, deep into the trees, where he'd constructed a small tent out of bamboo and silk. Outside its opening, he'd set up a small fire pit, already stacked with firewood. He set me on my feet and, taking the burning log from me, lit the fire.

As the fire grew strong, its warm light illuminated the white silk, and I crawled inside. I was delighted with the wool under my hands overlaying a bed of soft moss. "When did you do this?" I laughed incredulously as he crawled in beside me.

He ran his finger along my cheek. "I can plan surprises too, you know… besides, in my dream…" he leaned in, "I could see what we were doing."

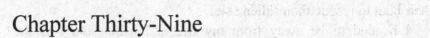

Chapter Thirty-Nine

"Oh A.J.!" Cece pulled me out of the passenger seat of Chris's Dodge Ram the instant we'd pulled into the driveway. "I'm so glad you're here. I've got the cabin on the lake all set up for you. You can stay as long as you want."

"AYAY!" Madison was at our calves, her little arms squeezing my legs.

"Hey munchkin," I managed, overrun with emotion as I hoisted her up into my arms, squeezing tightly and burying my tears in her mess of wispy golden hair. "I missed you." I held her there too long, her little arms wrapped securely around my neck, forcing my heart to shatter.

"Chris," I heard Cece behind me, "how are you guys holding up?"

I rocked Madison from side to side, listening to their voices as I tried to collect myself.

"It's been hard on her," Chris responded. "I really appreciate you guys letting her stay. I've got to head back on Sunday, but I'll be back every weekend until she's ready to go home."

"You brought her laptop? I had a router installed in the cabin so she can work."

"Yes, it's in the bag. She's still got another week before she's supposed to go back. They gave her maternity leave and bereavement and have been extremely understanding. She needs to get her mind off of it though, might be good for her to start back up a week early."

Madison squirmed in my arms and I released her reluctantly, turning to face the massive lake my cabin overlooked. I hated when they talked about me as if I wasn't standing right there with them.

"Here, give me those and you get the big one and I'll show you the cabin. A.J., are you coming?"

"I'll be right in."

I breathed in the fresh pines that surrounded the campground and the lake, watching a family far out on the water as they turned their boat to rescue their fallen skier.

I needed to be away from my life and Minnesota was the furthest I could get. Somehow, my grief had morphed into an attack on everyone around me. I was tired of being told how I needed to pull myself together... how I wasn't being fair to the people who loved me... I was tired of the sadness that surrounded me being taken personally.

I'd called Cece and asked if I could stay on their campground for a while. She was more than happy to accommodate me with my own small cabin. I imagined I would lock myself in and grieve without the burden that doing so might be hurting someone else. I needed to fall apart before I could ever be whole again.

Chris had been reluctant to let me go, arguing with me for hours about how he needed me, but he would always follow that need up with an *'I'm hurting too'* that validated all my reasons for leaving. It wasn't a competition. This wasn't about who was hurting more... it was about her and the complete void that losing her had left inside me. I didn't want to have to justify my sadness anymore.

After much debate, he'd agreed to drive me up there.

The car ride had been mostly silent. Eleven hours of silence sat heavy on me as I watched the skier on the water reposition and go again.

'Could I ever be that happy?'

It wasn't just sadness that consumed me. I was angry. I was angry at the world for taking her from me and angry at myself for having been so naïve when the doctors had all warned me that this very thing would likely happen.

I was angry at Chris for getting so excited. *'He knew the risks... and he let me get excited, too. Why hadn't we taken the warnings more seriously? Why hadn't we discussed the possibilities? Why hadn't he ever brought it up?'*

I wrapped my fingers around the necklace, sighing as I watched the boat and their skier disappear to the other side of a large tree-filled inlet far out on the lake.

"You must be A.J.," a deep male voice said behind me.

I turned to see a tall, tan, athletic young man in bright red swim trunks approaching, a set of water skis under one arm. He smiled under his short brown and auburn beard—a contrast to the much lighter inch of light brown and blonde hair on his head, his big green eyes full of playfulness. "I'm Doug. Owen's cousin. Wanna' come out with us?" He nodded toward the water.

"No." I smiled. "Thank you."

"It'll be fun," he teased, looping an arm through mine and pulling me toward the dock where there were already three young ladies in brightly colored bikinis waving us over to a shining yellow boat. "And you look like you could use some fun. I promise, if you don't laugh within five minutes out there, I'll bring you right back."

"No." I set my heels, stopping us short of the wooden dock. "I can't today. Thank you, though." I unhooked our arms.

"Okay," he sighed. "Fine. Do you fish?"

I frowned. "No."

"Have you ever tried?" He grinned. "I can teach you. Look." He pointed at an old man fishing on the far side of the dock. "We don't even have to leave the dock."

"Really, Doug, I should unpack. I just got here and I'm exhausted."

He leaned in scandalously. "I have pot." He pulled back and bounced his eyebrows.

I actually laughed at him then, surprising myself. "Maybe another time, kiddo, I really should get back."

He pursed his lips, looking up at the cabin. *"Kiddo?* What are you, like four years older than me?" He rolled his eyes. "Come on.

You really wanna go in there right now and play the pitiful houseguest?"

Taken aback, I scowled at him. "What's that supposed to mean?"

He raised his eyebrow, adjusting the skis under his arm. "Oh, like I'm not supposed to know what happened? Cece told me all about it. We've all been ordered to go out of our way to make sure you're comfortable. You go up there now, she's going to smother you with pity and pamper you like a child. If that's what you want, go ahead, but like I said, I have pot... And you might even have fun. Besides... winter comes fast here. You won't get more days like today."

"I don't know..." I eyed the girls in the boat as they giggled amongst each other, sneaking glances at Doug every so often. "I don't think—"

"Don't think." He looped his arm through mine again and pulled me onto the dock. "Just come for a ride and forget about it for an hour or two."

I looked back up toward the cabin. "I should at least let them know where I'm going..."

"Oh, you need permission to go on a boat ride?" He dragged me along the dock to the boat, winking at one of the two blonde girls as we got closer.

As he stepped into the small speedboat, I looked reluctantly back up toward the cabin.

Doug sighed, pulling two beers out from a cooler that sat in its center. "I'll text Cece and let her know I stole you away for a bit. Would that make you feel better? Ladies, this is A.J." He extended a beer to me as I stood on the dock debating.

"Your hair is gorgeous!" A short girl with bright blonde hair tied in a knot at the top of her head looked up at me from her seat. "I'm Meghan, and this is my cousin Brittany." She tapped the brunette on the shoulder, forcing her to look up from her phone long enough to smile at me. "And this is my sister Amanda." She affectionately pulled the straight blond hair of the other girl, who was reaching down to grab her own beer. "Now get in here, girl! Let's have some fun!"

I smiled at her as Doug presented his phone, typing like a professional with his thumbs, then waving the text screen at me as evidence. "Satisfied?"

I sighed and stepped down into the boat. *'What the hell are you doing, Alaina?'*

I hugged the cold beer against my chest as I self consciously sat down at the front of the boat on the bench seat opposite the three girls.

Doug started the motor, and the boat rocked as Meghan pushed us off from the dock. I looked back up at my cabin to see Cece and Chris as they exited the patio door to watch me from its private dock.

'This is a horrible idea.'

"So, A.J.," Meghan sat down next to me, both of us being pressed against the seat as Doug hit the deep water and opened up the motor. "Have you ever been to the cliffs?"

Water sprayed over me and despite the warm late August sun, I shivered as the wind hit the wet skin on my bare arms. "The cliffs?"

She nodded as she opened my beer for me. "You're gonna wanna drink that."

I brought the cold can to my lips, wincing as the bittersweet liquid hit my tongue. I had never really had a taste for beer and cheap domestic wouldn't have been my first choice.

"Back on the other side of these islands," Doug shouted over the boat's roaring motor, pointing far off across the water, "there's a cliff we make all our newcomers jump off of."

He laughed as my face distorted in horror. "Trust me, you're going to love it."

I took a large gulp of beer as the boat bounced on the choppy water. "I don't jump off cliffs," I shouted.

"You do today." He winked at me. "It's our tradition and you have to do it if you're going to stay here."

"Come on, seriously." I took another large swig. "I'm not doing that."

"Don't be such a prude." He grinned. "Trust me. You, of all people, *need* to do this."

"I'm not wearing a bathing suit!" I argued, "And I'm not that great of a swimmer, and I thought…"

He turned the boat sharply as we approached the small cluster of pine covered islands and we slowed to an almost stop once we were behind them and out of sight of the campground. "Here." He smiled, reaching into the steering column and producing a joint. "You need to chill out."

He lit it, standing to join us at the front of the boat, and its pungent smoke filled my nostrils, suddenly making me feel like I was fourteen again. He held the joint between his finger and thumb, extending it to me.

"Oh, I don't—"

"It's weed, not heroin," he laughed, "just smoke it and stop being such a prude."

I scoffed. "Stop calling me a prude!"

"Well then, stop acting like one!" He pushed the joint at me, urging me to take it.

I snatched it from him and brought it to my lips, inhaling deeply and holding the smoke in my lungs while I passed the joint to Meghan, who happily followed suit.

'This was definitely a terrible, terrible idea.'

I exhaled and coughed violently, bending over as they all laughed around me.

"Better?" he beamed as I straightened and downed the last of my beer.

"This is going to be fun," Meghan coughed beside me, passing the joint to Brittany before she reached in the cooler to grab another beer.

'I'm too old for this.'

She handed me the can and Doug sat down on the other side of me. "See, look." He pointed to an inlet ahead of us as we bobbed on the water. "See those rocks there? They're not that high."

I looked out as he took the joint from Amanda, noticing the tall orange rocks covered with spots of green bushes that grew between them. "Not that high?" I opened my beer. "That looks like, what… fifty feet?!"

He inhaled, nodding as he held the smoke in his lungs and extended the joint to me. "Maybe even sixty," he said with his breath still held. He blew out and giggled. "It's fun."

I took another hit, closing my eyes as the acrid fumes filled my lungs and nostrils. As I exhaled, I felt the muscles in my entire body relax, as if my whole body had been clenched like a fist for years and had finally let go. I offered the joint to Meghan and sighed.

"What do you think, old lady?" Doug closed one eye. "Ready to go for a swim?"

"Old lady?!" I laughed, "I'm twenty-eight!"

He whistled, shaking his head. "Twenty-eight. What's it like to be ancient?"

I rolled my eyes. "That's not that old."

"No?" He took the joint from Amanda, holding it near his lips. "Well I didn't think it was either until I met you and you're all *'no I can't do this or that cause I'm tired and scared and unadventurous!'*"

I narrowed my eyes as he puffed the joint audibly. "I'm not scared."

He handed me the joint, a small bit left, which I promptly brought to my mouth to inhale. "Let's go." I exhaled the cloud of smoke. "I'll prove it to you."

"That a girl," Meghan giggled, sticking a tongue out at Brittany. "See, I told you she'd do it."

Brittany's eyes were completely glossed over as she inspected me. "We'll see," she sneered.

"She's a redhead." Meghan smoothed a hand over my hair, "God I love your hair… And redheads aren't afraid of anything."

I laughed at that as Doug returned to his seat and steered us toward the cliffs.

'This is crazy.'

I chugged my beer as we pulled within swimming distance of the towering cliffs and Doug killed the motor. "Scared yet?" he teased, diving headfirst off the side of the boat and into the water. "Come on then, grandma!"

"This is nuts…" I looked over the boat as Doug swam toward the rocks. "You've all jumped before?"

"Oh, yes." Meghan grinned. "We had to. It's tradition."

"Dougie, wait up!" Amanda called after him as she dove into the water.

I watched them both swim to the shore and begin to climb.

"Told you she wouldn't do it," Brittany smirked, looking up from her phone. "You're chickening out, aren't you?"

I swallowed, watching as Doug straddled a rock and sat, waving me to join them. "No."

I blew out and stood, kicking off my sandals. *We're doing this. Oh God, we're doing this.* I plugged my nose and jumped feet first into the freezing water.

By the time I'd reached the rocks, the momentary euphoria I'd experienced from the marijuana had worn off and I stood with my arms crossed over my chest, shivering in my tank top and shorts as I stared up at the steep climb.

"Come on, chicken!" Doug teased, standing in his bare feet on the rock just above my head.

"I'm coming," I mumbled, climbing with my hands and knees and following him up the jagged path to the top, Amanda already standing in position on the ledge waiting for us.

"I'll go first," Amanda said. "Show you how it's done."

She winked at Doug and took three steps back, blowing out several times before she shrieked and ran, leaping high into the air and free falling feet first into the deep water below. My heart was in my throat as I watched. Her head emerged seconds later, and she extended both arms up. "Woooo!"

"See." Doug put a hand on my back and walked us to the edge. "It's fun! Your turn."

I peeked over the cliff nervously, imagining myself chickening out just before I jumped and tumbling over the rocks to my death.

Would it really matter? I shivered, the soaking wet clothes clinging to my body.

"We could jump together," Doug offered, "if you're scared."

Nothing matters.

I closed my eyes and blew out, taking a step back.

'Nothing fucking matters.'

I sprinted, screaming at the top of my lungs, enraged, as I launched myself over the edge. As my stomach met my throat during the free fall, I relived her death; held her in my arms, and felt her tiny fingers around my thumb. She'd lived, even momentarily, she had lived. And I had been blessed to know her. The cold water enveloped me, pulling me back to reality, and as I surfaced, I laughed wholeheartedly.

"Fun, right?" Doug shouted down from the top.

"Can I do it again?" I called back.

It was nearly dark by the time we pulled the boat back into the camp's dock. Cece and Chris were there waiting for us, her arms crossed over her chest as we all stumbled out of the boat.

"One hour," she scolded Doug. "You said you'd be back in *one* hour!" She wrapped her arms around my shivering, wet body. "Oh God, A.J., you smell like cheap beer and skunk weed."

I fell into her, freezing as the night temperatures dropped significantly. I hiccuped.

"You got her drunk?" she scoffed. "Douglas, this isn't funny. Where have you been? We've been worried sick."

Doug giggled. "Chill. We took her to the cliffs. She had fun."

"Jesus, she's frozen." She took her hoodie off and draped it over my shoulders. "Come on, let's get you inside."

"I'm not a baby," I laughed. "I'm fine."

Chris stood frozen in front of me, frowning.

"Oh, don't look at me like that." I hiccuped again. "Like you're some kind of fuggin' saint."

"Come on, A.J." Cece hurried me past him toward the cabin. "Douglas, I will deal with you tomorrow."

"Okay, *mom*," Doug teased, the girls giggling behind him.

"And girls," Cece turned slightly, "I wouldn't laugh if I were you. Your parents aren't going to be thrilled when you come back to camp stinking like weed and beer."

Once inside and changed into fresh, warm pajamas, I curled into the bed to avoid the spinning room around me.

"So you come up here because you need to be alone to grieve," Chris said, sitting heavily on the edge of the bed, "and then you immediately take off to get stoned and drunk with a bunch of strangers? I don't understand you."

"Well then, that makes two of us." I curled the blanket up to my chin. "Cause I don't understand me either."

"Is this what you're planning on doing up here while I'm gone?"

I hiccuped again, miserably. "Does it really matter?"

"Yes, dammit!" He pulled the blanket from me, resting his hands on each side of my hips as he looked me over. "Why won't you just talk to me? If you want to get drunk and stoned, I'll get drunk and stoned with you. Why did it have to be with strangers? Why can't it be me?"

I rolled my eyes. "Because you always do exactly what you're doing now. You're making this an attack on you."

"How could it not be an attack on me, Ally? You won't talk to me. You won't even look at me! You won't get out of bed for me but the minute we get out here, you get on a boat and go swimming with a bunch of twenty-year-olds! How do you think that makes me feel? Who the hell are you lately?"

"I don't know," I huffed, closing my eyes.

"Well, you need to figure it out." He removed his hands and turned away from me. "Because this person you're becoming is breaking my heart."

Chapter Forty

"Details, all of them." Lilly grinned. She'd changed into her shorts but was still swimming in Jim's "Mama tried" t-shirt as she looped her arm around mine.

"Lill," I yawned, "I need to wash off and change clothes." I turned her toward the cave opening, desperate to change out of the silk dress and into my shorts and boots.

"I'll go with you." She squeezed my arm and gasped suddenly as we reached the cave to find Jim modeling her flowy white dress at the entrance.

"How you like it? Eh?" He spun around, holding the fabric out at his legs. "Ain't so fun watchin' someone else traipse around in yer' clothes now, is it?"

"James Lee Jackson, you take that off right this instant." She let go of my arm to smack at him but he dodged, dancing around her, the dress threatening to burst where he'd pulled it up to his chest.

"Good morning." Phil appeared at my side, still smelling heavily of whiskey, his hand touching my lower back, a little too low for my liking. I shifted out of his reach, pretending not to have noticed as I kept my attention on Lilly and Jim.

"You take mine off first!" He circled. "Y'aint get to grab up a man's clothes whenever ye' like. I done told ye' last night it ain't happenin! Take off my dang shirt!"

She growled in frustration and lunged at him, grabbing a handful of his hair. "Take it off before you rip it!" she hissed.

"You sing beautifully," Phil continued, running a finger over my arm and once again hovering too close for comfort.

"Thank you." I forced a smile, quickly moving my arm away. I saw the loneliness in his eyes when he looked at me and I swiftly looked away.

"Ay ay ay!" Jim squirmed, then froze, his face shifting from playful to serious. "Shhhh! What's 'at noise?"

We all froze, and our eyes shifted upwards.

"Birds!" he shouted, freeing himself of Lilly's grip. "Sweet Jesus, it's birds!!!"

Thousands of them flew over and we all stood dumbfounded as their shadows passed over us for what felt like an eternity. There hadn't been a single bird on the island. The sound of them now was deafening.

"Hot damn!" he shouted, wiggling the dress down his legs so he stood in his white boxer shorts. "Eggs! By Got, we're gonna have us some dang breakfast!"

He bolted back inside the cave as Jack came running from the creek, his hair soaking wet and his shirt balled up under his arm. "Did you see them?"

"We saw them!" I shouted back, smiling with relief as I moved away from Phil to wrap my arms around Jack when he'd reached us.

"Get up, Kyle!" Jim's voice bounced off the cave walls, and he reappeared, hopping from one leg to the other as he pulled his jeans on. "They'll be headin' for the clearing—for the tall grass up 'er." He sat with a thud to shove his feet into his boots. "Shirt, woman!"

Lilly still stood, looking up. "Where'd they come from?"

"We call them Kolea," Magna informed her, emerging from the side of the cave with a pile of clothes under one arm. She knelt to pick Lilly's dress up off the ground and added it to her pile. "They migrate to the islands from the north when it gets too cold."

"They taste good?" Jim asked, standing and extending his palm to Lilly. "SHIRT."

Lilly absentmindedly slid her arms through the sleeves, removing the shirt to stand in her white tank and shorts, handing it to him while keeping her eyes focused on the sky. "How long will they stay?"

"Few months." Magna pursed her lips. "Sometimes longer."

Jim popped his head through his shirt. "Gonna get up 'er and set us some traps. We'll be havin' squab kebabs for supper, yes ma'am! Kyle! Get yer ass out here, we got work to do! You comin' Hoss?"

Jack slid his shirt over his head. "Right behind you." He kissed my forehead and jogged to catch up with an already sprinting Jim. Kyle and Phil followed behind them.

I stretched my arms wide over my head. "Alright, Lill," I wrapped my arm around her, snapping her back to reality, "let's go clean up. I've got some questions of my own for you."

At the creek, against the delightful soundtrack of birds chirping in the distance, I dove headfirst into the cool water, letting it wash over my tired body. I emerged to see Lilly tip toeing into the water slowly in her underwear, one arm protectively covering her breasts. "Stop rolling your eyes at me," she hissed. "It's cold."

I splashed the water over my face and down my hair. "Just get in already. It's not gonna get any warmer."

"Ah ah ah," she breathed as she lowered herself down, careful not to wet the hair she'd knotted on the top of her head as she moved to my side. "Alright, I'm in." She grinned with chattering teeth. "Tell me about last night."

"I will, but first," I tilted my head to one side, "you tell me. What are you after with Jim?"

She rolled her eyes. "I have no idea what you're talking about."

I splashed water at her. "Don't play innocent with me. What are you up to?"

She touched her hair to ensure it was still dry. "Nothing." She let out a long sigh. "I'm just... I don't know... he's not terrible looking when he's quiet. And it's fun getting him all worked up... and I just thought, I don't know, it might be fun... to do... other stuff."

"Lill," I shook my head, "I don't think he sees you like that..."

"He could though... and I..." She softly scrubbed her arm under the water. "Oh, don't look at me like that. You have Jack.

Anna and Bruce have been dancing around it for months...
Gramma has Grandpa... I have needs too, ya know."

"Oh honey, I don't know. I don't want to see you get hurt."

"Hurt?!" she scoffed. "By *Jim?* Pfft." She raised her hand out
of the water to inspect her nails. "Alaina, please. He's got needs
just as much as I do and he'd be lucky to have me."

"Just..." I sighed as I saw the desperation cross over her face.
"Don't get your hopes up, love."

I could see her hopes were already up though, and I knew Jim
well enough by now to know that beneath all the flirting and rough
exterior, he was a perfect gentleman; one who looked at Lilly with
the affectionate adoration of an older brother—not a potential
lover.

"I'll be fine." She pulled her cupped hands to her face and let
the water wash down her cheeks. "Now..." She rubbed her closed
eyes, opening one in my direction. "Your turn. How was he? How
many times... where?"

I tilted my head back, letting the cool water soak my hair and
cover my ears before I returned to eye level. "Oh, he was amazing,
Lill. I can't remember the last time I've smiled this much. It was
all so... perfect."

She grinned, singing, "You loooove him."

"Stop." I laughed as she circled me.

"Is he big?" She dramatically demonstrated size with her
hands, eyes wide.

"Lilly!" I splashed her hair.

She lowered her mouth under the water and bounced her
eyebrows, coming back up to spit water in my direction. "He is,
isn't he?"

At that, I placed my palms on her perfectly knotted bun and
dunked her below the water. She came up spitting and gasping,
laughing loudly with her eyes squeezed shut. "Oh, Jack!" she
mocked, curling her forearms over my head to dunk my head under
water. "Take me now with your giant—

"Can I..." Anna's tiny voice caught our attention, and we both
looked toward the edge of the water where she stood. "Do you
mind if I join you?"

Lilly dunked my head under water as she pushed off toward Anna. "Not at all!" she said as I came up. "Come in! I was just trying to pry all the dirty details out of Lainey! Perhaps you can help me!"

Anna smiled and pulled her t-shirt off. I'd never seen her without clothes before and noticed, as she turned to remove her capris, she had small pink scars all along the milky white skin on her back and legs.

"Oh, Anna," I gasped, coming closer as she lowered into the water. "What happened?"

"It's nothing." She sank down quickly into the water, covering her shoulders with her hands as she joined us.

"That's not nothing," Lilly insisted, touching a scar that ran down her shoulder, an action that caused her to flinch. "What happened here?"

"Really, Lilly, it's nothing." She moved away from Lilly's reach to my side. "It was a long time ago."

"Your husband?" Lilly persisted. "He did that to you? You mentioned you were divorced..."

Anna sighed. "Yes, but it was a long time ago, and I left him for it."

"That sonofabitch." Lilly's face turned red. "How could anyone do that to someone like you? Oh, let me get back home so I can find him and kill him."

Anna laughed nervously. "I'm alright now, and that's what I wanted to talk to you about... going home, that is. We're all well enough to travel now... and... well, I'd like to get back to Liam. We have a lifeboat... and a raft."

I hadn't thought of how hard our time here had been on Anna. I could see the bags under her eyes; the wear of it all. She'd kept herself occupied caring for all of us, but no one was caring for her. She looked pale and she was too thin.

"That boat is rotten, and the raft is too dangerous." Lilly tilted her head to one side. "Don't you think we're safer here watching for ships?"

She looked anxious. "That's the thing. No one's watching for ships... I'm scared we're getting too comfortable here... and maybe *you* want to stay." She looked at me, her eyes welling with tears. "But I *have* to get back. I have to get to my son. His father... if they think I'm dead, his father might push to take him."

I could see the worry for her son on her face, and seeing the scars his father had left on her, I knew she was terrified he might do the same to Liam.

I touched her shoulder. "I had no idea. We'll talk to everyone tonight. We'll figure something out."

"Its too dangerous," Lilly continued. "Gramma and grandpa couldn't get back on the water. What if there's another storm?"

I narrowed my eyes at Lilly, pleading with her to stop. I knew we couldn't get on the lifeboat or the raft, but my heart ached for Anna. If I'd been in her shoes, I'd have insisted we go the first day, but she waited for us to heal. She healed us and giving her hope was the least we could do. "Maybe we could build something stronger," I suggested. "A boat. We have tools and fabric for a sail. There are plenty of materials to work with."

Anna nodded, wiping her wet lashes. "You think they'd be up for it?"

I squeezed her shoulder. "I *know* they will. We'll build a boat, Anna. We'll get you home to your son. We owe you that."

Chapter Forty-One

The sun was setting behind me as I hoisted the wicker pack of coconuts over my shoulder. "I'm heading back!" I called down to Lilly and Anna, who were at the water holding spears patiently.

I turned into the trees and started uphill when an arm wrapped around my waist and hauled me off to one side behind a cluster of boulders. Before I could process what was happening, Jack's lips came down over mine and his arms curled around me.

I raised on my toes and returned the kiss, parting his lips softly as I let the basket of coconuts slide off my shoulder and folded my arms around his neck.

"I've been waiting to do that all day," he breathed, grinning as he curled a piece of my hair around his finger, "You know," he ran his thumb over my lips, "I've never wanted anyone the way I want you. I miss you the instant I can't see you... and I dream of nothing but you all day and all night."

Jim's head poked out over the rock wall behind Jack's head. "Ye' gonna have to dream a little longer, Romeo." He grinned at me when my eyes met his. "We got feathers to pluck."

Jack groaned as Jim's head disappeared beyond the rock, his voice echoing back as he made his way toward camp, "Come on wit' yas!"

"I swear," Jack blew out, kissing my forehead, "if I don't kill that man by the time this is all over, it'll be a miracle."

"Well, we might need him for a little while longer." I smiled, unwrapping my arms from him and sliding my hand into his. "We should catch up. I need to talk to both of you."

He eyed me cautiously as he knelt to pick up my basket, slinging it over his shoulder before letting me lead him up toward camp.

We caught up with Jim about halfway up. He was carrying a basket that was overflowing with fat brown and white feathered birds. "Jim." I placed myself between him and Jack, breathing a little heavily with the effort. My legs were shorter than his and my leg was still healing. "I'll help with these. I want to talk to you." I looked up at Jack. "...both of you."

Jim looked at me, then Jack. "Told ye' she'd come lookin' for the more experienced man some time." He winked at me. "Didn't think it'd be so soon though, bless your heart."

I laughed and squeezed Jack's hand. "I actually wanted to talk to you guys about building a boat."

"A boat?" they both asked in unison, the two of them looking down at me as if I'd proposed building a rocket and flying to the moon.

"Well, why not?" I snapped, feeling defensive. "We have rope, wood, fabric for a sail... Now that Bruce is healed, we need to figure out a plan to get off the island. Jim, you were the one who wanted to get back out on the water as soon as your arms healed."

"Well," he looked around, "I wasn't in my right mind. I don't think we ought to be puttin' ourselves in harm's way when we got an island full of resources right here. Might be best we wait it out."

My cheeks flushed. "You don't want to go home?"

He stopped, spinning to face me. "Not rightly, no ma'am." He looked at Jack. "You gonna lift her off that damn ankle or you waitin' for me to do it?"

"I'm fine," I assured him and spun toward Jack who was already shifting the basket on his shoulder to prepare to lift me. "And you? You don't want to go home either?"

Jack looked helplessly toward Jim, then back down at me. "Well, no... " He tilted his head to one side. "Why now, all of a sudden?"

He positioned himself to lift me and I moved a step out of his grip, scowling up between the two of them. "Anna needs to get home to her son, Bud and Bertie need medicine we don't have— have you heard her coughing at night? Magna has a husband and daughter waiting for her, and Isobel and Kyle have their whole lives ahead of them. Lilly's just graduated college." I looked at Jim. "You'd deny her of the fashion career she's dreamt of her whole life? We can't ask them to stay here because we're comfortable."

Jim kicked the dirt at his feet. "Well... hell, I don't know squat about buildin' a boat or sailin' one neither."

Jack cleared his throat. "I do. Well, not about building one, but I have a sailboat. I could draw up a diagram of what we'd need to build one."

Jim kept his head down. "We won't never see lil' Izzy again." He glanced at me. "You know that, right?"

I touched his arm. "We don't know that."

"Assuming we don't drown, I reckon I won't never see most of y'all again." He turned and continued walking toward camp.

"Jim," I hopped to catch up beside him, "that's not true." I folded my arm around his. "We're a family now. We'll see each other all the time."

"Oh, quit feeling sorry for yourself, Jackson," Jack mocked from the other side of me. "On top of your lottery winnings, do you have any idea what kind of money you're about to come into from the lawsuit we'll have on our hands when we get back? Phil says we'll never have to work a day in our lives again. We'll all be able to travel anywhere we want, anytime. And if I have to spend that money to drag my ass down to some podunk town in the middle of Oklahoma in order to smack you around, I will." He stifled a smile in my direction. "Now... if the woman wants a boat, we're going to have to build her a boat, might as well quit moping about it."

Jim huffed, shifting his basket and freeing himself of my grip. He walked a few more steps before stopping. "Now dammit, Hoss, she ain't even gonna be able to get *on* the dang boat if you don't get her off that Got damn ankle like I told ye!"

At that, Jack hoisted me over his free shoulder, forcing me to giggle wildly as he quickly caught up to Jim's side.

"Pain in the ass women," Jim mumbled, taking several more steps before he sighed. "It'd take time…"

He pondered it as we approached camp. "We'll wanna build it big enough to be able to handle the worst of 'em storms… with room enough for all of us and plenty of supplies. Wonder if we cain't catch and keep some of 'em birds.. Maybe even some piglets… and crab… if we can figure out a way to keep 'em alive, we'd be better off. Even better off if we could breed 'em. And I sure as shit don't wanna be sailin' off in no Wilson-Castaway-raggedy-ass raft that falls apart the minute we get out there. We cain't use that rotting lifeboat… we'll wanna start over. If we're doin' this, we're gonna take our sweet ass time to build it right."

Bruce appeared at Jim's side, pulling a bird from the basket and whistling. "Now this I can work with! What are we *building right*?"

"A boat," I grunted, my voice competing with Jack's shoulder against my abdomen. "Put me down now."

He set me lightly on the sandy dirt before slipping the basket of coconuts down his other shoulder.

"A boat?" Bruce raised an eyebrow, sitting down on a rock near our fire pit and beginning to pull feathers from the bird he'd stolen.

"Yes, and before Anna gets back," I placed an empty basket at his feet and snagged a bird of my own before sitting down beside him, "there's something else."

I filled them in on my conversation with Anna; told them about the scars, her ex-husband, and her worry over her son.

"Christ," Bruce said under his breath, ripping the feathers from his bird more violently. "Who could do that to her?"

"A soon-to-be-dead summbitch if I got anything to say 'bout it," Jim snarled, tossing a handful of feathers into the basket.

Jack nodded in agreement. "We've got a lot of work to do." He tossed the bird he'd been plucking into a clay pot and reached in the basket to pull another, holding it out to Jim and grinning as he pointed to a spot on its neck. "This one's mine too."

Jim waved him off as he continued. "We'll want to store as much water as we can hold, smoke a hell of a lot of fish, and cut down a whole mess of trees."

"And we need someone up on the summit keeping an eye out," I chimed in. "We've been down for two days now with no one keeping watch. We can't keep doing that. What if another ship comes while we're all down here?"

Jim straightened. "We're gonna need to set up a schedule and stick to it now. It's my turn to go up still and I'll go first thing, but 'for I do, let's get this figured."

"No, no," Bruce interjected. "It's my turn to go up. I'm walking just fine now. It might take me a little longer to get there, but I'll go. There's no sense in me being down here with so much to do that I can't help with yet."

"Where are you going?" Anna asked, her arm in Lilly's as they approached, both beaming as they showed off their two fresh groupers.

"To the summit." He grinned at her as she held the fish out to him. "I can't help build you a boat, but I can sit up there and watch for ships."

Her eyes glossed over and she looked at me. I smiled and nodded.

"We'll get ye' home, I promise," Jim said as he struck the flint and steel to start the evening's fire. "And so help me Got, I'll kill 'at summbitch dead if he's laid a finger on your boy when we get there."

"And I'll hide the body," Lilly added, depositing her fish at the cleaning table and taking her usual seat next to Jim.

"Oh," Anna sniffled, a tear rolling down her cheek as she sat down hard beside Bruce, "thank you."

"It's gonna take time," Jack said softly. "We want to build a real boat, something strong, sturdy. We can't risk going out on those waves in something that might fall apart. You'll have to bear with us. Be patient. We don't know how long we'll be out there so we'll have to stock food, water, and supplies."

She nodded, her lip quivering. "Thank you. Thank you."

"It's gonna be alright," Bruce said, petting her head as she curled into him. "We're going home."

'*Home,*' I thought to myself as the fire roared in front of me.

'*Where is home to me now? Where would I go? I can't go back to the house I lived in with Chris. Not now... Not with Jack...*'

Jim flung his bird in the basket and rose to grab a stack of skewers near the cave's entrance. "We'll have to do it like the vikings did it. We got tools but no nails. Gonna have to overlap the boards and rivet em' together. Fill any gaps in with moss."

'*Would I go to my mother? To Jack's home in L.A.? What will life with Jack even look like outside the island? Would he want to live with me? He's still Jack Volmer... the Jack Volmer. Will he love me the same outside the island or will I just be another one of his ex-flings once he's suddenly returned to the limelight?*'

Bruce shifted, pulling out the knife to begin gutting and skewering the birds. "There's nails in those cases in the cave. Maybe we could pull those?" He carefully balanced the skewers over the fire, one by one. "What about the dinghy?"

'*Will it be my face smeared across the tabloids—Jack Volmer back from the dead with a redhead at his hip—What home would I go to?*'

"Well, first I thought maybe we might use it as a base fer whatever we build, but I think we orta' keep it intact as a lifeboat in case somethin' goes wrong out there. Then we'd have the lifeboat and the raft."

Phil and Kyle approached with another basket, this one full of eggs, momentarily distracting me from my thoughts. Phil leaned heavily against Kyle as they came into camp, dropping the basket and falling onto his butt near the fire. He hiccuped. "I fuggin' hate this island."

He was drunk again, and the sun had barely set. I wondered if this was an issue we would need to address sooner than later.

"Well, that's good." Lilly rolled her eyes. "Cause we're leaving it soon. We're building a boat."

"PFFT. You can't build a boat." He hiccuped again. "How are *you* gonna build a boat?" He reached into the basket and pulled out the almost empty bottle of port.

"Shut up, dad," Kyle groaned, taking a seat next to Bertie. "Jim, can I help?"

At this, Phil burst into laughter. "You're gonna help? With your one little spaghetti arm?"

"Shut up dad, you're drunk."

"'Course ye' can, son." Jim shook his head at Phil. "We'll start drawin' up plans in the mornin' and then we'll need yer help haulin' wood down to the beach. That one arm'll do just fine."

Phil laid his head back against the rock of the cave and closed his eyes, a soft snore emitting from his limp body within minutes.

"Did he always drink like 'at?" Jim closed one eye as he observed Phil's unconscious body. "I noticed he's been takin' pretty heavy to it since we found it."

Kyle nodded. "He's always been in and out of the twelve-step program. He left us when I was about seven. This trip is the first extended amount of time I've spent with him since then. My mom didn't want me spending more time than I had to around him when he was drinking. I've seen him drunk more than I've seen him sober."

Jim made a "tsk" noise and reached for a skewer from the fire. He cautiously bit into one, breathing audibly against its heat as he moved it around his mouth. "Oh, that's damn good Bruce, DAMN good. Tastes just like chicken."

Bruce grinned proudly, pulling skewers off the heat and handing them out to each of us.

"Ye' want me to try to set him straight in the mornin?" Jim took another bite. "Christ almighty, that's hot!" He breathed dramatically.

"Honestly," Kyle spun the skewer in his hand, "it's best to just let him be. Arguing or attempting to reason with him about it has never done much good. If anything, it makes it worse. He only quits when *he* wants to."

Jim nodded. "Alright then. You steer clear of him, though. Ye' don't need to be dealin' with it on yer own. You stick by me. Now, Hoss...." Jim opened up the journal he'd been carrying around with him, flipping to a place he had marked, "I been readin' this journal and there's this part that don't make no sense."

He turned a page, frowning over it as he moved his finger to find the words. "*The storm has caused significant damage to the ship's hull. We've lost most of the crew with no signs of them in the ocean. The only of us left still on board are myself and my two New York guests, Frankie and Dutch. Even the crew below deck seem to have just vanished. Perhaps most disturbing, however, is our location. Before the storm, we were roughly 27°39'14"N, 143°50'33"W, but we are now showing a reading at 9°33'52"S 150°30'10"W. Initially, I believed the chronometer might be faulty, but then I confirmed this reading with the astrolabe. This puts us almost two thousand miles Southwest in a matter of fifteen minutes. There is no logical explanation for it. I've lost my entire crew and I am afraid my guests will not be pleased that we will not only have to find a place to dock and unload their merchandise in order to repair the hull, but that we are nowhere near docking on the west coast by their deadline.*"

Jim looked up from the journal. "Two thousand miles... that storm took 'em two thousand miles off course in less than fifteen minutes. How ye' think that's possible and what if it did the same to us? What if we're further south and further west than we think we are?"

I blew on the little charred pieces of meat on my skewer, cautiously biting into one. It tasted exactly like chicken. I closed my eyes and let the familiar flavor fill me.

Jack pondered as he took a bite of his own meat. "It's *not* possible. Maybe he was mistaken? You said he was sailing from Hawaii?" He frowned. "If he was about halfway into his trip like you say he was that would've put him pretty close to where we would've flown over when the storm hit, don't you think?"

Jim nodded. "Yeah, I do. Ye' think we mighta' got sucked up into some kind of Pacific Ocean version of the Bermuda Triangle?"

Jack laughed. "No. If I had to guess, I'd say the chronometer was broken and maybe he wasn't using the astrolabe properly. I'd bet we are probably very close to his initial readings—between Hawaii and California somewhere. It takes between two and three weeks on a boat to get from Hawaii to California... and that's *with* a motor... I figure if we can average five knots with good wind, assuming we're halfway there, maybe we could make it in ten or eleven days?"

"Well, that's to the shore." Jim bit off a huge chunk of his meat, moving it to one side to continue talking. "We'd have to hit some kind of shippin' route long before then. Don't ye' think?"

Jack nodded. "Definitely."

"Still… this man was a lifelong sailor." He frowned, re-reading the page in the journal. "And he knew the ocean well. He'd know how to use the astrolabe, wouldn't he? If he says he was off course, we orta take it into account. What if we're closer to his second reading?"

Jack sighed. "Then we'd be headed for South America. They seemed to be mostly off course to the south… we'd still make land in maybe… twelve days… then we go home."

'Where's home, Alaina?'

I took another bite, trying to avoid my nagging thoughts.

Jim shook his head, tossing his skewer into the fire, "I don't know Hoss… somethin' just feels strange about the whole thing."

'Where's home? And who will I be to him when we get there?'

Conversation around me grew muffled as my ears began to ring. The smoke from the fire mixed with panic and the air became suddenly too thick. I rose and excused myself, walking to the backside of our cave to lean myself up against the cool rock.

I closed my eyes and exhaled, cheeks burning.

'What am I doing here? With him? What if he created a fairy tale with me to distract himself from the severity of the situation we're stuck in? And I fell for it…. What if we go back and I'm tossed to the side? Did I let go of my life to be someone's fling? What am I even going back to?'

I could do the island. I could live a fairy tale here just fine, but home… the word had no meaning now.

I paced. *'You're being paranoid… right? Yes, he's an actor, but that doesn't mean it's all an act… you're not that naïve. Are you?'*

I closed my eyes, and my heart stung. I pictured his arms around me on the raft, his hands on my forehead, the sudden sweetness he'd taken with me by the fire and on the summit as I fell apart… Had he targeted me from the beginning? And had I let myself fall for it? Had I fallen completely in love with an illusion he'd painted me?

I ran my hands through my hair. *'It can't be fake... can it?'*

"Red?"

I stopped pacing and turned toward his voice. I could just make him out in the fading light. He was leaned casually up against the cave, watching me with his lips slightly curved up on one side. He crossed his arms at his waist, holding his skewer of half eaten meat to one side. "You keep doin' that, we're gonna have to pull you out of the hole you make in that sand."

I hugged my arms over my heart, feeling exposed and vulnerable as he scanned me. "What happens now, Jack?"

He tilted his head to one side as he crossed one leg over the other in front of him. "Well, I had a mind to come back here and steal you away but... apparently I'm interrupting. Should I maybe come back later?" He grinned.

"Stop smiling at me like that, you know what I mean."

His lip twitched, and he straightened. "I assure you, my dear, I haven't the slightest idea what you mean."

I huffed, my arms stiffening. I'd never felt so self-conscious before, and I didn't like it.

"I mean, what happens to us when we get back home? Who will I be to you when you're suddenly Jack Volmer again and we're not alone on this island anymore?"

He laughed playfully. "You say my full name like it's a bad word."

He pushed himself off the rock and stepped forward, but I backed away. "Jack, I'm serious. Is this..." I swallowed. "Is this real? If it's not, you have to tell me. Please tell me... Am I just something to pass the time here with?"

His expression shifted to mischievous as he came closer, scanning me from head to toe. "Oh, I could think of much worse ways to pass the time here."

He reached out to touch my arm, but I jerked away. "Did you bait me? Did you rehearse *all* of it? Was it all some scripted narrative to get me to fall for you?"

He smirked. "Did it work?"

I growled. "This isn't a joke to me!"

He wrapped an arm around my waist. "Aw, come on Red, tired of playing already?"

I squirmed against him but he held me in place, tossing his skewer into the dirt.

"Jack, stop it, I'm not playing. What happens when we build the boat? What happens to us if we get rescued? Where would you go? Where would *I* go? I don't know how to be this... this... what am I to you?"

I tried to wiggle free of him, but he held me there, smiling down at me. "Dammit, are you so dense that you can't see what you are to me? Have I not shown you what you are to me? How much I love you?"

His smile faded as he searched my face. "If you wanna get on a boat, I'll build you a boat and go anywhere you want to be. If you wanna stay on this island, I'll stay on this island forever with you."

His grip eased, and he ran his thumb along my shoulder, his expression softening. "I didn't bait you, and I didn't script any narrative for you."

He slid his palm up to cup my face. "Alaina, I *love* you. And nothing else matters to me. NOTHING matters but you. I'll go where you go, live where you live." He smiled. "Hell, I'll even change my name if that's what you want. Your happiness is my happiness and wherever you are is home to me. I don't know what happens next but I know I'll be next to you for it."

I let my arms relax and slid my palms up to rest on his chest. Was I being ridiculous? I'd never felt so vulnerable, so exposed... I'd only ever really loved Chris and was so confident he wouldn't hurt me that when he actually did I'd been knocked completely off my feet. Jack... he *could* hurt me far worse in the real world, and that terrified me.

His lips hovered over mine. "I'll go where you go, Red," he whispered. "Assuming I'm not just something for *you* to pass the time with? Tell me you really do love me too?"

I closed my eyes and nodded, sighing as his lips unlocked mine, soft and tender, his fingers delicately cupping my face and gradually erasing the panic that had filled my heart.

He ran his fingertips softly up my forearm, "I can't presume to know the life that led you to me," he brushed my cheek with his thumb, "but I swear, I'll never let you forget that you're loved or doubt that you deserve to be again."

Chapter Forty-Two

"We're going out to dinner, get dressed," Cece announced from the screen door of my cabin.

I lowered the book I'd been reading and stretched my legs against the arm of the loveseat, peering out over the back of the couch to see my sister dressed in her finest new black Marc Jacobs dress, her bright blonde hair perfectly curled with diamond earrings glistening in the afternoon sun. "Out? Where?"

"To a pizza place down in Cook. I have to get out of here for a while before I lose my mind and so do you."

The idea of leaving camp did sound promising. I hadn't gone anywhere in weeks. I'd spent that time falling into a routine at the camp, spending my days helping Cece clean cabins, checking in the guests, running the little store, or babysitting Maddy. I'd put off going back to work, enjoying the simplicity of helping around camp in contrast to the high-stress environment of agency ad design. Chris hadn't been thrilled with me for it, but my bosses had assured me my job would be waiting for me when I was ready.

Chris had been true to his word, driving the eleven hours to visit me every Friday, then the eleven hours back home alone every Sunday. It was always the same. He'd try to play or laugh or talk to me, and for reasons I couldn't explain, I kept him at a distance. I tried to force it, tried not to tense up every time his hand grazed mine, but I just couldn't fully get back to being the person he'd married. He'd notice every time and by the time Sunday would roll around, we were both fed up with the fighting that would result from it.

If I was honest, I had stopped crying for Evelyn the first time I'd watched his truck disappear into the trees leaving the camp. I'd even allowed myself to laugh, spending evenings on the lake with Doug and whatever campers were up on any given day. But every weekend Chris's truck would pull back in, and with it, the pain of having lost her would fill me all over again. I didn't think I'd ever be ready to go home.

"You're wearing *that* to a pizza place in Cook?" I laughed, sitting up and stretching my arms.

"You're damn right I'm wearing *this* to a pizza place in Cook!" She turned to one side and the other, checking herself out. "Where the hell else am I going to wear it?"

I smirked. "Alright, let me change."

"Meet me at the big house." She began to turn around, but stopped short. "Oh! Stop and light the sauna on your way over. Cabin nine booked it for five o'clock."

I frowned. "Why can't you light the sauna?"

She groaned. "Because I didn't spend the last two hours getting dolled up like this to stink like a campfire when we get there. Just do it."

I rolled my eyes. "Fine. I'll be up in a bit."

In stark contrast to my sister, my process of getting ready consisted of rolling my hair up into a bun on the top of my head, throwing on a pair of jeans, and applying a small amount of mascara to my very light eyelashes so I at least looked somewhat feminine. I grabbed a sweater, slid my feet into my tennis shoes, and jogged down to the small log sauna that sat in the woods off the lake.

I loved jogging in Minnesota. The air felt different, fresher and sweeter with the pines, making me somehow feel lighter.

I quickly circled to the side of the sauna, stacking my arms with the wood we kept there, then awkwardly fumbled against the pile to open the door, cursing Cece as the logs scratched at my forearms.

As I entered, a female shrieked, and I squinted against the darkness to find the newest young blond camper in a questionable position on the bottom bench beneath a shirtless Doug.

"It's just A.J.," he laughed down at the girl, sliding his hand out from under her shirt to wave innocently and blow me a kiss.

"Didn't mean to interrupt." I blushed. "Cabin nine has this booked for five. I'll just let you finish up here and be on my way. You can light it when you're... ah... done." I dropped the logs noisily on the floor near the stove, avoiding looking at them.

"You going to get pizza?" Doug asked casually, resting his cheek on his palm when I'd looked back toward them.

I cleared my throat, lowering my eyes as the girl buried her face in his shoulder. "Yes. We're leaving in about ten minutes."

"Oh, I'll come with." He giggled, grabbing his shirt and hastily sliding it back over his head. "Sorry, Lauren." He kissed her cheek. "I'll find you later."

She whispered something to him and he scoffed. "Who, A.J? She's not going to tell anybody! It's fine. Go head back to camp and I'll come find you when I get back."

He stood up and extended his hand to her, pulling her up hurriedly and smoothing her very messy hair before he nonchalantly walked her to the sauna door and opened it for her.

I rolled my eyes after she'd kissed him goodbye and the door closed behind her. "What's she, like sixteen?"

"I would never!" he teased, "She just turned eighteen." He smiled proudly, kneeling to pile wood into his arms.

"I don't know how you do it," I laughed.

"Do what?" He stacked the logs into the small stove that sat beneath the rocks.

"Manage to treat these girls the way you do and still have them drooling over you."

He sighed, adjusting the stack and feeling around for the lighter. "They're on vacation. I'm one of the attractions. They go home all giddy and doe-eyed until a week passes and they've forgotten all about me to move on to the real guys in their life."

"Well, that doesn't sound like much fun for you."

He smirked, the spark from the lighter lighting one side of his face. "Did you not see where my hand was? Or more importantly, where *her* hand was? It's plenty fun for me!"

"You're terrible."

As we exited the sauna to head up to the big house, Doug looped his arm through mine. "I don't sleep with them you know… well, not all of them… mostly we just fool around. I'm quite good at fooling around."

"I have no doubt you are," I laughed. "What with all the experience. How old are you anyway?"

"Twenty two." He turned us off the trail and onto the dirt road that wound up to the big house.

"And you don't ever think about maybe sticking with one girl, something that lasts a little longer than a week? Falling in love? Maybe even getting married someday?"

"I've considered it." He nodded. "But I'm not in any hurry. I like the freedom of being able to go where I want when I want without having anyone to ask me where I've been. I like that I can just be me without someone finding faults in it… wanting me to change… trying to fix me."

"You know, not all relationships are like that."

He shrugged. "Yeah, they are… you just don't see it when you're in one. There's always something you could be doing better or something you're not doing that they want you to do… or you go out to have fun and you get that look of disappointment when you're not back at a time they deem reasonable. I'll get married someday, sure. But right now, I just want to enjoy being utterly and guiltlessly me for a while."

'Utterly and guiltlessly me.'

He had a point. Chris had never made it a point to list out my faults, but he didn't need to list them for me to see his acknowledgement of them. I knew the look of disappointment well… particularly in the past few months.

"There you are, I'm starving!" Cece waved us up as she stood impatiently at the passenger side of their Land Rover, the four-inch heels of her black Louboutin pumps digging into the gravel.

"Where's Maddy?" I asked as we approached the vehicle and she opened her door.

"Owen's parents are keeping her overnight." She grinned. "Mama's having some cocktails tonight!" She looked up at the house and shouted aggressively, "Come on, O!"

"Mind if I tag along?" Doug batted his eyes at her while Owen hurried out the front door. "If I have to eat fish again tonight, I'll just die."

Cece frowned at him, then looked at me. "A.J., if he bats those eyes at you, you run! He's always up to something. Please tell me he hasn't tried to make a move on you?"

"EW!" Doug shouted, much to my horror. It wasn't that I wanted to be flirted with, but I didn't expect the notion of flirting with me to warrant an *'ew.'*

"No! He's been a perfect gentleman!" I laughed and pulled the hair on top of his head. "And what do you mean, ew?!"

He leaned close and whispered, "Just a tactic to drive her off our scent, my *dearest* love. I'll bat my eyes at you all you want." He straightened and grinned. "Now, can I come eat pizza with my favorite cousins?"

Cece, now half inside the SUV, pointed at him. "Yes. Just so I can keep my eye on you, you little man-boy-slut. I know you've been getting handsy with little Lauren Burkhart too. You do know her father is a marine and will absolutely kill you, don't you?"

I laughed out loud and opened the back passenger side door, sliding in across the tan leather to find myself wedged between Maddy's bright pink, crumb-filled car seat and Doug, who immediately stretched out his long legs.

As Owen backed us out and put the vehicle in drive, I watched as Cece laid her hand effortlessly over his on the center console, her bright diamond tennis bracelet and wedding bands shimmering in the sunlight that shone through the sunroof as he curled his fingers around hers. For the first time since I'd arrived, I felt a small stab at my heart as the action made me suddenly ache for Chris.

I looked back to Doug, who was staring happily out the window at the blur of green pines; a pair of earbuds wedged into his ears. What did *I* need? To be utterly and guiltlessly myself or the familiarity of laying my hand over my husband's? Did I want to be comforted, or did I want to be distracted for a little while longer?

Several hours, an extra large pizza, and far too many vodka-cranberry drinks later, we arrived back at camp. Cece had removed her shoes and fell out of the SUV, giggling loudly as Owen hurried around the front of the vehicle to assist her.

"You're so handsome," she cooed as he pulled her up to stand by her underarms. "Isn't he just so handsome, A.J.?"

I laughed, wobbling a little myself against the gravel driveway. "Sure he is."

"I'm gonna get you so naked." She tapped his nose with her pointer finger and began to topple over. "You won't even know what hit you, you'll be so naked."

"Okay then." Doug shook his head. "Goodnight freaks." He placed a hand on the center of my back and urged me in the opposite direction. "I'll just be out walking A.J. home and avoiding all the..." he snarled, "naked."

"You don't have to walk me back," I said between us as we stepped onto the dirt road. "I know the way. We wouldn't want to keep Lauren waiting!"

"The waiting is all part of the appeal," he said proudly. "Besides, she's camped way back in the woods and I don't want to miss this." He pointed ahead toward the lake.

"Miss what?" I hiccuped loudly.

"See that haze in the sky?"

I squinted out past the trees to the lake where I could indeed see a faint white-green haze forming over the water. "Yes."

"That's about to turn amazing. Have you ever seen the northern lights?"

My heart raced. "No. Am I going to?!"

"In a few minutes, yes. Come on!" He took my hand and pulled me toward my cabin, speeding up into a jog, forcing me to stumble awkwardly behind him until we reached the steps. "I'll grab a blanket. You go sit on the dock and prepare to be amazed."

Obediently, I split off at the front door to take a seat on the small cushioned couch that sat on my private dock, shivering against the cool night air as I stared up in anticipation. I'd always wanted to see them. So had Chris. My heart stung that he wouldn't be here to experience it with me. But then the sky lit up in a dance of green and purple, and I was mesmerized.

I felt a blanket come over me but was too entranced to look away. I forgot who I was, forgot who Chris was. Even Evelyn disappeared momentarily so that there was nothing but the exquisite rays of light whirling across the sky amid a blanket of stars.

My phone vibrated in my lap, pulling me from my stupor, and I looked down to see "Chris" on the phone's window. I closed my eyes and blew out, knowing that if I answered and told him what I was experiencing in that moment, he'd make me feel guilty. Guilty for experiencing it without him... Guilty for experiencing it with someone else... Guilty for being gone so long... Reluctantly, I hit the side button and focused my eyes back on the sky.

"Are you amazed?" Doug whispered, his shoulder brushing up against mine beneath the blanket.

"It's beautiful." I smiled, not looking away as the green streaks expanded upward, filling the sky with their glow.

"So are you when you smile like that."

I froze, slowly lowering my gaze. "Doug, this isn't a thing. I'm not going to —"

"Woah, woah," he put his hands up in surrender, "take it easy, grandma. It's a compliment. Nothing more. I'm not a saint, but I'm no home-wrecker."

I sighed in relief, my shoulders relaxing. "Oh, good."

"Although I am going to need to sleep here." He frowned. "*On the couch,* of course... I can't go back to the big house. Owen and Cece get creative with the dirty talk when they've had a few drinks. It's bad. REAL bad."

I giggled, looking back up at the sky. "That's fine."

I imagined Chris's disapproval if he'd walked up right now and seen me sitting with another man, sharing a blanket and watching the northern lights... He'd be disappointed... suspicious even. But this was just me being utterly myself, enjoying the entirely platonic friendship I'd formed with this man, and even though I was doing nothing wrong by it, he wouldn't see it that way. Doug had been right... it was there, and I didn't want the guilt... not yet. I'd stay a while longer and enjoy the distraction.

Chapter Forty-Three

The next morning, before the sun had risen, we were awoken by voices nearby our tent. Quickly, I draped the thin silk fabric we'd been using as a blanket over my and Jack's naked bodies.

"Oooh, I hate you, Jim Jackson," Lilly growled as their voices grew near enough to make out the words. Jack made a move to raise up, but I was curious, so I laid my arm across him and motioned for him to be quiet.

"Are we snooping?" he whispered, kissing my forehead.

I grinned. "It's not snooping if they wandered into *our* camp. Now hush."

"Oh, is 'at right? Ye' hate me now? Cause five minutes ago you was sangin' an entirely different tune. Somebody drop you on your head and knock a few screws loose or somethin'?"

She growled again. "You..." There was a shuffling of feet. "Son of a Bitch!"

"Ow ow! Quit woman!"

I stifled a laugh in Jack's shoulder.

"Why Jim? Just tell me why!" Her voice cracked a little.

"Woman, I done told ye.' It ain't right and I ain't doin' it. Now lower your voice 'for someone hears ye.'"

Lucky for me, Lilly had no concept of lowering her voice when she was angry.

"What's not right about it?!"

"Well, for one, I'm fifteen years your senior!"

"SO?!"

I curled into Jack, squeezing my eyes closed and whispering, "Oh no..."

"So, that ain't right!" Jim lowered his voice slightly. "What you want with this old man, anyway? Yer young and beautiful and I ain't got nothin' for ye."

She huffed. "I'm not asking you for a marriage proposal, you stupid idiot. I have needs and so do you."

"And that don't make it right."

"WHY NOT?"

His tone shifted to playful. "Listen, I know I might look like just a piece of meat to ye,' but I got feelings too, and I won't be used for my body."

"Stop grinning like that, it's not funny. Do you have any idea how small you made me feel back there?"

"Aw come on now, Princess, it ain't like that."

"Don't touch me."

"Now quit, ye cain't just wake a man up like 'at. And I wasn't turnin' ye down to be mean. I did it 'cause I care about ye.' I couldn't live with myself if ye' couldn't look me in the eye for lettin' ye do somethin' ye'd regret."

She sighed heavily. "I knew what I was doing. I'm twenty-three years old. I'm not a child."

"Oh, believe you me, ye made that *perfectly* clear this mornin,' but still... Yer gonna get on that boat and I'm gonna get ye' home. Maybe it won't be tomorrow, but some day ye'll wake up next to yer doctor or lawyer husband and bury yer head in the pillow rememberin' that time ye' went slummin' with some old man on the island. And I ain't gonna be that to ye."

"Thirty-eight is not that old, and I wouldn't be slumming."

"Yeah, ye' would," he said softly. "I love ye' girl. You're my family. Only family I got and look at ye. You ain't even done nothin' and you cain't hardly stand to look me in the eye. Come on now, let's just forget this happened."

"HA! *You're* going to forget this happened?"

"Well," he blew out, "not likely. Still, let's pretend we gonna forget it happened. How bout that?"

There was a long pause before Lilly finally answered. "Fine. For now."

"Aight then, what do you say me and you get some breakfast started for everyone? ...fer now?"

Their footsteps shifted back toward camp and their voices muffled as they moved further away.

Jack pulled his arms tight around me and he kissed the top of my head as his fingers combed through my hair. "Poor Jim," he sighed.

"Poor Jim?" I traced his collarbone. "Poor Lilly! It takes a lot of courage to throw yourself at a man. Even more to face him once he's turned you down."

"Oh?" He pulled me up to face him. "Do you speak from experience?"

I kissed his palm as it came to my cheek, nodding. "I do."

He looked at me incredulously. "Well, whoever he is, he's an idiot. I could never. We could be screaming mad at each other and I wouldn't be able to turn you down."

I smoothed over the split in his eyebrow. "Easier said than done. You've never seen me at my worst and I've never pushed you to your worst."

His thumb crossed over my lips. "Even then, I'd still want you."

I laughed. "We'll see about that."

He spun us suddenly and pinned me to the ground, grinning down at me. "Come on and try me. I'll fight with you if that's what you want this morning. Better make it quick though, wouldn't want my breakfast to get cold."

I giggled as his lips came down over mine. After a moment, he rose back up, looking at me quizzically. "What do you think she did to wake him up?"

I smiled, curling my arms around his neck. "I haven't the slightest idea, but as soon as we're done here," I kissed his lips and moved my hips against him, "I have a mind to find out."

About an hour later, we came strolling into camp hand in hand, the smells of pork, Fe'i and fried eggs overwhelming my senses.

The sun had just barely begun to rise and, although its light hadn't quite reached our camp, it was still bustling with activity.

Bruce and Anna were huddled over a case, packing items to head to the summit. Jim sat to the side of them with his nose buried in a journal. Lilly cracked eggs on a thin slab of rock over the fire, and Magna pushed clothes into a large wooden cask we'd been using as a washbasin. Isobel sat sleepily to one side of the fire in an oversized t-shirt and bare feet, her head resting against the arm of a still groggy Kyle. Bud and Bertie came out of the cave behind them with plates and forks.

My heart warmed at the sight of them and I wondered if I could be just as happy staying on the island with them as I would be stepping foot on American soil.

"Mornin' lovebirds." Jim grinned up at us from the journal. "Fix yuns a plate. Ay, get this." He waved his hand over the page he'd been reading. "Them two New York boys he was talkin' about? They was bootleggers... had ties to the mob. Neither of 'em knew a damn thing about sailin' neither. Zachary was not in the business of bootleggin' himself. He made an honest living pickin' up goods shipped from China in Hawaii and movin' 'em to San Francisco. These boys had an outfit get taken down on the east coast so they moved the whole operation west. Dragged him into it. Paid him a hefty sum of money to provide the transportation— figured since he was well known and well liked in the area, he'd be able to stay under the radar."

Jim took a bite of his eggs and squinted, bringing the journal closer. "He was right scared of this Frankie fella.' Says here, they had *three* lifeboats and Frankie wanted to load the booze up on 'em and paddle home. Zachary knew there was no way 'em boats would hold on the Pacific. I'm bettin' 'em two boys took off in the other two... but why shoot him?"

He closed the journal and stretched, looking up at us. "Well, whatcha' waitin' fer?! Fix ye' a plate, we got work to do! S'gonna be all assholes and elbows today! How fast ye' think you can draw up 'em plans this mornin' Hoss?"

Jack yawned and stretched tall beside me, stepping forward to grab a plate and load pork onto it. "I was thinking about it this morning. Got an idea of what we'll need in my head. Shouldn't take long to get it on paper." He scooped up a few eggs and handed me the plate, then reached down to grab a new one for himself.

I took a seat next to Bruce, who grinned at me. "Morning hot stuff." He took a bite of his eggs. "I've been talking to Magna," he leaned in. "And there's a plant up by the water on the summit we can pull for its roots. Very starchy, but since we have eggs, I'm going to try to grind it down into a flour, see if I can't come up with some kind of way to make bread. I think I could use the Fe'i in place of yeast. We could make a jam out of the guava we found. Could be useful on the boat when resources get low."

My mouth watered at the idea of bread and jam. "Oh, that'd be wonderful."

"I'll take some of the pork fat up with me too." His eyes ventured far off as he licked his lips. "Make it kinda like a Cuban bread... There's that metal drum we found in the cave... I bet I could turn it into a sort of oven. Fingers crossed, by the time I come down from the summit, I'll have the perfect recipe."

"Bruce," Jim stood, "you come down with bread and jam and I'll kiss ye' right smack dab on the mouth."

I smiled at that, shifting my focus to Lilly, who was dazedly looking into the fire. She'd managed to pull every detail of my relationship with Jack out of me, and I'd be damned if I was going to let her have secrets of her own. "Lill, I've been thinking about trapping and keeping some of the Kolea for the trip. You want to help me gather bamboo to build a birdcage this morning?"

She glanced over at me, and I raised an eyebrow, curling my lip to one side. I could see realization wash over her face and her eyes went wide. Her cheeks turned bright pink as she quickly shifted her focus to avoid my eyes, rising to grab a plate of her own. "Yeah, I'll go with ya. Let me eat first."

"Can I come?" Kyle asked.

"No!" we both said in unison.

"You need to help with the boat plans," I said to him.

Jack sat down beside me. Jim and Phil followed at the other side of him and they knelt over their breakfasts in conversation about the boat. "We'll need to build it on a platform by the water,"

Jack was saying, "that can act as a ramp to slide it in when we're ready to set sail. We'll need to secure it for storms, though. I think we should put all our effort into building that first."

On the other side of me, Bruce was still talking about flour and all its possibilities to Anna who gave him her undivided attention. "...and I bet those birds would be just perfect in a pot pie... or breaded and fried... the fish too... I can almost taste it."

I kept my eyes on Lilly as she poked at her eggs, glancing up at Jim every once in a while from her place next to Bertie opposite the fire. I wondered where their conversation had left off. Would she avoid him the rest of the time we were here, or would she persist? She wasn't one to be told no. I wondered if anyone had ever told her no before... I could see her thinking about it as she slowly chewed her pork and sipped her water.

I turned my attention back to Jim, who was deep in conversation with Jack and Phil, holding his hands out to convey whatever he was saying.

He wasn't unattractive. He had strong features, thick, dark eyebrows and long lashes over his gray eyes; a firm jaw, a full head of thick brown hair, and a bright smile. He was manly enough to take charge when he needed to; could hunt, fish, and build better than any of us and had a good heart. Still, he was Jim... and she was Lilly... I couldn't think of two people more opposite.

I scooped up the last bite of egg with the last strip of pork and washed it down with the last of my water. I kissed Jack's shoulder as I rose to deposit my plate in our wash basket. Lilly was on my heels in a heartbeat.

"How much did you hear?" she hissed in my ear.

"Enough," I assured her, "and you'll tell me what I didn't."

I picked up two full bags of water and handed her one, turning back toward the fire to make eye contact with Jack. "We're heading down. I'll see you down there." I glanced over at Anna and Bruce. "I'll see you two in a week!"

I looped my arm through Lilly's and dragged her off.

Outside of earshot, she leaned in. "It's not polite to eavesdrop, ya know."

I scoffed. "I wasn't eavesdropping. I was trying to sleep, and you two were screaming bloody murder right outside my tent."

She growled. "You should've said something. I didn't realize your tent was over there. Oh God, did Jack hear it too?"

"It's alright, Lill."

"UGH... That means they'll be talking about it..." She blew out. "Oh God, Lainey, I'm such an idiot. You were right."

I squeezed her arm. "You're not an idiot and neither of them will be talking about anything but the boat today. What happened?"

"I..." She swallowed. "I crawled into his bed."

"Lill, you've tried to crawl into his bed every night since he *got* his own bed... *and?*"

"And... well..." She sighed. "I didn't have any clothes on."

I didn't mean to, but I laughed out loud. "Oh, Lilly! What did you think was going to happen?!"

"Well, I didn't think he'd run out of there! Shut up, it's not funny!" She pulled my hair.

"Ow!" I laughed harder. "Is that all? Lill, he probably didn't even see anything!"

"No, he didn't *see* anything... but it's a small bed and I might've... crawled on top of him."

I wrapped my arm around her neck and kissed the top of her head. "I told you it wouldn't work."

She curled her arms around me and laid her head against my shoulder. "I don't know, Lainey. There was a second there... before he realized what was happening... the man's got needs..."

"Lill, let it go now."

She walked for a while with her head on my shoulder, quietly thinking. "He's not likely to look at me quite the same ever again. I'm a woman in his eyes now. This changes things."

I laughed. "Seriously, *woman*, have you ever accepted defeat?"

She narrowed her eyes. "No..." She stopped as we reached the field of bamboo. "I need to steal some of this bamboo for myself. We're going to add curls to my hair... and lipstick... I'll make him come to me now."

"Lill, you're impossible."

She smiled, breaking off a small piece of bamboo and wrapping her hair around it as a trial. "Impossible is fun. It keeps things interesting."

Chapter Forty-Four

We'd spent the duration of the evening and night drawing up plans for and arguing about the boat. We'd need to get swiftly to work chopping down bamboo. After much deliberation, it was decided that bamboo would work best since it was easier to bend when it was green and would harden in whatever shape we'd created when it dried out. We'd chop those first and soak them in the ocean while we worked on the platform.

For the size of the boat we'd finally agreed upon, we'd need to construct a massive platform at the edge of the water to house it so when it was ready to set sail, we could easily roll it into the water.

The boat needed to be large enough to weather the big storms, with a hull that could house sleeping quarters and a storage area for food and water, but it also needed to be light enough that we would be able to collectively paddle ourselves out past the shallow water.

We would carve pegs and joints into the bamboo after we'd bent and dried it, a task we would all need to help with, then we'd bind them together with rope and fill any gaps with moss and clay. Lilly and Bertie would work on the sails.

I'd tossed and turned throughout the night in anticipation of getting started. Jack had too, and as I laid across him in our little tent in the early morning, I couldn't bear the thought of waking him once he'd finally fallen asleep. He snored ever so softly and his face looked completely at peace, the corners of his mouth curled up slightly.

What had I done to deserve the love of this beautiful man?

Carefully, I slid out of the tent, pulling my shorts and boots on just outside before I crept back toward camp.

Jim was the only one awake, sitting on a log with his nose buried in the leather journal. I sat down beside him, but he didn't look up.

"Listen to this," he said in a far-off tone as he frowned over the journal, scratching his head. "From the night of the storm... *'According to our position, we should be close enough to reach the Marquesas Islands by morning. I will attempt to dock in Ua Pou to repair the hull. I've instructed Dutch and Frankie to begin loading the lifeboats just in case we have to bail out. Since Frankie has pointed his pistol at me twice already when he's been delivered bad news, I've decided not to tell them that I'm going to have to rely solely on the stars to navigate since none of the ship's navigation appears to be functioning. Even the needle on the small desk compass has frozen on north. Oddly enough, the skies are now completely clear, with no sign of the storm that just hit us on any horizon. The waves that once threatened to capsize us have suddenly gone completely calm.'"*

He quickly turned the page, his attention focused on the fine cursive. "But then here... he says, *'I have successfully navigated to the Marquesas. I can see the jagged cliff peaks of Ua Pou. I've been here once before and I know with all my heart that this is Ua Pou. I can see the distinct pillars of its twelve pinnacles shrouded in mist. Towering high above them all and hidden in the clouds is Mont Oave. I know this is Ua Pou and I know that is Mont Oave, but where there once were docks and ships and houses around the bay, there is now only infinite wilderness. I have checked the chronometer, and it confirms that this is indeed Ua Pou. But there is no one here. I could continue northeast and attempt to dock in Ua Huka, but I'm worried the hull may not make it the three hours it would take to get there. And what if there's no one there either? God be with us.'"*

He glanced at me then back at the journal, "So then he goes on to argue about it with Dutch and Frankie and they insist he head to Ua Huka... they need to fix the ship and they need people to do it... and then here," he flipped the page, running his finger over the words. "*'We have traveled for roughly three hours, Ua Pou is gone from sight and I'm afraid we are sinking faster than I thought. I can see land ahead but it is not Ua Huka. I'm afraid we went off course somewhere. This is smaller and it's not a known location on my map. I will have to turn the ship into its shore.'*"

He slid his finger down the page, his eyes rapidly dancing over the words. "So they get it to the shore then... *'We need to lighten the load of the ship if I'm going to stand any chance at repairing it. Frankie, Dutch, and I have successfully unloaded the bulk of the whiskey and port in the three lifeboats. I've taken a moment alone to catch my bearings before I attempt to unload the rest of the supplies, as they have refused to help unload anything that is not theirs. Were it not for the two of them, I might consider myself lucky to have landed in such a beautiful place. In all my life, I've never seen anything quite so extraordinary. I only wish Dorothy could've been here with me to see it. One massive jagged pillar stands tall at its center, shrouded in mist and almost as tall as Mont Oave. I'll need to climb it to get up higher to search for life or signs of the other islands - they have to be close by, a task that will be difficult at my age but one that I doubt Frankie and Dutch will volunteer for since they have both found a comfortable spot in the shade to take a nap.'*"

Jim reached to one side and unfolded a worn map that had been tucked away inside another journal. Its coloring had faded to a dim yellow with time and the once thick paper now molded like fabric over his knee.

"So that means we've *got* to be here." He pointed to a small spot that had been circled and marked with an 'X' by our predecessor at the northeast part of a group of islands marked *'Iles Marquises.'*

I frowned as I peered over the map. "If we're here..." I pointed, dragging my finger the short distance to Ua Huka, "then we're surrounded by other islands... maybe *we* could make it to Ua Huka? Maybe we could find help there?"

Jim nodded. "Maybe, but the man had been sailin' this water for fifty years... and if he says there should've been people on Ua Pou at that time, I believe him. Which makes me think... well, what if there's nobody *anywhere*? What if that storm wasn't a storm at all? We need to talk to Magna... she would know what shoulda' been there."

I stared into the fire. I knew nothing of the Iles Marquises. I'd barely ever travelled outside Chicago, and I'd never been a person to study up on places of the world, unlike Chris, who was fascinated by reading about the world and its most exotic destinations. He would've known about Ua Pou if he were with us...

"What ye' doin' up so early, anyway?" Jim asked.

"Oh..." I shrugged, "I couldn't sleep. I guess I'm a little anxious?"

"You and me both." He poked the fire with a stick, leaning back a little and stretching. "Ye' scared?"

I nodded, "I was... I was scared of what would happen next... after we found rescue... who we'd be to each other once we got home... but *now*..." I glanced at the map, "I'm terrified."

He let out a long sigh. "Me too."

I laid my head against his shoulder. "Maybe we should wait to tell the others about this finding... until after we've talked to Magna."

"May be a good idea. No use in gettin' everyone worked up just yet." He folded the map and tucked it back into the journal then laid his head against mine, "I got half a mind to go wake her ass up... if *she* didn't terrify me more."

I laughed, raising my head to look beyond him at a shadowy figure approaching. As she grew closer and the dull morning light shone upon her, I realized it was Lilly returning from the waterfall, and I laughed to myself at the sight of her.

She hadn't wasted any time in holding true to her word. Her hair was perfectly curled, she'd applied a dark smokey eye makeup and sported bright red lipstick, making her appear suddenly older. She'd pulled out the very tight little black cocktail dress we'd found in one of the suitcases and altered it to fit her just right. Her legs were smooth and tan, she'd put on four inch black high heels, and had impressively managed to pull off walking across the sandy dirt in them.

"James…" she said as she came up on my side, placing both hands on her hips and standing at an angle that made her legs look exquisite.

He looked up at her, frowning, then looked behind him and back. "Woman, who in the Sam Hill are you talkin' to?" He glanced at me. "Is she addressin' me?"

"That's your name, isn't it?" She raised an eyebrow, crossing her arms in front of her.

"Not one that I answer to, thank ye' ver—

He narrowed his eyes at her and cocked his head to the side, seeming to notice her appearance for the first time as he observed the length of her. "What… in… the hellllllll have ye' got on? Have ye' gone completely out of yer gourd? Ye' know we're cuttin' and haulin' trees today, don't ye? You're like to break yer dang ankle in 'em shoes."

"I'm not hauling trees." She flipped her hair behind one shoulder and cooly folded her fingers to study her nails, "I'm sewing sails."

He laughed out loud. "Not today ye' ain't, sweetheart. Today, those of us that's able are either cuttin' wood or haulin' it to the beach. Now, I suggest ye' go put somethin' else on lest ye' get a splinter somewhere unmentionable. "

Lilly scoffed. "You want *me* to cut and haul trees? Look at me." She looked down at her petite figure and back to Jim. "Do I really look like I could carry a tree?"

He folded his lips inward to hide his smile. "Well, not in them shoes, ye' don't. And ye' ain't carryin' trees anyway, yer helpin' me drag bamboo down to the beach. Now go put somethin' else on."

She growled, spinning on her heel to stomp back inside the shelter, leaving me and Jim alone to quietly giggle.

"Did ye' see that dress she had on?" He shook his head. "Ye' could just about see clear to Christmas!"

"I think that was the point, darling."

"Lordt Almighty. I swear she's drivin' me nuts."

"Oh, go easy." I patted his leg. "She's just looking for a bit of romance is all."

"I wasn't born yesterday. I'm well aware of what she's lookin' for. And she'd best start lookin' elsewheres."

"Good morning." Jack appeared across the fire from us, stretching tall and yawning before circling around to kiss the top of my head. "I didn't hear you get up."

"I didn't want to wake you. You seemed peaceful."

"Must be nice," Jim teased, reaching over to neatly stack the journals behind the log. "I ain't had me a second of peace since 'at damn woman set her sights on me."

Jack smirked, kneeling to one side to grab a handful of eggs from the basket. "Better you than me, buddy. You guys want breakfast?"

"Both of you be nice—Yes, I'll have two please—It's lonely out here." I stood and grabbed a water from the opposite side of the fire, hobbling against the stiffness in my ankle, then sat back down between them. "Anyone should be so lucky."

"Ay, listen up, freckles." Jim took a drink of his water. "I've seen ye' limpin' on that leg more often than not. Ye' gonna have to sit this one out today. Hang around camp and relax. Else 'at leg ain't never gonna heal."

"I'm fine," I insisted.

"No, you're not," Jack chimed in. "It's not healing because you're always up on it. You need to stay off it today. Keep Bertie and Izzy company."

I sighed. "Really Jack, I'm alright."

"That may be, but you're not going." He cracked the eggs onto the hot metal skillet. "Jim, you want eggs?"

"Yeah, I'll take two."

"And since when do you get to tell me what to do?" I huffed.

"Since now." He bounced his eyebrows at me, cracking two more eggs onto the skillet to sizzle.

"I want to help." I raised my chin. "I can't sit here all day with all the work that needs to get done."

"Oh, but there's work here you can do. You can work on that birdcage you've been talking about... or help Bertie with some of the bedding she's sewing... just stay off the ankle."

I rolled my eyes. "Really it's almost completely healed now."

"Woman," Jim nudged my shoulder, "yer stubborn as a dang mule. Now I know ye' think yer indestructible, but obviously," he looked down at my wrapped ankle, "ye' ain't. Stay up here on yer scrawny ass so he ain't worryin' about ye' all day. We ain't gonna be able to get shit done otherwise."

He leaned in close to whisper in my ear, "I'll tell Magna she orta stay here, watch out for you and Bertie. I'll leave the journals. Ye' can get some answers while we're out workin.'"

One by one, the others joined us. Lilly had accepted defeat and changed into a pair of khaki shorts and tennis shoes. Bertie, Bud, and Izzy joined her as Magna collected clothing and bent over our wash barrel. As they all finished up their breakfasts and left for the day's work, I recruited Magna to help me with our birdcage, leaving Bertie and Isobel near the fire to work on the day's lessons.

Outside of earshot, I sat on the grass, urging Magna to join me in front of the pile of bamboo. I held a piece of bamboo in one hand and leaned in, speaking in a hushed tone. "Tell me what you know about the Marquesas Islands."

She smiled her warm, motherly smile. "So you've figured out that we are here?"

Taken aback, I blinked. "Here?"

"Well, there's nowhere else in the world quite like the Marquesas." She tilted her head skyward, as though she could see the summit from where we sat. "I don't know this island, but I know the land and the fruit and the way the peaks grow and climb into the clouds. I know there are plants here you can only find in the Marquesas. I know there are fish we've caught that you can't find anywhere *but* the Marquesas. We *are* in the Marquesas... but at the same time, we are not, are we?"

I pulled the journal from my side and opened it, removing the map which held the page we'd marked, and handed the opened book to her.

She held it close to her face, squinting as she read the fine writing. I watched as her dark brown eyes scanned the words. When she'd finished, she sighed and lowered the open book to her lap, nodding. "There would be no mistaking Ua Pou for anything else. If he'd been there once, he knew where he was. And there should've been people there. Plenty of ships and docks and houses in the twenties... plenty more now... from where he landed—from *here*... we should see ships in every direction... cruise ships and merchants, sailboats and fisherman..."

"Where do you think they all went?" I asked, intrigued.

She shook her head and opened her mouth as if to speak, then closed it abruptly.

"What?" I begged.

"It'll sound silly..." She blushed, looking down at her pudgy fingers as she smoothed over the pages of the journal in her lap.

"Sillier than Jim's Bermuda Triangle theory?" I smiled. "I don't think anything would be silly if it offered an explanation as to what happened to us."

"Well," she spun a piece of bamboo between her hands, "there's this old legend Islanders used to tell that I've been thinking about since we got here... It's about Maui, the demigod... It was said that when storm clouds would gather over the volcano Haleakalā in Hawaii, the people would hide in fear that Maui might hurl them so far they could never return. Since I have no other explanation, perhaps we should consider that there could be some basis of truth to the folklore. And perhaps we might've just flown too close to Haleakalā when storm clouds had gathered."

It did sound silly, but the story was the first thing that offered any resemblance to our circumstances. What if the legend was based on some kind of fact? "What would happen to them?" I asked. "If they did get caught in the storm?"

She shrugged. "No one knows."

I unfolded the map, laying it across her lap and pointing to our spot. "Zachary thought we were here in the middle of all these islands... And Jim thinks our plane was here when we hit the storm." I tapped a spot between Hawaii and California. "Which would mean the storm hurled us all the way here. Do you think there are people on these islands?"

She traced the lines of the map with her fingernail. "There's an airport here." She circled Ua Huka with one finger then dragged it down to Ua Pou, "...and here." She slid her finger up to Nuku Hiva. "...and here." She shook her head and frowned. "We should see airplanes... we should see boats... even far out on the water or airplanes high in the sky... but we've seen nothing. Why? This area," she tapped the 'X' on the map, "should see all the travelers going to and from each of the surrounding islands... Tourists galore.... Local fishermen... Where is everyone?"

I furrowed my brow. "You said you often see sailboats between islands? What if we could put a sail on the lifeboat? Do you think we could make it to Ua Huka? How fast do you think we could get there? Maybe we could just explore it and see if anyone's there?"

She pursed her lips. "Well, we'd be relying on the wind. If we could get up to five miles an hour... we might make it there in four or five hours... but we could miss it and be lost or we could find it and..."

"And what?"

"Well... this is going to sound even crazier than the Maui bit, but it ties the Maui story to a potential truth. What if the reason we haven't seen airplanes or satellites or cargo ships is because they don't exist..." She swallowed and looked up from the map at me, "...yet."

I tilted my head, intrigued. "Yet?"

"It's a theory I've been playing around with in my head." She raised her eyebrows. "Think about it... The location... the lack of airplanes or tourists or satellites, the pirate ship Jim swears he saw..."

She smiled. "I remember when my daughter was in high school, she became completely obsessed with the theory of general relativity and the possibility of time travel. She had several books shipped to the island, and she was always talking about the possibilities over dinner. None of it ever really made the mathematical sense it made to her to me, but one thing did make sense. Why spend so much time, money, and effort on the study of time travel, particularly on the subject of traveling backward through it, if it didn't have some bit of mathematical possibility? So again I say, it's just a theory... but if it's the correct theory and we try to find life on Ua Huka or Ua Poa, well..." She looked around to make sure no one was listening. "The native tribes... they weren't welcoming of strangers... they'd tear us apart."

"You think we travelled back in time?" Outlandish as it was, it did make sense... but then again, most conspiracy theories tended to make sense when there was no other logical explanation for unexplainable events in history.

"Or..." She closed the journal and handed it back to me, seeming to read my mind as she reached out to grab a handful of thin bamboo. "We're not in the Marquesas at all... and we just happen to be so far removed that no one has crossed our path yet."

I grabbed my own stack of bamboo and followed her lead as we began weaving them together. It felt strange that the least logical of the two theories made more sense.

We spent the better part of two hours weaving and bending the thin bamboo together to form the walls of the enclosure. With most of it complete, Magna left me to finish so she could hang the clothes out to dry. As I pulled the last piece, I debated whether or not I would be asking for trouble if I walked the short distance to the field of bamboo to pull enough to finish.

The ankle was almost completely healed. The bruising and swelling was almost all gone, and it only hurt at the end of the day when I'd spent too much time standing or walking. I could go to the bamboo field and be back within a half hour. That wouldn't hurt it. I'd spent almost the entire day walking and standing on it the day before.

Decided, I stood, brushing the sand and dirt off my legs.

"Where are you off to?" Magna asked as she draped Jack's navy shirt over the thin rope.

"I'm just going to walk down to get a handful of bamboo so we can finish. Really quick. It's not far."

She frowned. "You're supposed to be resting, honey."

"I know, but it's really not that far. And it doesn't hurt."

Bertie shook her head, looking up at me from her sketchpad. "Can't it wait, dear?"

I looked at the nearly finished birdcage. "Please? I'm so close to being done. I just need a little more bamboo. It'll be like I walked around the cave a few times, which I've already done today... I'd love to have it finished when they come walking up."

Bertie let out a long sigh, coughing a little as she tended to do. "What do you think, Magna?"

Magna rolled her eyes, grabbing a pair of jeans out of the barrel. "Oh, alright, but be quick."

"Thank you!"

At that, I hurried off before she could change her mind.

The late afternoon sun shined brightly through the green canopy above me, warming my skin. I hummed as I walked, smiling to myself as I envisioned Jack's face when he walked up to see my craftsmanship. Oh, to make him proud was so gratifying. To be honest, to have him look at me in most ways was gratifying.

I pondered Magna's theory. What if she was right? Had we been pulled from our time to another? It made sense with the strange looking boat Jim spotted and the lack of satellites... It would make more sense if I could confirm our location. I wondered if we could find the astrolabe and figure out how to use it.

"Hey gorgeous." I heard Phil's throaty voice behind me and cringed. I could tell by his breathing he'd been drinking heavily already and wondered if the crew working on the boat hadn't sent him away just to be rid of him.

"Phil." I cleared my throat, turning around to face him and forcing a smile. "What are you doing out here?"

He narrowed his eyes, scanning me slowly as he swayed. "Following you."

He took a step toward me and I stepped back, laughing nervously as I looked around to see if anyone else was nearby. "And *why* are you following me?"

Before I could grasp what was happening, he'd lunged forward, grabbing both my hands and pinning me against a large tree.

"What are you doing? Get your hands off me!"

"Come on, Alaina," he growled, licking his lips as he pressed me further into the jagged bark of the tree, the bitter scent of whiskey on his breath wafting over me. "You have to know how bad I want you..."

"Are you crazy?!" I squirmed against him, surprised at how strong he actually was. "Phil, this isn't funny!"

"I want you so bad," he continued as if I hadn't said anything, his pudgy face coming inches from mine, forcing me to turn my head away. I tried to knee him but he was too close. Tried to wiggle free, but he was too strong. "I've wanted you since I laid eyes on you."

"Phil, stop it! This isn't happening!" I started to panic as he pressed his body against mine, bile rising in my throat as I felt his penis harden through the fabric of his pants against my leg. "PHIL, STOP!"

But he didn't stop. Suddenly, I felt the sloppy wetness of his mouth on my throat. "I SAID STOP IT!" And as the terror swept over me that he had a mind to actually go through with it, I dug my teeth into his shoulder, biting down as hard as I could.

"AAAAH, YOU FUCKING BITCH!" He released my wrists and slapped my face—hard enough to knock me off my feet and onto the ground in front of him.

He fell heavily onto me, pinning me against the ground with all his weight. His eyes were completely glossed over and unrecognizable. He'd gone completely mad. I wiggled and screamed in a pile of rustling leaves and dirt, but the fight only seemed to excite him more.

He sat up, pinning me between his legs as I tried to claw, slap, or punch any part of him. He caught my arms in his hands, stacking them on top of each other and pressing them hard to the ground over my head. The other hand quickly ripped the button-up shirt wide open, exposing my bra before he fell forward in a frenzy of groping fingers and an anxious mouth that moved hurriedly over my exposed skin.

I tried to knee him. I tried to bite him, but he wound his grubby fingers in my hair and pulled my head back against the dirt. His mouth came down over my breast and he bit me hard, his body moving excitedly against me.

"PHIL, STOP IT!!!" I kicked my legs, digging my heels into the ground and bucking, trying desperately to injure him in some way. He let out a growl and flipped me onto my stomach, releasing my hands as the full weight of him pinned my body to the ground.

He moaned, pulling my hair as he bit down on my shoulder. "You fight all you want, baby. I like it rough."

"HELP!!!" I screamed frantically as I felt his hand reach down and around my waist to rip the shorts open. I tried to head-butt him with the back of my head and he dodged; tried to reach back and grab his hair, but he laid his forearm across my shoulder blades, forcing me into the dirt as I heard his belt unfastening.

I screamed at the top of my lungs as I felt his hand slowly sliding beneath the elastic on my underwear.

'Please, God, no.'

And then, as if God heard me, I heard the familiar click of a gun being cocked… and Phil froze.

"Get off her." Kyle's voice was stern and suddenly very deep. I looked toward the sound and saw him standing there with the old pistol aimed straight at Phil's head.

Phil made no move to release me. Instead, he narrowed his eyes at Kyle, and laughed. "Whatcha' gonna do with that, boy? You gonna' shoot me? Ha!"

"Give me one good reason not to." Kyle's eyes were bright red, and his chest heaved, but his one arm remained steady.

"Because I'm your father. You're not gonna shoot your father. Come on, I didn't go after the one you like. Put that thing down."

"Get off her," he repeated in the same stern tone, the barrel of the gun still pointed steadily at the center of Phil's forehead.

But Phil didn't get off. Instead, he smiled, lowering himself ever so slowly to lick the side of my face, the hand beneath my shorts sliding lower.

"STOP IT!" I screamed at the top of my lungs, writhing beneath him, trying to get some part of me free enough to do damage.

"You're not gonna do anything, boy. Now go on. Get out of here."

"Get off her," Kyle said calmly, moving a step closer with the gun, "or I'll shoot you, I swear."

"You're not gonna—"

"I'm going to count to three… and then I'm going to shoot you in the head. Just like I've dreamt of doing since I was a little kid… since you beat my mother over and over… since you beat *me* over and over… since you've spent your entire worthless life belittling, bullying, and beating everyone who ever loved you… And now you've moved on to what?? Rape?! I knew I hated you for good reason. You sonofabitch, I *will* shoot you… and I won't regret it, do you understand me? Get off her."

"Kyle…"

"One…"

"Kyle. You can't be serious." Phil's voice started to shake.

"Two…"

"Alright. Alright." Phil shifted to his knees, raising both hands so I could scurry away from him, crawling forward several feet and folding my arms over my bra.

"I'm getting up. Don't shoot."

"Why shouldn't I?" Kyle narrowed his eyes, stepping a little closer with the gun still steadied as Phil stood.

I wiped at the saliva on my cheek and neck, disgusted. My cheek burned, and I tasted the familiar tang of blood, realizing my mouth was bleeding. I'd never been hit by a man before. I'd never been abused in any way and I suddenly felt smaller, frail, and devastated for having been so helpless.

'What if Kyle hadn't shown up?'

"Now, come on… I wasn't actually gonna rape her," Phil tried to backtrack, both his hands raised in surrender. "I just had too much to drink… got away from myself… put the gun down before someone gets hurt."

"I hate you." Kyle's eyes watered and his voice cracked slightly as he circled Phil, facing him with the gun extended and aimed at the center of his skull. "I fucking hate you. If I pulled this trigger, the whole world would be better off."

"You don't mean that." Phil's voice shifted from nervous to angry. "Put the gun down. NOW."

"Why? So you can beat me for it? Then jump back on top of her and finish what you started?" Kyle's arm followed Phil's movement as he tried to move out of harm's way. "No."

In one quick move, Phil lunged toward Kyle, and Kyle's eyes went wide as he squeezed the trigger.

Click.

Both of them stood dumbfounded, frozen in place, a foot of ground between them. Kyle's arm started to shake for the first time as his eyes welled with tears. The gun had been pointed at Phil's head and he'd pulled the trigger.

"You," Phil growled, "you were gonna kill *me*?" He leapt at Kyle's small figure and they rolled onto the ground in a mess of dried palm and sandy dirt.

Before I could get to my feet, the gun went off, this time sending an ear piercing "bang" through the jungle around us. It echoed across the rock walls of the cliffs behind us, sending nearby birds fluttering off in a frenzy. The sound reverberated in my body for several seconds as I tried to process what had happened.

Far below us, toward the beach, I could hear yelling.

'Jack heard it... he'll come to see what happened...'

I looked over at the two of them and saw both bodies moving as Kyle shuffled out from beneath him to stand shakily on his feet, the gun still in his hand. Panic momentarily rose in my throat. *'Did he kill Phil?'* I hated Phil at that moment, but wasn't entirely sure I wanted him dead... not at the hands of Kyle, anyway.

But then I heard Phil groan loudly and just as soon as I heard the noise, I saw him roll onto his back, slowly sitting up and holding his left arm. "You shot me."

"Don't—don't mo-move or I'll shoot you again," Kyle stuttered, tears streaming down his reddened cheeks. He held the gun out again, its barrel shaking as he started to break down.

"You shot me," Phil repeated breathlessly, staring up at Kyle in disbelief.

A new voice came from behind me, calm and even toned. "Give me the gun, son."

I recognized it as Bud and turned to look up at him. He was standing straighter than I'd ever seen him, stoic with his hands in front of him and his eyes focused solely on Kyle. Self consciously, I pulled my shirt closed and curled my knees into my chest.

"He was trying to r-rape her." Kyle sobbed, keeping the gun extended.

"We'll deal with that," Bud said evenly as he slowly approached Kyle. "But you're gonna have to give me the gun now. Killing him won't make things any better."

"Wouldn't it?" Kyle sniffled, shaking his head to clear the tears. "What's he ever done for any of us? Aside from getting drunk day and night and eating all the food?"

I couldn't move. I sat on the ground, shivering, as I watched the scene unfold and wondered what could've happened. *'Could I have fought him off if no one came? He'd been so close... and he'd had no weapon. No weapon and I couldn't stop him.'*

"Look at me, son." Bud moved closer, positioning himself between Phil and Kyle, seemingly unafraid of the gun that was now pointed at his chest. "Killing a man does something to you. It changes you in a way you can never get back. You remember it forever. You dream of it and relive it over and over for the rest of your life. It eats away at you day by day and you're lesser for it. I wouldn't wish it on my worst enemy. Killing your *own father*... come on now, you don't wanna live with that kind of weight on you."

Kyle closed his eyes, letting the tears wash over him as he lowered the gun, trembling with emotion.

"That's a good boy." Bud stepped closer, resting his hand on the barrel at his side. "Let me have it now, and you go on back to camp. You don't need to worry about him anymore. We'll deal with him now."

"Come on, son, give it to me," Bud encouraged, wrapping an arm around him as he took the gun in his other. "You leave this to me now." He squeezed him tightly as the boy shook and sobbed against his shoulder. "He can't hurt you now."

"You fucking shot me," Phil repeated angrily as he held his shoulder and began to rise.

"Take her back to camp," Bud continued, slowly turning him to peer past his shoulder at Phil. "It's over now."

Kyle looked at me then, his face distorted as he fought to get above the tears, and just as he began to step toward me, Jack appeared at the tree line beside them.

Chapter Forty-Five

Jack scanned me, then Phil, then Kyle and Bud, and I could see him put it all together. His eyes grew dark, his muscles tense, and without a word, he took two quick strides toward Phil, grabbed him by the hair, jerked him onto his feet and punched him in the nose, blood spraying out in every direction.

As Phil fell backward, Jack caught him by the upper arm, his expression cold and focused, and he straightened him out, promptly delivering another blow precisely where the last had landed.

"What in the hell's goin' on?" Jim panted, glancing around as Phil fell to the ground. Jack knelt over him, pulling him up by the shirt and rearing his arm back, delivering two very quick and very hard blows to the face that seemed to knock Phil out cold. His body went limp and his eyes rolled back as Jack released the shirt and Phil's body fell back into the dirt.

But he wasn't done. Jack wrapped both hands around Phil's neck, and I could see the muscles on his arms tighten.

"Ay, Hoss, ye' gonna' kill him!" Jim darted toward them, grabbing Jack's upper arm and pulling, but was unable to move him. "Ay, what's got into ye? Yer gonna kill him!!"

I crossed my arms over myself and rose. "Jack," my voice quivered and cracked, "you have to stop now."

His fingers remained curled around Phil's throat, but he looked up at me then, shaking his head slowly. "Say the word, Red. Say the word and I'll do it."

"No." I took the few steps to his side, careful to avoid eye contact with Phil, whose eyes had opened wide in the struggle for air. "No, he didn't..." I swallowed, "I'm alright. Kyle stopped it in time... I'm alright..."

Jim's eyes narrowed as he took in my torn shirt, ripped shorts, and bloodied lip. "Mother fucker..." He fell down to his knees beside Jack, removing his grip on his arm. "Whatever ye' wanna do, Hoss, I'm with ye.' Kyle," he looked over his shoulder, "you go on back to camp now."

"Are you gonna kill him?" Kyle sniffled, turning in the direction of camp.

"Whatcha wanna do, Jack?" Jim whispered.

Phil tried to wedge his fingers beneath Jack's palms, pulled at his hands and kicked his feet as he tried to get air. Jack stared up at me. "What do you want me to do?"

"I don't know," I sighed, "not this though."

"You're sure?" Jack raised an eyebrow.

I nodded, disgusted with myself. "I'm sure."

Slowly, Jack's grip loosened and Phil wheezed, curling into himself as he rolled onto his side.

"What's going on?!" Lilly ran through the trees, her voice raised an octave as she tried to catch her breath. "Grandpa?! What on earth are you doing with that gun?"

Bud was standing still, the gun pointed at Phil as he waited for Jack to finish.

"Go back to camp," Bud said cooly. "Take Kyle and Alaina with you."

"But what's—Alaina!" she shrieked when she noticed me. "What happened?" She scanned me up and down, then took in Phil's bloody wheezing body beneath Jack, "That son of a—"

"Go back to camp, Lillian." Bud raised his voice only slightly.

"What should we do with him, Boss?" Jim whispered. "We cain't take him back to camp with these women."

Lilly reached her arms out toward me, motioning me to her. "Come on, Lainey, let's get you out of here."

"No..." I whispered, shaking my head.

My heart burned as I looked down at Jack. His hands shook as they balled into fists and hovered over Phil. The only thing I wanted was to pull him to me, wrap his arms around me, and shut out the world... Shut out the whole day... The whole year... My whole life... To forget about rescue and just be at peace here... with no concern as to where *here* actually was.

He stood, flexing his hands at his sides as he looked down at the bloody mess that was now Phil's face. He glanced at me, his eyes welling with tears.

I saw his chest heave before he screamed out at the top of his lungs, balled both hands into fists and punched the tree over and over, his knuckles wearing down almost to the bone.

I pulled his arm while he continued to punch with the other, still screaming out. Jim raised on the opposite side and tried to grab the other arm.

He fell to his knees over Phil and landed blow after blow to his face, stomach, legs—anywhere he could reach. He was crying, tears pouring down both cheeks as he wailed on Phil's lifeless body. "You fucking bastard!"

I swung my arms around his shoulders, squeezing with all my might. "That's enough now. Come back now."

I tugged him and we fell over, rolling onto our butts as he heaved in my arms. "How am I supposed to.... What am I supposed to...?"

Jim stepped forward, grabbing Phil's discarded belt from the ground. "I got him now, Hoss. We'll tie him up and figure out what to do with him. You stay here and tend to yer woman 'for ye' come back to camp. I promise ye', he ain't goin' nowheres lest ye' say so.'"

Jim pulled Phil's shoulder hard, forcing his limp body to roll onto its back. He jerked his hands up and bound them with the belt. Dropping his bound arms, he then wrangled Phil's feet. "Come on ye' son of a bitch." He dragged him through the dirt toward camp. "Yuns come on with me. Leave them to their business now."

Slowly their footsteps disappeared as they made their way to camp, leaving Jack and I alone and shaking on our knees in the dirt.

"Jack," my throat tightened, "I'm sorry."

His face distorted then, and he shook his head. "I..." But he couldn't speak. The word cracked, and he trembled with the effort of containing his anger. I wrapped my arms around his neck and buried my face in his shoulder.

He was stiff, but his arms folded around me, one hand sliding up into my hair as he pulled me against him. I felt him exhale and then he rested his lips on the crown of my head. "My beautiful, wonderful girl, I'm the one that's sorry. Jesus, you have nothing to be sorry for."

Ever so gently, he peeled me from him and his hands immediately swept over my face, fingers lightly touching my lip where it had been busted. "Tell me what he did... where he touched you..."

"I'm okay."

He ran his fingers down the sides of my ripped shirt, his face twisting with the effort of not breaking down. "Did he..."

I stopped his hand and held it over my heart. "He didn't."

He pulled the shirt to one side, exposing the teeth marks on my breast, and he raised the back of his shaking hand over his mouth, "Oh Jesus... that fucking—"

I brought his hand to my lips, curling his fingers over mine to softly kiss his knuckles. "It's over now."

He lightly gripped my upper arms, and I winced at the bruising that had formed on them.

"I would've killed him," he said. "I would kill him *still* if you ask me to. Just knowing he's still breathing is killing me... knowing he put his hands on you... his mouth..."

"Shh..." I smoothed both hands over his hair.

"I should've known what kind of man he was... should've been watching him like a hawk..." He moved my shirt down my arm to expose the bite mark on my shoulder. "I should've never let him anywhere near you. I don't know what to do now. Do I kill him? Tell me what you want me to do."

"You know what I want you to do?" I cupped his face in my hands.

"Whatever it is, it's yours."

"I want you to take me to the waterfall so I can wash this off me. Once I'm clean, we'll figure out what to do with him. Then, after we've done whatever needs to be done, I want you to teach me how to fight. Show me how to never be that vulnerable—that helpless ever again."

He laid his cheek against the top of my head. "I promise you, you will *never be* helpless again. Never again, I swear." He pulled my legs into his lap and stood, cradling me in his arms.

I closed my eyes against the setting sun, burying my face in his chest as he carried me toward the sound of the rushing waterfall.

"Wait!" I heard Lilly shout from behind us, and I buried my face deeper into him as I heard her footsteps rustling against the dead leaves on the ground. "Here," she said breathlessly, and I felt his arm shift under my knees. "There's soap and shampoo in there and some fresh clothes for her. I put the robe she likes in there too."

Just as quickly as she'd shown up, I heard her scurry off. She knew me well and knew exactly what I'd need. She knew I wouldn't want to speak to anyone and hadn't tried to force it. I knew her well enough to know that it'd taken all her willpower to not ask me what happened, how it happened, and how I was feeling. And I loved her that much more for it.

Silently, Jack walked us the rest of the way to the waterfall, its rushing water drowning out the sound of my heartbeat. He didn't stop to remove our clothes, but merely grabbed the soap, dropped the pack on the ground, removed the one boot I had left and walked us waist-deep into the water before setting me on my feet in front of him.

Gently, he peeled the remnants of my shirt off me, shaking his head slowly as he scanned the dark blue imprints of Phil's fingers on my upper arms and wrists. "You know," he said softly, tossing the shirt onto the rocks, "I thought you were pretty indestructible too."

His hand hovered over my arm before he touched the bruises lightly with his fingertips. "You've had your ribs broken, head sliced open, you fought a boar with your bare hands... and none of that seemed to shake you..."

He slid my shorts down my legs and tossed them to the side. "I never thought to worry about where you were or what might happen if I wasn't watching over you... because you're Red... This indestructible, independent, stubborn woman."

He scooped up a handful of water and let it fall over my shoulders. "But I should've been watching out with him here. We knew there was something off about him. I shouldn't have forced you to stay behind when you'd asked to come with... I should've noticed when he wandered off... What happened today is my fault."

"Don't say that." I shook my head. "I wouldn't let you *watch out* for me if you'd tried. I *am* independent and I like that about me and you. What happened today is nobody's fault but his."

"Alaina, I don't know if I can control myself... when I see him. I never thought myself capable of murder, but I didn't want to stop until he was dead. Wouldn't have stopped if you hadn't asked me to. And now..." He touched the bite mark on my shoulder, "Now that I've seen the damage... It's all I can do not to turn back to camp and finish what I started."

"One thing at a time." I smoothed my hands over his chest and sighed heavily. "First, soap."

Gently, Jack washed my body, wrapping me in a strip of wool fabric Lilly had packed to dry me off. I stepped into the long loose yoga pants she'd sent, happy she'd thought to send pants instead of shorts, and slipped the tank top on over my head, wrapping the gold and red silk robe around me and feeling finally safe and clean.

The night had fallen, and as we approached camp, I could just barely make out the hunched over body tied against the tree beside our cave. I quickly diverted my eyes to the ground near his feet, not ready to look at him, where I could see a taut rope extending from the lump into camp. My heart warmed when my eyes followed the rope to find it securely affixed to Jim's ankle.

Jim was leaned against the wall of the cave with his legs spread out in front of him, his head back and his eyes closed. I smiled at Lilly, who, of course, was curled up against his shoulder, her arms wrapped around his upper arm as she stared into the fire.

The rest of our island family was busy inside the cave. I could hear the sound of dishes, silverware, hushed voices, and shuffling feet.

"James...?" Lilly asked softly, her eyes still focused on the flames.

He groaned. "Yes, Lillian?"

"What if it would've been me out there?"

He frowned, keeping his eyes shut. "It wasn't never gonna' be you."

"How do you know?"

He brought the other arm up and scratched the top of her head. "Because I know where ye' are at all times. Always got my eye on ye.' And if I cain't see ye,' ye' ain't never far enough away from me I cain't get to ye.' It wasn't never gonna' be you."

She sighed and nuzzled her face further into his shoulder. "I really don't know why you fight it. You obviously *love* me."

"Don't start, Lilly. Not now."

"What the HELL do you think you're looking at?!" Jack's voice bounced across the cave walls as we circled into camp, causing Lilly and Jim to jump. He glared down at Phil, moving closer and closer to him as he spoke. "You don't look at her! You don't speak to her! You don't even think about her! You understand?"

Phil's nose squeaked and whistled as his breathing grew heavier. He struggled against the restraints as Jack got closer.

"As a matter of fact," Jack closed the gap between them with one long stride, speaking through gritted teeth, "you don't move unless I tell you... you don't eat or sleep or breathe unless *I* let you. And if you so much as take a piss without my permission, I *will* finish what I started."

"Jack," he struggled, "I didn't—"

"DO NOT speak to me." Jack's shoulders tensed up. "There is not a single thing you can have to say to me that'll change anything. What's done is done and you'll pay for it for the rest of the time we're stuck here. Do not speak. I don't want to hear anything you have to say."

"Ay, Hoss." Jim shook himself from Lilly and rushed to the tree, draping one arm heavily over Jack's shoulders. "I took 'at bullet out of him." He grinned down at Phil. "Took my sweet time doin' it, too. Ain't that right ye' sasquatch lookin' summbitch?"

He turned Jack around to face away from Phil, walking him the few steps back to the cave entrance. "What ye' thinkin' we orta' do with him?"

"I vote we throw him on a log and send him out into the ocean," Lilly said, joining Jim at our sides and wrapping both arms around me. "I'm so sorry Lainey," she whispered close to my ear, "I can kill him if you want."

I laughed at that. "No, that's alright. Thank you for the soap and clothes."

"We could exile him," Bud offered, joining our little circle. "Send him up to the summit permanently to watch for ships."

Jack shook his head. "No. I have to know where he's at at all times. Can't risk him sneaking back to camp."

Jim nodded. "I agree. Cain't turn him loose. He'd find a way back... couldn't go without the drink, and once he had it... well... we've seen who he is."

"We should kill him," Kyle said, sitting with a thud on his butt by the fire, "and be done with it."

Jim shook his head. "No... we ain't killin' him... not yet anyway.... We *could* cage him... I could dig a pit close to camp. A deep one... like we do for the rest of the pigs... we could take turns guardin' it, shoot him square between the eyes if he tries to figure a way out."

Jack ran a hand over the short stubble of his quickly growing beard. "That could work. It's gonna slow progress on the boat. I don't want to leave any of the girls up here alone with him, so that means one of us..."

"I'll watch him," Bud offered. "I can't help much with the boat, but guarding him, I can do."

"What about at night?" Lilly demanded, her arms still wrapped tight around my waist. "You can't guard him around the clock."

"We could keep him tied up just like he is now." Jim glared down at him. "Wouldn't need to worry about him escapin' if we kept him tied like the hog he is and then none of us'd need to be guardin' him and we could focus on the boat."

"That seems pretty extreme." I frowned. "Even for him... Do you think..." I swallowed, knowing what I was about to say wouldn't be well received. "Well, what if it *was* just the alcohol?"

"No," Bud said pointedly. "I've been drunk plenty of times in my life—so drunk I couldn't remember my own name, and never once tried to force myself on a woman. A man capable of that, no matter how drunk he may have been, is beyond rehabilitation and is a danger to all of us."

"It's not the alcohol," Kyle assured us. "I saw it in his eyes—that same excitement he'd get when he'd beat my mother. He knew what he was doing and he was enjoying it. He's an evil man. If you give him the chance, he'll do it again."

"I'm telling you," Lilly insisted, "we should hollow out a tree and ship him out on the ocean. Then we won't have to worry about feeding him *or* watching him, let alone listening to him plead to get out. He'll just be gone with no chance of coming back. And maybe he'll run into a ship and go home... maybe he'll grow a conscience and send help... or maybe he'll die of dehydration or starvation... Either way, we'd be rid of him. If we watched him disappear, we wouldn't need to worry about him escaping a hole or sneaking back to camp, he'd be gone."

"I agree with Lilly." Magna appeared from the cave, her shirt filled with fresh spaghetti algae. Bertie made her way out at the side of her with a basket full of crab.

"Alaina, baby," Magna met my eyes, an apologetic grimace filling her round face, "I shouldn't have let you go out on that ankle, should've insisted you stayed put."

"I'm alright," I assured her.

Her eyes shifted to the discoloration on my cheek, and she shook her head. "You all come sit down now. Bertie and I are gonna fix you some dinner."

I wouldn't be able to eat. I was too disgusted to have an appetite. I smiled at her fondly, then returned my attention to the task at hand. "If we send him out on the ocean with no food or water, that's as good as shooting him in the head. I hate him, I mean I *really* hate him, but I don't want his death on my conscience."

"So what then, we dig a pit?" Jim looked at me for confirmation.

"Now wait a minute." Lilly stomped her little foot, looking up at Jack and then back to me. "If we dig a pit, then we're going to have to babysit him around the clock. And we'll have to pull him out in the rain if the pit starts to fill up... We'll have to bring him food and water... which means, after he's eaten and drank, he'll need to... well, let's just say he'll be living in his own filth unless we want to pull him out every time he needs to go... and I'm assuming we won't... which means that hole will start to stink... which means we can't have it close to camp. And that means whoever's babysitting is going to be away from camp. I don't like that. I don't like the idea of us being separated both at camp and up on the summit on account of this fat rapist bastard. I really think we should consider sending him off—with food and supplies," she rolled her eyes, "on the ocean. He could find help..."

"And what makes you think he'd send help?" Jack twisted his mouth in thought. "After everything that's happened?"

"He probably wouldn't. Maybe we could carve a message into the wood of whatever we send him out on? It's not like he'd be able to remove a carved message... we wouldn't send him out with a knife..."

"Actually," Jim smiled proudly at her, "that ain't a bad idea. We could put him on the lifeboat; patch it up, attach a sail and he could be gone in the mornin.'"

Phil wheezed and coughed. "No, please. I—

"Ay," Jim reached down and pulled the rope connecting them hard, forcing Phil to cry out in a strangled throaty sob. "Not another word out of ye.' Yer lucky yer even still breathin' you piece of dog shit. You'll take whatever we decide ye' get and ye' ought to be grateful for it."

"I do like the idea of never laying eyes on him again," Jack noted, shaking his head, "but to send him out on the only boat we have right now?"

"Would ye' spend weeks buildin' somethin' for him?" Jim spit to one side. "I ain't spendin' no more time than I got to on this piece of shit. That lifeboat's just about rotted through, anyway. We could patch it up enough for one person, but not the lot of us. We'd have a better chance in the raft than on that thing."

Jack sighed and placed his hand on my shoulder, his tone softening. "What do you think, Red? We wouldn't let him starve and we'd send plenty of water. We wouldn't necessarily be sending him to his death so it would keep your conscience clear."

I finally looked over at Phil then. His face was a swollen mess of purple and blue, caked with the dried blood that had spilled from his nose. How small he suddenly seemed to me. The thought that this small man had gotten so close to inflicting damage on me —emotional damage that might have been irreparable—seemed surreal. He disgusted me, not only in his actions, but more so for the way he'd made me feel about myself. I hated myself for having been so entirely incapable of fighting him off of me. I didn't ever want to be in that position again. Slowly I nodded, "I think that could work."

"Did you hear that, pervert?!" Lilly shouted down at him. "You're gone."

Chapter Forty-Six

"A.J.," Cece bit her lip and frowned as she tucked the sheet corners under the queen-size mattress opposite me. "I talked to Chris last night... he's not coming today."

As the mid-October chill had settled in, the normally busy campground was almost desolate. She and I took that time to deep clean all the cabins in preparation of the winter rush.

I frowned. "Why wouldn't he tell me that himself?"

She shook her head, eyebrows high on her forehead. "He's not coming the week after that either. He says he can't keep doing this."

I sighed. *'Well, you've officially shut him out. Are you happy now?'*

"Sweetie, you need to talk to him. He loves you and this is killing him."

I growled. "You think I don't know that? I hate this and I don't know how to fix it. Cece, I can't even look at him! And I hate myself for it." I groaned as I felt my eyes well with tears. "I want to be me again. I just can't get above this."

She exhaled slowly. "Alright, look, I know you don't like the idea, but what if you talked to someone? Maybe take a light antidepressant until you can beat this depression?"

She held up her palm as I moved to protest, "A.J., you are self-destructing. You're about to lose your job, your husband, and the life you worked so hard to build... You need help. Bigger help than what I can give. You can't stay distracted up here forever."

"Cece, I don't want to rely on a pill to make me happy."

"Well then, you'd better find something you *can* rely on fast. You've got an amazing life you're about to just throw away. I get that it hurts, believe me, I *know* it hurts, but it happened and what will happen if you don't get over that will hurt so much worse. You can always try again or adopt, but you'll never be able to get this life back, not after you've thrown it away. He's going to divorce you unless you do something to fix this."

I froze. "What are you saying? Did he say that?"

She looked down, tediously folding the duvet over the sheets and avoiding eye contact with me.

"He said the word *divorce* to you?" I demanded.

"A.J., what do you expect him to do?" She threw the pillows back into their places at the head of the bed, looking up then. "You've been up here for almost two months now. You won't talk to him, and you have shown him absolutely nothing to indicate you're ever going home. The man's a mess."

The lump in my throat was suffocating. Quickly I fetched my jacket from the dresser and sped out the back door, waiting until I was deep in the woods to pull the phone from my pocket, hit Chris's name, and break down when his voice hit my ear.

"Come get me," I sobbed, "I wanna come home. I wanna fix it. I'm sorry. Please don't leave me. I'll get help, I promise. I'll get help and we'll go back to normal. Please, please don't leave me."

"Ally, I'd never leave you," he said sweetly. "Never."

I sobbed incoherently, dropping to my knees in the fallen Autumn leaves. "Chris, I know we fight every single time you're here, but seeing your truck pull into this campground is the only thing I look forward to. I know I've been awful and I don't deserve you, but I don't wanna lose you."

"You're not going to lose me, I promise."

"But Cece said you're not coming and…"

He laughed. "Ally, baby, I couldn't not come. I was upset last night. I'm halfway there already."

I sobbed harder, folding over myself, "Oh, thank God. Oh, thank you, thank you, thank you. I'm coming home with you.

We'll fix this. I don't wanna be like this anymore. I want to be me again. I don't want to mess this up any more. I miss you so much."

His voice shook. "Ally, I miss you with all my heart. I'm driving as fast as I can."

I nodded, warm tears pouring down my cold cheeks as I cried out loud. "I love you."

"It's gonna be okay. We're gonna be okay," he breathed shakily. "I'll be there soon. There's lots we need to talk about. I love you, honey, and everything will be okay."

I sat on my butt in the dried yellow leaves, hugging my knees to my chest. "Stay on the phone with me until you get here? Tell me something... anything... everything."

"There's so much I need to tell you, but I don't want to do it over the phone."

"Why not?" I begged, sniffling loudly as the tears continued to pour from me. "We used to sit on the phone for hours."

He coughed. "I need to see you. Need to talk in-person. I don't want to do this over the phone."

"Do what?" I shook. "Oh God, you *are* going to divorce me, aren't you?"

"No, I'm not. I swear. We'll talk just as soon as I get there, honey. Everything's going to be okay."

I wept loudly, panic sweeping over me. "Well, what don't you want to do? Did something happen? Did someone die?"

"No, baby, nothing like that."

"Is someone sick? Please tell me you're not sick?"

"No, Al. We'll talk when I get there. Just a few more hours."

"Well, what is it, then? Did you sleep with someone?"

The dead silence on the other end of the line was deafening, and my entire body trembled. I straightened, wiping the tears from my eyes. "Chris... did you sleep with someone?"

"Not exactly," he finally said.

Fresh tears filled my eyes. "Well then, what *exactly*?"

"Al, please don't make me do this over the phone."

"Is this why you called Cece instead of me last night?" My breath hitched as a new breakdown overtook me. "Is this why you told her you weren't coming? Because there's someone else? Who is she?"

"There is no '*she.*' I got drunk and…"

"And what?" I sobbed, "and what?!"

"And I kissed a woman—hell, I made out with her for an hour outside the bar. And then…"

"AND THEN??"

He sighed. "She took me home, and it got more heated… we undressed and I was gonna…. But I couldn't. Ally, I couldn't do it, I swear to you. I held her in my arms and slept and wished she was you. Then I woke up and I ran out of there in a panic. I got in my truck and started driving to you. I had to see you. Had to tell you. Ally, I swear, that's it."

I nodded, my lips quivering as my heart broke in two. I'd done this to him. I left him, pushed him further and further away from me. He drove countless hours to come up here and have me turn away from him every time he tried to touch me. He'd lost a child, and I'd run out on him. How angry was I possibly allowed to be?

"Ally, please say something."

"I don't know what to say… Just… hurry up."

I hung up the phone and sat there, staring off into the woods, my heart pounding in my throat. Closing my eyes, I could see his lips on hers. I didn't know her, but in my mind, she was stunning. I could see her hands undressing him, pulling the shirt over his head and rushing to press her lips back onto his.

I buried my face in my hands, picturing his hands in her hair, his lips on her skin, his body laying naked next to hers, his arms wrapped tightly around her. I imagined her hands on his bare chest… touching him softly, the way I used to…

I curled my fingers up into my hair and pulled, trembling with tears as I pictured his hands on this beautiful, faceless stranger, caressing her the way he would me.

He said he couldn't go through with it, but was this just as bad? I needed to know more. I needed to know how he'd touched her… how and where she'd touched him…

I shook my head. Could I ask those questions after all I'd put him through? Would the answers be any less devastating than what

I already knew? Would it change the image in my mind in any way?

I squeezed my eyes tightly shut.

"A.J?" Doug's voice came up from ahead of me. "A.J., are you okay?" I could hear his running feet rustling through the leaves. "What happened?"

I sniffled, shaking my head of the tears. "I'm fine. I'm going home."

"Home?" He tilted his head, kneeling in front of me. "Are you sure?"

"Yes." I blew out, wiping my eyes with my thumbs.

"When?"

"Today... tomorrow... I don't know."

He took my hand in his, smiling. "Well, you seem real happy about it!"

I could feel new tears trying to come, and I inhaled deeply as I pulled my fingers from his grip. "Doug, I'm not really in a great place right now. I'm sorry, I kinda need to be alone."

He shook his head. "Well, I'm not really in a great place, either. What am I gonna do up here without my best old lady friend?"

I crumbled again, tears spilling down my cheeks. "I really need to be alone for a while."

"Not happening, grandma." He sat on his butt beside me, wrapping an arm around me. "I can't let you sit up here in the woods crying by yourself. What if a bear comes? Who will defend you?!" He chuckled at himself.

I sniffled, hiding my face in my hands. "Go away, Doug."

"Why don't you tell me what you're crying about and I will work my Doug magic to make it better?"

"Everything," I snapped, "I'm crying about everything."

"Well, that's dumb." He nudged me. "You need to break that down into smaller, bite-sized pieces. Everything is way too much to cry about in one sitting. Where do you wanna start? Ooh, you know what makes me cry? The Chicago Bears. Let's cry about them first, yeah?"

I rolled my eyes, wiping the tears from beneath them as I huffed. "You're ridiculous, you know that?"

He grinned, his eyebrows bouncing up and down. "I know. It's fun though."

I shook my head, my nostrils burning and tears spilling over me as I tried to catch my breath.

"Come on, A.J., talk to me." He smoothed his hand over my back. "What's going on?"

My voice wobbled with the words. "Doug, someday someone's going to love you in a way you'll know is forever the minute you meet them... Don't mess that up."

"Is that what you did? You messed up your forever?"

I nodded. "Yeah," I shook with tears again, "I really think I did."

"Well," he shrugged, "seems like a pretty simple thing to fix... *forever*, I mean. So much time to work on it..."

I smiled, laughing between sobs at the profoundness of such a simple comment. "That's pretty deep for you."

He scratched my back. "I smoke a lot of pot and spend a lot of time alone in the woods. I'm all kinds of deep."

I stared off toward camp, the momentary smile fading as I tried to imagine what I might say when he finally pulled in the drive. "He cheated," I whispered.

"Chris?" Doug shook his head. "Didn't see that coming... At all."

"Me neither. Not ever. He was always this man who would never hurt me in my mind. I never doubted anything he ever said or did because he's Chris and he's just... good. Good to me especially. There was no amount of terrible he wouldn't take from me because he just loved me that much. And now? I don't know what to do or feel or say or how to even react because my heart is broken, but I did this to myself."

He sighed. "You didn't do this. You were just trying to figure out a way to cope with the shit hand you got dealt... Maybe he was too."

I nodded. "Maybe." I closed my eyes and saw them, once again wrapped up in a kiss, his fingertips exploring the length of her spine. "But how many more shitty hands can I get dealt before I go broke just trying to stay in?"

My eyes were swollen and my nose was red. I'd paced the campground and my cabin at least a thousand times, rehearsing possible responses to things he might say, twisting the situation in my mind to try to understand whether I was angry with him, with myself, or at the world.

I stood at the living room window that looked out toward the tunnel of trees lining the entrance to the campground. Any minute his truck would come through them. What would I do? What would I say?

Part of me wanted to run into his arms and forget everything. I wanted my marriage back. I wanted to forget everything and go back to the sweet couple we'd been that made each other coffee and cuddled together on the sofa.

Could I forget? Could he? Would I ever be able to lie in his arms without wondering about her?

I chewed my thumbnail, watching the dirt road.

Would he still smell like her? Would there be marks on him where her lips had once been? Would he look different to me? Would he kiss differently after he'd kissed another?

What if she was beautiful? What if she was wonderful and sweet? What if he pulled in, looked at me and decided I was no longer worth the effort?

And then I saw the shimmering black paint of his all-too-familiar truck and bolted out the door. I ran down the stairs of the cabin's porch and stood in the driveway as he placed the truck in park and leapt from the driver's side.

He collapsed to his knees at my feet and stared up at me through bloodshot eyes. He didn't look different... he was still Chris—*my* Chris—and somehow he wasn't Chris at all. He was the most familiar person in my life, but at that moment, he was a complete stranger to me.

A hint of his familiar cologne filled my nostrils and, knowing he only wore cologne when he went out, I realized he was still in the clothes he'd worn the night before. She'd touched this shirt... she'd pulled this shirt off him... had her hands on his skin, in his hair... I took a step back as my heart began to race and my hands began to shake.

"Please, Ally. Please, forgive me," he wept.

I'd never seen him cry—not really. I'd seen his eyes water a time or two, but I'd never seen him sob. His entire face was swollen with it. He'd been crying as long as I had, maybe longer.

"It was a mistake and I'll do anything." He put his hands together to beg. "*Anything* to fix it. Please let me fix this."

I stood straighter, folding my arms over my midsection, determined not to break down.

"Please, Al. Tell me what I can do to fix it."

"Strip," I commanded.

"What?" He looked around the empty campground and out at the lake.

"Strip," I repeated with the same authority. "You said you came straight here." My nostrils flared as I took a deep breath. "And you're not coming inside in those clothes."

Slowly, he stood, glancing around again before he pulled the black t-shirt up over his head.

I extended my arm, and he handed it to me. He looked around once more before he kicked off his boots, unbuttoned his blue jeans, and pushed them down to the ground. He knelt and grabbed them, placing them into my still-outstretched hand.

"All of it."

He blushed, shivering a little in his thin white boxers, but he didn't argue. One last time, he scanned the campground for observers then stripped naked, handing me his boxers with one hand while the other promptly covered his manhood.

I spun on my heel, adjusting the pile of clothes in my arm as I walked to my cabin's fire pit and threw them in. I knelt, grabbing the lighter fluid and matches, careful not to look back at him as I doused the clothes in fluid, struck a match and dropped it in. The sudden whoosh of the flames engulfing the clothing was more satisfying than I'd imagined and I smiled to myself before I turned back to my naked, shivering husband.

"Now you can go shower. *Then* we will talk."

I stood at the fire for a good long while, watching as his clothes became ash and the sun crept down to cast a warm red glow over the lake. When I finally stepped inside, I found him sitting on the green plaid loveseat of my cabin, wearing only a towel. His dark hair still dripped onto his broad shoulders and his face contorted with the effort of not breaking down. He shook, both from the cold October air coming through my open windows and from the fatigue I could see in his body.

I cleared my throat as I leaned against the cabin's front door, facing him. "I'm tired, Chris."

"I—"

I placed my hand up. I didn't want to hear him apologize anymore. "This fucking hurts. Knowing that someone else..." I swallowed, my eyes welling. "Knowing that *you*..." I paced, sniffling. "You... my home... my heart... MY WHOLE HEART... YOU, *my* person... with your hands on someone else... with your mouth on someone else's. I can't un-think it. I can't get it out of my head. And it hurts."

"Ally, I—"

"Just let me talk." I paced, crossing my arms over my chest. "But the thought of you leaving me hurt more... What we have... You and me, this isn't like everyone else. You don't get to walk out on that. You don't get to give up on that. I remember and I promised you I wouldn't... but then I *did* walk out on you. I did give up... I walked out when you needed me most, and I pushed you out of my arms and straight into hers."

"Al..." he stood, holding his towel in place at his hip.

"Chris, I'm tired of being broken." I let myself break down then, warm fat tears spilling as my breath hitched and my nose ran endlessly. "And you're the only person who can fix me. I wanna go home."

He reached for me then, pulling me against his bare chest. I collapsed into him, sobbing uncontrollably as his arms tightened around me.

"I'll do anything to make it right."

"Swear to me," I pulled back, looking up at him. "Swear you'll never ever do anything like this to me again."

He cupped my face in his hands, his eyes red with tears as his face drew closer. "I swear it."

I looked at his lips as if I would kiss them, as if kissing them would erase all the pain we'd caused each other; as if all the comfort I desperately needed was right there within reach if I just kissed his lips.

But I couldn't.

All I could see was someone else's lips on his, and my stomach turned. I closed my eyes and buried my face in his chest again, letting his familiar arms curl around me. He held me tight, but his arms offered no comfort.

Had he held her like this? Would I ever be able to un-think it? Could we ever be the people we were before we'd ripped each other's hearts out?

What if forever wasn't enough time to fix all we'd broken?

Chapter Forty-Seven

"Just me, Red," Jack whispered against the back of my head as I jumped awake—visions of Phil still looming in my mind as the nightmare I'd been trapped in slowly dissolved in the faint blue morning light.

I sighed with relief, all my muscles relaxing as I rolled to face him. His eyes were bloodshot and dark circles had formed beneath them. "Have you slept at all?"

He closed his eyes for a moment and shook his head, running a hand over my hair. "Not yet." He gingerly traced the bruising I could feel on my cheek. "You relived it in your sleep... over and over. I couldn't fall asleep for fear you might relive it again and I wouldn't be able to wake you."

He took a deep breath. "I wish I could—

"HE'S LOOSE!" Jim shouted nearby, his voice full of panic, "Get up! EVERYBODY GET UP!! That summbitch got loose!! HE'S LOOSE, GOT DAMMIT!!!"

Jack leapt out of the tent, his bare feet rustling in the leaves near my head. "What do you mean he's loose?" he shouted. "HOW?"

"I don't know! I tied the rope myself. Wasn't no gettin' out of 'em knots. I dozed off for a second. A SECOND!! Opened my eyes and he's gone! KYLE! KYLE! GET YER ASS OUT HERE WHERE I CAN SEE YE! LILLY? GRAB IZZY AND COME ON!"

"Red," Jack knelt at the tent's opening, "we're gonna have to go look for him and I'm not letting you out of my sight. Can you manage?"

I nodded, my heart racing. "My boots..." I searched the tent, coming up with one and realizing I had no idea where the other was.

"LILLY?!" Jim continued on his rampage, his voice moving away from us.

"We'll have to go up and get the other one later," Jack insisted, extending his hand to me. "We have to catch up to him before he gets too far."

I crawled out of the tent to find Jim grabbing Lilly's hand and tugging her behind him in the direction of camp. "Where the hell you been?!" he growled. "Don't you never just go off like 'at where I don't know where ye' are."

"I was just—"

"Phil's loose, dammit. Ye' had me worried sick. Where's Izzy? KYLE! KYLE, GET OUT HERE AND BRING IZZY!"

I jogged awkwardly on my bare feet alongside Jack as we caught up to them and circled back into camp.

Jim knelt to inspect the frayed rope that sat in the place of Phil's body against the tree, running his palm over a set of footprints in the dirt. "If that boy turned him loose... I swear..."

Jack knelt beside him, inspecting the ground. "He couldn't have gotten far. He's got to be hiding out nearby."

"He went that way... they *both* did." Jim pointed uphill. "See 'em prints there? Looks like Phil and Kyle... and they's another set here... That's gotta be Magna?"

Jack nodded, rising and calling into the cave, "Bud? Is Izzy in there? We're gonna need that gun."

Silence.

"Bud?" Jack frowned, cautiously stepping toward the cave entrance. I followed him inside.

Bertie sat on the floor with Bud wrapped in her lap. She smoothed over his hair and rocked, weeping as she looked up at us. Izzy was standing over them, staring wide-eyed, one little hand resting on Bertie's shoulder. He was breathing—I could see his chest moving—but he had a large welt on his forehead and was completely unconscious.

"How could he do this to us?" Bertie asked, coughing as she held Bud against her.

"Did you see them?" Jack asked.

She shook her head, sniffling. "No. I... I woke up and found him like this."

"GRANDPA!" Lilly rushed past me and threw herself on the floor with them, smoothing her hands over the large bump protruding from his forehead. "Wake up! Wake up!" She shook him by the shoulders.

Bud's eyes fluttered as he struggled to open them.

"What happened?" she asked.

"He took the gun," he said to her, wincing as he touched his forehead. "I'm sorry."

"Shh, it's alright," she assured him. "We'll find him."

"Was Kyle helping him?" Jack asked.

Bud frowned, opening one eye. "No. Kyle was asleep right..." He pointed at the empty bed across from him. "...there."

"Shit," Jim said under his breath, his silhouette filling the cave entrance. "He'll be after three things: revenge, a place to hide out, and a drink. If he was in here, he's got the drink... now he's got Kyle and will be out lookin' for a place to hide... We gotta find 'em 'for he kills the kid."

"We can't leave them alone," Lilly whined, wrapping her arms around Bertie. "What if he comes back here?"

I knelt at the suitcases in the far corner of the cave, pulling out a pair of flip-flops that were slightly too big and sliding them on my feet.

Jim groaned. "He ain't comin' back here. And the longer we wait, the harder it's gonna be to find him. Now grab Izzy and come on."

"I'm not leaving them." She set her jaw and raised her chin.

"Dammit, woman, I cain't leave ye' here." He hopped from one foot to the other, looking outside the cave and back in.

"We'll be alright," Bud assured her. "You take Izzy and go with them."

"But—"

"We'll be alright," Bertie echoed. "You go and stay close to Jim."

Lilly spun around to face us. "I'm gonna kill him for this." She extended her hand to Izzy. "Come on, Iz."

Jim had already turned to go, the machete in one hand.

"You grab that axe and get behind 'em," Jim instructed Jack as we crossed camp and stopped at the tree to inspect the footprints. "I can track him. You make sure he cain't creep up on us from behind."

Silently, we followed Jim as he followed the tracks up into the shade of the canopy.

I watched the ground, positioning Izzy between my body and Lilly's, each of us taking one of her hands.

There were three distinct patterns in the dirt. The largest set was Phil's. I knew this from the fine line pattern and distinct heel impression his loafers left behind. I noticed one foot tended to drag slightly and wondered how far he could've gotten with a limp.

The second set was similar in size but left a deeper impression, the zigzag of the soles of Kyle's tennis shoes intertwined with Phil's steps. Had Phil taken him hostage, or was Kyle in pursuit?

The third set was the clearest of the three, Magna's bare feet, her wide toe impressions and the lack of heel in many of the steps told me she'd been running.

The tracks turned and led into a much more dense jungle to the west, the thickness of the overgrowth making navigation more difficult and following footprints impossible. As we turned with them, I pulled Izzy up into my arms to better keep my eye on her.

I noticed a broken fan palm dangling from its plant, and just beyond that, another. "Look." I pointed at them. "See the broken leaves? Magna must've left them."

"Oh Lordt bless ye', Magna." Jim hurried through the plants, following each new signal left behind as we continued further inland and upward.

The signals stopped at a clearing. We stood there circling, looking for any sign of them—no footprints in the dirt and no more broken branches. To one side of us was a large grouping of boulders and lava rock that climbed up a steep incline toward the summit. On another side was more dense jungle. Thick vines and wet vegetation obstructed the path forward. Directly ahead of us was wet clay.

There was no sign of them in the clay ahead. To go up the rocks didn't make any sense.

Jim shrugged his shoulders and turned toward the bush, "It ain't gonna be—"

In a flash, Phil leapt from the rocks behind me and pulled Lilly in front of him to face us, positioning the pistol at her temple and wrapping his other arm across her chest. "Nobody move."

I lowered Isobel to the ground and shielded her with my body, keeping one hand behind me to hold on to hers.

His nearly swollen shut eyes darted from Jack to Jim to me and back as he squeezed Lilly against him with his forearm. His face was shades of black and blue and his nose was triple its normal size, his breathing labored as he backed away from us.

"You can't put me out there to die." He turned to face Jack as he made a move to step forward. "DON'T MOVE OR I'LL SHOOT HER, I SWEAR!"

"Ay, easy now..." Jim raised his hands and spoke evenly. "We ain't movin', are we, Hoss?"

Jack shook his head as he glared at Phil.

The desperation in Phil's eyes made me freeze in place. I remembered his panic on the raft; his hand reaching for the rope every time the raft would bob. He was afraid of the water—so afraid he'd do anything not to go out there alone. He would shoot her... He would shoot all of us if he had to.

"I can't get on that water... I won't," Phil continued, his nose whistling as he tried to breathe between words while he fought to keep a furious, kicking Lilly still. "You can tie me up, put me down in a hole, put me up on the summit... but you can't put me out there to die." His attention shifted to Jim. "I've been shot and beaten nearly to death. I can't survive out there." He looked at me. "I would die out there. And that'd be on *your* conscience."

Jack tilted his head to one side. "Why don't you let her go and point that gun at me and we'll talk about it?"

Phil pulled Lilly tighter against him and pressed the gun harder against her head. "Hold still!" he reprimanded as she fought to free herself. "I'll shoot you. Don't think I won't do it!"

"Lilly," Jim shook his head in warning, "Quit squirmin.'"

Lilly wouldn't be deterred. "Fucking coward." She opened her mouth wide, struggling to bend her head far enough to bite. "You fucking coward!" She kicked her legs, attempting to hit his shins.

"Lilly, quit," Jim advised, keeping his eyes focused on Phil. "What's the next move then, Phil? Ye' cain't hold that gun to her head forever. What's it gonna' take to let her go?"

Phil pulled her tighter against him. "I need a guarantee you won't put me on the ocean."

"Coward," Lilly spat.

Phil cocked the gun, his nose squealing as he inhaled excitedly.

"Alright! Alright, easy easy." Jim pushed his hands in the air in front of him. "What do ye' want then?"

"I'm no fool. I let her go, you'll either kill me right away or put me on the water, anyway. I need a guarantee."

"What kind of guarantee?" Jack asked through gritted teeth.

"*You* go out on the ocean." He looked between the two of them. "Both of you."

"That's not—"

"Alright." Jim nodded, his eyes darting upward and back to Phil. "Alright. Tell me how it's gonna work. We all walk down to the beach and pull the lifeboat into the water while you hold that gun at her head the whole time?"

"No." Phil turned them to face Jim. "You'll take the raft. I'll hold this gun until I feel like putting it down."

"Well, I'm gonna' need a guarantee then too." Jim raised his eyebrows, glancing up again and back down to Phil. "How do I know ye' won't shoot her as soon as I get on that raft?"

Phil breathed loudly. "You don't."

"Well, seems to me we got us a Mexican standoff then, don't we? I need a guarantee before I'll step on that raft."

Phil glanced between the two of them, his muscles tensing as frustration flushed over him. "I'VE GOT THE GODDAMN GUN!

I'LL SHOOT HER RIGHT NOW! THIS ISN'T UP FOR NEGOTIATION."

"Alright, alright, take it easy. How ye' wanna go about gettin' down there then? Ye' want me to go first?" Jim continued all too calmly, and then I noticed what he'd been looking at.

Behind Phil, Magna was creeping down the rocks, one step at a time, a large boulder held high over her head with both hands.

"You are not getting on the raft!" Lilly kicked her feet.

"Yes we are," Jim assured her as Magna took another step forward. "Now, do we get to stock up the raft before we ship out?"

"Wasn't it you who suggested they send *me* off with no food or water?" Phil hissed against Lilly's ear. "It's only fair I treat them the same."

"Hold on a minute." Jim raised an eyebrow at him as Magna took another step. "We said we'd send ye' with supplies."

"After what you've done to me, the raft is more than you deserve. I ought to just shoot you both now and be done with it."

Lilly jerked hard to one side and bit down on Phil's arm, causing Phil to cry out loud. At the sound, Magna launched the large rock with all the force she had, and it crashed down on Phil's skull with a "clonk" that knocked him off his feet and out cold.

Jim and Jack leapt forward, Jack kneeling to grab the gun from Phil as Jim pulled Lilly into his arms. "Ye' stubborn ass woman. If I tell ye' to quit squirmin,' ye' quit, Got dammit! Ye' almost got yourself killt."

He squeezed her tightly with both arms and rested his cheek against the top of her head, looking up at Magna as he rocked her from side to side. "Ay Momma, ye' got one hell of a throw. Thank ye.' You seen Kyle?"

Izzy bolted from my grip and ran to Magna as she climbed down from the rocks. "He's alright." She lifted Izzy up into her arms. "Took a nasty hit to the face with the butt of the gun but he's alright. I'll get him back to camp. What you gonna' do with him?"

Jack stood over him as he nodded slowly, deciding. "We stick to the plan. We put him on the ocean… like we said we would." There was a sinisterness to him as he said it—a satisfaction in knowing how terrified Phil was of the ocean. It'd be a punishment worse than shooting him now. He met Jim's eyes. "I'll paddle him out there, you'll follow me in the raft."

Jim bowed his head in agreement, rocking Lilly to one side. "Alright then. Still gotta' rig a sail on that lifeboat. I reckon he'll wake up 'for I do."

Jack glared back down at his lifeless body. "Red, you and Lilly go ahead down, grab some fabric for a sail and some food and water while we get him tied back up. We'll meet you down there."

Chapter Forty-Eight

Lilly and I loaded up a duffle bag with coconuts, Fe'i, guava, and what remained of the smoked grouper. We'd gone to the waterfall and refilled all the resealable emergency ration bags with water and loaded them into Izzy's suitcase along with several yards of fabric.

She curled her arm in mine as we walked toward the beach, resting her head on my shoulder. "I haven't had a chance to ask you about what happened. Are you alright?"

"I'm fine," I assured her. "Kyle stopped it before anything could happen."

She sighed. "Thank God."

"Are *you* alright?" I asked, realizing being held at gunpoint might've been just as traumatic.

"Me?" She laughed. "I'm great. Did you see the chunk I took out of his arm?"

I snickered. "I did."

She raised her head from my shoulder and lifted the suitcase as the ground became too unstable to roll it. "It happened to me in college, ya know."

"What did?"

She blew out. "A bunch of us were hanging out at my apartment having a few drinks, playing beer pong." She twisted her lips as she remembered. "There was this guy there, Stephen Bass. I didn't know him. He didn't go to school with us but he was friends with one of the other guys there and he was my partner for a game."

She shook her head. "And he had that same thing as Phil where he stood too close... touched too often... looked at me a certain way." She met my eyes. "I should've known."

She took a deep breath. "Anyway, when I finished the game, having never really played it before, I was pretty drunk, so I decided I was going to bed. My roommate was still up, so I figured she would usher them out—it's what we did. Whoever was up last dealt with the stragglers. They'd started a new game of beer pong and I guess no one was watching Stephen... He waited a while, of course, until I was asleep before he crawled into my bed."

She narrowed her eyes and pursed her lips. "I was nineteen... and he made me feel like it was my fault... like I'd led him on all night and owed it to him. I kept telling him no... stop... kept trying to push him off me, but he was too big.... too strong... and eventually I just gave up and let him. I didn't scream or fight... Because deep down I felt like maybe I did lead him on... That son of a bitch really did make me believe it was my fault. I never told anyone about it until now."

"Oh Lilly, I'm so sorry." I wrapped my free arm around her.

"I'm tougher than I look." She smiled sweetly. "I'm telling you this because I know it's hard right after... the nightmares that haunt you even when you're awake, asking yourself what you could've done or why you didn't do something different. It's not your fault he's a pig. And it gets easier. Those nightmares go away faster than you think, probably even faster if he didn't...."

I nodded, pulling her against me and kissing the top of her head. "What ever happened to Stephen? After..."

She grinned. "Well it never sat well with me, what he did, but that nagging little nineteen-year-old inside me still felt a hint of fault that prevented me from going to the cops. So I got my own justice."

"What'd you do?"

"I waited. Two years after, Stephen Bass bought a gorgeous five-million-dollar house on Long Island right after he got engaged. And I paid a significant amount of money to a friend to drop off a few little packages for me."

I tilted my head. "Packages?"

"Do you know what a milk-chicken bomb is?"

I laughed. "No! But it sounds dreadful!"

"It is. You take a glass jar and you stuff it with raw chicken and milk that's already started to go bad. You fill that jar to the brim and you seal it. Then you stick it in the air ducts and you wait. Over time, after repeated exposure to heat and pressure, the glass will eventually break or the top will pop off. After that, every single time the heat kicks on, the most vile stench you'll ever smell gets released throughout the entire house. It gets worse and worse until the home becomes unlivable."

She beamed innocently. "And poor Stephen Bass ended up having to sell that house far below what he paid for it just four short months later."

I curled over in laughter. "Oh Lilly, this is the greatest revenge story I've ever heard! Serves him right!"

She laughed and leaned into me. "Men are idiots... Well, some of them. Jack's alright. And Jim... Did you see the way he reacted?" She kept her eyes ahead, her brows furrowed in thought. "The way he held onto me?"

"Lill... I don't think it meant anything."

She shook her head. "I don't know... it felt different. I think maybe I'm onto something..." She smiled. "I think he might cave sooner than I thought."

"What's with your sudden obsession with him? Why do you insist on pursuing him?" I raised an eyebrow. "We're going to build a boat. You'll be able to *fulfill your needs* soon enough."

"That's not the point anymore though, is it?" She bit her lip. "It's a challenge now... one I very much intend on winning."

We arrived on the beach, my shoulder burning from the weight of the duffle bag against my bruised skin. I could see Jim and Jack far ahead of us in the lifeboat attaching a mast that would hold its sail, the large yellow raft re-inflated at the side of it. I moved the bag and adjusted the strap over my other arm.

"He is kinda sexy, ya know." Lilly grinned as we got closer, her eyes focused on Jim. "In a weird, obnoxious hillbilly sort of way."

I laughed heartily. "Lilly, you're maybe the most interesting person I've ever met."

She tilted her head, still concentrated on him. "I *am* pretty great. Adorable too. I don't know why he insists on fighting it."

"I'M BEGGING YOU, PLEASE." I could hear Phil sobbing as we got closer. "I'LL DO ANYTHING. ANYTHING! PLEASE. PLEASE DON'T PUT ME OUT THERE."

Lilly stopped and reached an arm out. "Here. I'll take it. You don't have to go over there if you don't want to."

"No," I shook my head, "I'm alright. I want it to be my face he sees when they push off on the water... to remember the bruises he left on me that put him there."

"Good girl," she whispered, taking my hand in hers and squeezing as we took the last few steps across the sand to the boat.

"Please," he wept beneath Jack's knee on his back, Jack and Jim seemingly unbothered as they continued to lash rope around the makeshift mast. "Please don't put me on the water. Just shoot me here and now. I'll die out there."

I dropped the duffel bag on the sand. "There's enough food and water for him to last a month out there."

"Alaina," Phil begged, "I'm sorry—"

"You don't speak her name," Jack hissed as he dug his knee harder into Phil's back, pulling a length of rope out from the top of the bamboo mast.

Lilly knelt and unzipped the pink suitcase, pulling out the roll of thick, gray fabric. "I brought the sail."

"I'M SORRY," Phil continued. "I can't swim. Please, please don't do this."

"Thanks, sugar." Jim took the fabric from her and unrolled it. "Here." He reached behind him and pulled out the bowie knife, extending it to her. "Carve somethin' big in the top there in case he gets rescued."

She looked at the front of the boat and back. "What should we put?"

Jack held the fabric between his teeth as he cut a hole in the two bottom corners with the small utility knife. "The wind is blowing east. Carve something to tell them there are more of us to the west."

She nodded, climbing into the front of the boat and dusting off the wooden ledge atop the bow. "More of us to the west."

I smiled as I watched her stab the large knife into the wood; her face set in concentration. She was so small and yet so fierce. My heart warmed as I watched them all working hard to get the boat ready... sending off a man in my honor. This was my family now.

Phil continued to weep beneath them on the floor of the boat. "There's got to be something I can do. I'm begging you. Have mercy."

Jack slid the fabric onto the rope attached to the mast. "Trade," he said simply to Jim, who immediately moved to kneel over Phil so Jack could stand, extending the fabric up to the top and wrapping a length of rope around it.

"Can I help?" I offered.

Jack smiled down at me, tying the rope tight. "It's done." He pulled the bottom of the fabric down and looped the rope through the holes, sliding the fabric to form a triangle against the horizontal piece of bamboo that would serve as a jib.

The wind immediately hit the fabric, inflating it to flap to one side.

"Be right back," he said to Jim, leaping over the side of the boat to land on his feet in the sand in front of me.

He took my hand in his and walked me down the beach, far enough that we could no longer hear Phil's pleas. The afternoon sun was warm on our backs. "I'm going to ask you one last time, Red. I will take him out on the ocean and watch over my back for him the rest of our lives if that's really what you want... or I can shoot him right now and be done with it."

I shook my head. "I don't want his death looming over us."

"You're sure? There's a chance he could come back."

"I'm sure."

He wrapped his arms around me. "Alright. I'm gonna take him now. I wanna watch him disappear long before it gets dark. You wanna wait here or head back to camp? You should eat something."

"I'll wait here." I stood on my tiptoes and kissed his lips. "Thank you… for everything."

He shook his head. "You don't thank me for this. You are everything to me and I'll do anything to keep you safe. I'll be right back."

We walked back to the boat then and Lilly joined me to sit in the sand as they pushed the lifeboat and the raft into the waist-deep water. Jack jumped into the lifeboat as Jim slid into the raft and they paddled out. I watched them grow smaller and smaller on the water until they were so far out we could only see a white and yellow dot separating the blue of the sky from the blue of the ocean.

I could just see the gray of the fabric sail being raised up and sighed as I watched it catch the wind and move toward the horizon while the yellow dot returned toward us.

It was over.

Reaching into the suitcase, I pulled out the journal, removing the map where I'd marked our last spot. I glanced up at the water once more, watching the yellow dot move toward us before I squinted down to the tiny intricate cursive of Zachary William.

Chapter Forty-Nine

'*Thursday, September 6th 1928*

We've managed to unload all the cargo and pull it far enough up the shore that it should be safe from the tide. The ship is anchored just off the bank in the shallows. She's sinking slowly, but I was able to slow the intake of water by stuffing the hole with the bedding from the hammocks. I will have to use whatever resources I can find here to try to repair it while also bailing out the water that seeps in each night. Frankie is growing impatient with waiting. He doesn't help much but likes to spit orders at Dutch and I. He's a loose cannon and if he didn't need me in order to get off this island, I'm pretty sure I'd be dead by now. My heart aches for Charlie and Walter. They were the best crew I'd ever had and if they were here with me, we would most likely be back on the ocean by now.'

'*Friday, September 7th 1928*

I am going to climb up the summit tomorrow to see if I can see the other islands from there. We should be close. If I can see them, I might be able to take a lifeboat out - although the waves coming into this island aren't conducive to paddling. Still, if we are close enough, perhaps we could find someone there to help us. I've cut and hauled bamboo into the hull and have been attempting to reconstruct the far wall. I've stuffed clay and debris in between and kept the bedding in place as an extra precaution. The water still seeps in a little, but it is much more manageable. Dutch has agreed to continue to bail the water out while I am up on the summit. Depending on our proximity to the other islands, we may even be able to navigate the boat to them in its current condition.'

'Sunday, September 9th 1928

I returned from the summit this morning where I found absolutely no signs of life anywhere around us. I can see neither Ua Pou nor Ua Huka, which tells me I must have drifted too far for too long. I will have to rely entirely on the resources on this island to repair the boat. I broke the news to Frankie and Dutch upon my arrival back at the beach. Frankie, of course, was less than pleased, particularly when I informed him that it could take weeks to repair it enough so that we actually stand a chance at making it home.'

'Wednesday, September 12th 1928

We were hit by a tremendous storm that brought rain pouring down on us for three straight days and nights. The waves did a number on the boat and caused the patchwork we'd done to-date to crumble, and the hull began filling rapidly once again. Dutch and I have put all of our energy into repairing it, but it's sinking faster than we can work. Since Frankie appears to be only concerned with his whiskey, I've put him in charge of finding a safe, dry place to store it while we work. At the very least, it keeps him occupied and away from us.'

'Thursday September 23th, 1928

The water in the hull is now almost as high as my head. Dutch and I bailed all day and night without sleeping. Even Frankie joined us for a while. The water is not deep enough for her to sink entirely, but I'm afraid I've lost the strength to continue on. I am too old for this type of labor. I need to rest, but if I don't get the water out fast, we won't be able to save it. I've successfully resealed the hole so the water is no longer coming in. Hopefully, we will be able to get the water low enough that I can reinforce the seal.'

'*Saturday September 25th, 1928*

We found a large cave inland where we decided to store the cargo. The storms here are too heavy and extended exposure to the salty rain will surely destroy what we have. Frankie's mental state has not improved with time. He is angry with the amount of time it is taking to fix the boat. He threatened to shoot us both if we refused to load up a lifeboat and paddle out. I am too tired to be afraid of him anymore. I will not paddle out on the ocean when I have no idea where I am and a perfectly good ship that I just need to get patched back up.'

'*Sunday September 26th, 1928*

Today was a hard day. Dutch is a fine young man, although a bit of a coward when it comes to Frankie. If Frankie tells him to do a thing, Dutch follows the order, however outrageous it may be. Today, despite the red morning sky that signaled storms to come, Frankie recruited Dutch to steal away on a lifeboat loaded with two barrels of whiskey. With no idea where they were going, they paddled out on the choppy water. I watched through the spyglass as they almost disappeared at sea, and I could do nothing when I saw the waves begin to crash over them as the storm blew in. Over and over, the waves pounded the boat until, at long last, there was nothing left of the boat or the whiskey. It took them hours to swim to shore. When they finally reached the beach, they were both too exhausted to stand. Dutch's lungs were so full of water, he could scarcely breathe and Frankie wept like a child.'

'*Tuesday September 28th, 1928*

We have finally begun to tip the scales back in our direction. After days of bailing, the water level is now just around our ankles and I have secured the hole. I want to add one final layer and test the ship around the shoreline to make sure it will hold before we set out. Dutch killed a boar today as well, and we had a feast. I even decided to break open some of the fine china and silverware to celebrate the occasion, since Frankie had been generous enough to share a bottle of whiskey with me. I learned a lot about these two men tonight as we sat around the fire swapping stories. Dutch served in France and was badly injured in the Battle of Belleau Wood. He was deemed unfit for continued service and was sent home. Over the course of three months, he lost his two brothers in the war. Feeling at a loss, he turned to his old childhood friends, who were all caught up in the gambling business. He joined Frankie running high-stakes poker rooms in the back of a small pool hall. When the war ended and prohibition started, they made their fortune in bootlegging operations until they got shut down last year. He recently met a girl named Elizabeth and was planning to propose when he returned from this trip. He showed me the ring he's been carrying around with him for the past few months. This was to be his final run - he and Frankie would make more than 50% of the profit on this job. He wouldn't need to bootleg anymore. He was going to play it straight from here on out. Frankie, on the other hand, although he has been a bit more tight-lipped about his past, enjoys the thrill of bootlegging. He's good at it and has no intention of stopping despite a wife and two children back home. I get a sense that there's something not quite right about Frankie, perhaps a mental condition of some sort. He seems conflicted on a much deeper level than any man I've ever met.'

'Wednesday September 29th

A strange thing happened this morning. When Dutch and I arrived on the beach, we found Frankie paddling to its shore. He said he'd gone out in the night to search for the nearby islands and that a demon had come upon him in a strangely shaped canoe. He described him as having the body of a man but completely black - not African, but black as though he had poured tar over himself. He said it - he consistently referred to it as an "it" - had bright white eyes with black pupils and horns that curled like a ram's toward the back of his skull beneath a crown of human bones. He said that it pulled its canoe up to his boat, then climbed inside and tried to kill him. He claims that, in a panic for his life, he shot the demon twice with his pistol, hurling its body overboard before he turned his boat back the way he had come. He remains in a state of terror and paranoia. He calls this the 'Devil's Island' and is convinced we all need to leave before the demons that surround it find us and take their revenge upon him. He is obviously delusional and I wonder, given his mental state, if he imagined something happening or if he actually shot someone who may have just been out sailing.'

'Thursday September 30th 1929

I woke up this morning to a pistol being pointed at the center of my head. Of course, it was being held by Frankie who I don't believe slept at all through the night. "We're leaving," he said and urged me out of the bed and down the beach. I told him that the boat wasn't ready, but he insisted on going. I told him that I still needed to do more patchwork to make sure that the hull could handle the heavier waves, but still he would not be persuaded. I asked about the whiskey and he said there was no time to load it. He said we needed to leave right then and there before the demons could return. I told him I would not captain a broken ship, that we would surely sink, and in an outrage, he shot me in the shoulder. I'm not entirely sure of the events that followed. I must've lost consciousness for a good length of time because when I woke up, the boat was far out to sea, both Dutch and Frankie gone with it. I have spent the last few hours doing my best to remove the bullet, a daunting task which has had me in and out of consciousness. I did finally pull it out though and have used a needle and thread to stitch the wound as best I know how. I am alone now and I debate what I'll do next. Without the ship I'm afraid I have no other option than to await rescue. Once I am well enough, I will move some supplies up to the summit to keep a lookout for ships on the sea. I truly believe Dutch will send help if he finds it.'

PART III

Eternally affixed.

Chapter Fifty

The next five months came and went quickly. Jack drew up plans for a boat. He, Kyle, and Jim had gone promptly to work chopping down bamboo and large trees.

They built a massive platform at the edge of the water and worked around the clock to finish the outer shell, leaving only the deck and hull's construction before we could set sail.

It was large enough to have a hull with sleeping quarters and a storage area for food and water. With nothing but some old rusty nails, Jack decided to carve pegs and joints into the wood, a task we all helped with, then he'd bound them together with rope.

In the mornings, if I wasn't helping with the boat's construction, I was with Isobel. We finished the birdcage and every day, she and I would go out to the tall grass to stalk the birds.

Isobel was perfect for stealing eggs and feathers while I snuck around to collect the babies that were too young to fly away but old enough to survive without their mothers. We'd bring them back to camp and clip their wings to make it easier for us to store and feed them.

Isobel was completely enamored with the Kolea. If she wasn't helping me catch them, she was gathering bugs and feeding them. Despite our disapproval, she'd stay cooped up in the cage with them for hours, humming despite herself as she took turns petting each one.

She had a favorite she carried around with her most of the time, and after a while, he'd become so attached to her he could roam freely outside the cage, staying at her ankles wherever she went. She named him Finn by pointing to the word in her favorite book —The Adventures of Huckleberry Finn.

Bertie had taught her to read, and the girl was determined to understand the book. She would often take it into the cage with her and come running out every once in a while to Bertie, pointing at a word for explanation.

Jack put Lilly in charge of sewing the sails. She set up a sewing station inside our old shelter at the beach and was constructing a large mainsail with a smaller jib, sewing additional backups just in case something went wrong at sea.

She was a determined flirt and stuck to her word, putting all her free time into attracting Jim. She would get up earlier than all of us and go out to the waterfall, coming back with her hair perfectly curled, legs shaved, and makeup so flawlessly applied, you'd think she was stepping out onto the red carpet.

We all noticed the change in her; the new look and the less playful demeanor she was trying to pull off; the sun dresses she'd altered and insisted on wearing—for comfort she claimed—every day. Her efforts caught the attention of us all, all but Jim, that is.

When he wasn't carrying logs or helping Jack with construction, he had his nose buried in the journals of Zachary Charles William, seemingly oblivious to her attempts to seduce him.

Kyle, on the other hand, was completely hypnotized. He drooled over her.

We'd worried about him after Phil left. In the months that followed Phil's departure, we'd notice Kyle looking out at the water more frequently. When asked about it, he claimed he was worried about his father returning with a vendetta, but deep down I thought he might be searching for signs of him.

We all were watching the water more closely, hoping for a sign of rescue that never came. I wondered constantly if Phil had made it. Had someone found him? Had they read the message? Were they searching for us? Or had Phil died on the water shortly after he disappeared from view?

Jack took Kyle under his wing, giving him tasks on the boat and showing him sailing techniques. He'd matured during our time on the island. His voice was almost permanently low, and he had a much less playful demeanor since the night he'd pulled the trigger.

We all had shifts for fishing and spearing. Bruce set up a smoking hut and would spend every night smoking whatever we caught. Jim built a crab trap in the water and we'd pull a handful out every week for dinner, but hoped to keep the remaining crab alive until we shipped out.

Bruce and Anna, Kyle and Magna, and Jim and Lilly took over the shifts on the summit. Everyone agreed Jack should stay until the heavy lifting was done, and since he wouldn't let me out of his sight, I stayed down, too.

Those that were up were in charge of collecting and grinding arrowroot into a fine powder for flour. Bruce had delivered on his promise and had come up with a delicious bread and jam recipe. We'd devoured it within minutes the first time he'd brought it down. With the flour, he was determined to keep bread on the boat.

Bertie's cancer had started to get the better of her. Her cough had gotten worse and worse over the past few weeks, at first coming only in the night, then growing to be consistent throughout the day as well. She stayed in bed longer in the mornings until she inevitably began spending full days without ever leaving the cave. Her weight had dropped, and she looked twenty years older than she had when we'd arrived.

Bud would not leave her side. Once she got too bad to walk to the beach, he'd insisted on staying at camp with her. Not being one to sit idle, he busied himself at her bedside, whittling long paddles that would navigate us into the deep water and studying Ole' Willie's journals and maps to try to get a gauge of where exactly we were.

My evenings and nights were spent with Jack. The love I shared with him was unlike any other I'd experienced before. Where Chris and I had been two halves of one whole, entirely dependent on the other to make up one personality, Jack pushed me to discover more of myself and made me feel truly loved for the things that were uniquely my own. With Jack, I was adventurous, emboldened, and unafraid to show him my whole heart, to cry when the urge hit me, and to let him comfort me.

While the five months had gone by swiftly, they'd also felt like an eternity in the times he and I spent alone together. We'd put together our own bed in the smaller back cave, a single candle off to one side of it. With no phones or television to distract us from each other, we'd spent night after night talking and laughing, getting to know each other on a deeper level than I'd ever known anyone.

"Will you hold still?" Lilly struggled to say against the flashlight she had balanced between her teeth. She jerked Jim's hand beneath the beam of light and bent closer, attempting to pull a splinter from his palm with the first aid tweezers.

In the last of the evening's light and the warm glow of the fire, she looked pristine—hair curled, makeup perfectly intact over a crisp new cream-colored dress she'd sewn, the gold and turquoise floral pattern glistening against the fire's light. You would've never known she'd spent the day sweating in the sun, impressively working shoulder to shoulder with the men helping to carry and position the last of the logs on the outer shell.

Jim rolled his head back and groaned. "Well hurry up, woman, if ye' moved any slower, ye' might catch up to yesterday. Ouch!"

She kicked his shin with her heel and pulled the hand closer, digging the tweezers in and then raising them with the sliver of wood between. "There." She pulled the flashlight from her mouth and grinned as he held his hand to his chest, narrowing his eyes defensively in her direction.

"Keep yer eye on this one." He looked at me while nodding his head in Lilly's direction. "She's got horns holdin' up her halo."

She smoothed over the pleats of her dress and placed her plate back onto her lap, ignoring him while she cut into the breaded filet of grouper. "Now that the shell is finished, how long do you think before we can get it on the water?" she asked.

Jack was sitting on the ground at my side, picking at his fish while he whittled a long branch that would serve as the boat's primary tiller. "Maybe a few more weeks."

He straightened one leg and let his back lean against the rock behind him. "I figure if you guys can get the top deck started while we're up on the summit, we should be able to put her in the water and see if she'll float when I get back. Assuming it doesn't sink, we'll keep it anchored there while we finish the hull."

With the bulk of the heavy lifting out of the way, we'd all agreed Jack should get a much-needed break on the summit, and we were scheduled to go up in two days. I'd been counting down the days in anticipation. We hadn't been up together since our first trip.

"What if something goes wrong?" Lilly asked, "Will we be able to get back, do you think?"

"Well," he started, pursing his lips, "we'll take the raft and have it ready should something go wrong. The wind's blowing to the east and if we can keep on a steady course heading that direction, we might be able to navigate straight west to come back should something go wrong on the first day. I think if we go much further, we're not likely to find our way back—not in the raft."

She looked out past the fire. "I'll miss it here. Do you think we'll ever see it again?"

He stopped whittling and thought for a moment. "I wouldn't count on it."

A gurgling cough echoed from the cave behind us and Bud rose, his expression exhausted. "I'll say goodnight now."

Magna stood with him, bending to pour a cup of her tea. "This'll help her sleep," she said, handing it to him.

Lilly watched him return to the cave and kept her eyes on the opening as the coughing grew more violent. I noticed Jim's fingers flex as though he would touch her hand where it sat next to his. He curled them back down as he thought better of it, opting to pat her back instead. "Ay," he said quietly to her, forcing her eyes to meet his, "we'll find a way back here again."

She sighed and laid her head on his shoulder until Bertie's cough settled.

She straightened suddenly. "Let's all go down to the beach for a while... like old times."

I yawned, "I don't know Lill—"

"Oh, please? We won't all be here together much longer. You two are going up to the summit, and then I'll be up on the summit, and we won't have many more nights together. I'll bring some blankets and a bottle of wine."

I looked at Jack and he smiled back at me before shifting his gaze to Lilly. "Alright, just for a little while."

She grinned, standing to take her plate to our wash basket and disappearing into the cave.

Maybe it was because he was seated beside me, but for the first time, I noticed Jim's eyes lingering on her when she'd returned with two blankets folded under one arm and a bottle of port in the other. I wondered to myself if I'd been wrong about his obliviousness to her daily efforts to get his attention. They'd spent a lot of their time together since arriving at the island—always paired up to go to the summit or spearing together, and while she'd made her intentions to fulfill her own needs clear to me, I'd never seen him show any signs of attraction toward her until this single fleeting moment. He caught himself staring and swiftly looked back down at his plate.

"Magna, Kyle," she started, handing me the bottle, "come with us?"

Magna smiled. "You all go on ahead. I'm gonna get Izzy to bed." She motioned toward Isobel who was leaning up against her side fast asleep, the Huck Finn book curled under one arm.

Kyle shook his head, staring blankly into the fire. "No. I think I'll stay here."

"Ji—James?" She spun to face him. "Come with?"

"Oh, alright." He stood with a grunt and stretched his arms, his elbows cracking as he did so. "We'd best bring some fire. It's coolin' off quick."

He bent and collected a log that was half burned from our fire and we all said our goodnights to Magna and Kyle before letting him and the orange glow of the branch lead the way down.

"Do you think we should go up early and send Anna down?" I whispered to Jack as we trailed behind them. "What if Bertie doesn't have much longer?"

He tightened his arm around me and I laid my head against him. "She's got a while still," he said between us, "but we'll go up early just to be safe. Besides, I don't think I can wait two more days to be alone with you."

I sighed and smiled at the thought of being alone with him for a week. An entire week without the bustle of camp or the constant work required to build the boat that kept us separate through the daytime would be like heaven.

As we made our way closer to the beach and the canopy thinned out, the moon shone above us, illuminating our path in a cool blue hue. I could hear the waves gently rolling in, and I watched Jim and Lilly ahead of us. She'd grabbed his hand with her free one and he led her, pointing the light from the log at the ground ahead of her feet.

When we'd reached the sand, she broke into a jog, pulling Jim behind her and forcing him to run awkwardly down the sand. She let him go when they were close to the water's edge to kick off her tennis shoes, laying the blankets safely in the sand above before making it the rest of the way down and inching her toes into the water.

Jim stood watching her as she walked along the edge of the tide, kicking at the water.

I watched their silhouettes as I stopped at our old shelter and knelt to remove my boots while Jack gathered firewood from the store we kept inside for cooking lunch.

I smiled over at him, his arms full of firewood. "I'll miss it here too, ya know."

He waited patiently for me to pull off the other boot and rise beside him, leading us down into the sand before asking, "Does it make me a horrible person if I don't want to leave? I want to keep you all to myself, right here on this island, without the world to distract you from me."

I ran my palm up his back. "Honey, I don't think there are enough distractions in this world to ever pull my attention from *you.*"

He grinned, letting the firewood fall to the sand when we'd reached the blankets and pulling me into his arms to kiss me once.

"I'm tellin' ye' right now, woman, I ain't pissin' on ye' if ye' get stung by a jellyfish. Get yer scrawny ass back over here and quit goin' so far in."

I buried my face in Jack's chest and giggled as Jim slowly backed himself up to us. "I swear to GOT she's tryin' to kill me."

He knelt down with the log and dug a small circle in the sand, stacking twigs and branches onto it and blowing at its base until a flame erupted. I unwrapped my arms from Jack and spread the blankets on the sand, blowing a kiss at him before I joined Lilly at the water, exhaling when I'd stepped in to let it dance around my bare ankles.

"Oh, Lainey," she wrapped her arms around me, "what if we just stayed here forever?"

It was a tempting idea as we looked out on a sky full of stars, the bright white light of the moon shimmering across the ocean's surface and the only sound between us, the soft static of the tide gliding over our feet. I squeezed her against me as I took it all in. "Lill, I promise, you and I will find a beach back home and we'll do this all the time."

"You're not going back to Chicago?" She pulled away to look at me.

I shook my head. "I don't know where I'll go exactly, but I want to start over somewhere new…" I grinned, "Maybe you can live next door."

"Ooh!" She took both my hands. "Yes! I like that. And we could have coffee in the mornings… And we'll go shopping and get our nails done on the weekends!"

I laughed, pulling her with me back to the sand as I made my way to the blankets and the warmth of the fire. "Perfect."

I took my seat next to Jack as he handed me the bottle of port. I sipped it and passed the bottle on to Lilly, who was smoothing her dress to sit beside me. She extended her legs out in front of her when she sat, crossing her ankles as she tipped the bottle to her lips.

"Do you think it'll be hard to go back?" She extended the bottle to Jim, who lowered himself to lie back on his elbows, looking up at the stars.

He took the bottle and held it in front of his lips. "It ain't never gonna' be this quiet again, that's for damn sure." He took a hefty swig and offered the wine to Jack. "I ain't never gonna' forget this place, though. And all of yuns. I think we's meant to find each other... and this place. Think the Good Lordt sent y'all to me 'for I could piss away all that money on booze and broads."

Jack took a sip. "Do you really believe all that? That there's somebody up there pulling the strings?"

Jim sat up straight to look at him. "Ye' don't?"

"Not really." He handed me the bottle. "I mean, it just seems a little far-fetched to me... the whole heaven and hell bit. Sounds like the stories you tell kids to get them to behave, like Santa or the Easter Bunny."

Jim tilted his head to one side. "Well, how in the hell ye' think we got here then? Aliens?!"

Jack chuckled. "No. I think we just became over time, evolution and all that."

I offered the bottle to Lilly as Jim scoffed. "Evolution. Pfft. Maybe *you* came from monkeys, but I sure as shit didn't. What ye' think happens when ye' die then?"

"Hell, I don't know." Jack leaned back on his palms. "I guess nothing."

"Well, ain't that depressin' as shit? You go on and look forward to yer nothin' and I'll await my mansion in the sky." He looked out at the ocean then back to Jack. "What if yer wrong?"

"What if you are?"

"Well, if I'm wrong and there's nothin,' then I wouldn't know I's wrong, would I? But if I'm right and yer wrong, ye'll sure as shit know about it when ye're standin' in front of them pearly gates gettin' denied entry."

Jack positioned himself behind me and wrapped his arms around me. "What about you, Red? You think there's a God up there striking planes out of the sky?"

I laid my head back against him. "I do. I don't know that he's striking planes out of the sky, but I believe he's out there."

"HA!" Jim grinned wide, taking the bottle from Lilly. "Don't worry darlin,' I'll keep ye' company while the big man's down 'er entertainin' the devil."

Jack ran his fingers along my upper arm. "You really think so?"

I smiled. "I *know* so. What about you, Lill? What do you believe?"

She flexed her toes. "I think maybe both."

"Both?" Jim tilted his head. "Whatcha mean, *both?*"

"Well…" She gazed into the fire. "What if God *is* a bunch of aliens and they put a bunch of elements together to create the big bang… then there was some bit of evolution but maybe they created humans by mixing their genetics with the monkeys?"

Jim laughed and leaned back on his elbows. "You been watchin' too much X-files, darlin.'" He took another big gulp of the wine and passed it along, looking back up at the sky and shifting his tone from playful to serious.

"This one time when I's about six or seven, I's over at my friend Tim's house. His daddy was a hunter, ye' see, and he had this big ole' buck mounted on the wall up over the TV in the front room. Well, me and Tim used to lay in 'at floor in front of 'at TV watchin' cartoons whenever I's over, and this one day, well I just got this feelin' that buck was 'bout to fall. Didn't look no different than it always did and I thought I might be crazy for it, but I pulled Tim back to the couch anyway. No sooner did we get on 'at couch did that damn thing fall down, antlers diggin' in the carpet right where we just was. Now how do you reckon I knew it was 'bout to fall if there ain't no God watchin' out for me?"

Lilly's eyes were wide as she focused on him. "That really happened?"

"Yes ma'am. And it weren't no little green men whisperin' in my ear neither."

I laughed at that as Jim looked around Lilly and narrowed his eyes at Jack. "Well hang on a minute, Hoss." He closed one eye. "When we's crashin,' are you tellin' me that ye' wasn't prayin' for God to save ye? While we's fallin' out the sky, the thought never entered yer head that *maybe* there might be someone up 'er could save ye?"

Jack coughed uncomfortably. "Well, that was different. I think anybody in that situation would do the same."

"Oh ye' think, do ye? And do ye' often pray to Santy-Clause or the Easter Bunny when times get hard too?" He snickered. "And here ye' are alive and well, all cuddled up with a beautiful woman on an island that's kept ye' fed and watered." He shook his head. "If it ain't the Lordt lookin' out for ye,' I don't know who is."

He laid back, crossing his arms behind his head and stretching his legs. "That's all I'm gonna say 'bout that."

Lilly spun to one side, lowering her head to use Jim's stomach as a pillow as she stretched her legs out in front of me. "James?"

"Lillian?" Jim mocked, doing his best proper English accent.

She giggled. "Will you go back to Oklahoma when we get back home?"

"I don't know." He tilted his head up to look at her. "Ain't much there for me now that mama's gone. Might just drift around for a while. Don't reckon I'll need to work again after I sue the pants off the airline."

Lilly balanced the nearly empty bottle of wine on her stomach, holding her hands to each side. "You should come be neighbors with us. Me and Lainey are buying houses next to each other when we get back."

Jack nuzzled his head into my shoulder, whispering in my ear, "Oh, you are, are you?"

I smiled, reaching my hand up to touch his cheek.

"Ooh," Lilly grabbed the bottle before it fell, "we could buy the island and build houses here! Giant houses since we'll all be filthy rich... and a helicopter so we can go get supplies and visit family... No wait... a jet!"

Jack chuckled. "Sounds like a good plan. What's the first thing you'd have flown in on your jet?"

She handed the bottle to Jim. "Potato chips," she said instantly. "I've been thinking about potato chips for weeks. My mouth is watering just thinking about them. What about you, Lainey?"

"Ice cream," I said, closing my eyes. "Chocolate chunk."

"A big fat steak for me," Jack laughed, "and potatoes."

"Hot wings and an ice cold beer." Jim raised on one elbow to drink the last swig of wine. "And then I'll be partakin' in some of that steak and ice cream too." He scratched the top of Lilly's head, then reached to his side to pull out one of the journals he kept with him. "Yuns remember that ship we saw a few months ago? Listen to this."

I perked up as he flipped the book open to a spot he had marked and cleared his throat, " *'Sunday, January 5th, 1930 - Up on the summit today I saw a strange-looking ship on the water. It was a massive wooden ship with big ivory colored sails. I thought my mind was playing tricks on me, but it came closer and I could see it clear as day through the spyglass - taut ropes like triangles wove complexly from the multiple thirty-foot masts down to the deck, a big red and blue flag waved at its stern, and the deck was busy with bodies. I lit the fire and threw every bit of greenery on top of it. I know they saw my smoke, but the ship did not turn, it merely continued on its path. I ran down to the beach, thinking I might be able to paddle out close enough, but by the time I got down there, they were too far gone. I cannot fathom what a ship like that was doing out here or why they would not come to call on an obvious signal of distress.'* And that's the end of this journal. I gotta' check the dates on them other ones to see where he starts fresh."

I shivered, Magna's theory returning to my mind.

"Ay, sugar," Jim smiled sweetly at Lilly who'd closed her eyes, "we probably oughta' head back up soon."

She turned to her side to face him, adjusting her head on his stomach and curling her legs into a fetal position. "Let's just sleep down here."

"Mmm, I don't know," Jim began to argue as he looked at us for help.

"I think we're going to head up to the summit in the morning," I said. "Send Anna down to help with Bertie. We should probably get packed. "

Lilly closed her eyes. "That's a good idea," she yawned. "But you should sleep. We'll all get up early and head back to camp. I'll help you pack in the morning. Please, let's just stay down here for tonight. I can't sleep up there with grandma coughing. The worrying keeps me awake."

Jim moved his hand gently over her hair. "Oh, alright, but don't get too comfortable. We cain't hunker down right here, the tide'll snatch us up. Let's go up by the old shelter where it's safer." He waited for her to sit up before he followed suit, grabbing a length of tinder from the fire before he stood. "Y'all comin'?"

I squeezed Jack's arms around me, not quite ready to go. "We'll be up in a little while."

He winked at me as he extended a hand to Lilly and pulled her up. "Alright then, goodnight." He coiled his arm over Lilly's shoulders. "Come on, Princess. Let's get ye' tucked in somewheres."

As they disappeared into the darkness, I turned in Jack's arms to lay my cheek against his chest. "When we get up there, can we just do this for a whole day?"

He kissed the top of my head, rocking to one side. "I was hoping to do this for a whole week."

I closed my eyes and hummed happily. "Earlier, you said Bertie's got a while still. How do you know?"

He continued to rock us. "My dad got lymphoma when I was about ten. It's slow. Lots of ups and downs. He'd cough like that for a month and then seem like he was fine the next. He refused treatment. When it finally got so bad he couldn't get up out of bed, it still took him almost a year to go."

I ran my fingers up his arm. "That must've been really hard for you."

"Not really." He laid his head on mine. "He was never home and when he was, he was like a stranger to me. He didn't really want much to do with Macy and me. That year he spent dying was the only real memory I have of him being home. I felt relieved when he died... like I could finally get on with whatever I'd been doing before he got there, ya know?"

I sighed. "I know. Mine was a stranger too. He left before I was old enough to even remember what he looked like. Ran off with some other woman, I guess. Once, when I was about eight, he wanted to meet my sister and me so my mom took us out to see him. He was nice enough, played games with us and took us out to see a movie and eat pizza. But I remember just wanting to get out of there so I could get back to my *real* life."

He smoothed a palm over my hair. "Did you see him again after that?"

I smiled. "No, it was all for show. I think he got lonely and wanted to see if my mother would have him back. She wouldn't, of course. She was much too proud for that. We didn't hear from him again after that day. I don't even know if he's alive."

"I'm sorry, Red."

"I'm not. Some people just aren't made to be parents."

He took my hands in his and curled both our arms around me. "Did it bother you?"

I thought about it for a minute. "Not really. I think it bothered my sister a lot more. She'd cry for him sometimes. I don't know, we always had my uncle there. I couldn't have asked for a better father figure. What about you? Did it bother you?"

His arms tightened around me. "At first, yes. When I was little, all I wanted was his attention. We had money and never wanted for anything, but my mom was terrified she'd be a bad mother if she didn't push us early. Instead of doing normal kid things, Macy was modeling kid's clothes for department stores and I was shooting commercials. Sometimes I just wanted to be a kid; play catch or go camping... As I got older, I don't know... I still wanted those things, just not with him..."

"Did you ever get to go camping?"

He laughed. "This is my first official camping trip. I have no idea what I'm doing out here."

I smiled. "Could've fooled me. You're a natural."

He nuzzled my neck and kissed my collarbone. "I should get you to bed. If we're going up in the morning, you'll need your sleep. I don't plan on doing much sleeping once I get you to myself for a whole week."

I giggled, turning my face toward his to meet his lips with mine. "I can hardly wait."

"What movie did you see?" he asked, "with your dad?"

I tucked my face into his shoulder and smiled. "Jurassic Park."

Chapter Fifty-One

I stood in the shower letting the hot water pour down my face. It'd been a year since Evelyn... since Minnesota... since... *her*. We'd left Minnesota determined to make things right, both of us naively hopeful we'd return to our previous selves in time.

That never happened.

The hurt we'd delivered to each other created an unspoken barrier that caused us to physically detach entirely. I'd abandoned him, and he resented me for it. He'd touched someone else, and I resented him for it.

Instead of talking through it, we both resumed our routine—a facade—and didn't look back.

I went back to work, as did he. I cooked and cleaned while he found projects around the house. We went out to dinner regularly with friends and family. We went on with our lives while we refused to touch one another, and worse, refused to acknowledge out loud that it was happening. We just lived with it.

First it was a month, then two, then six, and before long, we'd gone a year without sleeping together; without touching at all. We would undress shyly behind locked doors, and crawl in bed together and claim to be tired. I knew both of our minds were trying to work out why our bodies wouldn't touch. We were still the people we once were; we laughed and talked as we had before, but the intimacy was gone.

Instead of cuddling on the couch together, we sat separately—he in the recliner scrolling mindlessly through his phone and I on the far end of the sofa with a book. Instead of a kiss at the door before he left for work, he'd say "I love you" and disappear before I'd even had a chance to look up from my computer.

I was tired of living that way. I didn't want anyone else; I wanted him. Why couldn't I touch him? He was my husband, wasn't he? I'd have to do something lest I end up never feeling intimacy again. I wanted that closeness back.

Decided, I turned off the shower, wrapping myself in a towel. I wasn't living like this anymore.

I flung the door open to our bedroom, letting the light wash into the blackness of the room as I circled the bed to stand at the foot of it and drop my towel.

He didn't open his eyes, but covered his face with his arm and whined, "Turn the light off."

I could feel a lump forming in my throat and I swallowed it.

With his arm still bent over his eyes, he groaned, "What are you doing? Turn off the light."

I rolled my eyes and crawled onto the bed over him, suddenly self-conscious and second guessing my decision to make the first move.

"Ally... what—"

He uncovered his eyes and looked up at me then, sitting up. "What are you doing?"

His face said it all... he was in a panic, just as I was. He was terrified and so was I, but I was determined not to live this way anymore, so I placed my hands on his face and brought my lips to his.

"Al," he breathed, "it's late... we should—"

I kissed him again, forcing his lips open and curling my arms around his neck. Finally, his mouth moved with mine and his arms came around my back, forcing tears to spill down my cheeks.

I kissed him with desperation, grabbing at his hair, pulling him closer, begging him to love me the way I needed him to. His mouth moved over mine but lacked the same enthusiasm, as if he were only responding to mine in an attempt to appease me. It didn't matter; I pushed deeper, moving against him in the hopes that the passion would come.

I cupped his face in my hands, crying as I tried to salvage our relationship, my mouth moving from his lips down to his neck, growing more eager as my palms slid down his chest. He breathed against me but his hands stayed still at my back, making no move to touch me further.

I sobbed to myself as I buried my face in the crook of his neck. "Why?" I whispered softly.

His hand came up to my hair, petting softly. "I don't know," he whispered back, laying his cheek against the top of my head.

"You don't love me anymore?"

"Of course I do." He pulled me against him, squeezing me tightly. "With all my heart."

"Then why is this so hard?"

He sighed. "I want to. I hate this. But…"

"But." I blew out and rolled off of him, covering myself with the blankets.

"Al, wait." He brushed the hair from my face. "You can't just push me away for almost a year and then suddenly expect me to just be able to… perform."

"It wasn't just me. It was both of us and you know it. And it shouldn't be this much work, no matter who pushed who… not if we love each other…"

"I know that," he huffed.

"I don't want to live like this anymore," I sobbed. "I can't live like this anymore. This… this… unspoken thing we've had… where we just avoid talking about it… avoid touching… I want to get back to who we were before it happened. I want that closeness back. I miss you."

He slid down to lie across from me on his side, taking my hand in his. "Al, I don't think I can ever get back to who I was before it happened. It broke me completely."

"So what then? We just never touch again? We live like this forever?"

"No." He ran his thumb over my wrist. "I just need you to give me some time. I gave you time when you needed it."

"Did you?" I asked, immediately regretting the venom with which I did so.

He narrowed his eyes. "Didn't I?" he snapped back, letting go of my hand. "I sat here alone in this house night after night while you traipsed around up there with Doug doing God only knows what. You think I didn't notice the way you laughed at him when he was around? The way he looked at you? The way you looked at him?! I'm not blind. I went to work day in and day out to keep this house for you, knowing what you were up to. I drove twenty-two hours every single weekend in the hopes that you'd come back home... in the hopes you would still *choose* me. I lost my daughter and my wife, but *I* was the monster for it. And now you want to throw yourself at me? Now you miss me?"

"You think I..." My fingers curled into fists. "You think I did something with Doug?"

"I talked to Owen every day. I know you spent a lot of time with him, and I know he spent several nights sleeping at your cabin."

I narrowed my eyes. "You were spying on me?"

"What the hell was I supposed to do?! Was I supposed to sit here and think someone like him wouldn't be all over someone like you?"

"You were supposed to ask me! If you think I'm doing something wrong, ask! I've never given you any reason to suspect me of lying to you! Or moreover, being capable of doing something like that!"

"I didn't know who you were at that time. You wouldn't speak to me."

"So you sat here thinking I'd been sleeping with Doug—a *kid* —the entire time I was away? And then... you... what? Decided to get revenge?!"

"I decided I was done."

"So then why'd you come back for me?"

"Because I realized I loved you anyway... I realized I loved you enough to forgive anything you could've done to me."

"Why did you never ask me? All this time, you've had this in the back of your mind... why have you never brought it up?"

He sighed. "I was hoping you'd tell me someday. You've never once spoken about anything you did up there."

"You wanna know what I did up there? ...with Doug??" I set my jaw and wrapped the sheet around my body, standing at my side of the bed. "I *talked* to him. Talked to him because I couldn't talk to anyone who knew me. Not you... not mom... not Cece or Bill... I talked to him because *he* didn't need to talk to me about my feelings. I talked to him because he didn't want to hash through the pain I was feeling or try to fix me. I talked to him because he didn't ask about Evelyn... or you... And despite all that, I still managed to talk to him night and day about *you mostly* because he was young and full of hope for the world and he offered advice that reflected that hope. I talked to him because I needed hope... because I needed the distraction... because I needed a friend. And that's *all* he was to me."

I crossed the room and turned back at our door. "Unlike you, I took the vows I made to you seriously. There's never been anyone but you since I met you. And this is what you think of me... I understand now why the concept of sleeping with me repulses you. Don't worry, I won't be throwing myself at you again anytime soon."

Angrily, I made my way downstairs and threw myself on the sofa.

'This is what my life is now. This is it. Forever.'

I huffed and turned to face the back of the couch, curling myself into it. *'How long will we do this before one of us leaves?'*

'Could you leave him?'

'No.'

'Could he leave you?'

'No.'

We were both holding onto this idea that we'd magically fall back into our old selves... but now... now that we'd said the words we'd held in for the past year; I was pretty sure our old selves were gone forever.

'Owen.' I turned again. *'Little smug bastard... who the hell does he think he is? Talking to my husband and making me out to be some kind of... harlot! Did he say the same things to Cece? Did she think the same of me?'*

I pulled the sheet up to my chin. *'Did Cece talk to mom about it? Did the whole family think this way about me?'*

I turned again toward the back of the couch, my heart beating faster. *'Did Chris talk to his parents about it? Did they think the same?'*

It all felt suddenly so insurmountable. I wanted to just disappear. How could we fix it if everyone was rooting against us? How could he believe a thing like that? How could any of them? *'That's not who I am.'*

I turned again to lie on my back, staring up at the ceiling and the dark wood beams that ran from the living room to the kitchen. *'But I did leave... I did act impulsively... I abandoned him when he was hurting... did he not have a right to assume the worst when I was at my worst?'*

I waited through crying eyes, checking the stairwell every few minutes for signs of him, hoping he'd come down to work things out.

He never did.

Eventually, I surrendered myself to sleep, welcoming the nothingness over the life I was suddenly trapped inside.

470 of us to the West   470

Chapter Fifty-Two

We came up on Bruce at the pond gathering arrowroot when we arrived at the summit the next morning. He was whistling to himself, knelt down near the cave's opening.

"Good morning, Bruce!" I called out, causing him to nearly jump out of his skin.

He smiled when he saw us, slowly rising to meet us halfway. "Well, aren't you a sight for sore eyes?! You're not supposed to be up here for another two days. Everything alright?"

Jack took the basket of roots from him as I looped my arm through his. "Bertie's getting worse," I explained, "Magna's been making her tea and it helps some. I figured we might want Anna and Magna to stay down for a while."

He made a 'tsk' noise. "Poor thing. I'll get packed right away."

We headed for the cave, Jack leading the way as I kept a snail's pace with Bruce. His movement was much better, but still slow.

"So," I leaned into him to whisper as Jack walked ahead. "You've been spending a lot of time with Anna. Are you two... ya know...?"

He snorted. "No, no. We're just good friends."

I frowned. "Does she know that? Cause I've seen the way she looks at you..."

"Oh, I don't know about that." He patted my hand. "She's too good and sweet for someone like me. Plus, well," he stopped us as we reached the small opening at the top of the cave to head up, "she's not you."

My cheeks suddenly flushed, and my stomach turned over in a panic. "What?!"

He laughed out loud. "You set it up so perfectly and I just couldn't resist! I'm just messin' with ya, of course! Serves you right for being so nosey, *Lilly!* Wouldn't that make for an awkward morning?!" He continued to giggle as he knelt and crawled into the darkness.

"Jesus, Bruce," I ducked down into the blackness behind him. "That's not funny!"

He looped his arm in mine again as we gradually navigated up. We all had made the trip so many times that we knew the path well in the dark, shifting with it as it narrowed and turned. "Anna's a sweet girl," he whispered, "but she needs someone with confidence; someone who'll make her feel safe. I can't do that. Hell, I can barely get myself out of bed most days. Sorry to disappoint you, but I'm not what she needs."

"And you?" I asked, unconvinced. "You're so sure what she needs. What do you need?"

He slipped in front of me as we turned the curve into the narrow passageway. "Honestly, Alaina, I'd be perfectly content with a cheeseburger and warm shower... speaking of needs, how's the battle of wills between Jim and Lilly?"

I chuckled. "She's still up every morning pulling the bamboo out of her hair and I'm pretty sure he's completely oblivious."

"Oh, he's not oblivious." He grunted as we shifted to side-step the rest of the way out, his belly pressed against the opposing wall. "Who are you rooting for?"

"At this point," I breathed, "Lilly. I was opposed to it at first, but the woman's sheer determination is impressive."

He came out into the wide open cave and exhaled, bending to catch his breath. "Oh, but if she won, she'd rip that man's heart out. I'm team Jim all the way."

"You think?" I smiled. "There are teams now?"

He straightened, crossing to the opposite side of the cave. "Oh, yes. Anna and I even have a wager—she's team Lilly—I'm tellin' you, I'll be a rich man when I get home."

He knelt down at his suitcase and began packing his things. "Jim plays dumb, but he's not. Deep down, I think he's smarter than most of us—if not all of us. He knows what she's up to. He won't budge."

I knelt to crawl up the tunnel to the landing, where I could hear Jack filling Anna in on Bertie and progress on the boat. "We'll see." I smiled and began to climb.

I hadn't considered what would happen after she won... would she break his heart? Could she? I'd been so amused by her attempts to get his attention, I hadn't really thought about what she might do with it if she'd finally gotten it. Would she even really let it play out or would winning be enough?

My head came out of the tunnel just in time to catch Anna as she touched Jack's bicep. "Thank you so much, Jack. You have no idea how much this all means to me."

I knew the look and the touch well enough, and based on my conversation with Bruce, I imagined after her time here, she gathered the love we'd hoped would blossom between them was nonexistent. It was lonely being stranded and here she was, standing in front of Jack Volmer in all his glory.

I couldn't begrudge her for it. It was easy for me to forget who he was in this life away from the rest of the world, but as I watched her smile at him, I was reminded that she'd probably had his posters on her wall just as I had. If the roles had been reversed, after ten months devoid of contact, I might've taken any opportunity to touch him as well... just to touch *someone*. The loneliness would've been overwhelming for anyone here. It'd caused Lilly to go to extremes. Why not Anna too?

I watched a moment longer, soaking in his broad shoulders, the clear blue of his eyes, the rugged beard... and I smiled with the knowledge that he was mine. She could have this momentary touch of his arm, but I could have it all. I *would* have it all within minutes of their departure.

I crawled the rest of the way out and cleared my throat. "Good morning! I smell bread!"

"OH!" She jumped away from him to head toward me. "We've made several loaves to bring down! Look!" She knelt at a basket full of fresh bread and my mouth watered as I joined her. "We'll leave a few for you. And you have to try this batch of jam. It's perfect."

She was talking fast and her cheeks were red. I touched her arm and smiled when her eyes finally met mine. "This looks perfect. Before you go down, maybe you can leave me the recipe? I'd like to try to make some."

Her shoulders relaxed. "Of course. Let me just pack my things and I'll write it down for you."

I nodded, and she disappeared into the tunnel toward the cave. I shifted my gaze to Jack, who was grinning at me. I rose and crossed over to him, pulling his mouth possessively to mine as I tangled my fingers in his hair and commanded his lips apart.

He bit his lip when I released my grip, raising an eyebrow. "I'm exclusively yours, Red. You know that?"

I wrapped my arms around his waist and nodded. "I know that. I just like to remind myself once in a while."

He tilted my chin up, his eyes on fire. "My darling, I plan to remind you *plenty* just as soon as I've got you alone."

"Well then," I kissed his lips quickly. "Let's bid them farewell, shall we?"

I spun on my heel and headed toward the tunnel, smiling as I crawled back down. He excited me in ways I'd never felt before. My heart would skip a beat every time his lips met mine.

When he was away from me, I would feel him still on my skin, taste him on my lips, and I wanted him constantly. I didn't think I'd ever stop.

"I left you some guava and Fe'i here." Anna pointed to a basket as I crawled out of the tunnel. "And I wrote down the jam and bread recipes for you." She handed me the notebook we all took turns jotting various notes in.

"Perfect." I looked it over. "And don't worry, Bruce, we'll have at least two more bags of flour ready when we come down."

He laughed. "*One* will do just fine. You two have fun up here." He winked at Jack and wrapped his big arms around me in a hug, momentarily expelling me of air.

He moved on to Jack, and Anna's arms came around me, her voice straight to my ear, "Alaina, I didn't mean to—

"It's nothing." I kissed her cheek. "I love you. Be safe, I'll see you in a week."

She squeezed me tighter. "I love you too. So very much."

They made their way into the crevice, and we stood at the crack and listened. Jack's fingers danced down my bare arms and I shivered, keeping my attention on the blackness until I heard their voices echoing back from the cave below.

We were alone.

He gripped my hips and turned me to face him, his expression mad with desire as he began backing me lazily up against the rock, where he gently raised my arms and pinned them over my head.

His eyes narrowed while his lips hovered over mine and his voice came thick and husky. "Do you know how bad I wanted you right here?"

His knees pinned mine, and I smiled. "How hard it was to have my hands on you and have to resist you?" He took both my wrists in one hand and slid the other down the length of my arm and side until it reached my thigh.

"Or to have your hands on me," he demonstrated by sliding his palm up my inner thigh as I had done to him that night, "...and have to tell *you* no?"

His fingers glided across the fabric of my shorts then shifted up under my tank top to climb between my breasts, "Do you know how many times I dreamt of it?"

He leaned in so his breath was hot against my ear. "And how many times I said yes in the dream?"

My body begged for him and I tried to pull myself off the wall, but he pressed me back. I tried to kiss him but he tilted his head further so his lips lingered over my neck.

"I've got you right where I want you, Red." His lips skimmed my collarbone. "And I intend to take my time."

My hips moved against him as his mouth came down wet against my skin and left me wanting as he removed it almost as swiftly. "I loved you already," he breathed, raising his face so his eyes met mine. "Did you know that?"

My eyes watered and I shook my head, my arms fighting his grip with the need to touch him.

"I loved you," he looked at my lips, "so damn much it hurt *not* to touch you."

I could feel his pain as I struggled beneath him, my body pleading to connect with his.

He watched me fervidly. "It still hurts. Christ, it's like I'm walking around starving for you when you're not with me."

His fingers glided up to trace the line of my neck as his lips laid damp kisses in their wake. "It's all I can do most days not to take you where you stand without mind to who'd see us the minute I walk up to the shelter and lay eyes on you."

My breathing grew heavier as his mouth became hungrier against my skin. "Jack—"

"Shh." He reached into my hair and pulled softly to one side, allowing his lips, tongue and teeth the full length of my neck to consume. I gasped against him, pulling my arms against his death grip over my head.

"I've never wanted anything the way I want you," his lips moved lower, "the way I crave you…" His hand slid out of my hair and over my shoulder so his fingers could curl around the collar of my tank. "The way I need you…" He pulled the fabric down and took my breast in his mouth, his tongue teasing as I arched into him.

His breathing was heavy when he rose back up, and he let his palm slide back up my arm to take both my hands in both of his. "I've never loved anyone *but* you." His lips finally covered mine, and I exhaled heavily as he released my hands to wrap his arms around me.

Chapter Fifty-Three

I sat on the summit with my feet dangling over the edge, grinding arrowroot into powder as I looked down on our beach in the setting sunlight. I could see the platform and the frame of the boat, our family on the beach—tiny dots against the blue sand preparing to head back to camp for the night.

I sighed. It was our last night together on the summit. The time up here had been a wonderful break. We'd spent every day wrapped up in each other's arms, making love at our leisure, and getting dressed only when we went down to the creek for arrowroot and fish.

"Did you bring what I asked you to?" Jack asked behind me.

I smiled and turned to see him kneeling at the tunnel's entrance. "I did."

"Do you think maybe you could go get it?" He grinned, holding both hands behind his back.

"What are you up to?" I bit my lip, raising from my spot.

"It's a surprise." He flashed his bright white teeth. "Now go get it and don't come up until I tell you to."

I giggled as I drew nearer, raising on my toes to get a glimpse as he shifted to one side. "Ok, Volmer, I'll play your little game."

I knelt to crawl back into the tunnel, giddy with excitement as I made my way down. What he'd asked me to bring was the navy silk dress Lilly made me. I happily stripped the instant I was in the cave, grabbing the dress and pulling it over my shoulders. It was dark in the cave and I hadn't thought to bring a mirror, but I blindly braided my hair to one side, letting it hang over my shoulder and knotting it where it draped over my breast.

I paced anxiously, looking up the tunnel every few minutes to see if I could get a glimpse of him.

God, I loved him. Not to say I loved him more than Chris... I loved Jack differently. It was a completely new kind of love from the one I'd shared with Chris, and I was glad of it. I'd been blessed with two great loves in my life. Two soulmates for two entirely different lives.

I wondered how I'd mesh those lives together once we sailed away from the island. How would Jack fit into my family when all this was over?

"Ok, you can come up now," he called down.

I grinned and hiked the dress up to avoid ripping it as I crawled up the sharp rocks to him.

I came up to find a candlelit dinner. He'd draped white silk fabric over our little rock and set out two proper place settings, each with a glass of wine and plates housing a filet of fish, Fe'i, boiled breadfruit, and algae. Two candles sat in the center along with a bouquet of pink and white flowers.

"Oh Jack, I love it!" I turned toward him. He was standing with a single flower, wearing his navy button-up shirt and the black blazer I'd sewn him. He took two long strides toward me and looped the flower behind my left ear, then bent to kiss me gently.

He folded my arm around his and escorted me to our little table, where I slid to sit on the ground and he took his place across from me.

"I can't believe you did all this." I picked up my fork and knife, inspecting the table.

"This is where I fell completely in love with you." He smiled. "Right here in this spot, over steak and red potatoes. I knew I was falling for you before that, but right here... this was the moment that changed me forever."

I beamed at him. "You know, that's one of my favorite memories on this island. It was the first time I felt like I really smiled..."

"I know." He sipped his wine. "It was the smile that did me in."

"You bring it out of me." I leaned across to kiss him.

I took a bite of my fish and leaned back, looking out at the ocean around us. "Jack... Let's say the boat works and we get home. In your perfect world, tell me what our lives look like there."

He set his glass down. "In *my* perfect world?"

I nodded.

"We drop the others off and sail back here and we never wear clothes again."

I chuckled. "That sounds pretty perfect, but seriously, we step off the boat and all of a sudden you're Jack Volmer again. What happens next?"

He leaned back. "Well, I wouldn't need to be an actor anymore. Acting was never something I wanted for myself. I did it because my mother pushed me into it, then I kept doing it because the money was good... I hated the publicity and I hated who I became because of it. But I wouldn't have to do that anymore."

He moved his food around his plate with his fork. "In my perfect world, I'd step off that boat and marry you instantly. Then we'd live somewhere secluded, somewhere away from the world, but easy enough to travel to and from. We'd surround ourselves with family—including the family we have here. We'd travel the world... come back to this island every year on our wedding anniversary with our children."

He smiled at me. "We'd get old together like Bud and Bertie. I'd hold your hand all the way up until the end and love you every day of our lives just the way I do now."

I closed my eyes and sighed picturing it. "Your world sounds pretty perfect to me."

I pointed to the big tree behind him. "Right there. Under that tree. You were lying about a foot from me and I knew right then, if I touched you, I'd love you."

He nodded. "I remember."

My lips curled upwards. "Turns out you're very hard not to love." I sipped my wine. "Mm, especially after that little ballet move you pulled."

"Oh, speaking of that." He raised an eyebrow. "There's one more thing." He stood and extended his hand to me.

"Are we going to do the move again?" I laughed and rose happily.

He walked me out to the center of the summit. "Okay," he said, circling me, "do your best ballerina impression."

I awkwardly obliged, giddy as he took his place behind me.

"Do you remember how to do it?" he whispered in my ear, the hairs at the nape of my neck standing on edge.

"Uh huh."

"Good. Close your eyes this time."

My cheeks started to burn from smiling. "Okay." I closed them.

I stood there grinning with my eyes closed and my arms held over my head, anxiously waiting for his touch, when suddenly the familiar voice of Otis Redding rang through my ears.

"These... Arms... Of... Mine..." and my eyes sprang open as the music kicked in and he lifted me up into the air.

"How did you—"

"Arch," he commanded.

I arched. "Jack, how did you—"

He pushed me upward with one hand. "Bend your leg."

I did and this time, when he swung me around, I curled my fingers in his hair and kissed him, letting Otis Redding and the love I felt overwhelm me. He straightened us, our lips still locked as he led me in a slow dance.

He broke the kiss and pulled me against him as he rocked us gently to the music. "Tell me, Red, what does your perfect world look like?"

I rested my head on his shoulder. "I think I like the sound of yours."

"Come on now, you've gotta have something in mind."

I swept my fingers over the hair at the back of his neck, "Well, I'd step off the boat and marry *you* instantly." I grinned. "And we'd build a small house in Tahiti off the single road that runs through it. Somewhere near Magna. We'd have coffee and baguettes on our porch every morning with Jim and Lilly. I'd write music and sing in the evenings with any new tourist friends we'd made that day. We'd have two children and a boat that we would take out frequently to come spend weekends on this island. We'd travel. And once we're too old to keep up, we'll come here to live out our last days together."

He took my hand in his, holding it near his heart and turning it over to run his thumb along my wrist. "Let's do it." He squeezed, releasing my hand to reach into his pocket.

I sighed, "If only it were that simple."

He tensed a little, pulling his empty hand back from his pocket and looking down at me. "Why couldn't it be that simple?"

I loved Jack, but there was a nagging thought that had been looming in my mind, growing more and more prominent as the boat got closer to being finished.

Coming home with him so soon... What would that mean to Chris's family? They loved me like their own and I loved them. I owed them time... time to grieve their son and to process my survival. Returning to them with Jack wouldn't be right... How was I ever going to explain myself? How could I ever look them in the eyes? Would they feel like I'd betrayed him? Like I'd never loved him at all? Would they hate me for it?

They'd become my family too, and I couldn't shut them out. I couldn't write them off. What would his father say? His mother? What would my own mother think? She loved Chris, too. Would they ever see Jack as anything but a betrayal?

"I'm afraid I have no idea how I'll ever be able to introduce you."

He ran a hand over my hair. "What do you mean?" he asked softly, turning us with the music.

"Well... How would I explain you to my family? To Chris's family?" My hand began to shake in his as he tensed visibly at the sound of Chris's name. "They wouldn't understand."

He stopped dancing, peeling me back from him as he narrowed his eyes. "*I* don't understand. What's to explain? We love each other."

I blew out. "Yes, but I was with him for ten years. His family became my family. If we get home, it's not like I can just write them off. What will they think if I come home ten months after their son died with you? How do I tell them that? What does that make me?"

He pulled me back into the dance, resting his chin on my head. "So we don't tell them for a while. We don't have to do anything until you're ready."

I shook my head. "That's just it... I keep trying to work it out in my mind. I've played out all the possible scenarios... It doesn't matter *when* we tell them, they'll still know it happened here... right after he died... they'll always think I betrayed him with you. They'll think I didn't love him."

"So you'll tell them the truth. Tell them how it all happened." He squeezed my hand. "They'll understand, eventually."

I raised an eyebrow, looking up at him as we circled again. "Would you? If it were Macy that died and Robert returned with a new girlfriend less than a year later, would you ever look at him the same?"

He shook his head, frowning.

"And if he returned with no girlfriend and then told you maybe a year or two later that he loved a woman on the island... would you accept that? Accept that knowing he'd loved her just months after Macy died?"

He cleared his throat. "No."

"So, there you have it. How do I introduce you?"

He stopped dancing and stepped back from me, his voice raising. "So what then, Alaina? What are you trying to say?"

I shook my head. "Wait, I didn't mean for this to turn into an argument. I'm just saying it's—"

"What the hell are you doing to me? Why now? After everything? You know I was going to..." He held up a hand. "Doesn't matter now. What was it you accused me of?? Using you as something to pass the time here with..." He scoffed. "And here we are close to going home, and it's *you* who suddenly doesn't know what to do with me?! So that whole *'I'd step off the boat and marry you instantly'* bit was just... what? For my amusement?"

"Jack, it's not like that." I reached out to touch him but he jerked away, Otis Redding still singing sweetly from the phone speaker beneath us.

"How is it then?" He hovered over me, breathing heavily as his eyes filled with tears. "You spend months telling me you love me, letting me open *my* heart to you, all the while avoiding any topic of Chris whatsoever... look at you now, you cringe if I even say his name!"

"Jack, I—"

"You refuse to let me in... You accused me of scripting a narrative for you, oh but look who's changing the script right when the boat is nearly finished! Suddenly now you're worried about what your family will think? Worried about what CHRIS'S family will think? Why now?!"

"No, I don't want—"

I reached up for him and he caught my wrist, squeezing tightly.

"What Alaina?" He leaned over me, eyes dark with hurt. "What do you want?"

Fresh tears filled my eyes. "YOU! I want YOU, but they'll never see you for who you are... and I can't just scrape them off! Not after all this. Not after they've lost their only son! Not after they find out their only daughter-in-law is alive! You tell me! What would you do? Huh?"

He leaned closer, his jaw set. "Do you love me?"

"Yes, of course I do." My wrist was starting to burn beneath his grip.

He shook his head, lowering his voice. "I don't know that you do. I'd write off my *own* mother if she didn't approve of you. I love you that much. I would've killed for you. I would still kill for you. All that matters to me is you."

He threw my wrist away from his grip, turning away from me and pacing to stand in front of the fire.

I followed him, flinging my arms around his chest. "I don't mean it! We'll figure something out!"

He made no move to touch me, only stiffened. "There's nothing to figure out, Alaina. You said it yourself. You can't go home with me, so I won't ask you to. Problem solved."

"No, Jack, please." I squeezed him. "This isn't what I want! I wanted us to talk about it... not this. Please don't—"

But he already had. He pulled my arms from him and distanced himself to the other side of the fire. "Figure out what you want and don't say another word to me until you know what that is."

He stuck his palm out as I made a move to speak. "Alaina, you've ripped my heart straight out of my chest with this. It's clear to me that you don't know what you want... you've acted impulsively, without thought to what you wanted long-term, where I've known exactly what I wanted since the beginning. I was naïve to think you could have the same confidence in us that I had, especially after all you lost... I can't blame you, but I'm *begging* you, don't say another word until you've thought about it. If I'm what you want, then that's that. Let anyone who doesn't approve go on with their disapproval. If I'm not, I'll live with that. But I won't live with the indecision. You're a grown woman, Alaina, and I'm not making your decision for you."

I stood frozen in place, tears pouring out of me.

"Go down to the cave," he said sternly, sitting on the ground in front of the fire. "I don't want to talk to you anymore tonight."

"But Jack—"

"I don't want to talk to you anymore tonight," he repeated, burying his head in his hands.

'*What have I done?*' I wondered as I turned toward the tunnel. I sobbed uncontrollably as I crawled inside, curling into a fetal position on the floor, and heard him turn the phone back off.

'*Is he right? Was everything impulsive instead of genuine? Was I so desperate to feel loved again that I threw myself into a fairy tale? Was Jack a means to escape the loss of Chris?*'

I turned, huffing. '*No, I love him. I love him very much. Why am I so afraid of what anyone else will think?*'

'*Because you love them too... Because you know that they'll feel betrayed and angry at you. Because deep down, you know you're going to have to give up one in exchange for the other.*'

'*Would they hate me forever for him?*'

'*Yes.*'

'*Could I live with that? Could I live happily with Jack knowing they'd never forgive me... knowing they'd spend the rest of their lives thinking I'd never truly loved Chris?*'

'*You'd beat yourself up over it. But could you say goodbye to Jack? Give up your own happiness for the sake of theirs?*'

'*No.*'

'*So what do you do?*'

'*I could just stay gone. Never go back. Stay here with Jack... Let them think I'm dead. They could get over death... they would never get over Jack.*'

'*And what about mom? Cece? Uncle Bill? You'd let them go on thinking you were dead?*'

'*No.*'

'*Well, then... what do you want?*'

'*I want Jack... without Jack serving as a means to discredit my happiness with Chris. I want my family—my whole family—to love him... to see him for who he really is... Couldn't I tell them the whole story? Wouldn't they come around someday?*'

'*If you told them the whole story and they didn't, would that be your fault? Would it really be Jack serving as a means to discredit your happiness, or would he merely be crediting their own unhappiness? You can't control that. What's going to make you happy? If you had to choose between them, who would you choose?*'

I tossed and turned and cried all night. No matter what I did, I was going to hurt someone. My indecisiveness had already hurt Jack, and I hated myself for not thinking it through beforehand. I would never be able to let him go, I knew that, and I kicked myself for having said anything in the first place.

As the night turned to morning, I'd cried myself sick, *literally.* The air felt thick, and I could feel the bile rising in my throat. I leapt off the floor and bolted to the mouth of the cave where I collapsed on the ground and vomited over the edge.

As I straightened, I could hear our replacements' voices echoing through the tunnel from the cave below.

"Awww, come on now, Princess, I's just havin' some fun, let's not fuss already."

"You're an asshole, James," Lilly snapped. "That wasn't funny."

I wiped my eyes and nose, rushing to our suitcases to grab my shirt and shorts as I slid out of the blue dress.

"Will you quit with 'at James shit? Ay, stop right there, I'm gonna grab us some hooch 'for we go up. Lordt knows we gonna need it."

"What's that supposed to mean?"

"Means that if I'm gonna sit up 'er for a week watchin' ye' traipse around in yer little dresses with that crap smeared all on your face, battin' your damn eyes at me, I'm gonna want to have a dang drink in my hand."

I pulled my shorts on and smashed the shirt over my head.

"Who the hell do you think you are?" she barked. "I'm not batting my eyes at you!"

"What, you think I'm some kind of dummy? If y'ain't gettin' all gussied up fer me to notice, then who in the hell are ye' doin' it for? Bruce? *Hoss*?! PFFFT."

"Maybe." Her voice was defiant. "Any of *them* would be grateful to have me."

"Woman, you're high as the nuts on a giraffe, you know that?"

I sat hard, checking the tunnel that led upward for signs of Jack. Nothing. I pulled my socks and boots onto my bare feet.

'What have I done?'

"Oooh, I must be. What in the world was I ever thinking coming up here with you? I can't stand you!"

He giggled, his voice becoming more muffled. "Ye know, you got your nose stuck up so high in the air, if it rained, ye' might drown."

She gasped. "I DO NOT!"

"Do so! Yer spoilt and ye' cain't help it! Someone tells ye' no and you throw a damn tantrum evra' single time. Just look at ye,' standin' there fixin' to throw one right now."

She growled and her volume increased. "OOH, I HATE YOU, YOU HEAR ME??? I HATE YOU!!! YOU BIG DUMB STUPID HILLBILLY IDIOT!!!"

The ground beneath me shook, and I heard Lilly shriek. "JIM?! JIMMY!!! HELP!!!"

I leapt up and called for Jack before I sprinted into the crevice.

"JIMMY!!!" Her panicked voice echoed through the blackness as I hurried downward.

I turned the corner and felt Jack's hand on my shoulder as he caught up. "What's going on?" he whispered as we began to jog side by side where the cavern widened.

"I don't know." My heart beat in my throat and I heard her crying out louder below us.

"JIMMY, TALK TO ME! I DIDN'T MEAN IT! I DIDN'T MEAN IT! SOMEBODY HELP!!!" I could hear her sobbing uncontrollably as the light from the small opening came into view.

"PLEASE TALK TO ME! PLEASE!"

I sprinted as fast as I could toward the light.

"I'LL STOP. I WON'T BUG YOU ANYMORE. PLEASE JIMMY!!!"

I came out of the crevice onto the ledge and rushed down the narrow passage that led to the cave floor.

I could see her then, at the far end of the cave, screaming incoherently and clawing at a pile of rocks and boulders stacked high where the opening to the tunnels had once been. She launched the smaller ones behind her and pulled herself up onto the big ones, pulling them with her entire body.

"JIMMY!" Her voice shook as she screamed out between sobs.

Jack raced past me as we reached the floor of the cave and he dodged a large rock as he came up behind Lilly, who was launching them wildly behind her. He went straight to work, dislodging boulders and clawing alongside her.

"Jim!" he called out. "Jim, say something, man!"

I climbed up beside them and hurriedly started launching rock. Lilly used her whole body, clawing with her hands and kicking at the rocks with her feet. Her nails were covered in blood, and her face was drenched with tears. "Jim!" I called. "Jim, please say something!"

We pulled and pushed the rocks, hurling them in all directions. Lilly's eyes met mine momentarily, glazed over and bright red, dark black lines from what had once been eyeliner spilling down her cheeks. "HE WAS RIGHT UNDER IT!!!"

I looked up then as I pulled with all my strength at a boulder, and I could see where the ceiling of the cave had crumbled... could see where it may crumble still. She continued, tossing a boulder half her size. "WE WERE BOTH RIGHT UNDER IT!!!"

"Lilly," I watched the ceiling above us as I spoke low, "stop yelling."

"WE WERE BOTH RIGHT UNDER IT AND HE PUSHED ME BACK!!!"

"Lilly," I squeezed her arm and pointed upward, "stop yelling."

She was looking at me, but she couldn't see me. She was mad with grief and she flung herself over the rocks, kicking her legs to dislodge a cluster and slide down it. "Jimmy, say something!"

I pressed my back up against the solid rock wall and used my full weight to dislodge a rock at the top of the pile. As it skipped down, it pulled several rocks with it to expose a boulder that was as big as all three of us put together.

Jack hurried up to the wall and put his feet on it, pushing his back against the wall as I had done. It didn't budge. Lilly and I followed suit on each side of him, all of us using our full weight to try to dislodge it. Still, it wouldn't move.

"I need to get some leverage. Stay here," Jack instructed and sprinted outside the cave.

Lilly curled herself over the dark rock and pressed her ear to the wall. "Please Jimmy," she shook with tears, "please say something."

Suddenly a muffled cough came from the opposite side of the rock, and Lilly jumped up, pulling at the boulder as though she could lift it off. "JIMMY!!! ARE YOU ALRIGHT?!"

He coughed louder and my heart skipped a beat. "Oh, thank God! We're coming, Jim! Hold on!"

Jack bolted back into the cave, pulling a large tree branch behind him.

"He's alive," I said as he reached the rock.

"Jim, hang on!" Jack called, wedging the branch into a crevice between the large boulder and several smaller ones.

He pulled down on the branch and the stone wobbled, but fell back into place.

Jim coughed behind it. "Ay," he coughed to a choke, "who…" he coughed again, "who taught ye' how to lift?? Yer grandma?!" He giggled and coughed violently.

Lilly sobbed at the sound of his voice as Jack repositioned the branch. This time we all three pulled with all our weight, Lilly hoisting herself on top of it, and the boulder lifted and rolled to one side.

I could hear his coughing clearly now as we all rushed to pull the remaining rocks out of the way, and in a cloud of gray dust, Jim emerged, limping to one side, covered from head to toe in the fine gray rock powder.

Jack grabbed his arm and helped him over the rocks to the floor of the cave where Lilly sprung herself on him, wrapping her arms around his neck and pressing her lips to his.

Jack and I stood dumbfounded as Lilly pulled him closer, sobbing frantically while her hands smoothed over his hair in a plume of dust, his arms hovering in the air around her as her mouth moved over his.

He made no move to stop her, but kept his hands floating a foot over her back. I watched as his eyes closed and I caught his own lips momentarily responding to hers.

She broke the kiss and curled her arms tight around him. "You stupid man… You stupid, stupid idiot man!"

He looked at us confusedly and slowly lowered his arms around her shaking body. "Hey now," his voice grew soft as he patted her head, "it's alright, come on." He pulled her from him to look at her face, running a thumb along her cheek. "I'm right here. What ye' squallin' fer?"

"I thought you were dead," she sobbed, catching her breath between words. "And the last thing I would've said to you is that I hate you. And I don't hate you, Jimmy."

He pulled back to get a better look at her face, running both palms along her cheeks as the tears continued to pour out of her, leaving streaks of pink as they dripped over his dust covered fingers. "Aww, come on, sweetheart. I know that… Look at me now. I ain't hurt. It's alright."

She tried to catch her breath but couldn't. "You stupid man." Her hands smoothed over his face and she kissed him again.

He shook his head, pulling her back, his thumbs attempting to wipe the dust off her face. "Ay, come on now, quit that."

Her voice hitched as she blubbered the words. "No. I'm done playing now. You either love me back or you don't."

He kept his hands on her face and his expression softened. "Love ye' *back*?" I could see him working it over in his mind, just as I was. "What do ye' mean, *love ye' back*?"

She sobbed, her words coming out in a jumble of high-pitched notes. "I mean I love you and you can't do this to me anymore. If you don't love me back, you tell me right now, James Jackson."

"You mean all this… the makeup and the dresses… the curls in yer hair… it's cause ye' wanted me to love ye' back?"

She sniffled loudly. "Uh huh."

"I thought ye' was just tryin' to…" He looked up at the ceiling, "Lordt help me." He met her eyes again. "Course I love ye' back, darlin.'"

He combed his hand down her hair. "Why ye' think I stay away from ye' when ye' come down showin' off 'em legs and lookin' at me the way you do? Ain't cause I don't love ye.' Hell, look at ye! Ye' could have any man in the world you wanted. What you want with someone like me, anyway?"

She angled her head into his hand, closing her eyes as she nuzzled it. "I love you."

He huffed, "Lilly, come on now, quit sayin' that. Ye' don't mean it… Not like that, ye' don't. Look at me and look at you. It don't make no sense."

Her voice raised another octave as she struggled against the lump in her throat. "I *am* looking at you and I love you… with all my heart."

He shook his head as he searched her face. "Maybe ye' think ye' do here, but back home… Hell, I'd ruin yer life and ye' know it. What's yer family gonna say when you come home wit' some ole' hillbilly truck driver on yer arm? Huh? *You*, an educated woman, goin' back to yer fancy fashion shows with some old low life high school dropout hangin' his arm round yer neck? What would they say?"

She gently wiped the dust from his face, shaking her head and sniffling as she did so. "The only family and friends I care about are right here, and they already love you. Anyone who doesn't can go straight to hell for all I care."

He stifled a cough, and his voice came out choked and hoarse. "No, Lilly. I cain't be that to ye. I'd embarrass ye.' I embarrass myself. "

Her palm smoothed over the dust on his lips. "No you wouldn't."

He tilted his head to one side and swallowed hard as she pushed the dust off his cheek. "Yeah, I would. Now, I ain't fit for ye' and that's just the way it is. What kind 'a man would I be if I let ye' throw away yer life like 'at?"

She rested her hands on the sides of his face. "Jimmy," she took a deep breath and straightened her shoulders, evening out her voice, "you're good in every single way a man is supposed to be good. You're smarter than anyone I know, and you make me laugh."

She sniffed. "You're the kind of man who runs three hours uphill and back down to save your friends. The kind of man who people want to follow... who *I* want to follow. I like who I am with you... Now, I'm telling you I love you. And I *know* you love me too. I can feel it and I want more of it. *You* make me happy, and if that's not fit, there's no such thing."

He shook his head slowly, lowering his eyes. "Ye' ain't thinkin' clear, sugar. I ain't got nothin' fer ye. Yer Lillian Renaud, for Christ's sake. Ye' got maids and fancy chauffeurs and shoes worth more than I am. I'm gonna' get ye' on that boat and take ye' home where a good man—a *worthy* man'll marry ye' and take care of ye' the way ye' deserve. I do love you, baby girl, and that's why I cain't do it to ye."

She stood tall, sniffling as she raised her chin. "Then I won't get on the boat. You can't make me go. I'll stay right here... with you. You won't leave me."

"Now just quit, woman."

"No!" She stomped her foot. "Do you think, *after all this*, I care about maids or fancy shoes? I don't need any of that now... And what the hell does *'more worthy'* even mean? You think some rich New York snob is more worthy than the man who saved my life? The man who pulled me out of that airplane and put me on the raft? The man who has taken care of me just fine since we crashed? You think anyone is more worthy to me than you? I don't want anybody but you."

"Lilly," he held her at a distance, "quit sayin' stuff like 'at. It ain't right. How can I say I love ye' and then go and take any chance ye' have at real happiness away from ye?'"

"Real happiness?" She sniffled. "*REAL* Happiness? You stupid, stupid man. Do you think I pair myself up with you to come up here because it makes me unhappy? Or snuggle up to you at night just for fun? Do you think I'd throw myself at you over and over, knowing you'll reject me, if I didn't think you would make me happy forever? Do you really think that I—*Lillian Renaud*—would ever *ever* spend months on end letting a man break my heart over and over and over if I didn't know with all my heart that that man was the source of my *real* happiness?"

"Now, Lilly—"

"You are breaking my heart, Jim." Her tears returned, heavier this time.

"Now, don't do that. Quit now." He ran his thumb over her cheek."I'm... I'm too old fer ye," he said softly.

She let one hand slide around his neck as the other pulled his chin to look at her, and she smiled as she drew closer. "I'll remarry after you're dead then."

He frowned, shaking his head as he tried to come up with more excuses. "Yer too beautiful. Come on, look at me. Ye' don't want me. Not really."

"I told you I *am* looking at you and I think you're beautiful." She let her fingers glide over the side of his face.

"People would talk. Yer friends back home... They'd say nasty, horrible things 'bout me. I ain't never gonna fit in with 'em." His voice softened and his shoulders relaxed.

"I don't want you to."

"Ye'd resent me for it…"

"I could never resent you." She shook her head, sniffling the last of the tears away. "Never."

He lowered his voice. "I ain't got nothin' to my name but an old trailer that leaks evra' time it rains."

She pressed her forehead against his. "Then I'll bring buckets."

"Lilly…" He blew out. "Oh, hell, I cain't do it no more, anyway." He let his arms glide around her and he kissed her, folding one arm up to let his fingers curl into her hair. I heard her sigh as he pulled her tight against him, and I recognized her happiness as my own.

I curled my arm around Jack's and smiled, turning us toward the cave's opening to give them privacy.

Outside, once we'd reached the water, Jack dusted me off, smiling down at me and speaking in a low whisper, "I thought it was just about sex."

I grinned. "Me too. I had no idea."

He sighed, looking back to the cave. "Well, they're definitely the most... interesting... couple I've ever met."

I laughed and wrapped my arms around him, burying my face in his chest as he pulled me against him. "Jack… I owe you an apology about last night. I didn't mean to ruin your romantic dinner."

"No." He pulled me closer. "I'm the one that should apologize. It wasn't fair for me to react that way. I had this idea of how the night was going to go, and when it didn't go that direction, I reacted poorly." He kissed the top of my head. "I'll never do that again."

I squeezed him tight with my forearms. "I'll tell you about him. Anything you want to know. I *do* love you. I didn't mean to make you doubt that. I don't care what anyone thinks. I just… I needed to talk it through."

"Shh." He rocked me softly. "It's alright. We'll figure it out. Let me look at you." He pulled me from him and I tried desperately to compose myself, wiping at my eyes and nose before he could see the puffiness the night of crying had left.

He smiled, "Jesus, you look terrible, Red. Come on." He pulled me toward the creek. "Let's get you cleaned up."

I leaned heavily against him as he walked us to the rocks at the water's edge. "I loved him so much for so long…"

He squeezed me closer. "I know."

My voice was hoarse. "And now I love you just as much… And the idea that anyone might look at our relationship and feel that it negates the one I had with him… it just feels like a disservice to both of you."

He nodded. "I know that too. I won't let it happen. We'll figure out a way. I should've listened to you. I was acting childish."

I sat on the rock, and he knelt in front of me, pulling off my dust covered boots and socks.

"I should've followed you down to the cave and held you in my arms instead of listening to you cry." He sat down beside me. "I shouldn't have taken a completely legitimate concern as a personal attack on me. It was immature and I'm sorry."

"I want that perfect world with you, Jack." I laid my head against his arm. "More than I've ever wanted anything."

Chapter Fifty-Four

Jim and Lilly emerged from the cave looking somewhat worse for wear. Jim was limping heavily with his arm over Lilly's shoulders, both of them almost completely covered in dark gray dust. Despite their rugged appearance, they both sported wide, bright smiles on their lips.

Jack sped to the opposite side of Jim to help him shift his weight, and Jim curled an arm over his shoulder, "All of yuns look like ye' been chewed up and spit out." He grinned as they came closer, winking at me before he looked at Jack. "Ooh boy and ye' smell bad enough to gag a maggot. I think we'd all best hop in 'at pond 'for we go back up."

They lowered him onto a boulder at my side and I wrapped an arm around him. "I'm so glad you're alright. You scared me to death."

"Oh, but the Good Lordt ain't done with me yet." He flashed his teeth at me while Lilly knelt in front of him and pulled the boot off his left foot, revealing a blood-soaked sock.

She looked at me then back up to him. "Jesus, Jimmy, this looks bad."

"Ain't but a scratch, darlin. I'll be fine."

She peeled back the sock and gasped at the protruding bones at the top of his foot. "Oh God!" Her eyes met mine, her face going pale white. "What do I do? Should we go get Anna?"

Jim glanced down at his foot and then to her. "Ain't nothin' she can do that I cain't. I been busted up more times than I can count. I know what needs done. Besides, no one's goin' nowhere with the storm that's fixin' to hit us. Did ye' see the sky this mornin?' I done told Bruce 'for we left to keep everyone at camp. It's gonna be a bad one."

She frowned at him. "Jim, this could get infected."

"Well then, sugar, we'd best get in 'at water right quick and get it clean." He pulled his shirt over his head, releasing a plume of dust. "I'll show ye' what needs done, then I'm gonna have to drink myself halfway stupid so ye' can do it. Now all of yas get in the water and warsh that dust off of ye' 'for it gets in yer lungs."

We all stripped to our undergarments and waded into the water. I dove down once I was deep enough and let the dust slide off my skin. When I surfaced, Jack's hands came to the top of my head, scratching softly.

He smiled down at me. "Lean back Red, you've got a whole mess of it in your hair." My lips curled, and I laid back against his arm, letting the water cover my ears and muffle the world as his fingers massaged my scalp.

I watched him as he concentrated on his fingers while they scratched and combed through my curls. His blue eyes were focused on his work, brow furrowed and jaw set. I wondered what it'd be like to be his in the real world. Would he always be this way with me? Would he always look at me like this or would we suffer the same fate I'd suffered with Chris? Would it fade away with time?

His eyes met mine and he grinned. "Good as it's gonna get for now." He pulled me up.

Behind him, Jim and Lilly had sunken down to their shoulders in the water. Jim held both of her hands in his, running his thumbs over the cuts on her fingers as he inspected them.

"Alright, Volmer," I tugged him down and leaned him back. "Your turn."

He obliged, laying heavily across my arm as I scrubbed at his hair, his eyes closing while I scratched his scalp. I bent and kissed his lips delicately, hovering there until his clear blue eyes opened. No, I wouldn't let this fade away. I couldn't. My heart was absolutely full over this man. Being loved by him meant everything, and I'd fight for this… Hell, *I'd* kill to keep it.

"I take it she said yes?" Jim giggled behind me, Lilly's arms wrapped around his neck.

I leaned Jack forward, frowning. "Said yes to what?"

Jack made a stern face at Jim and shook his head.

"You were going to propose…" I gasped, covering my mouth with both hands. "And I ruined it… That's why… The music… the candles…" I searched his face, my chest tightening as my heart sank. "Oh God, Jack. I didn't—"

He cupped my face, pressing his forehead against mine to whisper, "It's alright, Red. It wasn't the right time."

"But I—"

"I'll ask when it *is* the right time." He ran his hand over my hair.

"But it *was* the right time," I panicked. "It was all so perfect… and I ruined it."

He shook his head. "You didn't ruin anything. It's alright."

"No." I pulled back, looking up at him. "It's not alright. I'm an idiot. Ask me now."

"Red—"

"Yes!" I ran my palm over his cheek, pleading. "Yes."

He laughed. "I'll ask when it's right."

I nodded despite my desperate urge to beg. "And I'll say yes. Over and over."

"I'm so sorry!" Lilly interrupted, smacking Jim's shoulder as she pushed off him to make her way over to us. "I told him not to say anything!"

Jack wisely moved away from the splashing water and joined Jim in the deeper end of the pond.

"So," she whispered once Jack was outside of earshot, "he didn't propose?"

I shook my head. "No," I said between us. "He was going to but then I started an argument. I'm an idiot."

"He'll try again," she assured me, looking back at the two men. "He's crazy about you, ya know. He had all of us working up code combinations to get that phone unlocked."

I sighed. He'd gone to so much effort to make the whole evening perfect. Why hadn't I kept my stupid mouth shut?

"We went through Frank's wallet..." she continued, "tried the date on a baby photo, his birthday, the last four numbers of his social, nothing."

I laughed at her. "How'd you get it open?"

Her eyes welled with fresh tears as she looked at Jim and smiled affectionately. "Jim guessed the code."

"He did? What was it?"

She cleared her throat and did her best southern impression. "Six-nine-six-nine!"

I howled at that, looping my arm in hers as she bent with laughter. "You know," I raised my brow, "you didn't tell me you were in love with him."

She lifted her chin. "*You* didn't ask."

I giggled, but then I straightened, lowering my voice. "Did you mean all those things? You really think he'd make you happy after we've left the island?"

She looked over her shoulder at him, and her lip twitched as he caught her eye. "Yeah, I really do." She turned back to me. "I've spent a lot of time alone with him, getting to know him up here. At first it was all a game... just trying to get his attention. Then, I don't know. I didn't mean to love him, it just happened. He's the complete opposite of everything I thought I always wanted. And now all those things I thought I wanted just don't make any sense without him. You know?"

I wrapped my arms around her and squeezed. "I know." I looked back at Jack, sighing. "Believe me, I know. I'm happy for you."

"Ay." Jim and Jack made their way across the water to us. As he came around the side of her, Jim slid his hand over Lilly's hair. "You two done jackin' yer jaws or ye' want to wait til my foot falls plumb off?"

Her hand slipped up the side of his cheek and she grinned as she kissed him softly. "You know what my favorite part of this is?"

He smiled. "What's 'at?"

She kissed him again, lingering over his lips. "Now I've got a way to shut you up any time I want to."

He snickered loudly, then dunked her head under the water. She came up gasping and peeling the hair back from her eyes. "Well, looky there! So do I!"

He spun and strode proudly toward the shore. "Come on then, we ain't got all day."

Lilly hopped through the water to catch up to him, punching his arm before she looped it over her shoulder to help him walk out.

Jack coiled an arm around my waist. "Oh, these two are going to be entertaining."

I squealed as he lifted me off my feet and dragged me to the shore.

Jack and I shook out our clothes while Lilly ran back into the cave to grab new clothing from her pack for her and Jim. He sat with his bloodied foot extended in front of him, staring at it. "'For she comes back…" He looked up at us. "One of yuns is gonna have to do this. That woman gets the vapors if ye' squash a bug. Prolly gonna have to be you, Sis," he glanced at me then at Jack, "cause I'm gonna need him to hold me down."

He bent forward and pinched the toes of his bleeding foot, pushing on each one and wincing. "I ain't got no nerve damage, so this should be pretty straightforward. You see this bone stickin' up right here and here?"

My stomach turned over as I forced myself to look at the protruding bones. I nodded.

"Them's supposed to be down like 'at." He demonstrated with his finger lying straight over his foot. "You gonna have to push 'em down and together and hold it there. Pour some of 'at hooch on it, then wrap it tight as ye' can. Then, ye gonna get some long straight branches—not big ones, but sturdy enough they'll hold, and run 'em on either side of the foot, like this," he held his hands to each side, "then ye' wrap that tight as ye' can—you gonna throw up?"

I shook my head, but dared not open my mouth for fear that I might.

"Now, I need to be able to get around on it, so the last thing we gonna do is make a boot so's I ain't gotta' be limpin' around up here with a crutch. You gonna take two more small branches up the ankle, and two more underneath and wrap 'at as tight as ye' can."

He cleared his throat. "All that's gonna hurt like a summbitch, so I'm gonna need some of that whiskey 'for ye' get started."

Jack pulled his shirt on over his head. "I'll go find some sticks. You wanna do this down here or should I carry you up?"

Jim scoffed. "Ain't nobody carryin' my ass nowheres. We'll hunker down here for a while. I'll send Princess up to keep an eye out till it's done."

I swallowed, staring at the foot. "I'll go up with her and grab something to wrap that with."

He narrowed his eyes at me. "Woman, you white as a ghost. Y'ain't gonna be able to do this neither, are ye?"

Jack ran his hand over my forehead and laughed. "Alaina, you're cold and clammy. Are you seriously about to faint right now?"

"I…" I swallowed, "I don't know."

Lilly walked quickly toward us, sporting a cute yellow cotton dress. She held a white t-shirt out to Jim and he slid it over his head. Unfolding a pair of orange swim trunks we'd found in one of the suitcases, she knelt, carefully sliding a leg hole over his foot, then holding the other out for him to slip his other through.

"Thanks sugar." He stood, balancing his weight on his good foot as he pulled them up and sat back down. "Aight, change of plans. Hoss, you and me's gonna have to do this. Both of them's too squirrelly."

"I can do it, Jimmy," Lilly insisted. "Tell me what to do."

He grinned at her. "You see 'em bones right there? You wanna push 'em down fer me?"

Her eyes went wide and she blanched, leaning against me.

"I didn't think so," he chuckled. "You two grab me some whiskey and some fabric to wrap this up with. Then both of yas go on up and keep a look out."

We both dazedly turned toward the cave. "Ay, and both of yuns keep yer voices quiet in there."

Whiskey and fabric delivered, Lilly and I waited at the summit as the morning turned to afternoon and then evening. We sat side by side, our legs crossed in front of us, looking out at the water and the storm rolling in far off on the horizon, bits of lightning shooting from its clouds to skip across the water.

"You should get married on the beach," she said, daydreaming. "It wouldn't be right to get married anywhere else... Doesn't have to be this beach, just *a* beach. And I'll have these same pink flowers shipped there." She twirled a flower between her fingers. "And we'll make bouquets out of them. Oh, and have one for each guest to place behind their ear!"

I sighed, laying my head on her shoulder and closing my eyes, letting her paint me a picture. "If he ever decides to ask me again."

"Oh, he'll ask you," she said. "Anyway, we could have Bruce play the violin as you walk down the aisle... at sunset... in a long white lace dress that's formed to your body... with a train as wide as the aisle... we'll put your hair in a braid, he likes that... and we'll weave little white flowers in it..."

I smiled. "All of that sounds beautiful."

"And the bridesmaids will wear long, flowy blush dresses..."

"Blush?" I giggled. "Like pink?"

"No, you're right... pink wouldn't be right for you... how about silver... or champaign?!"

"Perfect."

"And we'll wear flowers behind our ears... white ones... how many of us are there?"

I raised my head and pursed my lips. "Three I guess. You, Anna, and my sister."

"You have a sister?" She looked at me incredulously.

I nodded and smiled, thinking of her. "Oh, yes, Cecelia. Cece." I laid my head back against her shoulder. "She's a year younger. We were very close growing up. She moved with her husband to Minnesota a few years ago. I think you'd like her. She's a very interesting character. She and her husband have this amazing campground up on the Canadian border that sits on a lake. It's beautiful. You can see every star in the sky, and if you go up in August and conditions are just right, you'll see the most beautiful display of the northern lights."

I could almost see my sister's face as I thought of her there. "It's perfect for her. She was always a tomboy. Didn't mind getting her hands dirty, which she has to do a lot of running a campground. Oh, but deep down, she's as girly as they come. When she's not helping chop firewood or chase animals out of the cabins, she's online ordering fancy purses, fine jewelry, and expensive clothes. I swear she has something shipped out there almost daily and nowhere to wear any of it, either. The campground is deep in the north woods with absolutely nothing but wilderness for miles. Still, she can't resist buying it, and every time I go up, she puts on a fashion show just for me."

She snickered. "I love her already."

We were interrupted by the echoing sounds of loud singing voices crawling up the tunnel. "OH A MAN AIN' NOTHIN' BUH A MAAAANNN…" They sang slightly off beat of each other and way out of whatever key they should've been in.

"BUUUUH MEH MEH SSSOMETHINNNNN…" They both howled with laughter and one of them hiccuped loudly.

Jim rolled out of the tunnel to one side, hiccuping to a burp as Jack crawled on his hands and knees out behind him, a nearly empty bottle of whiskey clanking on the ground in one hand.

They both rose to their knees, and Jim curled an arm around Jack's neck. They grinned at each other as they both filled their lungs and nodded a tempo. "I'D DIE WITH A HAMMER IN MY HAAAAAAND!!"

They balanced on their knees, arms draped over each other's shoulders and wobbling as they looked at us.

"Have a couple drinks, did ya?" I laughed at them.

Jack tried to make a straight face. "Ssnot right tuh let a ma-aan drink whisssey by hiiiissssselfff…. You-You're not the boss-a-me Woah-man." He made a high pitched 'hree' noise as he hiccuped.

I stifled a laugh as he closed one eye.

"Yeah, woahhhhhman." Jim giggled wildly at the word as he swayed and burped. "You teller who'ssssa bosss, Jick."

"You guys are hammered," Lilly chuckled.

Jim straightened tall, and he beamed at her with eyes almost closed. "Well haa-aay, shhhhuga…" He leaned over to Jack and pointed toward Lilly. "Ain't she"—his cheeks filled and collapsed —"Ain't shhhe ssssome'in? Lookiter… Jick.. Jick.. Jick, look… It… her…."

Jack squeezed one eye closed, then opened it and squeezed the other closed, giggling like a little girl as he slowly tilted to one side, pulling Jim along with him. "Oh… He-ey. You ladiesss come here offffen?"

Jim laughed a low guttural laugh and snorted. "Ohhho ma-an, thaasss good. Thass why I love ye' Hossss."

They had leaned so far to one side they were almost horizontal and Jim's eyes lit up as the bottle of whiskey in Jack's hand crossed in front of his face. "Oh… wass a-at? Don' mind if I do!"

He unwrapped his arm from Jack and snagged the bottle, leaving Jack to fall completely over on his side. He opened the bottle, closing one eye to look inside. "You alrigh, Hu-Hoss?"

Lilly leaned into me. "What the hell are we supposed to do with them now?"

I laughed, shaking my head slowly. "I have no idea."

Jim took a swig, then lowered on his hands and knees and crawled over to inspect Jack's face. He poked Jack's forehead and tried to whisper. "A-ay Jick ma-an, you goin' asleep fer tomorrow?"

Jack's eyes were closed and his lips curled into a smile as another high-pitched "hree!" hiccup escaped him. "No mannn, jusss for a second. Jusss five minn-uhs."

Jim lowered his face next to Jack's. "Ok bru-other… Get your resss caussse then Imma kick yer a-assss later." He snickered and collapsed onto the ground beside him, curling the whiskey bottle to his chest and letting his eyes close as he rolled onto his back.

"Sooooo…" Lilly tilted her head to one side, still staring at the two men. "Problem solved?"

I sighed, laughing to myself as Jack's arm draped over Jim's chest. A crack of thunder rolled in behind us. "Almost... let's get them down in the cave before they pass out completely."

Chapter Fifty-Five

We'd managed, with some effort, to get Jack and Jim down into the cave and propped up against the far wall just in time for the storm to beat down on us. The wind howled through the cave's openings and the rain poured overhead, dripping down through the tunnel and blowing into the mouth to soak the cave floor.

The combination of wind, thunder, and rain bounced off the rock and was so loud we couldn't hear each other even if we yelled. I'd gathered the flour and food, propping them up on our suitcases farthest away from where the water was rushing in.

I curled myself into Jack's lap and wrapped his unconscious arms around me, praying the storm would pass while he snored against my shoulder. Lilly and Jim were at our side. She'd pulled his arms around her body and we were close enough I could feel her shaking.

The storm had cloaked the cave in blackness, only the second's flash of lightning providing us a glimpse of each other.

I could hear the branches of the tree above us cracking just before the pressure of the wind filled the cave and caused my ears to clog.

With the world momentarily muted, I was reminded of the crash and the look in Jack's eyes as the plane fell toward the ocean in complete silence. My ears popped, the sound of the storm returning as I squeezed my eyes closed and buried my face in Jack's chest, reaching across to grip Lilly's hand.

Lightning struck close by, and the sound made me jump. I thought of the cave crumbling below and panicked. My heartbeat quickened. Would this one hold up against the thunder and wind or would we all get crushed beneath the rocks?

Another crash of lightning came, and Lilly squeezed my hand as Jack stirred beneath me, his arm around me pulling me against him. I felt him kiss the top of my head, and my heart slowed a little.

Water gushed down the tunnel now, pouring over our legs in a growing rush as it made its way to the crevice. I shivered as the cold water soaked my lower body.

"WHAT DO WE DO?" Lilly shouted, inches from me.

Jack squeezed me tight against him. I could feel his head moving above me, trying to assess the situation.

I looked up at him. The rush of water had completely filled the tunnel that led up, spilling out now like a waterfall, the sound of it drowning out the wind that blew in from the mouth. The crevice that led down filled rapidly with the cascade of water. We were all soaked now as the water grew stronger, and I could feel Jim moving next to us as consciousness found him as well.

"JUST HANG ON." Jack pressed his back against the wall and crushed me against his chest with one arm as the other reached for something to grab onto. I clung to him as the torrent pushed so strongly against me it threatened to take me with it. His legs wrapped around me and I felt Lilly's arm hook through mine.

Jim shouted and spit as the water sprayed over us. "WE GONNA NEED TO GET UP HIGHER."

Jack's legs squeezed as the water pushed us both toward the crevice. "YOU GOT A HOLD ON SOMETHING OVER THERE?" he shouted.

"FOR NOW." Jim reached out, gripping my upper arm.

"I GOTTA STAND UP AND SEE IF I CAN GRIP SOMETHING. YOU GOT HER?" Jack shifted and Jim curled me into his arm, wrapping one leg over me where Jack's slid out. I curled my arms around Lilly as he circled us with one of his, the other holding on for dear life.

I clung to them as we bobbed against the water, holding my breath as each new wave spilled over us. The water was rushing steadily now at my chest, fighting against our grip on each other and threatening to pull us away.

"I GOT SOMETHING," Jack informed us.

I felt his shin at my shoulder and looped my arm around it, holding my breath as I shifted to pull Lilly and Jim toward him. I kept her arm wrapped in mine as we each grabbed hold and Jim's arms came around the back of us. We all slowly raised up to stand against the current, swaying as we fought against it.

Jim on one side, Jack on the other, they smashed Lilly and I between them, holding us in place as the water raged against our thighs.

We held onto each other for what felt like an hour, listening as the thunder came less frequently and the howling wind faded to a dim whistle. The water slowly eased and drained down as the storm passed, allowing us to finally loosen our grip, our tired bodies collapsing as we all gradually lowered to the cave floor.

My arms were fatigued, my body shivered, and my teeth chattered from the cold that the wind and water had left on my skin.

Jim spoke quietly to Lilly next to me. "Shhh, I got ye' now." He cleared his throat. "Hoss, yuns alright?"

Jack pulled me to him. He was shaking and cold, but he ran his palms rapidly up my arms to warm them. "We're alright. Freezing."

"I don't reckon they's any coals left up 'er still burnin. What's up 'er would be soaked right through. 'Cept maybe the innards of the signal platform… if they's anything left of it. Ye' still got flint and steel on ye'?"

In a panic, Jack's hands went to his pockets then eased. "Yeah. I'll go up and see what's left." He squeezed me once more and kissed my temple before he left me shivering in the blackness.

I could hear Lilly shivering nearby. "Is your foot alright?" she asked.

"Don't ye' worry 'bout me now," Jim said. "I got ye' wrapped up in my arms, don't I? I'm right as rain."

"Lainey? Are you ok?"

I smiled to myself. "I'm fine."

We sat quietly for a minute before Jim sighed heavily. "Well shit. That'll sober ye' up *real quick*."

We all laughed out loud and I felt my body relax.

I heard the spilling of wood on rock as Jack returned. "Not much left up there. I might be able to get this lit long enough to dry off. It won't last the night, though. We're gonna have to rebuild the signal fire."

"Ye' think we lost the boat?"

The cave lit with each brush of the flint against steel as Jack attempted to light the fire. "Most likely. We secured it pretty good, but I don't think any amount of securing would've held in that wind."

A small flame appeared, and I watched it grow as Jack threw twigs and thin branches onto it.

"Ye' think camp did alright?"

Jack looked over at Jim and pursed his lips. "I don't think it'd be as bad there. The trees would shield them from the worst of the wind. As long as everyone stayed inside, they should be fine."

Lilly slid across the floor, towing Jim behind her as she positioned herself close to the small fire. She wrapped his arms around her and leaned her head into his shoulder.

I looked around and got my first glimpse of the cave as Jack took his place behind me. The bags of flour and suitcases were gone along with all of our food and water supplies, notebooks, bedding, and books. I assumed they'd washed down either to the cave below or the side of the ledge that climbed up to the mouth. "We'll need to track down our cases in the morning." I sighed. "Everything's gone."

"Ain't no matter." Jim laid his cheek against Lilly's head, rocking from side to side. "Y'all are alright. Everythin' else can be replaced."

We sat quietly until the fire burned out, all of us fatigued from the events of the day. Once we were enveloped in darkness, Jack gradually lowered us down to the damp cave floor where I curled my body into his and closed my eyes.

"Ye' know," Jim spoke softly, "I do believe the Good Lordt's tryin' to kill me after all."

Chapter Fifty-Six

"I went to see Doctor Moore today," I stated from the kitchen as I stirred the spaghetti sauce on the stove.

"Doctor Moore?" Chris echoed from the sofa, muting the television and looking over the island at me. "What for?"

"I read an article online… about my condition. Women have been able to conceive with IVF."

He stood suddenly and took two long strides to stand at the counter. "Ally, we're not doing that. We talked about this."

"No," I tapped the wooden spoon on the edge of the pot, setting it down in its holder, "*you* talked about it."

"Al, we can't go through that again." He shook his head, sitting down at one of the bar stools. "We're finally recovering from it just now and you want to start it all over again?"

"Are we recovering?" I crossed my arms over my chest. "When was the last time you kissed me? Can you even remember?"

He frowned. "When was the last time *you* kissed me? That goes both ways you know."

"Doesn't matter." I dismissed the impending argument. "We can't start over even if we both wanted to. Apparently the first pregnancy puts me at risk for rupture. I now have a *'thin uterine wall.'* So…" I waved the conversation off.

"Why didn't you tell me you were going?"

"I just wanted to know." I turned around, reaching into the cupboard to grab a box of spaghetti noodles. "I needed to know if I could. I was going to talk to you after."

"So talk to me now." He reached across the island to grab my hand. "Tell me why now?"

I sighed. "I'm thirty years old, Chris. I want a child... otherwise... what's the point?"

"What's the point of what?" He tilted his head to one side.

"Of all this..." I waved around the room with my free arm. "This big empty house that we stay separated in most of the time, the stressful jobs we both kill ourselves doing, this charade of a marriage..."

"It's not a charade, Al. I love you."

"Yes, I know that." I sighed, unlocking my hand from his to fill a pot with water. "And I love you, but there's no passion between us. And I get it, that happens sometimes... but maybe it's because something's missing. Maybe we were supposed to have a child to keep that spark between us alive... maybe we never would've lost the spark if she'd lived... Most couples have at least one child by the time they're our age. Look at us! What are we doing here? Just mindlessly wandering around doing the exact same crap every day... and for what?"

He lowered his eyes. "Well, what do you want to do, then? Adopt?"

"What do *you* want to do? Don't you want a child?"

"I mean... that was the plan." He traced a line in the marble with his thumb. "I guess so..."

"You guess so?" I scoffed. "This isn't like deciding whether or not you want a goldfish. You either want kids or you don't. This isn't a decision you can meet halfway. It would change everything about our lives."

"I want you to be happy," he said simply, finally looking up at me. "And if children are what you need to be happy then I'm on board all the way."

I sighed. "I want us *both* to be happy. We can always change the plan. Tell me what you want."

"I don't—"

"HELLLOOOOO?"

We were interrupted by the arrival of my mother for dinner. The conversation would have to wait. We had appearances to keep up, after all. I watched as Chris turned it on—the charade. His face changed in front of people. It was like he put on this perfect-husband mask the minute anyone walked through that door.

"Hey ma." Chris smiled sweetly, standing to remove her winter coat as she appeared in our living room.

"Hey babies." She turned and let him take the coat, watching as he disappeared into the foyer so she could lean across the counter and whisper, "What'd the doctor say?"

I poured the spaghetti noodles into the boiling water, sighing. "It's a no."

She clicked her tongue and shook her head. "Oh, I'm sorry, honey."

I pushed the stiff noodles with the spoon as they softened in the water, staring dazedly. "I'll live."

"It's not fair." She sat on the barstool in front of me. "What about adoption? Or a surrogate?"

I reached into the cabinet beside me and pulled out a bottle of cabernet and two glasses. "I don't know, ma. Maybe I'm just not meant to be a parent."

"Don't say that." She laid her hand over mine. "You'd make a great mother, and that's why you've always wanted to be one. Don't give that up."

I pulled my hand away to continue pouring the wine. "I don't think Chris wants kids anymore."

"HELLOOOOO?" Uncle Bill's animated voice shouted from the foyer.

She met my eyes. "Don't give that up." She spun in her seat. "HELLLOOO?"

Bill circled around the living room, Chris walking ahead of him to join me in the kitchen as Bill took a seat at the counter. "Smells good in here."

Chris wrapped his arms around me and kissed my cheek. "You want a beer?" he asked Bill, squeezing me tightly. I laid my head back against his shoulder and smiled. If I was honest, I liked the mask. He'd put it on and suddenly he'd be the man I married all those years ago—the one that would come up behind me and wrap his arms around me just because he needed to kiss my cheek. He would look at me the way he used to—like he really enjoyed me. He laughed when I spoke and I laughed when he did, and to all the world we were the picture of the perfect marriage.

"Sure, I'll take one." Bill smiled his cheeky smile as Chris spun around to retrieve said beer from the fridge. "You Graces ready to lose again this evening?"

We'd made a tradition of getting together twice a month to play Euchre with my mom and uncle and had lost a consecutive six times in a row. I twisted the corkscrew over the wine bottle and laughed.

"Oh, you think we lost those games?" I pulled the cork out. "We just didn't want to make you guys feel bad since you're old and you don't have many years left!"

"Hey!" My mother frowned, tossing her bright red hair over one shoulder. "*I* am not old."

I handed her a glass of wine as I poured my own. "Oh honey, look at them… they even have signs of dementia!"

"Alaina Jane, I will come right across this counter and beat you, don't think I won't!"

I giggled, sipping my wine as I stirred the noodles.

Chris smoothed his hand over the center of my back, and my heartbeat quickened at the touch. I'd been starved for any kind of affection and I ate up these small moments when people were around. "Be nice to your mother."

"Yeah," Bill teased. "It's not nice to pick on the elderly!"

My mother kicked his chair. "You know, I don't have to take this abuse!"

Bill chuckled and reached his hands out to me. "You want me to set the table?"

"Sure." I spun around and picked up the stack of plates, forks, and knives I'd placed on the counter earlier and handed them to him. "There's napkins in there."

My mother's phone rang loudly, causing me to jump. "Jesus ma, that ringtone is awful."

"Oh, hush." She stuck her tongue out at me. "It's your sister. I gave her the loud one so I can hear it from the other side of the house." She grinned as she pressed the screen and placed the phone to her ear. "Hello, my only good child!"

I rolled my eyes as I turned off the burner and pulled the noodles to another burner.

"WHAT?" My mom's face morphed in terror, her eyes wide and her head shaking as my sister's high-pitched voice rambled on the other end. "HOW?!"

"What?" I asked in a panic.

"Uh huh…" She held her finger up to me. "What hospital? What'd they say?"

'Hospital… Did something happen to Owen?'

"What?!" I nervously danced from foot to foot. "Is it Owen?"

My mom frowned and shook her head. "And then what?"

"Maddy?"

My mom nodded.

'Oh God, Maddy. What could've happened?'

"Alright, just calm down," my mom said shakily. "We'll be there soon. It's gonna be alright… uh huh. I love you too. Try to calm down now. I'm leaving right now. I'll call you when I get close. Bye."

She hung up and looked at me, her eyes suddenly welling with tears. "Maddy fell through the ice. They air-lifted her to a hospital and rushed her back. It doesn't look good. I need to get up there."

"We'll drive you," Chris insisted, grabbing his keys from the counter. "I've driven it so many times I could do it in my sleep by now."

"What happened?" Bill frowned at the door of the dining room.

"Maddy fell through the ice," I explained as I rushed to the foyer to grab my coat. "We need to go now."

Bill sped through the kitchen, checking that the burners were off as he switched off the lights and joined us in the foyer, grabbing his coat from the closet. "You want me to drive?"

"I got it, maybe halfway?" Chris swung his coat over his shoulders. "You guys go ahead and get in the truck, it's running. I'll lock everything up and shut everything off." He looked up the stairs at the light coming from our bedroom and rushed up, taking two steps at a time.

Chapter Fifty-Seven

The sun had barely begun to rise when we all groggily made our way up through the tunnel to the landing. None of us had slept in the cold, wet cave. Jack and I had tossed and turned, shivering against each other, and I could hear Jim and Lilly doing the same throughout the night.

Jim fell heavily to one side when he came out on the summit. The makeshift cast had come apart at the sides and the white fabric we'd wrapped it in was now pink and red. He pulled himself up to sit, leaning to one side and spitting. "Christ, I feel like death warmed over."

Lilly laid a hand across his forehead and he closed his eyes. "Sugar," he breathed deeply, "y'ain't gonna wanna be standin' so close. Last night's meal ticket was round trip, if ye' catch my drift."

Jack was in a similar state. He rushed past me and knelt behind the big tree. I could see one hand holding onto its trunk as the whiskey came up.

Acid formed in the back of my own mouth, and I ran to the opposite side of the landing and fell to my knees to retch painfully. My body shook as I recovered, running the back of my hand over my mouth. *'I didn't drink any—Oh God...'*

Slowly, I stood, glancing from Jim to Lilly to Jack. Lilly was rubbing Jim's back as he heaved dramatically and Jack was still kneeling down near the tree. None of them had seen. I closed my eyes. When had my last cycle been? *'Think backwards.... We were*

*up here for a week... then the week before we worked on the hull...
the week before that I put together our bed in the back cave... the
week before that I didn't have it either... The last time was... Oh
God, this can't be happening...'*

I blew out and walked across to the edge to look out on our
beach. My heart sank. Five months of back-breaking work was
now scattered across the sand. There was nothing left of the
platform or the boat, just broken logs and bamboo littered up and
down the shore from the water to the tree line.

'I can't be... not here... not now.'

I saw Jack stiffen when he came to my side and looked out.

I squeezed his hand.

'I needed that boat... I need it now more than ever.'

He ran his other hand through his hair, turning around to
inspect the landing. The twigs and branches from the signal
platform were mangled into mulch and strewn across the moss.
Branches from the big tree had fallen and blown from one edge of
the landing to the other.

I could see the fatigue and defeat in his eyes as he took it all in.
He was tired, which I knew meant he was also cranky. He needed
water and food and we had neither. I slid a hand over his back and
rubbed softly. "It'll be alright. Why don't you sit down for a bit
and I'll go see if I can get some water and scrounge up a fish or
two from the pond?"

He shook his head. "We need to get back down. Make sure the
others are alright."

Jim wretched loudly near the tunnel's opening, sending Lilly
scurrying in our direction. Her eyes were red and her shoulders
were hunched over. "I need to figure out a way to get water up here
fast. All the bottles are gone. We need to re-splint his foot too. It
looks worse. Oh God, Lainey, I don't know how much more I can
take."

'Lilly, you have no idea.'

I smoothed her hair. "It's alright. The bottles are probably
down in the crevice and in the lower cave along with everything
else. Hopefully, they didn't all break against the rocks. We'll get
his foot wrapped back up before we go." I focused on Jack, who

had turned back to the beach. "Let me just help her get water and see if we can retrieve a few of our lost items and we'll head down. We can't make the trip without water."

He slowly nodded, reaching into his pocket and handing me the flashlight, eyes still focused on the devastation below. "Be careful."

"Come on, Lill," I said quietly, my heart aching for him... and for myself. "Let's go see if we can find our things."

We left them on the landing and headed down, navigating into the narrow crevice, collecting debris—bottles and fabric—that littered the path.

At the small opening that led into the large cave, we found a suitcase plastered against one side. We poured our findings into it, then slid out into the cave. Sprinkled down the cascading boulders were the contents of our second suitcase, an entire roll of fabric, pieces of the bamboo bed frames, shattered bottles and Fe'i bananas strewn here and there.

"You go down and fill whatever bottles are intact," I instructed, handing her the case. "I'll grab what I can from up here."

She peered down the spilling rocks. "I don't know if you should be crawling on those rocks with the luck you've had."

I tested one with my toe. "I don't think I should either. I'll stay at the top and grab only what I can reach. I'll be careful."

Reluctantly, she took the suitcase and headed down while I eased myself over the edge onto the boulders.

I kept my head no more than a foot lower than the ledge, side-stepping from one boulder to the next, heaving fabric, clothes, and Fe'i up over my head. I could hear Doctor Moore's voice in my ears as I did, repeating over and over: *'The live birth rate in women with your condition is only about twenty-nine percent.'*

My heart beat in my throat. *'Twenty-nine percent... and stuck on this island...'* I shook my head, focusing on the task in front of me. When I'd recovered all I could reach, I headed down to the cave floor, where I grabbed all I could from the bottom of the rocks, including the second suitcase.

'Maybe I'm wrong... it could be stress. I've been under a lot of it.' I tried to convince myself, but even as I thought it, I recognized

the heaviness in my breasts and the fatigue that had taken over my body.

My bones ached and my eyes were heavy by the time Lilly returned and we made our way back up to the upper cave with full suitcases in tow.

I crawled out of the tunnel onto the summit to find Jim propped up against the tree, his leg extended and his foot in Jack's lap. Jack had removed his tank top and tore it into strips, using the fabric as he re-wrapped the cast on Jim's foot.

Lilly and I headed in their direction and Jack stood. "We should get going," he said as he plucked one of the two glass bottles out of my hand and took a huge gulp.

My body protested, but I nodded. "Okay."

'I won't tell him... not yet.... he's got enough to worry about right now.'

Lilly wrapped her arms around me. "I miss you already. Be careful."

I curled my arms around her. "Have fun up here." I kissed her cheek and grinned. "I know you will."

She smiled at me, and her cheeks flushed ever so slightly before she pulled Jack into a hug. "Thank you for everything. I don't know what I would've done if you hadn't been here."

I knelt beside Jim as he watched Lilly. "You gonna be alright up here?"

His lip curled to one side as he turned his eyes from her to me. "Darlin', I don't think I'll ever be better. Y'all get home safe."

We turned and headed toward the tunnel. While Jack crawled inside ahead of me, I looked back to them one last time, watching as Lilly curled herself into Jim's lap and pressed her forehead against his, a bright smile lighting both their faces. Content, I slipped into the passageway, excited for the stories she'd have when they returned.

The trek down was slow going. It was muddy and slick with downed trees everywhere. Given the events of the previous day, we were on high alert, watching warily with each step we made, both of us stuck in our own minds as we navigated downward.

'I will lose this baby.' My mind raced. *'How could I not? I spent my entire first pregnancy loaded with vitamins and the healthiest foods, getting plenty of rest, visiting the doctor almost weekly, and I still lost her. Here, I am vitamin deficient, limited only to the food we can hunt or gather, my body is under constant stress, and I have no doctors, no ultrasounds, no way to know what's going on. How could I not lose it? Or die in the process of trying? The doctors all reminded me constantly of the threat to my own life... I have to get off this island.'*

It was afternoon by the time we got to camp. We were both caked in mud and clay, our bodies exhausted, but we were delighted to see smoke at the fire and only minor damage to the birdcage despite the downed trees surrounding it all.

Isobel came running up to greet us, Finn chasing at her heels. As we approached, Jack scooped her up into a hug and carried her the rest of the way to the cave.

My heart warmed at the sight of her little arms around his neck, and I begged my body not to betray me. *'Please don't take this from us. Please be alright. Let it all be alright.'*

Magna shook her head as she rose from the fire. "I'm glad to see you both. We were worried sick over you in that storm. Jim and Lilly are ok?"

I smiled as Jack lowered Isobel back to her feet. "Everyone's alright. Jim's got a broken bone in his foot but he'll manage. How did you do here? Where is everybody?"

She looked apologetically at me, then at Jack. "Everyone's fine. Bertie's inside. She's been doing a little better the last few days. The rest of them went down to check the damage on the beach."

Jack nodded, scanning our camp as he ran his hand hard through his hair. "I saw the damage from the summit. It's all gone."

Magna made a 'tsk' sound as she grabbed a stick to pull the steaming clay pot from the fire. "It's a shame. All that hard work."

She sighed. "Nothing can be done to change it right now. Come sit down and have some tea. You both look exhausted. I'll fix you a plate." She looked at Jack, who was gazing in the direction of the beach. "Come on, honey, sit down now. We can worry about it later."

Magna was the most maternal woman I'd ever met. She radiated a motherliness that was unparalleled to anyone in my life. She was our island mother, and if she instructed us to do something, we did.

He glanced at me, then back at her, and his shoulders slumped in resignation. "Just bread and jam if we have it, then I'm gonna get cleaned up and head down." He led me to sit by the fire.

I touched his arm. "Maybe we should rest for today. Go down in the morning. I don't think there's much we could do right now. We're both exhausted."

Magna poured tea from the clay pot into two of the blue and white porcelain teacups, carefully handing one to each of us. "I'll go fetch you some bread and jam and fresh clothes."

Jack sipped and closed his eyes. I followed suit, letting the hot, sweet liquid fill me. For the first time since the storm, I felt warm.

'Please be okay.'

"I want to get a look at the damage up close," Jack insisted, curling his hands around the cup. "See if there's anything that can be salvaged. You can lay down in the cave while I'm gone."

I laid my head against his shoulder, yawning. "No, I'll go where you go."

He slid his arm around my back and massaged my shoulders. "You should get some sleep, Red."

I closed my eyes. "So should you. I'll sleep when you do."

Magna appeared with two small saucers, each sporting a hefty serving of bread and jam. She had a fresh change of clothes for each of us draped over her forearms. "Eat up now. I've got hot rocks heating the wash bin, why don't you two wash off here with some warm water for a change and then go lay down inside for a while?"

My stomach growled as I took the saucer from her. I immediately bit into the bread and my tastebuds rejoiced. With my mouth half full, I thanked her. "A warm shower sounds amazing right now." I took a sip of my tea to wash it down. "Don't you think, Jack?"

"Oh, thank God! Is Lilly alright?" Bud shouted from behind us.

I spun around. Bud was walking ahead of Bruce, who had his arms around a sobbing Anna.

"She's fine," I said, watching Anna attempt to compose herself. "Everyone's alright."

'I need to tell Anna.'

I saw Bud's shoulders ease and he leaned over us, wrapping an arm around each of us. "Glad to see you both. We were terrified of what that storm would do up there."

Bud took a seat on the opposite side of me and Bruce replaced him while Anna split off in the direction of the cave. "It's all gone, Jack. All of it in pieces."

Jack nodded. "I saw it from up there. We're gonna have to start over."

"Or…" Bruce knelt between us. "What if one of us went out on the raft?"

Jack shook his head, "We've already been over this—"

Bruce held up his hand. "Now, hear me out. I could go. We've got the compass from the kit, oars, a canopy, and we could make a small sail. I could make sure I stay east, just like we planned with the boat."

Jack shook his head. "It'd be too hard to stay on course in a raft, and it'd be almost impossible to find your way back here. Besides, Phil's been gone for months with no word back. We all go together so we *all* make it out. That was the deal."

Anna spun on her heel, barreling back toward us, her eyes full of tears. "It took us five months just to build what we had!" she sobbed. "We'll be here at least another five if we try to rebuild now!"

Jack took a deep breath. "I'm sorry. I really am. We're going to have to tough it out a little while longer."

Bruce straightened. "Well, what if another storm takes the next one before it's done? And the one after that? I'm tired of waiting, Jack. I feel worthless here. And she needs to get home to her son. I can't help with the boat but I could get on the water and try to find help. If I tried to stay headed in one direction, tracked it, then I'd know the vicinity of the island, wouldn't I?"

He frowned. "If I get home and tell them there are survivors out here, there's got to be some kind of technology they can use— satellites or something to find it, right?"

'There are no satellites.'

Jack furrowed his brow. I could see frustration welling up inside him as his shoulders stiffened. "I don't know. But let's say they don't. What then? And say you go, what happens when you sleep? How are you going to track movement then? Or say a storm destroys the raft, then we lose you, the raft, and the only compass we've got. It's not a good idea."

Bruce persisted. "I could take someone with me. We could take turns sleeping and navigating."

"I'll go with him! Please!" Anna sniffled.

Jack shook his head. "It's too big of a risk. We all need to go together."

Bruce's cheeks were red as he stood. "Well then, why don't we *all* get back on the raft?"

Jack stood and his nostrils flared as he looked down at Bruce. "Dammit, it's too dangerous. Did you not get hit by the same storm I did last night?"

Bruce raised his chin. "You and Jim don't get to make all the decisions. We all should have a say here."

Jack's hands balled into fists at his side. "You think I want to make any of these decisions? You think I want to tell *her* no? That she can't get on a raft and try to get home to her son? I don't want that kind of responsibility. I didn't ask for that. You want to take that responsibility, go ahead. Good riddance. It can be on you if we never make it back."

I could see the weight of the world on his shoulders then. He hadn't asked for any of this. He'd crashed just like the rest of us, had been ripped from his life just like the rest of us, but he'd been expected to solve every problem that'd come our way.

He worked day in and day out to build a boat strong enough to get us all safely home, and now he faced the knowledge he'd have to start over.

He'd planned a perfect proposal, and I'd ripped his heart out by questioning him. He'd done the bulk of the lifting to save Jim, set and splinted his foot when no one else could, and then had literally given him the shirt off his back after he'd held onto all of us to keep us from washing away in the storm.

He hadn't slept and had barely eaten for worrying that something might've gone wrong back here. His knuckles were bruised and his hands were covered with calluses. He'd taken care of all of us. Who was taking care of him?

I stood, my cheeks on fire. "Enough!"

I looked from Bruce to Anna. "That's enough. We're not having this conversation right now."

I took Jack's arm in mine. "Come on, I'm going to get you cleaned up and then you're going to lie down." I looked back at them. "Once this man—*who's been breaking his back for all of us for months*—has gotten some rest, then we'll talk about it. Until then, if you're feeling worthless, find something that's broken and fix it."

I pulled him off toward the wash bin at the side of the cave, fresh clothes stacked under one of my arms.

"Wait here," I demanded, handing him the clothes and spinning around to return to the cave. Inside, I rummaged through Lilly's secret stash of toiletries to steal a bar of soap and a cloth. I grabbed a clay bucket, threw the soap, cloth, an empty bottle, and a roll of fabric inside, then stole a bamboo chair and headed back to the side of the cave, avoiding eye contact with the others as I passed.

He tilted his head and smiled as I handed him the soap, fabric, and chair. I dipped the large clay pot into the warm water and marched toward the cover of the trees. "Come on."

About fifty yards from camp, I stopped and set the bucket on the ground, taking the chair from him. I launched the fabric over a branch overhead and stretched it on each side to create a temporary shelter, then placed the chair inside. I took a deep breath and let my heartbeat settle, taking his hand in mine and leading him inside.

"Alaina, I should —"

"Shh." I knelt to remove his boots. "You're done today."

I pulled his mud soaked boots and socks off, then stood to unbutton his jeans. He smiled down at me, letting his hands glide down my hair as I stripped them off. I pressed him gently into the chair and kissed his lips. "It's my turn to take care of you now."

I moved behind him, stripping my own clothes off before I tilted his head back, positioning the pot of warm water beneath him, then dipping the bottle in and pouring it over his head. He closed his eyes and sighed heavily as I repeated this over his face, neck, chest, and arms.

I dipped a piece of cloth into the pot and wrapped the bar of soap in it, turning it in my hands until bubbles formed between my fingers. I worked the soap into his hair, scratching and massaging his scalp, working my way down behind his ears and scratching softly at the nape of his neck. I filled the bottle again and let the warm water wash over him. I could see his shoulders relaxing with each pour.

I brought the cloth to his face and lathered, massaging the soap into his beard, over his nose and cheeks, and down his neck. He laughed as I pinched his nose and poured the warm water over his face until it was clear.

I bent over him to kiss his forehead as I slid my thumbs down and massaged the knots from his neck and shoulders.

I dipped my hair into the pot, working the soap into my curls as I came around to the front of him.

His head tilted forward and he watched me patiently, his hands sliding up the backs of my legs as I stood between his to lather his chest, arms, and torso, then my own. I pulled him up out of the chair and wrapped my arms around him, scrubbing his back and shoulders, working my way down to scrub his bottom half while he observed my every move.

I raised on my toes and kissed his lips before I circled around him and dipped my bottle again, pouring the water down his back over and over, laying kisses along his spine as I pushed the water to each side.

"Turn," I said softly, and he obliged so I could repeat the process on his arms, chest, and legs.

"Ok, best part." I grabbed the clay pot and carefully balanced on the chair, rising slowly to stand and pour half the remaining warm water over the top of his head and down his shoulders. I poured the last of the water over myself.

He smiled at me and took the pot, wrapping his arms around my back and pulling my mouth to his, kissing me deeply as he lowered my feet to the ground. He pressed his forehead against mine and twisted a piece of my hair around his finger. "You're a force to be reckoned with, Red."

I grinned up at him. "Honey, you have no idea. Now, let's get you to bed."

"But I—"

I shook my head and stuck my finger to his lips. "I'm taking you to bed." I bit my lower lip. "Where I'm going to *finish* taking care of you."

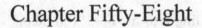

Chapter Fifty-Eight

We slept the rest of the day and through the night, until the sound of Finn's flapping wings at the foot of our bed forced my eyes open. I grabbed the flashlight from the bedside table and shined its light at my feet to find Isobel standing at the edge of the bed while Finn hopped around on top of my ankles.

I sat up abruptly, causing Jack to jump up as well. "What is it?" He looked around in a panic then settled when he saw her.

I rubbed my eyes and signed to her, "What's wrong?"

She signed back. "Come. Fast." Then she plucked the bird off the bed and carried him out of our cave and into the big one.

I leapt out of the bed, grabbing a pair of shorts from the ground and pulling them on as I followed her through the cave and outside. Jack was right behind me, jumping as he pulled his jeans up and fastened them, a shirt hanging from his teeth. Before he could pull the shirt on, Isobel took his hand in hers and led us in the direction of the beach, Finn hopping hurriedly alongside her.

It was very early. The sun had not risen high enough to light our camp, leaving everything shaded in a cool blue.

About halfway into the canopy, we saw them, Bruce and Anna, holding the inflated raft between them, loaded with supplies and drooping in its center.

"ANNA, WAIT!" I shouted, sprinting ahead to catch up to them.

They stopped and set the raft on the ground.

Anna spun around to pull me off to one side as Jack reached Bruce.

"Alaina," her tone was sharp, "you shouldn't have dismissed us like that."

I blinked hard. "Anna, please, just wait a minute. I wasn't doing it to be mean. We were tired, and it was getting heated fast."

She shook her head. "Doesn't make it alright. Look, I've been gone far too long and I can't take the risk of being gone any longer. I *have* to get back to Liam. Waiting another however many months is not going to work for me. You don't understand what he could do to him."

"Anna—"

She held up her hand. "I get it. You don't think it's a good idea, and that's fine. I don't need you to agree with it. I thought about this a lot. Bruce and I are getting on the raft and we're going to try to get home. You can keep the compass and the flare, but we'll be taking some food and water."

"Anna—"

"Alaina, you can't change my mind on this or Bruce's. It's the only thing either of us feels like we *can* do"

"Anna!" I covered my mouth. Bile had risen up my throat, and I rushed into the trees and fell on my knees to vomit miserably.

"Oh, Alaina..." She knelt beside me. "Tell me you aren't pregnant?"

I placed a finger on my lips and looked over at Jack and Bruce, both of them arguing heatedly ahead of us.

I stood, grasped her hand, and pulled her just outside of earshot.

"And I need you." I looked up, dismissing the tears that wanted to come. "Do you know what a unicornuate uterus is?"

She blinked, looking down at my midsection and back up to me, nodding slowly. "I don't know a lot, but I read about it." She placed her knuckles against her lips and paced. "Oh God, Alaina, there are so many risks..." She looked behind us and back, lowering her voice. "You know that. Miscarriage... preterm... breech..." She paced and turned. "Sepsis... Blood clots... There are so many... How far along are you?"

I shook my head. "Maybe seven weeks? Eight? I don't know."

"And Jack doesn't know?"

"No."

She paced again. "Jesus. You should've been more careful... This is really dangerous for you."

I hugged my arms around my chest self-consciously. "I know that. I just... didn't think it was possible." My eyes did water then.

"Oh, honey." She wrapped her arms around me. "You're going to need a *real* doctor... ultrasounds... access to hospitals and medicine we don't have... you can't do this here. *I* can't do this here."

She sighed heavily, letting go of me to pace again. "We need to find help. We have to go. *Now.*" She looked back toward Bruce and Jack who were both still arguing, although they had lowered their tone.

"Anna, I can't get on that raft. Not now. If we ran into another storm... or if no one found us... I can't take that risk. Not now."

She paced again. "No, you're right. But someone needs to get out there and find help. And you don't have time to wait for us to rebuild the boat. You *can't* have it here... You could die. And I can't help you... Unless...?"

"Unless?"

"Well," she cleared her throat, "we *could* resolve it now... before it's too dangerous."

I shook my head. "No. Absolutely not. I can't do that."

She persisted. "Alaina, you have to consider it. Phil's been gone for five months. *Five months* with that message carved loud and clear for whoever might've found him. You don't have the luxury of time. Abortion might be the only safe option."

"There's nothing for me to consider. The answer is no."

She shrugged her shoulders, evidently frustrated. "Well, I can't help you otherwise... If you won't consider it, the only thing I can do is try to find help. Let me go find you help."

I squeezed my palms together to stop them from shaking. "I can't stop you. Will you stay at least long enough to show Magna and Lilly what to do if..." I swallowed, wiping my eyes.

"If we don't make it," she whispered, looking back out at the beach.

I nodded nervously. The only person here who could help me was leaving for her child's sake, and I couldn't guilt her into staying for the sake of mine.

She softly touched my shoulder. "Alright, we'll stay just a little longer. Just until we've lined out all the possible scenarios."

She turned us toward the men, and I took a deep breath to compose myself. "And please don't say anything. I'm not sure I'm ready to tell Jack just yet. He has enough to worry about."

"I won't."

As we approached, Jack was pleading. "Bud and I are the only ones here who know anything about sailing. We can't leave yet. Not with Bertie. Please... I'm begging you. If you go out there, you're as good as dead. Give me one month. One month to build something stronger and I'll take you myself."

Anna took Bruce's hand in hers. "We're staying. But not for a month. Two weeks. Jack, you'll teach us to sail and build something stronger by then."

"Anna," he shook his head, "I can't tell you what to do or keep you from going but—"

"But nothing," she said. "We're leaving in two weeks."

Jack sighed, but nodded. "I'll get started right away. With what's left on the beach from the platform, I should be able to build a stronger raft."

"I'll help you," Bruce insisted.

"We'll take Izzy back." Anna wrapped an arm around Isobel, glancing out at the ocean one last time, her shoulders slumping in acceptance of her defeat. "I'll send Kyle down to help but I'm keeping Alaina with me. I'm going to put together some instructions on how to treat various injuries and show her some techniques to help with Bertie."

She turned Izzy back toward camp and paused, spinning back toward him. "You're a good man, Jack. We'll find help and we'll come right back for all of you. I promise."

As we began to trek uphill, my mind returned to Zachary, to the map, and Magna's words echoed in my thoughts. *What if the reason we haven't seen airplanes or satellites or cargo ships is because they don't exist yet?'*

What if there were no doctors to go back to? What kind of world would we find when we'd left the security of the island? Would it be any safer than the world we'd created here?

"Alright." Anna blew out, glancing over her shoulder to ensure we were far enough outside of earshot to converse freely. "You know you have a unicornuate uterus, which means you've been diagnosed? You need to tell me everything you know so I can form a plan for all the possible risks."

I squeezed Isobel's hand between us as she took Anna's in her other and swung her legs out from beneath her, oblivious to the conversation going on over her head.

"I was pregnant once before. They coined it a "miracle" that I'd conceived at all. But they laid out the risks clearly. Miscarriage, breech, pre-term." I raised my arm to support Isobel's weight as she launched herself off the ground again.

"I lost her at twenty-seven weeks." I was surprised at how easily the words came. I'd never been able to talk about it without breaking down.

"A few years later, I returned to the doctor to see if I was a candidate for IVF and they told me that my uterine walls were thin and I would be risking rupture if I tried to conceive a second time."

Isobel giggled at Finn as she swung her legs out and Finn flapped his wings, chasing her kicking feet. I smiled down at her, then made eye contact with Anna.

"I know the risks. I really do. And I know that I should consider…" I swallowed. "You know… But I can't. I have to give it the chance. I can't willingly lose another child… no matter how dangerous it might be."

"I understand that Alaina, I really do." She laughed as Isobel swung again, giggling audibly as we both accelerated the force by raising our arms higher, forcing her tiny legs into the air in front of her.

"I know it might seem like a miracle, but out here…" she shook her head, "it may be more of a curse. This really could kill you. Just take the week to consider all the risks thoroughly, okay?

And I will, in turn, come up with every possible outcome and plan for it."

I nodded, and we walked along in silence for a while, enjoying the little happy sounds of Isobel as she swung between us, evidently delighted Anna was not leaving her.

Just before we got back into camp, I looked back at Anna. "The journals... and the storm.... The lack of planes or ships... What's *your* take on it all?"

She squinted her eyes for a moment, looking forward as Isobel unwrapped her fingers from ours and ran ahead to join Magna at the fire. "I think we hit a storm and crashed in a very remote place in the middle of the Pacific. I don't think there was anything more to it."

"Really?" I furrowed my brow. Everyone had their own theories about the crash and none of them were so cut-and-dry. "You don't get the slightest sense that something bigger happened to us?"

"No." She took a deep breath, then met my eyes. "Traumatic events can make your mind go into all sorts of creative coping mechanisms. I really believe everyone is trying to make the cause for the trauma bigger than it is. It makes the damage that much more bearable—like we had to go through the crash because of some higher power, some apocalyptic event, some kind of paranormal phenomena, or some fated destiny. But really, we just got unlucky... our plane got hit by lightning and crashed into the ocean. It didn't make any noise because of the effect the sudden loss of cabin pressure had on our ears. I think I'll get on that raft and run straight into a ship and get home to my Liam and the world will be just as it was before."

"I really hope you're right."

I yawned, stretching my arms as she moved ahead of me to join Magna and Izzy. Her theory was the most likely, I knew, but the idea of the world being just as it was seemed much more far-fetched to me than any of the conspiracies the rest of us had come up with. In my gut, I truly felt there was more to it, but for the sake of the child that grew inside of me, I prayed she was right.

While Bruce and Jack stayed back at the beach attempting to salvage the wreckage to form a new raft, I spent the rest of the day out of the burning sun and inside the cave with Bertie, happy she was feeling well enough to converse.

I listened to her stories, a welcome distraction from my nagging thoughts, as she whisked me away to the sixties and seventies and her various travels around the world with Bud.

She told me about their trips to Italy and Greece; to India and Africa, about how they'd seen the world as a family and never missed an opportunity to go some place new.

Her openness with Bud was endearing, and it was something I recognized developing between myself and Jack. I didn't hide myself from him the way I did with Chris. And he didn't hide himself from me. I wanted to always be honest about our thoughts and feelings. And I knew I couldn't keep this secret from him any longer. I had to tell him.

That night, after he'd returned late, Jack paced the small back cave, the firelight of our two candles dancing off the tensed muscles of his arms.

"If I worked late... maybe I could build a smaller version of the first boat..."

He spoke in a low tone so no one in the front part of the cave could hear. "One we could all get on. They don't know the first thing about sailing."

He leaned against the wall near our bed, his eyes narrowed and his shoulders stiff with worry. "If they hit a storm... or if they veered off course... I'd be sending them off to die out there... Maybe we could move back to the beach? Work later? Maybe we could all go with them. I can't stop her but maybe I could stall her for a week or two more... we need more time. What do you think, Red?"

I was sitting on the edge of the bed, my hands shaking in my lap. I'd spent the entire afternoon and evening playing it out in my head, but now he was here and I was terrified.

"Hey, what's wrong?" He knelt in front of me, the orange glow of the candle highlighting the concern on his face.

I smoothed my palms over his warm chest and down his shoulders, noticing in his closeness that his body was burned from spending the entire day working in the sun. My voice began to tremble. "There's something I need to tell you."

He kissed my lips softly, taking my shaking hands in his. "What is it? What's going on?"

"I'm…" I breathed out shakily; there was no turning back now, "…pregnant."

"Pregnant?" he breathed, his face lighting up as he said the word. He made a move to kiss me again but stopped short, searching my face until his expression shifted back to concern. "This isn't good news?"

I shook my head. "It's very likely…" I couldn't contain the tears any longer and began to sob. "I'm going to lose it."

He pulled me against him, stroking my hair. "Don't say that. You don't know that."

"Yes, I do," I blubbered.

He pulled me back, sweeping the hair from my face. "How do you know?"

I sniffled, trying to catch my breath as it hitched. "The doctors told me." I shook my head. "I didn't think I could even *be* pregnant again… otherwise I would've been more careful. I should've told you this before."

He kissed my lips again, pressing his hot forehead against mine. "It wouldn't have made any difference. I'd have loved you all the same." He let his hands fall to my stomach. "And whatever happens next, I love you still."

He pulled back, searching my face. "Did you tell Anna? She can't leave now."

I nodded. "Yes. And there's nothing she can do. This is all the more reason they *should* go. They've got to send help before…" I swallowed.

He curled his arms around my waist and laid his head against my stomach. "I'm right here with you for all that comes next. Tell me everything I need to know. What are we up against?"

I let my fingers glide through his hair, evening out my breath as I leaned back on one arm to get a better look at him. His hair had grown too long and was beginning to curl at the ends. The sun had lightened it in the time we'd been here. I took a deep breath, determined not to break down. "Well, first, there's..."

'Rupture.' My mind echoed the dire warning Dr. Moore had given me. However honest I wanted our relationship to be, I wouldn't tell him that... He had enough to worry about.

"Miscarriage. Most women miscarry in the first trimester. And with a miscarriage, there's the risk of sepsis."

His palm swept over my belly, and he raised his head up to look at me.

I combed the hair from his face and continued, "Then there's breech... From what I was able to find on the internet the first time around, for most women with my condition, the babies come early and their feet are down... so if my uterus did somehow hold up, I'd most likely have to have a cesarean... which Anna is going to leave instructions for Magna and Lilly in case of an emergency."

He tensed visibly, shaking his head as I proceeded. "And even if they could pull that off, there's the preterm aspect. It's very rare to ever go the full nine months. Usually the baby comes somewhere between thirty and thirty-five weeks. And that small, there are health risks that come with an underdeveloped baby that we wouldn't be able to treat here. I'm about seven or eight weeks now... so that leaves us with about five months to get off this island."

"Jesus," he whispered under his breath. "Could we..." he looked down at my belly and ran a thumb over it. "Is there something we could do now... to prevent...?" He looked back up at me, his eyes glossed over.

I shook my head. "I won't do it."

"But—"

"I won't do that. I know what the risks are, but there's still a chance our baby could live and I won't take that away..." I blinked the fresh tears away.

"Our baby," he repeated, looking back down at my midsection. "I'll build a boat. I'll work round the clock—night and day. I can't leave your fate in their hands. We have to go too. We've got to get you to a doctor."

"Jack, I can't add any more risk to this pregnancy than I already have. I can't take this baby away from a food and water supply to take the chance at finding rescue. What if we don't find help? What if the boat capsizes? What if we run out of food and water before we find a ship or land?"

He gently guided me to lie back on the bed, sliding in beside me as I rolled to face him, the heat radiating off his skin. "I'll go. I'll get help. I know how to sail and we know where we are now. I can get help."

"No," I said flatly, placing my palm on his chest. "You can't leave me. The plan was to go east. They don't need you to go east. I need you to stay here with me. Phil's been gone for five months with no word back. I can't risk losing you for that long."

He kissed my forehead, then my lips, running his thumb over my cheek. "I have the map and I can try to make it to one of the other islands. If I can find one of them, then I can confirm our location, sail between the islands in search of a ship. I wouldn't go any further. I'd be close enough to get back within a few days."

"No," I pleaded. "I can't do this without you."

He combed the hair from my face. "Sweetheart, I have to go. I have to find help. Look at me." He pulled my chin up so my eyes met his. "I will come right back. I swear. I have to try."

"What if the map is wrong?"

"If the map is wrong and I head toward Ua Pou, I would know within two days it was wrong and would turn right back."

"According to Zachary's map, Ua Pou is west of here," I argued. "How would you make it there sailing against the wind?"

"I'll paddle," he said simply. "If it's as close as we think, I should be able to see Mont Oave long before I'm anywhere near it. I'll take the telescope with me."

"And what if you find it and there's no one there?"

"Well," he sighed, "I'd come back to report it and then try for Ua Huka. I'll spend as much time as I have to circling between the three islands until I spot a ship. I won't go any further. I'll be close by."

Resigned, I blew out. "Promise you'll come right back?"

"I promise." He pressed his forehead against mine.

"What about Anna?" I frowned, pulling my forehead away to search his face. "She doesn't believe we're in the Marquesas and she has her heart set on going home. If you make it to Ua Pou and no one is there, she'll want to keep going. She won't want to come back here."

"She's not going," he said matter-of-factly. "There's no way in hell I'm going to let the only person on this island that could save you if something went wrong leave it."

"If you tell her she's not going, she's likely to sneak away, anyway. You saw what they did this morning. How would we stop her?"

He raised his eyebrow. "We aren't going to tell her."

"Oh, I don't think—"

"Will you marry me, Alaina?"

Taken aback, I smiled, my heartbeat quickening. "You're not obligated to ask me that now."

"I know that. I'm not asking you out of obligation."

I squeezed my eyes closed. "Are you sure you really want to marry me? Knowing this? If I lose this baby, I will probably never be able to give you a child… and in your perfect world, you wanted children."

His hand left my stomach, forcing me to open my eyes as he rustled around in his pocket, producing a small gold ring and holding it between us. "I want to marry you more than I've ever wanted anything. *You* are my perfect world."

I studied the vintage gold ring as he held it between us, its round diamond glistening in the candlelight among the intricate silver swirling pattern that encased it. "Where did you get this?"

He smiled. "I found it in Zachary's bag that day we found the bones. I thought I might like to hang onto it in case… well, in case of you. I've known I wanted to marry you since then. I'll buy you a new one when we get back, it's just… if you don't like it—"

"No, it's perfect." I pressed my palm against his heart. "I love it."

"So," he raised one eyebrow, smiling, "will you marry me then?"

I nodded. "Yes, I'll marry you." I pulled his chin to bring his lips to mine. "Of course, I'll marry you."

He smiled against my lips, kissing my forehead as he gently pulled my left hand toward him. I looked down at the hand and the braided silver diamond Chris had given me. It had been there for so long, it felt like a part of me. I'd developed a habit of touching it with my thumb and I panicked suddenly at the thought of taking it off.

As if he'd read my thoughts, Jack curled his fingers around mine and kissed my knuckle over the ring, pulling my right hand up between us to slide the ring onto my right ring finger. "He'll always be a part of you and I will never try to take that from you. I'm just happy to be in there somewhere too."

"Jack," I breathed, "if something happened to you out there... if you got hurt... I..."

"I promise you," he swept his thumb over my lips, "I will *swim* back to you if I have to." He pressed his lips against mine, then whispered softly, "there is nothing that will keep me from coming back to you."

Chapter Fifty-Nine

The week went by fast. Jack, Magna and Kyle had spent twelve-hour days constructing a large log raft which would house the inflatable one. It was sturdy, with two-foot walls lining its frame. The inflatable raft was positioned to one side and would carry their emergency supplies.

They'd attached a sail and a rudder and had taken it out on several test runs to ensure it could navigate the choppy water. Anna and Bruce were all packed and ready to set sail in one week, and it broke my heart that we were going to betray them.

Kyle had insisted on joining them, but after a week of arguing reasons why he shouldn't, he caved in and agreed to stay. He and Magna said their goodbyes that morning and headed up to the summit.

Anna had taken over one of the blank journals, drawing diagrams and extensive instructions for Magna should something go wrong.

The sun was now high in the sky, and I paced the sand outside our shelter in anticipation of Lilly and Jim's return. I missed them. I longed to hear all about their time together on the summit and was anxious to tell Lilly my own news.

I wanted to be more worried—more cautious. I didn't want to get attached to the thought of having a child when the odds were stacked so heavily against me. I'd done that once and it had broken me entirely. But despite the odds, I was a little excited—naively so —that I might someday hold a child of my own, and I was desperate to share that naivety with someone who wouldn't meet it with more worry.

Jack had been a mess. He'd spent every hour of daylight at the beach working on the raft. When he'd return each night, he'd inspect me and inquire as to how many times I'd eaten and whether I'd drank enough water.

Anna and Magna too had hovered around me, insisting I stay off my feet, not lift anything, and always questioning where I was going if I made a move to rise from my seat.

I missed Lilly and Jim more than I thought I would, and my heart skipped a beat when I finally heard their voices coming down the path.

"Oh yeah? Well, you can go ahead and get glad in the same britches you got mad in, sugar! We's just about home free so I'm done fussin' with ye' about it."

"Oh, no you don't. We're done fighting when I say we're done fighting." Lilly's voice echoed down the trail. "I'm not doing it."

"Yes, ye' are, dammit."

I could see them, coming down toward me, Jim's arm wrapped around her as he limped heavily to one side. She pulled his hair hard. "No I'm not, and you're not going to make me."

"Ah ah ah." He grinned at me when his eyes met mine. "Let go, devil-woman. We got company."

I smiled and laughed, walking up the hill to greet them. "Oh, I've missed you both!" I wrapped an arm around the other side of Jim, helping him downhill. "What aren't you doing?"

Lilly rolled her eyes. "He wants me to keep us a secret!"

Jim huffed. "Oh, quit bein' so dramatic. It ain't like I'm embarrassed of ye.' I'm doin' it fer yer own damn good. Bud'll wring yer neck over it."

"He will not, and I'm not hiding. End of discussion. How are you, Lainey?" She looked past him at me.

"Will too and yes ye' are, dammit. NOW it's the *end of discussion.*"

She looked at me and mouthed, *"No, I'm not,"* behind his head. "Kyle told us about Anna and Bruce. They're really going?"

"Well…" I started to explain.

"There's my angel." Bud smiled at Lilly as he caught us at the bottom of the hill.

"Hi grandpa," she beamed at him, "how's gramma?"

"She's doing much better." He escorted us into camp, inspecting Jim's foot as we neared the fire. "Eager to see you. I'll go get her."

"Oh, I'll get her." She grinned mischievously at me before she pulled Jim's lips to her own, holding him there as she kissed him passionately. "Be right back, *honey*." She skipped toward the cave and disappeared into the opening, leaving Jim and Bud staring dumbfounded at one another.

Bud's cheeks flushed red. "You... son... of a bitch."

He marched toward Jim faster than I'd ever seen Bud move, causing Jim to retreat behind me.

"Now, wait, wait," Jim pleaded, backing us away and using me as a shield.

"I trusted you." Bud rolled up his sleeves. "Trusted you like you were my own blood. Sure, I saw what she was up to.... But never in a million years did I think you'd lay a hand on her!"

We continued backward. "Bud, let me explain..."

Bud's nostrils flared, and he moved with us, hands balled into fists at his sides. "I don't want to hear anything you've got to say. She's too good for you. Too smart... too pretty... too young, dammit!"

Jim hobbled backwards, circling the fire as Bud pursued. "Y'ain't tellin' me nothin' I don't already know. I done told her all of that!"

Bud stomped. "Quit hiding and face me like a man."

Jim let go and rose, gently pushing me out from in between them. "I love her... sir."

Bud spat to one side. "I don't want to hear that. She deserves better. If you loved her, you'd know that. I oughta knock your damn lights out."

Jim sighed and dropped to his knees in front of him, closing his eyes as he placed both hands behind his back. "Go on ahead then, do it. I know what she deserves and I know it ain't me. I shoulda' told her no, but I couldn't. Go on and do it. I won't fight ye.'"

Bud narrowed his eyes, inhaling as he reared his fist backward.

"BUD!" Bertie gasped, coughing into a small piece of cloth as she and Lilly came out of the cave. "What on earth are you doing?"

He kept his fist in place and Jim dared to open one eye. "I'm about to knock some sense into this fool," Bud huffed. "Do you know what he's been doing up there with your granddaughter?"

Bertie smiled as Lilly hurried to place herself between them. "Darling, I know she's been up every morning before dawn putting curls in her hair to get his attention, just like I walked two blocks out of my way to pass that garage every day and get yours."

Bud frowned but kept the fist ready and his eyes focused on Jim. "It's not the same, Bertie. He's too old."

Bertie walked calmly toward them. "I know she's talked about nothing but him for months when she's sat alone with me, just like I spoke about nothing but you to my mother."

Bud shook his head. "She's too good for him, Bert."

Bertie gently laid her hands on Bud's shoulders. "That's Jim you're talking about, darling. He's a good man and you love him and so does she. What are you gonna do?" she laughed. "Punch him until she changes her mind?"

Bud considered it and stifled a smile. "I could try. Your dad sure as hell tried to get you to change yours."

Bertie grinned. "And you can see how well that worked out for him. Come on now, look at them!" Lilly'd wrapped her arms protectively around Jim's neck. Bertie placed her hand on Buds fist, lowering it. "Let them be happy. You're too old to be starting fights, anyway."

Bud's shoulders relaxed marginally, but his fists remained at his sides as his eyes continued to pierce Jim's. "I swear to God, Jim, you so much as make her frown, I'll knock you into next week. Don't think I won't."

He shifted his focus to Lilly, his expression softening. "This is really what you want, angel?"

She nodded. "More than anything in the world."

Jim swallowed. "I know I ain't what ye' want for her. I ain't who I want for her neither... She deserves better and I'm gonna' do everything I can to be better for her."

Bud shook his head and exhaled, letting his fingers relax. "No one could ever deserve her." He turned toward Bertie, escorting her to a seat by the fire before disappearing into the cave.

Lilly pulled Jim off his knees to stand beside her and Bertie smiled up at them. "Don't worry about him." She coughed into her fist. "He's stubborn as a mule. Give him a day or two. He'll come around."

Lilly wrapped both arms around Jim's waist and he ran a hand over his hair, tilting his head toward Bertie. "I'm real sorry I'm not more, ma'am."

Bertie laughed heartily. "Aren't we all, honey?"

"Well, I'll be a sonofabitch," Bruce teased as he, Anna, Jack, and Isobel approached camp, he focused on Jim. "You caved."

"Ay, I got some choice words fer both of yuns," Jim shouted toward them, "but for' I start yellin' at ye' for desertin' us, Blondie, I'm gonna need ye' to look at this foot. It's hurtin' like a summbitch."

Lilly unwrapped her arms from Jim to leap at Anna, curling them around Anna's petite figure and squeezing her tightly. "I'm so mad at you."

Anna smiled as she squeezed back. "I won't be gone long. I'll find help and we'll see each other soon."

Lilly pulled back and punched Anna's arm playfully. "I'm not mad at you for leaving us. I'm mad that you're taking our Bruce away." She made her way to Bruce to wrap him in a hug. "Who will cook for us if you're gone?"

Jack assisted Jim into a sitting position near the fire as Anna kneeled to unwrap his foot. "You know," she tilted her head to the side as she began to unravel the shirt we'd wrapped it in, "you're all going to have to start being more careful." She narrowed her eyes up at Jim. "Especially you. You've just about broken every bone you've got since we met."

He winked at her. "Ay now, I broke them other ones keepin' yer scrawny asses in the raft. Them don't count."

"You what?" I gasped. "I thought you broke them on impact?"

"No, ma'am." He grinned. "Me and Hoss was holdin' on for dear life. We come down the backside of that wave and my arms was straight when we hit the bottom. I felt 'em crack."

I remembered the wave and I remember the two men above us. I knew one was Jack. I'd never thought to ask who the other was.

Anna laughed. "Well, I guess I owe you a thank you then."

"No, darlin.'" He looked down at her. "All of us owes you a thank ye.' I cain't think where we'd be without ye.' That one fightin' boars and this one hollerin' till rocks fall on people." He winked at Lilly. "Lordt knows what condition we'll be in when y'all come back for us."

She looked down at the foot, pinching the toes and feeling along the healing skin over the broken bone. "By the looks of this, you should do just fine. This is impressive work. The bones look good. I don't see any signs of infection. You said it's hurting? Show me where."

He touched the top of his foot where the new skin was forming. "Right there, just when I'm up on it."

She smoothed her palm over it. "Well, that's going to happen. You need to stay off it completely if you want it to heal. I'll re-wrap it with bandages and that'll hold a lot tighter than the shirt, but you're going to want to build a crutch and actually use it for a while. I don't want you to put any weight on it." She rose. "Don't move, I'll grab the bandages."

I sat down across from him and Lilly joined me. "Did you know he broke his arms on the raft?" I whispered, still staring at him as Isobel inspected his foot in Anna's absence.

"Yes," she whispered back. "I saw him above me, holding on that night, put it together a few days later that his arms couldn't have been broken before then."

Isobel touched his toe and he fell to one side, faking death and causing her to giggle wildly.

"Lainey, I have so much to tell you," she breathed, sighing as she watched him fake die again after Isobel touched another toe.

"And I have so much to tell you too." I leaned against her.

She raised an eyebrow at me. "Wanna go for a swim?"

We waded into the creek until the cool water covered our shoulders. We stood close to speak over the roaring of the waterfall behind us. She looked different to me, more at peace than I'd ever seen her as she let her head fall back to dip her hair in the water.

I watched her patiently as she brought her head forward and smoothed her dark, straight hair back. Her eyes met mine and she smiled mischievously. "You go first."

"Oh no." I splashed her with water. "It's definitely your turn to go first."

"Lainey," she tilted her head back and sighed audibly, "once I start talking about it, I won't be able to stop. You'll never get a word in. *You* go first."

I giggled. I *was* anxious to tell her. "Alright. But it's not good news... necessarily...."

Her eyes went wide, and she leaned in, captivated by the possibility of something dramatic about to unfold. "What is it?"

I cleared my throat and pulled water up over my arm. "Well... I've been a little... sick."

She narrowed her eyes. "What do you mean sick?"

I looked down and shrugged. "Every morning this week."

"You're pregnant?!" She giggled, bouncing up and down in the water.

I nodded but put a hand up before she could shriek. "Lill, now hang on... like I said, this isn't necessarily good news yet."

She frowned. "How could this not be the best news ever?"

"Well," I took her hands in mine, "I have this condition that caused only half my uterus to develop, which is why I couldn't carry Evelyn to term. Because of this, the doctors said I would most likely never get pregnant again. And if I did, I could have multiple miscarriages or carry another child that would be born too soon. Being pregnant in general is scary for me, but being pregnant on this island, well, it's horrifying."

She squeezed my hands softly, "Alaina, it's going to be fine." She nodded. "We'll pray. Every day. We'll come right here every day and I'll pray with you."

This is why I had missed her. There was no horror in her eyes —no suggestion of abortion, no doom and gloom. She just smiled excitedly at me.

"Oh Lilly, I want to be excited. You have no idea how long I've wanted to have a child… and with Jack?" I shook my head. "I keep telling myself not to think about it… not to get attached to it. Not to love it already… But I do."

"And you should!" She combed her fingers through my curls. "Lainey, this is wonderful news, and you should treat it that way. I know you're scared, but *I* have a feeling. And my feelings are never wrong about these things. We'll come out here every morning and we'll pray. And you'll see. Everything's going to be fine."

I smiled. "Thank you. It's been so hard without you here. Anna and Jack are always so worried… makes it hard to stay positive."

She tapped the side of her head, grinning. "Oh, but Anna and Jack don't have the gift." She closed her eyes and pressed her finger against the side of her forehead, waving the other arm in a circle as she shifted her voice. "I see a little girl… and you name her Lilly... after your best friend… and she's fabulous."

I chuckled, wrapping an arm around her shoulders, "This is why I love you, Lill. Now… I've told you my news. I want to hear all about your time up there with Jim."

She swooned. "Oh God, how am I supposed to follow that kind of news? Where would I even start?"

"You can start," I nudged her, "by telling me precisely how and when you went from wanting to fulfill a need to being in love and how you failed to mention this little detail to me!"

She raised an eyebrow and exhaled. "Well, I wanted to tell you. I just… didn't know how. I felt like you'd think I was ridiculous."

I shook my head. "I'd never think that about you, Lill."

"Oh, you would've." She raised her eyebrows. "It's ok. I *am* ridiculous sometimes. To be honest, I even thought I was being ridiculous at first. I mean… it's Jim… but," her expression lightened and she smiled, "he's different when we're alone... when he's not putting on the Jim-show and being loud and obnoxious. He's sweet, honest.... Thoughtful. There was this day, back when we started building the boat, everyone had gone back to camp because it had started to rain, but I stayed behind at the beach shelter finishing the stitching on one of the sails. He came and sat with me, reading one of the journals out loud while I sewed. Ooh, and I was looking good that day, too. I was so sure that would be my moment," she giggled, "especially when the wind picked up."

She grinned. "I was wearing that little green dress, you know, the one with the thin straps? And the rain started blowing into the shelter. Lainey, it was so cold I could see my breath! So, Jim being Jim, he came to sit with me. He said, *'don't get any ideas'* as he wrapped my arms in fabric, then pulled me against him. With his arms tight around me, he rested his head against mine, holding the journal out and he kept on reading it to me... asking me what I thought here and there... and," she shook her head slowly, "that was it. The feel of his voice against me, his arms around me, his smell even. I didn't just want him for fun anymore. I wanted all of him... for good. I wanted that moment over and over."

Intrigued, I pressed further, "Then what happened?"

"Well, we stayed like that for hours. Long after the rain stopped and he'd finished reading... and I thought... maybe I could have him right then, you know? It just felt right... but I was terrified if I moved, he'd snap out of it and tell me again how he was too old or too poor or too whatever he could come up with... so I stayed there in his arms until he decided it was time to go back. Neither of us talked about whatever that moment was for us in the months that followed... but I loved him then and every moment after. He loved me then too... that's why he avoided me. He said he knew he wouldn't ever be enough for me and couldn't handle having to let me go someday. He avoided me like the plague for a few weeks after that... but there were these brief moments... the rare occasion that he'd meet my eye and he looked at me differently."

She smoothed water over her arms. "I didn't push him, though. Even the few times we went up to the summit after that, I kept my distance. But even at a distance, it was there. I never had a man ask me my opinions and genuinely care to hear them. But he did. We talked about everything. I told him all about my life and he told me about his…" She wiped her eyes. "Lainey, I've never been so interested in someone else's life. Never cared enough to really know anybody this way. And once I knew him… how could I not love him?"

I smiled and nodded, genuinely happy for her. "And what about this time? On the summit? Did you… fulfill your need?"

She glowed as she recounted it in her mind. "Oh, it was so much more than that. All that build up and anticipation… all the emotion… it just… I can't even describe it. First, there's the kissing… amazing. He kisses me like he was made just for me to kiss… Like… his lips were shaped just for mine. And when we made love… Have you ever just felt so entirely completed by someone else you can barely stand to be without them? I mean… it took some convincing after you left… he's so hard on himself and was so sure he wasn't what I wanted… but once I got him to let his guard down," she sighed heavily, "Lainey, I've never felt more loved in my life."

I could see the happiness radiating off of her, but she was so young still, and I couldn't help but wonder what would become of them if we ever got off the island.

"Lill," I cleared my throat, "all those things he's afraid of… when you get home… have you really thought about them? I know you're happy and I can tell you love him, but, back home… in your world… they won't approve. You know that."

She nodded. "I know that. The people in my world never approve of anything. My whole life, they've constantly reminded me that I was too rich or not rich enough… too pretty or not pretty enough…. Too smart or not smart enough… I spent far too much of my life feeling like I needed to change something in order to be perfect… Well, now I have someone who makes me *feel* perfect and I'll be damned if I'm going to let any one of them take that away. I don't need that life or those people. I don't care what they think. I'm going to marry him someday and the only people I want there are the ones who support us; the ones who love us just as we are. To hell with everyone else."

"Planning the wedding already?" I chuckled.

She raised her chin. "Oh, yes. I'd marry him right here, right now on this island if he'd ask me."

"Speaking of that," I raised my eyebrow, "there's one other thing..."

"What? Oh God, what?" She looked at me worriedly.

"Jack proposed."

At this, she did shriek, wrapping both her arms around my neck and squeezing.

"He's leaving though," I whispered, looking around to make sure no one could overhear. "Don't tell Anna. Jack's going instead. He wants to sail between the islands in search of a ship. No farther though, which I know she wouldn't be happy about."

Lilly's eyes went wide. "Now, that's some drama. She's going to be pissed."

I nodded. "Lill, I don't want him to go. Part of me wants to tell her just so she'll sneak off and I can keep him here... where I know he's safe."

"Lainey, he's Jack. If anybody's gonna' find us help, it's him. He'll be alright."

"I know. I'm just... being selfish, I guess. What am I going to do without him?"

Lilly bounced her eyebrows. "Plan a wedding?"

I giggled.

"Oh God, please please let me make your dress!" Her eyes went wide as she looped her arm in mine and turned us back toward the shore. "I have all the fabric and lace and thread... and I can already see what it should look like. Please let me do this for you."

"That sounds wonderful."

Arm in arm, dripping from head to toe, Lilly and I happily made our way back toward camp.

"There you are!" Anna shouted, placing her hands on her hips as she stood. "Alaina, you can't just take off and not tell anyone where you're going. Not in your condition..."

Lilly squeezed my arm. "She wasn't *alone,* Anna. I was with her the whole time."

"What you mean *condition*?" Jim squinted one eye at me. "What condition? Christ almighty, did ye' go and get yerself hurt again??"

"Lainey's pregnant!" Lilly grinned, laughing as we came into camp.

"Aw well, hell." He smacked Jack hard on the back and stood shakily on his one foot, grinning as he extended his arms to me.

Anna shook her head, keeping her eyes on me as I passed her. "Jim, this isn't exactly news to celebrate. There's a much higher chance of her losing it than having a healthy baby. We have to be prepared for the worst, so I need to walk you all through some things before I go."

I knew it already, but to hear her say it out loud so matter-of-factly burned at my throat, erasing the momentary excitement I'd allowed myself to have at the creek with Lilly.

"Now just hold on one minute." Jim wrapped his arm around my shoulders and pulled me to sit down on the log between him and Jack. "We don't know what the Good Lordt's got in store for her. We cain't just be throwin' out words like 'at!"

"Jim, this is serious." She knelt in front of us. "Without me here, there's a lot I need you all to know. The chances she'll have a healthy baby are slim and if we don't find help in time, you all need to be ready. She's got this condition—"

He squeezed me against him, ignoring her to speak directly to me. "Do ye' know how slim the chances were that ye' fell out of the sky and lived to tell about it? Had your skull cut wide open and not a soul among us thinkin' ye'd make it and here ye' are with nothin' but a itty bitty scar we cain't hardly see? Or that we come upon an island with plenty of food and fresh water right when we's all fixin to die of dehydration? Or that we found a cave full of supplies on that verra' same island? Or that ye'd fight a boar with nothin' but a stick and come out alive? Woman, if anybody's beatin' 'em odds it's you."

"Jim, it's not that simple," Anna insisted. "She's—"

Jim held up his hand. "It *is* that simple." He leaned in, addressing both me and Jack. "Now, yuns can sit here and listen to those odds all ye' want but I'm tellin' ye' the Good Lordt wouldna' brought ye' through all that mess if he didn't have somethin' bigger planned for ye.' I reckon this might just be it."

Jack took my hand in his and squeezed it.

"Now, Blondie, I don't think she needs to be listenin' to no more of this. I don't know much about havin' babies, but I know ye' cain't stress a pregnant woman out if'n ye' want her to stay pregnant. You can tell me, Jack, and Lilly all 'em odds and what needs done just as soon as she runs off to bed. By the looks of her, seems to me like ye' ain't tellin' her somethin' she don't know already. We'll handle her just fine while we're waitin' on ye,' won't we Princess?"

Lilly smiled proudly. "Of course we will." She pranced around the fire to launch herself into Jim's lap, nearly knocking him over as she wrapped both arms around his neck. "Besides, we have more important business to talk about tonight. Lainey and Jack are getting married!"

Anna squeezed my knee and nodded. I needed a break from the constant state of worry we had been in this past week, and she understood. There needed to be a little hope, and she would give me that tonight.

Lilly beamed at Jack. "And I'm making the dress. We're getting started this week. I have plenty of work for all of you."

Anna forced a smile. "I think that's a beautiful idea. How can I help?"

"Come." She grabbed Anna's hand and stood, "I'll show you what I have in mind." She pulled Anna behind her and disappeared into the cave.

Jim smiled after her as he watched her go, then turned his attention back to us. "Ye' know she ain't gonna let none of us sleep until she's got that dress lookin' like somethin' out of a magazine."

I giggled, curling my fingers into Jack's as I listened to Lilly explain the shape of the dress as she pulled out fabrics to present to Anna in the cave behind me. "She really is a force to be reckoned with."

"Don't I know it." Jim stretched his legs out in front of him. "That woman's tough as a pine knot, I tell ye." He sighed and stared into the fire, his smile fading. "And she's gonna tear me to pieces when she finally comes to her senses."

I laid my head against Jack's arm. "You really love her?"

"Yeah. Lordt help me, I *really* love her." He glanced at the cave behind him. "And that's why I'll let her do it, too."

I smiled at him. "Well, *she* really loves you. And once she's made her mind up about something, I can't see anyone or anything convincing her otherwise. Not even New York."

He snickered. "She is stubborn as all get out. I'll give ye' that. But someday she's gonna' see what we all see. And I cain't stop her runnin' fer the hills the minute she does."

"I highly doubt she will." I laid my free hand over his. "I'm afraid she's already planned *your* wedding."

He laughed out loud at that. "I don't doubt that neither. I don't know if I'm comin' or goin' half the time. One minute I'm thinkin' she's surely gonna' run and the next I'm pickin' out flowers for our wedding…"

"Speaking of weddings," Jack added, "Jim, I've got something I want to ask you."

"Whatcha' need, big man?" He grinned over my head at him.

"Well…" Jack shifted uncomfortably, clearing his throat. "I was wondering if maybe you would be my best man?"

Jim's face lit up then. "Ye' serious Hoss?"

"Well… yeah." Jack frowned. "You're the best friend I've got and I can't imagine anyone else I'd rather have standing next to me."

"I'd be honored, brother." His eyes watered a little as he looked between us. "Well hell, ye' got me all choked up now. 'Course I'll stand witcha.' I'd do just about anything for ye. I love you, both of ye.'"

Chapter Sixty

My mother and I rushed through the automatic doors of the hospital as Chris and Bill stayed behind to park the truck amid the blizzard that had formed over us about three quarters of the way into the trip. Mile by mile, the snow on the road grew increasingly hazardous, causing us to slow to a crawl the last fifty miles. It was almost 9AM by the time we got to the small front desk of the hospital's lobby.

The trip up was a long one. All of us were terrified for Maddy. My mother was constantly checking her phone for updates, begging Chris to drive faster, and calling Cece every hour to let her know where we were and ask if there'd been any change.

Throughout the duration of the trip, we'd learned that Maddy had been with Owen on the dock when she'd stepped out onto the ice and fallen through. It was mid-December and the unseasonably warm weather had prevented the lake from freezing thoroughly, leaving it thin in some areas.

Owen had struggled to pull her out. She'd immediately slid beneath the dock, so he'd had to jump into the frozen water to retrieve her. When he finally retrieved her, she'd stopped breathing. He performed CPR and got her breathing before help arrived.

At the hospital, both Maddy and Owen had been rushed into the Emergency Room. Both of them were hypothermic and the oxygen levels in Maddy's blood were dangerously low. They'd spent hours rewarming her and working to restore her circulation to normal. She'd gradually stabilized, but had a severe case of pneumonia and was unable to breathe on her own.

She'd been intubated and there was concern over potential brain damage or organ failure from a prolonged lack of oxygen in the blood. Both she and Owen were sent to the ICU, leaving Cece a nervous wreck as she endured several hours alone, pacing from room to room until Owen's parents were able to get there.

When we stepped off the elevator, she was standing in the hall waiting for us.

Throughout our entire lives, Cece had been the type of person who would spend an hour perfecting her hair and makeup just to pick up a gallon of milk. Now, standing under the unforgiving fluorescent lights of the hospital with her bright blonde hair matted in all directions and makeup smeared amid the dark circles under both eyes, I hardly recognized her.

She sprang into my mother's arms, sobbing uncontrollably. "She's just so tiny in there hooked up to all those machines… and she still isn't breathing on her own…" She squeezed my mother and shook, her voice raising higher. "And now Owen's got something wrong with his heart and they took him down for a CT scan… and what if it's bad? Mom, I don't know what to do!"

"What do you mean something's wrong with his heart?" I blurted out, forgetting my manners with the lack of sleep.

She let go of our mother and her bloodshot eyes met mine. "They say he's got atrial fibrillation and they think it's a result of the cold shock. They're running some tests to make sure he's not at risk of heart failure or stroke!"

"Owen's strong," mom said calmly, wrapping an arm around her. "He'll be just fine. They're both gonna be fine. Come on, let's go see Maddy."

Maddy's room was dimly lit and the three of us sat quietly around the bed, listening to the beeping of the heart monitor and the constant rhythmic flow of air from the ventilator filling her lungs. The bed looked enormous in comparison to her small body, and there were tubes and wires hooked up to her in such a way that you could hardly make her out aside from the curly bright blonde hair and the little lump under the blanket of her body rising and falling with the oxygen.

I fidgeted anxiously in my chair, not knowing what to say or do to offer any kind of comfort to the situation. The seconds passed slowly, then turned to minutes that turned into an hour when I could take it no more and stood. "I'm just going to go check on Chris," I offered, stretching my arms. "Cece, should I get you something? Water? Food? Anything?"

"No." She swept her hand over Maddy's, not looking away. "I'm fine."

I made my way out of the room and down the hall toward the ICU waiting room where, turning the corner, I ran straight into Doug, nearly knocking us both over and forcing him to juggle with the glass vase of bright yellow flowers to avoid dropping it.

"Doug!" I smiled, assisting him to regain his grip on the flowers, genuinely happy to see him after so long.

"Grandma!" He grinned, balancing the flowers against one shoulder as he wrapped his other arm tight around me in a hug.

"How are you?" I laughed. "How's camp?"

He twisted his lips to one side. "*I* met someone."

"Oh?" I raised an eyebrow. "Settling down, are you?"

He nodded. "For this one, absolutely. She's really incredible. I'd love for you to meet her. Maybe once this is..." he frowned, apologetically shaking his head, "once Maddy and Owen are better, I mean, maybe we could get dinner? Before you go home?"

"I'd like that very—"

Before I could say more, Chris forced his way between us, one large hand on Doug's chest forcing him back several steps. "What the hell do you think you're doing?"

Doug laughed uncomfortably, raising his free palm up in surrender. "Woah, woah, take it easy, man, I was just saying hello."

"Chris!" I jerked at his arm. "What the hell do *you* think *you're* doing?"

Chris didn't look at me. His eyes remained narrowed at Doug. "Did you sleep with her?" He asked through gritted teeth.

"Oh my God," I groaned, trying to keep my voice down. "Are you seriously doing this right now? I already told you—"

"Did you sleep with my wife?" He raised his voice slightly and I noticed a few people in the waiting room behind us had started to look in our direction.

Doug looked confusedly between Chris and me, backing up as Chris stepped closer, "No! I would never—"

"Don't you dare lie to me," Chris persisted, his fingers curling into fists at his sides. "I know you did something. I can see it!"

"Chris!" I placed my hand on his shoulder, pulling. "What's gotten into you? Are you crazy? You're gonna do this *here? Now?* I already told you nothing happened!"

"I didn't," Doug started, but I could see his demeanor shifting from having been caught off-guard to instantly angry. "Oh, but I wanted to!" he taunted. "And I dreamt of it every night, if you know what I mean."

"Doug!" I shrieked.

But Doug continued, setting the flowers down on a table at the entrance of the waiting room to provoke him further. "And I would've made my move that last day if you hadn't come up here to save your own ass. You and I both know she deserved better. If I would've had one more night, I'd have made her forget all about you!"

Chris wound his fingers around Doug's upper arm and jerked him toward the exit.

I ran in front of them, pushing on Chris's chest. "Are you nuts?"

He plowed past me, pushing through the ICU double doors and out to the elevators, where he roughly released Doug's arm, pushing him to one side as he hit the button.

"Seriously!" I stood between them. "Stop it!"

Doug sneered. "What's a matter, Chris? You trying to justify what you did by reflecting it back on her?"

Chris glowered at him over my head. "You slept at her cabin. Did you touch her?"

Doug smirked. "Oh, I touched her plenty."

I spun around. "Doug. Stop it!"

Doug shook his head. "No. This is ridiculous. He comes up here after what he did and has the nerve to accuse me of being the same type of man? No. He wants to settle this outside, that's fine, I'll go." He winked at me before he matched the scowl on Chris's face over my head. "Even if I can get one good punch in, it'll be worth it. You're better than this accusation and you know it."

The elevator bell rang and the big silver doors slid open to reveal my uncle Bill, his arms loaded to his chin with various bottles of water, soda, bags of chips, and candy bars. He stepped carefully out of the elevator, oblivious to the scene surrounding him as he chuckled. "You guys want some snacks?"

Chris breathed heavily to one side of him as Doug did the same on the other. I nervously began to unload his arms. "Can you do something with these two?" I begged. "They've both lost their damn minds."

Bill frowned, the chip bags crinkling as he adjusted what was left in his cradled arms. "What's going on?" He looked between the two of them.

Doug shook his head. "This idiot thinks I slept with Alaina."

Bill laughed dubiously and looked back at Chris in disbelief. "Are you serious? With *him*?"

Chris's face flushed red. "He slept at her cabin when she was up here. What am I supposed to think he did there?"

Bill shook his head, eyeing Doug and then me. "Nah. He could've tried, but she'd have turned him down. You know that." He bent to one side to prevent a bag of Cheetos from slipping through.

Chris grabbed a handful of the chip bags from him, visibly trying to work out his emotions. "Do I?"

Taken aback, Bill knitted his brow. "*Don't you?* You've been married to her long enough, you certainly *ought* to. Come on, kid, you're better than that. Look at him. She wouldn't do that to you… not with him."

Doug saw an opportunity and took the cheap shot, raising an eyebrow at Chris. "Yeah, she's not like *you.*"

Bill twisted his lip to one side and glanced apologetically at me. "Both of you knock it off. You," he looked at Doug, "get the hell out of here. And you…" he faced Chris, "we're here for Cecelia and Maddy and Owen. This is not the time or the place for whatever this is you're doing. Here, I'll settle it now..." He looked at me then, smiling slightly. "Did you sleep with that kid?"

I shook my head, rolling my eyes. "No. And I've told him that."

"Well," Bill nodded at Chris, "there you have it. Drop it and be done with it. Come on, both of you, before my arms fall off."

We followed him silently, neither Chris nor I looking up from our feet until we'd reached the waiting room and unloaded our arms of their snacks onto a small side table.

Bill reached into his back pocket and pulled out an orange card. "Here. It's your hotel room key. I checked us all into the Marriot down the street. Both of you go work out your business and take a nap."

He held his hand up to me as I moved to argue. "You both need to sleep and you definitely need to work out whatever this was. Go. I'll call you if there's any change."

I took the key abashedly, and Chris and I left, walking in silence through the crisp morning snow storm toward the hotel a few blocks down.

The snow was a welcome cold on my burning cheeks and I tried to level out my breathing, our feet crunching the snow beneath them the only sound between us until we'd crossed the hotel lobby into the elevators. Ironically, Billie Holiday's "I'll be Seeing You" was playing through the small elevator speaker and the memory of who we once were stabbed at my heart once more.

I exited the elevator in a hurry, avoiding eye contact with him as I stormed down the long hallway to our room, sliding the key into the door and pushing it open. Only once I heard it click locked behind him did I spin on my heel, heart racing, "How dare you—"

He pulled me to him and pressed his lips against mine. "I'm sorry," he breathed, curling his fingers into my hair and kissing me deeper. "I'm so sorry." He pressed his forehead against mine. "I'm an idiot. I've been an idiot for so long."

He hadn't kissed me like that for so long that I was torn between the argument I wanted to finish and the need to be touched with the kind of familiarness with which he was touching me. I missed him more every day we went without it. My heart ached as we grew further and further apart, and when his lips found mine again, I sighed in relief, pulling him closer.

We didn't speak, and what happened next wasn't the love I'd hoped we'd make to each other. Instead, it was anger, sadness, frustration, and pain. I buried my face in his shoulder and he did the same in mine, and we clung to each other, moving blindly with each other, hoping relief would come.

It wasn't passionate but methodical, obligatory even, like we owed it to each other. I was lost in my mind and he in his. Once it was done, he wrapped me in his arms and I wept quietly, mourning the life I'd never have again.

And we never made love again after that.

Chapter Sixty-One

"Now, don't move," Lilly commanded as I held my arms out and she pinned white silk fabric at my waist.

At the insistence of Anna and in an attempt to keep up the charade, Jack had taken her and Bruce out on the raft to show them how to sail it and practice various scenarios. They wouldn't be back for hours still, which proved the perfect opportunity for Lilly to scheme wedding dress plans. Without much else to do, having been ordered not to lift anything or venture outside camp, I was happy to oblige.

"It's going to be beautiful," Bertie said from her bed beside us, her breathing labored as she wheezed between words. "Did I ever tell you about our wedding?"

Lilly smiled up at me as I shook my head. "You'll love this story."

Bertie coughed softly. "It was 1969," she spoke slowly between audible breaths, "I was in my sophomore year in college, an all girls' school about thirty miles from Bud's school."

She smiled fondly. "My father didn't approve of Bud and had hoped the all-girls school so far away would separate us. It didn't, of course. We were mad about each other. He'd drive up every day to pick me up and take me to dinner or just to bring me flowers."

Lilly stood and circled to the other side of me, my arms starting to burn from holding them out.

"That December, they were holding the first lottery for the draft and since Bud was nineteen, we were both terrified his date might get chosen early. He picked me up, and we went down to my aunt Edna's house since she had a television. I remember it like it was yesterday. There were about thirty of us there. We all stood in her living room around the tv holding hands with family, friends, and strangers that were our age, and we all held our breath as they drew out the first date, then another, and another. We all collectively sighed each time it turned out to be no one there's birthday."

She coughed, then shakily continued. "I remember my cousin George going ghostly white when they called his birthday. My aunt Edna fell apart, crying and holding onto him. She made quite a scene... And I remember I'd been looking at them when I heard them call the very next number—April eleventh... Bud was number fourteen. His number was picked early, and he was going to Vietnam."

She held a fabric to her mouth and coughed against it, taking a deep breath when it passed. "That was the longest ride home of my life. It had started to snow and I can remember both of us being so silent that the sound of the snowflakes hitting the windshield was almost deafening. And when he'd pulled into the parking lot of my dormitory, and placed the car in park, I looked up at him and I said to him, 'Lloyd Bud Renaud, you're marrying me. And you're *going* to come back to me.'"

Lilly giggled, "Gramma wasn't gonna wait around for him to ask!"

"That's right," she smiled, "and he agreed. We had seven months before he'd land in Vietnam. We spent every day together all the way up until he left for basic training. Then we wrote to each other every day while he was in there. I spent all my time planning the perfect wedding, and I wrote to him in detail about the exact flowers we'd have on the altar, where we'd say our vows, and who would be in attendance. My father still didn't approve, but I'd convinced my mother and she'd forced him to come around. We'd be married at my grandparents' estate in Connecticut. I would wear my mother's wedding dress."

"Bud had a ten day leave after AIT before he'd get shipped out and that's when I'd planned the ceremony. My father insisted on picking him up and driving him straight there to be wed the very next morning, and they'd given us the guest house to stay in afterward."

Bertie sat forward and coughed violently then, causing Lilly to rush to her side with a bottle of water. Bertie waved the bottle off and laid back, taking several deep breaths. "Go on. I'm alright."

Lilly cautiously turned back to me, kneeling at my waist to resume pinning while her eyes remained on Bertie.

Bertie smoothed the fabric over her chest and cleared her throat. "We were hours away, and I'd been forced to go to sleep long before they arrived. That next morning, I woke up in my grandparents' guest bedroom, a complete mess. What if he didn't show up? What if my father scared him off? My mother was worried too. She hadn't seen my father all morning and hadn't remembered him coming to bed the night before. All through breakfast and while they got me dressed, I was a nervous wreck. I was sure something happened and any minute they'd come tell me to change out of the dress and go home."

She laughed. "But they didn't. My father knocked on the door, clad in his finest suit, and extended his arm to me. When I took it, he whispered in my ear *'I can't stop you from loving him so I won't try anymore.'* He walked me down the hall to the winding staircase," she smiled wide, "and I looked over the rail... and there was Bud at the bottom waiting for me in his green formal military suit. I hadn't seen him in months and it was all I could do not to run down those stairs."

I closed my eyes and could picture the two of them.

"That whole wedding..." she beamed, shaking her head softly from side to side as she closed her eyes, "all that planning... All that work picking out the food and arranging the perfect table settings... I never noticed a single thing but him standing there looking up at me. I can't remember the flowers... or the dresses... or who was in attendance and who wasn't... Oh, but I can remember him. His face as I came down the stairs, his eyes when I spoke my vows... his hands shaking over mine as he said his. That kiss... the kiss that made me his forever..."

Her eyes watered a little. "And I remember thinking I only had nine days to be his wife before he would leave—nine days to be the kind of wife he needed to get back to. Nine days to be the kind of wife whose face he would see before he'd jump in front of a bullet or volunteer on some mission that would surely get him killed."

She held her hand over her heart. "So the wedding reception went on without us. I was told the dinner was wonderful and the flowers were beautiful... but nothing was as beautiful to me as the time we spent in that little guest house as Mr. and Mrs. Renaud. We said '*I do*' and we didn't leave that house until the morning he had to ship off. Richard was conceived right then and there." She opened her eyes and looked fondly at Lilly. "And it's been the greatest story of my whole life."

She coughed harder then, sitting up and holding the fabric over her mouth. I noticed the bits of blood on it when she pulled it away from her lips.

"You see, time will go on and you'll forget the little details... the flowers and the food and the music... the patterns on your wedding dress... you'll forget the words you said to the people around you... but you'll never forget him. You'll remember every little detail about him on that day... *his* clothing... his smell... the words he says... The kiss. You'll never forget the day you become his forever. Cherish it and be the wife he always *needs* to come home to. I wish I could be there to see it myself."

Lilly dropped the fabric she'd been holding. "What do you mean? Of course, you'll be there!"

Bertie shook her head and smiled, "I can feel my body dying now."

"No gramma." Lilly crawled across the floor to lay her head on Bertie's lap.

Bertie caressed her head. "It's alright. It's time for me to go now. I've lived an amazing life. I've shared it with an amazing family, traveled to places most people could only dream of, and I've come to my end right here in this heavenly place with people I've come to love dearly. I'm not afraid and you shouldn't be either. I don't want to be sick anymore. I don't want my amazing life to be overshadowed by an extended death."

"Gramma no," Lilly wept, "not yet."

"Hush." She swept her hands over Lilly's hair. "I'll live on— through you." She pulled her ring from her finger and offered it to Lilly. "Besides... you've got someone here watching over you now. I feel like I can go and I'll know you're okay."

"Gramma no," Lilly whimpered. "I can't take your ring. You should have it with you always."

Bertie kept the ring held out. "Don't be silly. I won't need it where I'm going, and it's too beautiful to be buried in a pile of bones. You take it."

"No..." Lilly sobbed, curling her fingers over the ring. "I need you still!"

"No, you don't baby. Look at you, you've become a wonderful, strong woman. You've got a man who loves you and," Bertie smiled up at me as I stood frozen, "the sister you always wanted. You'll be just fine and so will I. Don't you dare be sad for me. I want you to keep working on this dress and make it as beautiful as I know you will. Take care of her and help her with the baby."

Bertie reached a hand out to me and I took it. "And you. You're going to have a healthy baby, I know it. You might think I'm just some old dying woman talking nonsense, but I'm close to death and I've seen it for you. You take care of that baby and you watch out for mine too."

I nodded, my own eyes burning. "I promise I will."

"Both of you take care of each other. You'll need each other more than ever in this place... In this time... You'll both live happy lives so long as you watch over each other."

"Gramma..." Lilly looked up at me, her lip quivering, "GRANDPA!" she called in a panic, squeezing Bertie's hand.

"You say goodbye to me now." Bertie swept her finger over Lilly's brow. "And promise me you won't stop living your life just because I stopped living mine."

"I won't. I promise." Lilly rose to her knees and wrapped both arms around Bertie's neck. I released Bertie's hand and took a few steps back.

"I love you so much, Gramma."

"What's going on?" Jim whispered as he joined me at the cave entrance, Bud rushing past us.

"Bertie's... going," I said softly, my eyes watering as I watched Bud kneel down beside Lilly.

Jim nodded, wrapping an arm around me as he turned me away. "Come on, let's give 'em some privacy."

We stepped out into the midday sun to find Izzy lying in the grass across from us on her stomach, her feet dancing from side to side as she stared at the pages of her book. Finn happily pecked at the surrounding grass.

"She told me last night she couldn't hold on much longer." Jim hobbled around me, gathering the ruched fabric I attempted to keep off the ground. "Ye' got clothes on under here?"

"Yes."

"Well, if we mess up this dress, there'll be hell to pay. Lift yer arms up."

I raised my arms. "She said she could feel her body dying," I said between us.

He carefully grabbed the top of the strapless dress near my armpits. "See if ye' can slide down and out. She told me the same."

I slid my body down and crawled out from beneath the dress as he looped it neatly over his arm. He shook his head, looking back at the cave. "It's the way I'd wanna' go. On my own terms... She said she didn't wanna' be sick no more and I don't blame her."

"Lilly's going to be a mess," I assured him, looking toward the cave.

"She's tougher 'n she looks." He searched for a safe place to lay the dress but resigned to hang on to it. "I can handle her. Ye' gonna' be alright?"

I nodded. "I was too young to feel the loss of my grandfather. Never lost anyone that I knew I was going to lose... it's strange to be both hoping for death and dreading it at the same time."

"I know the feeling well." He hobbled to the big tree and draped the dress across a branch. "Went through it with my momma. Go on and sit down now. I'll fix us somethin' to eat."

"I'm not really—"

"I ain't fixin' it fer *you*." His eyes darted to my midsection and back. "Besides, it's gonna' be a long day fer us all. We're all gonna need to eat."

Jim proceeded to limp around camp, gathering three birds from the cage and plucking them of their feathers, meticulously cutting them into legs, thighs, wings, and breasts, rolling them in egg and flour and frying them like chicken on the metal skillet over the fire. He skewered enough Fe'i bananas for us all and would rise to pace near the cave entrance every so often.

As if on cue, the moment he pulled the meat from the fire, Lilly and Bud emerged arm in arm, their eyes red and swollen.

Bertie was gone, and the emptiness I suddenly felt was overwhelming.

Jim stood and Lilly leapt into his embrace, burying her face in his chest. He folded his arms around her shaking body and laid his cheek on the top of her head. His eyes followed Bud, who walked with a heavy heart to the side of the cave and swung the old rusty shovel up over his shoulder, then turned in the direction of the beach.

Jim whispered to Lilly, running his hand over her hair and kissing the crown of her head. "I gotta' go help him. I cain't let him do this by his self."

She unburied her face and looked out at Bud, sniffling loudly as her voice raised two octaves. "I told him to wait. I told him he didn't need to do that right away!"

"You take care of her fer a minute?" Jim looked at me, and I nodded. Then he focused back on her. "There's some things a man's just gotta' do when he gets it in his head he needs to do 'em. I'll go help him and be back 'for ye' know it, I promise. It's gonna be alright."

She raised on her tiptoes and kissed him as she shook with tears.

"And eat somethin.'" He held her chin between his thumb and finger. "Ye' ain't gonna wanna eat but ye' need to and so does she." He tilted his head toward me as he wiped the tears from her cheeks. "Both of yuns eat somethin.' I'll go get this sorted and be right back."

She nodded, lip quivering as she turned to join me by the fire.

She exhaled audibly as she sat, watching as Jim half-jogged, limping heavily, to catch up with Bud.

"I love that man." She wiped her nose with the bottom of her dress, glancing back at the cave's entrance as her breath hitched. "I really thought I was ready for this, but it's so much harder than I thought it'd be. She was my person, you know? My mom died before I was old enough to remember her, so gramma was more my mother than grandmother. And I knew she would go soon but…" She sniffled loudly. "I'd give anything to have had her just a few more years."

I laid my arm over her shoulders as she leaned her head against me. "I think you'll have her plenty more years looking down and watching over you."

She nodded. "Lainey, you're *it* now in terms of women in my life. Promise me, when we get off this island, you won't disappear?"

I squeezed her shoulders. "Not in a million years. We're family now."

Chapter Sixty-Two

We'd wrapped Bertie in fabric and Bud insisted on carrying her, despite opposition from Jim, Bruce, and Jack, all the way from the cave to the beach where he and Jim had spent the afternoon digging her grave. We all followed behind as he made his way down, her small lifeless body pulled tightly against his chest.

Where Bertie's body had worn away on the island, her figure nothing but skin and bones in the end, Bud's body had grown stronger. He was seventy, but a young seventy. He could still get around just fine and he helped with the boat and the heavy lifting as if he were still in his twenties. He'd mentioned it a few times, how he wished his body would show signs of aging... of getting sick... so he could know he would follow her soon. It hadn't though, and I could see his devastation from behind, the tenseness in his muscles, the slumping of his shoulders as we walked the twenty-minute hike down to the beach without stopping.

They'd selected a spot near the tree line where a large stone pillar towered high above our heads. Bud spent over an hour earlier that day carving an inscription into the rock:

'Alberta 'Bertie' Renaud
Beloved mother, grandmother,
And the greatest wife a man could ask for.
I will count the days until we meet again.'

The three of them laid her inside and we all pushed the sand over her body until the ground where she lay was once again even. We all took turns laying stones around the outline of her and Lilly placed a bouquet of pink and white flowers under Bud's inscription at the head of the grave.

We all stood heavy-hearted, silently looking down at the sand as the sun set at our backs. Lilly sniffled and whimpered as she held the hands of both Jim and Bud.

Anna laid her head against Bruce's shoulder, wiping at her eyes every few minutes.

I leaned heavily against Jack, who held Isobel in his arms, mindlessly running one hand over the center of her back as she rested her head against his shoulder.

We hadn't taught her a sign for "death" or "heaven" and I wondered if she was too young to understand what was happening or if she had a better grasp than all of us. Despite her young age and lost hearing, she was extremely perceptive. She'd spent every day of our time here with Bertie—loved Bertie the most of all of us —and there was something about her demeanor that told me she understood Bertie was sick and wouldn't be around much longer.

She would stare at her sometimes for an extended amount of time, as if she were trying to commit her to memory. As Bertie's health deteriorated, she spent less time in the birdcage and more time at the foot of Bertie's bed with her book. She was exceptionally smart for being so young—she'd learned to read without sound, had learned an entire made-up language in months, and she had adapted to our predicament better than any of us.

I looked up at her, her small face squished against Jack's shoulder, her big hazel eyes watching her fingers as she picked at a loose thread on the seam of his shirt. I wondered what could be going on in that remarkable brain of hers.

Bud finally cleared his throat, drawing us all to attention. He forced a small smile, his eyes damp and reddened, then he spoke and his voice did not waver.

"Bertie had this favorite bible verse... and of course, I later learned it was her favorite because she loved the song that was inspired by it so much. She would reference it any time anything bad... or good... or sad would happen in our lives. She'd even sing it on occasion... and no matter the circumstance, the verse always seemed to fit... always offered inspiration... which is fitting of

Bertie. If she was anything in this world, she was an inspiration... as a wife... as a mother... as a teacher... as a friend... she was the kind of human being people aspired to be."

He glanced down at the sand that housed her as he fondly recited, "There is a time for everything, and a season for every activity under the heavens: a time to be born..." He closed his eyes and sighed. "And a time to die, a time to plant and a time to uproot, a time to kill and a time to heal, a time to tear down and a time to build, a time to weep and a time to laugh, a time to mourn and a time to dance."

He took a deep breath. "Today we mourn you, Bert, but tonight we will dance for you... like I promised you we would. We will celebrate your life and achievements and we won't cry for your death but rejoice that you lived... It's been my absolute honor in this life to have been able to share it with someone so wonderful as you. You were my best friend and I miss you." His voice cracked but he straightened, clearing his throat. "I'll miss you every day and I have no idea how I'll ever manage without you... But since you forbade me to lay down in this sand beside you today, I promise you I will find a way to manage and when it's my time, I'll come right back here to you."

He sniffled softly and blinked the tear from his eye. "I promised you I'd watch over Lilly." He took Lilly's hand in his as the mention of her name had her falling apart. "And I will... although," he swallowed, decidedly reaching his other hand out to Jim who took it, "I think someone else is doing a fine job of it."

Bud nodded proudly toward him, shaking his hand in a gesture of his approval. "We're all better people for knowing you Bertie, and the generations that will descend from us will be better people for the lessons you taught us... Lessons that will be passed down long after we're all gone. Thank you for being who you were to all of us, for the meaning and inspiration you brought to all of our lives. We love you and, God willing, we will be with you again soon."

Bud looked up at us all then. "I'll leave you all to say your own goodbyes now. Dry your tears here and let that be the end of it. When we return to camp, we will have a drink in her honor. It's what she wanted and if I don't do it exactly how she wanted, well… she'll be letting me know about it when I get up there." He smiled, glancing skyward.

"Jim," he cleared his throat again, "I can't thank you enough for today. You're a good man and I'd be proud to one day call you my family."

Jim stood straighter, and his lip twitched as he fought with his own emotions.

"And Lilly, your grandmother left this for you." He reached into the front pocket of his shirt and pulled out a folded piece of paper. "It says right there on the top you're not to read it until your wedding day. There weren't any envelopes to seal it in, so I trust you'll abide by her wishes and wait."

Lilly pressed the paper to her heart, Bertie's ring shining on her right ring finger as she did so. "I will. I promise."

"I'll see you all at camp." Bud turned and began the lonely trek uphill.

Anna and Bruce knelt at the grave, whispering their final sentiments before they each walked up behind him.

Jack lowered Izzy to her feet in the sand and I sank down to my knees to face her, pointing to the grave and signing, "You know this?"

Izzy nodded, her lip pouting as she inhaled bravely, then put her two hands together in the form of a bird flapping its wings. It was her sign for both the birds and for Bertie, and it felt profoundly right in that moment.

I smiled, my eyes burning as I watched her little face distort with the effort of holding back the tears that filled hers. She slowly flapped the wings of Bertie's symbol with her fingers and then she looked at me and signed, "Goodbye."

I signed back, "Yes, goodbye. You say goodbye?"

She looked toward the stone; her face turning red as the tears slid down her cheeks. She kept her hands together in the symbol of a bird, her fingers flapping its wings as she slowly approached the edge of the rocks that surrounded the grave.

She knelt at the edge, sniffling loudly. Then, though she couldn't hear it, she spoke, the words not quite right but close enough to understand. "Bye bye, bird."

She flapped the bird's wings and slowly rose to stand, raising the bird high over her head before she separated her fingers and spread her arms wide, gazing up to the sky. Then she shouted upward, "I love you!"

It was such an insightful gesture for such a small child that I became overwhelmed with emotion, my body shaking as tears poured from my eyes and laughter poured from my heart.

It wasn't sadness that filled me, but rather, an immense sense of harmony, as if Bertie herself had somehow shown us in that moment that she, as well as the rest of us, were exactly where we were all meant to be. For the first time in as long as I could remember, I had no doubts about myself or the people around me. I wasn't afraid of where we were or where we would go. All that was meant to happen had happened, and I was utterly at peace.

I think Lilly felt it too because she laughed through her tears and smiled as Izzy spun in a circle with her arms outstretched over her head. Lilly proceeded to raise her own arms over her head, tilting her head to the sky as she joined her, her green dress swirling outward while she spun in a circle and closed her eyes. "Bye bye, bird," she echoed, smiling.

Beside me, I heard Jim's breath tremble, his lips curling both upward and downward as he watched them spin and wrestled with what appeared to be a similar feeling washing over him.

Jack wrapped an arm around my back and pulled me against the side of him. I looked up at him and smiled when his watering eyes met mine. We'd all felt it. "Should we head up?" He asked.

I looked back as Lilly and Izzy continued to spin and I smiled, Bertie's voice in my ear repeating: *'You're going to have a healthy baby, I know it. I've seen it for you.'* I nodded, glancing at the engraved stone. "Bye bye, bird," I whispered, "Thank you... for everything." Then I took his hand in mine and we turned toward the path. "You'll be alright?" I asked Jim.

"Yes ma'am," he whispered back, his eyes still focused on Lilly and Izzy. "We'll be just fine."

Back at camp, the mood shifted to a happier tone. Bud held a glass of wine. It was the first time I'd seen him with a drink since their anniversary dinner. He shared stories of his and Bertie's lives. He told us about his return from Vietnam and how they'd started the Renaud Boot Company. He laughed as he remembered Bertie holding a crying Richard against her shoulder as she helped him stitch the boots by hand.

Bertie had made an impression on all of us and we all had our own stories to share, all of them a testament to the inspiration she truly was.

"You know," Bruce blushed, swirling the liquid in his glass, "when we first got here and I couldn't walk, she would sit with me every day. And I was downright miserable—hot, injured, immobile, and hungry. But she'd sit there anyway and ask me about my life and get me to laughing."

He took a sip from his glass. "This one day I was really down, thinking about my wife and how things had ended... Thinking about all the things I could've done differently. I was feeling right sorry for myself, to be honest. It was one of those depressions that just consumes you, you know? It had me so low, I was contemplating crawling straight into the ocean and just being done with it all. But she said something to me I don't think I'll ever forget. She said, *'It's easy to mistake a dream of happiness with real happiness because it feels so similar. A dream can feel so real that we miss it when it's over. But it's silly to waste so much time grieving for something you never really had.'* I don't think I ever thanked her for it, but she saved me from myself that day. The very next day is when I stood for the first time."

Bud closed his eyes and grinned. "That's my Bertie." He laughed. "She always had the perfect words to say the moment you needed to hear them."

"To Bertie." Jim raised his glass.

"To Bertie!" we all echoed, raising ours.

The night progressed and several more bottles of wine were passed between them. I was excluded, of course, from the drinking, but enjoyed the stories nonetheless. Everyone got a little louder, a little looser, and before long, the entire camp was slurring and stumbling around, forming smaller groups to tell stories and smile.

"Jimmy," Lilly burst between myself and Jim where we stood near the cave, "you take this." She pressed the letter Bertie had written against his chest. "I can't have it without reading it. You hold it and you don't let me anywhere near it until the day you marry me."

Cautiously, he took the folded paper, holding it as if it might break between his fingers. "Sugar, are you sure ye' want *me* to have this? What if ye' change yer mind?"

She narrowed her eyes as she swayed. "When have you ever known *me* to change my mind?" she scoffed, placing her hand on his chest to balance herself. "As a matter of fact," she took Bertie's ring off her finger and held it out to him, "you take this too... and you use it to ask me."

"Nope. Ain't doin' that." He crossed his arms and turned his head to one side. "That's yer grandma's ring and I ain't takin' it from ye.'"

She raised her eyebrow as she fell into him and shoved the ring into the front pocket of his jeans. "Yeah, you are and if you don't want to take it, then you'd better ask me sooner than later."

"Now dammit, I done told ye..." He reached for the pocket and she gasped dramatically.

"James Jackson, don't you even think about pulling that ring out right now! I don't want to see it unless I'm surrounded by candles in a romantic moment. You hand that ring back to me now and I'll dedicate my whole life to making you regret it."

"Lilly..."

She rolled her eyes. "*James...* You might as well just accept that my mind is made up now. No one—not you or anyone else—is gonna change it so quit questioning it and just go with it. Now give me a kiss and go away so I can talk to Lainey about *her* wedding."

I fidgeted nervously. "Lill, we don't have to do that now. After all this..."

She turned slowly, her expression shifting to disbelief. "*You* too?" She looked from me to Jim and back. "Why does everyone think I can't make my own decisions? If I say I want to marry you, then I do." She spun to face me. "And if I say I want to go on with planning your wedding, then I do. Have you all suddenly forgotten who the hell I am? I am Lillian goddamn Renaud and I don't do anything I don't want to do. Now..." She whirled back around to face Jim, whose face was lit up with amusement. "*You* kiss me and go away."

"Yes ma'am," he said, wrapping both arms around her and lifting her off her feet. I noticed Bud noticing them as Lilly pressed her palms against Jim's cheeks and pulled his lips up to hers. He held her there for a moment. "Ye' know, yer just about as pretty as ye' can be when ye' get all worked up about somethin."

She sighed as he lowered her back to her feet. "I know it. Now go away. Find us someplace to sleep where we're not surrounded by other people."

At that, he released her and smiled back at me. "My momma used to tell me if I wasn't a little bit scairt of her, she wasn't the right one." He winked, combing his palm over the top of Lilly's head once before he wandered off to join the others.

She watched him for a moment before she turned back toward me. "Alright." She hiccuped delightedly. "Tomorrow, we'll finish the dress. Let's talk about the location."

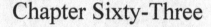

Chapter Sixty-Three

Long after my eyes had become too heavy to keep open and I'd excused myself from the festivities to curl into bed, I felt Jack crawl in beside me in the darkness.

"Red?" he whispered softly, the faintest hint of whiskey still wafting off his breath.

"Mmhmm?"

His fingertips danced across the scar on my forehead as he swept the hair from my face. "Anna told me about rupture and what that could mean." He leaned over me. "Why didn't you tell me?"

I swallowed, a ping of betrayal stabbing at my heart that Anna would share my secrets. "I didn't want to add another reason for you to worry."

"I *am* worried though." He kissed my temple. "I'm terrified. Terrified for each day I wait to get on that water. Horrified the ship I need will pass by while I'm still here and something could happen to you before another comes along. I spoke to Bud. He wants to go with me. I think we should leave right away, and he agrees. The longer we wait, the worse things could get without a doctor."

I smiled as his fingers swept over my lips. "Do you know what Bertie's last words to me were?"

"What?"

"She said, *'You're going to have a healthy baby, I know it. I'm close to death and I've seen it for you.'* And I really believe her."

He blew out. "I truly hope she did see that for us, but it's not enough for me to stay on. Every day the risk to you weighs heavier on me. I can't sit by any longer. Bud and I are leaving.... tomorrow."

"Tomorrow?" I gasped.

"Tomorrow. Bud's loading the raft as we speak. Red, a ship could be out there right now. I could miss it. I can't take that chance anymore. Not with all the risks that are already stacked up against us. The raft is ready, and it doesn't make sense not to go now."

"But..."

"I'll be back in a week, two at the most." He took my chin gently in his grip and pressed his lips against mine. "I promise I'll come back to you. I was leaving either way, it's just a few days sooner than we thought."

"Could we send Jim with Bud instead? Or Kyle? Or Bruce?" I knew I was reaching for alternatives he would never agree to, but I had to try. I was desperate to keep him with me. "Does it have to be you?"

"You know it does," he said softly. "I don't *want* to leave you. I'd much rather stay right here like this forever, but..."

I groaned, nuzzling my face into his chest. "I know."

He pulled me away and kissed my temple. "There are some things I need to say to you before I go."

"No." I took his hand in mine and placed it over my heart. "This isn't goodbye. You're coming straight back."

"Alaina, I can't leave without saying them."

"No," I repeated, gently caressing his fingers where they laid over my racing heart. "You say them when you come back."

"If something happens, I need you to know..."

"Please don't," I begged. "Don't say goodbye to me."

"...that I've meant every word... That what I've found here with you has been life-altering. I can only imagine that a year spent with me might seem abbreviated in comparison to the ten you spent with him, but—"

"Jack, don't—"

"Let me finish," he said, clearing his throat, "...*but* for me, it has been a lifetime—the most amazing lifetime any man could ask for. Now, I've spent the night trying to find the right words to leave you with, so forgive me if this is rehearsed and corny. I can't remember a world without you in it—don't want to remember my life before I found you. Everything before that plane was mindless and without meaning... Like I was wandering blindly in search of you. You brought me to life right here on this island. Your lips found mine and suddenly I knew the God I'd never believed in. How else could I possibly explain my soul's recognition of yours?"

His fingers danced effortlessly down my sternum to rest upon my stomach. "And the knowledge that my child grows inside you... Alaina, it is everything. You are my world—both of you—and you have *always* been. There is not a word you could speak or a blow you could deliver, no amount of distance or even death that could ever prevent my soul from being eternally affixed to yours. Thank you for this life. If I lose it, I want you to know it has all been worth it for the time I've spent with you. I love you, *unequivocally*, and I will love you far longer than the rest of my life could allow for."

At that, he pulled my mouth to his, his kiss an assertion of his words, his lips moving softly at first, and then with an unyielding intensity that made me cling to him. He pried my lips open, rolling over me to add exclamation to the sentiments he'd spoken, deepening the kiss as his hands swept over my cheeks. When he came up for air, at long last, he pressed his forehead against mine.

"Jack," I whispered into the darkness, feeling his eyes over mine. "It is everything *but* you that seems abbreviated in comparison."

Without another word uttered, our bodies spoke on our lips' behalves, making promises to each other as we held on to our final hours together; each of us testifying before the other, declaring the depths of the love we held for one another. We made love without concept of time, moving endlessly in unison, each of us moulding around the other until we became but a single beating heart in the darkness.

We lay silently afterward, listening for the first signs of morning, unmoved until a whisper jarred us from our trance. "Ay Hoss. It's time."

We crept down to the beach under the darkness of the canopy, the faint morning light shrouding us all in shadow. At the shore, the sky lightened in preparation of the sun's arrival and we all stood with heavy hearts at the water's edge, watching as Bud and Jack secured the last of their provisions inside the raft.

"We should go before they wake up," Bud insisted, quickly folding his arms around Lilly and laying his head over hers. "You take care of her while I'm gone." He glanced up at Jim.

"Yes, sir." Jim nodded.

Jack hopped off the raft and grasped Jim's hand in his. "Take care of all of them."

"Ye' know I will, Hoss."

Jack quickly moved past him to pull me into his embrace. "Two weeks at most," he whispered, his breath heavy in my ear. "I'll be back before you know it."

I sniffled and nodded as he gently tilted my face up to lay one final, fleeting kiss on my lips.

How empty my arms felt when he turned to join Jim and Bud to push the raft into the water. I reached for Lilly to fill them and she curled her body into mine as we watched the three men push the raft chest-deep into the water. Jack and Bud climbed inside as Jim waded back toward us.

The three of us sat in the copper sand and watched them disappear over the course of an hour into the infinite blue abyss.

"No, no, no, no!!!" I heard Anna screech from the tree line behind us.

We all turned to see her sprinting down the beach, her blonde hair spraying to one side as it fought against the breeze.

"How could they??!" She collapsed breathlessly to her knees on the sand beside us, her eyes welling with tears as she scanned the horizon. "Why??! WHY?!"

"It's alright, Anna," Lilly cooed, raising on her haunches to pet Anna's head. "They're coming right back. They went to search for Ua Pou... to see if they can find help there. They promised they'd come right back."

"ARE YOU ALL CRAZY?!" She swatted Lilly's hand away, rising up off the sand to pace, her cheeks flushed bright red. "UA POU ISN'T OUT THERE!!! WE'RE NOWHERE NEAR THE MARQUESAS!!! IT IS IMPOSSIBLE THAT YOU COULD THINK WE WOULD BE!!"

"Anna," I said calmly, "Jack said that—"

"Wait.. wait..." She held one hand up to us, plastering the other over her heart. "You knew?"

I nodded. "Yes, but—"

"How could you do this to me?!" she sobbed, her face mangling as she fought between the rage and sadness that filled her. "Do you have any idea what you've done?!"

"If Ua Pou's not out there, they'll come right back," Lilly said sweetly, "and then we'll know for sure. They had to go, Anna... They had to know before you went."

"They have the compass?" She crossed her arms over her chest.

"Yes." I stood and made a move to console her, but she jerked out of reach.

"And the life raft?"

"Yes."

I could see her fingers curl slowly into fists over her chest, and she narrowed her eyes at me. "And what will we do if they never come back?"

I reached a hand toward her, but she took another step backward. "Anna, they'll come back."

"You don't know that." She forced her fingers through her hair as she groaned. "They've screwed us... you've all screwed us. We're completely stranded with no way out!"

"What's the difference between them going and you?" I argued defensively. "They're looking for rescue and are no less capable of finding it than you would've been!"

She glared at me, lowering her voice. "They're looking for an island that's not out there. All of you bought into this nonsense about strange lightning that threw us thousands of miles off course and now… now they're headed the wrong direction on the Pacific ocean. If I would've gone, I'd be going east. And I would've stayed east until I hit land and sent help!"

"What's going on?" Bruce appeared behind her, resting his palm on her heaving shoulder as Izzy skipped happily ahead of him to throw herself onto Jim, tipping him over in the sand.

"They've all screwed us," Anna said, spinning back in the direction of camp. "They've stolen the raft and any chances we had at finding rescue. I'm going back to bed and I pray someone wakes me up from this nightmare."

Chapter Sixty-Four

I paced the water's edge, endlessly watching the horizon for signs of Jack. *'Two weeks,'* he had promised the day he'd shipped off. But it hadn't been two weeks. The two weeks became three, and then three weeks became six, and then six weeks became *two whole months* without a single trace of him.

Had they capsized and drowned? Had they found a ship and then couldn't find their way back? Had they drifted too far and died of dehydration? Had there been truth to Frankie's story of the demon? Had something slithered onto his boat in the night to kill him?

I flattened my hands over my stomach, urging my heart to settle as I walked barefoot along the damp sand and stared out while the sun crept up over the water.

At seventeen or more weeks pregnant, I'd formed a noticeable bump in my midsection; one that Lilly, Magna, and Izzy couldn't seem to keep their hands off of, and I lavished in the early morning solace of walking the beach alone.

I would stay there all day, of course, as I had done since the day he left, and when the others woke up, they would join me. We'd moved most of our cooking supplies down to the old beach shelter and spent our days there, all of us with little else to do outside of watching the horizon.

Anna was never far from me. She stayed close solely out of duty and not because of any affinity she held for me. She was still angry, and as the days passed, her resentment toward all of us for having betrayed her only grew stronger.

Bruce, not being capable of holding a grudge, had quickly softened and had encouraged her to forgive us, but she wouldn't.

I didn't blame her. I wouldn't have forgiven us if it were me in her shoes. They'd taken the raft and the compass and, with Phil gone in the lifeboat, we were utterly stranded with no way to get to her son.

I sat down in the sand, my back already aching, and leaned on one hand as I ran the other over my growing abdomen.

Being pregnant on the island was much different than being pregnant before. The first time, I had the internet. Every cramp, headache, muscle spasm, or craving got placed into Google for confirmation that it was all normal. I would track common symptoms on a weekly basis and every week, I'd know the rough size and stage in development of Evelyn.

On the island, I had nothing but my intuition, and that was something I'd completely overlooked the first time around. Intuition was a powerful thing. I could feel my body changing; the baby growing stronger; could sense the normalcy of it all. My intuition told me he—and he assuredly was a *he*—was fine.

And where my intuition about our child seemed secure, my intuition about Jack, on the other hand, wasn't. I had a nagging suspicion something had gone terribly wrong. Nothing would've kept him away from me for so long. The others, too, had grown more and more wary, forcing fake smiles of encouragement in my direction in an attempt to keep my already panicked mind at ease.

"Good morning," said a deep voice behind me.

I turned to see Kyle a few feet from me in the sand. He stood taller than he had when we'd arrived; his shoulders broader, his outward appearance manlier even without the one arm. Like the rest of us, his skin was darker, his hair had lightened in the sun to an almost blonde color, and he'd begun to grow facial hair around his jawline and lip in thin patches of glistening blonde and brown hair.

He stood patiently, holding a coconut bowl overflowing with boiled Fe'i, bread, and guava jam in his single hand. "I thought you might be hungry, so I fixed you some breakfast."

I smiled up at him. I was *always* hungry. A sense of pride washed over me at the man he was becoming. With Jim on the summit, he'd placed the responsibility of looking over me in Kyle's hands, and Kyle had taken on the role of protector proudly. He was always going out of his way to make sure I was fed, calm, and comfortable; never letting me lift a finger or want for anything; the perfect model of chivalry. I patted the sand beside me. "God bless you, Kyle. I'm *starving*."

He bent his knees to sit without the aid of a second arm in the damp sand beside me, handing me the coconut as he settled back onto his behind. "How are you feeling?"

I dipped the bread into the jam and took an enormous bite. "Better now," I said with my mouth full. "You want some?"

"Take food from a pregnant woman?" He giggled. "I'd like to keep the hand I've got, thank you."

I smirked and mixed a bite of Fe'i into my still full mouth, groaning as the mixture delighted my demanding taste buds.

"I'm heading to the summit this morning," his low voice was still something I was adjusting to, and it never failed to make my head turn toward him just to be sure it was still in fact him that was speaking. "Do you need anything before we go?"

I breathed out heavily through my nose as I chewed and swallowed. There was a single rotation now on the summit between Jim and Lilly and Kyle and Magna. I was always sad on the days they switched, as it left me alone for hours with only Anna, Izzy, and Bruce.

Anna avoided speaking to me and Bruce danced awkwardly around it, trying to make us friendly with small talk. Those days were the longest. Hours passed like days and amplified the strain between us. I would always breathe a sigh of relief when the returning duo finally arrived. "A boat would be nice if you have one."

He attempted a smile that was all apology. "He'll come back, you know. Whatever it is that's holding him up, you know he's fighting it with all he has to get back here."

"But it's been too long." I followed his gaze back out to the horizon. "What if he can't get back? What if he's stuck on Ua Pou and needs our help? We could get there. We could build another raft. I just... I have a feeling. A bad one. And I don't think I can sit here and do nothing anymore."

"He's alright," Kyle soothed. "He'll come back. I know it. You wouldn't want to get out on that water and risk missing his return? With no compass and no way to know for sure the way back..."

I huffed. "But what if he's in trouble?"

He shook his head. "There's no amount of trouble Jack and Bud couldn't find a way out of. They'll be back. We just have to be patient."

"I just feel so helpless." I looked down into my bowl of food. "I don't know what to do with myself. I can't lift anything or fish or go up to the summit... I'm useless."

"Well," he grinned, "you *could* work with Lilly to sew some maternity clothes." He held his hand up playfully in surrender. "Don't kill me, but the button on those shorts looks like it's going to come flying off any day now!"

I looked down at my waist and could feel the sting of the waistband I knew was getting too tight. "I *could* use something more comfortable... Although I could've done without *you* pointing it out!" I punched him softly on the shoulder, then stuffed the last bit of bread and jam into my mouth. "I'll walk you back and grab some fabric to bring back down with me."

I rocked to one side as if to raise up, and Kyle gallantly rose to extend his hand to me. I took it with my free hand, still holding my coconut in the other, and as I rose, the softest zapping sensation bubbled in my midsection.

"Oh!" I released his hand to place mine over my belly.

"WHAT?!" He panicked, putting his hand on my lower back as I straightened.

I laughed. "He kicked." It was the first time I'd ever felt him move, and my eyes watered at the reassurance he was alive and well inside me. I quickly pulled Kyle's hand to my stomach as the sensation came again; a small, faint tickle. "Do you feel it?"

Kyle's eyes went wide, and his face lit up with amusement. "I feel it!!" He laughed breathlessly. "Oh my God!"

We stood there, frozen in time, both our hands over the small swell that housed him until the sensation passed.

"You said '*he*...' How do you know it's a *he*?" Kyle asked when we'd recovered from our trance, looping his arm through mine to lead me up the beach.

"Oh," I twisted my lips, "I don't know how to explain it. I just woke up one day and knew it was a boy."

We spoke casually about pregnancy and all the little sensations that came with it: heartburn, backaches, unrelenting hunger, and the feel of him all the way back to camp, stopping conversation every few minutes to continue snacking on my breakfast.

At camp, Magna was balanced on her haunches, leaning over a suitcase to stack preparations for their trip while Bruce plucked feathers from two birds which would serve as both lunch and dinner. My morning nausea had worn off, but the smell of fish was something I still couldn't handle, and so I was forced to a diet of strictly birds and fruit for the time being.

I navigated my way around the fire and into the cave where Anna still laid in her bed. I'd noticed her eyes were open when I walked inside, but she promptly closed them and pretended to sleep as I passed by to the trunk that housed our fabrics. I wondered just how long she would go on with the silent treatment.

I rustled around the trunk for a fabric we hadn't already tore into, very much aware of her eyes boring into the back of my head, and pulled out a roll of lightweight cotton that sported a simple navy, turquoise, and white print resembling peacock feathers stacked one atop the other. It would suffice for the extremely simple dress I had in mind to sew.

Having never attempted to sew much of anything in my life, I was sure it would be a disaster, but one that would keep me occupied for a little while. I plucked up the needle and thread and the surgical shears from the survival kit, then quickly made my way out of the cave to avoid the weight of Anna's glaring eyes.

"That's a pretty pattern," Magna beamed, zipping up the carryon and rising. "What are you going to do with it?"

I shrugged. "I'm going to attempt to make a dress. If nothing else, it'll keep my mind busy." I frowned, scanning the birdcage and camp. "Where's Izzy?"

Magna swung around in a panic. "She was just here."

"Relax," Bruce said cooly, not looking up from his work. "She's in her secret spot."

"Her secret spot?" I echoed, raising an eyebrow.

"I've been watching her wander off just beyond those trees whenever we're up here." He pointed to the woods at the side of the cave. "Look up."

I followed his finger and my eyes darted upward, where, about twelve feet off the ground, Izzy was nestled into the crook of a fat branch on an oversized tree, her two little legs dangling beneath her as she balanced a book across her lap. I smiled fondly at the sight of her.

"You know," I bit my lip, "you don't all have to come down to the beach with me today. I don't mind being alone for a while. I'm alright. Between sewing and the journal, I've got plenty to keep me occupied. Besides, Izzy could use a day out of the sun." I smiled at his bright red cheeks. "So could you, honestly."

Bruce glanced back at the mouth of the cave. "I doubt she'll approve, but we could use a break from the beach. I'd really like to get a few loaves of bread going today, too. We're down to one and it's much easier for me to make them up here."

He pondered for a moment. "There's no chance I could talk you into staying at camp, is there? We do have other lookouts, you know." He glanced skyward in the direction of the summit.

"No," I said simply. "I have to be down there when he comes."

He sighed. "I know. I'll see what she wants to do. If we're not down when you get hungry, come up for lunch?"

I nodded. "I will." I smiled at Kyle and Magna. "You two have a safe trip up."

I headed back down to the beach, hopeful that I'd be left alone. I set up an area in the old shelter out of the sun to sew and spent a few hours attempting a simple dress. It was indeed a disaster.

When the afternoon sun beat down and I'd had enough, I held my dilapidated creation out in front of me.

'You are definitely no seamstress.'

I decided, with Jack's long white tank, what I'd haphazardly put together could serve as a long skirt; a much more comfortable alternative to the shorts that plagued my gut, and I could pull the tank down over the top to hide the horrible attempt at spaghetti straps. I glanced up at the path that led to our camp and, finding it clear, rose to slide my shorts off and my "skirt" on. It was ridiculous, but it was the most comfortable I'd felt in weeks.

My back ached from sitting so long on the bamboo floor, so, despite my growling stomach, I decided to lie in our hammock for a little while longer before I headed back. Pulling out Zachary's journal, I scanned the horizon once more, then opened the little leather book to the page I'd left off on.

May 15th, 1932

My Dearest Dorothy,

As time passed, Zachary started opening his journal entries with "My Dearest Dorothy."

Today is my birthday. I am 71 years old and am most assuredly going to die on this island. I couldn't help but remember my 65th birthday - it was the last birthday I spent with you before you got sick. You and the kids surprised me with cake and champagne. Peter and Mary announced they were pregnant with little Helen. Margaret played piano and we danced in the living room.

God, I miss home. I spent far too much of my life away from it. I'm sorry for that. I miss Peter and Margaret. How I would've loved to see my grandchildren grow up. Most of all, I miss you, Dorothy. I still carry your ring with me everywhere I go. With the weight I've lost since arriving here, it fits my finger now and I wear it to remind myself that you are with me.

I do wish I could hear the sound of your voice, though. In contrast, I also carry the bullet Frankie shot me with. It's a reminder of the cruelty of the world I've escaped from. In some ways, knowing I am in a world free from greed and savagery gives me peace. But most days I think I prefer the cruelty of the world to the silence of this island. It's deafening.

I miss people. The chatter... the little nuances of their everyday lives they always wanted to discuss. What I wouldn't give to hear someone complain about their wife's cooking for even a moment. I'd even settle for Frankie's unpredictable mood swings and random urges to point his pistol at me over the solitude and silence.

I wonder how long I will live? Can I will myself to die? I have considered taking my own life, but I don't have the courage. I don't even have the courage to starve myself. I thought about taking the lifeboat out on the ocean. Out there I could most certainly die if I don't find rescue. I am constantly caught between paddling out to sea or climbing back up the summit to await death.'

"Alaina?" I was pulled from the fine cursive to find Anna standing at the edge of the shelter with a clay bowl. I could smell the freshly fried Kolea and breadfruit, and my stomach grumbled in anticipation. "You should eat."

"Sorry." I wobbled with the hammock, struggling for balance until I managed to swing my feet over the edge. "I lost track of time."

She said nothing more and extended her arm, holding the bowl toward me. I rose and took it, mindful of her dismissive body language. "Anna, please talk to me. I don't expect your forgiveness, but we can't go on like this. What can I do to fix our friendship?"

She crossed her arms over her chest. "We are not friends, you and I. We never were."

"That's not true. We're family."

She met my eyes then, her shoulders tensing visibly. "I do wish you would all stop throwing out that term as though it means anything. You don't know what *family* or the love of one even means. My *family* is out there probably getting beaten and mentally broken night after night. What kind of man will he grow into? Huh? Will he become his father... or something far worse? Will he develop rage and shoot up a school or a shopping mall as the result of years of mental and physical abuse? Will he turn to drugs? Alcohol? Will he develop depression? Will he take his own life as a means to escape the nightmare I left him with? These are the thoughts that plague me. You didn't just steal the raft, Alaina, you stole my son's future with it."

"Anna, I'm—"

"Save it." She spun on her heel in the direction of camp. "I will help you with this baby because it's not the baby's fault, but as soon as the birth is done, I am done. I will find a way to get on that ocean, and if I die out there, at least I've tried. As far as you and I are concerned, the expectation that anything you could do or say could *'fix'* our relationship is unconscionable. I would've preferred to be stuck here with Phil. At least he didn't hide his selfishness behind fake niceties and the word *'family.'*"

At that, she stormed off, and I followed behind her. My heartbeat quickened, and a lump formed in my throat. It hadn't been my idea for Jack to go. In fact, I'd begged him to stay. I'd begged him to stay for selfish reasons: I didn't want to be away from him. I had never considered the life her son might lead as the result of her being stuck here. I'd never once thought of him growing into a man—a *damaged* man—as the result of us never finding rescue.

Too ashamed to meet Anna's eyes, I kept my head down as I entered camp, hurrying into the cave and blindly navigating my way to the solitude of the back cave before I collapsed on our bed.

I picked at the food for the sake of the baby, but her words left me with very little appetite. I sat there, humbled, replaying the events over and over in my mind, wishing I'd stopped him, wishing I'd let her go instead, praying that God would send us a way home.

I laid back in the bed, utterly deflated and guilty, closing my eyes to let the fatigue pull me away to dream.

Chapter Sixty-Five

I was sitting at the kitchen island finishing a logo design that, upon completion, would wrap up the week's work. I sipped my coffee and curled my leg up onto the barstool, shivering a little despite the heater blowing just beneath my seat. I had meatloaf in the oven and was waiting for the timer to go off before I could retreat to the quiet of my office.

Chris sat on the couch behind me, his long legs sprawled the length of the sofa. With the holidays behind us, the winter weeks had been dreadfully drawn out. The snow forced Chris's work to slow down and the two of us were cooped up together for almost a month in the house.

He sat casually in sweatpants and bare feet with the television on and his phone in hand, scrolling the internet, completely oblivious to the five o'clock news that was blaring through the house and forcing my attention span to become shorter and shorter.

"...*were shot, two of them fatally, on the city's south side, including a wounded 11-year-old boy...*"

I shook my head, forcing myself to focus on the happy pink logo looking back at me from the computer's screen. It was a woman-owned bakery called "SunFlour" and they had insisted on incorporating pink into their brand.

I huffed. *'Focus... Just a little longer...'* I moved my cursor around the lettering, hoping for some creative inspiration.

"...*and found a 41-year-old man unresponsive in an alley with gunshot wounds to his back and chest, Chicago police said...*"

I rolled my eyes, leaning closer to the computer screen in the hopes that by being closer I could somehow drown out the television and muster up something more creative than a wheat stem.

'Actually... The wheat stem could work... maybe if I use it inside the wordmark in place of the L.' I excitedly began moving the symbol over the word. *'We could be onto something gen—*

"BEEEEEP!!!" The timer on the oven made me jump nearly out of my seat. I stood, my fingers still on the mousepad as I positioned the little leaf perfectly.

I skirted around the counter, pulled out the meatloaf and wrapped it in foil.

'If I change the wordmark to a thinner freehand cursive, then I could make the wheat look hand-drawn and we could spell out bakery in a smooth all-caps sans-serif...'

"Did you hear me?" Chris asked, standing now at the counter and looking annoyed.

I blinked. "I'm sorry, what?"

He sighed, shaking his head, "I *said*, we need to talk."

"SMOKE!" I heard Lilly scream, my eyes popping open. "WAKE UP! THERE'S SMOKE ON THE SUMMIT!!!"

I leapt out of the bed.

'Jack.'

I pulled a nearby sundress on, relieved to find Lilly had placed it there after altering it at the waist. I grabbed my boots and socks in one hand and ran out of the cave to the campfire where everyone was scurrying to put their shoes on to head for the beach.

"Lainey!" Lilly's watering eyes met mine. "They've come back to us." She wrapped both arms around my shoulders and squeezed.

I looked up toward the summit and could see the thick black plumes of smoke rolling off the top and out toward the water.

I dropped the boots and ran down the path that led to the beach, Jim and Lilly at my heels.

"Slow down, woman," Jim heaved. "Ay! Yer gonna hurt yerself!"

But I couldn't. My heart raced at the promise of holding Jack once again in my arms. As the days added up, my mind had tortured me with images of violent waves tipping the raft, sharks circling to devour them the moment they'd fallen overboard. I'd imagined him drowning, dehydrating, starving, being set upon by modern day pirates... My dreams were relentless in their creativity and had me worried sick.

I sprinted down the path, my bare feet sending sand flying out behind them as I picked up speed.

I ran blindly, my eyes welled with tears, my heart beating out of my chest, completely ignoring my aching sides and labored breathing. All of it would disappear the minute I was back in his arms.

I could hear voices ahead of me as I gained momentum, and as the beach came into view from the top of the hill, I could see a massive wooden ship far out to sea, its sails blowing high in the sky with the breeze, looking like something out of an old painting instead of the reality before me.

I saw people on the path running toward me. The rising sun behind them blinded me and cast them all in shadow. As he grew closer, I could make out Bud, already halfway up the trail and running at full speed despite his age, three men still on the beach jogging far behind him.

"GRANDPA!" Lilly shouted down to him as she and Jim caught up to me.

Bud made quick work of the distance between us, panting as he stood before us.

"Where's Ja—"

"All of you, be silent until I tell you. Don't say a single word," he huffed, pulling his wedding band off his finger and presenting it to Jim, glancing behind his shoulder suspiciously. "Put this on and don't ask any questions. DO NOT SPEAK, do you understand? Lilly, do you have your grandma's ring?"

"Uh huh," she said, evidently frightened.

"Put it on your left ring finger and don't say anything." He looked at me then. "Alaina," he shook his head and met my eyes, his expression full of solemn warning. "There's something—"

Before he could say more, the three men caught up to him, all of them looking as though they'd stepped out of a revolutionary war reenactment, clad with double-breasted navy coats lined in intricate gold braid and brass buttons. They all wore cream waistcoats over matching breeches, and their calves were all bright white in stockings over shining black shoes. Atop their heads were three-pointed tricorne hats. I blinked several times as I tried to clear the sun from my eyes enough to make sense of them.

I looked back at Bud, whose eyes were nervously darting from Lilly to me and back to the men. I noticed he had a cut above his eye that had been stitched and his clothing was torn in several places. He mouthed silently, "Do not speak."

The two frontmost men looked up at me as they approached, and I held a hand up to shade my eyes, squinting to make out their faces against the unrelenting sun, searching for Jack. I didn't recognize them and they didn't seem to recognize me. They each stepped to the side, clearing the way for the tallest of them to stand before me.

He towered a good foot over my head, and as he slowly removed his hat, my heart stopped entirely.

His big green eyes came into focus and my husband breathed out, "Ally?"

Printed in the USA
CPSIA information can be obtained
at www.ICGtesting.com
LVHW031536060424
776655LV00011B/95